STILETTO

DANIEL O'MALLEY graduated from Michigan State University and earned a Master's Degree in medieval history from Ohio State University. He then returned to his childhood home, Australia. He now works for the Australian Transport Safety Bureau, writing press releases for government investigations of plane crashes and runaway boats.

Also by Daniel O'Malley

The Rook

STILETTO

DANIEL O'MALLEY

First published in United States of America in 2016 by Little, Brown
and Company, a division of Hachette Book Group, Inc.

First published in the United Kingdom in 2016 by Head of Zeus Ltd
This paperback edition first published in 2017 by Head of Zeus Ltd

9 7 5 3 1 2 4 6 8

A catalogue record for this book is available from
the British Library.

ISBN (PB): 9781781853948
ISBN (E): 9781781853931

Typeset by Adrian McLaughlin

Printed and bound in Great Britain by
CPI Group (UK) Ltd, Croydon CRO 4YY

Head of Zeus Ltd
Clerkenwell House
45–47 Clerkenwell Green
London ECIR OHT

WWW.HEADOFZEUS.COM

For Mollie Glick
and
for Asya Muchnick
with tremendous thanks

If you had taught her, from the dawn of her intelligence, with your utmost energy and might, that there was such a thing as daylight, but that it was made to be her enemy and destroyer, and she must always turn against it, for it had blighted you and would else blight her;—if you had done this, and then, for a purpose, had wanted her to take naturally to the daylight and she could not do it, you would have been disappointed and angry?

—*Charles Dickens, Great Expectations*

Optometry is the discipline of vision. What its boundaries will be depends upon what the word vision *means to the profession.*

—*A. M. Skeffington, May 1974*

STILETTO

*To Felicity Jane Clements, Pawn of the Checquy Group
and ward of HM Government:*

*You are herewith called forth by the authority of the
Lord and Lady, in accordance with your obligations
and your oaths, to give service, in secret, for the
protection and security of the Monarch, the People,
and the soil of the British Isles.*

*On this day, you are to proceed with all haste into the London
borough of Northam, to the location commanded. There, you
will bend the abilities instilled within you to the task ordered.*

*To ensure that you remain unknown and that none
remark upon your presence, you will be given clothing
to blend in among the populace.*

*To discourage civilians from approaching you,
you will be sprayed with urine.*

Bring milk and chocolate biscuits.
— *Odgers*

1

The woman was crouched in an alley, her back against the wall and her hands pressed awkwardly to the bricks behind her.

She was not an appetizing sight. A tangle of dirty dirty-blond hair hung down over her grubby face. Behind it, her eyes were open a slit, showing white. A string of drool dangled from her mouth. Apart from her ragged breathing, she was utterly still. She was dressed in several layers of filthy clothing and a pair of trainers whose mesh sides had rotted away almost completely and whose soles were peeling off as if trying to escape.

She was also not an appetizing smell. There was a pungent odor coming off her, one that suggested an ongoing lack of access to bathing facilities. And laundry facilities. And toilet facilities. She was actually pretty enough behind the dirt, but to discover that would require several minutes' concerted attention with a damp sponge and, possibly, a trowel. As she was, she fit into her surroundings perfectly.

The alley was terribly narrow, more of an incidental gap between two sets of row houses. Hypodermic needles, feces of unspecified provenance, improperly disposed-of prophylactics, and general domestic rubbish were the primary topographical features.

For a few minutes, rain drizzled in and soaked her, but still she did not move.

A rat scurried between the rubbish, presumably on its way to somewhere more salubrious.

Finally, she moved her hands away from the wall behind her and opened her eyes wide. She took a deep breath that would have been cleansing had she been in a place that was slightly less vile. She licked her lips, felt the drool that had dripped down her chin, and moved to wipe her face with her sleeve before realizing how disgusting her sleeve was. She sighed and, still crouching, swung her arms about stiffly. Then she looked up blearily at the sound of someone approaching down the alley.

That someone was a tall redheaded man with lily-white skin and freckles that had cornered the real estate market on his face. Behind him was another someone who looked much the same except that he was bigger and had shaved his head so there was only a corona of orange fuzz. Both of them were dressed in clothes that did not look at all out of place in the alleyway.

"Oh, hello," said the first man. The woman squinted up at him and grunted. "Look at this, Petey," he remarked to his associate. "We're looking for something to do, and here something is."

"What?" she said.

"Shut up," said the man easily. Then, just as easily, he punched her in the face. Her head slammed back against the wall, and she fell onto her bottom.

"The fuck?" she spat, pressing her hand against her jaw.

"I *told* you to shut up," said the man mildly. "Now, me and my mate are gonna have a bit of fun right here, and you're not going to give us any trouble unless you want another fist to the face."

"And that'd be just for starters," said the other man, Petey.

Rather than being terrified by the prospect of a vicious assault upon her person, however, the woman seemed unperturbed and somewhat incredulous.

"Are you serious?" she said. Her accent was not one you would have expected to come out of the mouth of a person in those environs. It bespoke an expensive education. "You actually want to do this? To someone who looks like me?" She glanced down at herself and then around at the refuse that filled the alley. *"Here?"* They didn't answer her, but apparently for these men, a blond woman was a blond woman, even if she smelled like carrion left out in the sun. The first man, the hitter, put his hands to his belt. *"Such* a mistake you're making," she said.

Then she reached out and grasped the man's ankle. The smirk didn't have time to leave his face before she'd yanked on his shin and kicked him, in dizzyingly quick succession, in the testicles, the stomach, the chest. He toppled backward into his colleague's startled arms, and she drew herself up. Moments before, her posture had been hunched and defensive, but now she held herself in the classic boxer's stance.

"Bitch, you've got to be kid—" began Petey, but his assertion was cut off as the woman stepped forward and briskly broke Petey's companion's nose with a smart right jab. The companion's wail of pain broke off as she punched him in the stomach and drove the air out of him. He sounded like a set of bagpipes that had just been stabbed. His knees buckled, and Petey staggered to keep him upright. The woman took a few steps back, sized them up, and was lunging forward when the toe of one of her shoes landed in something vile and squishy. Denied any purchase, her leg shot out from under her, and she lurched violently to the side.

"Bugger!" She bounced off a wall, fell against a pair of rubbish bins that were, ironically, completely empty, and ended up sprawled on her back on the ground. Then the breath rushed out of her as Petey, who had apparently jettisoned his friend in favor of subduing her, dived onto her and pressed her into the pavement.

The man who had hit her seemed to have righted himself.

"Stupid bitch," said the hitter in a sort of wheezy falsetto as he came down the alley to them. "It'll be bloody now. So much worse now."

"Yeah," said Petey. He was lying across her, his weight holding her down, and he pressed his face into her vile hair.

3

"You know," he said, "under all that hair and muck, you're not bad-looking. But you will be when me and Joe are done with you." She struggled, but he had her well and truly pinned. She sighed and looked up. Joe was staring down at her, and the expression on his face was terrible to behold.

"I really didn't want to do this," she remarked. "Pawn Cheng?" The men exchanged confused looks.

"Uh...I got your porn right here, slut," said Joe, grabbing his crotch.

"I'm not talking to you," she said coldly.

Then Joe clapped his hands to his head and seemed to fling himself backward. As Petey and the woman watched in fascination, he fell onto the ground, revealing a petite Asian woman. She was wearing a black yoga outfit and a grim expression. On her feet, somewhat incongruously, was a pair of heavy boots that looked suitable for undertaking construction work or possibly some sort of hate crime. It appeared that to pull Joe down, she had simply buried both her hands in his thick red hair and yanked with all her strength. There had been no sign of her a minute before.

"Joe!" exclaimed Petey.

Then Joe was up again, and he was roaring with rage. He flung himself at his diminutive assailant. There was so little room in the alley that there was simply no way she could dodge a man that big. He charged toward her, his shoulder dropped to slam into her.

It was almost as if the Asian woman *burst* under his bulk. Streamers and strands of black material erupted from the point of impact, spreading out and then fading away completely. Joe kept barreling forward until he collided with the wall, hitting it so hard that he bounced off it a little.

Petey, at this point, actually held tighter to the woman splayed out underneath him.

"What the *fuck*?" he whispered. "What the fuck what the fuck what the *fuck* is going on? What is that?"

"That's my colleague," the woman he was lying across said

pleasantly, and then she initiated a wrestling maneuver referred to by some as "the dump truck." From beneath him, she crooked one arm around his neck and the other around his torso, then she arched her whole body high, rolled him up and over her head, and dumped his arse firmly on the ground before snapping to her feet.

Joe, meanwhile, had been so absorbed by the Curious Incident of the Sporadically Vaporous Asian Woman in the Alleyway that he'd missed his friend's discommoding behind him. Before his eyes, the air in the center of the alley roiled, and the aforementioned Asian woman suddenly reappeared. However, she didn't seem in the least bit interested in him.

"Felicity, did you need me for anything else?" she asked in a thick Birmingham accent.

"Nah, I'm fine, thanks," said the other woman. His heart thundering with anger and bewilderment, Joe reached into his pocket and drew out a knife, which he flicked open. His hands low, he lunged forward again, but the short woman was already evaporating away with an unimpressed look on her face. He turned around and saw Petey getting painfully to his feet. The blond bitch was tying her hair back from her face. She gave him a look that said he had gotten himself into this situation and really had only himself to blame.

"You—you..." Words failed him. This was *not* how it was supposed to go.

"Hey, I'm right here," she said, and the complete lack of concern in her voice ignited something in him. He barreled toward her, his knife clutched in his fist, shoving past Petey. She swayed to the side, then turned, stepped back against his chest, and caught his knife arm. Before he could think, she had flipped him over her shoulder. He went down on the ground, the knife clattering from his hand, and seemed disinclined to get back up.

Petey came a little more cautiously, but as he moved toward her, she snapped into swift, dizzying motion. She swung her leg with mechanical precision and kicked out at the side of his knee. Under the combined force of her strength and her complete lack of hesitation or mercy, his leg simply crumpled. He fell into the mud and the rubbish, shouting and clutching at his leg. She stepped carefully over the trash and delivered a meticulous kick to the jaw that left him facedown and unconscious in the remnants of a pizza that someone hadn't wanted anymore. The alley was quiet except for the sound of Pawn Cheng condensing out of the air.

"Well, that was nicely done," said Pawn Cheng. "You all right?"

"Yeah, I'm okay," said Felicity sourly. She dusted off her clothing, which did not make an appreciable difference to its appearance.

"Honestly, I can't believe you needed me to step in to help you with two chavs."

"Give me a break, Andrea," said Felicity. "I just spent three and a bit hours squatting against a wall. Plus, I'm wearing these ridiculous leper shoes." She looked down at the men on the ground. At any other time it would have given her profound satisfaction to break every bone in their bodies, or at least to put the boot in a couple of times. But there was the danger here that she might attract unwanted attention, not least from the house she'd been observing.

However... she mused.

"What the hell are you doing?" asked Andrea. "Are you *robbing* them?"

"I'm not going to keep it," said Felicity reasonably. "But I think that losing their mobile phones and their wallets will teach them a valuable lesson about...um...you know...respecting the homeless."

"You don't think they learned that by having the crap beaten out of them by a homeless woman?" asked Andrea. "To say nothing of a chick who can turn into oxygen?"

"You know what would make this lesson extra-special?" said Felicity after a moment. "We should take their shoes as well."

The Asian Pawn shook her head disapprovingly, then shrugged.

"Yeah, all right."

Two minutes later, Felicity was humming cheerfully as she sauntered out of the alley.

God, I love this job.

2

Wake up and get out of the bathtub. If you're late for this cocktail party, the British will take us all out to the parking lot and shoot us in the back of the head. Plus, we need to get the slime out of the tub before the hotel maids come in for the turndown service."

The voice came thundering into Odette Leliefeld's sleeping brain by way of the waterproof headphones that were clamped to her sleeping ears. She was jolted awake, and opened her eyes. The light at the bottom of the bathtub was dim and lavender, and it really was tempting just to snuggle down in the warmth and return to a nice therapeutic stasis. But then Alessio's voice came back into her ears. "Room service will be here in seven minutes, so hurry up."

Odette grimaced and set about speeding up her heart rate from its restful one-beat-every-three-hours tempo. She pushed herself up out of the depths of the ridiculously large tub. The designers of the bathroom had apparently thought the hotel guests would be either engaging in group bathing or traveling with their exotic pets, because there seemed to be enough room in the tub for a party of six good friends, seven *extremely* good friends, or fifteen pedigree jellyfish. Instead of a bijou orgy or some purebred Olindias formosa, however, it currently contained Odette and about fourteen hundred liters of thick, viscous slime.

She surfaced with a little difficulty, the sludge holding on to her, and sat up, taking her first breath in five hours.

"I hate sleeping in a swimsuit," she remarked weakly to the world as she wiped the gunk out of her eyes.

"If I have to come wake you up all the time," said her younger brother, "then you are not sleeping naked in the tub." She felt the headphones get plucked off her head as he bustled by, presumably tidying up the clothes that were still scattered on the floor.

"Did you order coffee?" she asked.

"Yes," he said, his voice cracking a little. "Although you're not supposed to have hot beverages or caffeine until all your new organs have settled."

"You know what? Don't lecture me until your larynx has settled," she retorted.

"Oh, would you like me to cancel the coffee?" asked Alessio.

"No, I'm sorry," said Odette hurriedly.

"Don't step on the floor yet," he instructed. "Otherwise you'll just get it everywhere. Here's the strigil." He handed her a curved rubber blade and then hurried out to the sitting room. She smiled at the retreating back of her thirteen-year-old brother as he closed the door behind him, then stood up and looked around.

"If any British government official is watching me," she said out loud, "I really don't care if you see me naked, but it's very tacky on your part."

No answer was forthcoming.

"Well, all right, then," she said to herself. She peeled off her bathing suit and set about scraping the slime off her body and back into the tub.

Once she'd transferred herself, mostly slime-free, to the shower, Odette carefully examined her legs, limbs, and torso. Coming along nicely, she thought. The scars along her limbs were now only faint lines, and a few more nights spent in a bathtub of goop would get rid of them completely. The Y-shaped scar tissue that ran down her chest to below her navel was taking longer to heal and was still a little itchy, but she stopped herself from rubbing at it. She held out her arm, her hand bent back, and flexed. A sculpted bone spur the size of her index finger slid out from the underside of her wrist. Okay, good. She tensed another set of muscles, and a drop of amber liquid appeared on the end of the spur. And good.

Then she turned on the water and set about the laborious process of getting the slime out of her hair.

So, what do you think of the place so far?" she asked Alessio as she sipped her coffee and swallowed one of her pills.

"What's to think?" he asked without looking up from his tablet computer.

"Well, the view out the window is nice," she said, taking two more pills.

"It's a very gray, cloudy kind of place," said Alessio.

"We're right opposite Hyde Park, and I just saw one of those red double-decker buses go by. I expect we'll get some time off from the negotiations. We can do London things. The Tate. Trafalgar Square. Harrods. And we could go to Buckingham Palace." Her brother looked at her skeptically over his computer. "I'm not saying that I want to meet a prince or anything, but it would be cool to see the changing of the guard." He shrugged. "And the hotel is very posh."

"Every room on this floor is probably bugged," Alessio said grimly, a little frown line appearing between his eyebrows. "And everyone we meet is probably from the Checquy. That woman who just brought up the food was looking around like she thought we'd have entrails on the floor for her to tidy up along with the wastepaper bins."

"She was probably aghast that a twenty-three-year-old woman has to share a suite with her thirteen-year-old brother," said Odette, swallowing another two pills.

"I'm aghast at that as well," said her brother. Odette made a little snorting sound as she looked at him thoughtfully. They both had the same heart-shaped face and the same dark brown hair, but Alessio's hair was dead straight whereas hers had a tendency to go curly unless she was concentrating. Thankfully, she was still a good deal taller than him, but people in their family often went through a growth spurt late in their teens, and she had no doubt that he would eventually be the one resting drinks on her head.

However, at the moment, he looked very vulnerable. There were still traces of puppy fat on his face, and in his little suit and carefully tied tie, he reminded her of a boy going to a funeral, forced to face adult things too soon.

"I really am sorry about all this," she said to him, and he looked up at her. "You shouldn't have to be acting as a diplomatic representative, you should be..." She trailed off.

"What?" he asked. "At home in Roeselare with my tutors, working on my surgical skills like a regular teenager?" He rolled his eyes. "Grootvader Ernst wanted me to come. He wanted both of us to come. He said it would help."

"Yes, but I'm actually going to be engaged in negotiations, albeit in some unspecified capacity," said Odette, pausing a moment to swallow four more pills. "You're going to be, what? Standing around looking harmless, showing them that we're not all monsters that have been so heavily modified that we're no longer human."

"Only because I'm not fifteen yet," said her brother. "At least you have some weapons inside you."

"Not enough," said Odette darkly. She popped three more pills in her mouth and slammed them down with the last of the coffee. "Now, how long do I have before the meeting to finalize the strategy for the cocktail party?"

"Half an hour," said her brother.

"All right, I'm going to go do my injections and get ready."

In the bathroom, Odette eyed herself closely in the mirror. I need to look businesslike, professional, and normal, she thought. Not overly attractive or unusual. Not threatening in any way. She concentrated, and her lips flushed slightly. Good.

Not too red, not too dark. Her eyelids darkened subtly, and she dilated her pupils a bit, flinching in the suddenly brighter light.

"Going for the belladonna look?" said Alessio as he came into the bathroom to brush his teeth.

"Well, we have to make a good impression, and people are attracted to dilated pupils," Odette said defensively. But she constricted them a little. "You're just lucky you don't have to go to this thing tonight."

She watched in the mirror as Alessio carefully rolled up his sleeve, slid his arm into the slime-filled bathtub, and fished around. He finally located the plug and yanked it out. A little dimple appeared on the surface of the liquid, but the slime did not seem to be in any hurry to vanish down the plug hole. They both stared at it in chagrin.

A couple hundred gallons of eldritch ooze probably aren't going to make a very good impression, Odette thought. Even if it is nectarine-scented.

"Try adding some hot water," she suggested finally. "And the shampoo from the shower breaks it down a little."

"I may simply have to try flushing it down the toilet," said Alessio. "I can use the rubbish bin as a bailer." Odette could all too easily imagine something horrible happening to the toilet as a result. A bathtub of evil somehow seemed much less embarrassing than a toilet of evil. With a toilet, people might think the evil had come out of her.

"Better not," she said hastily. "I think we should just leave it. And since you think the maids are with the Checquy, they aren't going to bat an eyelash at a slowly draining bathtub full of biochemical soup."

"Well, I'm not positive they're with the Checquy," said her brother, the little line appearing between his eyes again. "You could help me with this, you know."

"This thing I'm doing right here? It requires a fair amount of close attention," said Odette. She pursed her lips in concentration and watched in satisfaction as her cheekbones shifted under her skin, moving up and out a little.

3

Five hours before her pied-à-tête with Joe and Petey, Felicity had been sitting in an office in the Hammerstrom Building, dressed in a suit and very definitely not covered in filth. The Hammerstrom Building, despite being the most boring-looking building in the City of London (it appeared to have been designed by a committee of depressive Puritans), was in fact one of the facilities belonging to the Checquy Group, the secret government department that employed the supernatural to protect the populace from the supernatural.

The Hammerstrom Building was the headquarters for all domestic operations of the Checquy, overseen by two executives known as the Rooks. As a result, it was affectionately referred to as the Rookery. It was where government strategists made the arrangements to acquire every child born in the British Isles with unexplainable abilities. It was where the course of those children's lives, including their rigorous education at the remote and heavily fortified boarding school known as the Estate, was planned. It was where the supernaturally gifted operatives, once grown up—the Pawns—received their assignments to stations across the country. It was the place to which intelligence was funneled from a thousand different sources. It was the place from whence elite soldiers sallied forth to combat the unnatural.

It was also where Felicity had arrived early that morning in an effort to catch up on paperwork. She had been sipping an inferior coffee and waiting for her computer to boot up when a courier trotted over and handed her the envelope containing the summons. The last part of the official message—the caution about the urine—had given Felicity a moment's pause, but then she'd shrugged. Service in the Checquy called for all sorts of unorthodox duties. Those duties tended to be especially unorthodox when one was a member of an urban assault team.

And if you want to climb higher, she told herself, you don't ever complain. You just show that you're ready and eager for any challenge.

The location to which she had been commanded turned out to be a house. It was not a particularly pleasant house, being both abandoned and in disrepair, but as a result it blended in perfectly with the surrounding area. It was in Northam, the least convenient district of the Greater London conurbation, too far from the city's center or any public transport for even the most optimistic of gentrificators, and too far from the edge of the metropolis for people to delude themselves that they were enjoying country living. Evelyn Waugh had once described it as "the perineum of the Empire."

Felicity had found the chief of her team, Pawn Millicent Odgers, tucked away in the kitchen at the back of the house sifting through the contents of some hard plastic cases. A plump woman in her midsixties, Odgers spoke with a pure Glaswegian accent. From the shoulders up, with her gray hair in a tight bun and her glasses on a chain around her neck, she looked as if she should be checking out books in a country library. However, the rest of her was swathed in a formidable coverall of dense black material that appeared to be several sizes too large for her. She was shod in boots that looked as though they could kick in a door or a rib cage with equal facility.

"Good morning, Chief."

"Morning, Clements. Did you bring the biscuits and the milk?"

"Yes, sir," said Felicity, holding up her shopping bag.

"Good. Buchanan is bringing the thermoses with coffee and tea."

"So where's the rest of the team?"

"They'll be trickling in. The sudden arrival of a horde of healthy people will draw attention in this neighborhood. Hopefully, they've all shown the same sense you have and dressed down a bit." Felicity, having noted the tenor of the area, had taken the precaution of changing out of her suit and into a pair of jeans and a rather grubby fleece. "Meanwhile, are you ready for work?"

"Always, sir."

"Grand to hear. I'll brief you after you've put on the clothes in that bag over there."

Felicity cautiously opened the bag and saw that it was filled with garments for which the most charitable description was "vagrant camouflage." She sighed. It wasn't the worst ensemble she'd ever been compelled to wear in the name of duty (one mission had called for her to put on a gillie suit composed entirely of well-manured poison ivy), but the clothes were all covered in filth and grease, and there was a pungent odor coming off them.

Gritting her teeth and controlling her gag reflex, she changed into the vestments of the damned. The shirt had several collars sewn in, so it looked like she was wearing multiple layers of old T-shirts and rugby jumpers. The jeans adhered to her legs in various places. She took a seat.

"Are you sitting comfortably?" asked Odgers.

"Are there lice in these clothes? Because—yes."

"Then I'll begin." Odgers took up a file and settled her glasses on her nose. "In the past three weeks, there have been a series of mysterious disappearances throughout London. Now, at first glance, they seem unrelated. All the subjects went missing on different days; they're of different races, different ages, different socioeconomic backgrounds. However, Checquy statisticians have identified a pattern. All the missing people have B-positive blood type."

"Any possibility it's a coincidence?" asked Felicity as she very deliberately did not scratch herself.

"I thought of that too," said Odgers. "However, in addition to being B-positive, they had all received organ transplants. Something like four people with new hearts, several with new kidneys, a skin graft. Pancreases, corneas, what have you. And all done in London hospitals."

"How on earth did they figure that out?" asked Felicity, impressed.

"Oh, you know the statisticians," said Odgers. "They're always trawling through all the information they can get. I think they identified this trend after the eleventh disappearance."

"What's the Checquy bait, though? Do we have any sign that this is something supernatural and not just, I don't know, an extremely specific and well-informed serial killer?"

"All of the missing people vanished from their homes in the middle of the night," said Odgers. "In most cases, it looks as if they went to bed and then, after a few hours' sleep, got up and walked out the front door. There were no signs of forced entry or violence. They just left."

"Did they all live alone?"

"No," said Odgers. "There were two teenagers who were living at home, and seven of the victims were married or living with a partner, but none of the parents or partners reported anything strange happening. One woman vaguely recalled her husband getting out of bed, but she assumed he was going to the loo. She just went back to sleep and didn't realize anything was wrong until she came down in the morning and found the front door open."

"They didn't take anything with them?"

"No. They didn't even change out of their nightclothes," said Odgers. "Didn't put on shoes or slippers or a coat. One man apparently left wearing just a T-shirt. It was like they were sleepwalking."

"And no sign of them afterwards?" said Felicity. "No witnesses?"

"Actually, the police managed to find a couple of witnesses," said Odgers. "In Green Park at three in the morning, two homeless gentlemen saw one of the victims walking across the grass. They said he was in his pajamas and staring straight ahead. He didn't respond when they called out to him."

"So something is summoning them?" Felicity asked. She shuddered a little at the thought.

"We don't know what's going on," said Odgers. "After our analysts identified the trend, they checked for connections between the missing people, but they haven't found any.

"The most recent disappearance happened last night. A man

15

called the police right away when he found his girlfriend gone. We got a team to the flat immediately, and one of the Pawns managed to track her scent twelve miles to a house near here. He caught traces of the scents of two of the other victims. We're assuming that all of them are there but that the traces of the others have dissipated or been washed away since they arrived. You're going to be scouting the house for us."

"So the reason that I look and smell like the inside of a dumpster is...?"

"You're going to be homeless," said Odgers, her eyes intent on the files.

"I see. I take it that a homeless woman is not going to get a lot of attention in this neighborhood?"

"We're less concerned about the neighbors and more about spooking the kidnapper, or the summoner, or whatever it is. The house you're scouting is supposed to be abandoned. In fact, all of the houses in the row are. But if there is something or someone malevolent in there, and you're spotted, you might get attacked. Or it might lure you in. Andrea Cheng will be providing backup, but obviously we'd prefer you to conduct your reconnaissance and withdraw without any incidents."

"Understood," said Felicity. "How long do I have?"

"I'll trust your judgment. I want the standard information —layout, traps, presence of any living entities, anything unusual. All right, I'm going to do your face now." She smeared some mentholated ointment under Felicity's nose and then under her own. "This will help you not throw up on yourself. It isn't really a smell you get used to." She briskly applied some specially blended military-grade filth to Felicity's face and blotted off the excess with a tissue.

When it came time for the promised application of the urine, it was something of a relief to find that she wasn't to be sprayed so much as lightly misted. It wasn't a huge relief, though, and there was another startling, somewhat unwelcome revelation.

"It's my urine?" Felicity said incredulously.

"Don't think of it as urine," Pawn Odgers advised her. "Try to think of it as an olfactory disguise." Felicity tried and was not measurably comforted.

"But where did you get my urine?" she asked.

"The Checquy has samples of everyone's everything," said Odgers cheerfully. "Remember, during your time at the Estate, they kept taking specimens of your every fluid and solid?"

"That was for scientific research!" exclaimed Felicity. "And it was years ago!"

"Would someone else's fresh urine be better?"

Felicity could think of no dignified response as she tugged her greasy forelock (Odgers had combed something like vegetable oil into her hair). She wiped her hand on her jeans, cringed at the result, and then left through the back door.

And now she was returning through the back door with Pawn Cheng. She noted that while the past four hours had left her looking even more disheveled (if such a thing were possible), the kitchen had been transformed into a cramped little command center. The cooker had been manhandled out of the room, and there were floor plans tacked up on the walls. Laptop computers glowed on the counter and the kitchen table. A flat-screen TV sat precariously by the sink showing camera feeds from around the outside of the house.

The main difference, however, was that there were now people bustling around. Some were examining the plans on the walls, some were perched on whatever surface they could find, staring at screens, and others were bent over plastic cases, checking the guns that glinted in their little foam beds. Felicity scanned them all, automatically noting their locations, but she was really looking for six specific people. It wasn't hard to identify them: four men, two women, all dressed in the menacing black coveralls that Odgers had been wearing, although theirs fit. They were all possessed of excellent posture and spoke in quiet tones. One of the men was in a corner doing the splits with his ankles raised up on stacks of phone books.

Everyone looked up as Felicity entered the room. There was a moment of appalled silence, and then a wave of laughter and hooting filled the kitchen. She ducked her head, blushing under her grime.

"Clements, you look fab!" one of the women called. "Are you coming from a date or going to one?" Grinning, Felicity raised a brisk two fingers in reply.

"You'll never make it to the Barghests if you show up to work looking like that," a large man tsked.

"Jennings, don't be hard on Fliss," said one of the men, "just 'cause she looks like she raided your wardrobe."

"Ah, he's just doing his best to flirt," said Felicity. "After all, this"—and she gestured at herself—"ticks all his fantasy boxes, doesn't it? We all know he's into that hobo porn." She paused as a short redheaded woman came over and stood in front of her.

"Pawn Clements, I note no difference in your appearance or smell from that of any other day," said the woman flatly.

"Nice one, Cordingley, that was an amusing remark," said Felicity. The woman nodded. She's been working on her humor, Felicity thought fondly. Someone pressed a cup of tea into her hands, and the team members continued to chaff her and one another as she moved into the room.

It was all comfortingly familiar. She knew these people as well as she knew herself—better, really. She'd been working with them for two years now, since she'd graduated from combat training, all innocent-eyed and nervous-shouldered and hesitant-voiced. They'd helped her gestate into a real soldier. Pawn Gardiner had held Felicity's hand while she pulled herself together after shooting her first eel-man hybrid, and she in turn had held Pawn Moore's head and left foot while he pulled himself together after confronting a man made out of scythes. With them, she had battled bunyips in the Barbican, hunted horrors on Hampstead Heath, been air-dropped into Acton, sloshed through the sewers under Soho, and served as sentry at Sandringham House.

They had all seen one another at their best and their worst. She'd seen them covered in spilled blood (mainly other people's) and spilled beer (mainly their own), and she'd stood as honor guard at Barnaby's wedding and as godmother to Jennings's daughter. They weren't just colleagues; they were her brothers and sisters in arms.

Odgers entered the room and the noise died away as everyone stood to attention. The chief was followed by someone Felicity did not know, a tall, strapping Indian man about her own age or perhaps a year or two younger. He looked vaguely familiar. I suppose I might have seen him at the Estate, she mused.

"Welcome back, Clements. Was your reconnaissance successful?"

"For the most part," said Felicity.

"That sounds half promising," said Odgers. "Oh, before you report, this is Pawn Chopra." She gestured to the Indian man.

He's rather more-ish, thought Felicity appreciatively.

"Sanjay," he said, stepping forward. Felicity shook his hand. Although he had long eyelashes and smooth elegant features, his grip was strong and his hands had a fighter's calluses on them.

"Chopra's been added to the team as of today," said Odgers. "This is his first mission; he's just graduated from combat training. Now, Clements, what did you find?"

"I went through the whole place, and of course there's the bad news, but there's also actually some good news. It turns out that we don't need to worry about witnesses, at least not inside. The whole row has been completely stripped. There's no furniture, no carpets, no lighting fixtures, no people in any of the houses."

"This is not license for us to cut loose with guns and gifts," said Odgers severely, and there were some disappointed noises from the team. "Not unless it's appropriate. Clements, the inevitable bad news?"

"Well, sir, the preliminary inevitable bad news is there have been some substantial modifications. Hallways have been blocked off, doorways have been cut between the houses, there's a few places where rough holes have been made through the floors and ceilings. It looks like something has created a little warren for itself in there." She moved over to the maps on the walls. "There's only one entrance that hasn't been walled up. The whole thing is a labyrinth with booby traps scattered throughout. I found trip wires hooked up to boxes containing mechanisms and vials of chemicals that I didn't recognize." She quickly marked up the floor plans, showing where the changes had been made and the traps laid.

"Little boxes of stuff..." murmured Odgers. "Chopra, what does that suggest to you?" she asked suddenly in a schoolmarmish tone that perfectly matched her schoolmarmish face and figure.

"Um, well, it implies that the source of this malignancy is probably an actual entity rather than some sort of geographical phenomenon," said Chopra.

"So what is the source of these booby traps?" mused Odgers. She turned to Felicity. "What did you see?"

"That brings me to the final inevitable bad news," said Felicity. "At the heart of the row is something I couldn't see. It's approximately five meters by ten meters. One story high. I expect that's where the target is, along with the latest missing person. Maybe all of them."

"You can't see it? What does that mean?"

Felicity shrugged helplessly.

"I couldn't see it, and I couldn't see through it. You know there are a few things my abilities don't work on. Water. The wood of the cedar tree. Salmon. Air."

"You think it's a barrier made out of cedar?" said Odgers, frowning. "Or ice? Or salmon?"

"I don't know what it is," said Felicity. "It could be something new, something I've never encountered before."

"Fair enough," said Odgers, seemingly unperturbed by the prospect of an Oblong of Mystery. "So, you can take us through the warren?"

"Yes," said Felicity confidently.

"Right." The chief stared broodingly at the plans for several moments. "I don't like it," she said finally. "Even if you know your way through a maze, simply by entering, you put yourself in the power of the maze maker." She pursed her lips. "We need to break the maze." She looked over at one of the support staff. "Gilly, you trained as an architect, right?"

An intense conversation ensued. Various people drew on the plans and scribbled over one another's drawings. Teeth were sucked. A new nomenclature emerged: everyone began referring to the enemy as "the Homeowner," and the Oblong of Mystery became the OOM. Calls were placed to sundry Checquy experts to consult on the properties of certain building materials. Finally, a plan was agreed upon, with only two people no longer speaking to each other.

"Good," said Odgers. "I'll advise the Rookery of the situation and request permission to commence infiltration. I want everyone ready to depart in eight minutes."

"Is this a rescue job, sir?" asked Jennings.

"That depends on what we find," said Odgers grimly. "So move quickly, but move right." The team snapped into action, everyone knowing what his or her role was. The support staff had backed up against the walls, opening a space in the middle of the kitchen for the soldiers to work. The team members began donning their dense black armor.

Felicity shucked off her filthy clothes and tossed them into the plastic rubbish bags that one of the support staff held open. Pawn Chopra flushed and lowered his gaze at the sight of Felicity in her underwear, but the others didn't react, and Felicity told herself she wasn't concerned. When you've seen someone cry and vomit and shower and shit, and they've seen you do the same, you don't feel shy around them. There wasn't a single person on the assault team that she hadn't seen naked at one time or another, although never in a recreational setting.

Still, despite herself, she rather wished that the first impression Chopra had gotten of her didn't involve her in her extremely sensible undies, her face smeared with essence des excréments.

"All right, on with the school uniform," she said hurriedly. Across the room, one of her teammates put a boot against a plastic trunk with Felicity's name stenciled on it and sent it skidding across the floor to her. "Ta."

First was a bodysuit of thin stretchy material with a built-in sports bra. Then a set of the black coveralls. Felicity rubbed Vaseline over her feet before she pulled on some tactical-grade socks. She stepped into a pair of large boots and laced them up tightly. Then came the combat armor that had been cast for her when she graduated from the Estate. Dense plastic greaves, vambraces, and rerebraces that would protect her limbs. A breastplate, one that made no attempt to acknowledge her gender. She thoughtfully brushed her fingertips over the marks that scarred it. It was festooned with little chips and divots, and a splashy stain was etched into the surface.

"Gauntlets?" asked an attendant.

"Fingerless gloves," said Felicity, pulling them out of her trunk. "I need to be able to initiate immediate skin contact." It wasn't unusual for Checquy soldiers to modify their outfits according to their individual requirements. Two of the other soldiers were also gauntlet-less. Gardiner's armor was all white, while Jennings's appeared to be made out of highly polished mahogany. Cordingley was wearing no helmet. Barnaby had a spiked flail Velcroed to her thigh and she had undone some zips and slid the entire right sleeve of her coveralls off, revealing a small but muscular arm. Buchanan was wearing only the coveralls and a pair of light canvas trainers.

A helmet with a transparent faceplate was squashed down over Felicity's head, and she made a grim mental note to shampoo the helmet's interior after the assault. She shifted through a few stretches to make certain that everything was fitted correctly.

"Will you need night vision?" asked the attendant.

"Uh, probably, yeah," said Felicity. "There's no electrical power in there." He undid a couple of catches and slotted a new, bulkier face shield on. She knew that when she slid the visor down, she would be presented with a couple of little monitors.

A steel combat knife was sheathed on one thigh, a dense industrial-plastic blade on the other. Felicity holstered her nine-millimeter pistol on her hip.

Now all the team members were girded in their battle dress.

They were a study in deadliness. As Jennings cracked his neck from side to side, the air above him wavered hot and green. Gardiner's white armor suddenly shimmered like mother-of-pearl. Pawn Barnaby tested her flail, and it swung with a tearing sound that cut through the space. Sparks crawled briefly and crazily over Pawn Buchanan's coveralls. With a swirl of air, Pawn Cheng condensed herself and appeared in the group. The others' calm stillness simply hinted at their potential for supernatural violence.

The team stood ready for the call to action.

Which didn't come.

And didn't come.

And didn't come.

Finally, one of the support staff poked his head through the door into the next room, listened a moment, and then looked back. He shook his head and held his hand up to his ear in the universal sign for She's talking on the phone. He grimaced and waggled his other hand in the universal sign for Might be a while.

"For Christ's sake," said Jennings. "I suppose we'd better sit down while we're waiting for the order."

"Bloody bureaucracy," grumbled Buchanan, settling down on his kit case. "They get us out here in the colon of London, all suited up, and then we have to wait while someone in an office finds the backbone to make an actual decision."

"Maybe it won't take that long," said Chopra hopefully.

"Doubt it," said Barnaby. She took out a cigarette and nodded thanks to Jennings when its end erupted in a small green flame. "Keep in mind, today's the day that the Belgians are coming into the country. The entire Rookery is going to be running around, all atwitter. Everyone with any real authority will be taken up with the preparations."

"Yeah, I'd much rather be doing an actual mission than standing guard duty for the fucking Grafters," said Gardiner. There was a murmur of agreement.

The Grafters, thought Felicity, and she shuddered in her armor. Bloody hell. The Checquy faced monsters every day, but the Grafters held a special place of horror in their hearts and their memories.

Begun around 1474 as the Wetenschappelijk Broederschap van Natuurkundigen,* the Grafters were Belgian alchemists. Rather than following the traditional alchemical pursuit of failing to turn lead into gold, however, they had directed their attention to the mysteries of the mortal clay. Somehow, working in primitive conditions, they had gained radical insights into biological science, developing techniques that still remained far beyond modern medical understanding. With their knowledge and capabilities, they possessed the ability to twist and warp living flesh to suit their purposes.

Apparently, the Grafters' original purpose had been simple research, but then, in the seventeenth century, they'd turned their brains to military applications. On the orders of the government of the time, they created monstrous soldiers and then mounted an invasion of the Isle of Wight with an eye to conquering the rest of the British Isles. It had taken the full supernatural might of the Checquy, and the losses had been horrific, but finally the Grafters had been subdued.

The British had not allowed the matter to rest there. Instead, they pressed their advantage, mustered up the shattered remnants of the Checquy, and dispatched emissaries to deliver some fairly pointed and undiplomatic messages to the Continent. Faced with the unimaginable forces that the British could apparently bring to bear, the ruling government had briskly given in, and the Wetenschappelijk Broederschap van Natuurkundigen was dismantled.

The Checquy had never forgotten, though, and over the centuries the Grafters had remained something of a bogeyman to new recruits. This was no mean feat, given that many of the new recruits themselves could be considered eligible for the title of bogeyman. But every Pawn was brought up to loathe and fear the memory of the Grafters.

* Which could be translated as "the Scientific Brotherhood of Scientists" if your Dutch wasn't great and you weren't keen on making the Grafters sound good.

As a result, it had been a matter of significant outrage and consternation when, a few months ago, it was announced by the executives of the Checquy that the Grafters, far from being utterly destroyed and consigned to the secret-history books, had been operating clandestinely for the previous few centuries. Even more outrageous was that the Checquy would not be mustering its power to smash them into oblivion once and for all. Rather, the Grafters were going to become part of the Checquy Group, pledging their loyalty and service to the nation that had once been their worst enemy. It was to be a new era, one of collaboration and camaraderie.

"It'll never work," said Pawn Buchanan.

"The Checquy and the Grafters?" Barnaby snorted. "Course not. I'm betting that VIP cocktail do tonight will erupt in magma and blood before they bring out the first tray of canapés."

"But how can the Court believe the Grafters could ever be trusted?" wondered Buchanan. "How can they even think about giving them the benefit of the doubt?"

"Not our job to worry about it," said Felicity. "That's a problem for the wonks swanning around Apex House." And they're welcome to it, she thought with feeling. The world of policy and diplomacy held no attraction for her. Never had. Ever since she was a little girl, she'd wanted to be a soldier. Give me an enemy I can fight, not one I've got to smile at politely over dinner.

"Yeah?" said Moore. "Tomorrow the Grafters will be walking in the corridors of the Rookery and the Apex. Just you wait until they're adding some Flemish Frankenstein to our team. Then it'll be our turn to worry about it."

"It will never get that far," said Buchanan confidently. "The Grafters are the opposite of everything we are. They may be negotiating today, but within six months, our little team here will be part of an army taking a trip across to the Continent to do a bit of smiting and pick up some tax-free wine."

"Enough chitchat," said Gardiner firmly. "At the moment, you need to be thinking about the mission. After we've reduced this wee beastie to ashes, written up the report, and had a pint, then we'll have a team meeting and you can bother Pawn Odgers with your concerns." There was an exchange of looks and a little bit of eye-rolling, but they all were guiltily silent. Then the door to the other room banged open, and everyone jumped.

"All right, children, time to move out!" shouted Odgers as she swept into the room.

4

W e've got the order, so stir yourselves! Transport's out the back," Odgers barked.

The soldiers hurried out, leaving the support staff to tidy up. As they went through the door, they were each handed a short-barreled submachine gun by a waiting attendant. In front of them was what appeared to be a very unhealthy moving van. They all hustled up the ramp and sat on the benches that ran along the walls. Chopra sat next to Felicity. Odgers came in last, and the door was rolled down behind her. The truck began moving.

Time to get into character, Felicity told herself. She turned her attention to the gun in her hands and automatically checked that the safety was on. Then she ran her Sight through it, confirming that it was full of bullets and that all the components were in good shape. Part of her training at the Estate had involved the laborious memorization of the specifications for (among other things) several dozen kinds of guns. "What good is it if you look at something and don't know what you're seeing?" one of her instructors had said reasonably when she'd balked at learning the structure of an internal combustion engine.

Around her, the rest of the team was getting ready. Chopra was breathing the slow, deep breaths of someone who was doing his utter best not to get unprofessionally excited. His armor caught her eye. The same basic model as Felicity's own, but much glossier; aside from a couple of scuffs, it had no real damage.

Not yet, anyway, thought Felicity. Maybe today it'll get some scars.

Felicity herself was beginning to feel the familiar creeping of nerves and excitement spreading out from her stomach. Still, the memory of that strange void at the end of the maze left her feeling uneasy. Focus, she told herself. Calm.

"Barnaby will open the door," said Odgers, "and I'll enter first." Felicity noticed Chopra looking skeptically at the older woman in her ill-fitting armor even as she laid out the strategy for them. She couldn't blame him. In the Checquy, they were taught not to judge by appearances, but with her multiple chins wobbling heavily, Pawn Odgers was not a sight to inspire confidence in a combat setting.

"Remember," continued Odgers, "we have to assume that the Homeowner will be aware of us as soon as we enter. So we move quickly." Felicity, who had the best knowledge of the layout, would lead the way, accompanied by Barnaby and by Cheng in her gaseous form. The rest of the troops would follow closely, ready to kill anything that appeared to be a threat.

"So if something eats Barnaby and me, at least it won't have time to digest us," Felicity remarked.

"Exactly," said Odgers.

"One minute, Pawn Odgers," the driver called back.

"Right," said the leader. "Children, be prepped." Beside Felicity, Pawn Susie Cordingley began quietly singing scales, limbering up her voice. The hairs on the back of Felicity's neck trembled as her comrade emitted tones that she couldn't hear but that she felt. To Felicity's surprise, Cordingley's voice caused her lip balm to evaporate off her mouth—she could actually see the mist curling away from her lips.

"My apologies, Pawn Clements," said Cordingley. "Are you using a new brand?"

"Yeah, but don't worry about it," she said sourly. On the other side of her, Jennings held his hands up as if he were carrying an invisible basketball. To Felicity's eyes, nothing actually happened, but Jennings nodded in satisfaction. Meanwhile, the other troops were checking their guns or their armor.

The truck stopped with a jolt, turned, and began backing up.

All right, here we go, thought Felicity. She looked to the back of the van, where Pawn Odgers had stood up. Felicity watched as the lead Pawn took off her glasses, lifted the chain over her head, and stowed them away in a case. She undid her bun and let her thin, graying hair hang free.

Then, as the team watched in fascination, the woman began to un-age. The first thing that caught Felicity's eye, as always, was the Pawn's hair. It suddenly grew thick and lustrous, and a startling auburn shimmered through it. The length altered, growing alternately longer and shorter, so that at one point it hung to her waist, and then it was snapping up to her ears. Odgers stood straighter and taller, her shoulders broadening. The uniform slid into place on her body as her stomach shrank and her biceps swelled. Her weathered complexion paled, the tan swirling away like clouds, and the skin on her neck and cheekbones grew tauter. Within moments, she stood before the team as an Amazon with a crew cut. She looked quite capable of seducing a movie star and then beating him to a bleeding pulp.

"Whoa," said Chopra under his breath.

"You should see her when she's eighteen," said Felicity.

"Okay, I've got forty-one minutes like this," said Odgers, "so let's get moving." The back door of the van was hauled up, revealing a ramp that led to the front door of the house. The driver of the van had erected a sort of canvas tunnel over the ramp to conceal the assault team from the prying eyes and mobile phones of any passersby.

In an effort not to alert the Homeowner, they had selected a door on the very end of the abandoned row. Felicity had informed them that, as with all but one of the front doors, a thick barricade had been erected behind the entrance, but they did not anticipate that being a problem.

"Clements, confirm there are no new alarms or traps on the door."

Felicity nodded and trotted down the gangplank to rest her palm on it.

"Clear."

"Barnaby, go," said Odgers. The petite Pawn stood up and marched down the ramp with her right hand out. Felicity hastily got out of the way as her teammate walked implacably forward. She did not stop, and her arm did not bend when it hit the door. Instead, the wood glistened and turned murkily transparent. She continued pushing her arm through, and the door and the bricks behind it tore in shreds and slopped down. Under her touch, the material had become gelatinous. Barnaby took a moment to wrench the trembling remnants of the jelly away. Dust drifted in from the opening. Beyond was darkness and the smell of long-abandoned rooms.

"Fix night vision," said Odgers, and all of them hastily flicked down their visors. The front hall opened up before them out of the murk, painted in shades of green and gray. Once you could actually see it, the place did not make any better an impression. "And move." They hurried up the staircase in front of them and clustered on the landing. The modifications to the row houses meant that they'd actually entered an area that was completely walled off from the labyrinth, but it brought them on level with the OOM.

"Barnaby, this is the wall," said Felicity. She held her breath as her colleague placed both hands on the bricks and tore a hole large enough for the biggest person on the team to scuttle through. It was the party wall connecting this house with the one next door, and all the experts had agreed that it was load-bearing. They had not all agreed, however, on whether transmuting some of the bricks into collagen would bring the whole thing crashing down. Apparently, it was not the sort of problem that was regularly addressed in engineering school.

Fortunately, Barnaby's control was precise enough that jellification did not spread out farther than she wanted it to. The wall did not come tumbling down, although there was some alarming creaking.

And thus they proceeded. Odgers had decided that they would cut directly through the maze with Barnaby slicing through any inconvenient walls that blocked their way. They moved as quietly and as quickly as possible.

As they cut across one hallway, Felicity pointed out a booby trap a few meters away. On Odgers's orders, they paused as Felicity sent her Sight along the floor and up into the interior of the device. Although it was connected to a simple trip wire that crossed the hallway at knee height, the interior was fiendishly complicated, with a multitude of little cogwheels nested around four bulbous, dense vials of mysterious fluid.

"Can you disarm it?" asked Odgers after Felicity had reeled her mind back into her brain.

"I don't know," said Felicity. "But I don't want to suddenly find out that I can't."

"That's fine, we'll just ignore it, then."

A few times, they found signs of those who had gone before: a torn piece of cloth on a jag, some footprints made by bare feet blurred in the dirt and dust. There were also many signs of the Homeowner's presence: Barricades that blocked off certain hallways. Crudely bricked-up doorways. And two more traps, both of them consisting of wires connected to those boxes. Felicity felt a certain amount of satisfaction that they were exactly where she'd remembered them, and Odgers gave her a nod of approval.

"Sir, it's around this corner, at the end of the hallway," said Felicity.

Odgers nodded and then addressed thin air. "Pawn Cheng, check it out and report back." There was, of course, no answer at all, but Odgers seemed satisfied.

"Did—did Pawn Cheng hear her?" Chopra asked Felicity in low tones. "Is she doing it?"

"I've no idea," admitted Felicity. "It's one of the extremely irritating things about working with her. But if we don't hear back within five minutes, we'll come up with something else." As it happened, it took only two minutes before Cheng swirled out of the air.

"The OOM's there. It's just a flat surface," she said. "It fills the hallway, like a wall."

"Then let's go ahead," said Odgers. "Clements, you move back a little. I want Jennings and Gardiner at the front. Then regular formation."

When it came time for her to step around the corner, Felicity tensed, but the hallway was quiet except for the sounds of the Checquy troops. She squinted, looking past the two Pawns ahead of her. At the end of the corridor was a smooth blank.

The Oblong of Mystery, which her powers could not read and her Sight could not seep through.

I'm going to be very interested to see what this stuff is. Provided it doesn't kill me. The team drew near the surface. Although her visor painted it green, Felicity deduced that it was a mottled gray in color.

"Team, take up positions," said Odgers. The Pawns laid themselves out in formation, two of them at the back scanning the area behind them, the rest facing the thing ahead. "Cheng, examine." Felicity nodded slightly. Andrea, with her ability to effectively become invisible and intangible, usually served as the team's point man. She could evaporate away from any sudden danger.

Pawn Cheng emerged out of the air by the OOM. She was still dressed in her yoga outfit and boots, but she was now wearing latex gloves as well. As everyone watched breathlessly, Cheng reached out cautiously and touched it, then snatched her hand back.

Nothing happened.

She pressed her hand against it, looked at the team, and shrugged.

Odgers gave the hold signal and then proceeded to the wall. Tilting her head in thought, she drew her knife and poked gingerly at the surface. It gave a little, and she poked a bit harder. She drew her knife back and examined it.

"Blood," she said. "It's...alive."

"How bizarre," Felicity said. "So that's why my Sight slid off it." To Chopra's questioning look, she explained, "My powers can't penetrate living things…and this creature actually fills two rooms, completely."

"Gardiner, Cordingley, keep your positions and alert me if it does anything. The rest of you, fall back around the corner," said Odgers. They retreated cautiously, unwilling to turn their backs on the unnerving surface. Even once they were out of sight of the thing, they kept their guns at the ready.

"This is a bit big for us. I want some advice from someone who makes more than I do," said Odgers. She stepped away from the group and put her hand to her earpiece. "O'Rourke, this is Odgers. I'm going to need a direct line to the ops center at the Rookery."

"What's happening, Jennings?" asked Barnaby quietly.

"Well, apparently it's a big fucking monster that's eaten some people, i'n'it?" said Jennings. "If we're going to kill it, we'll need some backup and preparation."

"You know, that thing doesn't look like it's doing anything," said Chopra. "Maybe it's asleep?"

"Until the chief poked it with a knife," muttered Barnaby.

"So, do we think that whole oblong thing is the Homeowner, then?" asked Buchanan.

"Well, I don't think it's part of the original decor," said Jennings. "But it doesn't look like it can go out and fetch the victims. It wouldn't fit through the door."

"Maybe it just summons people?" suggested Felicity.

"Maybe the Homeowner feeds these people to it?" suggested Pawn Chopra.

"I don't see a mouth," said Jennings. "But that doesn't mean anything. Pawn Rutledge at the Annexe doesn't have a mouth most of the time."

"I can't see this thing laying down traps and motion detectors," said Felicity.

Odgers tilted her head as she listened to voices coming down her earpiece, and then she rejoined the group. "Okay, well, they want to send a science team to examine it. We'll be escorting them when they arrive."

"So, what now?" asked Chopra.

"We've found it, and it doesn't appear to be doing anything interesting. I don't think shooting it is going to help much, especially since we don't even know where its head is. So we'll just fall back, nice and quiet and careful, and then once we're out, we'll secure the street." The team was arranging itself to retreat when Cordingley held up a hand.

"Do you hear that?" she asked. They all held their breath and listened carefully. Nobody heard anything. "It's coming from inside the OOM."

"What do you hear?" asked Odgers. "Stomach rumblings?"

Or screams, thought Felicity, although she didn't say it. Everyone was tense again, guns once more at the ready.

"It's music," said Cordingley.

"Music?" repeated Odgers. "What kind of music?"

"Instrumental," said the singing Pawn. "Like orchestral. I don't know the composer."

"We'll have to check it," said Odgers. Once again, the team moved around the corner and drew a little closer to the OOM. The flat pale surface did not appear any different.

Well, I'm not putting my ear against that thing, Felicity thought firmly. She watched with interest as Odgers tried to think through the implications of the music. Then Felicity saw the wall of the OOM shiver.

"It's moving!" she shouted. Six guns and three hands were immediately pointed at the surface. Out of the corner of her eye, Felicity saw Cordingley open her mouth and take a deep, controlled breath.

"Move back!" yelled Odgers. "Jennings, if something comes at us, torch it! Barnaby, on my word, you make us an exit."

As they backed away, lines appeared on the object's surface, marking out a large X. They grew broad, and Felicity realized they were actually seams in the flesh. Where they met, the corners began to curl out, and from the chinks, light poured into the hallway, flaring in their night vision. Wincing, her eyes burning, Felicity hastily flipped up the visor.

She squinted as the triangles hinged open, like the valves of a heart. Light and music filled the corridor. It was not clear whether this development warranted a retreat. Felicity kept her gun trained on the opening and waited for her orders.

Oh, that music is Bruckner, she thought absently. Symphony no. 8. She resisted the urge to point this out to Cordingley, as it didn't seem like the best time. The Pawns were braced for something disastrous to happen, but instead, the music grew quieter, and an amused-sounding voice emerged from the opening.

"Please come in, we should talk."

The Pawns looked at one another and then at Odgers. Odgers looked at her watch and then at the opening. You've got to be kidding me, thought Felicity. This seemed like the easiest decision in the world to make.

"If you come in," said the voice, "then we can talk about this lovely young lady who wandered in a few hours ago. Perhaps we could work out some sort of deal. Before things get too messy." Everyone looked to Odgers again. She had her hand to her ear, was talking quietly into her mic. She shook her head at what she heard and then straightened her shoulders.

"Chopra, Clements, Jennings," said Odgers. "We're going in."

"Are you insane?" asked Felicity incredulously. Everyone looked at her. "I'm sorry, sir, but it's a living creature and it just invited you into its mouth!"

"There is a civilian in there," said Odgers. "A British civilian. And there is the possibility that we can save her life." Felicity looked down, ashamed. "Plus, we need more intelligence."

Well, on that we can agree, thought Felicity.

"So, yes," Odgers said firmly, "we are going in. We are the troops of the Checquy, we are trained, we have supernatural powers, and we have big fucking guns. This is what we do." The team nodded obediently. In hushed tones, she gave instructions to the Pawns who were to remain outside, outlining the circumstances under which they should act as backup and the circumstances under which they should get their arses the hell out of there and report everything they'd seen to the Rooks.

"And only the Rooks," she said firmly.

"Understood," said Gardiner uncertainly.

"Be sure to follow the route we took exactly," said Felicity. "Remember the traps." He nodded.

Meanwhile, Odgers was eyeing the valve-door-thing grimly. "That entrance is terrible," she said. "Irregular doors and hatches are always a bitch—you see how it tapers down at the bottom? It means only one person through at a time, and you all be careful, I don't want anyone tripping." She chewed her lip thoughtfully. "Clements and Chopra will enter first, in that order. Clements, you'll slide along the wall to the right; Chopra will take the left. Clear your corners immediately. Then me. Jennings, you don't enter until called."

Felicity nodded slightly at this. Jennings was the team's heaviest hitter—if necessary, he'd be able to clear the room completely, but he had a tendency to simply unload everything he had.

"Understood?" They all nodded. "All right!" Odgers shouted toward the opening. "We're coming in!" She muttered something to herself, but Felicity couldn't make it out. And then Odgers led the three of them down the hallway.

As they drew nearer, Felicity saw that a thin translucent membrane was draped down the inside. It retracted up silently, clenching itself in bunches.

"Go," said Odgers, and Felicity stepped through.

Her eyes swept quickly across the room: clean, white, with metal benches against the sides and empty in the middle. She turned to the right and moved along the wall as Chopra came in behind her and covered the left half of the room.

"First corner clear!" Felicity shouted. Then: "I have a target!" In the far right corner of the room was a man, a white figure, his back to her. For a moment, he'd blended in with the white walls and floor. "You! Hands in the air! Hands in the air!"

"Jennings, enter!" barked Pawn Odgers as she moved next to Felicity. Both had their guns pointed at the man's back.

Jennings came in and there was a pause as it sank in that the man was naked and urinating into a metal rubbish bin. He did not seem even slightly discommoded by the armed soldiers shouting in the room.

"You! Hands on your head!" shouted Odgers. "Go down on your knees and cross your feet over each other!"

"Do you mind if I finish here?" said the man languidly, without turning around. "I have some important business to hand." Felicity frowned, trying to identify his accent.

"Finish," said Odgers calmly. "If anything unexpected happens, I will shoot you in the spine. Chopra, Jennings, keep the room covered. Clements, can you scan this place?"

Felicity turned to take all of it in. The first thing that struck her was how clean everything was. She'd expected, well, the inside of an animal. Flesh pulsating. Liquid dripping. Maybe some huge organs, or bones supporting everything. At least a smell of some sort.

Instead, she was in a large white chamber whose smooth rubbery walls curved to meet the ceiling and the floor. The lack of edges actually left her feeling a little dizzy, and the effect was compounded by the fact that light glowed gently from the entire inner surface. On the metal benches that lined the sides were several closed metal suitcases. The music was coming, so far as she could tell, from the walls and ceiling, although it had gotten much quieter as they'd entered.

After the derelict grubbiness of the row houses, the bright antiseptic nature of this place was disorienting. To the left of them another membrane hung down, obscuring the area beyond. Chopra and Jennings had it covered.

She crouched down and put her hand on the glowing floor. Odgers darted a look at her, and Felicity shook her head. As she had suspected, she could not read it at all. It's all alive.

"You! Pissing guy!" snapped Odgers. "What's behind the curtains?"

"The living room," said the man drily.

"Is there anyone in there? Anything I need to be worried about?"

"No."

"Jennings, that curtain makes me uncomfortable," said Odgers. "We'll be going there next, and if anything comes out, you smite it."

"Yes, sir." Jennings slung his weapon over his shoulder, lifted his arm toward the membranes, and flexed his fingers wide.

Felicity kept her gun and her eyes firmly pointed at the man. Unfortunately, that meant that she got a good look at his backside. It was hairless, but then, so was the rest of him. Or at least, the parts that she could see. There was no hair on his scalp, but there was a set of curious bony ridges ringing his head. His skin was paper white and shone like glazed porcelain. As she peered closer, she saw that he was actually covered in tiny, perfect, polished scales. He was tall and slim.

The man finished and took his foot off the pedal of the rubbish bin, sending the lid down with a clang. To Felicity's consternation, he then turned around. He didn't look over his shoulder, and he didn't cover himself up. Despite herself, she looked at his penis.

Okay, that's... unorthodox.

Instead of any form of genitalia with which Felicity was acquainted, the white man's groin sported a smooth skin of those tiny white scales that shivered and locked together seamlessly before her eyes.

The rest of him was similarly nonstandard. Like the back of him, the front of him did not have any hair. His skin glistened white in the light, and he was fairly muscular-looking. A ridge of scales rimmed his face, which looked normal and smooth apart from its pallor. Felicity guessed him to be in his late twenties.

The most eye-catching thing about him (apart from the weird nodules on his head, the odd quality of his skin, and his lack of such traditional accoutrements as clothing and genitals) was the large crimson splash of blood on his torso. There was also blood on his arms, from the middle of his forearms up to his elbows.

"Kneel," said Odgers. "Hands on head."

"Of course," he said as he knelt down smoothly. "I expect you are from the Checquy?" he asked, his accent seeming to skitter around the globe, as if he'd lifted pronunciations from multiple different languages.

He knows about the Checquy!

"We're from the government," said Odgers firmly, and the man smiled. He was not at all perturbed by the guns pointed at him. "Where is Melinda Goldstein?"

"Through there," said the man, jerking his head to the far side of the room, where the membrane hung down.

"Is she alive?"

"Ish."

Alive-ish, thought Felicity. Jesus.

"Fine," said Odgers grimly. "Now lie down with your face on the ground." The man nodded and cleared his throat.

"Skreeoh," he said.

"I beg your—" began Odgers, and then the music stopped and a horrendous shrieking sound began to rip forth all around them. It hammered through their heads. Automatically, Felicity began to hunch down, but—

"Keep him covered!" shouted Odgers.

"We're clear!" shouted Jennings. "It's coming from the walls!" Felicity saw the man tense his face, and then the floor beneath his feet and the ceiling directly above his head darkened, and the light was swiftly extinguished throughout the entire chamber. She caught a glimpse of him beginning to move just before the place was completely shrouded in darkness.

"He's bolting!" she shouted.

"Shoot him!" barked Odgers, and the two women opened fire at the corner the Homeowner had been kneeling in. The rest of them held their positions as the muzzle flashes lit up the room for a moment. The screaming noise of the walls mercifully cut off with a tortured squeal, leaving everyone's ears ringing.

The strobing of the gunfire left afterimages glowing in Felicity's eyes against the darkness, and she hurriedly slapped her visor down over her face.

The room had apparently not taken well to getting peppered with bullets; the screaming had ceased, but a cloud of acrid black smoke was swirling through the space, along with the smell of burned hamburgers. Felicity could just make out that the corner of the chamber had been somewhat shredded, and the thick walls were oozing a viscous liquid. The rubbish bin of urine had been knocked over, with vile results. There was not, however, any sign of a white naked man or a white naked corpse. There weren't even any white naked fragments.

"I don't see him!" she shouted. "Scan the room!" She peered around, gun raised, and saw that the others had flipped down their visors too. The valve-door had closed itself tightly; not even a trace of the seams remained.

Then Felicity saw that Pawn Odgers was lying on the ground, her throat cut.

"Oh no," she breathed.

"Clements, Chopra, flank me!" ordered Jennings. His tone cut through her horror, and she nodded obediently. The two of them moved to either side of the Pawn, trying to cover every direction the enemy might come from.

"No radio contact with the team," said Chopra grimly. "The door is shut."

"No sign of the target?" Felicity asked.

"Maybe he escaped out the door?" wondered Chopra. "And then shut it behind him?" They looked around, peering through the smoke, and saw no trace of their quarry. The chamber was silent, apart from the dripping of the wounds in the wall.

"Or he went into the other part of the room," suggested Felicity quietly. "That bit behind those membranes, where he said the civilian was."

"We'll take it," said Jennings. "Burst through and secure the area. Standard trident assault pattern. If that sneaky fuck's there, we kill him. Don't hold back. Ready on three?" They nodded.

"One."

Felicity's hands tightened on her gun.

"Two."

She took a deep breath.

"Thr—"

There was a swirling in the smoke, and the unexpected figure of Pawn Cheng manifested just in front of Felicity.

"God, Andrea! Don't do that!" Felicity gasped. That must have been what Odgers was muttering before, she thought. Ordering Cheng to accompany us. "I almost shot you." Pawn Cheng, who had opened her mouth to say something, paused and gave her an incredulously pitying look. Then she shook her head and got straight to the point.

"He's on the ceiling!" the Asian Pawn shouted before evaporating away. As one, all of them looked up and saw the man crouched above them. Then Felicity's visor flared blindingly as a horrendous torrent of green flames surged up out of Pawn Jennings's open hands. The fire roared as it engulfed the ceiling, and the entire cube squealed and shuddered.

Felicity ducked down automatically, away from the flames, and tore her helmet off. The heat was tremendous, and sweat was bursting out of her skin. She squinted and saw that Jennings had both his arms raised and his head thrown back. A deluge of emerald fire flowed out of his skin, even gushing up from his face and neck to spread across the ceiling. Felicity tried to shield her eyes from the glare. Beyond him, Chopra was also crouching away from the inferno.

"Jennings, stop!" screamed Felicity. "Or we'll all be killed!"

"I couldn't agree more," said a voice in her ear. She jerked away and saw the naked man was now crouching by her. He scuttled forward, moving swiftly even though he was bent double. She caught a flash of a white blade in his hands, and then he was standing behind Jennings. He swung and in one movement sliced through both the Pawn's forearms.

Jennings's hands, and a good portion of his lower arms, spiraled away, green fire still spurting from them in little bursts.

Felicity squeaked as sparks hissed in her sweaty hair, and then she fell back on her bottom when one of the hands landed right in front of her. The fingers clenched spasmodically, and small flames danced for a moment on the fingertips before dying away.

The conflagration on the ceiling did not die, but it was no longer being fed by the Pawn's will. The deafening roar faded, and there was only the sound of cracklings and Jennings's labored, gulping breaths. Felicity looked up, dreading what she might see. Her comrade was staring, wide-eyed, at his newly curtailed limbs.

Then he began to scream, and blood sprayed out of his wounds and across the room, igniting in the air into liquid green fire. She flung up her arms to protect her face and felt burning drops patter across her armor. When she brought her arms down, she saw that flames were pouring out of Jennings's forearms and flowing onto the floor. They were spreading out swiftly, like pools of water. Felicity and Chopra hastily scrabbled backward, away from each other. The naked man vaulted back too, up and onto one of the metal benches, and leaned against the wall. The flames were reflected in his strange, glazed-porcelain skin.

"That really ought to have worked," said the man to himself, looking a little crestfallen.

"What are you?" Felicity spat. He didn't even bother to look at her, just surveyed the scene with a mildly displeased expression. The flames did not seem to be exhausting themselves; they were climbing higher and spreading across the floor. The place had become an inferno. She looked around wildly for some way out.

The ceiling was still ablaze, and the smell of cooking meat had given way to an acrid black smoke. Peering through the smoke as best she could, Felicity could see that part of the flesh had been completely burned through, and now the structure of the house was ablaze. The wall with the valve-door was covered in those lapping green tongues of fire, and the flesh seemed to have melted.

We're not going to get out of this, she realized. The flames were climbing the walls. Jennings fell to his knees, and though his clothes began to smolder, the fire did not touch his skin or hair. His screaming tapered off, and now he made a weak, moaning sound that was almost lost in the crackling of the flames.

What do I do? Should—should I shoot him? wondered Felicity. It was far too late to stop the fire, but it might be a mercy of sorts for her comrade. The pool of fire had almost reached her feet. The heat was unbelievable; it burned in her lungs, and her armor seemed impossibly heavy.

The metal of her gun scorched her fingers, and her control over her Sight splintered for a moment. Sensation and memory washed into her mind, and, despite herself, she briefly saw the gun's inner workings.

And then she saw movement out of the corner of her eye, and Chopra was dashing in her direction from the far side of the room. He ran through the fire, past Jennings, and she could see that his clothes were alight. Flames splashed around his boots, and he was yelling from pain and determination.

Chopra flung himself the last few meters toward her. He reached out his hand and she automatically grasped it. Even though he was aflame, she pulled him closer. She knew that her own clothes and hair were catching fire, but she wouldn't let go. She did not want to die like this. Not alone.

"I'm right here," she whispered. "I've got you."

"It'll be all right," said Chopra into her ear.

Around them, burning fat and flesh fell like glowing rain. Chopra's arms tightened and the room wavered before her. Darkness rose up on the edges of her sight, and she felt her knees buckling.

The last thing she saw was Jennings slumped in the middle of the fire. His armor and shirt had burned away while his skin remained untouched. Flickering green light still poured out of his wounds. I'm so, so sorry, Richard.

The last thing she heard was the naked man musing to himself, "If I were to cut his head off, would that make things better or worse?"

And then the darkness took her.

5

Once upon a time there was a little girl who lived a nice normal life. She liked to read and she liked to run and she liked stories about monsters. Her parents, who were university professors, were sometimes away doing research or giving lectures, but she was never lonely because she was part of a big family, with cousins and uncles and aunts and cousins once removed and great-uncles and great-aunts and cousins twice removed and great-great-uncles and great-great-aunts and a grandfather with so many greats that she lost track of them, and so she just called him Grootvader, which is Dutch for "Grandfather."

And she was very happy.

Then, one day, Grootvader sat her down in the garden and explained that their family was not like other families. There were members of the family who were very, very clever, and knew all sorts of secrets, and made all sorts of discoveries, and created beautiful things. And because she was a member of the family, and a clever girl, she could, if she wanted, learn all the secrets, and make her own discoveries, and see and do and think things that no regular person ever would.

If she wanted.

It wouldn't be easy, he warned her. She would have to study hard, very hard, and sometimes what she learned might be scary. And he would not love her any less if she decided that she didn't want to do this. Her father had decided he did not want to learn the secrets, and instead he had learned all about fossils and married her mother, and he was perfectly happy.

And if she decided that it was what she wanted, she would never be able to tell any outsiders about her studies or her discoveries or the family, because there were bad people in the world who would try to steal their knowledge, or take advantage of them, or make them into slaves.

And if she decided that it was what she wanted, she would make enemies. There were monsters, real ones, that hated the family. The monsters had once tried to destroy the family utterly, and it was only by living in secret that the family could survive.

And finally, if she decided that it was what she wanted, they would have to cut her open and make some changes inside her. And it wouldn't hurt, or at least not very much, but it might be frightening.

And she decided, after a bit of thought, that it was what she wanted.

Twelve years later, the wisdom of that decision seemed somewhat questionable.

I could literally be incinerated and devoured at this cocktail party, Odette thought. It could actually happen. I could get torn to pieces or turned into a starfish or smeared across the ceiling. All it would take is one of these Checquy monsters to have a little too much to drink and start thinking about how much he hates the Grafters, and I'm suddenly an echinoderm.

There was a definite tension in the air as the party of Grafters emerged from the lift and looked around warily. The designer of the hotel had apparently liked the idea of people making an entrance via a staircase, because even though the elevator had just lifted them to the top floor of the building, they were looking down to the skyline bar on the twenty-eighth floor.

It was a sophisticated space, with dark polished wood and elegant antique mirrors. At the far end, a massive curtain of glass looked out onto the city. It was an ideal place for the young and wealthy to stand around and eye one another over kumquatinis. Currently, however, it was closed to the public, and the patrons consisted entirely of Checquy executives.

Some rather reluctant applause floated up the stairs once the Checquy noticed the arrival of the Grafters. This is so awkward, thought Odette. We're having drinks with the very monsters that Grootvader warned me about. She could almost smell the hate radiating through the room. The new arrivals made their way down the stairs with all eyes upon them. When she reached the bottom, however, rather than following the rest of her delegation into the fray, Odette edged around the gathering until she reached the window. If I just stand here with my back to everything and look like I'm admiring the view, no one will bother me, she thought.

Although her plan had been to pretend to marvel at the panorama, she found herself actually marveling at the panorama. The city spread before her to the horizon. I cannot believe I am in England, she thought. In London. I never in my life thought I would be in this country, in this city. It just wasn't possible.

She gazed at the skyline, at buildings she'd only ever seen in films or books. There was the London Eye. There was the jag of the Shard glittering in the last of the light. That top-heavy building whose nickname she couldn't recall. The Cheesegrater. The gigantic Fabergé egg that they called the Gherkin. The BT Tower. Her eyes tracked back across the landscape, cutting through the dusk, picking out the dome of St. Paul's. Big Ben. Westminster Abbey. And hundreds and hundreds of rooftops.

Amazing.

Then her focus shifted so that she was not looking through the glass but rather examining the reflections. In the foreground, of course, was herself, an image she regarded without any particular enthusiasm. Her dress bugged her. It was not a cocktail dress. An uncharitable (but accurate) observer would have described it as more of a cocktail shroud.

It was certainly not a dress Odette would have picked under normal circumstances, but it was politic. It hid her scars. Unfortunately, that meant covering most of her. As a result, she gave the impression of being someone's disapproving maiden aunt.

Behind her reflection was the movement of the cocktail party. She studied the guests critically. Men in suits and women in nicer dresses than hers. Some of the women wore business suits, but even those were exquisitely cut and tailored. Waiters passed through the party carrying trays of drinks and food. At first glance, it seemed quite a normal affair. But every once in a while, a shimmer of light would erupt from someone's head, or a figure would vanish abruptly, or a guest would turn and reveal a set of stegosaurus-type plates emerging from the back of a tailored suit. She shuddered.

And then, approaching her in the reflection, came a tall, handsome man.

"Odette," said a voice behind her. She felt a light hand on her shoulder and turned to look up into stern blue eyes.

This was Ernst, formerly the Duke of Suchtlen and the undisputed lord and master of the Wetenschappelijk Broederschap van Natuur-kundigen. His body, which looked only about five years older than Odette's, represented the most cutting-edge biotechnology on the planet. His mind held centuries of statecraft, espionage, and military insights. His hand held an hors d'oeuvre that had apparently suffered a catastrophic loss of structural integrity, leaving him awkwardly clutching the shattered remnants of a piece of toasted pita and some ground-up tuna and onions sprinkled with expensive herbs.

"A beautiful view," he said appreciatively, and for a moment they both looked out over the city. "I have waited centuries to look upon it." He turned to her. "I can see how you could lose yourself in the vista, but" — he paused, and she tensed, knowing what was coming — "you are not being polite to our hosts." She sighed. "Now, I realize you are nervous. I understand your concerns."

Odette looked at him. "You do?"

"Come, now, over the course of my centuries, I think I have come to comprehend the minds of women a little bit. This gathering is many things, serving many purposes, but it is, in the end, a party. And so you are worried about your dress and the thing with your hair."

"The thing with my hair? What's wrong with my hair?" asked Odette.

"But," he carried on blithely, "our hosts have organized this soiree as a way for us all to meet informally before tomorrow's work begins, and so it is important that we take this opportunity to be diplomatic."

Odette nodded reluctantly. "Yes, I understand," she said. "I've just been mustering up my enthusiasm and reviewing appropriate conversational topics."

"Very sensible," he said. "Are you ready, then?"

"Sure," she said. She briefly envied her little brother, who was still in their hotel suite, one floor down.

"I am not entirely certain what to do with this, though," he said, holding up the remains of the inadvertently deconstructed canapé. "There is no way to eat it with any sort of dignity, and this is my handshaking hand."

"Just dump it in that plant pot," suggested Odette, gesturing to a nearby palm.

"Excellent thinking." Graaf van Suchtlen looked around and then gingerly dropped the remnants into the pot. "Now, come. It is your duty to mingle." He offered her an arm, and she took it, allowing him to lead her to a little group of Checquy.

Just calm down, she told herself. These people may be monsters, but they're professionals and they're upper-class and British, so they'll be polite.

"Ladies, gentlemen," van Suchtlen said easily. "Allow me to present Odette Leliefeld." There was a chorus of greetings, and she smiled to each person as she was introduced. She was so nervous that she failed to remember any of their names. None of them were in the Court of the Checquy, and so she assumed they were simply high-ranking managers of the covert government organization.

They were certainly not your standard-issue humans, even if they were all dressed in expensive clothes. One of the men had a birthmark on his face that oozed around slowly, like the contents of a lava lamp. There was a woman who seemed to waver like the air over a hot highway. When one older man moved, light and color shifted briefly behind him, as if he were sporting a holographic peacock tail. Another man's breath steamed, even though the room was, according to Odette's skin, exactly 20 degrees centigrade.

You do not need to be afraid of them, Odette told herself. You are here under a truce. And while these people may have abilities that defy all the laws of physics, biology, common sense, and good taste, you are a scion of the Broederschap. You have training beyond any surgeon in the world. Your body is an exquisitely crafted tool. You have repaired limbs and delivered babies and saved lives. You have climbed to the top of the Eiffel Tower and touched the deepest bottom of the Mediterranean Sea and danced on the underside of the Bridge of Sighs. With an effort, she dragged herself back to the conversation.

"You two have the same eyes!" one of the women was saying. "Graaf van Suchtlen, is she your sister?"

"No," said Odette, smiling despite herself at the thought.

"Not your daughter, surely?" said the woman, looking uncertainly at the two of them.

"No," said Odette. "I'm his descendant." By, what, six generations?

"And my protégée," said Graaf van Suchtlen. Odette looked at him and kept her face deliberately blank.

"So, Miss Leliefeld is the first in line, then?" one of the Checquy men asked.

"No, there is no line," said the graaf matter-of-factly. The Checquy people exchanged confused glances.

"Grootvader—I'm sorry—Graaf van Suchtlen has no intention of dying," explained Odette. "Ever." She expected to see a raised eyebrow or two, but they nodded sagely.

"We have a Bishop like that," said one of the women. "In fact, he's right there. Bishop Alrich! Yoo-hoo!" Odette's stomach flipped over. Bishop Alrich. That was definitely a name she'd managed to remember.

Bishop Alrich wasn't a church bishop. The Court—the leaders of the Checquy Group—had a hierarchy based on chess pieces. It was ridiculous, probably one of those archaic British traditions that made no sense to anyone else. The two Rooks were responsible for domestic operations. The Chevaliers oversaw international affairs. At the top of the tree were the Lord and

Lady (they weren't called the King and Queen, as it would have made the real British monarchy a little antsy). And just below the Lord and Lady were the Bishops, who, from what Odette could gather, oversaw everything.

As a result, Bishop Alrich was incredibly important and powerful. But that wasn't why she felt a sudden bolt of dread go through her. It was because of what he was. If the reports were correct, then he was actually a vampire. A blood-drinking, apparently immortal entity who preyed on human beings.

And he's behind me.

Despite herself, she turned. Oh, she thought. Gosh.

The dossiers she'd read on him had not included photographs because the Bishop did not register on any photographic equipment, either digital or chemical. There had been a few sketches and a copy of a rather idealized watercolor painting, but they hadn't done him justice.

He stood tall, in a suit of exquisite cut. And he was striking, so striking, with features that might have been sculpted by Donatello and eyes that could have been painted by Blake. His hair poured vermilion down to his waist. Odette felt the blood rising in her cheeks. And then she wondered if he could sense it. When their eyes met, his expression was one of dry amusement.

"Bishop Alrich," said the woman. "You've met Graaf van Suchtlen, of course." The two men nodded to each other. "And this is Miss Odette Leliefeld." He took her hand, and his skin was warm. Suddenly she was simultaneously very glad and very regretful of her dress's dowdy high neck.

"Good evening, Miss Leliefeld," he said. "It's a pleasure to meet you."

"Thank you," she said, and the strength of her own voice took her aback. "I've heard a great deal about you, sir."

"Indeed?" he said.

There was a long pause, during which Odette flailed around in her mind for something to say. This is why I don't like going to parties.

"It's a lovely party," she said finally.

"Yes, and there have been no atrocities committed yet," remarked the Bishop, looking around.

"Oh, Bishop Alrich, you are bad," said one of the Checquy women fondly.

"It's not out of the question, Pawn Titchmarsh," said the vampire. "The last party I was at ended very badly. And didn't you once attend a dinner in Bhutan where everyone except you left having been rendered completely sterile?"

"And they all became allergic to rabbits," said the lady with some satisfaction. "But that was for work."

Isn't this evening also for work? thought Odette.

"And have you been enjoying your time here in London, Miss Leliefeld?" asked Alrich.

"We got here only this morning," said Odette, "so of course I haven't seen much. But the hospitality of the Checquy has been very..."—she hunted frantically for an adjective that wouldn't cause an international incident—"welcoming."

In point of fact, the hospitality had been almost smothering. It had still been dark when the delegation of sleepy Grafters stepped off the jet at Heathrow. They had been met by a group of extremely alert-looking people from the Checquy headed by the imposing Bishop Raushan Attariwala. He had greeted them cordially and escorted them through the bowels of the airport, bypassing customs and immigration. Odette had noticed that none of the hallways they'd passed through had any security cameras and that none of their escorts were carrying any obvious weapons.

Then they'd been ushered into large black cars with tinted windows and driven through a maze of service lanes and hangars. Gates were opened and wary security guards waved them through until they emerged on a service road that segued into a back road that segued into a street that segued into an actual highway. Despite her exhaustion, Odette had been glued to the window during the trip to the city. Her squeal at the sight of her first proper London cab woke Alessio.

And then there was the hotel, tall and grand, where they had been checked in and shown to their rooms. For all Odette knew, Graaf Ernst had attended meetings with the senior members of their delegation all day, but she and Alessio had been told to get some rest and not to leave the hotel. The cocktail party would be held at six thirty, and she was to attend the strategy meeting beforehand. Any time she or Alessio had opened the hotel room's door, those grim Checquy operatives were standing guard in the hallway, and so she'd elected to stay in the suite and have a long nap in the bathtub.

"Yes," said Odette. "They've taken very good care of us."

"Good to hear," said Alrich. "I hope you're looking forward to working with us."

"Oh, I hope so too," said Odette. It took her a couple of moments to realize that what she'd just said made no sense. Mercifully, he didn't comment, just smiled a little smile, bowed his head, and excused himself.

That didn't go too badly, she thought. She relaxed a little and watched as the vampire moved smoothly through the crowd. She couldn't help but appreciate the fact that his hair stopped strategically right at his waist.

"It's enough to make you wish he were an incubus, isn't it?" said an amused voice next to her. Odette turned and saw a short woman in her thirties. She was a rather unremarkable-looking person, but she was wearing an astounding cocktail dress of ebony cloth and leather. Judging from the unorthodox cut and fit, it had to have been made specifically for her. Indeed, it seemed to have been sculpted around her. Tight curves swept up her body to sharp points that spread just beyond her shoulders and elbows. She looked as if she were wrapped in elegant black flames. The sleeves were connected to the dress at the middle of the rib cage, which made for an arresting silhouette, although it was not terribly practical—the woman had trouble lifting her glass to her lips.

It was, in short, the dress to which Odette's own gown was the ugly stepsister who had taken vows of chastity and poverty.

Beyond the dress, though, there was something about the

woman that set her apart despite her plainness. She had an air of command, but she also gave the odd impression that she did not quite belong, even among the Checquy. Then Odette recognized her and felt genuine fear—even more than she had with the vampire.

Rook Myfanwy Thomas. My God.

Rook Thomas was the reason they were all there that evening. One night, months earlier, Graaf van Suchtlen had presented himself in her office in the Rookery, having strolled easily past every security measure in the place. He introduced himself to the Rook, his habitual courtly manner unhampered by the fact that he was completely naked, and then made the astonishing proposal that their organizations should put aside their centuries of enmity and join together.

Rather than responding as any other Checquy soldier would and doing her utmost to destroy the intruder, Thomas had offered him a cup of coffee and a bathrobe and listened to his proposal. Given the legendary hatred between the two organizations, it was an extraordinary reaction, but then, it was somewhat in keeping with Rook Thomas's apparently unpredictable nature. Odette had pored over the Grafters' dossiers on the woman and found herself utterly confused.

The records described an almost pathologically shy woman who, despite her timidity, had somehow risen to a high rank. But Thomas had overcome her shyness, as well as her inculcated loathing of the Grafters, to become the driving force of this merger. She had argued strenuously for peace and faced down the protestations of the highest in the land. If not for her, the Checquy and the Grafters would, at that very moment, have been at war.

From what Odette had read, Rook Thomas had traditionally been unwilling to use her powers, but then again, she had also recently single-handedly subdued not one but two biological weapons of mass destruction.

Thomas's unpredictability, however, was not the reason that Odette was afraid of her. Or at least, it was not the main reason. Alone among the Checquy, Rook Thomas possessed the supernatural ability to completely control other people's bodies. With a touch, she could turn a person's flesh and organs against him, bending them to her will. Odette was far too aware of her own organs to feel anything but revulsion at the idea. And the greater implications were even more frightening.

All our resources, she thought, everything that sets us apart from normal people. Centuries of knowledge, weaponry, augmentations—they would all be rendered completely useless with one caress by this woman. For all she knew, the Thomas woman could make the Grafters' implants tear themselves right out of their bodies.

"I won't ask you to shake hands," said the Rook drily. Evidently, Odette had not concealed her horror very effectively. The other woman's smile had gone from amused to wry, and she was not displaying any of her legendary shyness.

"Myfanwy!" boomed Graaf van Suchtlen from behind Odette.

"Ernst," said Thomas with a little archness to her voice. To Odette's astonishment, the Grafter lord leaned down to kiss the Rook's hand. "Good evening, I've just been making the acquaintance of your great-great-great-great-great-granddaughter."

"Ah, yes, we are very proud of young Odette," said the graaf, resting his hand heavily on Odette's shoulder. "I expect great things of her." Odette resisted the impulse to cringe.

"I'm sorry that I couldn't be at the airport to welcome you this morning," said the Rook. "Bishop Attariwala felt that it would be more appropriate for a higher-ranking and more important member of the Court to greet you."

"Is that how he put it?" asked Graaf van Suchtlen, raising an eyebrow.

"Pretty much," said Thomas blithely. "Apparently there's a long-standing awkwardness between the two of us." What an odd way to phrase it, thought Odette. An older woman appeared at Thomas's shoulder and spoke to her in low tones. The Rook made a face. "Please excuse me, Ernst, Miss Leliefeld. It seems that something absolutely horrible has happened, and it needs my attention." She moved away, accepting a mobile phone from the older woman and putting it to her ear.

"An intriguing woman," mused Graaf van Suchtlen. Before Odette could think of a response, the Rook returned and spoke quickly to her assistant.

"Any problems, Myfanwy?" the graaf inquired.

"Not with the party," said the Rook. "But word has just come to us through the London police that there's been an incident. Multiple civilian fatalities. The local constabulary have secured the site, but they've found some very unusual elements. Someone called their boss, who called their boss, who called my office. I've just authorized a team to go there and examine it."

"Do you have to go?" asked the graaf.

"It's not obligatory," said Thomas, "not at this level. But I think I will make an appearance. It turns out that the incident is just around the corner." She hesitated. "Would the two of you like to come along?" Odette looked at her ancestor in surprise. "Your perspectives might be useful."

"It would give Odette a good opportunity to see the Checquy in action," said van Suchtlen thoughtfully. "But would our leaving raise any eyebrows?"

"I shouldn't think so," said the Rook. "You've greeted every-one, and I'll inform my head of security if you inform yours." The two leaders separated to find their respective underlings, leaving Odette standing alone. Despite herself, she found the prospect rather exciting. Rook Thomas's invitation had an air of adventure about it. Not only would she be escaping the dire party, but they would be going out and actually doing some-thing important.

Unless, of course, this is some sort of ambush, a paranoid part of her brain suggested. They lead the head of the Grafters and the girl they think is his protégée away from the gathering, kill them, slaughter the rest of the party, and then have a celebratory drink. She firmly instructed that part of her brain to shut up, lifted a glass of orange juice from the tray of a passing waiter, and took a defiant swig. Seriously, you have got to calm down, she told herself.

"Miss Leliefeld?" It was the older woman who had brought the phone to Thomas. "I'm Ingrid Woodhouse, Rook Thomas's executive assistant."

"Hiya!" said Odette, still caught up in her determination to relax.

"Yes, hello," said the lady, mildly taken aback by her enthusiasm. "Um, the Rook advised me that you'd be coming to the site."

"Yes, apparently that's what I'm doing," said Odette.

"Marvelous. Come with me, please."

As they approached the lift, the doors opened to reveal Rook Thomas and Graaf van Suchtlen. Also inside was Odette's cousin Marie Lemaier, who was the head of security for the Grafter delegation, and a tall black man who Odette assumed was the Checquy chief of security. The two leaders were looking distinctly uncomfortable as their underlings engaged in some highly courteous but highly vigorous bickering.

"Pawn Clovis, what guarantees can you provide regarding the safety of Graaf van Suchtlen and Odette at this site?" Marie asked as Odette and Ingrid got on the lift. Her hair was auburn, shot through with streaks of black—a sure sign that she was getting irritated.

"None at all," replied Pawn Clovis calmly. "Of course, there will be a full team of Checquy investigators, all of whom have combat training and many of whom possess special abilities. There will be a small internal security team present, and local police are providing external security. Plus, Rook Thomas and, I gather, Graaf van Suchtlen both possess significant abilities of their own. But there are still no guarantees. Something killed those sixteen people, Miss Lemaier, something mysterious. A manifestation site is not a safe place. But then, this is not a safe business that you are entering into."

"We shall be fine, Marie," said Graaf van Suchtlen as the lift doors closed. Marie gave him a cool look, and, for the first time

Odette could remember, he seemed a bit nervous. Although she was only twenty-nine, Marie had a strength of will that the entire Broeder-schap respected and even feared. It was that strength of will, combined with her fierce devotion to her job, her talent for multitasking, and her ability to kick a man's head clean off his neck, that had led to her assignment with the delegation.

"If something happens to you, Graaf van Suchtlen, do you realize what sorts of questions I will be asked by my superior?" Marie inquired.

"I am your superior," the graaf pointed out.

"You're not the chief of security," said Marie dismissively.

"I'm his superior too," said the graaf, a trifle plaintively. Marie made a noise that suggested that, even if true, the fact had no bearing on the argument. The lift was silent for a moment. Odette was profoundly relieved when the doors opened on the lobby. They all stepped out, and van Suchtlen turned to Marie.

Before he could speak, she said loudly, "Fine. Go, then. Strive not to get killed. You've no idea how much it would inconvenience me!" She patted Odette absently on the shoulder—apparently Odette's death would not be an inconvenience worth mentioning—and moved back into the lift. Pawn Clovis joined her, looking slightly intimidated. The door shut on them.

6

It dawned on the group that all the occupants of the lobby— receptionists, civilian guests, bellmen, concierge—were staring at them. The four of them proceeded through, ignoring the wary looks of absolutely everyone.

"Ah, good, the car's already here," said Mrs. Woodhouse briskly.

They all regarded the car thoughtfully. It was not what any of them had expected. Not only was it minuscule, with only two doors, but it appeared to be quite unwell. The black paint was badly scuffed, and one of the doors was white with a cartoon rabbit wearing sunglasses and smoking a cigarette drawn on it in marker. The front bumper seemed to have been tied on with twine, and there were the peeling remnants of old bumper stickers on the back. The uniformed driver who got out looked as if he had been cut-and-pasted into the wrong vehicle.

"I don't mean to sound like a diva here, Ingrid," said the Rook finally, "but this is a very small car." Odette thought it was rather charitable of her to comment only on its size rather than its general insalubriousness. "And I know I was distracted on the way here, but I'm fairly certain this is not the car I arrived in."

"That's right, Rook Thomas."

"So...were we robbed?"

"No, but the deaths at the site have already caught the attention of the press. They're hanging around outside, so we'll have to go in the back. I thought a stretch limousine might draw some attention."

"I suppose that makes sense," said Thomas grudgingly. "Good thinking." She sighed and looked at the diminutive and disreputable vehicle. "Where did we even get this car? Whose is it?"

"Pawn Thistlethwaite's. He said we could borrow it."

"Pawn Thistlethwaite came in this?" asked the Rook. "That can't be right, I know what his salary is. Make a note, Ingrid, we should have him screened for drugs."

"It's his son's car," said the EA. "I gather his is at the mechanic's."

"Oh, all right, then." The driver opened the passenger door and triggered the little lever that was supposed to hinge the seat forward. The seat did not slide up automatically, and he had to struggle a little with it. The resulting aperture to the backseat was not encouraging, and the four of them looked at one another. The Rook sighed heavily. "I'm the shortest, so I suppose I had better go in the middle." She glanced down at her dress and bit her lip. "Ingrid, can you help me here?" The executive assistant stepped forward and gripped the points on Thomas's dress's shoulders to help her get into the car without crumpling the couture.

It took the Rook some undignified wriggling and a strategic shimmy, which elicited an appreciative whistle from a passing pedestrian (who promptly and mysteriously tripped over nothing at all), but she managed to slide awkwardly to the center of the backseat. "Well, come on!"

"Graaf van Suchtlen, you're the tallest, so you can take the front passenger seat," said Mrs. Woodhouse. The graaf offered his hand to help the older lady in, while Odette hurried around to the other side. As the driver opened the door for her and attempted to move the driver's seat forward, Odette noticed a young man across the street. He was looking on with amusement as the people in expensive clothes squeezed themselves into the dilapidated little car. He was a young man, about her age, and the sight of him made her breath catch in her chest.

Don't be ridiculous, it's not him. And yet she could not drag her eyes away from the boy. Maybe it was something about the way he stood, so casual and at ease. He was not worried about the supernatural. He was not worried about the intricacies of diplomacy and negotiations. He was not worried about anything but the pleasure of an evening in the city. And he was not her boy.

It will never be him, she told herself mercilessly. No boy will ever be Pim. Pim is gone. Forever.

"Miss?" the driver asked hesitantly.

And besides, that guy doesn't look anything like him. So just stop being silly.

With an effort, she tore her eyes away from the boy and everything he was and wasn't. She eased herself into the backseat, which seemed to be completely full of Rook, executive assistant, and other detritus.

The driver shut the door firmly, and Odette was crushed against the Rook. She felt her hip bones accordioning together. Matters were made worse when Graaf van Suchtlen began moving his seat back.

"Ernst, if you keep doing that, I will call off the whole merger," said the Rook tightly. Her feet were up on the hump of the transmission, and Mrs. Woodhouse's knees were already crushed against the back of the seat.

"Maybe we could make some legroom by moving some of the rubbish from the foot wells," suggested Mrs. Woodhouse. With difficulty, she retrieved a discarded fast-food bag from the floor. Cold, dead french fries showered from a tear in it onto the Rook and Odette.

"So, here's the plan," said the Rook conversationally. "After we've attended the site, we'll track down and kill Pawn Thistlethwaite's son for being a complete slob, and then we'll head back to the party. Pawn Wheatley, let's go." The driver pulled away into London traffic, the car's engine making a protesting noise that sounded like a walrus asked to do improvisational theater. "Ladies, do put on your seat belts."

"I can't find the seat belt," said Mrs. Woodhouse.

"Me neither," ventured Odette.

"Try not to crash, then, Wheatley," the Rook said to the driver.

"Especially since I have just found the marijuana of Pawn Thistlethwaite's son in the glove compartment," remarked the graaf.

"I would have thought—" Odette began, then stopped herself.

"Go ahead," said the Rook cheerfully. "My elbow is lodged in your rib cage, so there's no point in being shy."

"I just thought that the police wouldn't be a problem for the Checquy," said Odette.

"The difficulty with being a secret organization is that no one has ever heard of us," said the Rook. "The cops would have to go pretty far up the ladder before it all got sorted out, and in the meantime, we'd be held up. And people remember that sort of thing. Questions would be asked. If we weren't on official business, we'd get the tickets and have to lump them, I'm afraid. Just because we're in the Checquy doesn't mean we're outside the law."

Their destination was not very far, and the traffic obliged them by clipping along at a reasonable pace. Eventually, they turned into a narrow lane lined with restaurants.

"There's the place, Rook Thomas," said the driver, and they all peered out as the car cruised by. It did not look like the site of supernatural malevolence. A cheerful Italian restaurant with red, white, and green awnings, it had a warm glow coming from the windows. It looked like a very nice place to dine, apart from the flashing lights of the police cars outside and the solemn constables standing guard at the door. There was a small crowd gathered, and Odette supposed that at least some of them were from the press. A woman in a serious suit and a serious hairstyle declaimed in front of a television camera, and a couple of men with large zoom lenses took pictures from across the street.

"Oh, bugger," said the Rook. "The Liars at the Rookery are going to have a hell of a time with this." The car swept them past without pausing, and Pawn Wheatley smoothly took them around a corner to the service alley behind all the restaurants, where two more policemen were standing as sentries by a temporary barrier. They eyed the car suspiciously as it approached. Rook Thomas hurriedly dug into her purse and took out an extremely thick wallet. She flipped through the various card sheaths until she found what she was looking for and handed it to the driver.

"Evening, lads," said Pawn Wheatley as he rolled down the window (which stuck halfway).

"Road's closed, sir," said one of the constables. "There's a crime scene back there."

"We know, Constable," said the Rook. "We're here with the investigation." Thomas didn't acknowledge the unprofessional mien of the car. "Wheatley, give him the card." The policeman examined it briefly and looked at her.

"You're a colonel in the British army," he said dubiously. The Rook made a small sound that suggested to Odette that she had produced the wrong identification card. The officer's gaze swept over the car, lingering on the Rook in her cocktail dress of sexy evil, which, Odette noticed, still had a couple of french fries on it. The suspicion lay heavy in the air, but Thomas rallied.

"Yes...I am a colonel. There are concerns that this may have military implications. Concerns at the highest levels." The policeman glanced at the other occupants of the car. "These are my staff," Thomas said haughtily. Odette prayed that he wouldn't ask their ranks. "Look, use your little radio and call through to the officer in charge of the crime scene. Tell him that I'm here. We'll wait."

She sat back, folding her arms imperiously—a process that, because of the cramped environment, involved her inadvertently elbowing both Odette and Mrs. Woodhouse painfully in their breasts. The constable exchanged a long look with his colleague but apparently decided it would be more difficult to argue with them than to call his superior, and he turned away. There was some electronic chatter on the radio, and then he turned back.

To Odette's disappointment, he was not profusely apologetic. But he did let them through. Down the service alley, two large police vans were lined up behind the Italian restaurant. Pawn Wheatley parked, and the passengers in the rear set about prying themselves out of the backseat.

As they all stretched the kinks out of their spines, they were approached by a pudgy man in Wellingtons and a rustling white hooded coverall that Odette recognized as made of Tyvek. The only visible part of him was his round face with its astonishingly luxuriant ginger mustache.

"Colonel Thomas, I presume?"

"Don't even think about saluting, Gadenne," said the Rook. "I managed to give them the wrong identification, and I thought that it would be even more ridiculous if I then found the card identifying me as a scene-of-crime officer." She introduced Odette and the graaf, and Pawn Gadenne greeted them with the very particular British demeanor that translates as I am absolutely appalled to have you here, but I am also extremely well mannered and so I shall conceal that fact from you. After the courtesies were exchanged, he described the incident.

"It's rather nasty, this one," he said. "Sixteen people were in the upstairs dining room of the restaurant. Normal evening, lots of chatter. The waitress went downstairs to pick up a tray of drinks, came back two minutes later, and found all of them dead."

"Hell," said Rook Thomas. Odette was inclined to agree with her.

Pawn Gadenne continued, "They were all lying about with expressions and postures of agony. No one on the floor below had heard a single sound. No screams. No voices. Not even thuds of them hitting the ground."

Odette felt the hairs on the back of her neck rising up. A real supernatural event had happened a few meters from where she stood. She looked up at the second floor of the restaurant. Floodlights were visible through the windows. Set up by the forensic team, I suppose.

"Was it one big party?" Rook Thomas was asking.

"No. Four groups, unrelated. Two couples out for romantic dinners. A gathering of five students, and a birthday group of seven. Some of them were already eating, some hadn't even ordered yet."

"All right, so the waitress found a roomful of abrupt corpses," said Rook Thomas. "What did she do then?"

"Dropped the drinks, screamed, and almost fell down the stairs," said Gadenne. "People rushed up to see what had happened, and the police were called."

"Did they try to offer any medical attention? Did they touch the corpses?"

"Rook Thomas, when you see these bodies, you'll understand why no one wanted to go near them," said Pawn Gadenne. "The manager put his hand on one of them to feel for a pulse, and he said the skin was like leather."

"Did anyone take pictures?"

"I gather some piece-of-shit student tried but a waiter punched him and smashed his phone."

"Good," said the Rook. "Well, that restores a bit of my faith in humankind."

"We're quite fortunate, really. Only six civilians and eight police officers saw the scene before we took over," said Pawn Gadenne. "Of course, with this happening in the middle of London, it was inevitable that the press would materialize."

"And what have you told them?"

"Nothing, yet," said Gadenne. "The Liars are trying to invent something that won't panic the populace or destroy the reputation of the restaurant."

"Let me know what they come up with," said the Rook. "Now, let's go take a look at this." Pawn Gadenne ushered them up into one of the vans where several people in coveralls were talking into headsets or bustling about with stainless-steel cases. When they noticed the Rook, they nodded to her respectfully but didn't break off from what they were doing.

"We've swept for radiation and gas, of course," said Gadenne. "Nothing. But you'll have to wear Tyvek suits when you go in." Coveralls were found for three of the party, Mrs. Woodhouse having decided that visiting roomfuls of corpses was not part of her duty statement. She did, however, produce from her voluminous handbag a pair of trainers for the Rook.

"Do you always carry running shoes around for her?" asked Odette in low tones.

"Her job requires her to dress like a professional," said the EA quietly. "It also tends to abruptly require her to move around frantically. I've found that it's best always to be prepared." Her preparation, however, did not extend to carrying around a spare outfit, and so Rook Thomas was obliged to pull her coveralls up over her cocktail dress, which made for an interesting silhouette. Graaf Ernst, once he had taken off his coat and removed his tie, fit comfortably into one of the larger suits, but in order for Odette to put on the suit, her hideous dress of frumpitude had to be bunched up to the tops of her thighs, which left her with a gargantuan bulge around her hips.

"We haven't detected any foreign materials in the air," said Pawn Gadenne, "but we still insist on goggles and filter masks." These were handed out, along with latex gloves. Well, now I'm actually starting to feel at home, thought Odette as she snapped the gloves on. She pulled the hood up over her hair, stood a little straighter, and waited as Pawn Gadenne crammed his voluminous mustache into a dust mask.

They were then led out of the van and in through the back door of the restaurant. The kitchen contained several white-suited people bustling around, taking samples from all the cooking pots and industriously sealing vegetables and plates in evidence bags. There were also two white-suited people standing in unoccupied corners. Odette eyed them warily. They didn't appear to be doing anything but staying very still and being very large.

In the main dining room, the tables were still laid with plates of food and half-drunk glasses of wine. Even more Checquy techs were doing their thing. As Odette watched, one of them chiseled paint off the walls while another appeared to be laboriously jarring samples of the air. Again, some figures stood around, not doing anything. It was hard to tell with their bulky suits, but they had an air of extreme alertness.

"I'm sorry, may I ask who the people standing still are?" Odette inquired timidly.

"They're security," said Gadenne after a pointed pause that implied she was wasting his valuable time. "Manifestation sites are not always safe. Even if an event seems to be over, there may be residual threats. Our scientists cannot do their work while worrying that eels are suddenly going to come squirming out of the ceiling or that the furniture is going to come alive and try to trample them to death."

"I see," said Odette. "And does that sort of thing happen often?"

"Yes."

"Ah."

64

"You—Garden—where are the civilians?" asked Graaf Ernst abruptly. "The ones who were present when the event occurred?"

"Erm, well, everyone, of course, gets questioned," said Pawn Gadenne. His tone was less snooty than it had been with Odette. There was something about Graaf Ernst that made people more polite. Possibly it was his air of authority or the undeniable weight of centuries that hung around him. Or it might have been his rudeness—he was in the habit of barking out commands and questions. "We have commandeered rooms at the local hospital and kept those who saw the bodies separate from those who were simply present in the building at the time. We'll take statements and blood samples. Those who saw the bodies are being x-rayed. They'll all be advised to contact us if they feel odd or if any symptoms appear. In six months, unless we have definitively identified the problem, we will reinterview them and take more blood."

"Six months?" said Odette, and she mentally kicked herself for asking more questions.

"Generally, we have found that if something is incubating inside a human being, be it a disease, an organism, or a psychosis, signs will begin to appear within six months. Of course, the people will also be flagged in the government computer systems so that if they are hospitalized or die, or if they are arrested or abruptly change careers, we will be notified."

With this cheerful assurance ringing in her ears, Odette continued on with the rest of the group. The entrance to the staircase was sealed off with a plastic curtain that Gadenne unzipped to reveal a narrow and steep flight of stairs. They squeezed up and had another curtain unzipped before them; it was closed as soon as they'd passed through into the dining room.

The scene was not pleasant.

As a woman of science, Odette had seen human bodies before. And as an apprentice of the Grafters and a frequent attendee of Parisian nightclubs, she'd witnessed her fair share of the unexpected and the disturbing. But what she saw in that room was unlike anything she had encountered before.

Do not show weakness, she told herself. Not in front of the Checquy. Do not bring shame upon your family and your brotherhood. You must be strong and you must—

"Jesus Christ!" exclaimed Rook Thomas in horror. She turned her head away for a moment, and her shudder could be seen even through the coverall. She pressed the back of her wrist against her mask and breathed hard.

Odette thought she had been prepared for this. Gadenne hadn't pulled any punches in his description, but this was gruesome. Corpses everywhere. And these were not corpses laid out tidily on examination tables. Some of them were slumped over on the ground, their bodies curled up tight, but others looked as if they had been turned to stone in mid-death throe. The people were frozen. All their features were caught in a moment of torment. She could play out in her mind exactly how it had happened.

People had been eating and chatting, and then suddenly they had all been struck by the most dreadful pain. A few must have expired almost instantly. They were still seated in their chairs, clutching at their stomachs or their heads. One man was slumped over, facedown in his meal. The ladies on either side of him had their heads thrown back, mouths gaping, teeth bared, fingers curled into claws. Their eyes were still open, staring blankly.

Other people had taken longer to die.

One woman had crawled across the table, dragging herself over the plates and food. She was now half hanging over the edge, spaghetti and sauce dripping down her hair.

There was a man on his knees; his body was upright, his hands pressed against his head. It appeared that he had been tearing at his own face, although there was no blood coming from the ragged skin.

Another man had clawed his way across the floor to the stairs and then arched his head and spine back as he died. His face was twisted in agony, and his mouth was petrified in midscream.

Gadenne said that no one had made any sound, a clinical part of Odette's mind thought. So this man must have been screaming silently. The nonclinical parts of her mind were doing a little silent screaming of their own.

There can only have been a few seconds of pain, she told herself. Even from the farthest table, for him to get this far would have taken fifteen seconds at most. Judging from the expressions of the dead, however, fifteen seconds must have seemed like a very long time.

What on earth could have done this? she thought helplessly. Was this place built on an ancient Pictish burial ground or something? And how many more things like this are happening every day? She realized that her hands were shaking. The restaurant was so mundane, so commonplace. She could have eaten there herself. And yet, in this normal place, something unfathomable had taken the lives of sixteen people.

For much of her life, Odette had loved living in a secret world. It was delicious, knowing things no one else knew. And while there had been the distant, theoretical awareness of the Checquy, the monsters from her childhood, they had been tucked away in history, on a little island.

Then, in the past few months, another secret world, that of the supernatural, had begun to impinge forcefully upon her life. Now it was right in front of her, and it was horrendous.

"We pulled everyone out so that you could see the bodies in situ, Rook Thomas," Pawn Gadenne said.

"Thank you, Roland," said the Rook absently. She appeared to have gotten over her initial horror, although her fists were still clenched tight. Her eyes had gone distant, and her brow was a little furrowed. Then she blinked and focused on him. "Well, they're all dead," she said definitely. "You can bring the team back in now, unless—Ernst? Anything?"

"I don't think I can add anything," said the graaf. "This sort of tableau is outside my experience. But Odette is more the scholar than I." He turned to her. "Do you wish to examine them?"

I'd rather take a cheesegrater to myself, Odette didn't say. Really, there was little on earth that Odette wished to do less than get closer to those bodies. Diseases and poisons caused no fear in her, but this was something else entirely. The Grafters' knowledge and abilities were based on science. Unorthodox science, admittedly, but at least they had an explanation for how everything worked. Odette was painfully aware that there might be no scientific explanation at all for what she was looking at.

If I point out that their fixed postures indicate a paralytic agent that locked their muscles and ligaments, the Checquy might open them and find that their bones have turned to obsidian or something. If I speculate on why they couldn't make any sounds, all my scientific theories will look ridiculous when it turns out the room was temporarily transported to the moon by the dreams of a five-year-old, and in an Italian restaurant in space, no one can hear you scream. I don't have any answers— I don't even know where to start.

And if these negotiations go through, she thought, I'll be doing this sort of thing for the rest of my life. Nothing will make sense.

"I, uh, I don't have any of my tools," she said finally.

"All right, then, I'll fetch the team," said Gadenne briskly. The white-clad investigators filed in and spread out. For the most part, they appeared to be engaged in a fairly standard crime-scene investigation. Cameras were flashing, and lots of things were being done with swabs and test tubes. Of course, there was also the boy carrying the forked hazel-wood wand, the woman holding a scrimshawed elephant tusk, and the man who'd stripped naked in the center of the room and was now levitating a few inches off the floor, an expression of profound thought on his face. Odette was somewhat pleased to note that even the other investigators seemed uncomfortable with that particular forensic approach. But apart from those, everything was reassuringly scientific.

"Pawn Gadenne, it looks like you have everything under control, so I think we'll shuffle along," said Rook Thomas. "I'll have your preliminary report on my desk in the morning?"

He nodded obediently. "And do you need me to sign off on any special acquisitions or requisitions for tonight?"

"No, I don't think so. Thank you, Rook Thomas," said Gadenne. "Oh, I tried to call in Pawn Clements. I thought her perspective might be useful, but she's not answering. I realize it's well below your responsibility, but you don't happen to know if she's on leave or something, do you?"

"Pawn Clements," said the Rook uncertainly. "I know the name, but, um, remind me?"

"Felicity Clements," said Gadenne. "Young, just a few years out of the Estate. She has touch-based abilities—she reads the environment and can look into the past. She's posted with an assault team, I believe, but she often gets seconded to us for the on-site portions of our investigations."

"Oh, I know why I recall her name," said the Rook. "I just saw it written down today somewhere." Her shoulders slumped abruptly, and her voice was solemn as she said through the filter mask, "Ah, hell, I'm afraid she was in the team that got caught in the fire this afternoon."

"No," said Gadenne. "The one in the row houses? With the disappearing sleepwalkers?"

"Yes," said the Rook. "I'm sorry to say the whole team was killed." Odette and the graaf remained respectfully silent.

"Damn," said Gadenne. "Do we know what the story is there?"

"Not yet," said Thomas. "One of the other forensic teams is picking through the wreckage, trying to get a handle on it."

"Well, I don't envy them. At least with this lot"—and he looked around the room—"it's not our own people."

"Quite," said the Rook. "And Gadenne, our London investigation resources are going to be spread a little thin for a while because of that fire. The labs have a billion samples, the historians in the Rookery and the Apex have already started researching the location, and the meteorologists are putting together a climatic portrait. You'll be able to send a few samples to our labs in other cities, but for the rest, I'm afraid you'll just have to wait your turn."

"I understand," said Gadenne. "We'll have our hands full here for a while anyway." He nodded to some team members who were preparing to check under a corpse that was sprawled faceup on the floor, its arms rigid above it.

"And lift and turn on three," one of the investigators ordered. "One...two...three." The team lifted, and Odette couldn't help but flinch as the body, utterly stiff, was moved. It looked like a mannequin being shifted. Then there was a collective gasp from the room as, under the force of its own weight, the skin of the face tore like wet cardboard.

"Fucking hell, put him down, put him down!" the investigator ordered. As they did, however, the rip grew larger, jagging down into the body's collar. Before everyone's aghast eyes, the head ripped away and hung from a shred at the nape of its neck. A torrent of black liquid poured out of the corpse. Everyone jumped back as the stuff spilled out and spread across the floor. Odette was not the only one to squeal in horror. Even the security guards scurried away. One of the investigators threw up inside her mask, which made for a brief but complex sideshow.

Despite herself, Odette crouched down, staring at the body. It was clear that everything inside the man had liquefied, turned into whatever that fluid was. All that was left was the husk of his skin crumpling into itself.

My God, what kind of business are we getting ourselves into? she thought weakly. Then she caught a wave of smell, strong enough to wash past her mask. There were minerals, strange compounds, and a trace of rot, but most of all, there was a strong presence of citrus. It hit her memory like a hammer, and she was suddenly terribly afraid.

"Does anyone else smell oranges?" said the Rook, sounding very perplexed.

No, Odette thought in horror. Oh God, no. She looked to the graaf, who shook his head at her, commanding her to be silent.

They've followed us here.

7

Odette's brain woke her up on schedule. She grimaced, and then, as memories of the previous evening presented themselves for inspection, she grimaced even more. The trip back from the crime scene to the hotel had been extremely uncomfortable, although Mrs. Woodhouse had managed to rustle up a slightly more reasonable vehicle. The three who had entered the crime scene had been obliged to discard their shoes after that horrible black liquid had engulfed their baggied feet and seeped through.

As a result, they had sat awkwardly in the back of a town car in their stockinged feet; their shoes had been shipped off to a special facility to be professionally destroyed. Odette and the graaf had been pointedly silent while the Rook spent most of the time on the phone, giving orders to hapless flunkies. After the Grafters were dropped off at the hotel, Odette had opened her mouth to say something, but the graaf had shaken his head.

"We'll discuss it tomorrow," he said, and they had gone to their rooms. Odette had drawn herself a bath, added various compounds, and watched as the water turned cloudily purple and gelatinous. Then she eased herself in, sank to the bottom, and fretted. Sleep hadn't come easily, and now that she was awake, the problems didn't seem any better. She curled up, hugged her knees, and brooded on how she'd come to be there.

Really, it was all the fault of that greedy bastard Carlos de Aragón de Gurrea, duke of Villahermosa.

In 1677, there was no Belgium. The lands that would eventually become Belgium were part of the Spanish Netherlands and were technically under the rule of Carlos II of Spain. Carlos the Deuce, however, delegated the responsibility of ruling them to a governor-general who lived in Brussels and tried not to lose any of the king's territory to that canny buck Louis XIV of France.

At that time, the Wetenschappelijk Broederschap van Natuur-kundigen was effectively a government agency in the Spanish Netherlands. The brotherhood had begun a couple of centuries earlier when two noblemen, Grootvader Ernst and his business partner and cousin Gerd, Count of Leeuwen, funded the efforts of some shabby alchemists. Said shabby alchemists had been unexpectedly, mind-blowingly successful in their efforts. The two noblemen had put money in, and unfathomably advanced biotechnology had come out.

In the beginning, the mission of the Broederschap had been simple research—pushing the boundaries of human knowledge, gaining a greater understanding of the glory of God's creation (with an initial emphasis on replacing the leg Ernst had lost in a riding accident), and extending everybody's life span to ensure there was enough time to get a really good understanding. Ernst and Gerd, being responsible members of the nobility, had informed the government of the brotherhood's work. The government had responded with the bureaucratic equivalent of some pocket money, an encouraging pat on the head, and an absentminded suggestion to run along and play, do.

Thus unencumbered by interference from the authorities, the Broederschap pursued their activities with an enthusiasm and focus almost as astounding as the results they produced. In a time without flush toilets, they unraveled the genome. In laboratories lined with hand-painted Delft tiles, men who bathed at most once a week cracked the secrets of immortality and developed surgical procedures that allowed them to twist the human form (and various other forms) into whatever shapes they pleased. Their work was based firmly on scientific principles and human intellect, but the results were nothing short of miraculous.

At which point, Ernst and Gerd decided all this could make them look very, very good to the government, and they finally wrote that status report they'd been putting off for decades.

The report raised a few skeptical eyebrows in Antwerp, but

after the government scoured the books and realized that, yes, they actually had funded a scientific brotherhood of scientists a while back, a minor bureaucrat was dispatched to check in on this obscure little group. Upon presenting himself at the gate of the nearest Broeder-schap facility, he was cheerfully welcomed, given a beverage, and shown around the place. His hosts assured him that they were not sorcerers and that everything he was seeing was the result of natural philosophy and thus perfectly aligned with God's will. He returned to his office with his acne all cleaned up, his piles a mere memory, and a troublesome allergy to gluten scrubbed from his system. The brotherhood's executives had sensibly kept the existence of the immortality project to themselves, but the military potential of their work was apparent to even the least visionary of quill-pushers.

Once he'd overcome his astonishment and nausea, the bureaucrat wrote up a detailed report and submitted it to his superior. His superior reviewed the report, asked his subordinate if he was feeling quite well in the head, and then passed the report to his superior, who took it immediately to the governor-general, one Carlos de Aragón de Gurrea, duke of Villahermosa.

The governor-general was delicately informed that, tucked away in a forgotten corner of his government, there appeared to be the ultimate weapon. The Most Excellent Lord (the honorific to which the duke was entitled as a grandee of Spain) reviewed the paperwork, looked incredulously at the drawings he'd been provided, poured himself a glass of Malaga sack, and had a think.

He could report these developments to his lord and master, the king. That would be the proper thing to do, bureaucratically speaking. But His Majesty Carlos II, king of Spain; duke of Milan, Lothier, Brabant, Limburg, and Luxembourg; count of Flanders, Hainaut, and Namur; and count palatine of Burgundy, the anointed sovereign to whom the governor-general owed his sworn allegiance, was, not to put too fine a point on it, completely fucking useless. Indeed, he was so inbred that he could barely function as a human being, let alone as a king.

Carlos II's ancestors had been marrying their close relations for so many generations that the scion of the line suffered from uncountable intellectual and physical disabilities and indeed was technically his own cousin, his own cousin once removed, and his own second cousin. All of his eight great-grandparents were descendants of the same couple, and his mother had been his father's niece, making his grandmother also his aunt.

For all that he was really qualified only to sit quietly, blink, and then expire, Carlos II did happen to possess a rather extensive kingdom, including a huge overseas empire. It was the kind of empire a governor-general might seize if he possessed drive, clarity of vision, faith in himself, and access to an unstoppable army.

So the governor-general very carefully did not pass word back to Spain about what had been unearthed and instead drafted a memo to Ernst and Gerd. In a time of verbosity and poetry, it was quite to the point. The memo stated that it was the will of the government (by which he meant himself) that the existence of the Broederschap remain a secret from the general public and that they turn their attention to creating a military force capable of conquering any nation on earth. If they accomplished this, the rewards for their work would be suitably and unbelievably lavish.

Ernst and Gerd were a little surprised that they weren't immediately invited to Madrid to receive the kingdom's highest honors or at least asked to see if they couldn't do something about the king's multiple disorders, but they shrugged. The promise of unbelievably lavish (if somewhat vague) rewards was sufficient incentive.

Overnight, the Broederschap's priorities shifted from general research to offensive applications. They were tasked with producing soldiers who could shrug off musket balls (or cannonballs, for that matter) without breaking stride. Soldiers who could build an empire.

The scientists set to work with a will. They had, of course, already done some exploration in this arena. The brotherhood's estates were guarded by the world's most terrifying watchdogs, and any ruffian who laid hands on one of their modified guards would have really regretted it—in the few moments before he was torn into little pieces. However, now the project consumed all their attention. The governor-general provided men, the sort of men who were willing to go under the knife, and the saw, and the chisel, and then spend several days in a sarcophagus of slime in exchange for might and future wealth. A general was appointed, a professional killer from outside the Broederschap whose loyalty to the governor-general was unquestioned and who had been promised unbelievably lavish rewards of his own.

In their workshops, Ernst and Gerd's fleshwrights created troops who would be unstoppable.

Each soldier was unique, a bespoke warrior equipped with living armaments. The troops were designed to operate in all conditions and to withstand all known weapons. Above all, they were designed to terrify, with all the artistry and cunning that the Broederschap could muster. An army of nightmares, led by a monstrous general whose new modifications gave him the appearance of having crawled out of hell.

This was strength that positively cried out to be used (especially after the labor of creating them had been so incredibly expensive), but the Grafters were still cautious, and, above all, they were scientists. They needed a proving ground, a contained area in which to test their strength. And so the Broederschap turned its eyes across the North Sea to the British Isles, with the avaricious blessing of Carlos de Aragón de Gurrea, who saw this as the ideal place from which to launch a conquest.

In 1677, the army of the Wetenschappelijk Broederschap van Natuurkundigen marched out of the waters of the British Channel onto the shores of the Isle of Wight. Van Suchtlen and de Leeuwen were present, but only as observers—it had been made very clear to them that the general appointed by Carlos de Aragón de Gurrea was in command. And so, mounted on creatures that might once have been horses, the cousins observed as the invading warriors brushed away the musket fire of the English soldiers stationed there. Then, at a signal from their commander, the Grafter troops briskly slaughtered their opponents and set about conquering the island. Against such an army, no earthly force could stand.

It turned out, however, that the British Isles possessed some forces that were decidedly unearthly.

The first the invaders knew of these forces was a man who stood in the middle of the road as they marched to Newport. A hunchback, empty-handed, barefoot, and clothed in crude homespun, he watched their approach not with fear but rather with pursed lips and an unflinching gaze. He held up a hand as they drew near, and the general at the head of the column called for a halt.

"Move aside," growled the general.

"I am here to deliver an ultimatum," said the hunchback. "If you cease your advance, you may live. This invasion is over."

"Vermoord hem," said the general. Murder him. The two huge soldiers flanking the general stepped forward. One carried serrated swords coated with venom that seeped down the jagged blades from glands in his hands. The other had a carapace like a beetle's and bore a giant war hammer covered in the same poisonous substance.

The hunchback stepped back and clenched his fists, and a curious thrumming reverberated through the air. Midstride, the two monstrous fighters fell to their knees and clutched at their stomachs. Before the stupefied gaze of their comrades, their torsos began to crumple in on themselves. The soldiers screamed briefly before their voices strangled off into nauseating wet gurgles. The chitin on one and the steel armor on the other cracked and were retracted into their bodies as they collapsed. No one made a sound as the two were compressed. What remained were two rough nuggets of flesh and armor, each about the size of a human head.

"So, you s—" began the man.

"Maak hem af!" shouted the general, and the rest of the troops rushed forward. The hunchback was swiftly engulfed and cut down.

Later, after they'd set up camp, eager Broederschap alchemists dissected the man's corpse and, much to their bewilderment, found absolutely nothing out of the ordinary. Every element of his frame was bog standard, unremarkable. His brain was not particularly interesting. His blood was tediously unoriginal. There were certainly no signs he'd received any modifications such as the Grafters had performed. Even his spine, they reported disappointedly, was textbook for a hunchback.

When they gingerly chiseled open the dense little ingots that had once been two of their comrades, the alchemists could not find anything to explain why the men had suddenly imploded. There were no chemicals, toxins, or mechanics. It appeared that every fiber of the warriors' bodies had suddenly felt the need to occupy the same space. That evening, when they made a report to Ernst, Gerd, and the general, the scholars gave a long, awkward description before calling the whole event "an inexplicable phenomenon."

"And what does that mean?" asked the general.

"It means they don't know what happened," said Gerd sourly.

"But how can they not know? What if there are more?"

"It is troubling." Ernst shrugged. "But one thing we do know is that they can die."

That night, there were more inexplicable phenomena. As a group of soldiers warmed themselves around a fire, the flames suddenly flared up and then leapt from the wood. They enveloped a warrior and could not be smothered or extinguished until he had died through a combination of burns and strangulation.

Then one of the scientists was found dead in his tent. A hurried autopsy revealed that every drop of water in his body had been transmuted into a coarse white powder that his colleagues identified with some bewilderment as talc.

As word got around the camp that night, the men began to feel decidedly ill at ease. Most of them were not sophisticated folk, and their understanding of their own augmentations and modifications was far from complete. They had been assured that not only was it all based on science and natural philosophy but it was reversible, and the power they had received had been enough to outweigh their concerns. The stuff with the fire and those men shriveling down on themselves, however, was worrying. It didn't make any sense.

The next day, as dawn broke, the invaders met the inexplicable phenomena on the field of battle.

When they came, they were not regimented troops marching in formation. They were not even a horde of hunchbacks. Instead, bewilderingly, it was as if a random selection of the populace had spontaneously decided that it was a nice day to attack an army of monsters. Out of the morning mist came men and women of all ages and social classes. They were dressed in clothes that would not have drawn a second glance on any European street.

The people were so unremarkable that for a few moments, the invaders did not react. Then a man in the black robes and mortarboard of an academic stepped forward from the small crowd. He ran his hand across a long pistol and wordlessly raised it at the invaders. A glowing torrent of molten metal burst out of the barrel of the weapon and screamed with the voice of a woman as it jetted across the field to engulf a soldier.

And the first battle commenced.

It was utterly chaotic and utterly hideous. The Broederschap troops' feet thundered on the turf and many of them vaulted high into the air to land in the midst of their enemies like mortar bombs. Their enemies struck back, some with conventional weapons and some with…not. Waves of force smashed out against the Grafters. Liquids and fumes spread and did harm. Twice, explosions blossomed on the field, sending fire and pressure washing out and devastating nearby fighters. These were all the more terrifying because they had no accompanying sound.

Their adversaries appeared to have been endowed with terrifying, inexplicable abilities according to no discernible rhyme or reason. A periwigged gentleman, gorgeous in lace and velvet, bounded toward the enhanced troops on all fours while razor-sharp tusks erupted out of his jaws. Meanwhile, the outthrust finger of a fat laundress puffing along through the wet grass caused a Broederschap soldier to turn on the comrade at his side and hack him to pieces.

The battle went on for over an hour until, to the surprise of the invaders, their attackers suddenly withdrew back into the fog. A couple of the troops, caught up in the frenzy of the battle, pursued them, but after fire flared momentarily within the cloud and a charred head came rolling out, no one else felt like following.

The field looked even worse than a post-combat battlefield usually did. There were corpses from both sides scattered across it, but none of the crows circling overhead appeared interested. All the bodies were gathered up. The brotherhood dead were harvested for any useful organs or appendages. The injured were repaired briskly, in some cases receiving the still-warm anatomy of their fallen comrades.

The British corpses were examined carefully. A few of the bodies showed unusual characteristics—a set of tripled pupils here, a polished mandible there; some unexpected orifices scattered the length of one man's spine. There was not, however, any sign that these characteristics had been added by human hands.

While the graafs, the scientists, and the general talked in low tones in a pavilion, the soldiers muttered amongst themselves. It was obvious that the scholars didn't have any idea what gave these British people their powers. But it wasn't natural, was it? A man could understand the concept of popping some extra muscles into a person, or even sewing on a tougher skin. You could wrap your mind around the idea.

But what enabled a gaunt old woman to punch her bare hand through steel armor and tear out both of a soldier's hearts? And that young boy, hardly old enough to be in breeches, whom they'd all seen hovering in the air above the battlefield and dropping grenadoes. How could such things be possible?

In a time of faith, the answer was obvious: Demons. Deals with the devil. Black magic. By the end of the day, a name had been given to the British monsters.

Gruwels.

Abominations.

There was no question of abandoning the invasion. The Broederschap had suffered some losses, true, but they had won the battle. They still vastly outnumbered the Gruwels, and if they could subdue the Isle of Wight, then the rest of the British Isles lay before them for the taking. And from there, who knew? The government had not shared its plans, but the potential for wealth and power was plain to see.

But first they would need to be strategic.

"Rather than proceeding directly to Newport," said the general, "let us be unpredictable. Our troops' speed and endurance mean that we can take as circuitous a route as we like. Let the Gruwels exhaust themselves chasing us. Our goal is to take it all, so wherever we go, it is profit to us."

And so that night the Broederschap soldiers activated the modifications in their brains that relieved them of the need to sleep. Their rods, cones, cubes, and tetrahedrons changed gears, their pupils dilated as wide as they could go, and the army sprinted off, not in the direction of Newport but toward the southwest. They took a couple of villages, detoured around the town of Yarmouth (just to confuse), and dashed into the island's center to fall upon a particularly prosperous farm and feast on its cattle and the thatch of its farmhouse (the troops having been modified to live off the land). Their movements were random and erratic, preventing any possible ambushes. Further conflict was inevitable, that was certain, but it would not be on the Gruwels' terms.

Two days later, the Gruwels fell upon them in some fields on the northwestern coast. There were more of the monsters, many more, and there were significant differences this time. For one thing, they were now arrayed in regular ranks. The columns were sometimes broken up to allow for a single hulking individual's whiplashing tentacles or a perfectly cylindrical column of indigo smoke that kept its position in the formation. But overall, they were far more organized.

The two armies regarded each other levelly for a moment, came to a decision, and then all hell broke loose.

It was bewildering, nauseating, disorienting warfare. Storm clouds gathered, although it was not clear if this was the work of the Gruwels or just the traditional cussedness of English weather, and combat played out in mud and rain. Swords clashed against swords and shattered on inhuman skin. Musket balls were snatched out of the air and sent hurtling back at their firers. Flames were projected across the battlefield, flashing the raindrops into steam.

There was no respite. The Grafter warriors did not need to sleep or eat. They fought into the night, the Gruwels lighting torches while the Grafters' vision showed the landscape clearly in shades of gray and orange.

Both armies were equipped with a myriad of unique abilities, and if the Gruwels did not appear to be bound by the laws of science, well, it was still damn difficult for them to kill a Grafter soldier. A limb torn off might give him pause, but he was likely to pick it up and use it to bludgeon his opponent to death. Being set on fire simply meant shedding a layer of cuticle from one's epidermis. Mortal wounds weren't.

The conflict continued through days and nights, with the Gruwel forces ebbing and surging as their soldiers were relieved and withdrew, presumably to snatch what sleep they could. The battle moved about as one side or the other gave way or pressed forward. They fought in meadows, and in marshland, and in the forests. Farms and villages were engulfed by battles, and civilians were cut down in the combat.

As the fighting continued, the Broederschap began to identify certain individuals. They learned to dread the presence of the girl whose long red hair floated about as if she were underwater and who could dive into the soil and emerge on the other side of the field, perfectly clean and calm, to put a blade in a man's back. They loathed the leper who let loose plagues upon them. And most hated of all were the three men and the woman who seemed to be acting generals for the Gruwel army. Early on, they became the targets of the Grafter attacks, the brotherhood taking the same approach to warfare that they took to a rogue experimental tortoise: that if you cut off the heads, the body would die. Through a concerted onslaught, with the Broederschap enduring painful losses, the woman and two of the men were killed.

The remaining general, however, seemed able to dodge every attack. No matter where a gun was fired, or a saber slashed, or venom spat, he managed to evade it perfectly. Eventually, through the shouted orders that crossed the battlefield, the invaders learned that he was called Crimson Rook Perry.

As the fighting wore on, it became increasingly apparent to Ernst and Gerd that the Broederschap could not win. It might take a dozen Gruwel deaths to kill a Grafter soldier, but some British demons—like Perry—also seemed capable of tearing through multiple invaders without pausing. The Grafters were outnumbered and outmatched. Slowly but surely, their forces were whittled down.

Their commander, however, was unwilling to acknowledge the possibility of losing. Whether it was the might that came from his implants, his avarice for the promised rewards, or some orders from his master the governor-general that he dared not disobey, he refused to yield. Instead, to the massive distaste of the cousins and over their objections, he turned to the tactics of atrocity. Under his direction, his soldiers carried out grotesque outrages against their enemies. He thought that the strategic use of depravity and brutality would break the will of the Gruwels.

He could not have been more wrong.

After seventeen days of continuous conflict characterized by monstrous barbarism on the part of the invaders, scores of soldiers and hundreds of civilians were dead, and only a handful of Grafters were left. From a hilltop, Graafs Ernst and Gerd watched as the Gruwel army closed around the remaining invaders clustered in the valley below. The cousins' eyes zoomed in, and they saw each of their warriors fall in turn. Finally, the only Broederschap soldier left was the commander, a hulking black-carapaced shape surrounded by enemies.

"Well, this should be interesting," said Ernst.

"How long do you think he'll last?" asked Gerd. Two Gruwels launched themselves at the warrior. Despite his size, he moved with dizzying swiftness and plucked the attackers out of the air to slam them down on the ground. A burst of musket fire erupted, and the reports echoed up to the ears of the noblemen. They could see the sparks as the balls ricocheted off him, but he did not fall or even hesitate.

"Very difficult to say," said Ernst. "He really does represent the apogee of our craft."

"I should hope so," replied Gerd. "After all the time and mon—good God!" Before their eyes, a wave of fire smashed out of the crowd and hit the general. As it faded, they saw him step forward unscathed to tear a Gruwel in half. "Perhaps we should have made all the soldiers like him."

"Yes, and bankrupted the kingdom," said Ernst. "Still, he is very good." In point of fact, for all his loathsome character, the commander was an outstanding warrior, and his Grafter enhancements seemed to have made him unbeatable. They watched for many minutes as he plowed his way through his assailants. He'd already killed over a dozen and showed no sign of slowing down. Then Crimson Rook Perry stepped up.

"Is he drawing a pistol?" asked Gerd.

"I think so," said Ernst. "How odd. They already know our soldier is immune to—oh."

The remaining Gruwel general had just put the gun against his own head and pulled the trigger. Perry collapsed instantly. There was silence—everyone was still—and then the massive figure of the Grafter general slowly keeled over to land with a heavy thud on the turf.

"Did—did that just happen?" asked Ernst faintly.

"I think it did," said Gerd.

Ernst zoomed in more closely on the body of Perry. There was absolutely no doubt that he was dead. Anything with that much brain sprayed across the grass had to be. "What did he do?"

"I have no idea. But now we have a new problem," said Gerd.

"Oh?"

"The surviving Gruwels have, in fact, noticed our presence."

"Ah."

"And they are coming toward us."

"Indeed," said Ernst. "I think we should vacate the premises."

And so the graafs mounted their huge steeds and fled, breaking through the enemy lines. They were pursued by several dozen Gruwels who witnessed as, without hesitation, the two noblemen spurred their horses off a cliff and plunged into the ocean.

Nine days later, Ernst and Gerd, still on their horses, emerged wearily from the surf onto a twilit beach by the village of Zeebrugge. It was the first opportunity they had had to exchange words, but they were too exhausted. With the water streaming off them, they grimly set off for home, intent on some bowls of cream-based soup, a few beers, and then bed.

The Broederschap held several estates dotted around the country. All of them were discreet, with high walls to conceal what was going on in them, and with outstanding security. They were the ideal places for the noblemen to rest and recover and plan how they were going to explain the situation to the governor-general. Gerd and Ernst proceeded wearily to the nearest facility, a country manor outside Bruges, only to find that the British had already arrived there. Even worse, they had sent a force more terrifying than the Gruwels: diplomats.

Emissaries of Charles II* of England had arrived in Brussels five days before and presented themselves to the governor-general. Although they were not accompanied by an army, or even a single bodyguard, they strode in as if they held all the power in the world. It was not clear if any of them were Gruwels themselves, but they presented Carlos de Aragón de Gurrea with an ornate box of polished English oak. Under their unwavering gaze, he opened it and found it contained the head of the Grafter general. It was incontrovertible evidence that the Broederschap

---

* Charles II of England was not Carlos II of Spain. Confusing one for the other would probably have earned you a backhanding from Charles and a bewildered stare from Carlos.

invasion had failed. He looked up at them hopelessly, and they made known their demands.

It was all very carefully worded in appropriate diplomatic and legal language with no mention of matters supernatural. The governor-general would be permitted to keep his life and his position. News of the debacle need never reach the court of Spain. (Carlos II might be an inbred idiot, but his wrath could be terrible.) But Carlos de Aragón de Gurrea's state-sponsored foray into alchemy would be destroyed. The possibility of empire that had hung appetizingly before him would be cut away.

He rolled over immediately.

That afternoon, a swarm of British clerks and troops arrived in the country, divided themselves into brigades, and set about the systematic and complete dismantling of the Wetenschappelijk Broederschap van Natuurkundigen. The governor-general told them everything he knew, but there would have been no point dissembling about the extent or distribution of the brotherhood's resources anyway — the British seemed to possess an encyclopedic knowledge of their affairs.

Belgian observers were attached to the brigades, primarily, it was suspected, to keep the governor-general aware of the implacable and meticulous ruthlessness shown by the British. The forces descended upon the estates, and startled scientists were rousted out of their laboratories to have guns, fingers, and legal documents pointed at them threateningly. A few put up a fight, even activating their implants, but they were subdued and executed on the spot. Every member of the Broederschap the British could find, right down to the most junior apprentice, was arrested and held in the most secure facility in the country. There, they were guarded by silent Englishmen, not all of whom carried guns.

Meanwhile, work proceeded on the orderly sacking of assets. Chattels were seized and coffers emptied as reparation for the destruction visited upon the Isle of Wight. In the laboratories, greenhouses, sties, kennels, aviaries, apiaries, stables, orangeries, and mews, all Grafter creations were killed and their carcasses destroyed. The local populace had learned not to pay too much attention to the doings of their reclusive neighbors, and that carefully cultivated disinterest, combined with the fortified nature of the facilities, meant that most of the destruction could be done in relative secrecy.

Ownership of the land was to be transferred to the English church as soon as every structure had been demolished, every animal put down, every plant uprooted, and all of it burned, regardless of whether or not there were obvious signs of "tampering."

As for the members of the brotherhood, they were to be put down as well. When Ernst and Gerd arrived at their own front door, they were taken into custody; their names were dutifully removed from the list of the dead and added to the list of those who would soon be dead. The two noblemen were imprisoned separately from their cohorts, although the conditions were no better.

For the cousins, the most astonishing fact was that the Gruwels were apparently in league with the British throne. Indeed, the monsters were actually a part of the government! That a Christian nation—even one that had schismed away from the Church in Rome—would knowingly ally itself to the creatures of the devil was almost incomprehensible.

The second most astonishing fact was that the British seemed to have no care for the possibilities the Broederschap's work held. It was only natural that the British would demand retribution for the invasion. The pillaging of the Belgian estates, the humbling of their ruler—such were the vagaries of war and the price one paid for losing. The two noblemen could even face the prospect of their own execution with a certain amount of equanimity. But the Gruwels were not destroying only the warriors and weapons of the brotherhood.

Gerd and Ernst looked out of their cells into the courtyard of their prison and saw their scholars and scientists being put to the sword. The most brilliant minds the world had known were beheaded like common murderers. Books containing centuries of insights were thrown contemptuously onto heaps and burned. Apprentices were swiftly executed, even the very youngest ones who had received no modifications, the children who had barely learned to read.

To the Grafters, wiping out such a priceless body of knowledge represented the grossest of superstition. The Gruwels were even killing some of the servants—men and women who'd had nothing to do with the Broederschap's work beyond occasionally cleaning up the laboratories or taking delivery of a consignment of sheep.

Finally, after their people had been killed and their life's work obliterated, Ernst, Duke of Suchtlen, and Gerd, Count of Leeuwen, were escorted at blunderbuss-point from their cells to the scaffold. Black ashes from the bonfires of books still blew about, settling on the wigs and hats of the great and the good of the land. All the significant nobility of the country had been gathered to witness the execution of their convicted peers.

The crimes of the two men were unspecified but clearly involved an outrage against Charles II, by the grace of God King of England, Scotland, France, and Ireland, Defender of the Faith, etc., since His Majesty the King had traveled to Brussels to observe the proceedings. He sat close by the scaffold, next to the governor-general, and the two noblemen were marched before him in shackles. The condemned evinced no fear; indeed, they gave no sign of knowing where they were or what was happening.

Was it terror? wondered the watching nobles. Or perhaps they had bribed the guards and drowned their fears in strong drink? There was some unsteadiness in their steps, and they both looked around blankly at the crowd. A priest offered to administer last rites, but the two men acted as if they did not hear a word. It took a soldier's firm hand to get them to their knees.

Chains were passed around the men's shoulders and secured to heavy iron rings on the floor of the scaffold in front of them and behind them, holding them upright. The massive executioner drew out a long sword and held it in both his hands. He looked to the King, who nodded assent.

The blade swept out and passed through Ernst's neck without pausing. Blood jetted messily in the air, but the blade was clean.

Again, the executioner raised the sword, and again it came down to behead a Grafter lord.

The heads fell from the bodies, and the crowd let out a breath. They were uncertain how to react. It was a time when executions were entertainment, but the presence of the kings and the status of the condemned made cheering inappropriate. It was meant to be a solemn occasion, but in fact the whole thing had an air of the absurd about it, with the chains still holding the bodies upright on their knees. And then the executioner raised his massive sword again and cut the left arm off the corpse of Graaf van Suchtlen.

This time there were gasps from the crowd, but he continued along like a workman, methodically chopping off the bodies' remaining arms. As the blade whipped up between strikes, blood flicked onto the crowd, and there were shrieks and cries of outrage. There were no true screams, however, until he swung the blade back over his shoulder and brought it down with unbelievable force to slice the duke's body in half with one inexorable blow.

Blood burst forth in a torrent; bits of torso thumped onto the platform. The same was done to the body of the count. And that was the indisputable end of the Wetenschappelijk Broederschap van Natuurkundigen.

Except, of course, that it wasn't.

Everyone stood and swarmed ingratiatingly around the King and the governor-general as they were ushered away to the carriages. Everyone except two gorgeously dressed men standing off to one side. They each held a flask of something alcoholic, and as they watched the dismembered corpses being gathered up into baskets, they both took a swig.

"Well, that was thorough," remarked one of the men. To anyone looking at him, it was abundantly clear that he wasn't Gerd de Leeuwen.

"Yes," said the other, who looked nothing at all like Ernst van Suchtlen even before he had been cut up into little pieces. "Although not really thorough enough."

They had been stripped of their estates and their wealth, and even of their bodies, but as Ernst had remarked, "You don't live as long as I have without learning that there's always someone who slashes your throat or your budget at the least convenient time possible."

Since the creation of the Broederschap, Ernst had been under no illusion that they would always be permitted to operate. The Belgian lowlands were strategically valuable, and different powers had claimed the territory over the years. When the brotherhood had begun, they'd actually been working for the Burgundian Netherlands, but power had shifted and the territory had become the Spanish Netherlands, and it looked as if it would become the Austrian Netherlands pretty soon. Admittedly, Ernst had not anticipated that the force to bring them down would be monstrous English bureaucrats, but the end result was much the same.

Accordingly, they had been prepared. Though they'd lost the bulk of their assets, there were resources and hidden monies that had never gone down in the books. Backup libraries of texts and of genetic stock had been established in facilities hidden in other cities, in other countries. And if one planned to kill a Grafter, one had better make truly certain that the body one was executing held the right brain. The majority of their scholars had been killed, but not all. Some had been working at secret remote facilities. A couple had escaped the British through luck or cunning.

The Broederschap regrouped and retreated, moving back even farther into the shadows. It would take decades for them to rebuild, but they had learned several vital lessons that would define their future.

First, they now knew that despite all their abilities and knowledge, they were not the ultimate force they had believed themselves to be. The world contained creatures of unfathomable and inexplicable power, creatures outside God's pattern that could destroy them easily. The British Isles possessed such monsters, but the Grafters could not be certain that similar demons did not dwell on the Continent. From then on, the brotherhood would operate under the strictest secrecy. No public profile, no seizing of power, nothing that might draw the attention of the Gruwels or something like them.

Second, Ernst and Gerd were determined that they would never again be subject to the authority of an earthly government. The invasion of the Isle of Wight had been done at the command of a man with no understanding of the brotherhood's value. Far from being a worthy leader, he was a greedy coward who had tossed them to the dogs when they became inconvenient. It was clear that if normal people learned of their abilities, they would try to use the Grafters as tools or weapons.

The Broederschap now had a new purpose, a mission that would burn within them and push them to far greater works: revenge upon the abominations that were the Gruwels.

They began to rebuild, establishing houses in various cities across Europe. Over the years they grew quietly in wealth, numbers, and knowledge. The wealth came from sensible investments augmented by substantial fees for discreetly curing wealthy individuals of incurable ailments. If they had revealed and marketed even a fraction of their abilities, they would have become stupendously rich, but there were several things that stood in the way of that. The most pressing deterrent, of course, was that if medical technology several centuries ahead of its time was suddenly to emerge, it would serve as a beacon to the Gruwels. There was also the fact that Grafter art was incredibly difficult to implement, expensive to fund, and labor-intensive. Besides, after watching themselves be executed without anyone raising any objections, they were not feeling particularly well-disposed toward mankind.

Their numbers swelled, but in a strictly controlled manner. It was understood that if the brotherhood grew too much, they would draw attention. Some new members came from the Grafters' own families, their potential identified while they were children. Outsiders were also enlisted, with talented scholars and scientists lured in by the promise of knowledge and (once sworn to secrecy) demonstrations of what was possible. Even as new Grafters were instructed in the science of the Broederschap, they were taught to hate and fear the monsters that lived in the British Isles.

Their work progressed. The Broederschap scholars believed in research and exploration, and while many devoted themselves to martial applications, there were just as many whose efforts were guided solely by their curiosity. Some sought to duplicate the abilities that the Gruwels had exhibited, and others simply worked to take their knowledge as far as it could go.

But even as Ernst and Gerd oversaw the rejuvenation of their brotherhood (and sisterhood; any thoughts of gender discrimination had been thrown out the window in 1554 after their greatest scholar had asserted there was no relevant difference between the male and female brains and had produced two brains as proof, offering to walk any doubters through the pertinent features—an offer hastily declined), they were carefully laying the groundwork for vengeance.

It would be more than two centuries before the Broederschap learned the true name of their enemy. Agents and money finally did their work and revealed the Brotherhood of the Checquy, an organization that coiled its way through the British government like a parasite. Another century and a half passed before the Grafters could place even a single agent in the enemy organization, and she was obliged to commit suicide just before she was discovered. The next agent took decades to penetrate the myriad of security checks surrounding the Checquy, but slowly, slowly, they gained more knowledge of their nemesis.

For Ernst and Gerd, it was simply a matter of patience. It might take centuries, but their revenge was inevitable, and their rage burned. For many of the other Grafters, however, those who did not seek or expect immortality, their hatred of the Checquy was abstract—still very real, but unconnected to their daily lives. That was how it was for Odette. She had known that one day, perhaps long after her death, the Broederschap would move against the Checquy. But she was not a soldier. Her purpose was to learn, to innovate. To create. She loathed the idea of the Gruwels, but they seemed very distant.

Distant, that is, up until a sunny morning a few months ago when Ernst had announced to the brotherhood that there had been a change of plans. Rather than wreaking their dire revenge upon the hated demons called the Checquy, the Grafters would be joining them as colleagues and allies.

Which brought Odette to the here and now, in the bottom of a hotel bathtub full of slime.

8

Trouble behind us. Trouble in front of us, Odette thought grimly. Staying at the bottom of the bathtub seems like much the best option.

Nonetheless, it didn't seem a realistic course of action, not least because room service was unlikely to deliver breakfast to the bottom of a tub of muck. Odette pulled herself out of the mire and began to get ready for her day.

Forty-five minutes and a cosmetic pupil-dilation later, Odette was flatly wished good morning by the Checquy guard at the elevator as she and Alessio passed by.

"Oh, uh, good morning," said Odette. Alessio walked a little faster until they had gone around a corner. "Are you okay?" she asked.

"I'm just creeped out. They're everywhere."

"Alessio, they're security guards."

"The difference between a security guard and a prison guard is one order from the boss," said Alessio darkly. They came to the door of the royal suite. Two men were standing sentry outside. One was their cousin Frank, the other was a Checquy operative.

"You can go ahead," said Frank. "The rest of the delegation

is sort of trickling in." Odette and Alessio exchanged raised eyebrows as they walked into a sitting room much larger and more opulent than the already impressive one they shared. *I wonder how big the bathtub in this suite is*, thought Odette idly.

A conference table was off to one side. Several members of the delegation were already seated there, reviewing documents. All of them were wearing suits and harried expressions. At the head of the table sat Graaf van Suchtlen, dipping a toast soldier into a soft-boiled egg and chortling over the latest edition of *Private Eye*. Odette walked over to him, Alessio trailing silently behind her. They stood wordlessly by the patriarch's side until he acknowledged them.

"Ah, Odette and Alessio! Good morning," he said cheerfully.

"Good morning, Grootvader," they said, almost in unison.

"I trust you slept well, surrounded by the guards of our allies?" he said.

"Absolutely," said Odette. Alessio smiled weakly.

"Alessio, you look very smart in your suit, but you won't be needing it today."

"Oh?" said Alessio warily.

"No, the Checquy have kindly made arrangements for you to be entertained. A group of students from their training facility—"

"The Estate," added Odette helpfully.

"Yes, a group of students from the Estate are in London for a field trip to visit various musea and landmarks. You will be joining them." Odette did not dare look at her brother, but she couldn't hear him breathing, which was not a good sign since he needed to do that in order to live.

There was a fraught pause.

"Oh, Alessio, you'll get to see London," she said encouragingly. "That sounds like fun." She nudged him.

"Yes. Such fun," he said woodenly.

"However, in order to fit in with them, you will have to be wearing the school uniform. Frau Blümen, the headmistress of the Estate, has thoughtfully sent one in your size." Van Suchtlen did not make any gesture, but his secretary Anabella, a plump older woman, immediately came over carrying a uniform on a hanger.

A blazer of lurid orange, lime green, and purple stripes burned Odette's dilated pupils. There was a tie in the same horrendous colors, which was apparently worn over a white shirt. A pair of gray trousers appeared to be trying to hide themselves so as not to be associated with the blazer and tie.

"And, of course, the hat," said Anabella, presenting a straw chapeau of the sort that Odette vaguely remembered was called a boater. It was adorned with a broad ribbon in the school colors.

"Well, that all looks very impressive," said van Suchtlen in the cheerful tones of a man who did not have to wear it. Alessio reached out and took the suit as if it were made out of the scrota of war criminals. "Go and put it on so that we can all see how it looks." Alessio tottered out of the suite, beaten down by the knowledge that he would be spending the day with the traditional enemies of his family while wearing a suit that might induce epilepsy in passersby.

"Grootvader, forgive me for asking, but will he be all right on this excursion?" Odette said.

"He'll be fine. It will do him good to get out and spend more time with children his own age."

"I meant, will he be safe with those people? Those children are already trained warriors. Are they going to know who he is?"

"They'll know," said van Suchtlen. "Their teachers will have advised them. Alessio is part of the negotiations. His presence is a sign of good faith on our side."

So my baby brother will be a hostage, thought Odette. Terrific. But she knew better than to voice any complaint. Really, they were all hostages, but the Checquy, for all its unnaturalness, was a government agency and could be trusted to keep visiting dignitaries safe. Probably.

Odette sat down at the other side of the table and woke up her tablet computer. She reached for a cup of coffee, but one of the aides moved the tray out of her reach with a disapproving look. As she reread the files on the Checquy's hierarchy, other members of the delegation entered the room. Almost all of them stopped to pay their respects to van Suchtlen, standing patiently until they were acknowledged. Her great-uncle Marcel, however, merely traded a nod with the head of the Grafters before walking directly to Odette. He pecked her on the cheek and sat down beside her.

He was still wearing his original body, so although he was several centuries younger than Grootvader Ernst, Marcel Lelie-feld looked as though he could be the graaf's grandfather. He was a dapper little man with old-fashioned side-whiskers and a suit that had last been in style during World War II. The nature of his enhancements was a matter of much speculation among the younger generation, but it was known that, in his prime, he had torn open a bank vault with his bare hands, and just last year he had broken the neck of a Komodo dragon that had escaped from its pen in his atelier.

"Good morning, my dear," he said. "Your eyes look lovely." Odette could feel herself blushing, and stopped it. "Did you have any coffee?"

"No."

He looked at her for a long moment. "Don't have any more," said Marcel. "Your throat needs to heal."

"Fine," said Odette.

"Doing some last-minute reading up on the key players?"

"There are still two spots in their Court that haven't been permanently filled," said Odette. "I don't understand why Rook Kelleher and Chevalier Whibley are only temporary. Especially since they replaced Bishop Conrad Grantchester right away. Clearly they can move quickly when they need to, and I would have thought his position would be harder to fill than the other two."

"Well, there's some speculation that they are deliberately leaving those spots open," said Marcel. "Perhaps a newcomer will be granted a role."

"One of us?" asked Odette, startled. The Court was the executive branch of the Checquy and possessed authority over enough supernatural individuals to destroy a nation with ease. Any nation.

"Or perhaps they just want us to think that it is a possibility." Marcel shrugged. "We are coming to them as supplicants, but we are not a power to be treated lightly. If this merger is to work, then both parties will be forced to change." Odette opened her mouth to say something, but at that moment the entire room fell silent as, at the end of the table, van Suchtlen shut his magazine and handed it to one of the hovering aides.

"There is one thing I would like to cover before Alessio returns," he said. "But first, we shall take some precautions. Lars, please check the room." One of the assistants bowed from the waist and opened a bulky plastic suitcase. Nestled in the foam were small black appliances that were handed out to several of the other aides. They immediately began passing them over the walls and fixtures, checking for electronic surveillance devices.

"Didn't they check for these last night?" Odette muttered to Marcel.

"Of course," said Marcel, "but the Checquy are extremely talented, and we are on their home turf. It is always best to be cautious." Van Suchtlen gestured to Harold, one of their financial executives. Harold removed his tinted glasses to reveal his extraordinary eyes. Irises lay within irises, green circling brown circling blue circling gold circling purple. Odette squinted to watch the circles in his eyes rotate around each other. She knew that some of their craftsmen had labored for months to construct them.

"No listening devices, Excellency," said one of the aides finally.

"And I don't see anything unexpected in the spectrum from gamma through microwave," said Harold.

"Thank you," said van Suchtlen. "That's very encouraging. I like to think that they respect us as a diplomatic party. Well, then, let's get started. To begin with, I understand there have been more attacks on the Continent?"

Odette braced herself. The attacks had started a couple of months ago, shocking the Broederschap with their randomness, their complexity, and their spite. Ever since the battle with the Checquy, the members of the brotherhood hadn't considered themselves truly safe; from then on, they had operated at a level of extreme paranoia and had a policy of keeping to themselves that had helped them avoid any significant conflicts. That had all changed as their facilities and personnel were suddenly subjected to a series of hit-and-run attacks engineered by a body they had come to call "the Antagonists."

The Antagonists were not a government organization intent on subjugating the Grafters. Nor were they a mindless group of supernatural monsters that wanted merely to kill. They were motivated by hatred and anger; their attacks were designed to cripple, to wound, to mutilate. They not only caused horrendous damage but also served to keep the Broederschap completely off balance. There was no pattern to their malice. One day, it was an elaborate act of vandalism at a private gallery of historic Grafter masterpieces; the next day, a strike on a lab that left people injured and equipment destroyed. And then for weeks nothing would happen, and dread grew in the ranks. With no idea where the Antagonists were based, the brotherhood could not strike back. And now there had been more attacks.

Marie, the (currently) short-haired (currently) blond head of security for the delegation, raised her hand.

"They are escalating their strikes against us. There have been three more attacks in the past six days. Several vats in Ixelles have been found befouled—irreparably. Their contents are being destroyed. One of the labs at Seraing has melted. And the head groundskeeper at the Madrid house...well, his arms and legs fell off yesterday evening without any warning. We're not entirely certain that the Antagonists are responsible for that, however. He may have been veering from his prescribed diet."

"And no progress in tracking them down?" asked van Suchtlen, looking grim.

"We have a few leads, extrapolating from where they've been striking at us." Marie did not sound hopeful. "You know, I think that the Checquy could probably assist us with this sort of thing," she said tentatively. "Their connections are much more extensive than ours."

"Absolutely not," said van Suchtlen sharply. "We are trying to court these people; we don't need to air our dirty laundry in front of them. When you're pursuing a woman, you don't tell her that you have the pox at that moment. You keep bringing her the flowers, and you dance the minuet, and the whole time, you are getting the treatment with the mercury."

A bemused silence ensued.

"They will not want to merge with us if we come bringing enemies," said van Suchtlen, apparently oblivious to the nonplussed expressions of his staff. "If we arrive at the negotiating table admitting this problem, then we are already weakened."

Oh, this is a great start to an honest relationship, thought Odette.

"And matters have grown even more complex as of last night," continued the graaf. "Odette and I were invited to visit a Checquy occurrence site, and there were unmistakable signs. The Antagonists have followed us to London, and they have killed at least sixteen people."

Reactions around the table varied. There were some gasps, and one of the assistants gave a little screamlet. Marcel simply closed his eyes. Marie's hair went from blond to white. Harold spilled his orange juice across the table.

"Why would they do that?" he asked. "Why would they come here? With the Checquy acting as the supernatural police, this is the most dangerous place on earth for their kind."

"They hate us," said the graaf. "They hate what we are, they hate our work, and they will not leave us alone."

"So what is our next move?" said Marcel.

"We can endure the strikes on the Continent," said van Suchtlen. "For a little while longer, anyway. Security must be increased at all the houses and facilities—Marie, inform your mentor." She nodded. "Their presence in London, however, needs to be addressed immediately. If the Checquy discover the truth about this, it will mean the end of everything we have worked for."

"I can't cover a city with what we have here now," said Marie. "This delegation is all lawyers and financiers." Some hurt expressions blossomed around the table, which Marie ignored. "They all have enhancements, but they don't have the training, and they don't have the time. All we have in terms of military is ten bodyguards. The only fleshwrights we have are Marcel and Odette. And all of us will be constantly under the eyes of the Checquy."

"Perhaps we could bring in some Chimerae from the Continent," suggested Marcel. Odette looked at him, surprised.

The Chimerae were the elite of the Grafters' soldiers—humans who had been completely transformed into weapons. They were rare, not only because they were recruited from the best but because they were fabulously expensive to create. Rigorously trained in combat, each one represented months of work by the Broederschap's most skilled artisans. Each had multiple offensive enhancements drawn from across the biological kingdoms. No two were alike, but they all, as a baseline, could easily break every human record for speed and strength.

In the olden days (which meant up until a few months ago, when Ernst had made his announcement), they had been stockpiled in preparation for the moment the Grafters brought their revenge against the Checquy. Until then, for the most part, they had served as guards of the brotherhood's most valuable holdings. In hidden vaults and strong rooms dotted across Europe, they stood vigil over hoards of wealth and precious biological specimens—though each of them was as much a treasure as the riches he protected.

On those rare occasions when they were unleashed, they solved problems.

For instance, in the eighteenth century, a brilliant young student from the University of Ingolstadt caught the eye of members of the Broederschap. His work with galvanism and chemistry was deemed to have tremendous potential, and they recruited him. He was given a thorough grounding in the core principles of the brotherhood's techniques, but he chafed at their restrictions and eventually went rogue, disappearing to pursue his own research. Agents scoured the known world for him, but it was years before five Chimerae were dispatched to the Arctic, where he had constructed and animated a monstrous being using cadavers and lightning. Four of the five troops were killed, but the rogue doctor and his creation also died out there on the ice.

In the late nineteenth century, a Grafter research facility stood on Noble's Isle, a remote island in the Pacific. The head of the facility designed and oversaw a private project in which more than one hundred animals were surgically altered and augmented with heightened strength, rudimentary intelligence, and opposable digits. In a development of outstanding predictability, the subjects rose up, briskly slaughtered the Broederschap staff, and began constructing crude vessels with an eye toward escaping. Seven Chimerae were sent to address the problem. None of the experiments left the island.

In the early 1990s, when a Colombian drug lord decided not to pay the Broederschap the agreed-upon price for a significantly extended life span (one unencumbered by cancer, male-pattern baldness, or impotence), he retired to a fortified estate and surrounded himself with a private army. After several increasingly emphatic invoices went unpaid, ten Chimerae descended on the fortress in the dead of night and systematically slaughtered almost everyone. (Graaf Ernst had felt that it would be inappropriate to punish the domestic staff, and so their memories were instead forcibly readjusted.) The Broederschap had then pillaged the drug lord's private zoo for some rare specimens, leaving only his hippopotamuses to gambol about freely in the jungle and terrify the local fishermen.

Despite the Chimerae's effectiveness, the Grafters' paranoia about the Checquy (and any other possible Continental equivalents) was such that their soldiers were deployed for only the most serious situations, and even then measures were taken to ensure that they left no trace. Odette assumed that substantial safeguards had been built into the Chimerae's very frames to guarantee that no incriminating skin cell or drop of blood would ever be left behind for examination.

"Deploying the Chimerae here is a terrible idea," Nikolina, the communications liaison, said flatly. "If the Checquy found even one Chimera trying to enter the country, they'd take it as a declaration of war." Odette nodded in agreement. The Chimerae were unmistakably the creation of the Broederschap; some of the Chimerae's organs would literally have Grafter fingerprints all over them, and the nature of their enhancements would leave no doubt as to their purpose.

"There are eighteen Chimerae in Cardiff," said the graaf. "They are in hibernation in an apartment there." The entire table was silent for a moment in horrified awe. If he had declared that he had a couple of nuclear weapons tucked away in Wales, they couldn't have been more startled.

Another one of his arrangements, thought Odette, impressed. The canny bastard.

Looking at him, one could easily forget that Ernst van Suchtlen was centuries old, with all the cunning and foresight these years had taught him. His strategies were hugely complex, spanning decades, and very few others in the Broederschap were privy to his plans. When he had announced that, as the culmination of years of work, the Grafters would be entering into negotiations with the Checquy, Marcel had been the only person she knew who was unsurprised.

It was only when she was told that she would be joining the delegation that Odette learned about the extensive preparations Graaf van Suchtlen had made before he presented himself to Myfanwy Thomas with his proposal. He had not been interested in simply throwing himself and his brotherhood on the dubious mercy of the Checquy, and so, while he had extended the open hand of peace, his other hand had been holding a selection of weapons—just to make peace as appetizing a prospect as possible. To that end, he had put in place two weapons of mass destruction in British urban centers. He had suborned Checquy operatives. He had even purchased the loyalty of two members of the Checquy Court.

None of his measures proved very successful—Myfanwy Thomas had smashed them all before he could even enter her office. But now it appeared that there had been other preparations, other contingencies.

Always planning ahead, mused Odette. But he wasn't prepared for the enemy behind us. He never foresaw the possibility of the Antagonists, and now they are threatening our future. She wondered what other schemes he had put in place. He might very well have more facilities and operatives dotted around the country. In the back of every Grafter's mind was the knowledge that, should the negotiations fail, they would need to fall back from the wrath of the Checquy.

"All right, then," said Marie, and for the first time that Odette could recall, she sounded uncertain. "So we'll activate the Chimerae and bring them here. But I'm still not convinced of the wisdom of this. Even with the soldiers, how will we find the Antagonists in London? This city is huge!"

"But it's a great deal smaller than Europe," said the graaf in a very reasonable tone. "I have utter confidence in you. This problem must be taken care of without letting the Checquy know that it ever existed." There were murmurs of subdued agreement around the table. "And if we are finished with this subject, then Alessio can come in, and we will go over the schedule for today."

Anabella scurried to open the door, revealing Odette's brother waiting in his Estate uniform. It was, if anything, even more ghastly when placed on a human being. He walked in stiffly, as if trying to make as little contact with his clothing as possible. Odette kept her face carefully blank.

"You look very nice," said van Suchtlen warmly.

"But you're not wearing the hat," said Odette in a helpful tone. Alessio shot her a look that promised retribution of the direst sort, and then, with absolutely no expression, he placed the boater on his head. The entire table clapped politely, Alessio closed his eyes in an effort to endure the agony, and Odette took the opportunity to snap some pictures with her phone.

"What a fascinating outfit," she said quietly when Alessio sat down next to her. "I'm sure it's full of historical and cultural significance."

"I'm sure it's so that I'll make an easy target if they need to shoot me," said Alessio.

"Is that a teapot on the crest? Why would there be a teapot?" asked Odette.

"To torture me," said Alessio. "This uniform is probably revenge for my ancestors' invading their country centuries ago and slaughtering their people."

In unison, they looked to the end of the table, where one of the ancestors in question was drinking a cup of tea and playing with his smartphone.

"Well, you can take it up with him if you like," said Odette. Alessio made a little moaning sound as he picked at his blazer. "It's not that bad," she said soothingly. "And Grootvader Ernst likes it."

"Grootvader Ernst was born in a time when men wore tights. And hats with feathers in them!" Great-Uncle Marcel shot them a look, and they both went quiet.

The schedule for the day was quite straightforward. The entire delegation would travel to Apex House, the administrative headquarters of the Checquy. They would be scanned and registered by a security detail before Alessio went off with his school group and the rest of the delegation was formally welcomed to the negotiating table by half the Court (the Lord was obliged to meet with the Prime Minister every Wednesday morning, Rook Kelleher had the flu, Chevalier Whibley was on his way back from a journey overseas, and Bishop Alrich would apparently crumble into greasy ash if he appeared during normal business hours). After that, everyone would split up into work groups to address various issues.

"And be polite at all times," said van Suchtlen. "They are as wary of us as we are of them. Be professional, be normal. Endeavor not to do anything that will result in them obliterating us."

9

Blackness. Blackness and cold, and a terrible weight pressing down on every part of her. That was all Felicity knew. It was everything. There was no room for any thought. All she could do was cling to the one warm thing that existed. She buried her face in its softness and felt arms closed tight around her. All around them, the cold darkness moved, surging, compressing, pushing them along. And it lasted for a long, long time.

Light!

It unfolded all around her. And it was not the terrifying green glare of Pawn Jennings's power but a soft, gentle warmth that soaked pinkly through her eyelids and stroked her skin. There was heat against her front, and the chill on her back was not as bad as it had been. For a few seconds, she floated in the light.

And then she fell, flailing, untangling, for perhaps a meter before she flopped down onto a softish, yielding surface. The smell of plastic and nylon was familiar. Crash mat, her brain supplied vaguely. Like in gymnastics at school. She tried to open her eyes, but they were sticky, and she had to rub at them before she could see. On her hands, she could see little crystals that melted away into water. Frost.

Felicity was exhausted, but she managed to lift herself up on her elbows and look around. She was sprawled on a blue Olympic-style crash mat in a white room with windows that looked out onto a gray sky. The crash mat appeared to be the only furniture. The whole place felt delightfully warm.

If this is the afterlife, then everyone has been extremely wrong about it.

Next to her was the curved brown back of a naked man. *Great, another one,* she thought weakly. *At least this one seems* to be a little more standard-issue. This naked man had a nice back, from what she could tell, but he did not seem to be doing well. All she could see of him was covered in a rime of frost, and he was shaking. The muscles in his shoulders and arms twitched violently. Well, that's not good, she thought. I'd better do... something. It took all her strength, but she sat up. She could feel her head wobbling on her neck like a baby's.

It was at that point that Felicity realized that she, too, was naked. Her armor and coveralls had vanished. There was no sign of her gun or her wristwatch. Even the smears of rubbish-based visual and olfactory camouflage were gone. All she was wearing was a thin, swiftly melting coat of ice and frost. She gave a moment's thought to spreading her Sight out beyond the room, but even the idea left her exhausted. I think it'll be easier just to stand up and open the door.

There was a door, and somewhere beyond it, a bell was ringing. She was just getting to her knees when the door opened and a woman in a nurse's uniform bustled in. She was black and in her late fifties or early sixties. The nurse's eyes widened when she saw the two naked people on the mat.

"Oh Lord," she said in surprise. "He's brought another with him!" she shouted back through the doorway. She spoke with a strong Caribbean accent. "You all right?" she asked Felicity, who nodded. The nurse cast a quick diagnostic eye over her and then descended on the naked, twitching man and hurriedly gave him an injection. His shuddering eased, then stopped completely, and the nurse carefully rolled him onto his back. It was Pawn Chopra. His eyes were closed, and his breathing was settling into an easy rhythm.

The nurse briskly toweled Chopra dry, spread a blanket over him, and kissed him on the forehead. Then she took a pair of glasses out of her pocket and put them on the mat by his head.

"His contact lenses will have been lost in the journey," she explained to Felicity. "And he always likes to wake up and find his glasses waiting for him. Now, let's dry you off and get you a robe."

"But I've got to let them know we're still alive!" exclaimed Felicity. "They'll think we all died in the fire. And the naked Homeowner in the OOM!" She stopped under the nurse's politely uncomprehending gaze. "Are—you are with the—" began Felicity, but the nurse held up her hand.

"I'm not with your little group," she said.

"You're a civilian?" squeaked Felicity, aghast. She was aware that not only had she mentioned highly classified matters to an outsider, but she also probably sounded insane.

"I'm just a nurse in the hospital, but don't worry, we called your people as soon as you came through. I'm Cedella. Please don't tell me your name, I don't need to know it, and I really prefer to keep my knowledge of you people to a minimum."

"I—yeah, okay," said Felicity, still slightly taken aback. "Um, you said this is a hospital? What hospital? Where are we?"

"This is the William Harvey Hospital," said Cedella. "In Ashford."

"Ashford?" repeated Felicity in bewilderment.

"In Kent," said the nurse helpfully.

"Kent. Why—how are we in Kent?"

"Him," said Cedella, patting Pawn Chopra gently. "This is the room that Sanjay was born in. I was here twenty-one years ago when he came into the world. And now, periodically, he comes back." Felicity stared at her.

"It was about four times the first year, and don't even ask me how much fuss that caused when he started popping up in the hospital bed with no explanation. For a while, people thought he was being kidnapped." She draped a tactful towel over Felicity's lap, and then started rubbing her shoulders and back dry. "Although I don't know what kind of kidnapper would keep delivering a child back to the one place," the nurse sniffed. "Especially since no one ever saw him being brought into the building. One patient woke up to find the baby crying in her lap.

"But then I saw him arrive here. He just appeared back in the bed where he was born, wriggling out of nowhere." She smiled and shook her head. "I didn't know what to do—no one was going to believe me. They might even think I was the kidnapper. The police had already asked me some questions because I kept finding him. Thank the good Lord another girl once found him when I was away on holiday." She draped another towel around Felicity's shoulders, then undid her braids and began vigorously toweling her hair. Felicity was reminded of being a child and having her hair dried by an Estate nurse after a bath. It was that same brisk, comforting intimacy.

"So, a hospital administrator sat me down, asked me what happened, and I was so tired of being interrogated that I told him the truth about what I'd seen," said the nurse. "A couple of days later, I heard that the little baby had died. And word came down that room four was not going to be used anymore.

"Then I was called up to the office of the chief of the hospital. He welcomed me and then he left the room. Two ladies came in, dressed very smart. They explained that the baby was not dead, that he was in the care of the government, and that there would be some more duties for me here at the hospital. If I took on those duties and kept it all secret, then I would receive a good deal of money and the gratitude of the nation. If I didn't—well, they never actually said what would happen. But I understood it wouldn't be nearly as nice."

"So you agreed," said Felicity, fascinated. The children of the Estate were rarely told how they had come to the Checquy. "And you...never talked to the parents about it?"

"No, that would have led to the ingratitude of the nation," said the nurse flatly. "Anyway, that night, men moved the furniture out of room four and put in a sports mat and the electrical eyes." Felicity looked around and saw the little red blinking lights in the corners of the room. "Those let us know when he's arrived. Otherwise, this room is kept empty. And you wouldn't believe how inconvenient that is—it's right in the middle of the hallway.

"Still, it's added something interesting to the job," Cedella said. "For the first few years they'd call us when he'd be coming through. I expect they found him missing and knew he was on his way. Me or one of the other girls would go in with a blanket and a bottle of hot milk for the baby and wait for him. He'd arrive, we'd warm him up and care for him for a bit, and then someone would come along and take him off in a car.

"Then, when he got a little older and could talk, they'd send us schedules for when he'd be coming. It was clear they were training him to do it on command. The little lad would pop in a couple of times a week, we'd put some pajamas on him, make a note of his vitals, and they'd come and get him.

"Sometimes he'd appear without any warning," she remembered. "I think he'd come if he got in trouble or wanted some company. Middle of the night, the bell would ring, and I'd go in to see him sitting there, shivering, wiping the ice off his arms. I'd call them, let them know we had him, and he and I would have a chat. I'd give him a bit of advice about school, or girls, or whatever was bothering him.

"Now that he's grown, he doesn't show up as much. And it's never easy when he does. He'll come through with wounds, and that makes it much worse. We've had to defibrillate him a couple of times. And the journey here isn't good for injuries either. But he's never brought anyone else through with him."

"The journey," said Felicity, trying to remember. "We were... somewhere else. He took us away from the fire, and there was a place." It all seemed like a dream that was fading away even as she thought about it. "A dark place. And cold."

"Sounds like it," the nurse said with a shrug. "Never been there myself and certainly don't want to go. He always comes out of there freezing cold and stripped of everything that isn't him. Clothes, deodorant, dirt, it's all gone." She finished drying Felicity. "On the bright side, though, your hair will never be cleaner."

Well, that's something, thought Felicity. She hadn't been looking forward to trying to get all the refuse-based camouflage out of her hair.

"What time did you go in there?" asked the nurse. "They like us to keep records."

"About four o'clock?" hazarded Felicity. She'd lost track of time, but she vaguely recalled they'd entered the house late in the day.

"In the morning?"

"No, the afternoon."

"Oh, my," said the nurse. "Eighteen hours. That's his longest journey ever. Poor boy." She patted the sleeping Pawn Chopra gently.

"Eighteen hours?" repeated Felicity incredulously. "You mean it's Wednesday?"

The nurse nodded. "Wednesday morning," she said, fetching Felicity a soft robe. "Now, do you fancy a cup of tea?"

And so, Rook Thomas, it appears that the man was strangled to death by his own beard."

"By or with?" asked Myfanwy, frowning.

"By."

"Well, that definitely sounds worthy of some attention," she said, jotting down a note to get her hair cut. "Initiate a short investigation, and if anything serious emerges, we can up the priority."

"Yes, ma'am." The voice came from a speakerphone in the middle of the boardroom table.

"If that's all you need at the moment, then I'll hang up," she said. "I'll be here at Apex House for the rest of the morning, and then, once we've finished the formal greetings, I'll come back to the Rookery. Call me or Mrs. Woodhouse if anything comes up." A chorus of agreement came out of the speaker, and then the call finished. "Ingrid, can you book me in for a haircut, please?"

"Certainly, Rook Thomas. And a coffee?"

"Only if you want to live out the hour," said Myfanwy. The previous night had gone far later than she had expected, and she'd had to be up early in order to reach the Apex before the morning traffic congealed. Now she was ensconced in the boardroom with a stack of papers, a pen, and a firm intention to get some work done.

She opened the folder that contained the overnight notifications. As always, she was amazed at the things that happened in the world. Every day, every hour, stories of the bizarre flowed into the Checquy. Reports came from a variety of sources—law enforcement, medical bodies, religious institutions, government departments, universities. All through the British Isles, people in authority were constantly confronted with unusual situations. Sometimes they saw things they couldn't explain, things that made no sense. Or a subordinate would go to the boss, confused or frightened by an occurrence he could describe only as "unnatural." At that point, the superior would remember the vague but disturbing briefings from the government and would dial the number officials had given out—a number that connected to the Rookery.

These reports were received by Checquy operatives who had special training in sounding sympathetic and not at all skeptical. The notifications were dutifully transcribed, checked, analyzed, reviewed, and passed on up the line. Many were identified as false reports or duplicates, but some continued to ascend through the ranks of influence until they were given the tick of approval and an official response was authorized. It wasn't Myfanwy's responsibility to approve anything other than the most exorbitantly expensive of activities, but at the opening and closing of every day, she received a summary of recent events, a distillation of the supernatural in the United Kingdom.

The reports before her included the previous night's fatalities at the Italian restaurant. The corpses had been carefully moved to the morgue in the Apex, although one more had torn open during its trip down the stairs, with horrible results. The scientists were not clear on the nature of that black liquid and hadn't yet determined whether it was dangerous, but it was unlikely that the restaurant would be reopening anytime soon. However, that massacre was not the only event that had occurred since the end of business yesterday.

There was a boy in Cornwall whose eyes had changed color overnight.

Salvage divers had examined a cargo ship that sank two weeks previously near the Port of Immingham and found tears in the hull that appeared to have been made by huge teeth.

All the reptiles in the Edinburgh Zoo had begun molting at the same time, and their shed skin was evaporating off the ground.

Two VW Beetles that had been reported stolen in Thetford had been found in a field outside town after nearby residents heard loud, increasingly frantic horn-beeping and the sounds of grinding metal. The police observed that one of the vehicles appeared to have mounted the other.

And there, at the bottom of the list, in red ink, was the one she'd been dreading. Another one, she thought. Damn it. And unlike the mating cars, which could just be a student prank, there's no doubt that this is genuine. She flipped through the photos.

Just like the others, it had occurred in one room of a house, this one a bedroom in the town of Wellingborough. It was a normal-looking room—double bed, framed Monet prints, a vase of dried flowers on the chest of drawers—except for the score of large crystals that had erupted from the walls, ceiling, and floor. They were meters long, razor sharp, and all projected out to the same spot in the room, in front of the chest of drawers, where they had transfixed the seventy-four-year-old Miss Audrey Dudgeon, owner and resident of the house. In the photos, wearing a nightgown and a bathrobe, she was slumped over but held in place by the shining blades. The crystals were murkily transparent except near her body, where they were stained red on the inside. No autopsy had yet taken place, but Myfanwy knew that Miss Dudgeon's blood would be found to have crystallized inside her body. Just like all the others'.

The Checquy had been pursuing this case since the very beginning, two years ago, when a man and his son had been found impaled by crystals in the dining room of their house in Daventry.

Initially, there had been two theories. Some had thought the phenomenon might be linked to the locale—there were precedents for that sort of thing. There was an estate in the

West Country, Yalding Towers, where the statues were said to walk at night. In Herefordshire, Ryhope Wood was apparently impossible to get through—the place would simply turn you around and deposit you firmly where you had begun, although there were rumors of some very strange things coming out of it on occasion. Even the old Deptford Power Station in southeast London had, for a while, appeared to be controlling the local weather before it was tactfully demolished.

The other possibility was that one of the victims had caused it, perhaps suddenly manifesting an ability he or she could not control. There were precedents for that as well—Checquy statisticians advised that a small but significant percentage of people who died from aneurysms were actually spontaneous telekinetics who'd accidentally tried to move something heavy with their brains. But then, over the next two years, five more crystal-skewering deaths occurred, two in London and the rest of them in the county of Northamptonshire. It was those two in London that had really put paid to both theories. The Checquy had decided that, indeed, an individual or an organism was causing these deaths, whether knowingly or unwittingly. Myfanwy was really hoping it wasn't deliberate, because otherwise she was dealing with a supernatural serial killer. Questions were being asked, not just from within the Checquy but also at the highest levels of the British government. Pressure was beginning to be applied.

And they're happening more frequently, she thought grimly. Before, months could go by between them, but it's been only five weeks since the last one. We need to stop this. She made a note to allocate more resources to that investigation, and then she snorted. Every so often, she caught herself, startled at the power and authority she wielded. Especially since, technically, she wasn't the Myfanwy Thomas who had been made Rook.

The Myfanwy Thomas who had been brought up by the Checquy and elevated from Pawn to Rook had been a shy woman, frightened to use her supernatural power or her authority. In fact, that was one of the reasons she had been promoted, so that she would not pose a threat to certain parties. Instead of taking command, she had focused her attention on being an excellent bureaucrat.

Then, to her bewilderment, she had begun receiving warnings from a variety of sources, each of them predicting that she would lose her memory, that it would be torn away from her. Most people would have scoffed, but this was the Checquy. People who scoffed at the impossible tended to look stupid fairly soon afterward. Instead of scoffing, she had responded like a true bureaucrat, allowing herself a few moments of grief and then preparing a series of briefs for her future self—the woman who would wake up not knowing who she was or what kind of life she had inherited.

In due course, the predictions had come true. Her memories had been stolen, and her amnesiac self had woken up in a park with no idea what was going on but with a couple of extremely informative letters from her old self in her pocket. The letters had outlined the situation and given her the choice of leaving the country or assuming the identity of Myfanwy Thomas without telling anyone she had no idea who she was. Possibly against her better judgment, she'd picked the latter option.

Armed with the notes of her pre-amnesia self, she had slid into the role of Rook. It hadn't always been easy, but so far, she had not caused any catastrophes, despite the fact that she was effectively masquerading as herself—a role for which she was not terribly qualified. Unlike her old self, she was not shy, and she was perhaps a little too eager to say what she thought and do what she wanted. The change in her personality had been noted by the organization, but only two people knew that she had lost her memory.

The first was Linda Farrier, the Lady of the Checquy, who had the advantage of being able to walk around inside other people's sleeping minds and poke into things that interested her. The second was Myfanwy's executive assistant, Ingrid Woodhouse, because there was really no way of concealing that sort of thing from your EA. Myfanwy suspected that the pet rabbit she'd inherited was also aware of the change, but she had not been able to establish it for certain.

"Rook Thomas?"

Myfanwy looked up with a start. She'd been musing on the oddness of her life and lost all track of time. Ingrid was standing at the door with a steaming beverage balanced on a saucer.

"Oh, thank God," said Myfanwy.

"You're going to need it," said Ingrid grimly. "Bishop Attariwala has sent down word that he'd like to meet with you in his office as soon as possible."

"Did he say what it was about?" Myfanwy asked. She had a sinking feeling in her stomach.

"I'm afraid not."

"So that means it's going to be bad."

"That means it's going to be very bad," agreed Ingrid.

"Fine," said Myfanwy. "But I'm bringing the coffee."

"Do you want me to see if I can find something alcoholic to add to it?"

"Probably best not. But I may want something for afterward."

Among the briefs the old Myfanwy Thomas had left for the new Myfanwy Thomas were dossiers on prominent members of the Checquy. In her early days, the new Myfanwy had focused on the people with whom she worked closely. Mostly, these had been the members of the Court. Unfortunately, one of the Court was promptly killed in battle, and two others were revealed to be traitors. One of the Rook's responsibilities was to help select replacements, and so she'd become very familiar with the histories of the candidates. As she approached Raushan Singh Attariwala's office, Myfanwy ran through what she knew about the newly minted Bishop.

Raushan's family, devout Sikhs, had emigrated from India to the United Kingdom when he was an infant and settled in Blackpool. Mr. Attariwala was a pharmacist; his wife was a secretary for the local government council. They had four children (Raushan was the eldest), all of whom grew up speaking with English accents and proudly wearing the tangerine strip of the Seasiders. However, they never forgot where they had come from and remained fluent in Punjabi and Hindi.

Raushan was a sober child who took his responsibilities as eldest son very much to heart. Studious in school, he had friends, but his teachers described him as reserved. Life proceeded along a relatively standard course until Raushan turned nine. At that point, while bowling at a school cricket match, he managed to throw the ball in such a way that, with an earsplitting crack, it shattered the opposing team's bat.

Nobody was injured, but the batsman started crying out of shock. There was some momentary consternation among the spectators, but then it was generally agreed that the occurrence was the result of a cheap bat getting hit in just the right spot by a lucky bowl. A one-off fluke. The batsman was told briskly to stop being soft, the wreckage of the bat was tidied up, a new bat was produced (the ball was never found), the game continued (Raushan's team lost), and for a few weeks, Raushan enjoyed some local celebrity.

However, two people knew that it hadn't been a one-off fluke. The first was Raushan himself, who had felt a powerful tingling in his fingertips as the ball tore itself out of his hand. The second person was one of the cricket umpires, who happened to be a retired Checquy operative. A keen cricketer and former commando, he was able to identify a cheap bat or a supernatural manifestation from a mile away, and he knew that only one of those had been present that day. He passed on his thoughts to some of his old colleagues who were still in the game (of Checquying—not cricket). They were intrigued and placed the Attariwala residence under surveillance.

Over the next few weeks, the Checquy observers watched as Raushan secretly experimented with his newfound abilities to manipulate kinetic energy. His efforts were crude but impressive. He flipped a coin through the roof of his house and threw a tennis ball two miles out to sea. When he kicked a football through the trunk of a pine tree, they decided it was time to acquire him.

It was an aspect of the Checquy that Myfanwy had

experienced some difficulty coming to terms with. Apparently, in the United Kingdom, the monarchy reserved certain rights for itself, entitlements known as "the Royal Prerogative." Many of these rights had to do with government policies, defense, foreign affairs, and judicial matters. They also included a few unexpected privileges, such as automatic ownership of all unmarked mute swans in open water and any whales, sturgeons, or porpoises that might turn up around the place. If you found an unclaimed porpoise, it belonged to the monarch.

But an unpublicized element of the Royal Prerogative was automatic guardianship of "any and all persons or creatures exhibiting traits and capabilities for which no explanation can be divined." If you gave birth to a child whose breath baked bread, it too belonged to the monarch.

Of course, the monarchy didn't want these people (and creatures) hanging around the palace, being all unnatural and touching the furniture. Thus, the throne delegated this authority of guardianship to the Checquy, so, by royal writ, the Court of the Checquy held the right and the obligation to take into its custody any person on the British Isles who was possessed of supernatural abilities.

In times past, it had been a fairly simple (if cruel) process. There were different approaches depending on the social class of the target. For the literate classes, a representative of the Checquy would present a flowery letter from the King or Queen ordering that the child be taken and impressing upon the parents the requirement for secrecy. There would be a discreet stipend and possibly some sort of medal awarded. For the illiterate (read: poor) classes, if they were lucky, they'd get a coin or a ham chucked at them before their kid got picked up. If the Checquy sensed that the parents were going to make an inconvenient fuss, they might just snatch the child away and offer no explanation at all, leaving distraught and bewildered families to mourn and wonder for the rest of their lives. In none of these cases would the parents ever see their child again.

But society moved on, and eventually it wasn't as acceptable to just bludgeon people with the authority of the Crown (which was becoming a trifle averse to its name getting thrown around in relation to stolen children). And so the Checquy adapted its methods. Families would be observed for weeks or months before the target was acquired, and an appropriate approach would be designed. Paramount, however, was the requirement that the families not raise a fuss. In the age of newspapers, radio, and outraged citizens, there could be no trail leading back to the government. Parents were left with the belief that their child had died, or run away, or been kidnapped. It was ugly, but it was necessary.

The acquisition of Raushan was not as smooth as others had been, owing primarily to the Attariwala family traits of suspicion and strength of will—traits that would serve Raushan well in his later career. But eventually, after some missteps, he was placed in the Estate school on Kirrin Island to be tutored in the use of his abilities. And while he would attend the Church of England-based services at the Estate with the other students, he was unyielding in his insistence that he would continue to receive instruction in Sikhism. It was one of a series of compromises he successfully negotiated with an organization whose usual level of compromise was along the lines of "We don't exist. Now do what we say or Claire from Accounting will bite your head off."

During his time on Kirrin Island, Raushan pursued his studies with determination and focus. Like all the students, he worked closely with the Estate scientists, exploring the extent of his supernatural abilities. Soon, he could flick a toothpick clean through an egg, toss an egg clean through a car, and shove a car clean through a wall. It turned out, after some painful experiments with tennis balls, that he couldn't drain the kinetic energy out of an object that was traveling toward him. Nor could he increase the speed of vehicles he was traveling in, although he could give them a hell of a push start.

Naturally, he broke all the Estate records for the throwing sports (except for the javelin, because one girl in his class managed to fold space so that her javelin landed in China).

He also became a master of the bank shot, sending his weapons ricocheting off walls and around corners before traveling much farther than they should have.

All of which was very nice and impressive, especially at school sports days, but proved to be of little use in his career with the Checquy (beyond getting him in the door). Though Raushan excelled in all his studies, he showed special aptitude for business and the law. At the age of seventeen, he underwent the amrit, the Sikh ceremony of baptism. There had been some concern among the Checquy higher-ups that this dedication to his faith might constitute a conflict of interests, but Raushan never wavered in his loyalty to the organization.

Upon graduating from the Estate, Pawn Attariwala did not go for initial placement within the Checquy or a cadetship in the regular government. Instead, he went to Cambridge to study law. He did well enough that the Checquy altered the career course it had previously mapped out for him.

After earning his degree, he worked for a year in the Rookery before being seconded to the Ministry of Defence. Unusually, he was not provided with a cover identity; he merely presented himself as Mr. Raushan Attariwala, on loan from some other government department. He spent the next twelve months working hard, making friends, and learning how things worked in the nonsupernatural civil service. Then he was recalled by the Checquy, who put him to work at the Annexe helping to coordinate foreign operations. After that, he was on secondment to the normal government again, this time to the Foreign and Commonwealth Office. His career continued in this vein for several years, Pawn Attariwala alternating jobs at the Checquy with jobs in the regular civil service. Apex House; the Home Office. The Checquy's outpost in Edinburgh; the Cabinet Office. The Comb; the Attorney General's Office. Always working under his own name.

At the end of the decade, Pawn Attariwala was transferred permanently to Apex House. By that time, he was familiar with most aspects of the Checquy and had extensive contacts throughout the regular civil service. He was also married and had two small children, neither of whom gave any sign of possessing unusual capabilities.

Attariwala spent decades in the higher echelons of the Checquy in the role he had been groomed for, working under the Bishops as the key liaison between the Checquy Group and the central government. A true mandarin, he was accustomed to dealing with the most powerful politicians and bureaucrats in the United Kingdom and to exerting the Checquy's authority.

His career was marked by impressive highlights. He fabricated an outbreak of meningitis so that the entire nation was inoculated against mind-controlling maggots. He drove a Gorgon out of the country, not through any supernatural or military means but rather by unleashing constant audits upon her personal and business finances. He argued successfully with the Treasury for a 5 percent increase in the Checquy's budget allocation.

Indeed, he was so adept that he was usually the person called upon to act in the role of Rook or Chevalier when the regular person was away. As a result, when one of the Rooks was promoted to the rank of Bishop, almost everyone in the Checquy expected that Attariwala would replace that Rook in Domestic Operations. There had been much surprise, and not a little outrage, when instead the young and notoriously timid Myfanwy Thomas was put in the role. Pawn Attariwala impassively accepted the massive injustice, went into his office, and, to the astonishment of his staff, didn't smash anything at all.

Even when Rook Thomas proved to be capable (if incredibly introverted), some resentment on Pawn Attariwala's behalf still lingered. When Bishop Grantchester was revealed as a traitor and discreetly assassinated, there was no question who would fill the vacancy. Bishop Attariwala was installed in his new office in Apex House and assumed his duties without hesitation or difficulty.

There was, however, considerable friction between him and Myfanwy. He still resented her for taking the position that should have been his. The fact that he now had authority over her only made it worse, and it would have done her no good at all to explain that it was a different Myfanwy Thomas who had taken his job. Whenever the two met, his manner was imperious, and Myfanwy, who felt a certain affection and protectiveness for her previous self, was disinclined to be diplomatic.

When Myfanwy entered Attariwala's office, the Bishop had his back to the door and appeared to be reading an extremely important and absorbing paper. It was so important and absorbing that he did not acknowledge her arrival even though she had knocked and his executive assistant had buzzed him to advise she was there. Myfanwy rolled her eyes and moved to the chair in front of his desk. She noticed that he was twirling a pen around his thumb, and she couldn't help but tense up. Given the Bishop's abilities, it was like anyone else absently twirling a loaded gun.

I'm not clearing my throat, Myfanwy thought, and she sat herself down comfortably in the chair. She opened her notebook and began industriously writing down a shopping list. The sound of her scribbling apparently made an impression because Attariwala put down his paper, turned, and acted surprised to see her there.

"Ah, Rook Thomas. Thank you for coming."

"Of course, sir."

"Now, I've asked you to come here because I have some very serious concerns."

"Sir?"

"Last night, you left the reception at the hotel to inspect a manifestation site."

"Yes, sir," said Myfanwy.

"Your absence was noted."

"That's hardly astounding, since I told several people, including Bishop Alrich and Lady Farrier, that I was leaving," said Myfanwy tartly. "And the heads of security for both the Checquy and the Grafters."

"I'll have to ask you not to call them that," said Bishop Attariwala. "It may be an offensive term."

"Excuse me? You mean Grafters?"

"Yes. We're not certain, but it may be a term of hatred."

"I think it's probably a term of hatred because of our long history of hating them," said Myfanwy mildly. "If we called them the Shimmery Pistachios, Checquy operatives would use that as an epithet."

"Be that as it may, until the committee comes back with a decision on it, kindly do not use that word. We must make every effort not to insult them, which is why your desertion of our guests last night was so ill-advised."

"But—" began Myfanwy. She was about to point out that it was hardly desertion of their guests since she had taken Graaf Ernst van Suchtlen and his apprentice with her, but the Bishop cut her off.

"And you took Graaf Ernst van Suchtlen and his apprentice with you! It was highly inappropriate and highly irresponsible." Despite herself, Myfanwy felt the heat rising in her cheeks. "Rook Thomas, you are well aware of how dangerous manifestation sites can be. Just this morning, one of the investigators encountered something at the burned-out row house. He was enveloped in a cloud of mist and his skin began to melt. What if something like that had happened to either of your guests last night? You could have done irreparable damage to the negotiations!"

Myfanwy couldn't think of anything to say. She'd taken down monsters and men, but she was having trouble mustering up an attack on a reasonable argument.

Crap, she thought, he's right. It was stupid. Unforgivably stupid. Of course, there was no way she would admit that to him, but it burned inside her. She kept her mouth shut and her expression unimpressed.

"Matters are even more complicated, however," said the Bishop. "I have seen the preliminary findings from the row-house investigation." Myfanwy felt her face twist a little at that. She hadn't had time to review those findings yet. "I noticed that the head of the assault team put in an encrypted request for consultation with the Rooks."

"Yes," said Myfanwy.

"What did she want?"

"I don't know," said Myfanwy. "By the time I got to the phone, the connection was broken."

"Hmm," said the Bishop. "So far, in the ruins, they have found huge sections of charred meat with human skeletons in the middle of it."

"Something ate our people?" asked Myfanwy.

"Possibly," allowed Attariwala. "It seems to have been occupying a rectangular space. So, this large entity may have swallowed them or tentacles may have come out of it and pulled them into itself, where they were absorbed." Myfanwy felt the bottom drop out of her stomach. The Bishop was describing one of the weapons the Grafters had mobilized against the Checquy a few months ago, before the overtures of peace had been made.

"What are you saying?" she asked weakly.

"Nothing, at this point," said the Bishop. "Although Pawn Odgers, the head of the assault team, was one of the few familiar with the flesh-cube weapon in Reading and she knew that it was deployed by the Broederschap. I wonder what she wanted to tell you." He shrugged. "The investigation will continue, and we shall see what it uncovers. But I am very concerned about the possible implications. After all, the Broederschap has proven itself capable of planning and executing a multifront war."

"But we're at peace," said Myfanwy. "The Checquy and the Graft—the Broederschap—are working to join together." Inside her head, she was frantically thinking through the angles. Was it possible that the Grafters had played her? That Ernst had played her, used the negotiations as a prelude to an attack?

Well, anything is possible, she thought. I'm an amnesiac with the power to control people's bodies with my mind. But it's just not how I read the situation. I was sure these negotiations were genuine.

"I certainly hope that is true," said Attariwala. "And, of course, the negotiations will continue in good faith. But until we have confirmation on this issue, you will do everything in your power to make sure that our Broederschap allies are kept safe from harm. And from doing harm."

"Yes, Bishop Attariwala," said Myfanwy reluctantly. Additional guards and measures would need to be put into place at the Grafters' hotel, and she'd have to have a quiet (and extremely distasteful) word with the heads of the security detachment about what kind of protection they might be called upon to provide.

"Now, unless you have anything you'd like to discuss, I have some preparations to make for this morning's meetings," said the Bishop.

Myfanwy shook her head and stood, still taken aback by the revelations. When she reached the door, however, the Bishop spoke again.

"My predecessor worked very hard to bring you into the Court," he said calmly. "And it suited him to afford you a great deal of independence."

"Yes, sir," said Myfanwy warily.

"However, my predecessor was also a traitor in the employ of the Broederschap."

Now she understood. Not only the Grafters were under suspicion; apparently, she was too.

10

The Checquy executives were pleased, if somewhat startled, to discover that Felicity and Pawn Chopra were alive. They assured her over the telephone that someone would come to pick her up shortly. In the meantime, Cedella procured her a cup of tea and some clothes (in that order, which reflected a very realistic set of priorities) and guided her to the room where Chopra was now awake, lying in a normal hospital bed. He would be remaining under observation for exhaustion for a while longer.

"Sanjay," said the nurse as she led Felicity in, "your friend has come to check on you."

"Thank you, Cedella," said Chopra weakly. He was tucked up in bed, and a decidedly nonregulation but extremely bright patchwork quilt had been carefully laid over him. The sight of him in pajamas was a little ridiculous. He didn't look sick, just tired and wan.

"Miss, you sit with him for a while, and I'll get you when your ride comes," said the nurse. She smoothed Chopra's hair and moved out of the room.

"Well," said Felicity. "She's pretty bossy."

"Isn't she marvelous?" said Chopra. "I was so lucky to have her and the other nurses to visit while growing up at the Estate." Felicity wandered over to the tray of food by his bed. It appeared to be rice and peas with spices, and it smelled absolutely heavenly. Apparently, knowing the nurses your entire life ensured you weren't subjected to the standard-issue hospital food.

"And how are you feeling?" asked Felicity.

"Knackered."

"You look terrible," she said lightly. "Nice pj's, though." From the look of them, they weren't standard-hospital-issue either.

"They keep a few pairs for me."

"So, you always have to rest here afterward?" she asked.

"Ah, well, it's always a bit of an effort," said Chopra dismissively. Felicity smiled weakly and looked away. The memory of the journey through that...place was unsettling. The complete darkness, the burning cold. And the two of them, clinging to each other, his warmth the only solid thing. She could easily imagine having been torn away from him there, left to flail helplessly in the frozen blackness until she died.

"Thank you," said Felicity. "Thank you for saving me, for taking me with you." He smiled and looked down.

"Have you heard anything about the rest of the team?" he asked. "The ones who didn't come in with us?"

"No, but I haven't really spoken to anyone yet," said Felicity.

"Do you think they got out all right?" he said. There was tension in his voice.

She sat down in the chair next to the bed and took his hand. His grip was surprisingly weak, but his fingers were warm around hers. "They're damn good," she told him. "They can handle themselves."

They didn't say anything else, just sat like that until the nurse came to tell Felicity her ride was there.

The silence was torturous.

Odette and Alessio sat in the back of a long car across from the glossy young man who had been assigned to escort them. At the hotel, the delegation had been divided up into seven groups, and each group put into its own black car. Their escort had introduced himself as Pawn Bannister from Apex House. He'd placed special emphasis on the "Apex House" part and had seemed a trifle disappointed when they'd failed to react.

Pawn Oliver Bannister was the youngest of the escorts, in his midtwenties, and the expression on his handsome face had become a little fixed when he realized that he'd been assigned to the youngest (and, therefore, least important) of the Grafters. His suit was well cut—Odette suspected it was from Savile Row, or at least wanted to be mistaken for being from Savile Row—and his teeth and hair were both extremely shiny. Conversation in the car had withered and died after some observations about the weather and reassurances that the hotel was nice and that they'd slept well.

"You'll notice that we aren't hitting any red lights," said Pawn Bannister finally. His accent could have cut glass. "None of the other cars are getting stopped either. They're opening up seven different routes through the city. It's playing merry hell with the rest of the traffic."

"And this is for security reasons?" asked Odette warily. In addition to the driver, there was also a Checquy guard in the front seat. Are they worried about some sort of assassination attempt? No one is supposed to know we're here. Or that we exist.

"It's for security, certainly, but also convenience," said Bannister. "After all, you're VIPs. We want to remove as many distractions as possible so that we can all focus on our goals and work toward a satisfactory and successful end result."

God, he speaks like a motivational-management course, thought Odette.

"It's very impressive," she said encouragingly. "Such...strategic capabilities." Bannister nodded happily. Apparently, she'd hit the appropriate level of jargon. "And you said that you're based out of Apex House?"

"Yes, indeed," he said. "I was placed there right out of the Estate."

"What's your role there?" asked Odette. "When you're not stuck escorting us?"

"Well, I'm in international affairs and relations," he said airily. "Diplomatic work." Odette made polite interested noises. To her dismay, he continued to talk about himself for the rest of the car ride. He spoke of reviews he'd worked on, junkets he'd traveled on, and meetings he'd attended with high-ranking officials. It was simultaneously the most boring and the most intimidating lecture Odette had ever received. I'm so far behind in my career, she thought glumly, having forgotten that she wasn't even in the civil service. By the time the car pulled up at Apex House, she was beginning to question if she'd ever accomplished anything in her life.

The door was opened by a security guard, and Alessio and Odette both slid out of the car as quickly as possible. Odette snapped out an arm and caught Alessio in an iron grasp.

"Don't even think of leaving me with him," she said between gritted teeth. She looked around for the other cars and saw that they were the first to arrive. Behind her, Bannister was talking loudly on his mobile phone. "Suddenly the excursion to the museum is looking a lot better, isn't it?" she said.

"I'm still wearing this uniform," said Alessio. "And according to your new boyfriend, it's a lot to live up to." Back in the car, Bannister had also mentioned his accomplishments at the Estate. He'd congratulated Odette's little brother on the outfit and then informed him that it came from a proud tradition. Alessio had mustered a sickly smile and, in the name of diplomatic relations, kept his mouth firmly shut. "What do you think his power is?"

"Why, to entrance us with his résumé," said Odette sourly. "Although apparently he possesses preternatural skills at rugby as well. Frankly, I'd have thought that someone who works in diplomacy would have mastered the art of feigning interest in other people." She looked around as the object of their conversation approached, shooting his cuffs so that his cuff links caught the light.

"Sorry about that," he said. "The rest of the cars should be here shortly. In the meantime, welcome to Apex House." He gestured grandly to the building in front of them. Odette looked up and took an involuntary step back. She'd seen pictures in the Broederschap's files, but standing before it in person, under the gray skies, she had to clench her hands into fists to keep them from shaking.

It loomed. A large white building with columns, it struck her as the architectural equivalent of Pawn Bannister's conversation — ostensibly there to be enjoyed, but really designed to intimidate. This was a structure that spoke of centuries of wealth and discreet influence. It had watched the rise and fall of an empire. It had tolerated the Great Stink of 1858. Pea-soup fogs had enshrouded it. Suffragettes and toffs and flappers and anarchists and mods and rockers and hippies and punks and a million others had passed by it, all unaware of the power that resided within. It had weathered the Blitz. It endured. The leaders of the Checquy governed supernatural Britain from within those walls. Apex House was the stronghold of her family's oldest enemies.

I don't want to go in there, thought Odette. *Everyone in that building hates me just on principle. If I go in there, I don't think I'll come out.*

It started to rain.

"Well, we'd better go in," said Bannister. "There's no sense in getting soaked." Odette looked around hopefully, but no other long black cars materialized and the rain was getting heavier.

"Fine, yes, let's go in," she said. "Alessio, put that damn hat back on." They hurried up the steps and through a massive rococo revolving door that deposited her in a semicircular marble-floored lobby. The walls were paneled in dark wood and rose very high. Large, impressive double doors stood at the head of the room, flanked by two sets of smaller, much less impressive doors. Behind each of two large marble counters sat two uniformed security guards. All of them were staring at her fixedly.

"Oh, hi," she said awkwardly. It wasn't immediately clear which counter she should be addressing. The guards at the right-hand desk stood up, and she turned to them.

"Good morning, Miss Leliefeld," said one of the guards flatly.

"Welcome to Apex House," said the other guard, equally flatly.

"Thank you," said Odette, taken aback by their foreboding expressions and the fact that they knew her name. Their eyes flicked to the door behind her as Alessio and Pawn Bannister emerged into the foyer.

"You'll be signing them in, Pawn Bannister?" asked one of the guards on the left-hand desk.

"Yes, might as well get started," said Bannister. "Getting everybody logged in will take ages. How far behind are the other cars?" The guard put his hand to the side of his head, and Odette saw with a shudder that he had no radio or earpiece.

"Next car should be here in about three minutes," he said.

"All right, well, let's get the paperwork out of the way, at least," said Bannister, sounding terribly bored. "Alessio, we'll do you first." Odette's little brother looked a trifle alarmed as he was ushered to the right-hand desk, but he nodded obediently.

Odette had not been at all certain what the process of entering Apex House would involve. She'd been braced for laborious computer entry, typing in massive amounts of personal data and history. Or a shadowy member of the Checquy would glance at her and then give a silent nod. Or maybe she would stand in a scanner and guards would look at her naked. She hadn't been prepared for a photocopied form on a clipboard and a piece of carbon paper underneath.

"Fill that in, please," said the guard to Alessio. "Full name, address, date, and time. Oh, and do you have ID?" Alessio, whose personal effects consisted of a chunky wristwatch that monitored various vital signs including glucose and hormone levels, a mobile phone, and the ugliest hat in the whole world, looked at Odette, panicked.

"I've got your passport," she assured him, and she retrieved it from her bag and handed it over along with her own. The guard examined the photos in the little burgundy booklets that were stamped with the Belgian coat of arms.

"Fine," he said, returning them to her. He typed away on his computer and printed out a flimsy piece of paper with the word visitor in big red letters. He slotted it into a clear plastic sleeve clipped to a bright red lanyard and gave it to Alessio. "Keep that around your neck while you're in the building," he said sternly. "And be sure to hand it back in when you leave." Odette was feeling a little torn—the guards were intimidating, but the casual security arrangements seemed almost absurd.

For heaven's sake, we're monstrous foreigners who have used our dark science and warped God's handiwork to suit our own twisted needs. We tried to invade your country, and my centuries-old ancestor infiltrated your organization. The least you could do is pat me down or take my fucking picture, she thought in irritation.

"I, uh, thought there was going to be some scanning?" she said to Bannister as she signed her name on the form.

"Oh, certainly, in the next room," he said. "This is just your visitor's pass."

"Thank you," she said to the guard as she hung her pass around her neck. The guard nodded back without smiling.

Bannister led them to one of the sets of smaller, unimpressive doors, which clicked and opened with a grinding noise. She felt slightly mollified when she saw that they were massively thick and made of layers of metal, wood, and stone sandwiched together.

Beyond the doors was a long, bland room with various pieces of bulky equipment dotted around it. The entire place—ceiling, floors, and walls—was covered in white tiles. A portly gentleman of African descent and wearing a lab coat approached them. Trailing behind him were a line of anxious-looking men and women in lab coats or scrubs.

"Good morning," the man said cheerfully, holding out his hand. Odette shook it cautiously. "You are the first ones?"

"We're the first ones to arrive," said Odette. "We're not, like, ranked first or anything."

"That's fine," said the man. "I am Dr. Francesco Hethrington-Ffoulkes, and I'll be overseeing the preparations for you." Odette introduced herself and her brother while Pawn Bannister tapped away on his phone in the background.

"Now, as you are formally guests of the Checquy here in the United Kingdom, and because several of your party do not legally exist, we are taking responsibility for your well-being and security. Accordingly, we will need to build a profile of your identifying characteristics. I'm afraid that it may seem a little intrusive," he said apologetically.

"We will be taking fingerprints, palmprints, toeprints, voice-prints, and impressions of your teeth, tongue, and ears. We will collect fingernail clippings, toenail clippings, strands of your hair, swabs from the inside of your mouth, and samples of urine and blood. Not to fret, young fellow," he said reassuringly to Alessio, "it will be just a few drops, and we'll be as gentle as possible." Alessio, who had been responsible for harvesting his own blood and bone marrow since he was nine, regarded him stonily.

"And that's it?" said Odette before she could stop herself. Dr. Hethrington-Ffoulkes looked at her, startled. "I'm sorry, but you're not even putting us through an MRI, or an x-ray, or, or one of those airport scanners..."

"Millimeter wave," said Alessio helpfully.

"Yes, that. Don't you want to run a Geiger counter over us? Or at least check my handbag?"

"Well, I suppose we could, if you like," said the Checquy doctor. "But it's not really necessary. You see, detailed descriptions of your, uh, enhancements were provided to us ahead of time. Although I would like a few drops of both the venoms that you carry in your system, Miss Leliefeld," he added hopefully, "if you wouldn't mind. I have to admit, though, that's just for my own personal research. I'm a bit of a toxicology buff."

"You know?" squeaked Odette.

"We exchanged dossiers weeks ago," said Bannister airily. "As a sign of goodwill. So, everyone knows who you are. At least, everyone who works in the Diplomatic section. We've got details of your education, your rank within the Broederschap, your surgeries. I do hope everything's healing all right, by the way. And don't worry, we've made sure to have lots of cold, noncaffeinated beverages available so your throat shouldn't be aggravated at all."

Oh God, thought Odette. So the entire diplomatic corps knows everything about me. They know about my spurs, they know I've got a sore throat. Hell, they've probably got a report on that time I wet my pants at the museum when I was six years old. Despite her best efforts, she was blushing furiously.

"You're our guests," said Dr. Hethrington-Ffoulkes in a reasonable tone. "It's important that we begin from a situation of mutual trust and security. And also that we verify everyone's identity."

"All right," said Odette. "That makes sense."

"Very good," said the doctor. "I'll be taking care of you, Miss Leliefeld. Pawn Winger will escort Mr. Leliefeld." Pawn Winger was a pretty doctor with red hair, and Alessio was so entranced by her that he didn't even seem to mind that she was a Pawn. Or that she looked absolutely petrified by him. She led him over to a machine on the other side of the room.

"We'll start with the fingers and toes, shall we?" said Dr. Hethrington-Ffoulkes.

"Certainly," said Odette.

"I'm afraid you'll need to remove your tights," said the doctor.

"Oh, okay," said Odette.

"There's a lavatory through that door, just over there."

The bathroom seemed to date back to the Victorian period, and unfortunately it did not appear to have been cleaned since it was built. There were all sorts of pipes that might once have been gleaming brass but now looked as if they were supporting several ecosystems. Odette felt distinctly unglamorous and unbusinesslike as she hopped about taking off her stockings while trying not to put a bare foot on the slick floor. So this is the world of high-stakes supernatural diplomacy, she thought grimly. She teetered on one high-heel-shod foot and fell against the sink. Great, just great. By the time she emerged from the bathroom, she was red-faced and her hair was somewhat less professional-looking than it had been. Dr. Hethrington-Ffoulkes escorted her to a corner of the room and helped her into a dentist's chair. "Comfortable?"

"A little ill at ease," admitted Odette as the chair rose up smoothly, presumably bringing her to a more convenient working level. The doctor smiled without looking at her. He was peering at her feet carefully. I wish I'd gotten a pedicure, she thought. But who knew? She realized, to her intense mortification, that there was a bit of dried slime from the bathtub under the nail of one of her big toes.

"There isn't going to be any problem with me taking a clipping of your toenails, is there?" he asked, looking up at her. "They can be cut, right?"

"Yes, of course," she said. She flinched a little when he touched her foot—his hands were much cooler than she had expected—and his assistant flinched in response, which made Odette flinch again. Whereupon the assistant flinched even more violently, and it took a real effort for Odette not to continue the cycle lest they both end up convulsing on the floor.

The assistant handed Hethrington-Ffoulkes a tablet computer, and he consulted it briefly before pressing it against Odette's left foot. "Now, if you could just flatten your foot as much as you can, please. We want as complete a scan as possible. Good."

The doctor looked at the result and nodded. "Nice, clear images of the toes," he said approvingly. He tapped away at the screen, and a frown grew on his face. "Oh, dear," he muttered to himself. "Oh, dear, oh, dear."

"What?" asked Odette nervously. "Is there a problem?"

"Not with your foot," he said absently. "I'm just checking the cricket scores, and the West Indies are thrashing us." He shook his head at the computer before pressing it against her other foot. Meanwhile, his assistant was gingerly using another tablet to take prints of her hands. Odette smiled and the woman looked away. "Now we just need to get some ink-based prints as backup, and then we'll move on to the casts," he said.

For the next half hour, the doctor and his jumpy assistant did their thing, scanning and copying and taking samples. Whenever new members of the delegation filtered in, there would be a pause in the proceedings as Dr. Hethrington-Ffoulkes stopped what he was doing and went over to introduce himself, leaving Odette gagging on a mouthful of dental putty or reciting the first stanza of "Ode on a Grecian Urn" into a microphone. At one point, she had to suffer the indignity of reentering the unpleasant bathroom and peeing into a container while a wide-eyed nurse watched to make sure she didn't substitute someone else's urine or give birth to some stoats or something.

Of course, the Grafter envoys submitted to the examinations without any complaint. They were accustomed to taking business calls even while undergoing thoracic surgery, so a few scrapings and clippings couldn't throw them off their stride. The Checquy doctors and nurses were careful in their work, although they seemed aghast at the fact that they were working on actual Grafters. There was a slight commotion when Grootvader Ernst's fingerprints insisted on changing even as they were scanned, and the nurses were somewhat at a loss when one of the visiting dignitaries turned out not to have fingernails or toenails, but apart from these setbacks, the proceedings proceeded without incident.

"You're quite thorough," remarked Odette as the doctor held a container of molding putty against her left ear.

"Ah, we'll be taking even more samples once our organizations are united," said Dr. Hethrington-Ffoulkes. "The Chècquy keeps very, very detailed records of all its operatives. All this is just for security and legal purposes."

"Legal purposes?"

"We need to establish beyond a doubt who is present at what meetings and who signs what. Now, we just need to take some pictures of your eyes."

The dentist's chair sank down, and Odette put her bare feet on the cold tiled floor. The eye machine was just a few meters away and she had watched as her colleagues had their retinas and pupils scanned and the insides of their eyeballs photographed. "It's pretty standard optical coherence tomography," said the doctor. "No unusual technologies. And after that, you're done." She sat in the chair offered, and there was a mechanical whining as the apparatus was lowered and closed around her head. "Right, now, if you can just look directly into the lenses." Odette obediently stared ahead, keeping her eyes wide open as a light erupted out of the machine. It flared with the force of a thousand supernova suns into her unnaturally dilated, gorgeously large belladonna-style pupils.

"Ow! Klootzak!" she shouted, flinching back and slamming her head against the equipment.

"What happened? Are you all right?" asked Dr. Hethrington-Ffoulkes in the frantic tones of a man who might have inadvertently sparked a diplomatic fiasco.

"Yes," said Odette sourly, holding her hands over her eyes. Her head was pounding as though she'd just walked into a wall, and there appeared to be a disco-kaleidoscope arrangement on the inside of her eyelids. Her tender rods and cones were screaming bloody murder. "It's my own stupid fault. I didn't even think. My pupils were bigger than they should have been."

"Oh," said the relieved voice of Dr. Hethrington-Ffoulkes, somewhere to her left. Then, with obvious curiosity: "Why?"

"I don't want to talk about it," said Odette, feeling that treacherous blush climb up her cheeks again. She concentrated, and the blood was sucked out of her face, leaving her even more light-headed. She cautiously took her hands away from her eyes. By now, her pupils had constricted as much as they could, but her eyes still felt like they were pulsating.

"Would you like an aspirin or something?"

"No, I'm not allowed painkillers yet, they'll interfere with my system," she said. "If you could just please get me out of this thing and let me sit down for a while."

"Of course," said Dr. Hethrington-Ffoulkes. He retracted the apparatus from around her head, put his latex-gloved hand in hers, and guided her to a chair. "Your shoes and handbag are right next to you," he said. "I'm going to go help the others finish up the exams. You're the first to be done, so you've got some time to recuperate."

"Thank you," said Odette, trying to keep the annoyance out of her voice. The noise of the examinations was muted, but it reverberated through her head. She heard the doctor move away and risked opening her eyes a chink. Even through her contracted pupils, the room was blindingly bright, but she could make out people moving about.

Squinting, she could just see the bathroom door immediately to her left. I'm going to sidle in there discreetly, she thought, throw some water on my face, put my stockings and shoes back on, and maybe have a quick therapeutic vomit. She fumbled for her handbag and shoes, stood up, and, keeping her hand on the wall, awkwardly made her way to the bathroom.

As Odette stepped through the door, her sullen brain made several observations in rapid succession:

1. There's much more of an echo in this bathroom than before.
2. It doesn't smell as bad in here as it did.
3. Someone has lowered the floor and added a step where there was no step.
4. I am falling forward uncontrollably.
5. Someone appears to have replaced the dingy tiles of the

bathroom with polished marble in a black-and-white-checkerboard pattern.
6. I am able to notice this because I am now lying sprawled on the floor.
7. My face really, really hurts.

All of these thoughts added up to the inescapable conclusion that she had, in her dazzled state, gone through the wrong door. Please, God, let me have gone into the men's room, she thought desperately. Let me look up and see several men urinating into a trough and looking at me quizzically over their shoulders. Let me not have gone through the door I think I went through. She took a deep breath and lifted up her face.

Wow. Thanks for nothing, God.

As she had feared, the elegant marble floor did not reflect a disgusting lack of equality in the standards of the Apex House lavatories. Instead, it reflected the fact that she was in the large, beautifully appointed foyer where the Checquy elite had gathered to greet their distinguished guests. She sighed and rested her cheek on the cool marble for a moment.

Finally, she got up on her knees and grimly waited for her eyes to reset. Slowly, details began to swim out of the blur of her vision. Through the clearing haze, she saw a small crowd of people standing at one end of the room. All of them were dressed in expensive-looking suits, and all of them were staring at her in astonishment.

They were not normal people. Quite aside from the fact that they all had exquisite posture, some of them were obviously not your standard-issue human beings. Odette's eyes had scanned the group and automatically picked out the four people she least wanted to see. The members of the Checquy Court. Her treacherous memory was helpfully presenting little dossiers on them and their positions in the Checquy's demented chess-based hierarchy.

The stately looking older lady with the dark chocolate eyes and disapproving expression is Lady Linda Farrier, one of the two heads of the Checquy. Viscountess in the British aristocracy.

Spent a couple of years as lady-in-waiting to the last Queen. She can walk into people's dreams and tinker about with their sleeping minds. Apparently, she once goaded an enemy of the Checquy into gnawing his own hands off in his sleep.

The blond man with the tan who is smoking a cigarette inside a government building is Major Joshua Eckhart. Chevalier— responsible for international operations. Superior tactician. Manipulates metal via touch. He can warp it, mold it, render it liquid. He killed Graaf Gerd de Leeuwen. Then he went out for a hamburger.

Next to him is the newest appointee to the Court, Bishop Raushan Attariwala.

And there's Rook Thomas, the only person who appears to be concerned about the fact that I just pitched face-first onto the floor.

Odette became aware of some flashes of distant light flickering in her vision. Maybe I have a concussion, she thought, and this is all a hallucination.

Instead, it turned out that some photographers were present in order to record the historic meeting of the Checquy and the Grafters. The photographers, who knew a good thing when they saw it, were immortalizing this moment for posterity.

Terrific.

11

The car that came for Felicity was driven by an older man wearing tweed and a dissatisfied expression. Felicity had a sneaking suspicion that he was actually a retired Checquy operative who lived nearby and who had been abruptly reenlisted into service to ferry her back to London. For one thing, the car was an extremely nice Jaguar, and for another, there was a set of golf clubs in the backseat.

You never leave the Checquy, she thought. You may get your farewell party, your gold watch, and your pension, but one day, you'll be called back out of retirement to smite evil or oversee an investigation or transport a girl in pajamas and two pairs of bed socks.

"Felicity Jane Clements?"

"Yes," she said.

He gestured for her to get in, and the car peeled off almost before the door was closed. She hurriedly put on her seat belt.

"Do you have my address?" she asked.

"You're wanted at the Hammerstrom Building," he said. "No detours."

"Dressed like this?" she asked incredulously. He shrugged and then proceeded not to say a single word for the entire drive. To make matters worse, traffic between Ashford and London had been held up by an accident on the M20. Apparently, a truckload of carbonated beverages had overturned, and the subsequent chaos had resulted in miles of backed-up cars. The driver kept sighing heavily in a way that suggested he blamed Felicity for the whole thing, and it took her some effort to resist the urge to apologize.

Much to her surprise, she fell asleep. She woke up forty-five minutes later with a jerk and a gasp only to find that they had moved approximately twenty-five meters and that her face was welded to the shoulder strap of her seat belt by the copious amounts of drool that had seeped out of her mouth. Peeling her face away from the belt made a mortifyingly loud noise, and the driver's mouth twisted in disgust.

Then, in the middle of Essential Classics on BBC Radio 3, it suddenly hit her. Perhaps she'd been unconsciously avoiding it, or perhaps the journey in Chopra's arms through that strange place had done something to her thoughts, or perhaps she'd simply been too exhausted to think about it. But now it filled her mind.

They're dead.

Her comrades Odgers and Jennings. Even Andrea Cheng, who, with her powers and her sharp mind, had always been able to escape any situation, was unlikely to have escaped the inferno. They'd been murdered in front of her. Now when she closed her eyes, Felicity saw Odgers lying on that floor, her blood pouring from her throat. Or else she saw Jennings, silhouetted in flames that boiled out of his own body.

I'll have to face their families, she thought helplessly. Odgers's husband. Jennings's and Andrea's partners. It was the thought of Jennings's little daughter, Louise—her own goddaughter—that really broke her. The knowledge that she would have to answer questions about Louise's father's death, and that she would have to lie. That girl would never know the truth.

"Nooooo..." She realized that she had actually made a sound, moaning softly despite herself.

Oh God, please make it not be true. Please, God.

To her horror and confusion, she started crying. Felicity was not a crier. If you wanted someday to be a Barghest commando, you did not cry. She had made a very deliberate decision never to cry again in her last year at school. She hadn't cried when her class graduated from the Estate, and everyone cried then. She hadn't cried last year when her boyfriend broke up with her because her schedule got in the way of their life. She hadn't even cried when one of the team died on a mission in Wapping—not at the funeral, and not when they all went out afterward and got completely drunk and told stories.

But now it wouldn't stop. Gasping sobs continued to bubble out of her. She tried to marshal her thoughts, to calm herself down, but she couldn't focus. Her mind kept presenting her with images of her comrades—mental snapshots—and at each new picture, another wave of grief would flood through her head, prompting more sobs.

The driver eyed her sidelong and handed her a handkerchief from his breast pocket. It was not clear whether this was an act of gentlemanly compassion or simply his fear of her getting more fluids on the upholstery. He didn't say anything at all, for which

Felicity was grateful. They kept driving, and as they finally came to the outskirts of London, she managed to stop crying. Maybe my body has just run out of water, she thought weakly, and she sat, slumped in her seat, not looking at anything.

Pawn George Korybut watched, disbelieving, as the group of men and women in suits were guided down the hallway past his office. They looked normal but he knew what they were. It didn't seem real. He'd known this day was coming, but he'd always secretly believed in his heart of hearts that the Court members would change their minds at the last minute and declare war on those abominations. They hadn't. Instead, the Grafters were walking about in Apex House, treated like honored guests. For a moment, he felt like a frightened child back at the Estate.

As a rule, Checquy children didn't scare easily. When your parents willingly give you to the government because you are inhuman, and your roommate has been known to inadvertently turn into a poplar during the night, and your mathematics teacher sometimes absentmindedly projects holograms of angry leopards during class, you become a trifle blasé. Horror stories tend to lose their impact when you are a horror. This effect was only amplified by the fact that much of the curriculum at the Estate was taken up with lectures on the various supernatural abominations they would be called upon to deal with when they graduated.

But the stories about the Grafters were different.

Those stories were a litany, passed down through generations of Checquy youth. They were history. They dated back to before the creation of the Estate, to a time when Checquy education had been based not on schools but on the tradition of master and apprentice. The stories told of the events of 1677, the year that the entire Checquy had been called to the Isle of Wight to defend Britain against invaders.

So dire was the Grafter threat then that the Rooks (at that time the military leaders of the Checquy) had rallied the entire organization. Not only the soldiers but the scribes and scientists, the craftsmen, the statesmen, and the men of the church — all of them had come to throw themselves at the invaders. Only the very youngest, the infants and the smallest children, remained on the mainland, guarded by unpowered Retainers. But there were child soldiers, apprentices still learning how to use their powers. They had marched alongside their masters, ready to do good toward their country. What they experienced would change them forever — those who survived.

There was never any question of quarter being given. The unannounced invasion, the inhuman army, and the atrocities committed upon the general populace had established that the rules of civilized warfare no longer applied. And so, unrestrained supernatural war commenced.

Events from the ensuing combat entered Checquy history. Pawn William Goode, after being disemboweled by a Grafter, haughtily re-emboweled himself and then backhanded his opponent, sending him flying nine miles. Pawn Morag Campbell ripped all the moisture from her foe, leaving behind nothing but dust, fractured bones, and a rather gaudy uniform. Bishop Rosemary Chuzeville summoned gouts of steam out of the turf and boiled Grafter soldiers in their shells like lobsters.

The child soldiers reached moments of glory as well. Twelve-year-old Sarah Jessup managed to hurl three hulking soldiers into the atmosphere. Henry Wright trapped one of the Grafter commanding officers in a pond — if one goes there and stands in the right place, one can still see his reflection, screaming to be released. Little Robert Savory, whose only power was the ability to increase the nutritional value of root vegetables, lured an enemy off a cliff through a combination of foot speed and sheer wits.

But for every victory, there were dozens of terrifying stories. Children were shot, stabbed, bludgeoned, burned. Christopher Madoc's skin and clothes were permanently dyed by his sister's blood as he tried to stanch the bleeding of her fatal wounds. Luke Hathaway's skull was crushed beneath the boot of a

Grafter foot soldier. Helen Murtaugh, brought face-to-face with the enemy, lost control of her own powers. Ribbons of black fire erupted from her spine, flogging the comrades around her and consuming her alive. Eventually, her master was called upon to put her down.

The Broederschap recognized the effect that the loss of each child had on the Checquy and began to target the youngest troops specifically. On the battlefield, they dispatched them as brutally as they could. At night, the Checquy camps were infiltrated and the children were snatched away, never to be seen again. The atrocities did not break the spirit of the British. Rather, they inflamed them. Rage drove the Rooks to throw caution to the wind and put their defenses aside to ensure that they brought their foes down. The Checquy moved forward, implacably, and scoured the land clean.

Three weeks after the Grafters set foot on British soil, the war was ended with a final gunshot. The enemy's leaders fled, bursting through the lines of Checquy soldiers and hurling themselves into the ocean. Their army had been smashed, wiped off the Isle of Wight. However, it had been at horrendous cost. The Checquy had suffered catastrophic losses, especially among their young. A generation of Britain's supernatural youth had been decimated.

Of course, that was not the end of the story. The Checquy Court traveled to Brussels to oversee the dismantling of the Wetenschappelijk Broederschap van Natuurkundigen. But for the apprentices of the Checquy, the war was over. Their wounds were stitched up, their comrades were buried. They went home. Some of them had lost their masters, and these went to new houses to resume their training.

They were changed, of course. How could they not be after what they had seen, after what they had done? Quieter, more solemn, utterly dedicated to their mission. But there was very little of the crippling residual trauma one might have expected. The children of the Checquy had never been coddled and had never labored under any delusions about what they were and what they might be called upon to do. When they came back, they were hardened, tempered. Hatred for the Grafters smoldered within them. They could still feel joy; there were still times when they could play and romp. Yet they all remembered what they had seen, and they made sure it was not forgotten.

When the new generation of children began their apprenticeships, they brought a little more light into the lives of their sober older siblings. It's remarkable what exposure to genuinely innocent happiness can do. Inevitably, the younger students adored the older, quieter boys and girls who patiently helped them with their lessons. When it came time for the older apprentices to leave their master's house, they would take the younger ones aside. They might sit in the master's library, or at the top of a nearby hill, or simply on the back stoop. And then the veterans of the Isle of Wight would tell their stories, remembering the names of their fallen comrades and recounting the events of those weeks.

The stories were all different, of course. Different soldiers had seen and felt different things. They had lost different people. But, as if by agreement, all the tales ended the same way.

"Remember," the older apprentice would say. "And pass the memory along to those who come after you."

And so it went, for decades, for centuries. Each generation passed the stories on to the next and instructed them about the debt owed to the dead. It was not a formal practice or a requirement. In the official histories they were casualties, figures, names, honors. In the stories, they were people, friends, comrades.

In the mid-twentieth century, when the Estate was established as a school, the very first students, former apprentices themselves, brought the stories with them to Kirrin Island. There, finally, all the memories and anecdotes came together, and a new chapter in the oral history of the Checquy began.

When students at the Estate entered year seven, the upperclassmen would sneak into their rooms in the dead of night and take them down to the echoing assembly hall. They would sit, silent in the dark, while the older students took turns telling them carefully memorized accounts of what had happened all those centuries ago. There might be a pupil with a gift for illusion who would fill the darkness with images or perhaps just a budding actor who could draw people in with the sound of his voice. But for hours, the memories of long-dead children would wash over them. When the sun came up, every student was shaken, wrung out, and exhausted. And they all came away with certain important lessons drilled into them.

You will face horrible things. Admittedly, this lesson did not come as a tremendous surprise to the students. But it had a certainty to it now.

You could die. This message struck home, hard. Up to that point, the Estate education had always emphasized triumphant victory. Their bedtime stories and lessons had revolved around adventures in which grown Checquy warriors always overcame the threat. But the children at the Isle of Wight had been called to duty, and many of them had not come back.

You will never be alone. The Checquy will always be there for you. Coming from the bigger students, this meant the world to the year-sevens. After the night they'd had, the lack of sleep, the litany of atrocities and warnings, this was the reassurance that would bond them to their siblings and give them courage to hear the final caution.

The Grafters were normal men. Normal men who wanted to be like us and made themselves into monsters.

All of the students came away from the experience with a smoldering hatred for the memory of the Broederschap. The Checquy generally didn't hate the monsters they hunted — it would have been unprofessional, and exhausting. But the brutality at the Isle of Wight meant that centuries later, Checquy dinner parties would still frequently end with a toast of "Fuck the Grafters, we're glad they're dead! Oh, and God save the King."

Except that now, apparently, they weren't dead. Instead, they were walking around the hallways of Apex House. Pawn Korybut's grip on his desk tightened, and a slick of something slid out from under his touch.

12

Well, I think that all went very nicely," said Lady Farrier. "Apart from your little tumble, Miss Leliefeld. How's your face feeling?"

"Fine, thank you," said Odette.

"And your throat?" asked Marcel.

"It's fine, really," said Odette testily.

Once she'd been picked up by the aghast executives, and all the scattered possessions from her purse (including those damned stockings, a tampon, some shiny and clattering surgical tools, and several dozen pills that had burst out of their containers and made a desperate break for it across the tiled floor) had been gathered up and gingerly returned to her, there had been a humiliating few minutes in which Marcel insisted on checking to make sure that she hadn't done herself any serious injury. He'd taken her pulse, made her say "Ahh" loudly for three minutes, and asked in a disconcertingly carrying voice if any of her sutures might have ruptured. She was sure the gathered VIPs now thought she was an invalid or an idiot or both.

An invalidiot.

Odette remained silent throughout the ensuing introductions and morning tea and was then given the petrifying news that she was to join Marcel and Grootvader for a little stroll around the building with the Court of the Checquy. The only bright spot had been the fact that Pawn Bannister was not approved to join them. They'd left him sulking by the little cakes and had been led away through some stodgy wood-paneled corridors to a much nicer corridor. And then they stopped.

"And here we are," said Lady Farrier.

"We are?" asked Marcel.

"We are," said Rook Thomas. "And now we need to have a little meeting."

It was a genuinely odd place to hold a meeting. The hallway ran around the courtyard; on one side of the corridor, there were huge, ancient stone arches, their openings glassed in, and on the other, the wall was completely tessellated in oil portraits of all sizes. There was absolutely nowhere to sit.

"This needs to be a very discreet meeting," said Rook Thomas. "It deals with some topics that we don't want on the record, so there are no stenographers or scribes."

The three Grafters—Ernst, Marcel, and Odette—looked at one another warily.

"Do you know who this is?" Thomas pointed at a portrait of a strikingly handsome man with a knowing gaze.

Odette looked at it, half ready for the man to step out of the picture. It was the sort of thing she believed could happen in a Checquy art gallery. As she examined it, however, she actually found herself wishing that he would step out of the picture and then maybe lead her to his Jag, drive her to 1967-era Annabel's, and buy her a gin martini. His eyes seemed to smolder at her. It was like the artist had mixed a whole load of pheromones and a hint of cologne into the paint.

"It is Bishop Conrad Grantchester," said Ernst finally.

"The traitor," said Bishop Attariwala.

"You mean our traitor," said Ernst.

"One of several," said Chevalier Eckhart darkly.

"Bought and paid for," said Ernst in a tone that showed absolutely no sign of remorse.

This is getting somewhat awkward, thought Odette. Apparently Rook Thomas thought so as well, because she cleared her throat, and when she spoke again, it was extremely calmly.

"Ernst," said the Rook, "the problem is that over the past several years, the Broederschap has suborned a number of Checquy operatives at every level of our organization. They were bribed, with money or, ahcm, augmentations. You purchased their loyalty, their services, their secrets. Our secrets. You told me that you had done this as part of your preparations to make an overture of peace."

"It was a gambit to help ensure that you would listen to us, that you would not simply destroy us as soon as we stepped forward," said Ernst.

"Along with the secret research and training facility that you established on British soil using embezzled Checquy funds," said Eckhart. "And the two biological weapons of mass destruction that were unleashed on British soil."

"To be fair, I didn't unleash them," Ernst said lightly. "My partner did. And then you, Chevalier Eckhart, killed him by putting a javelin through his head. If I can move beyond that, then I would expect you to be able to come to terms with the actions I took to safeguard my people."

"And we are," said the Rook hastily. "We've come to terms with them. And look, there's precedent for this sort of thing. One of my colleagues? He and his, um, family killed a whole bunch of Checquy personnel before he joined up with us. And now he's on the Occupational Health and Safety Committee, among other things. So, yes, we can move beyond the violence and the crimes. But your people within the Checquy swore oaths of obedience, loyalty, and secrecy to us. They broke those oaths. And we can't have that."

"I was anticipating that there would be some sort of amnesty," said Ernst. "Now that we are all friends."

"No," said Lady Farrier, and her voice, though low, was cold enough that they all turned to look at her. "There will not be." Odette shivered, and she was certain that she was not the only one.

"What will happen to them?" said Ernst after a pause.

"The traditional punishments for Checquy oath breakers are very old," said Bishop Attariwala, "and very detailed."

"However," said Rook Thomas, "we've been exploring some more merciful alternatives." The Bishop was looking at her fixedly, and Odette noticed that the short woman seemed to be avoiding his gaze. "It could be as simple as being imprisoned for life in a Checquy facility or going to the gallows."

"That's merciful?" asked Marcel incredulously.

"Compared to the law, it's incredibly merciful," said the Rook.

"Plus, we'd save a fortune on sourcing narwhal ivory and importing lynxes." Everyone looked at her, and she shrugged. "They're very intricate punishments, with all sorts of symbolism. They haven't been performed in centuries. No one's dared betray us like this in a long time."

"Regardless of what their punishments will be," said the Bishop, "we cannot permit these vipers to remain nestled within our bosom. You must provide us with a complete accounting of every person within the Checquy whom you enlisted. They will be taken into custody, and any augmentations that you provided will be removed, either by our surgeons or by yours under supervision. Then they will stand trial."

"Before a jury of their peers?" asked Marcel.

"No," said Lady Farrier grimly. "Before us." Her tone left little doubt about the outcome.

"So my agents—people I employed—will be punished while I and the other members of the Broederschap are welcomed in?" asked Ernst.

"They were our people first," said Lady Farrier. "They allowed themselves to be turned. There must be consequences."

"This is not up for negotiation," said Chevalier Eckhart.

Odette watched her ancestor as he mulled it over. Despite herself, she could muster up nothing but contempt for the Checquy turncoats. They've shown what people will do to gain the power of the Broeder-schap, she thought. They'll betray whatever they hold dear just to profit from our work. So how can we believe the Checquy won't do the same? What are we doing here?

"Very well," Ernst said finally. "But it will take a few days."

"A few days?" exclaimed the Bishop.

"Yes. Unlike every intelligence organization in every movie ever, we do not maintain a single list of all our agents and their home addresses. That would be bad security. The information will be compiled and submitted as it is retrieved."

"How many are there?" asked Eckhart.

"I am not certain." The graaf shrugged.

"You don't know?"

"I deliberately ensured I would not know," said Ernst. "I gather that in certain company, not even the secrets of one's mind can be considered secure." Odette watched with interest as Lady Farrier flushed. Rook Thomas seemed a trifle amused. "There are not too many moles, however. Not anymore. I understand that the majority were killed during a Checquy drinks reception."

"And when will we have the names of these double-crossers?" asked Lady Farrier.

"Within a week," said Ernst. "You have my word."

"Very well, then," said Farrier. "By this time next Wednesday." She looked at her watch. "Well, with that settled, I believe this little tour is over. We all have meetings to attend. Rook Thomas, can you escort our guests to where they need to be?"

"Certainly, my Lady," said Rook Thomas. The other members of the Court departed, leaving the Rook and the three Grafters in the gallery. "I think that went quite well."

"You and I had discussed the possibility of a pardon," said Ernst stiffly.

"I broached the subject with the Court," said the Rook. "They didn't go for it. I suppose it's easier to forgive an enemy than a traitor. Those people bound themselves by oath. If they were willing to break it before, there is no way to be certain they will not break it again. And nobody leaves the Checquy. Not alive, anyway."

"You know, we are able to remove people's memories," said Marcel. "Do you think that might be a way to a compromise? You don't look enthusiastic."

In fact the Rook looked like she might be ill. Odette couldn't blame her. She'd seen footage of the Grafter operatives who could steal people's memories. They were very rare and represented a tremendous investment of time, labor, training, immunosuppressant drugs, and flunitrazepam. They were among those highly specialized constructs that required the investment of an infant. In order to produce one, a Grafter had to look at a baby and say, "I will perform a lot of surgeries on this small person, for years and years, and eventually it will be a tool that I can use to affect other people's minds." Odette was not at all sure that she was the sort of person who could do that.

"I'll think about it," Rook Thomas said finally. "But Ernst, if any of those turncoats should disappear before the list is delivered, or if any Checquy operative is later discovered to have undeclared augmentations, all bets are off. Do you understand?"

The graaf nodded.

"Excuse me, Rook Thomas," said Odette. She was again looking at the portrait of Grantchester. "May I ask why his picture is still up on the wall even though he was a traitor?"

"Everyone in the Court gets a portrait," said Rook Thomas sourly. "It doesn't matter what atrocities you've committed. We've had incompetents, murderers, and rapists. Rook Hal Carpenter"—and she pointed to a picture of a man in a large red wig—"incinerated an entire village because he thought a boy there was making the soil infertile. It wasn't the boy. And it turned out to be the wrong village. His portrait is still up on the wall.

"We've had plenty of skeletons in our closets," continued Thomas. "Hell, one of our Rooks was a skeleton. And he was in the closet as well, come to think of it. But we don't hide our history. At least," she amended, "we don't hide it from ourselves. As a result, I still get to look at Conrad Grantchester's smug face every day." Odette nodded meekly. "And I get to look at them as well," the Rook added, gesturing to another picture.

It was a group portrait, three blond men (two of them identical twins) standing around a chair on which sat a blond woman. All of them were extremely attractive, and all of them were wearing the same stern expression.

"The Rooks Gestalt," said Thomas. "Hive-minded siblings, a brilliant collective warrior, and a complete pain in the arse to work with. Honestly, of all the members of the Court, Gestalt may have been the easiest for you to buy, but you got yourselves a poisoned chalice. Or possibly a poisoned tea set."

"Where are they now?" asked Odette.

"Theodore, Robert, and Alex are in separate maximum-security prisons, and Eliza fell out of a window on the top story of the Apex," said Rook Thomas. It might have been Odette's imagination, but the petite woman appeared to be a trifle cheered by the thought.

"Is that why you held this meeting here, so you could use these portraits as visual aids?" asked Odette.

"No, that's just a bonus," said Rook Thomas. "We had it here because it's one of the few interesting places in this building that we could justify going on a tour to see and that no one would walk by. But we should be moving along." She began to lead them away.

"So, wait, how did Eliza Gestalt fall out of the window?" asked Odette curiously.

"Hmm? Oh, a small girl shot her in the head," said the Rook. "Anyway, now that the issue of the traitors is being addressed, we have important work to do."

As the car drew near the Rookery, Felicity's reluctant driver spoke. "What in the name of God?"

"They're the protesters," said Felicity tiredly. "They've been there for ages." A tribe of activists had been bivouacked on the footpath outside the building for several months now, attempting to enlighten the pedestrians of the City of London about the secret government conspiracy that lurked within. The secret government conspiracy that lurked within was appalled but was doing its best to ignore them.

"Outrageous," snorted the driver. "Such a thing would never have been permitted when I was in the Rookery. I'm astounded that the Pawns haven't done something."

Felicity opened her mouth to tell him that Checquy operatives were strictly forbidden to interfere with the protesters, no matter how much they shouted or how many eggs they threw at operatives' cars. Then she shrugged and closed her mouth.

The injunction had been laid down after a certain Pawn Willet, who worked in the Governance section of the Rookery, had been deliberately jostled one morning by several of the demonstrators, causing her to spill coffee all over her suit. She retaliated that lunch hour by strolling through the middle of the Occupy Sir Rupert Faunce Lane encampment humming at a pitch that induced severe digestive problems in those around her. The results had been frightful, especially since the protesters had refused to leave their camp, even in the face (as it were) of dire intestinal distress. Pawn Willet had been suspended from work for a month and had also been billed for the power-washing of the pavement.

Since then, the staff members of the Checquy had restrained themselves, gritted their teeth, and submitted their dry-cleaning receipts to Accounts for reimbursement. Also, a car-washing station had been added to the underground parking lot.

When he pulled up at the Rookery, the driver was unwilling to brave the gauntlet of protesters. "I'm not getting any eggs on this paintwork." To Felicity's horror, he insisted on depositing her at the front of the building. He barely even brought the car to a complete stop, and upon alighting, Felicity promptly stepped in a puddle. Marvelous. That's just marvelous. Her socks soaking, she sloshed through the protesters, accepting pamphlets and bumper stickers, and arrived in the foyer only to realize that she had lost her security pass during the trip through the void between the OOM and the hospital.

Fortunately, the security guards in the lobby recognized her, and once they'd run her fingerprints, they issued her a temporary pass. She ignored the lifts and walked through the small, unassuming door beside them and then through various security measures before coming into the real lobby of the Rookery.

Felicity suddenly found that she did not know what to do or where to go. She had walked through that lobby a thousand times, but now everything felt alien. Should I just go to my desk in my pod and sit? she wondered. Her team leader was gone. Do I report to the general manager? Is—is there a form to fill out? "Death of Team—Application for Replacement." A hysterical laugh bubbled up in her and she fought it down. Standing by the entrance in her hospital scrubs and socks, she felt completely at a loss.

13

Odette discovered that she had no important work to do. All the Grafter representatives had splintered off into their various sessions, and she had found herself without a session into which to splinter off. Originally, she had planned to sit in as Graaf Ernst was briefed on some aspects of Checquy operations, but Bishop Attariwala had delicately pointed out that her security clearance was not yet processed. So instead she was being guided around the offices by a bored-looking Pawn Bannister. *I've gone from the most high-level secret meeting possible to the diplomatic children's table,* she thought glumly.

To make matters worse, all the people they passed looked at her warily and then hastily averted their gaze. It was evident that her photo had been shared around the building. Occasionally, Pawn Bannister would make a point of introducing her to someone, usually someone much older in an extremely nice suit. Apparently he had decided to make career lemonade out of the lemon that was Odette.

"May I introduce Miss Odette Leliefeld, one of our guests today," he would say, raising his eyebrows meaningfully. "I'm just escorting her around the facilities." Odette would smile and automatically offer her hand and would then be treated to a brief look of horror and a reluctant handshake. Some meaningless chitchat would ensue, Odette trying to be reassuringly normal and polite, and finally they would move on. She very deliberately did not look behind her, but she was certain that if she had, she would have seen her new acquaintance wiping his hands on his trousers. After each introduction, Pawn Bannister smirked for a little while in a self-satisfied way.

I'm being used to build his damn CV, she thought resentfully. *He just wants everyone to know that he's been entrusted with the Grafter chick.* She kept a pleasant expression on her face and looked around curiously at the offices. Most of what she saw was disappointingly normal, with people working in cubicles. She could actually track the spread of the e-mail alerting people to her presence as heads popped up, looked around, and then ducked down again. One thing that caught her eye was that each cubicle was equipped with large cupboards that ran the length of the dividing walls.

"What are those for?" she asked. "They're not filing cabinets?"

"No, those contain go-kits," said Bannister airily. "Every member of the Checquy has a kit. They include clothes for different environments and conditions, survival gear—sleeping bag and so on—and tools. Also a laptop. Satellite phone. Emergency beacon. And, of course, body armor, in case they're called to a combat situation."

"You said this was the Payroll section," objected Odette.

"It is," said Bannister. "But every Checquy member, Pawn and Retainer alike, must be ready for the call to duty. We are all weapons, and at any time we may be summoned forth to stand between the people of these islands and the threats that rear up against them."

This was delivered in a tone of the utmost pomposity, and it washed over Odette unpleasantly, like an upended bathtub of dog slobber. She had to lock her facial muscles in an expression of polite awe.

"And besides," continued Bannister, "many of us possess a specific ability that may prove useful in a specific scenario. There's a man who works in the mail room who is always getting called out because he can deflect lightning back into the sky. And Rochelle, who works down in the motor pool—her presence increases people's fertility, so she's often brought in to attend, um, events."

"Oh, we can probably help with the fertility thing as well," said Odette brightly. "I'm very good at in vitro fertilization—you can even pick the gender of the baby if you want to." She had to give Bannister credit—he managed to conceal almost all of his revulsion at the thought of the dreaded Grafters tinkering around with Checquy genetic material.

"Yes, that does sound very helpful," he said, his mouth twisting a bit over the words. "Speaking of medical affairs, here is the medical center." He guided her through a pair of double doors, and she breathed in the familiar antiseptic smell of a hospital. "I expect your people will be doing most of their work either here or in the Comb." Behind her, there were carpets and walls with pictures; before her, there were gleaming tiles and people in white coats moving about purposefully. She immediately felt more comfortable and relaxed a little.

"What's the Comb?" she asked absently.

"The Comb is our major research center," said Bannister. "It's out in Oxfordshire; lots of labs and technical facilities."

"Sounds nice," said Odette. "So why do you have a medical center in a government office?"

"A number of reasons," said Bannister. "All the Pawns have to have regular checkups in case our powers change. Many of us have entirely unique physiology, so we can't just go to the local hospital if we get hurt or sick. One of the boys who used to be at the Estate didn't bleed blood if he got cut. Instead, a sort of sentient arsenic mist would come out and chase people around the cricket pitch."

"Gosh."

"And if they identify a civilian woman who's pregnant with a Checquy-style baby, they'll usually try to pull some strings and have her give birth here," Bannister went on airily. "They tell her it's a private hospital and that it's a high-risk pregnancy that only the experts can deal with. Which is true."

"And then they take the baby?" said Odette.

"It depends." Bannister shrugged. "They have many different ways of getting kids. And then, of course, there's trauma."

"I bet," said Odette. "Losing a child would be hard."

"No, the combat-trauma department. If any of our troops get injured, they try to transport them here or to the Comb."

"I thought the Hammerstrom Building was the place for domestic operations."

"I think the traffic isn't as bad around here," said Bannister. "Oh!" he exclaimed. "There's Dr. Crisp." He pointed down the hallway at a gaunt-looking man. "He's usually at the Rookery, but he's very important in the Medical section, and I know he'll want to meet you."

"I don't know, he's probably awfully busy," said Odette. "And, look, he's just going." The doctor had vanished around a corner. "Oh, well, perhaps next time." Thank God; I can't take another point-scoring exhibition.

"No, no, I'll just get him," said Bannister, trotting off. "Wait there, we'll be right back." Odette gave a little sigh and looked about. Standing in a hallway, with her large visitor's pass dangling around her neck, she felt extremely conspicuous. Across from her was a break room with a little kitchen, some chairs, and a table. When Bannister failed to return after a couple of minutes, she moseyed in casually to have a little snoop. I wonder if they have supernatural coffee, she mused.

As it turned out, they had disappointingly mundane coffee, and there were no miniature cafeteria workers toiling in the fridge or cupboards. A notice board hung on the wall, and Odette recoiled when she saw that, between a flyer warning about flu and an advertisement for a set of bunk beds, there were pictures of several of the Broederschap delegation (including herself) with a note explaining that they would be visiting and should be afforded every courtesy. This charming and hospitable sentiment was spoiled by the fact that someone had modified the portraits with a pen, providing them with hats, horns, and a selection of unlikely dental abnormalities. Odette's own picture had been augmented with goat eyes and a long mustache in the style of Fu Manchu.

Lovely, she thought. That's just lovely. Then she spun around as two Checquy workers entered the room, chatting easily.

"...And I said, 'I don't doubt that you're the reincarnation of Pawn Muskie who died in 1934, but the Checquy is not going to be paying his pension to you because pensions stop when you die.'" The speaker was a skinny, unshaved man with long, tangled hair that seemed to float after him as if he were in space. Odette hurriedly stood in front of her portrait and tried to look casual.

"So what did he say?" asked the other Pawn, a plump man with compound eyes that glittered beautifully behind an extremely intricate pair of eyeglasses.

"He asked what the point of reincarnation was, then. Morning," he said to Odette.

"Good morning," she replied. It was clear he had no idea who she was. They probably didn't recognize me without my mustache and goat eyes, she thought sourly.

"Morning," said the insect-eyed Pawn as he started pouring coffee. "Well, meanwhile, the Cheltenham branch is operating out of the Hyatt for three weeks while their office is cleansed of asbestos."

"That's a brand-new building, though," objected his friend.

"Oh, it's not the building. The office manager started shedding without realizing it. Three people ended up in hospital, including a civilian janitor. So now the whole place has to be cleaned, and he's down at the Comb, getting his new traits examined and cataloged." They finished making their coffees and strolled out, nodding to Odette.

Well, they can be perfectly pleasant when they don't know who you are, she thought as she wandered back into the hallway to wait for Pawn Bannister to appear. She leaned against the wall, and immediately the lights above flickered, and an alarm blared out of hidden speakers.

Christ! She scrambled to stand up straight. Do they have Grafter detectors in the paint or something? She looked around frantically in case a team of armed guards was coming to punish her for leaning with malicious intent.

"Code Heliotrope," said a calm Scottish voice over the speakers. "Incoming wounded. Code Heliotrope. All medical personnel proceed immediately to the reception area and operating theaters. Code Heliotrope."

Doors were opening along the hallway and people were rushing out. Odette found herself being swept along by the crowd, and in moments she was in a sort of round lobby with a circular nurses' station in the middle and corridors coming off it like the spokes of a wheel. People were hurrying about, and no one seemed in the mood to stop and help a visitor. She pressed herself up against the nurses' station, as much out of the way as possible. There were three nurses there, typing away on computers and talking frantically on phones. One of them, a bald woman with eyes ringing her skull, looked at Odette questioningly, and Odette shook her head, indicating she didn't need anything. The nurse nodded, and Odette went back to watching the chaos.

"What happened?" one nurse called out to a medic.

"Something at a kid's birthday party over at Gants Hill," he said. "We don't know exactly what, but bad things went down."

People were getting wheeled in on gurneys, and it did not look as if they were coming from a child's birthday party. For one thing, all of them were wearing body armor in various states of disrepair. Grievous wounds were much in evidence, and there was a good deal of screaming. The smell of blood filled Odette's nostrils, and she found herself mentally conducting triage on the victims rolling by in front of her.

The injuries were weird. One woman had a spiderweb of cuts that sliced across her chest and through her armor, but rather than blood, rivulets of silver, like mercury, oozed out of her body. Two men hurried by carrying a stretcher on which an unconscious youth was foaming indigo at the mouth. As they passed, the paint on the walls around them turned a virulent turquoise and then shifted back to white. She watched them hurry away and saw that the temporary redecoration followed them down the hall.

Another medic came in pushing a gurney on which lay a man who appeared to be half turned to glass. Odette couldn't tell if this was the result of the malevolence at the birthday party or if he was meant to be like that, but the man did not seem at all happy.

"What happened to the kid whose birthday it was?" asked Odette.

"Whole family got eaten by the cake," said the medic, and then he rushed on. Odette and the nurse exchanged horrified glances. Then a painfully loud sound, like an air horn being fed into a wood chipper, tore through the hallways, and Odette and the nurse and everyone else clapped their hands over their ears.

Are we under attack? Odette wondered. Her instincts were itching to pop out her spurs, and she had to actively keep them in check lest she puncture her own face and poison herself. The noise grew louder and more painful, and then a medic wheeled in a stretcher carrying a man whose combat armor was drenched in blood. Restraints crisscrossed his body, his right arm had been crudely splinted, and Odette saw that his left leg had been torn off at the knee and was in a plastic bag at the end of the gurney. The horrible wound had been carefully bound up with white gauze, but some blood had seeped through.

The torturous sound was coming from the patient. It was his voice that was warbling and shrilling up and down inhuman scales and setting Odette's teeth on edge. The medic was wearing a bulky set of ear protectors and a grim expression.

"Get some painkillers into that man now!" bellowed a doctor. He was just barely audible over the man's screaming.

"They don't have any effect on him!" the medic shouted back. "It's in his prep file!"

"Then sedate him!" yelled the doctor.

"He doesn't respond to any sedatives!" came the answer. "You'll be operating while he's awake!"

"I definitely think you should be having this conversation right here in the lobby!" screamed the bald nurse with all the eyes. The surgeon and the medic turned to look at her, and just then, the patient shifted. His arm twisted against the splint, and a jagged bone cut through the skin. Blood squirted up into the air and then began to pour out, and the man's painful screaming faded away to a weak moan.

Without thinking, Odette scrambled to the gurney, leaned

across the man's body, and applied pressure to the spurting wound. She could actually feel the force of the internal fluids pressing against her fingertips, and hot gore continued seeping out under her hands, although it was much slower.

It had been an automatic response on her part, but in retrospect it seemed like a terrible idea. The patient's eyes were still open, and he was looking at her pleadingly. A normal person would be unconscious, she thought. I suppose there are disadvantages to some inhuman abilities.

"I'm right here," she assured him. "I'm not leaving you." She turned her head over her shoulder. "You may wish to move quickly here, before this man bleeds out." They were all looking at her. "Now!" The doctor's head moved in a figure-eight pattern as he scanned the situation.

"We can't arrest the bleeding here," he said. "We'll need to get him to surgery. Are you okay to keep pressure on his arm?"

"Yes."

"All right, then," the doctor said. "You're not going to be able to walk, bent over him like that, so I'm going to lift you up onto the gurney," he said. "Maintain pressure." Odette nodded and kept her grip tight as the man put his hands on her hips and lifted her gently. She straddled the patient awkwardly, careful not to jostle his injured leg. "Now move!" he barked at the medic. Several people pushed them down a hallway and through a series of heavy doors. The patient was still looking up at her, his eyes wide with pain and shock.

He's my age, she realized with a jolt. And cute. Grievously wounded, she admitted, but cute. Sandy-colored hair cut short, nice features, and pale blue eyes. Say something comforting, thought Odette.

"So, painkillers have no effect?" she said sympathetically. "That's really got to suck. Especially right now."

Brilliant. Nice job.

"I'm immune to all drugth and poithonth," he said thickly. "Thatth why I'm on the firtht-rethponthe team." He frowned. "Why am I talking like thith?"

"Blood loss and shock," said Odette. "You might be about to pass out."

"I wish," he said ruefully. "But it'th nithe to meet you. Thankth for thtepping in to, you know, thave my life."

"My pleasure," said Odette, swaying slightly as they went around a corner.

"I'm David."

"Odette."

"Nithe t'mee'choo," he slurred.

I wonder if Pawn Bannister has noticed that I'm gone? she mused as they entered the operating theater.

Around her, people bustled about. Despite the organized chaos and the critical damage to the young man, Odette felt in her element. The intense focus on the problem at hand, the stripped-down surroundings, the blood—I could be back at home, she thought.

David, however, did not seem quite so at ease. He winced away from the surgical lights and regarded every development warily. Odette tried to reassure him as the nurses carefully removed the man's armor. He winced as the blood-soaked cloth was pulled away from the cuts on his chest and the tender area where his leg had been severed.

"Sorry, Pawn Baxter, but you leave your dignity at the door," said one of the nurses as she cut off his clothes.

"I din't think thith mission wath gonna end up with me naked and a cute girl straddling me," joked David weakly.

"Oh, yes, this is hot," said Odette, eyeing the cuts on his chest with a clinical eye. They appeared to be shallow, but they were long. "Nothing like having a lot of people standing around swabbing up your blood to get you in the mood."

"You seem fairly cool about it," said the nurse.

"It's an operating theater," said Odette. "Not terribly remarkable. I'd shrug, but I don't want to loosen my grip on David here."

An Indian gentleman in a suit and tie came in and peered carefully at the patient for a few moments.

"Fractured radius and ulna on the right," he said, "although

I expect you know that, since the young lady has her hands clamped around the injury. Nice little blades you have tucked away in there, by the way, miss," he said to Odette, who smiled at him tightly. "And, of course, there's the severed leg. Apart from those two things, several of the ribs on the left side are cracked, and his left scapula is fractured. No major organ damage that I can see."

"Thank you very much, Pawn Motha," said a nurse. "We appreciate your coming out of your meeting for this."

"Always glad to help," said Pawn Motha, "and always glad to get out of a budget meeting." He sauntered out and a careful piece of choreography ensued in which Odette and the patient were transferred to a fresh, nonmobile operating table. Odette clambered down awkwardly, still keeping pressure on the man's arm. Bags of blood were hung and began to percolate down into his body. Special foam braces were secured around him to prevent him from making any more sudden moves.

"Okay, Pawn Baxter," said the surgeon, who had reappeared, scrubbed and gowned. "I've been reviewing your records, and I'm afraid that we won't be able to sedate you. And I see that you don't ever sleep or lose consciousness, which means that you're going to have to tough it out."

"I knew that would happen," said David weakly. "It alwayth doth. Getting my withdom teeth out wath a bitch. Do you think I'm going to..." He trailed off and looked at Odette with frightened eyes. She smiled reassuringly.

"We're going to do everything we can," said the surgeon. "In a few moments, I'm going to ask this young lady to remove her hands from your injuries. I will immediately clamp the severed arteries, and then we shall set about repairing the wounds to your arm. Meanwhile, Dr. Jurwich and her team will tend to your leg." He nodded toward the foot of the table, where a voluminous woman swathed in an equally voluminous operating gown was peering dubiously at the leg in the bag. "These restraints should prevent you from moving, but do try to keep as still as possible. Do you understand?"

"Yeth, thir," said Baxter.

"Do you understand?" the doctor asked Odette.

"When you give the word, I'll move back and out of the way as quickly as possible," she assured him, and he nodded in approval.

"Pawn Baxter?" said Dr. Jurwich from the foot of the table. "I'm sorry to have to tell you this, but I'm afraid that we won't be able to reattach your leg." David closed his eyes, and Odette saw tears seeping out. "I'm very sorry, but the damage is just too severe."

"I can probably get it back on," said Odette.

I have simply got to stop doing things without thinking them through first, she thought. Everyone was staring at her incredulously. But I could do it; I know I could. She could gather up the gory trailing wounds and connect everything meticulously, and even without the equipment back in her hotel room, she could reattach this man's leg. She could have him walking in a month, running in three, and the scars would completely vanish within a few weeks.

"I . . . beg your pardon?" said Dr. Jurwich.

"Well, I mean, I can't guarantee it," said Odette awkwardly, "but provided he doesn't have any unorthodox anatomy and the ends aren't contaminated by anything . . . um . . . supernatural, I think I could probably do it."

"Wait a minute, who are you?" asked the head surgeon. He peered at her and noticed the visitor's pass slung around her neck, and for a second she was afraid that he was going to have a heart attack.

"Don't worry, I'm not a civilian. I'm Odette Leliefeld," she said shyly. This revelation failed to have any impact. Some people haven't been reading the flyers in their kitchens. "I'm an apprentice with the Broedersch—with the Grafters."

Odette suddenly felt unsafe. The abrupt silence was profound —even the various hospital machines seemed to have halted. Several of the nurses stepped back. Both doctors were holding scalpels, not in the surgeon-approved palmar or pencil grip, but rather in a grasp that lent itself to briskly stabbing someone in the trachea.

163

David Baxter was staring at her with a look of utter revulsion.

"Y'rra Grafter?" he slurred, and on the last word, his voice took on that pain-inducing pitch from before. Odette flinched.

"Yes, but I'm a guest," she said. She would have held up her visitor's pass, but both hands were occupied on David's arm.

"Get 'er off me," said Baxter, his teeth clenched.

"David," began Odette, "I can—"

"Get it off me!" he shouted, and this time his voice reverberated through the room like a thunderclap. Odette felt the sound punch through her bones. One of the monitors cracked and shattered.

"I think you'd better go," said the doctor quietly. Odette nodded. She was shaking, but her hands were dead still.

"Are you ready?" she asked. The doctor wordlessly held up the equipment he would need. "Okay, then. On three?"

He nodded. "One. Two..."

She had to give the doctor credit—he had fast hands. By the time she took her hands off the wound and scrambled off the bed, he had already clamped the arteries. She turned and the nurses and attendants parted before her, opening a path to the door.

Stand tall, Odette told herself. Do not show weakness. Do not cry. Do not bring shame upon your family and your people. She walked out of the room, her head held high as, behind her, the Checquy surgeons began to save David's life but not his leg.

Odette stood in the hallway, her hands clenched. This is never going to work, she thought. They hate us. They hate us even more than we hate them. She realized that she was garnering curious looks from passersby and glanced down at herself. From her elbows down, she was dripping with Baxter-blood. It was splashed liberally across her blouse and blazer, and she had a distressing conviction that there was more in her hair. Plus, despite her best efforts, her eyes were burning and her nose was running.

I look like I just helped deliver a baby walrus, she thought grimly. I should find a bathroom and at least wash my hands.

But first, she would find Pawn Bannister. If she was lucky, maybe the sight of her would completely ruin his day.

14

Felicity had been standing in the lobby of the Rookery in her hospital scrubs and sodden socks for almost ten minutes when one of the receptionists at the central desk waved her over.

"There's a call for you, Pawn Clements," said the receptionist. "From the office of Rook Thomas." Felicity took the phone.

"H-hello?"

"Pawn Clements?"

"Yes."

"This is Ingrid Woodhouse; do you know who I am?"

"Um, yes."

"Rook Thomas would like to speak with you. Can you come up to her office?"

"I'm, uh, not really dressed for a meeting with the Rook," said Felicity. "I don't even have any shoes on." She realized that her feet were freezing, and that she'd left wet footprints across the floor of the lobby. Then she remembered that she'd changed into street clothes before going to meet with Pawn Odgers. It seemed like something a different person had done, years ago. "I have a suit at my cubicle, though, if she can wait a few minutes."

"Really, it would be better if you came immediately," said Mrs. Woodhouse. "It doesn't matter what you're wearing."

"All right," said Felicity uncertainly. "I'll come right up."

"I'm sending someone down in the executive lift to fetch you," said the EA. "And Pawn Clements?"

"Yes."

"Don't talk to anyone until you've spoken with the Rook."

Felicity had not spent much time on the executive level of the Rookery. It was far nicer than the other levels. Rather than carpet tiles, there were polished wooden floors, and the paintings on the walls were much more valuable. The portraits seemed to be looking down at her disapprovingly as she left wet footprints behind her.

"Ah, good," said Mrs. Woodhouse as Felicity entered the reception area. At that moment, the door to the Rook's office opened and four people in finely tailored suits emerged. Felicity recognized them as the Rookery's heads of Legal, Finance, Governance, and Communications. They were all looking rather startled to be leaving.

"I really am terribly sorry to cut this so short, ladies, gentlemen," the Rook was saying. "But something extremely important has come up. Mrs. Woodhouse will reschedule our meeting."

The four executives made polite if somewhat befuddled sounds and then noticed Felicity. They took in her hospital scrubs and wet socks, her messy hair, and the unmistakable vestiges of her earlier bout of weeping. Four pairs of eyes and a pair of nostrils narrowed (the head of Communications had unorthodox sensory capabilities). Unspoken was the obvious sentiment that she did not look, in any way, extremely important. Nonetheless, Felicity was beckoned into the Rook's office, and the door was firmly shut behind her.

It was a large, pretty room with broad windows looking out on the City and imposing portraits lining the walls. A tasteful arrangement of roses in one of the corners filled the room with perfume. There didn't appear to be any other exits. But it wasn't the setting that Felicity was interested in. This was the first time that she had seen the Rook close up.

Of late, the Checquy had been rife with gossip about how Myfanwy Thomas had changed. In the past, she'd reportedly had trouble confronting telemarketers, let alone evil fleshcrafting alchemists. The few times Felicity had seen Rook Thomas in person, in the hallways, during all-staff meetings, or at the Rookery Christmas party, she'd gotten the impression of a woman desperate to avoid all human contact. Then, recently, word had trickled down that Rook Thomas was no longer self-effacing or shy. She'd actually been involved in combat and had acquitted herself rather impressively. Now when people did the wrong thing, she called them into her office and shouted at them rather than sending apologetic e-mails.

She looked like the old, unassertive Rook Myfanwy Thomas. In her early thirties, she was shorter than Felicity and had an unremarkable face and shoulder-length brown hair. But something had changed.

Interesting, thought Felicity. She holds herself differently. She's no longer trying to make herself smaller. I wonder what happened to pull her out of her shell.

"Pawn Clements, thank you for coming," said the Rook.

"Of course, ma'am."

"You have my sincerest sympathies for the loss of your comrades. This is a horrendous tragedy." To give the Rook credit, she looked Felicity in the eye and sounded really sympathetic. None of that stuff where they claim they know how you feel.

"Thank you. I actually haven't been told anything yet, Rook Thomas. Is it—are they all gone?"

The other woman pressed her lips together for a moment and took a breath. "Our investigators are still examining the wreckage. However, they have found ID tags from six Checquy people, and some remains have already been identified. We have confirmation that Pawns Gardiner, Buchanan, and Cheng are dead. For the others, it may be some time before we can say for certain."

"Oh," said Felicity. She felt empty. All the tears inside her had been shed, and the last little flame of hope had just been extinguished. Gardiner and Buchanan had been two of the soldiers who'd stood guard at the entrance to the cube. They had been intended to carry word back to the Checquy if no one emerged from the OOM, but apparently they had never made it. And Andrea Cheng. Her powers had not been enough to save her. "I can confirm that Pawns Odgers and Jennings are also dead," she said, her voice wavering a little.

"I am very sorry," said the Rook. "I'd better let the appropriate people know." She made a quick, quiet phone call and then turned back to Felicity. "You will, of course, be required to undergo an official debriefing from the head of your division and give a formal statement for the record."

"Yes, ma'am."

"But first I want you to tell me about it. And then we will decide just how comprehensive your official debriefing and formal statement will be," said the Rook.

"I—okay," said Felicity warily. Suddenly, this sounds complicated. The Rook gestured, not to the chairs in front of her desk but to the couch off to the side.

"Please, have a seat. Would you like something to drink?" The Rook put a call through to her EA, who brought in two pots of tea (Earl Grey for Felicity, peppermint for the Rook), a selection of biscuits, and a large fluffy towel for Felicity's feet. "Thank you, Ingrid. I won't be meeting with anyone for the rest of the day, and I would prefer not to take any calls."

"I'll push anything nonapocalyptic to tomorrow," promised the EA, and she closed the door as she left.

"Now, Pawn Clements, I need you to tell me everything that happened. I will be recording our conversation and taking notes. We will each retain a copy of the recording and the notes, but I want your word that you will not share that material with anyone unless I instruct you to do so or unless you are called before an internal tribunal."

"Rook Thomas, what is going on?" asked Felicity.

"We are still gathering information, but it is possible that what happened to you and your comrades has political implications. If so, the details must be kept off the official files. I may need to act on that information in a manner that...is not within normal parameters, which may expose me to formal disapproval. I do not want you left without any protection. This material will demonstrate that whatever action is taken as a result of your testimony, it is my responsibility and done on my orders."

"Very well..." said Felicity cautiously. This was beginning to sound like the kind of political shenanigans she'd always tried to avoid. I'm just a soldier, she thought. That's all I've ever wanted to be. But her general was there, right in front of her, asking for her trust. "I give you my word."

The Rook sat down on the couch, set her tablet computer to record, and spoke clearly. She noted the time, date, and location and stated that she, Rook Myfanwy Alice Thomas, was interviewing Pawn Felicity Jane Clements. She asked Felicity if she would confirm those facts.

"Yes, that is the...situation?" she said uncertainly, looking to the Rook. The other woman nodded and smiled.

"Then let us proceed," said the Rook. "Oh, but look, for God's sake, take off those socks and dry your feet."

It was a very odd debriefing, really, not at all like the clinical process that had always followed Felicity's deployments. Rook Thomas held her teacup in both hands, and kept her notepad on her lap. After a while, she kicked off her shoes and nestled back in the corner of the couch with her feet up. Sometimes Thomas would interrupt to ask questions, and she scribbled notes, but mainly she just listened, nodding occasionally. She was a very good listener. At one point, when Felicity found herself getting a little teary, the Rook provided her with tissues.

As she recounted the events of the day before, Felicity forgot who she was talking to. Unconsciously, she brought her legs up and sat Indian-style on the couch, hugging a cushion.

"So, the uh, Oblong of Mystery—it was a room?" Thomas asked.

"Yeah."

"And your team just walked into it."

"Yes," said Felicity. "Why?"

The Rook leaned back, frowning. "This is not to be shared with anyone," she said finally. "But in the months leading up to the negotiations, the Grafters deployed several weapons throughout the country. One of them was a gigantic cube of living matter. A flesh cube."

"And it summoned recipients of organ transplants?" said Felicity, mildly confused.

"No," said Thomas grimly. "It consumed people—tentacles came out and pulled them in."

"Well, there were no tentacles, but I think Pawn Odgers had concerns," said Felicity. "She ordered the team to report to the Rooks—and only the Rooks—everything that happened. But they died."

Thomas nodded, and Felicity continued with her story.

Hours passed as the Rook took her over every detail, again and again. At one point, Mrs. Woodhouse brought in two delivery pizzas, one vegetarian and one that was the antithesis of vegetarian.

"What time is it?" asked the Rook, looking startled.

"Six o'clock," said the EA.

"All right," said Thomas. "Thanks, Ingrid, it's fine for you to go home. We'll be finishing up soon."

"I can stay if you need me."

"No, we're almost done, but thank you. Give my best to Gary." The EA nodded and left. As they ate the pizza, the Rook continued to ask questions, and then she drew a firm line in her notebook. "Okay, I think that's it, unless you have anything to add?" Felicity shook her head. "Then thank you. I'll make a copy of the recording and my notes and give them to you before you go home."

"What should I say in my debriefing with the division head?" asked Felicity.

"Tell him everything," said Thomas. "It will all come out in the investigation of the ruins, or it might prove important for him to know. I just ask you not to mention the possibility of the Grafters being involved. If he figures it out, he'll come to me, and if he doesn't, well, even better." She got up, picked up the tablet computer, and padded over to her desk.

"Do you think Pawn Odgers was right?" asked Felicity. "Do you think it was the Grafters, that they're betraying us?"

Thomas's shoulders slumped a little. "I don't know," said the Rook. "Maybe." She sounded tired. "But maybe it was something else, completely unrelated."

"You need more information," said Felicity.

"Yes," said Thomas, plugging the tablet into her desktop computer. For all her authority and confidence, at that moment, the Rook seemed very unsure, almost lost.

"But you can't tell anyone else your suspicions," said Felicity. She felt a growing sense of certainty. "Not even the rest of the Court. That's why you've just gone through all this to get my story. If word were to get out about even the possibility of the Grafters leading us up the garden path, everything would fall apart. People here will jump at any excuse to stop the negotiations, and dead Checquy agents would just make it worse."

The woman watched her with no expression on her face, and suddenly Felicity made a decision. "Let me help you." For a split second, she had the satisfaction of seeing the Rook look completely flabbergasted before she mastered her features.

"Help me? Why?" asked Thomas, her eyes narrowed. "For vengeance? To punish the killers of your team?" Under that intent gaze, Felicity felt a shiver go through her, as if a hand had closed gently around her entire body.

"We don't know that they're the killers of my team, not for certain," said Felicity. "And I won't be a party to injustice. I hate the Grafters, but I won't hold them responsible for something they didn't do." The other woman was still looking at her suspiciously. "Rook Thomas, you need help. You are a Rook of the Checquy, and I am your soldier. Let me be of service."

The Rook regarded her for another long moment.

"Normally, after this sort of event and this sort of trauma, you would be removed from combat service to receive counseling," she said finally.

"I don't want that," said Felicity. "I can't sit at my old desk and look at all the empty chairs where my people used to sit. Or go on anguish leave, where I'm paid not to come in to work. I'll wander around my flat and watch television and go mad." The Rook sat back in her chair and steepled her fingers. Her eyes were distant, and Felicity could almost hear her future being decided.

"All right, then," said Thomas. "I accept. Thank you." Felicity felt a rush of relief.

"What do you want me to do?"

"I already have an idea. Do you know Pawn Oliver Bannister?"

"In the Diplomatic section? Yes, he was in my year at the Estate," said Felicity. "He's a wanker—pardon my language."

"No, it's fine, that's the impression I've gotten as well," said the Rook. "He was assigned as minder to one of the Grafter delegation—Odette Leliefeld. Today he managed to lose track of her, and she wandered into the Apex medical wing, where she stirred up some trouble and freaked everyone out. The whole organization is buzzing about it. Apparently, she has abruptly become the poster girl for anti-Grafter sentiment. You'll be replacing Bannister as her minder."

"What? I mean, I beg your pardon?"

"You're going to be accompanying her, keeping her out of harm's way, and observing her. You will report regularly to me."

"How are you going to explain my replacing him?"

"I don't have to explain anything. I'm the Rook," said Thomas comfortably. "But the official reason will be that, because of Miss Leliefeld's newfound unpopularity, she needs to be accompanied by someone who is more equipped to protect her. I know you don't have any bodyguard experience, but you have greater combat training than Bannister does. Plus, you're a woman, so you can keep a close eye on her even in more...sensitive settings. The unofficial reason, which I will allow to percolate through the Checquy, is that Bannister's incompetence put his charge, and therefore the negotiations, at risk. It will be believed because it happens to be true and because he is a dick."

"So, I'm going to guard her but also spy on her?" said Felicity warily.

"In a sense," said Thomas. "You look perturbed. You did say you wanted to be of service."

"Yes, but I didn't expect—"

"What were you expecting?"

"I was really just thinking that you could use me to beat information out of people. I'm not an espionage kind of girl."

"You are now. But maybe we can arrange for some beatings

later." The Rook flipped through the pages of a file. "I'll have a briefing package on Leliefeld put together for you, and you can spend tomorrow reviewing it. I'll need to make arrangements for your reassignment, so the earliest you'll be able to start is the day after tomorrow. Will that be enough time for you?"

"I—yes, I can do that," said Felicity. She was beginning to wonder what she'd gotten herself into.

"You'll still need to go to counseling," said Thomas. "That's nonnegotiable, but we'll schedule the sessions around your duties with Leliefeld."

"Very well," said Felicity glumly. The prospect of talking about her feelings filled her with almost as much dread as the idea of hanging around with a Grafter.

"You look a little dazed," said the Rook kindly. "I know it's a lot to take in, and the fact that this operation has undercover elements might make you uncomfortable."

"Maybe a little."

"I've found that in these under-the-table arrangements, there can be a lot of vagueness. People won't say exactly what they mean, and that can lead to misunderstandings. Someone is ordered to arrange a warm welcome for a delegation, and instead of hiring a chocolate fountain, he sets the guests on fire. But you and I can't afford any misunderstandings. So I'm going to be very clear."

"All right," said Felicity.

"You will be acting as a bodyguard to that girl. It is a real responsibility. You will keep her safe. You will be discreet—people will ask you about her, but you won't talk about her personal life to anyone...except me. And, most important, you do not take any action against any of the Grafter delegation without my word."

"Yes, ma'am."

"If you do anything unauthorized, it could mean war."

"I understand."

"But if I give the order, you will need to kill Odette Leliefeld."

★　　★　　★

That should have been it, but it then transpired that Felicity's car had been towed from the Rookery parking lot the day before, when they thought she was dead. It was not clear where her wallet with her credit cards, money, and Oyster card was—she had left it with the support team when she entered the row of houses. The Rook did not have any money on her for a cab and was not certain where her EA kept the petty cash.

"Well, we'll get you home tomorrow," said Thomas. "For tonight, we'll just put you up in the Barghest watch barracks."

At this, Felicity's heart jumped in her chest, and she made a little gasp. She watched, tense with excitement, as the Rook called the watch manager, Pawn O'Brien, a broad man with a crew cut, who appeared and took custody of Felicity. The two women shook hands, and then Pawn O'Brien guided Felicity through the warren of corridors and to a lift that took them down to the fourth floor.

"Have you ever been to the barracks?" asked O'Brien. The Barghest sections were pretty much off-limits to regular Checquy staff, mainly because the special operations teams were obliged to spend so much time there that it was considered polite to afford them some privacy.

"No," said Felicity, "but I've been working toward joining the Barghests, so I'm very interested."

"Well, they're right in the center of the building," he told her. "Equal distance from the parking garage or the roof if they're taking a helicopter." Felicity nodded. Despite her exhaustion, she couldn't help but feel a little thrill at the thought that she'd be sleeping in the same dormitory as actual Barghests.

The Barghests were the Checquy's elite soldiers. A combination of SWAT, knights, ninjas, and Swiss army knives, they carried a dizzying array of weaponry (some of it decidedly unorthodox) and were trained in various esoteric martial arts that were tailored to their specific inhuman abilities. These were the warriors called in when something disastrous occurred and when at least one of the regular assault teams (who were themselves no slouches) had been unable to subdue the threat. They were soldiers of mass destruction. They were the best.

Every child on the Estate grew up on stories of the heroism and badassitude of the Barghests. Every child on the Estate wanted to be a Barghest, until they found out that most of the coffins at Barghest funerals didn't contain bodies. Instead, they contained parts of bodies, jars of puree, bits of rubble, or, in one memorable and bewildering case, the shattered remnants of a Louis XIV chair.

Felicity was one of the few who wasn't put off by the stories of proud warriors being dismembered, ground into a pulp, turned to stone, or transmuted into valuable antique furniture by malevolent forces. In fact, ever since she had learned about them, she had desperately wanted to join the Barghests, to be one of the real guardians of last resort. There was a mystique about them; they were defending Britain from the very worst dangers.

There were several Barghest squads scattered around the globe, and they could be activated only by a member of the Court. Nevertheless, there was always a team on call at the Rookery. And I'm going to actually hang out in their actual barracks! thought Felicity. Maybe she'd get to shoot some pool with them, ask questions, and make a good impression.

Instead, it turned out that they were all asleep. Pawn O'Brien led her through their barracks, which were equipped with a weight room, a sprung-floor movement studio, a sprung-ceiling movement studio, an indoor shooting range, a sauna, a steam room, a fog room, a small cinema, a large lounge, and a medium-size woman who stood up from a desk to greet them.

"Major Somerset, this is Pawn Felicity Clements. She'll be under your care for the night. Someone will collect her in the morning," said O'Brien, and he departed. Major Somerset was a motherly looking woman, and Felicity knew from her title that she was a Retainer, rather than a Pawn, and that she had been recruited from the military. The attendant guided Felicity through heavy frosted-glass doors to the actual dormitory, which was dimly lit. There were two rows of beds, and slumbering forms were curled up in all but one of them. Wow, she thought in awe. Actual sleeping Barghests. By each bed was a pair of large combat boots, ready to be stepped into.

"No armor?" whispered Felicity. "I always thought they had armor standing ready for them."

"The suits of armor are in the van downstairs and in the helicopter on the roof," said Major Somerset. "They get armored up on the way — saves time." She gestured toward the one empty bed, which was already made. "You'll be sleeping there."

"Whose bed is that?"

"Oh," Somerset said quietly, shaking her head. "That's Pawn Verrall's bunk."

"What happened to Pawn Verrall?" Felicity asked warily.

"Her Labrador started whelping, so she got the night off."

"Ah," said Felicity. "Okay."

"We still have a full complement of troops," the attendant assured her. "There's always an understudy on call." She supplied Felicity with official Barghest pajamas (navy blue, with no emblems whatsoever) and an official Barghest toothbrush (in no way distinguishable from a normal toothbrush). "Would you like a hot-water bottle?" she asked.

"Thank you," said Felicity gratefully. By the time she fell into bed, the chill had been taken off the sheets, and she nestled down comfortably. As she drifted off, her mind was filled with delight that she was so close to her heroes, mingled with sorrow that her team could not share her excitement.

Thirty minutes later, she was jolted out of her sleep by a torrent of noise. It sounded like someone was cramming a metric ton of live weasels into a phone box, and it was coming from a spot only a few centimeters from her face. With no time for thought, she launched herself out of bed before she was even properly awake, flailing away at whatever was attacking her. The sound seemed to be coming from everywhere, and shapes were moving about in the dim light. Then the sound cut out, and the lights in the room flared into brilliance, blinding her. She stumbled back with her hands pressed against her eyes and bounced off a Barghest of indeterminate gender who was lacing up its boots.

"Watch out!" said the Barghest. All around them, people were rushing about madly. Bewildered, Felicity fell back on her bed and watched as all of the soldiers ran out of the room. The lights assumed a more normal intensity, and Major Somerset came in, accompanied by two men who began making the beds.

"Oh, darling, I'm very sorry about that," said the attendant. "They got the call, you see. Had to bolt off to Neath. Something about a computer that's eating the Internet. Good riddance, I say—it's all smut and people whining. But we can't choose our assignments, I suppose."

"But what in God's name was that noise?" said Felicity weakly.

"The Rookery has been experimenting with different sounds to rouse the troops," said Somerset. "I believe that one is a recording of baboons fighting over a Mars bar." She gestured toward Felicity's bed. "See the speakers in the headboard? Gets them awake immediately."

I'll say, thought Felicity.

"Course, it's a problem for some," mused the attendant. "Pawn Sutton keeps punching them out on instinct. She's gone through four headboards so far. But it wakes her up sharpish. Anyway, you get yourself back into bed," she said. "You won't get woken up again until it's time to wake up."

Four and a half hours later the Barghests charged back into the barracks, loudly singing some sort of victory song in Latin. Apparently, the computer had been successfully killed or turned off or negotiated with. Felicity buried her head under her pillow.

15

A chauffeur-driven car, clean and discreet, ferried Felicity through the London traffic to her home. She was dressed in the suit that had been retrieved from her locker and had a stack of files on her lap. Grenadier, her Pomeranian, was seated next to her, gnawing contentedly on a new toy. He was black, with the wide-eyed stare of a lemur or a celebrity caught wearing old holey sweatpants by the paparazzi. She'd had to swing by the home of a Checquy operative to retrieve him.

As soon as Felicity was declared dead, a representative of the Checquy had gone by her town house. He had emptied the fridge of all dairy products, picked up her dog, and re-housed him with a loving family that had happy, laughing children. Said children had been in tears at the loss of their new pet. Grenadier, however, had trotted away from them without a backward glance.

The driver turned the car into Felicity's lane, a few streets away from Kensington Gardens. It was paved in bricks and, a hundred or more years ago, had been the back alley that served the carriage houses of the big expensive terraced houses on either side. Now all the carriage houses had been converted into little town houses that cost the earth. The driver held her files and stood on Grenadier's leash as Felicity fumbled with her keys. She thanked him, and then she and her dog went inside.

The floor of the onetime carriage house had been dug out so that the living room sat half a story below street level, and the kitchen a story below that. A tight spiral staircase led up to a landing and a bedroom with no windows. Because it was the largest bedroom and had its own bathroom, it generally went to whichever of the three housemates currently had a boyfriend. At the moment, it was Felicity's, not because she had a boyfriend (she didn't), but because she was the only one in a position to use it. From the landing, more stairs led up to two tiny bedrooms and the world's smallest bathroom.

Grenadier trotted across the living room and vaulted onto the couch. He nestled himself into his accustomed corner and closed his eyes. Felicity placed her files on the coffee table and went downstairs to make herself a cup of milkless tea.

The house was quiet. One of her housemates, Priscilla, was out of the country, posted to Okinawa, where she was meeting with one of the four other supernatural organizations the Checquy had diplomatic ties with. Kasturi, the second housemate, was hibernating on a plinth in her bedroom. I must remember to go in and dust her, Felicity told herself. Then, with her cup of tea, she settled herself on the couch and closed her eyes for a moment.

It had been a busy morning. Early, well before the sun came up, she'd been woken by the attendant with a summons to Rook Thomas's office. All the Barghests were still asleep, and Felicity had tiptoed out reverently. Her suit had been waiting for her, and she'd dressed quickly before scurrying up to the executive floor. Mrs. Woodhouse had waved her in, and Felicity had found the Rook wearing pajamas and a dressing gown and participating in a conference call about snipers. It was evident that she had been roused from her private apartment upstairs to talk with some far-flung outpost of the Checquy. Thomas had excused herself from the call, muted the phone, and handed her the Odette Leliefeld files.

"Where did we get all this material?" Felicity asked.

"Most of it was supplied to us by the Grafters themselves," said Rook Thomas. "They sent us an insane amount of information. We can't decide if it's a strategic attempt to bury us in paperwork or if they're just really, really anal."

Flipping quickly through the files, Felicity was inclined to believe the second option.

The Rook told Felicity that she was to report to her division head, attend a therapy session, and then go home and prep for her placement with the Grafter girl. She gave Felicity the direct number for her mobile phone, wished her luck, and was back on the conference call before Felicity had gotten a chance to sit down.

The head of her division was waiting for her when she arrived. Her special placement on the orders of the Rook had raised a couple of eyebrows, but it had a certain logic to it, and because it was an order from Rook Thomas, it was accepted. Felicity did as Rook Thomas had ordered and recounted every detail of the events in the row house without mentioning any speculation about the Grafters. The division head had nodded thoughtfully and was sad at the loss of his people, but there was no indication that he linked the events to anything more significant. As far as he was concerned, it was just another inexplicable supernatural atrocity that had flared in the heart of the city. Tragic, but unremarkable.

Then came the session with the therapist. Felicity had been braced for a horrible surge of emotions, but in fact the time had passed quite quickly and easily. It was partly because she had vented so much grief during the car ride to the Rookery, and partly because she was now focused on her new mission. There was still sorrow in her heart, of course, but there was so much to do and think about and plan for that she could not spare the time to be traumatized.

It happened, she thought. It all happened, and now this is happening. She sat quietly for a moment, then took a sip of tea and opened the first file.

A picture of the Leliefeld girl stared back at her. It was not the typical ghastly ID photo, nor a surveillance photo with a fuzzy image of the subject as she walked down the street. Rather, it featured Leliefeld groomed and polished and smiling right into the camera. It was the sort of photograph that you would send to your grandmother or feature on a Christmas card.

And then there were pages and pages and pages.

Everything had been meticulously folioed and indexed. It's as if they included every piece of paper they could find. Photocopies of driver's licenses and student-ID cards. A birth certificate. Math tests. Felicity winced at notes from surgeries—some that Leliefeld had performed and some that she'd undergone.

Much of it was in Dutch, a little was in French, and what English there was had been written in the laboriously stilted language of someone not completely fluent. There was a list of the medications Leliefeld was taking now and lists of the medications she'd taken at other times in her life. Diets she'd been put on. Fingerprints, toeprints, tongueprint, x-rays, and an image with streaky lines that Felicity vaguely recognized as a DNA report.

She skimmed over a checklist of all the samples the Grafters had submitted to the Checquy. Samples of Leliefeld's blood, saliva, bile, urine, tears, mucus, stool, skin, venoms, hair (scalp, underarm, forearm, nostril, leg, pubic), toenail clippings, fingernail clippings, breath, flatus, vitreous humor, bone marrow. *I'm glad Rook Thomas didn't give me the reports of those as well,* she thought.

Still, despite the chaos of the documents, Felicity found that she was building up a mental profile of the subject.

Odette Louise Charlotte Henriette Clémentine Leliefeld, born on the first of September twenty-three years ago in Ghent to the hoogle-raren Drs. William and Ludmilla Leliefeld.* There were copies of the parents' résumés, which Felicity flicked through, noting that they were both paleontologists with a few books under their belts.

There was an extensive family tree. Odette's mother's side went back only four generations, but the lineage on her father's side more than made up for it. It extended back to the court of Charlemagne and showed connections to the noble families of France, Spain, the Netherlands, and Bohemia, as well as to the seven noble houses of Brussels. Felicity noted that Leliefeld was the direct descendant of Ernst van Suchtlen, leader of the Wetenschappelijk Broederschap van Natuurkundigen.

Great, so she's like the princess of the Grafters.

There was a list of vaccinations for the infant Leliefeld. Felicity knew most of them—diphtheria, tetanus, polio, and so forth—but some were unfamiliar. Apparently, they had been

---

* Some thoughtful soul had added a footnote explaining that a *hoogleraar* was a professor.

unfamiliar to someone else too, because they were highlighted and had question marks scribbled next to them.

Leliefeld had attended ordinary, which was to say non-Grafter, preschool and primary schools, with all their attendant bits of paper. There was a finger painting of a happy smiling girl under a happy smiling sun. A school photo of a little Leliefeld, missing her two front teeth. A soccer team with Leliefeld sitting in the middle, holding the ball. Thank God they included her spelling tests, Felicity thought drily.

And then suddenly there were no more records from schools but rather reports from private tutors and long handwritten essays on anatomy. Sketches she'd done of bones and musculature. More inoculations. Surgeries—there were x-rays of her hands, photographs of the insides of her eyes, before-and-after MRIs of her brain. Felicity squinted at the brain pictures, unable to identify the significance of the changes.

Photocopies of every page of every passport Leliefeld had ever had were included, each page certified by a justice of the peace as being a true duplicate of the original. Felicity saw her age from infant to child to gangly adolescent to the woman she was today. The passport pages told a story too. Leliefeld had traveled quite a bit, but only in Europe. It looked as if she had asked for stamps even though, as an EU resident, she hadn't needed them.

She had studied, under assumed names, in non-Grafter institutions. Six months at the Karolinska Institutet in Sweden. A course at the Paracelsus Medizinische Privatuniversität of Salzburg. Art classes at the Accademia di Belle Arti di Firenze.

Apparently, the trips hadn't all been for academic purposes. Leliefeld, along with some other Grafter students, had been rebuked by the Broederschap security office for getting arrested in Stuttgart. Drinks in a nightclub had segued into a fight with locals (which ended when two of the locals mysteriously went into anaphylactic shock from a previously undiagnosed allergy to their own leather jackets), and the local constabulary had stepped in. Nothing serious, but evidently the Grafters saw any official attention as a dangerous failure to remain covert.

There were also holiday trips to Venice, Barcelona, Grindelwald, Marseille.

So, something of a party girl, Felicity mused.

She found some photos of a teenage Leliefeld wearing just a pair of shorts, her hands demurely covering her breasts. There were livid red scars running down her chest and spiraling around her arms and legs. One curved out of her hairline, down her jaw, and back up the other side. In another picture there was a long row of sutures running up her spine and disappearing into her hair, with other lines jutting off across her back like tributaries. Most jarring, however, was the proud smile on the girl's face in all the pictures.

There were DVDs with ominous labels, surgeries that Leliefeld had performed.

O. Leliefeld—Appendectomy on subject B7245

O. Leliefeld—Mini-asymmetric radial keratotomy on
   subject UT633

O. Leliefeld—Gastroduodenostomy on subject RR274

O. Leliefeld—Femoral-head ostectomy on subject RP898

O. Leliefeld—Salpingo-oophorectomy on subject LK
   N555555

O. Leliefeld—Caesarean section on subject 187, subject
   187(a), subject 187(b), and subject 187(c)

O. Leliefeld—Harada-Ito procedure on subject 07224

I don't think I need to watch these, Felicity thought queasily. Then she noticed that Leliefeld had performed these surgeries while she was still a teenager.

She turned to a different section of the file. Leliefeld had a younger brother: Alessio Léopold Albert Pépin Leliefeld. Felicity skimmed his records and saw the same sort of history, but ten years behind. A standard childhood except for some nonstandard inoculations, and then an abrupt transfer to a life of private tutors. No surgeries, Felicity noted. Yet.

Then she came to the part that was of greatest interest to a member of the Checquy: what Odette Leliefeld was capable of, the enhancements that set her apart from regular people. To begin with, her eyes had been almost completely rebuilt; additional lenses had been inserted and the rods and cones "accelerated" by means of some long process explained in Dutch. There was a note about the inclusion of a negative lens, which apparently gave her eagle-like vision when she wanted it.

Changes had also been made to the musculature running from Leliefeld's shoulders down to her hands. These changes did not, to Felicity's surprise, appear to give her any superhuman strength. Rather, the alterations granted her unparalleled fineness of touch and control. That control, combined with her outstanding vision, enabled her to perform microsurgery with her bare eyes and hands. She could conduct operations on living tissue that were well beyond the capabilities of the most advanced (non-Grafter) hospitals in the world.

A sealed pouch in her left thigh held two surgical scalpels that had been grown from her own bone. The description noted that her body sterilized the scalpels, thanks to Leliefeld's highly modified body chemistry and bespoke gut flora, which not only rendered her impervious to most toxins but also gave her a ridiculously healthy immune system and scented her perspiration with jasmine.

They don't say what her poop smells like, thought Felicity sourly.

And that was pretty much it. Pretty much.

Despite herself, Felicity felt a bit of pity for the Grafter girl. Really, it was almost as if Leliefeld had been designed for a specific purpose. They had taken a little girl and decided that she would be a surgeon.

Say what you like about the Checquy, but at least you get to pick what kind of job you do. Her own abilities were not particularly combat-relevant, but she had known she wanted to be a soldier, and her teachers and the organization had supported her. Of course, she still got pulled in to provide insight on crime scenes and artifacts, but they'd never said, "You will do the job your abilities are ideally suited for, and only that job." As far as she could tell, the Grafters had told Odette Leliefeld, "You will do this job, and we will ensure that your abilities are ideally suited for it."

Leliefeld seemed to possess only two augmentations that were not directly linked to performing surgery. The first was the modifications to her facial musculature and skin, which apparently conferred some cosmetic advantages. The file was quite adamant that the changes did not allow Leliefeld to alter her appearance so much that she would be unrecognizable, which left Felicity quite certain that they did allow that very thing.

The other modification was the two retractable spurs sheathed tidily away in her forearms, one spur in each. They were connected to little reservoirs of chemicals tucked up near her elbows. According to the notes, each spur could deliver one dose of octopus venom and one dose of platypus venom before they had to be refilled with hypodermic needles.

To Felicity, who hadn't even realized that platypuses had venom, it sounded like the most ridiculous defense mechanism ever. She knew that the Grafters were capable of constructing utterly lethal weapons and had been doing so for centuries. But this woman had restricted herself to the equivalent of a pair of dueling pistols or a stiletto dagger.

The spurs were lovely, though. There were photographs of them, and sketches that looked like the work of Leonardo da Vinci. They were elegant little things, almost art deco in their design. If they weren't tucked away in someone's forearms, you'd want to have them on your desk as the world's most exquisite letter openers.

Finally, Felicity turned to the itinerary of events that would be held for the Grafters over the next few weeks. Presumably, she would be attending them as well.

"Great," she said aloud. "I'm going to have to buy a hat."

Odette sat at the Apex House conference table and tried to ignore the looks of passersby. That morning, after the meeting in the graaf's suite, Marie had pulled her aside to deliver the good news that she would no longer be escorted about the place by Pawn Bannister. It had been swiftly followed by the bad news that it was because the Checquy thought she needed more protection.

"Protection?" she asked incredulously. "From what?"

"Apparently, the Checquy feels you are in need of more protection from, well, the Checquy," said her cousin apologetically. "It seems that your jaunt to that operating theater has made their people...dislike you a bit."

"They already hate us!" exclaimed Odette. "You know that."

"Yes, well, now they hate you a bit more than the rest of us." Marie shrugged.

"But I only offered to help," said Odette helplessly. "That boy was going to lose his leg, and I could have saved it."

"Actually, he did lose the leg," said Marie. "I checked."

"Damn!" spat Odette. "What a fucking waste!"

"I couldn't agree more. I gather that it was a traumatic amputation of the leg, perfectly simple to repair. Even I could have gotten him walking."

"So who am I getting as a replacement?" demanded Odette. "Some huge thug who's going to follow me around?"

"Actually, no," said Marie brightly. "You get a girl this time. Here's the file the Checquy gave us on her." She passed over a slender manila folder. "And here's our file on her." She passed over a morbidly obese manila folder.

Although Odette apparently had no purpose to serve in the negotiations that day, she was not allowed to stay in her luxurious hotel room or go exploring in the city, because she would have no bodyguard until tomorrow. So she went to the Apex with the rest of the delegation and was given a room in which she could sit and study. Being a Grafter meant you always had homework, and so she dutifully lugged along her laptop, books, and notes. But once they had settled her in the empty conference room, she shoved her homework to the side and opened the folder Marie had given her.

Pawn Felicity Jane Clements. Who are you?

According to the Checquy, when Clements was born, twenty-three years earlier, there had been no indication of anything wrong or unnatural. Ten fingers, ten toes, no teeth, no pedipalps. Standard-issue Anglo-Saxon girl child. She slept, she cried, she cooed, she pooed.

Then, when she was three months old, her parents tried to give her some solid food. The instant that the pureed carrots passed her lips, Baby Felicity began screaming like they'd set her on fire. She kept it up for twenty minutes, crying piteously, then settled down to a prolonged whimpering that didn't stop for hours. Finally, she fell asleep. Her parents, who had tried everything and were on the verge of calling an ambulance, were immeasurably relieved. They were less so when she started whimpering again immediately upon waking up.

A pattern emerged. Baby Felicity could not bear to consume any food but breast milk. Anything else left her screaming and trembling. When she was awake, she did not stop mewling unless she was placed, naked, in a bath of water and held in the center of the tub. If she even touched the sides of the bath, she began complaining again. The Clements parents were frantic, convinced that their daughter had some sort of hypersensitive skin. The family doctor and the physicians at the local hospital were bewildered. Pain medication was prescribed and made no difference whatsoever. The parents made appointments with experts, and waited in agony.

Two days before she was to see a Harley Street specialist, Felicity went into a coma. Her mother found her lying in her crib, eyes open, pupils shrunk to the size of pinheads. The baby was breathing shallowly, but apart from that, she was utterly still. Horrified, Mrs. Clements picked her daughter up. She had lifted the infant no more than four centimeters off the mattress when Felicity went into violent convulsions. Mrs. Clements was so shocked that she actually dropped her child back into the crib. Immediately upon the baby's returning to the mattress, the convulsions stopped.

A few minutes before the ambulance arrived, Felicity's pupils dilated; she blinked, wriggled, and started whimpering again. Distraught, her mother still took her to the hospital, where scans of her brain and heart revealed nothing unusual. The details of the coma were added, a trifle skeptically, to the baby's medical files, which were forwarded on to the Harley Street specialist.

The specialist had never seen or heard of anything like it. He consulted a number of colleagues, and none of them had ever seen or heard of anything like it. But the Checquy had. In fact, they had seen it in 1552, 1585, 1634, 1827, 1884, and 1901. The symptoms afflicting Felicity were strong indications that she possessed the power of psychometry—the ability to read the history of any object she touched.

To the Checquy, it all made sense. Felicity's unwillingness to eat was the result of her powers reaching into the history of the food. To her, it would have felt raw, or covered in dirt, or perhaps as if someone were touching it even as it was inside her mouth. Worse, it might have felt like it was still alive. Her aversion to clothing was much the same—a deluge of images and experiences pouring into her mind. Even the most mundane items would have foisted their histories on her. And the seizure, well, the Checquy had seen that before too. It was a textbook example of a psychometric who'd been deeply immersed in the experiences of an object and then torn away before she'd had time to reel herself back in.

Psychometry could be a terrifically useful power with many practical applications, and the Checquy were eager to have it at their service. So, once they learned of Felicity through their contacts in the medical industry, they made their move.

The dossiers were tactfully silent as to the means by which Felicity had been extracted from her family. They didn't even mention whether she had any siblings. If, one day, Felicity were to marry a civilian, the Checquy would pull the relevant files to make certain she was not marrying a relation.

She'd retained her birth name. The Checquy's policy, it seemed, was that if you'd been christened with a name, you kept it. (Although, to prevent anyone from tracking down their members, the Checquy did provide new National Insurance and National Health Service numbers, and new official dates of birth. Operatives were also usually posted in different cities from any immediate family members who might recognize them.)

Thus, at the age of four months, Felicity Jane Clements was brought to Kirrin Island, enrolled in the Estate, and, incidentally, was legally made a Taurus instead of an Aries. She was installed in the nursery and given various treatments that an Irish peasant woman had come up with several hundred years earlier for her child's psychometry. Primary among these ministrations was the regular application of an ointment made out of moss and yogurt (the original recipe called for fermented goat's milk, but yogurt worked just as well). It smelled terrible but did have the effect of numbing Felicity's powers somewhat and letting her function. It also left her skin looking terrific.

One of the unexpected problems was that, unlike the Checquy's previous psychometric operatives' powers, Felicity's abilities were not limited to her mouth and the skin of her hands. In fact, they were activated through all of her skin, which meant that she spent the first few years of her life almost completely covered in a thick, green, constantly cracking coating of crud. She also subsisted on raw vegetables that were specially cultivated on the island by one person, in order for them to have as little history as possible.

There was, of course, tremendous incentive for Felicity to gain complete control of her abilities as swiftly as possible. Quite aside from the potential benefits to the nation and the distressing odor of the ointment, there were dangers associated with psychometry. The records of the Checquy told of two operatives and three infants who had fallen into deep comas from which they could not be awakened. Popular theory held that they had gotten tangled up in the histories of some object they had touched and could not find their way out again. They had been discreetly put down, rather than being allowed to linger and rot. The Checquy did not want to lose Felicity.

Fortunately, like all Checquy operatives, her predecessors had left behind copious notes about their powers. These journals were stored in high-security vaults and archives around the British Isles. Researchers immediately began trawling through the documents to sift out useful tips and techniques. As soon as she was able to understand words, Felicity was rigorously taught the mental exercises that would allow her to turn off her powers at will. Some were physical routines akin to yoga, but most involved strict mental discipline, constantly keeping her powers in check and shutting herself off from the world.

The Estate, which took a dim view of its students relying on crutches of any sort, weaned Felicity off her lactose/lichen lotion as quickly as possible. The process was exhausting, especially since she had to maintain her barriers even while she slept lest she lose herself in dreams filled with the past experiences of a bed frame or a set of sheets. But her powers did not penetrate water, and every Sunday she was permitted to sleep in an isolation tank. Drifting gently, she was, for once, at rest, her mind unclenched, untroubled by her dreams or those of the furniture.

The scientists and philosophers at the Estate were fascinated by Clements's abilities and urged her to explore the boundaries of her Sight. They discovered that it was not limited to the past and that she could use it to augment her perception of the present. Her Sight could spread out to give her a perfect awareness of everything approximately three meters from her skin. In that area, with her eyes closed, she could describe the nature and position of items placed around her. More, she could see through them, whether metal, stone, or plastic. If they placed a gun at her feet, she could read its every component, every bullet.

Under the enthusiastic prodding of her instructors, Clements discovered that she could push her Sight out even farther. Her consciousness would leave her body as an invisible probe that she sent out of herself, taking up about the same amount of space as a basketball. Kneeling blindfolded in a room, she could send it down through her bare hands, across the floors, up the walls, and along every object in the place.

There were blind spots, however. Certain materials were impenetrable to her Sight and key among them was anything that was alive. There was something about living things that caused her powers to slide off them. They were invisible in the present, and she could see their echoes in the past only through the history of nonliving things. She could shake a person's hand and get nothing at all (unless the cuff of his coat brushed her hand). But give her a corpse and she could read its past from the moment she had zipped open the body bag, through the person's murder, and back into his life. (The Checquy hadn't killed someone so she could try this, the file noted, they'd just happened to have a corpse handy.) Decant some blood out of a healthy boy, give the cells a few minutes to die, and she could draw you a picture of the donor.

There were other limitations as well. Her powers would skip automatically over anything that had occurred in the forty-eight hours surrounding a solstice, and there had been a couple of shells and a fork that, for some unknown reason, she couldn't read at all.

Fascinated, Odette read a transcript from an interview with a nine-year-old Clements as she'd tried to explain her Sight to a group of eminent scholars, including a Nobel Prize-winning physicist, an Oxford don specializing in the philosophy of consciousness, three mathematicians, and the bishop of Bath and Wells, all of whom had been sworn to secrecy under the Official and Unofficial Secrets Act.

It's sort of like swimming. Everything is an ocean. When you're exploring the present, you're swimming along the top of the water, getting farther and farther away from your body. And then, when you want to go into history, you dive down.

The scholars went away and wrote lots of academic papers about physics, space, and the memory of reality that no one outside the Checquy would ever see. Meanwhile, Felicity got used to being pulled out of class to read the history of the occasional murder weapon or blood-drenched obsidian altar stone lifted from the inner sanctum of a dark temple in downtown Plymouth.

She'd done well enough at school, her grades not outstanding, but respectable. Her hobbies included tae kwon do, cross-country running, and a couple of failed attempts at bulimia. The file contained some records from Felicity's counseling sessions, and Odette hesitated guiltily before opening them. They were unremarkable, which was simultaneously disappointing and reassuring. Rather than stemming from any form of demonic possession or psychic backwash from her abilities, the bulimia had been an attempt to assert some control over her own life. The counselor judged that it was due to Felicity's being obliged to maintain a constant rigid hold on her abilities combined with normal teenage angst and the fact that she would never be permitted to leave the Checquy. She'd grown out of the second problem and come to terms with the first and the third through some traditional talk therapy.

Early on in Felicity's schooling, the Estate had noted her fascination with stories of warriors and soldiers. She displayed a marked aptitude for martial arts and strategy. Her sessions with the Checquy career counselor had established that she was very interested in joining the Barghests. And so, after graduating from the Estate, Clements underwent intensive training in armed and unarmed combat, and then moved into active service with an urban assault team based in London. She had nine confirmed kills of people and two confirmed kills of creatures who, although they wore trousers, were not counted as people by the Checquy.

And this violence-obsessed killer is the woman responsible for my well-being, thought Odette weakly.

So do you have a cure for cancer, then?"

Startled, Odette looked up from the file to see a tall man looming over her. She hadn't heard him enter the conference room, but the door was closed behind him. She tried to pull her thoughts together and out of the files.

"I'm sorry, what?" said Odette.

"Your lot are supposed to be masters of biological science, right?" said the man, a Checquy employee who looked to be in his forties. He was wearing a gray suit and carrying a leather briefcase, which he put down so that he could cross his arms.

"Well, I'm still learning," said Odette. "But we don't generally get cancer unless someone makes a mistake. My name's Odette, by the way." She thought about offering her hand to shake, but he was standing very close to her.

"You can alter people's bodies?" he asked, ignoring her attempt to be polite.

"Um, yes."

"You're the best surgeons on the planet."

"I suppose."

"So does that mean you have a cure for cancer?"

"Uh...which cancer?" asked Odette, who didn't like being loomed over.

"Any cancer," he said flatly.

"Oh. Then yes," said Odette tartly, and she felt triumphant for a moment as the man took a step back. He rallied, however, and stepped forward to loom again.

"And will this cure be made available to the British people?"

"Well, one dose of the cure involves slaughtering seven adult sea turtles and about three hundred cattle in such a way as to render the meat and hide unusable," said Odette. "Basically, it leaves the corpses as a form of toxic waste. Making it is very labor-intensive. And it results in the recipient becoming sterile."

"How convenient," sneered the man. Odette could feel her eyebrows wrinkling in confusion.

"I'm sorry, English is only my fourth language," she began, "but I don't think that's the right—"

"Shut up!" he spat at her. Odette noticed that his hands were clenched tight.

He's not just being a jerk. He's spoiling for a fight, she realized with shock. She looked around anxiously. One wall of the conference room was glass, and throughout the day she'd had to make a conscious effort to ignore the stares of the passing Checquy staff, but now the corridor seemed to be empty.

"You Grafters can do a lot, can't you?" he asked. "You can make soldiers bigger and stronger. You can make a man whose skin eats other people until he fills the room. And then tentacles reach out and pull people in and dissolve them." Odette didn't answer. There was a strong smell of ozone building in the air. She kept her hands in her lap, petrified of saying or doing something that would push him to act. Inside her forearms, she felt her spurs twitch. Why doesn't someone come?

"That meat cube in Reading?" said the man in a fierce whisper. "One of my friends got pulled in by that thing before Rook Thomas ripped it to pieces. I saw his corpse, bleached white and eaten away." The smell of ozone was burning her nose by this point, and she had a sense that something absolutely horrendous was about to happen.

"I'm very sorry to hear that," said Odette softly. "But that wasn't—"

"Sorry? You're sorry?"

Odette's hands slipped off each other, and she looked down. An orange-tinged clear oil was covering her skin, as if it had condensed there. As she watched, shiny orange drops appeared on the sleeves of her suit coat. He's using his powers on me! she thought wildly. What's happening? What is this? She shifted under his enraged gaze and felt herself slide a little on the seat, which was also suddenly slick with grease. She could feel more oil sweating onto her face and sliding under her clothes. The conference table was swimming in the stuff, and it was soaking into the papers scattered across it. It dripped down from the ceiling and oozed onto the walls.

"That wasn't me," she whispered. "That wasn't us."

"Of course; that was the other Grafters, wasn't it?" snarled the man. There were tears in his eyes, and his face was red. Odette felt a pinch all over her skin, as if the oil were tightening around her. "The ones that invaded my country and killed children."

"I—" began Odette.

"But don't you live forever?" said the man. "Hasn't your boss been walking around for centuries?" There was a jolt under Odette, as if the seat had been jerked suddenly. Except that the man still had his arms folded. "Centuries."

What do I do? she thought. If I attack him or scream for help, he might kill me. So stay still, she decided. Don't do or say anything that might provoke him. Maybe someone will come. Maybe he'll calm down.

"It might have been a long time ago," said the man. "But we remember, and we pass the memory along." He stared at her, and her skin prickled sharply.

That wasn't my nerves, she thought. That's him. She tried to lean back a little and found that it was difficult, as if she were wearing rigid clothing. She could practically taste the hate in the air. Her legs felt stiff, pinioned in her own skin and a shell of oil.

You're holding my exterior, she thought. But there's more to me than what you see.

She concentrated and engaged some nerves that were tucked away deep within her torso. The moment he brings violence, I am not going to pull any punches. Unless he calmed himself down, the man in the suit was going to be receiving a dose of venom that was normally found in the crural glands of the male platypus. It wasn't fatal, but it was supposed to be excruciatingly painful.

That is, if he'll even let me get a punch in. She felt as if she were being held in a vise, the oil gripping her.

"Pawn Korybut," said a voice. A woman's voice. With an effort, Odette turned her head. There stood the small figure of Rook Myfanwy Thomas.

"Rook Thomas," said the man, Korybut, not taking his eyes off Odette.

"Stand down," said the Rook. Her voice was calm, mild even, but under that cool tone was the promise of dire consequences if she was not obeyed.

There was a horrible pause as Odette was transfixed by Pawn Korybut's gaze. There was no change in his eyes. The rage and madness didn't grow fainter. There was simply a man who was deciding what mattered most to him.

"Yes, ma'am," he said finally. Odette felt the prickling tightness on her skin easing, and she was suddenly able to slump.

"Now go," said Rook Thomas. "You're done for the day. It's time to go home." He picked up his briefcase and backed away. "You don't talk about this to anyone, Pawn Korybut. You and I will discuss this tomorrow." He nodded. Finally he turned and walked out the door. The goop, however, failed to mystically evaporate.

Odette buried her head in her hands; the oil squished on her palms and burned her eyes. It was not immediately clear, even to her, if she was crying. There were some gasping breaths and a fair amount of emotional turmoil, but no actual sobs. She looked up and saw Rook Thomas standing by her, looking sympathetic.

"I'm not crying," said Odette, trying to muster up some dignity. "Whatever this stuff is, it's in my eyes."

"It's everywhere," said the Rook. "Let's go get you cleaned up. I'd pat you comfortingly on the arm, but I don't want that crap on me."

"I can't," said Odette helplessly. "I can't walk through the halls like this."

"Oh, I've attended meetings looking far worse," said Thomas dismissively. "No one will look twice at you."

Persuaded by her practical tone and the fact that the liquid covering her was getting unpleasantly cold, Odette gingerly stood up, slipping a little on the floor. The Rook was staring, stony-faced, at the conference table. Odette looked down and saw several large cracks running through the wood. "Well, at least he vented most of his frustration on the furniture," said Thomas. Odette shuddered. "Anyway, there are showers and spare tracksuits at the gym, so let's get going."

Rook Thomas led her, squelching, through the hallways of Apex House to the ladies' changing room. There were more than a few curious glances, but Thomas ignored them, so Odette tried to do the same.

I'm making such a wonderful impression, she thought.

"Did—did you use your powers on that man Korybut?" she asked finally.

"No, that was just me being his boss," said Thomas. "Although I would have." She opened the locker-room door, peered in, and then gestured Odette through. "No one else is in there, and I'll wait here in the hallway to make sure that you're not disturbed. Tracksuits are on the shelves by the towels," she advised.

"Thanks," said Odette, walking hurriedly into what might have been the nicest locker room she had ever been in. A thick red carpet covered the floor, leather couches lined the walls, and the lockers themselves were made of dark wood. She felt a trifle gauche to be trailing oil across the carpets and scurried to the showers. When she caught a glimpse of herself in a mirror, she flinched.

Oh, marvelous, she thought grimly. I look like a whale sneezed on me.

To her immense relief, the stuff washed off easily—far more easily than the slime she'd been sleeping in. Under the hot water, her muscles relaxed, sliding back into their normal positions. She took the opportunity to have a private little cry, and then, once she was dressed in a nondescript gray tracksuit, she spent a laborious few minutes staring in a mirror and draining the redness from her eyes. She crammed her greasy suit into a plastic bag she'd liberated from a rubbish bin and wiped the better part of the oil off her shoes with handfuls of wadded-up toilet paper.

As she walked out of the bathroom in her sweat suit and high heels clutching her bag of clothes, Odette was secretly hoping that the Rook had left. That way, she could slink through the hallways, avoiding everyone, catch a cab to the hotel, and go straight to bed without having to talk or think about anything that had happened.

However, in keeping with the tone of the day, Rook Thomas had failed to leave and was leaning against the wall. She had stepped out of her heels and, as a result, was a good deal shorter. She was squinting at her phone and tapping away at it.

"What a fucking day," said Thomas. She sighed and tucked the phone away in a pocket. "Miss Leliefeld, I am aghast at Pawn Korybut's actions. His behavior was inexcusable, especially toward a guest and most especially toward a diplomat. On behalf of the people and the Crown of Great Britain and Northern Ireland, please accept my formal apology." Odette blinked. The ritualistic language was somewhat at odds with the stockinged feet.

"Of course I accept," said Odette.

"I realize we must tell Graaf Ernst," Thomas said.

"Yes, I have to," said Odette.

"I don't know how he'll take it," said Thomas, "but the last thing we need in secret negotiations between secret organizations is more secret secrets. I'll come with you when you tell him, and I'll apologize to him as well." Odette raised her eyebrows a little at the woman's assumption that she would decide what would happen but found herself nodding in agreement. The Rook had that kind of authority.

"I saw how much that man loathed me," said Odette. "He loathed the idea of me. And it's not just him. People have been giving us poisonous looks since we arrived."

"They've been brought up to hate the memory of the Grafters," said Rook Thomas mildly. "I can't expect them to stop overnight."

"You were brought up to hate the memory of the Grafters," said Odette. "And you seem all right."

Thomas gave an odd little smile. "They'll come around," she said. "Now, let's go talk with your ancestor, and then I'll see about getting your bodyguard brought into service immediately."

Oh, good, thought Odette glumly. I feel safer already.

16

That evening, Felicity knocked on Odette's hotel-room door. It opened and a short youth whom Felicity recognized as the brother looked up at her.

"Hello, I'm Felicity."

"Hi," he said. They stared at each other warily for a while. "So, I, um, I ordered a hamburger?" he said finally.

"I'm not room service," said Felicity curtly, somewhat irritated by the way his gaze had paused on her breasts. "I'm looking for Odette Leliefeld."

"Why?" he asked suspiciously.

"I'm her new roommate." This revelation appeared to lie completely beyond his comprehension because he continued to stare at her. But at least he was staring at her face. She sighed heavily. "Is she here?"

"Odette!" he called, turning slightly but not taking his eyes off her. The girl Grafter appeared and looked over his head, her eyes widening in surprise.

"You're Felicity Clements." She did not sound delighted to have the Pawn on her doorstep. In fact, she sounded as far from delighted as it was possible to be without having a chain saw at one's throat or genitals.

"I am. It's a pleasure to meet you, Miss Leliefeld."

Odette pushed her brother to the side, and they shook hands gingerly. Odette tried not to imagine Felicity's powers seeping into her skin and reading her history, while Felicity tried not to brace herself to get stabbed by those spurs. Both women let go gratefully and discreetly wiped their hands on their legs.

"She says that she's the new roommate," said Alessio.

"I think you misunderstood," said Odette. "She's actually my new..." She trailed off as she searched for an appropriate word, eventually settling for "bewaarder."

"What happened to Bannister?" asked the boy. "Did he fulfill his life's dream and climb up his own asshole?"

Odette winced and cast an apologetic look at Felicity. "Alessio, please try not to be disrespectful about our hosts."

"Don't worry about it," Felicity said. "I know Oliver Bannister. The greatest tragedy of his life is that he went to the world's most exclusive school and he can't tell everyone about it. He's a complete twat," she assured them. She noticed the boy mouthing her words, filing them away for later use. *Marvelous, I'm such a good ambassador for our culture.* "Anyway, in addition to being your new bodyguard, I'm also your new roommate."

"You're what?" said Odette.

"I'll be staying with you."

"You can't be serious!" The words were out before she could think about them, and she flushed at her own rudeness. The Pawn's eyes narrowed a little, and she spoke before Odette could apologize.

"Quite serious," said Felicity. "The Checquy rooms in this hotel are all full, but I understand there's a spare bedroom in this ridiculously large suite they've given you."

"There isn't," said Odette. *I don't care if I'm being rude, I don't want this killer staying with us. Bad enough that she'll be following me around all day.*

"Well, we kind of have a spare bedroom," said Alessio, who, now that they'd established Felicity wasn't there to kill them or deliver a hamburger, seemed quite intrigued by the development. Odette gave him an evil look.

"That doesn't sound good," said Felicity. "Wait—we?"

"Yeah, Odette and I share this suite."

"That sounds even worse. So, may I come in?" They drew back to let her in, and she picked up the backpack she'd brought, stepped inside, and took in the room. "Crikey," she said without thinking. "This place is bigger than my whole house." *And who is footing the bill for this? The British taxpayers?*

"You're getting a bodyguard?" Alessio asked Odette. "Why?

Is this related to the fact that at the end of every day, you're wearing a different outfit than the one you started in?"

"Don't be ridiculous," said Odette. "I haven't been doing that."

"Yes, you have," said Alessio. Odette tried not to think of the two suits that she had wadded up and hidden in her luggage. One was stained with the blood from that injured Pawn and the other covered with that horrible orange oil that had congealed all over her. I should just buy new suits, she thought grimly. I'm down to three that aren't stained with unacceptable fluids.

"I've been assigned to protect your sister because she's managed to alienate the entire organization," said Clements. "There are concerns that if she's left unattended, she may be subject to harassment or violence." The two Grafters looked at her in shock.

Damn it! thought Felicity. This is why I should not be working in any sort of diplomatic role.

"But you don't need to worry," she said in an effort to be reassuring. "I will make sure that no one kills you. Or, if they do, that they'll regret it." Judging from their still-dropped jaws, this guarantee did not allay their concerns.

"So, don't I need a bodyguard?" asked Alessio, which both women understood to mean Why don't I get a hot woman to follow me around?

"No one hates you that much," Odette told him absently. "Except me."

"I see only two bedrooms," said Felicity, turning back to them. "Is he sleeping on the couch?" Or are you sleeping upside down in a closet? she thought.

Then she realized that, in addition to thinking this, she'd actually said it. Alessio appeared amused, but Odette looked distinctly annoyed.

Felicity tried to recover, drawing her lips back in what she hoped was a charming smile. They did not look particularly charmed.

"That's Alessio's room," said Odette finally, nodding toward one of the doors. "And that's the bedroom I've been keeping all my things in, but I don't sleep there. I actually sleep in the bathtub."

"Oh," said Felicity. Odette was mildly entertained by the warring expressions on the Pawn's face as the allied forces of courtesy and professionalism battled with the axis of disgust and incredulity.

I don't think I need to enlighten her any further, Odette thought. Let her imagination run riot.

"Anyway," she said, "Alessio's current room has its own smaller en suite with a shower and a toilet. I guess we'll put Alessio in my bedroom, and you can have his. Alessio, start moving your stuff into my room. I'll call housekeeping and let them know we need the sheets changed. And the porters are bringing up your luggage?" Odette asked.

"This is my luggage," said Felicity flatly, holding up her back-pack.

"Oh."

For the next few minutes, the suite was a scene of frantic activity. In short order, Alessio's hamburger and the chambermaid with the sheets arrived. Alessio frantically moved armloads of clothes, textbooks, and equipment from one room to the other while Felicity unpacked. Odette, after being politely (to her relief) rebuffed in her offer to help Felicity, contributed by staying out of the way, tipping the hotel staff, and eating Alessio's french fries.

All the while, Odette watched the Pawn out of the corner of her eye. Her augmented vision gave her an excellent view, and she noted all the details she could.

Dirty-blond hair pulled back in a nondescript ponytail. Excellent skin, thought Odette with a flush of envy. Without any help from makeup. Pleasant features, even as she scanned the room for threats with a suspicious expression on her face. Felicity Clements was taller and more muscular than she was, but she was not bulky, not a bodybuilder. Instead, she gave an impression of extreme fitness. As an anatomist, Odette knew that her musculature would combine strength and flexibility.

The Englishwoman moved carefully, like a cat in an unfamiliar house. Each time someone new came to the suite, Clements was present, evaluating, and Odette noted that she did not return to her unpacking until the person had left and the door was safely shut.

Then she remembered, with a jolt in her stomach, that the Clements dossiers—which not only discussed the intimate details of her new roommate's life but also constituted classified government material that had been obtained illegally—were, at that moment, actually on the coffee table, not five meters away, where she'd been reviewing them. Oh, crap. She moved her eyes minutely and zoomed in.

Yes, the files were definitely there, spread about, painfully obvious for all to see. In fact, they were open to a picture of Clements in her teenage years, snapped while she was running in an Estate athletics carnival. It was not a flattering picture—she was pouring with perspiration, her red face caught in an expression that suggested she was dying of asphyxiation. As far as incriminating evidence went, it would possibly be the most awkward discovery in the history of espionage.

She cursed softly in Flemish.

Extremely calmly, and extremely casually, Odette got up from the couch and moved over to the table. She began gathering up the pages gently, trying not to rustle them at all.

Quickly, she told herself. Quickly.

"Odette?" said a voice behind her, and she literally jumped into the air with a little shriek. She turned to see Alessio standing there. Then Felicity bolted out of her room, her fists clenched and up. Presumably she'd been summoned by the sound of her protectee's shriek.

Conceal the files! Odette's instincts screamed at her, but they did not offer any useful suggestions for doing that. She froze, her fingers inexplicably spread in the "jazz hands" formation. Fortunately, the other two people stared in utter bemusement at her to the exclusion of all else, including the dossiers.

"What is wrong with you?" asked Alessio.

"You startled me, is all," said Odette. "What do you want?"

"I need the code to the room safe." She gave it to him, warning him not to tip over any of the vials that were in there. He went into the bedroom, and Clements gave her a long, measuring look before returning to her room.

Well, I've certainly justified any preconceived notions she might have had about my being a freak, thought Odette. She hurriedly gathered all the papers up and cast about for a place to store them. With Alessio now occupying her bedroom, any possibility of concealing them there was effectively quashed. And if I hide them in this room, Clements or the maids might find them. A solution occurred to her.

"Where are you going?" asked Felicity, her eyes narrowed. She had poked her head out of the bedroom before Odette had even put her hand on the doorknob.

"Just next door," said Odette. "To see Marie—the head of security. I'll be right back." The Pawn looked at her for a long minute, and then nodded her head.

Damn right, you're nodding your head, thought Odette with a flash of irritation. You don't get to tell me where I can and can't go. Especially since I've already been told I can't go anywhere.

Felicity stepped out of the bedroom and watched her go, biting her lip. She had no experience as a bodyguard, so she had no idea how paranoid she ought to be. But there are guards all over this floor, including at the lifts and the fire stairs, she told herself. So she's not going to be wandering out into the city.

That said, she and I are going to have to sit down and go over the rules, she resolved. She is not going off this floor without me. No harm is supposed to come to her.

Unless I bring it myself.

And that was the real issue floating in the back of her mind. At any moment, she might get the call to kill that girl. Felicity knew how to do it, but she'd never been asked to kill someone with whom she was sharing a front door. Felicity was firm that she was not going to get attached to this woman.

It helped, however, that she was not predisposed to like Odette Leliefeld anyway. Quite aside from the whole Grafter issue, she gave off the vibe of a rich, spoiled Eurotrash girl. Maybe it was the fact that her outfit cost as much as Felicity's entire wardrobe, or maybe it was the way she seemed completely at ease in the ridiculously luxurious hotel suite. It wasn't that Felicity would take pleasure in killing her, but disliking the Grafter might take some of the sting out of doing it if she had to.

Then she turned to see Alessio looking at her.

And he's a weird little guy too, she thought. *According to the files, he hadn't had any surgeries yet, although apparently there were some Grafter-type chemicals and inoculations already in his system. Jesus, I hope I don't have to kill him too.* He didn't even look like he'd committed to puberty, let alone evil.

"Yes?" she said.

"Have you finished unpacking?"

"Yes."

"Do you want me to show you around?" he asked.

"I suppose that's a good idea," said Felicity. *I should reconnoiter the place.*

"Well, to begin with, this is your room," he announced grandly, heading toward the room she'd just been unpacking in.

"You don't ever come in here," she told him flatly, shutting the door. *Establish boundaries.*

"What if I need to use the lavatory, and my sister is in the other one?" he asked cunningly.

"Then you hold it. I am obliged to prevent harm from coming to your sister," said Felicity. "No one said anything about you."

"I see," he said. "Well, then, this is the sitting room." He gestured around at the room they were currently occupying. "You may be familiar with it, since you've already been in here for quite a few minutes."

"Yes," said Felicity, "but I haven't taken a close look." It really was a beautiful place, large, bright, and modern. There was a dining area with a polished table large enough to host a fairly big dinner party. The sofas were plush, the sort you could sink

205

into for a good long hibernation. An enormous television was attempting to hang discreetly on the wall and failing miserably. Glamorous coffee-table books lay artfully displayed on glossy coffee tables. You felt more sophisticated just for being in the room.

The current occupants had added a few touches, however, which detracted a little from the fashion-shoot vibe of the place. Distinctly unglamorous copies of anatomical textbooks, bristling with bookmarks, lay splayed amongst the (seemingly aghast) coffee-table books. There were partially filled-out government forms on the dining table. A small fern in a pot trailed tendrils of green and glittering copper. And on a sideboard stood a large clear plastic box containing a thick layer of wood shavings and a pair of flamboyantly patterned...

"Mice," said Felicity.

"Those are mine," said Alessio.

"I didn't think that a hotel would let you bring pets," said Felicity. "My dog is with a sitter."

"I told them that these were my seeing-eye mice."

"What?" asked Felicity, looking at him.

"Not really," said Alessio. "And they're not pets, they're part of my studies."

"How did you get them into the suite?"

"They're mice," said the boy. "It's not like I had to smuggle in a pair of aardvarks. And besides, in a hotel this expensive, they're used to privileged guests bringing their pets. If it's not some celebutante with her Chihuahua, it's a movie star with his angora goat or a pop musician with a large man on a leash."

"All right, so what are their names?" asked Felicity. She was trying not to be intimidated by the fact that the kid was obviously much more familiar with a life of luxury than she was. She peered down at the rodents, which were extremely peculiar-looking. Their left sides were pure glossy black while their right sides were a flat, spotless white. The line that divided the colors could have been drawn with a ruler. Their right eyes were red, their left eyes black. Apart from their chromatic bisection, they appeared to be perfectly normal and were engaged in the traditional mouse activities of wandering around and squeaking.

"They're Mouse A, and Mouse A(i)," said Alessio, somehow managing to convey through speech the presence of parentheses and a lowercase Roman numeral one.

"Catchy. Explain."

"Mouse A is the latest in a long line of mice that has been bred by the Broederschap. They're designed to be highly distinctive in appearance."

"And what do they do?"

"The mice? You're looking at it. They run around, they squeak. They're mice. But Mouse A(i) is one of my assignments," said Alessio. "I've grown him as a clone of Mouse A. He's a copy."

"You copied a mouse?" said Felicity.

"Good, isn't it?"

"How?" asked Felicity, unable to take her eyes off the Grafter-mice. She kept expecting them to extrude talons and antlers, break through the plastic of their enclosure, and scuttle off in search of cheese and human blood.

"Do you have any knowledge of microbiology and cellular formatting?"

"No."

"Are you interested in learning about them?"

"God, no," said Felicity.

"In that case, I took some mouse blood, put it in a tub of magic Grafter-slime, added some starch, and a new mouse grew out of it," said Alessio.

"How do you know which mouse is which?" asked Felicity.

"At the moment, I don't," said Alessio in a satisfied tone. "Not by looking. No one does. Mouse A(i) is a perfect copy."

"So, could you copy a human being?" said Felicity.

"Yeah," said Alessio. "I mean, I couldn't, but the Broederschap could." She looked at him questioningly. "That description about the slime and the starch, that was a drastic simplification. Mouse A(i) has taken me months of work. A person would be a lot more difficult to make. And, yes, you can make a copy of a person, but you can't make a copy of memories. Mouse A(i) started out as a fetus, then grew into a baby mouse, and then grew into what you see today. Four months ago, you could have easily told the difference between the two, just by size."

"So, you could make a fetus that would grow into an identical copy of a person?"

"Genetically identical," said Alessio. "But we don't."

"Why not?"

"Um, because why would we? Odette says that anyone who wants a clone of himself is the last person you would want more of."

"So I'm not going to wake up and see a Stepford me standing over me with a blank expression and a knife?" said Felicity.

"Like an adult? No," he said definitely. "I mean, we can speed-grow a clone to be an adult, it's an extrapolation of Podsnap's Technique, but it still doesn't have any memories. It's like a fetus. I think a Stepford you would stare at you with a blank expression and then fall over because it hadn't learned how to stand yet." Felicity nodded, still entranced by the identical mice.

"Show me the rest of the suite," she said finally.

"There's the other bedroom," said Alessio. "Which I suppose is mine now." The other bedroom proved to be a little bit larger than hers, with a gigantic bed and various artsy bits of furniture. There was also a goodly amount of expensive-looking luggage lined up against the wall. Felicity examined it enviously. Then with incredulity. Then with a mild sense of horror.

"I didn't know Louis Vuitton made a biological-specimen quarantine case," she said faintly.

"I think it's bespoke," said Alessio. The room had its own little fridge tucked away in a cupboard, but when Felicity opened it, it contained none of the standard minifridge drinks. Instead, it held some decidedly nonstandard minifridge vacuum flasks that were, she noted, each monogrammed with an ornate O and L. Well, I won't grab anything to drink out of here. There were also some hypodermic needles in sterile plastic wrappers.

In front of the window, there was a desk with a laptop, a few notebooks, and some large leather-bound books that looked incredibly technical and tedious. There was also a series of framed photos that caught Felicity's eye since they clearly belonged to Odette and not the hotel. She moved closer.

The first was a picture of Odette and Alessio with two pleasant-looking people who were obviously their parents. One showed a West Highland terrier smiling from a pile of golden leaves. And there were lots of pictures of Odette with a group of six people her own age.

"Who are they?"

"Those are Odette's friends," said Alessio quietly. He came up beside her.

"They're all Grafters?"

"Yeah, they all studied together," explained Alessio.

From the look of the photos, that wasn't all they did together. Every photo seemed to have been taken in some glorious location. In one picture, they were all dressed in ski clothes and goggles, and the Alps reared behind them. In another, they were underwater, their mouths drawn open in grinning subaqueous roars. One of the pictures showed them having dinner in a restaurant, holding up enormous steins of beer in a toast to the camera. And then there was a night shot of them clinging to a jagged stone sculpture atop a horrendously steep roof, the lights of a city far behind and below them. It had clearly been taken at arm's length by one of the men, who was reaching out to the edge of the picture.

"That's the cathedral in Cologne," said Alessio. "They climbed it in the middle of the night."

There were pictures of the group in tuxedos and ball gowns, in bathing suits, in nightclubbing clothes, and in cloaks and Venetian masks. It looked as if they had toured all of Europe, always laughing or smiling or perhaps pouting ironically. There was a shot of Odette, in a bathing suit and sunglasses, braiding the hair of one of the other girls as she lay on the sand. In another, Odette was asleep in a rail carriage, her head cradled in the lap of a boy with dark curly hair. Felicity noticed that in many of the pictures, that same boy had his arms around Odette.

"Who's that?" she asked.

"That's Pim," Alessio said. "He was her boyfriend." Felicity noted the use of the past tense but didn't comment.

"And none of them are in the delegation?" she asked. "They're all back in Europe?"

"They died a few months ago," said Alessio.

"All of them?" she asked, startled. The boy nodded.

"That's Saskia, and Mariette, and Simon," he said sadly, pointing to each one in turn. "That one's Claudia. And that's Dieter. He was actually Odette's and my uncle, but he was only two years older than Odette."

"I'm, uh, I'm very sorry for your loss. Was it some sort of accident?" she asked hesitantly.

"No," said a voice from behind them. They both turned to see Marcel, the older craftsman, standing in the room. "I'm afraid, Pawn Clements, that they were murdered."

17

"The Checquy aren't the only enemies the Broederschap has faced," said Marcel conversationally. "What do you know about the supernatural on the Continent, Pawn Clements?" Alessio had introduced the two of them—although they each already knew who the other was—and they had shaken hands and moved into the sitting room. Alessio set about making coffee with an incredibly expensive machine that had been concealed in a cupboard.

"Um, not a great deal," said Felicity uncomfortably. She

wasn't certain how much information she was allowed to share with the Grafters.

It doesn't help that they all look so normal, she thought irritably. Whenever Felicity had pictured Grafters, they had always been disturbing, muddled images—disgusting, twisted, with strange limbs sprouting from their torsos. As a child, she'd been shown some of the surviving armor from the Isle of Wight invasion. It consisted of heavy, asymmetric plates that looked like sheet metal that had been bent around a giant that was part octopus, part wolf, and part musketeer. During her final studies, she had been permitted to read some of the older files, the ones that contained detailed descriptions and a few eyewitness accounts.

Finally, when she graduated, she and her class had been taken to the Apex and shown the few carefully stuffed corpses that had been retrieved from the Isle of Wight. The students had pretended sophistication and insouciance. A few had claimed to appreciate their design, the cunning that had twisted sinew and muscles around blades and bone. Someone had remarked that the layers of varnish on the one with the scales really captured the quality of the slime that must have dripped there when it was alive. But the few jokes cracked were weak and trailed away uncertainly. By the end, everyone was silent, and that night, no one slept easily.

So Felicity thought she knew what Grafters looked like.

But these people looked normal—their skin, their bodies, their hair. None of them would catch her eye on the street.

She realized that she'd gotten caught up in her own thoughts, and she hastily rejoined the conversation.

"Right, the supernatural in Europe," she said carefully. "Um, the Checquy doesn't maintain any offices on the Continent. We have some outposts in parts of the old British Empire, but we don't have the mandate—or the numbers—to have people everywhere. Our responsibility is the security of this country. So we rely on the regular civil service—the Foreign Office and the British intelligence agencies—to provide us with information, but they don't have much to do with the supernatural."

"I'm afraid we know very little ourselves," said Marcel.

"How is that possible?" asked Felicity. "You live there."

"You have to understand, Pawn Clements, that when the Broederschap was begun, they had no idea there was a supernatural..." — he seemed to search for an appropriate word, then shrugged— "anything. The supernatural is always secret, always discreet. Up until it eats you.

"The brotherhood, however, is not supernatural," he said, fixing her with a piercing gaze. "Except perhaps for the genius and the insight that can flare in the human mind. I suppose that can be considered as miraculous as anything in this world. But for everything we do, there is an explanation. Our work is based on a system, on an understanding of the world. The foundations of that understanding were built by our first alchemists, who gained it with no mystical advantages.

"Over the course of centuries, they built on those foundations and learned a tremendous amount about the nature of biological life," he continued. "Their understanding of the science was unparalleled. And then, when they marched out of the sea to take the Isle of Wight, they were confronted with something completely outside that understanding." He paused to accept an espresso from Alessio. "You."

"Me?" said Felicity, bewildered.

"Well, the forces of the Checquy," he said. "People like you. People for whom there is no explanation at all. Of course, you know what happened next." Felicity did but expected that the Grafters' telling of the story differed quite a bit from the Checquy's. "Can you imagine their horror? When the gaze of a child in a smock un-aged a soldier back to infancy in a moment or an old woman's gesture sent a battalion flailing upward to vanish in the sky? The Broederschap had worked so hard to leave the superstitions of the age behind, and now those superstitions were slaughtering them."

"They didn't surrender, though," said Felicity.

"No," agreed Marcel. "Not at first, but eventually. And then, of course, they had the disconcerting discovery that these demonic forces were actually servants of the British Crown. Not only did these monsters attack us on the battlefield, but they came at us through diplomatic and legal channels! They forced the dismantling of the brotherhood, wrung out financial reparations—substantial ones, by the way—bound our country with secret treaties, and then vanished back to their island."

"The dismantling wasn't as thorough as the Checquy thought," remarked Felicity, and Marcel shrugged.

"Perhaps not, but it left the Broederschap reduced to a fraction of what it had been. They were decimated. The next few centuries were spent rebuilding, and they did it under a cloak of stifling paranoia. Those generations were defined by their fears. To begin with, there was the fear that the Checquy would discover they had survived and would come back to finish their extermination.

"Then there was the fear that there might be more monstrously unnatural people, perhaps not affiliated with the British government, wandering around Europe, ready to destroy the brotherhood.

"And finally, there was the fear that some other government might find out about them."

"Why were they so afraid of that?" asked Felicity, who had been brought up to regard the government as everyone's friend.

"Their experiences with the governments of Spain and Britain had demonstrated that tangling with the affairs of common men was too dangerous. It could lead to the loss of one's estates, to the slaughter of one's colleagues, and, eventually, to watching one's own body be dismembered." Marcel took a sip of coffee. "And so paranoia became our policy. It defines us almost as much as our work does."

The Grafters kept themselves to themselves, Marcel went on to explain. They did not seek out the supernatural. However, sometimes, much to their horror, the supernatural sought them out. It was not clear if there was something about the Grafters that attracted these elements or if the Grafters encountered a standard number of them but were slightly better equipped to survive them than normal people. Regardless, every experience was isolated, and inevitably violent. Sometimes the Grafter would triumph, sometimes all that remained was a smear, or some bones, or a crater.

From what the Grafters could tell, throughout Western Europe there was no equivalent of the Checquy. European supernatural manifestations were not policed in any way, not by the supernatural, not by any government, and certainly not by any supernatural government. Whether through sheer luck or some other factor, there were very few large-scale manifestations. Rather, there were people and creatures who deployed their unnatural abilities discreetly. They might use them for profit or to do horrible things, but they were circumspect enough that the normal population didn't know about it.

"Without the protections and the order imposed by something like the Checquy, the European continent is, secretly, a savagely dangerous place," said Marcel. "These people—these things—are free to do what they want. They have the power to indulge their whims and their tastes. People get killed; children go missing. They can act without fear or consequence."

"It sounds dreadful," said Felicity. The old man gazed at her for a long moment. Without taking his eyes off her, he spoke to Alessio.

"Alessio, would you please go to your room? I need to talk to Pawn Clements privately." The boy left the room, closing the door behind him. "Let me tell you a story."

In 1914, Marcel Leliefeld was born into the world, delivered expertly by his father with some expert direction from his mother. He was joined ten minutes later by his twin brother, Siegbert. From a young age, the two boys were completely aware of the Broederschap. This was unusual. As a matter of policy, the Grafters kept their true occupations (and their physical capabilities) a secret from everyone, including their own families. Merely being the spouse or child of a Grafter did not automatically qualify one for a membership. The most that such a relationship guaranteed was a seemingly lucky immunity to various infectious diseases, a lack of cancer, and blessedly perfect offspring who were conceived and delivered with an abundance of ease. To become a Grafter, one needed to demonstrate exceptional aptitude.

Marcel and Siegbert's knowledge of the Grafters was a result of their parents' unorthodox approach to, well, pretty much everything. The parents in question, Hendrika and Arjan, were both Grafters. Important Grafters.

Arjan was the son of a Grafter, and Hendrika had been brought into the organization as a child from Delft when a neighbor, who was also a Grafter, had been struck by her facility with a paintbrush. The neighbor's justification had been that anyone with that level of unorthodox imagination and such fine motor control would make a marvelous Grafter. Hendrika and Arjan had served their apprenticeships at the same time and, after the (predictable) period of intense competition and mutual loathing, had (predictably) fallen in love (slightly less predictably) over an autopsy table of Siamese quintuplets (who had been longtime friends of the Grafters, as they would not have been born without some Broederschap assistance, and who had died simultaneously after living a good, long collective life, leaving behind three widows, two widowers, thirteen children, a wardrobe of intricately tailored clothes, and a well-established mercantile business).

Arjan and Hendrika were married in Amsterdam in a huge church full of well-wishers and then promptly moved to Paris, where they embarked on dazzling careers of experimentation and research, constantly on the cutting edge (as it were) of innovative surgery. Their home was renowned, not only among the Grafters but also among the artists, intellectuals, and scientists of Paris as the place to come and talk and argue and drink.

It was a salon unlike any other, where the good and the wicked, the rich and the poor, the unearthly and the earthly came to meet and disgust and inspire one another. At any given moment, there was a wide variety of visitors.

In the parlor, one might find a debate involving Arjan, a Turkish cabinetmaker, a Catholic priest, and a drunk individual whom no one seemed to know but who kept muttering about some goddamn beekeeper and the dynamics of rocks in space.

Lounging on the front stairs, a centuries-old Grafter drinking oolong tea might be discussing scissor technique with an apprentice hairdresser, while on the back stairs, one might find an Oxford don locked in a passionate embrace with a Cambridge don (both dressed in full academic robes). In the kitchen, one could come across a cellist and a boxer smoking opium and staring fixedly into each other's eyes as the cook and the scullery maids bustled around them, laboriously sewing the front end of a dead pig to the rear end of a dead peacock in preparation for cooking.

In the library, Baron László Mednyánszky had painted a now-famous portrait of a hermaphroditic Grafter cousin.

In her studio upstairs, Hendrika had once removed the Spanish ambassador's appendix and put in a fresh one before descending to have afternoon tea with Marie Curie. Architects fought in the garden, mathematicians and sculptors folded origami in the gazebo, and rosellas and parakeets flew freely through the rooms, never relieving themselves on guests' heads, since they had been altered to subsist entirely on sunshine and secondhand cigarette smoke.

In that house, children and theories were conceived. Lectures were given and drawings drawn. Venereal diseases were contracted and then effervesced away after the infected person drank some of Arjan's jasmine tea. Symphonies and viruses were composed, and hypotheses and cadavers were deconstructed. There were fabulous dinner parties in which the guests feasted on meats from animals that had never existed and drank wine that glowed faintly in their mouths and left them in states of heightened creativity.

This was not to say that Arjan and Hendrika were indiscreet. Or rather, they were not indiscreet about the fact that they were Grafters. They were indiscreet about most other things, but as far as their non-Grafter guests were concerned, the Leliefelds were a naturalist and a (woman!) surgeon, both possessed of great wealth and intellect. The glorious nature of their hospitality always carefully straddled the line between the improbable and the impossible, and guests who caught a glimpse of the unexplainable were left to doubt their own eyes and swear off drink.

Above the second floor of the house, however, all doubt would have been removed. In their separate studios (they maintained that the key to a happy marriage was being able to get away from the other person), Arjan and Hendrika developed startling new techniques and pushed biology to its limits. In the bedrooms, Grafter guests slept, hanging from the ceiling or cocooned in the closets.

And in a vast rooftop greenhouse of wrought iron and stained glass, two identical little boys romped amidst flowers that nuzzled them like kittens, beneath vines that gave off perfume that hung in the air like trails of smoke and tasted sweet on the tongue.

Siegbert and Marcel grew up surrounded by the preposterous. Their mother might come down to breakfast with feathers cascading down her back instead of hair. Their father was usually surrounded by a choir of chirping dragonflies and had been known to vault down the side of the building rather than using the stairs. The family dog, a West Highland white terrier named Chloe, did not age. Visiting cousins would excuse themselves to the bathroom to shed their skins and reemerge as members of a different race.

The boys themselves did not receive any enhancements. Like ballet dancers who had to wait for the bones in their feet to ossify before they could go up en pointe, they were kept completely and perfectly human. However, they often observed their parents' projects and might be called upon to put a finger on some sutures, drip compounds into a subject's eyes, or reach their little hands into an incision and tweak something that Mama could not reach. When they were twelve, their understanding of anatomy and medicine would have placed them in the highest echelons of normal surgeons. That, plus the fact that they were direct descendants of Graaf Ernst, meant there was no question that they would become members of the Broederschap.

Except that Marcel questioned it.

He was well advanced in his apprenticeship as a Grafter when he made the decision. Under Marcel's care, a somewhat startled dog had given birth to kittens, and he'd had several useful organs added to his system. However, two weeks after his nineteenth birthday, Marcel canceled his appointments and retired to his bedroom, where he spent several days meticulously removing all the alterations that had been made to his body. He emerged several pounds lighter, sporting his original cheekbones and teeth, and calmly announced to his startled parents that he was enlisting in the French army.

Why?" asked Felicity.

"I was dissatisfied with the direction my life was taking," said Marcel easily. "I did not care for the person I was at that point. I judged that a drastic change was needed."

Marcel's parents were distraught at this rejection, and the Broederschap was shocked, but in the high ranks there was no tremendous concern. Marcel had made it clear that he was not severing connections with his family, that he held no resentment toward them for their lifestyle, and that he had no intention of revealing any secrets or using their knowledge for his own gain. No one doubted his character or, more important, his discretion, and so they wished him the best of luck as he began his career as a private in the VIIe Armée.

Marcel did well in the army, rising at a respectable clip and acquitting himself with valor on every occasion where it was appropriate. Though his appearances at family functions were always welcome, and he and Siegbert corresponded on a regular basis, relations with his parents remained painful and awkward, even after he married his second cousin Claudette, who was a Grafter. Siegbert, meanwhile, had married a sensible lady named Aimée who was not a Grafter but who had figured out her new family's capabilities through the simple strategy of observing them and being willing to accept that the impossible might not be.

Marcel's letters to Siegbert grew more and more concerned as the political situation in Germany became increasingly turbulent. Marcel urged his brother to pass his disquietude on to the heads of the brotherhood. The disquietude was duly communicated, but if any action was taken, it was not apparent to Siegbert.

In 1939, Marcel was posted to the northern front under Giraud. He saw serious battle against the Germans and was promoted to lieutenant. When Giraud's army was crushed in Belgium in May 1940, an injured Marcel could not face the prospect of evacuation to Britain—his Grafter upbringing and the terrifying stories of the Checquy prevented him from even entertaining the possibility. Instead, he deserted and took refuge with family members in Antwerp. He reluctantly permitted them to repair his damaged leg on the firm understanding that it would be restored to standard leg specifications with no convenient weaponry or storage pouches added.

At that point, the leaders of the Broederschap, Graafs Ernst and Gerd, arrived, word of Marcel's situation having been passed along the family grapevine. They sat down with their descendant and, after some cursory inquiries after one another's health, the talk turned to current events. Thus, over tea and pfeffernüsse, Marcel learned that the Grafters were in a state of crisis.

It seemed that while the members of the Broederschap were more than willing to eschew earthly affairs, earthly affairs were unwilling to render them the same courtesy. This did not astound Marcel, but most of the Grafters were completely taken aback. The graafs and the elder members had lived through a number of conflicts, including the Kettle War, the Napoleonic Wars, la Guerra de los Agraviados, l'Insurrection Royaliste dans l'Ouest de la France, the Austro-Prussian War, and the Austrian

Civil War, but none of them had proven to be terribly disruptive. Even the Great War had not really done much more than mildly inconvenience them. As a result, while some preparations had been made, they had anticipated that this squabble, like so many others, would wash on by.

Instead, the weight of modern war had descended upon the brotherhood just as it had on all the normal people in Europe, bringing with it all the attendant problems: supply shortages, armed conflict, general chaos. Lines of communication between the chapter houses were constantly disrupted. No contact could be made with the Grafter relatives in Germany, and it was feared that they had been arrested or killed. There had already been casualties among them—an errant bomb blast had consumed an important laboratory with a group of apprentices inside; soldiers had gunned down a two-hundred-year-old master crafter of lungs. Most dire of all to Marcel, Paris had fallen to the invaders, and they had received no word from the Grafters who lived there.

Paris, home to Claudette, Siegbert, and Aimée (who, last anyone heard, had been pregnant with their first child), as well as Marcel's parents.

In Marcel, the graafs saw a man who was fully engaged in the world. A man who knew the brotherhood, who was bound to them, and who could be trusted. They asked for his help and struck an agreement. Two Chimera soldiers, equipped with some of the most deadly weaponry in their arsenal, would accompany Marcel to Paris. They would ascertain the status of the seventeen Grafters known to reside there, including Arjan, Hendrika, Claudette, and Siegbert. The graafs' greatest priority was to prevent any Broederschap technology from falling into the hands of the Nazis. Marcel's greatest priority was to get his family somewhere safe.

If the Parisian Grafters were dead, their corpses were to be incinerated and every trace of their work removed or destroyed. If they had been imprisoned, they were to be rescued or, failing that, rendered useless to the enemy through any means necessary. If they were alive and free, Marcel and his team would bring them to Belgium, which, though occupied, was where the Grafters were consolidating themselves. Then, provided he survived, Marcel would take the security of the Grafters in hand and bring them through the war, however long it lasted.

Marcel and his two hulking soldiers, Hans and Henk, set out for Paris. There were few cars or trucks available—most of the private vehicles had been commandeered by the military—but the Broederschap had provided them with a wagon and a draft horse named Angus who had received modifications that gave him the strength and endurance of four normal horses, night vision, and the tracking abilities of a bloodhound. They joined the hundreds of refugees on the southern road, a stream of people with wagons, prams, and barrows loaded with possessions.

Despite their efforts at disguise, they had to spend a goodly amount of effort avoiding enemy troops. The three of them were unmistakably warriors (Henk and Hans, in particular, had literally been designed to wreak havoc), and just the sight of them seemed to provoke antagonistic feelings in the occupying authorities. After three days, they had already been in several fights, and word had gone out among the Nazi authorities to be on the lookout for the three men, although their apprehension was a comparatively low priority; there was a war going on, after all. Still, whilst evading a patrol near the French border, the three were forced to abandon the wagon and set Angus free to either make his way home or end up in the possession of some incredibly lucky farmer.

In early July, when the three men entered Paris, the circulated descriptions of the outlaws were no longer accurate. In addition to having dyed their hair and shaved off their mustaches, Marcel was sporting a black eye and missing several teeth, Henk had been obliged to regrow his left arm and right leg, and Hans had lost his wallet. But if they were changed, so was the city, which was saturated with tension and fear. There were shortages and curfews, and patrols of soldiers moved through the streets checking identities.

Marcel and his cohorts (Hans and Henk were each big enough

to count as a cohort) made their way cautiously and were obliged to evade several patrols. Upon arriving at Marcel's home, they found that his wife, Claudette, had barricaded herself in the flat and was relying on her chlorophyll tattoos and the water in her bathtub to keep herself alive. The reunion of the happy couple was necessarily restrained, since there was much news to share, and none of it good.

The Parisian Grafters had not been entirely unprepared for the coming of the Nazis. Reclusive scholars they might be, but no one in Europe at that time could help but be aware of what was happening in the world. The Grafters had seen newsreels of the German bombing of Warsaw and read the news that the French army was preparing in the north. They had watched as the wealthy and well-informed quietly departed the city for the south. They had heard of the defeats suffered by the French armed forces at the hands of the Germans and then seen the hundreds of thousands of refugees flocking from the Netherlands, Belgium, and northern France.

Some of the Broederschap had argued that they ought to join the masses fleeing Paris before the invaders, but they had decided against it. If they were to go anywhere, it would be north to the home of their leaders, and it would be impossible to go in that direction and keep a low profile. So instead, they would wait. There was no question that the Nazis would come, but the manner of their coming, and how they would be met, was unclear. There was talk of a defense, that soldiers and police would stand against the invaders, but the concept of an "open city" had also been spoken of. It was entirely possible that the Germans might simply march in unopposed and without conflict. The Grafters made plans for all of these eventualities.

But there were things that they had not planned for, things they could never have known would happen.

"I did not lock myself inside the flat because of the Nazis," said Claudette. "I fortified our home because a new threat has arisen in Paris, something that is targeting only the members of the Broederschap."

On June 9, as the Germans drew nearer to the city, Claudette had gone to meet with a colleague named Anne to discuss the details of their plans. Upon arriving at Anne's house, however, she had found the back door forced open and her friend dead on the kitchen floor.

"All the fluids had been drained from her body," said Claudette with a shudder. "All that was left of her was a husk." Claudette had fled and sent word to the other Grafters. Three of them had not replied, and cautious investigation had revealed their desiccated bodies in their residences. At that point, panicked, the remaining Parisian Grafters had sealed themselves in their homes.

A few days later, the invaders entered the city with tanks, trucks, and motorcycles rolling unopposed down the boulevards. Swastika banners hung from the buildings and flew from the Eiffel Tower. While German soldiers established themselves in commandeered houses and the führer himself visited the city, the Grafters remained sequestered.

"My parents?" asked Marcel. "Siegbert?"

"I've had no word, beertje," said Claudette. "The telephone system has been unreliable, and none of us have dared to go out." No one knew the cause of these desiccations. Some Grafters believed it was a deliberate policy by the new regime, which must somehow have found out about them. Others feared that the Checquy had tracked them down and were taking advantage of the chaos to finish them off. They had elected to keep separate and quiet so as not to present a single target.

"Well, this adds a new level of complexity to the mission," said Marcel. They agreed that there was no time to waste. Within half an hour, the four of them were proceeding on foot down the nighttime streets of Paris toward Siegbert's house. It was not an easy journey—a strict curfew had been established and the streets were dark. The streetlamps were off, and the few cars that passed them had blue cloth across their headlights, permitting only the barest of illumination. Citizens were under orders to keep their windows and shutters closed with no light showing. The darkness posed no real problem to the eyes of the Grafters, and Claudette led Marcel by the hand, but the empty streets added a strange, haunted quality to the city.

Occasionally, roving patrols would stop them and demand to see their identity cards, whereupon Henk and Hans would briskly beat them to a pulp and steal their money. By the time they arrived at Siegbert's home, Hans had seven new wallets to replace his lost one.

No one answered their quiet knock, and so Claudette picked the lock with some hastily grown fingernails, and they proceeded inside. The place was dark, but there were sounds coming from the back of the house—a low murmur, and the occasional clink of glass. Cautiously, the four made their way down the hallway. Ahead of them, the wavering glow of candlelight seeped out around the edges of a door.

In the dining room, they found a barely conscious Siegbert lying on the table. Wooden stakes had been driven through his wrists and ankles to secure him, and a middle-aged woman was in the process of draining his blood into some demijohns. It was not clear who was more startled, the Grafters or the woman, but it was apparent that this was one of those situations where polite conversation would not suffice.

For a few moments, no one moved, and then the woman drew herself up, and a low, throbbing growl bubbled out of her mouth.

The Grafters, not unreasonably, took this as a sign that violence was the order of the day and so moved forward. Hans's muscles appeared to grow as he walked, and the flesh of his neck and shoulders plumped out, lending him an arresting pyramidal appearance. With an audible tchok, curving blades erupted from Henk's wrists. They projected forward and around his hands, so that his fists were surrounded by cages of sharp bone. Whipping tendrils burst out of Claudette's shoulder blades and punched through the back of her dress. They flailed around, cracking in the air. Compared to these figures of biological violence, Marcel's unholstering of his (admittedly rather small) pistol was a trifle anticlimactic, so the woman could be forgiven for focusing on his companions.

Still growling, the woman took a cautious step back, and her jaw unhinged itself like a snake's. Her snarl rose in pitch, shivering up through the scale until it could no longer be heard, only felt. The sound hit Marcel like a cudgel, and he staggered back and clutched his head (although he did not drop the gun). It felt as if his skull were being beaten briskly with some very small hammers. He looked around, and saw that it seemed to have affected his comrades very differently.

The other three Grafters gasped as they felt strange lurchings in their bodies. Then, as one, they screamed as their implants flared in agony. Marcel watched in astonishment as his compatriots' legs buckled and they keeled over. They lay there, twisted like puppets whose strings had been cut.

Henk and Hans, who during their journey to Paris had each shrugged off several bullets to the chest and head without complaint, were wailing like infants as the sound rippled through their bodies. Claudette lay curled in the fetal position, her face contorted in agony. On the table, Siegbert was whimpering weakly, arching his back and fighting helplessly against the stakes that impaled him. The woman kept screaming, her breath seemingly inexhaustible.

As Marcel watched, his companions' implants began to break down. Several of the blades surrounding Henk's hands fell away, trailing little strands of flesh. Alarming black blotches expanded across Hans's augmented muscles. Claudette's tendrils lay limp, with occasional shivers rippling through them. All three of them were incapacitated.

The mysterious woman seemed to be smiling as she regarded the three people lying on the floor. Then she took in Marcel's failure to collapse in agony. He was in pain, there was no doubt, reeling, barely on his feet, but he was on his feet, and he still had the pistol in his hand. She began to move toward him, and he raised his gun.

She couldn't smirk contemptuously, because her mouth had to stay open, but she gave a little shrug and stood still with her arms spread out. The message was clear: Go ahead. Try and shoot me. As Marcel shakily aimed his weapon, she actually rolled her eyes. His arm wavered, weaving back and forth in a figure eight as he tried to focus. He took a deep breath and then fired two rounds square into her torso. Her eyes opened wide. I didn't think you would actually do it.

She gave him a slow round of applause. Not that it makes a blind bit of difference.

She moved forward.

And then she halted.

An expression of confusion washed over her face. Then, mercifully, she stopped screaming. The horrible throbbing pressure in Marcel's head faded away, and he could see the woman clearly as she clapped her hands to her chest. A black liquid began to trickle out around her fingers. Bewildered, she looked up at Marcel, who remained impassive. Then she collapsed, and a pool of the black liquid washed out of her.

18

M arcel fell to his knees beside his wife and tried to help her sit up. "I'm here, mijn lief, I'm here," he said to her frantically. "It's all right."

"Oh, thank God," said Claudette weakly. "That was... horrible...like being torn apart...from the inside." She turned her head and spat out an alarming mixture of blood and slime. "I think...that thing...has done some serious...damage."

"Can you move?" Marcel asked gently.

"I don't know," said Claudette with some irritation. "Make sure...that fucking thing is dead...and then...check the boys."

Upon examination, the fucking thing in question seemed to

be dead, but by that point Marcel was taking no chances, and so he used a carving knife to carefully remove its head, which he then placed several feet away. Henk and Hans were clutching their stomachs and seemed to be having trouble making their limbs do what they wanted, but they didn't appear to be in any danger of expiring immediately. Siegbert, however, smiled weakly at the sight of Marcel, and then a little blood foamed at his mouth.

"Siegbert!" exclaimed Marcel. He hurried to his twin and cradled his head gently. He was in extremely bad shape and could barely move. Marcel did not dare to remove the stakes that pinned him to the table.

"Siegbert, where is Aimée?" asked Claudette urgently.

"Dead," said Siegbert. "She's dead."

"No!" whispered Marcel.

"That thing killed her when it entered the kitchen. It simply broke her neck." He closed his eyes, and tears trickled from the corners.

"I am so sorry, Siegbert," said Marcel. "Your wife and baby."

"The baby is fine," said Siegbert through labored breaths. "We felt that now was not the time to bring a child into the world, so a few weeks ago I removed him from the womb and placed him in stasis. He is in a thermos upstairs in a locked cupboard in our bedroom. Please, mon frère, you must promise to take care of him." Before Marcel could answer, Siegbert lapsed into unconsciousness.

"Can you help him?" Marcel asked his wife frantically. It had been years since he had utilized his Grafter training, and Claudette was the only proper fleshwright there.

"Well, I can't sit up," said Claudette, who had regained some of her color. "But we'll see what we can do. I know he has some spare blood in the wine cellar. Go get that, beertje, and we'll replace some. Also, while you're down there, get some wine. And don't get them mixed up. And then go and find the thermos with our nephew in it."

The rest of the night was spent with all of them lying about sipping wine while blood dripped back into Siegbert's body. Marcel brought the woman's head over to Claudette, and she carefully examined it, exclaiming over the bizarre growths that lined the woman's throat.

Meanwhile, Siegbert slowly regained a bit of his strength. In addition to having lost all that blood, and his wife, he had been exposed to the woman's anatomy-shredding scream twice, since she had struck him down with it earlier. Once he could speak properly, he demanded to know how Marcel had killed the woman. "I emptied my gun into the bitch, and she shrugged it off," Siegbert said weakly.

"Plague bullets," said Marcel, cracking open his revolver to reveal chambers holding some extremely odd-looking cartridges. They were made of a transparent chitin, and strange squirming organisms were just visible inside. "Aunt Coralie whipped them up. So, who is the bitch?"

"I have no idea," said Siegbert feebly. "She walked into the house, broke Aimée's neck; I shot her, she ignored it, and then she screamed. I woke up staked to the table."

"So who fabricated her?" Marcel eyed the head carefully—she didn't look familiar.

"No one fabricated her, Marcel. Those weren't modifications. She was born with those powers, like something out of the Checquy."

"Mon dieu! Do you think that's what she was?" asked Marcel, eyeing the corpse with a newfound wariness. "Have the Gruwels tracked us down?"

"She never mentioned them," said Siegbert. "And she was quite chatty. Although I am certain the Checquy would have loved to have her. None of the stories I ever heard involved someone who could do this to Broederschap implants."

"And not a Nazi, or even the French government?"

Siegbert shook his head.

"So, nothing to do with the war?" said Marcel.

"No. In fact, she said all the fighting had proven very inconvenient for her," said Siegbert. "She complained that she couldn't transport me back to her place. Apparently she has some sort of juicing press there." He shuddered.

"Who else has she taken?" asked Marcel.

"I don't know," said Siegbert. "She said that there had been several, but she didn't say how many exactly." Claudette knew only who the first four victims were. After that, all the Parisian Grafters had tried to barricade themselves in. To Marcel it seemed like the height of foolishness, but his relatives were scholars and scientists, not soldiers. They'd been conditioned by the tales of the Checquy always to retreat and hide from threats.

Unspoken between the brothers was the possibility that their parents had been consumed by the woman.

"We'll need to ascertain the status of all Broederschap members in Paris," said Marcel.

"You may need to do that by yourself," said Claudette from the floor, where she was propped up on cushions and peering carefully into the neck of the woman's corpse. "Whatever that woman did to us, it's been very bad for all our implants. I think some of the materials in my joints have actually dissolved, and a lot of my internal connections have been severed." She held up one of the tendrils that drooped lifelessly from her shoulder blades. "We're going to have to do some repair work, and it will take several days." Marcel glanced questioningly toward his brother and then back to her, and she shrugged sadly.

I don't know if we can save him, she didn't say.

And so, as morning dawned, Marcel had to venture out by himself into a strangely subdued Paris. There was a tension in the air, and people did not meet each other's eyes. It was not the gay metropolis he had grown up in. Hitler's soldiers moved through the city and did not hesitate to question any man of military bearing. Marcel hurried through the streets and was prompt in providing his (forged) identity card when stopped. Tucked into the small of his back were two pistols, one of them carrying normal ammunition, the other with the modified rounds he'd been given.

Against his first impulse, he hadn't gone straight to his parents' house, which was the farthest from Siegbert's, across the Seine. Instead, he was methodical, plotting out routes that would take him to as many homes as possible each day while still permitting him to return to Siegbert's house before night fell. In addition, he was responsible for obtaining food and supplies for his crippled companions.

The first few houses yielded heartbreaking results. In three of them, Marcel found the drained corpses of his relations. A fourth was empty, although from the wrecked furniture and punched-in doors, it was apparent that the three Grafter residents had been taken by the screaming woman. The fifth house, however, held Richard van Eijden, a distant cousin who had replied to Marcel's knocking with some shouted threats and a spray of some pungent spores under the door. It had taken Marcel several minutes to persuade Richard who he was, and all the while his skin had been itching madly from the spores. Eventually, however, he was permitted inside and given the antidote before his skin peeled off.

Richard's relief at seeing Marcel and hearing about the demise of the screaming woman was palpable. When he learned that they would be evacuating to Belgium, he was ecstatic. Upon arriving at Siegbert's house, he immediately set to work on the injured.

Marcel continued to visit Grafter houses but found only two more survivors: Alphonse, a master, and his apprentice, Pauline. They were both so caught up in their studies that they had barely realized there was a war on, let alone that some supernatural entity had been stalking them. They acceded, with very poor grace, to Marcel's command that they accompany him back to Siegbert's but insisted on bringing several suitcases of documents and samples.

"So, to recap, we have ten members of the Broederschap horribly dead, yes?" said Alphonse. All the Grafters had gathered in the library of Siegbert's house. Those who had been struck down by the woman's voice were propped up on couches or lying flat on the floor. Upon hearing no disagreements, Alphonse made a little note in a little notebook. "And we have two whose horrific deaths have yet to be established." He looked up to see everyone else staring at him. "What?"

"Ahem, those two unestablished deaths—" began Claudette.

"Horrific deaths," interjected Alphonse helpfully.

"Thank you," said Claudette. "You are talking about the parents of Siegbert and Marcel, and Siegbert and Marcel are sitting right here in the room with you."

"...Yes?"

"Never mind," said Marcel. It was clear that Alphonse, while possessing an unparalleled understanding of biochemical interactions, was useless when it came to the human kind.

"I have examined Claudette, Hans, Henk, and Siegbert," said Richard to Marcel. "We cannot repair them without access to significant facilities and more expertise. I will need help, from either your parents or our brethren in the north."

"I'll go to the house tomorrow morning," said Marcel. It had been the sensible thing to leave them until last, but in his heart, he was afraid to go, afraid of having his fears confirmed. In the past few days, a dozen different scenarios had floated through his imagination. The memories of the drained bodies that he had found in those other houses were always in his mind. He envisioned his parents sprawled lifeless on the floor of their parlor. At night, he had been tortured by nightmares of the house in flames or demolished. In his sleep, he had walked through the ruins, and in every room, his parents had lain dead.

It was raining on the morning that he went to his parents' home. He had an umbrella, but his legs were soaked from the knees down by the time he reached the house. Still, he stood across the street for several minutes, staring through the downpour at the place where he'd grown up. No lights were on that he could see, no sign of anyone inside.

I've gone into battle, he told himself. I've watched my friends die around me. I've fought and killed a monster. It seems a trifle ridiculous that I should be afraid of knocking on my own front door.

Eventually he mustered up the courage and crossed the road, the wind buffeting his umbrella.

Little seemed to have changed in the years since he'd left.

Pots of flowers stood by the door. They were flourishing, but that meant nothing. Thanks to his father's tinkering, those plants could flourish without human care. They could probably flourish on the surface of the moon. He rang the doorbell several times, but there was no answer.

That doesn't confirm anything, he told himself. They could be in hiding, afraid to answer the door because of that screaming woman. He moved around to the back of the house and retrieved a hidden door key from within a beehive whose occupants had been engineered by his parents to be deadly poisonous but also to recognize the scent of their family members. But as Marcel climbed the stairs, something caught his eye, and a feeling of doom swept through him. The door was ajar, and, judging by the leaves and dirt that had blown inside, it had been that way for at least several days.

At that moment, Marcel knew in his heart that his parents were dead. Whether they had been killed by the screaming woman or something else, they were gone. Walking into the house would only bring him pain. But he had to do it. The house was not only their home; it contained a myriad of samples and technology. His parents' work. It couldn't be left here to be found by anyone, least of all the occupying forces, who had been undertaking some extremely thorough investigations of people's households.

Holding both guns, Marcel checked each room. Outside, the growing storm battered against the windows. All through the house, there were signs that preparations had been made. The storage bins and cold containers of his parents' laboratories did not contain samples, constructs, or strange animals. Their tools had been carefully sterilized. Many documents and books were missing, and, given the copious amount of ash and fragments in the fireplaces, they would never be found. Of his parents' portfolios and journals, there was no trace. The house had been methodically stripped of any Broederschap materials. Oddly, much artwork was missing from the walls, and quite a few pieces of the more valuable furniture had gone. Marcel hoped this did not mean that the authorities had taken his parents and their work.

But surely the Nazis would have emptied the house completely, he thought. And there would be soldiers or officials billeted here. He looked through the bedrooms and saw that all the beds had been stripped. He paused in his old room and retrieved a few mementos of his childhood. There was no sign, however, of his parents.

He finally found them in the rooftop greenhouse, sitting together on a bench, surrounded by flowers that had clustered around them. Except for their white skin, they could have been asleep. Corruption did not touch them. Possibly it was a quirk of their genetics, but he suspected that his mother had arranged it that way. She would never have wanted to rot, and his father would have indulged her fancy. The air was lightly touched with the perfume of dried flowers, and when Marcel trailed his hands along the blossoms, they crumbled away, as if they had been dead and preserved for years.

Marcel walked toward his parents, his eyes wet. He pressed his arm to his face, blotting away the tears, and then drank in the portrait of them both. When he reached out to touch his father's shoulder, both Arjan and Hendrika fell away to powder, as if they were themselves dried flowers.

He sat for a while and remembered his life in that place. Then he got up and opened the doors at either end of the greenhouse. The wind swept through. It picked up the dust and the flakes of all the plants and whipped them away, up into the skies of Paris.

Good-bye.

As he left the house, he noticed a troop of soldiers down the street. They were going from door to door and did not seem overly concerned with courtesy. He sighed and turned his back on them.

Getting away from Paris proved even more difficult than getting there. Whereas before they had been three warriors well equipped for combat and stealth, they were now a party consisting of one warrior who had an unorthodox gun, three alchemists whose implants tended toward the scholarly, and four horribly crippled invalids. In addition, they were transporting various documents, equipment, and samples that could not be easily replaced or safely destroyed. Vans, trucks, and automobiles were still in short supply, and they again ended up in a wagon (this one stolen) pulled by a horse (this one legally purchased). Now they were moving against the flow of refugees, which made them stick out even more. As a result, they were obliged to travel on meandering back lanes and often went across the countryside—a strategy that kept them out of sight of soldiers but slowed them considerably.

Partway through the journey, they discovered that the damage that the screaming woman's voice had done to Henk's, Hans's, Siegbert's, and Claudette's insides had been far greater than anyone had realized. If Richard and the other two Grafters had not been with them to administer first aid, it was highly doubtful that any of them would have survived the first two days of the journey. The woman's cry had attacked their Broederschap implants like a virus, shredding the patterns within, leaving them in a state of ongoing liquefaction.

To Marcel's despair, Siegbert was in especially bad shape. The double exposure to the woman's scream had increased the effect, and Marcel could actually see his brother wasting away in front of him. Every hour melted flesh off his bones. His breath rasped painfully in his lungs and throat.

"He's dying," Marcel said to his wife.

"I'm afraid he's not the only one, beertje," she said, and she patted him weakly on the cheek. "Unless we do something, the four of us won't make it to the border. But he won't survive another twelve hours without help."

And so that night, in a field near Amiens, the hale Grafters were driven to crack open their comrades' bodies and set about some frantic jury-rigging. They dealt with the comparatively easy ones first. Henk and Hans submitted to their operations with stoic silence. Claudette provided testy instructions even as they opened up her chest. All three of them seemed a trifle better after their procedures, although none of them could yet sit up.

Then Siegbert was laid down on a bed of dingy straw. Richard confided to Marcel that his twin was too weak to receive any form of painkillers, but it hardly mattered. Siegbert had passed into a delirium and had no idea where he was. His fingers trembled, and his breath was shallow, but other than that, he lay still.

"I don't know what I can do for him," Richard confessed.

"Just try," said Marcel. "Please."

Several desperate hours ensued. They were hardly the best conditions in which to undertake emergency surgery. The cows whose field the Grafters were occupying had moved off to a distant corner, but a fox watched the operation from the hedge. Marcel held his twin's hand and prayed that the animal hadn't been drawn by the smell of carrion. Rain fell, trickling into the incision in the patient's belly. Pauline, the apprentice, hurried to the containers they had brought with them and fetched new organs that dripped with preservatives and oils. Clipped instructions passed back and forth between the two master Grafters, and their hands and tools moved frantically.

Finally, despite their best efforts, Siegbert's hand went limp in Marcel's and a last, labored breath eased from his mouth. They were all silent, and Richard drew his hands out of the abdomen.

"We can't leave his body here," said Richard finally.

"I know," said Marcel softly as he closed his twin's eyes and then closed his own.

I'm sorry," said Felicity, and Marcel opened his eyes.

"Thank you," he said. "It was very difficult at the time."

"What did you do after that?" she asked.

Siegbert's body was wrapped in a coat and placed in the wagon along with the three surviving invalids and the thermos containing his son. The rest of the journey was punctuated by more abrupt surgeries as the patients variously went into seizures or cardiac arrest. In addition, the party were continually obliged to evade troops, refugees, and the inhabitants of the countryside they were traveling through. Along the roads there were smoldering vacant villages, and violence was always imminent. To cross the border meant going miles across rough country and through forests to avoid sentries.

By the time they made it back to Belgium, Henk, Hans, and Claudette were all three hanging on the edge of death, as the implants in their brains and spines had broken down completely into a foul-smelling syrup. Upon arrival at a Broederschap chapter house in the city of Roeselare, they were immediately taken into surgery and then spent several months in therapeutic comas as their bodies were carefully repaired by some of the Grafters' most capable fleshwrights.

I would have liked to go into a therapeutic coma myself," said Marcel, "or at least take a nap, but there were important things happening."

"What things?" asked Felicity.

"The Second World War. The brotherhood sent me on various missions. There were family members scattered around Europe, many of whom needed help escaping the violence. There was much running around. A great deal of derring-do. Nazis were fought and dissolved." He shrugged. "It was an exciting time."

After the war, Marcel and Claudette decanted their nephew from his thermos and raised him as their own. A bright and cheerful boy, young Arjan would go on to be the father of Odette and Alessio and a respected paleontologist, though not in that order. For Marcel and Claudette, four other children followed in their own time, although only the youngest would become a member of the Broederschap.

Marcel resumed his studies with the Grafters, partly as a way to honor his parents and partly because he felt he needed to make up for the loss of Siegbert. In the Leliefeld home at

Roeselare, grandchildren played with a reclaimed (and un-aged) Chloe. It turned out that Marcel's parents had heeded their estranged son's warnings and placed the dog in a stasis of her own in a bank vault in Switzerland, along with all their notes and artwork. Marcel and Claudette continued their work until Claudette passed away. "Only three years ago," Marcel said.

"The woman who killed your brother, and your relations..." began Felicity.

"Yes?"

"Did you ever find out about her? Where she came from? Why she wanted to kill your people?"

"Actually, yes," said Marcel. "After the war was over, I returned to Paris and spent some time tracking down her history. It wasn't easy, but I was very curious."

"I imagine so," said Felicity.

"I found where she had been living," said Marcel. "No one had entered the place in years. It contained various upsetting things: A sort of mangle that was stained with blood. Human bones. Large containers of blood and other fluids. But nothing was as upsetting as the journals I found."

Her name was Béatrice Mermier. Born to farmers in the northwestern part of France, she had apparently enjoyed a relatively ordinary childhood. The only thing that stood out about her, the only odd thing her neighbors could remember, was that she did not like to eat anything except meat. No fruit, no vegetables—she simply couldn't stand them. But her life continued normally enough, even when her parents passed away and she sold the farm and moved into town.

At the age of twenty-four, however, she had woken up one morning possessed by a ravenous hunger and tortured by the scent of something unutterably delicious. Her body was shaking, and she was actually drooling. She emptied the larder and devoured a haunch of lamb, but nothing would satiate the gnawing emptiness inside her. All the while, there was that smell, driving her frantic, leading her out of her house to the door of the slightly startled neighbors.

They welcomed her in, and she apologized for disturbing them, it was just that...she didn't quite know. She couldn't explain it. She was so hungry. The wife, knowing her tastes, brought her some sausage and watched as she ate it. Béatrice thanked her, still looking around for the source of that tantalizing smell. Then she kissed her neighbor's cheek and tasted her sweat.

"She wrote that it was like lightning in her mouth," said Marcel. "The most delicious thing in the world. She couldn't stop herself from tearing the woman apart." Suddenly, she had a strength that she'd never known, a strength so great that she tore the neighbor to pieces with her hands. The husband came at her with a knife and she screamed, instinctively. He reeled back, clutching at his head.

"I know the feeling," remarked Marcel. "She wrote that most people just felt the pain. But her voice had a terrible effect on members of the Broederschap—something she discovered later. It seemed to liquefy some of the crucial components in our augmentations."

After Béatrice murdered her neighbors, she fled to Paris, thinking it would be easier to hunt and avoid notice in a large city. A lifetime's upbringing in the Catholic faith had been swiftly jettisoned, replaced by the glorious high that came from other people's fluids, that lightning in the mouth. She was completely untroubled by what she had become, and it was not clear if her lack of concern was a result of her physiology or just plain wickedness. Regardless, she stalked the arrondissements of Paris, taking people when she hungered. After the first murder, that terrible hunger had ebbed a little—she could go weeks without feasting. But then she encountered a Grafter in a café and was entranced by the unique savor of his perspiration.

"It seems we were addictive to her," said Marcel. Some elements of the Grafter technology made them absolutely irresistible to Béatrice's already monstrous palate. "She tracked Cousin Jean-Baptiste from the café back to his house and bled him out in his bathtub. After that, she tracked down the other Parisian members of the Broederschap by scent. Well, scent and the contents of their address books. I gather that once she'd drained all Siegbert's blood, she was going to tap his spine, brain, bones, and bladder for everything they contained, and then, after a couple of days of bingeing on Siegbert-extract, she'd be on to the next one of us."

"Charming," remarked Felicity.

"She was terrifying," confessed Marcel. "But my point is this, Pawn Clements. I have no doubt that if Béatrice Mermier had been born in this country, she'd have been recruited into the Checquy."

"Or killed by us," pointed out Felicity defensively. In her secret heart, she felt a stab of pity for the long-dead woman with the uncontrollable hunger and no one to help her. The thought of coming into your powers and being enslaved by them was very frightening to her. Thank God the Checquy found me.

"Yes," he said grimly. "It seems that the line can be very thin between the monsters and the ones that protect us from the monsters."

"And monsters killed Miss Leliefeld's friends?" asked Felicity hesitantly. He nodded slightly.

"They were murdered in front of her," he said. "In broad daylight. They were all staying at a beach house in Marseille, and a thing came in the back door and tore them apart. Odette only just escaped with her life." Felicity's eyes opened wide. "She was able to summon help, and when our people arrived, all they found was the scent of oranges and a series of bloody footprints going out the back door and across the sand into the ocean. No explanation of who did it or why."

"You're sure the attackers were supernatural?" asked Felicity.

He nodded. "We are not talking about defenseless victims," said Marcel. "All of them had augmentations that provided them with inhuman strength and agility as well as concealed weaponry." Felicity nodded, thinking of Leliefeld's deadly little spurs. "One of them was my youngest son, Dieter."

"I'm so sorry for your loss," said Felicity, horrified.

"Thank you. It has been difficult for all of us, but Odette was left significantly scarred, both emotionally and physically.

The loss of her dearest friends has been extremely painful for her, but most especially the death of her lover. Alessio knows to avoid talking about them to her, and I would ask you to do the same."

"I won't bring it up," said Felicity. But I will tell Rook Thomas about this.

"Thank you. It was difficult for Odette to come to this country. I think that she is haunted by the idea that we are tying ourselves to the same sort of beings who killed those she loved best."

19

Security Vetting Form

Duplicates of the personal documents requested must be certified by a justice of the peace to be true and accurate copies.

1. Surname:

2. Christian names (Please note any family members after whom you were named or, if known, any other factors that prompted the selection of these names):

3. Gender (at birth, and current):

4. Date of conception (in Gregorian calendar):

5. Date of birth (in Gregorian calendar):

6. Time (in Greenwich Mean Time) at which the umbilical cord was cut:

7. Location (if known) of placenta:

8. Western zodiac sign:

9. Eastern zodiac sign:

10. Location of birth (including latitude and longitude and, if born above ground, feet above sea level). Affix copy of birth certificate:

11. Country (or countries) of citizenship; provide current passport number(s). Affix duplicates of every page from every passport ever possessed, regardless of whether stamped or not:

12. Mother (if applicable):

   a. Full name (include maiden name in parentheses):

   b. Birth date:

   c. Citizenship(s):

   d. Date of death (if applicable). Affix copy of death certificate and location (in latitude and longitude) of interment. If cremated, provide receipt of cremation and, if possible, sample of ashes:

13. Father (if applicable):

   a. Full name:

   b. Birth date:

c. Citizenship(s):

d. Date of death (if applicable). Affix copy of death certificate and location (in latitude and longitude) of interment. If cremated, provide receipt of cremation and, if possible, sample of ashes:

14. Siblings (if applicable). Provide names and gender of any and all full, half, step-, or foster siblings. Include current addresses. Please list in order of birth and note, with a red asterisk, where you appear in the birth order:

a.

b.

c.

15. Sexual partners (if applicable):

a. Current. Provide name, gender, contact details:

b. List all previous partners, including name, gender, contact details, and the estimated level of acrimony (on a scale of 1 to 14) that they currently feel toward you.

(Page 1 of 168)

20

O dette stomped angrily but carefully through the hallways of the hotel. In an effort to muster every shred of authority when interacting with Pawn Clements, she had put on her tallest, most expensive stiletto heels and her third-best suit (the best and the second-best no longer constituting appropriate business wear except in abattoirs, séances, or, possibly, highly specific erotica). That morning, she had sailed out of the bathroom armored in her elegance, intending to show that she was not cowed. Her confidence had lasted for approximately thirty seconds, at which point Clements had sat her down and given her a half-hour soul-withering lecture on how this whole bodyguarding arrangement would work.

It was apparent that, in the eyes of the Checquy, Odette Leliefeld had come to represent a tremendous liability. They did not trust her to walk in the hallways of a Checquy facility without threatening the negotiations. They did not trust her to cross the street without getting harmed. They barely trusted her to dress herself. And so Clements would be accompanying her everywhere for the foreseeable future.

"I will escort you from this hotel to the various places they are sending you," Clements had explained. "If you go to Apex House, or the Rookery, or the little field office in Lancaster, I will be standing right with you. When you go to the various social occasions and junkets that they have organized for you, I'll be frocked up and rolling my eyes right behind you.

"Now, all this responsibility doesn't fall just on me. It's going to require a new way of thinking on your part. From now on, before you leave a room, you make certain that I'm with you. If you need to go to the toilet, you let me know, because I'll be outside the stall door, making sure no one comes in to bother you. If you decide that you want to go out to Harvey Nichols and get some new shoes and a spot of lunch, you run it by me, and you book a table for two, because I'll be there, not carrying your bags for you.

"You do not try to ditch me. You do not absentmindedly get lost in a crowd. You do not ever, ever, fail to have your mobile phone with you and turned on. If I call you, you take that call. And if I give you an order, you follow it.

"All of this is not just because your safety is at risk. It's because if anything happens to you, it will affect my career. And I like my career.

"In short, if you even leave this floor of the hotel without me, I will make certain that you regret it."

It was patronizing, humiliating, and frightening. Alessio had listened, wide-eyed, presumably deciding that he didn't really want a bodyguard like Clements, even if she was a hot woman. At the end, Odette had nodded weakly and then gotten permission to attend the Broederschap planning meeting. Clements had grudgingly allowed her to walk down the hallway by herself, but only because there were guards stationed at every corridor junction.

Now, as she walked angrily down the hallway, she was aware that her choice of footwear and the elaborate caution it required in order for her to stomp effectively meant that she looked somewhat like a dressage pony, or possibly a dressage praying mantis. She was too pissed off to care.

It was bad enough that they dragged me here to interact with these horrible people. These horrible Gruwels! But now I'm supposed to have one of them trailing around after me like Frankenstein's bossier monster?

Well, forget it! she thought, and her fists clenched. I'm going to tell them I don't need or want this bodyguard! I don't care what the Checquy says. I am not having that woman stalking around after me, holding a leash!

Odette ignored the wary looks that the guards in the halls gave her and marched into the graaf's suite, where people were already gathered. Filled with righteous indignation, she looked around for Marie in order to deliver her edict and saw that she was reading through a stack of fax paper. Judging from her furrowed brow and the flat blackness of her hair, Marie was not getting good news. Odette hesitated. Righteous indignation was all very well, but dealing with Marie in a bad mood was an even more dire prospect than having Clements looming over her.

Maybe I'll talk to her afterward.

Great-Uncle Marcel smiled good morning at her, and she smiled back weakly and sat next to him.

"About this Clements woman," she began.

"I think it's a splendid development, don't you?" he said.

"What?"

"It will give you a very good opportunity to get insight into the Checquy, and it may provide you with some excellent contacts."

"But I hate her," protested Odette.

"Oh, I'm sure you think you do," said Marcel cheerfully, "but you're still young. It takes decades to really hate someone." Odette sighed heavily. "I'll tell you what, if, after fifteen years, you still think you hate her, we'll do something about it."

"She's not going to be my bodyguard for fifteen years," Odette objected.

"Then quit your complaining," said Marcel. "And stand up."

They all stood as Grootvader Ernst entered the room accompanied by his secretary Anabella.

"Sit," he said. They sat. "Before we move on to the bad news, let's just review the good news. Yesterday went well, for the most part," he said, looking only briefly in Odette's direction. "Our meetings were productive, and the transcripts are in the folders in front of you. We will be reviewing these before we depart for Apex House. Please indicate if there are any amendments that you feel need to be made.

"I was particularly pleased with the excellent presentation that Reinier gave on our latest developments in ergonomic office furniture. Rook Thomas has advised me that, in the end, only two of the sick bags provided were used." Reinier smiled hesitantly. "And now, Marie will share the current situation on the Continent," Ernst said. "Marie?"

"It's extremely bad," she said, looking up from her faxes. Odette was shocked to see that she had been crying. "The... the Antagonists killed another house. The Vienna house."

"No!" exclaimed one of the lawyers in shock. All around the table, people looked stricken.

"Are the residents all right?" asked Marcel.

"They're fine," said Marie. "Everyone got out okay, but the house is...it's gone. They lobotomized it before burning the place down." The lawyer who had cried out before was now sobbing quietly in his seat. Marie looked to Graaf Ernst. "Sir, we have to move up our schedule. These attacks are escalating."

"And they will continue to escalate," rasped an unfamiliar voice.

Everyone's eyes turned to Anabella, the graaf's secretary. A plump woman with a hairstyle that could probably resist a blow from a hatchet, she was always calm and composed. Now, however, she was slumped over and trembling in her chair next to the graaf.

"Anabella?" said Ernst cautiously. A curious choking sound, as if she were trying to cough up a tarantula, came from the secretary's mouth. And then the entire delegation jumped in their chairs as she abruptly lurched upright.

The woman's lips had peeled back from her teeth, and her eyes were staring straight ahead. She was breathing rapidly and Odette could see sweat pouring from her skin.

Is she sick? thought Odette. Is she having a seizure? Shouldn't someone do something?

Then, before Odette could move, Anabella caught her breath and made a pained straining noise. Her hands, gripping the edge of the table, suddenly spasmed, making the table shake and sending cups toppling. Documents were engulfed by beverages, but no one noticed as their drinks waterfalled into their laps.

And then Anabella's features changed. Before the horrified gaze of the delegation, the muscles of her face rippled, shifted, and rearranged themselves, pushing certain areas out, hardening the soft curves of her face into a longer, more angular visage. Her arms gave little jerks as they came up to cross her chest and she looked around the room.

"Anabella," said Ernst again, and he reached out a hand toward her.

"Keep away!" she barked, and her voice was not Anabella's but rather that of a young male. "The sow is mine." She smiled, baring her teeth. For a moment, her eyes met Odette's, and then Odette looked away. "Nobody? No reaction?" Anabella's body gave a labored shrug. "Anyway, you are correct. The attacks are escalating and we will continue to strike until this is finished. Until you are finished."

My God, thought Odette. It's them. Aghast, she stood up, knocking over her chair. Everyone else around the table also stood and stared incredulously at Anabella.

"You have brought this upon yourselves. When one beholds an atrocity, one cannot stand by and allow it to continue," said the voice. "You are become atrocities. You must be ended."

"It is not your place, or anyone's, to judge us," said Grootvader Ernst. Rage boiled in his eyes, and his hands were curled into fists, but he kept his voice calm. "You must cease these activities immediately."

"You do not give us orders," said the voice, sounding amused. "You saw our work the night of your little party? The restaurant?"

"We saw. Your stupidity in coming to these islands is unfathomable," said Ernst flatly. "Is it possible that you do not understand the forces that dwell here? The Checquy exists to destroy your kind."

"Oh, we know. But it exists to destroy your kind too. You need to be more afraid than we do."

"This conflict between us is not necessary," said Marcel soothingly. "Surely you understand that we want only peace?"

"There cannot be peace," hissed the voice. "You delude yourselves if you think it is possible. This proposed alliance between you and the Checquy: the ridiculous marrying the profane. You despise each other. Sooner or later, one of you will turn on the other, and the conflict will consume you both. But we are not willing to wait. We are going to make it happen sooner than you can believe."

"If you do not cease these hostilities," said Ernst, "you will know pain and sorrow unlike anything you can imagine."

"We know what your threats are worth," said the voice in a tone thick with contempt. It paused, and Anabella's body shuddered for a moment. Her hands clenched the arms of her chair, and then she vomited violently down the length of the conference table. Her head came up, and there was a look of triumph in her eyes. "It is you who should be afraid. It is going to get so much worse for you, and you will not be safe anywhere. Not even in your own skins."

The face smirked, and then the features sank back into the shape of Anabella's familiar ones. Her eyes rolled back in her head, and she crumpled to the floor.

21

What in the hell happened to you?" asked Felicity as Odette entered the hotel room. Odette looked at her blankly.

That's right, she thought, dazed. She's staying here with us. In the frenzy of what she had just witnessed, Odette had completely forgotten about the Pawn's presence.

"I—what?" she asked.

"Why are you wearing a too-large bathrobe over your clothes?"

"I was cold?" hazarded Odette. The Pawn gave her a long, level look. She got up from the couch, walked over until she was uncomfortably close to Odette, and abruptly reached out and opened the robe.

"Bloody hell!"

Odette looked down at her suit. In the course of forty-five minutes, it had gone from being her third-best suit to her third-worst suit. Not only had it picked up some mingled coffee, tea, orange juice, cranberry juice, splashes of Anabella's projectile vomit, and a torrent of Odette's terrified sweat, but there was also blood splashed liberally up the sleeves and some arterial spray across the lapels.

"I was cold and we had to do a bit of emergency surgery," amended Odette.

After Anabella collapsed, the entire delegation had stood frozen for a few long seconds. Then everyone had proceeded to freak out completely. However, with the Checquy guards outside the door, ready to overreact, the freak-out had been necessarily hushed. Ernst barked orders that no one listened to, Marie called her superior in the Netherlands, and the lawyers and the accountants fluttered around like agitated flamingos.

Since Odette and Marcel were the only actual medical practitioners in the party, it had fallen to them to provide first aid to the unpossessed secretary. However, they had to elbow their way through a confusion of milling and squawking professionals in order to reach her.

They discovered that the possession had left more lasting results than a dismayed delegation, a soiled table, and several beverage-stained designer suits. Patches of blood were spreading rapidly on Anabella's white blouse. Marcel tore open her shirt to reveal lacerations all over Anabella's body. Jagged lines spelled out obscenities and threats, and blood flowed out at an alarming rate.

"Apply pressure!" Marcel barked to Odette. She swept up some coffee-stained but mercifully vomit-free linen napkins from the table and bent over Anabella. The secretary was still unconscious, and Marcel brushed one of his fingers lightly over her carotid artery.

"Chemical glands in my fingertips," he explained to Odette. "To keep her asleep. You know, they're far more discreet than spurs."

"Is now really the time to critique my implants?" asked Odette tightly. "Implants that you know were a gift."

"Fine," said Marcel. "We'll need to disinfect and suture." He looked around and caught the eye of the least panicked functionary. "You! We need surgical needles, disinfectant, antimicrobial thread, and tissue adhesive, statim!"

"Where am I going to get all those?" asked the functionary in bewilderment.

"They're in my handbag by my seat," said Odette. They pressed into service the two largest accountants, who carried Anabella into Ernst's gigantic and luxurious bedroom. Marcel laid some gigantic and luxurious towels on the bed. It was a relatively routine procedure, but the necessity for speed and the lack of facilities meant that there was no time to use Grafter techniques or for Odette to activate her operating musculature.

"These are going to be the worst scars ever," remarked Odette.

"Don't be so hard on yourself," said Marcel. "You're doing a very nice stitch."

"That's not what I meant," said Odette. "I was talking about the word monster on her belly."

"We'll take care of that later," said Marcel dismissively. "The main thing is to ensure she doesn't bleed to death."

In the end, she didn't bleed to death, but it wasn't tidy, and afterward, Odette and Marcel looked exactly as if they had conducted emergency surgery in a hotel room.

In order to leave the suite without sending the Checquy guards bursting in as soon as they got one look at her, Odette had washed her hands and face thoroughly and wrapped herself in Ernst's gigantic and luxurious robe. It had trailed behind her as she walked down the corridor, which had garnered some startled looks, but the hallway guards seemed to put it down to Grafter-style eccentricity on her part.

Unfortunately, Clements did not seem to be so asinine.

"You performed surgery?" exclaimed Felicity. "At a staff meeting?"

"Um, yes," said Odette, trying desperately to behave as if this were a perfectly normal occurrence. "One of the assistants had some problems with her implants. She was sick all over the table, so we opened her up in the bathroom," she added in a fit of inspiration. There was really no way to prevent news of the vomiting from getting out.

"I see," said Felicity. She looked appalled at the idea, but to Odette's relief she seemed to buy it. Apparently, she was willing to believe anything of the Grafters—a thought that depressed Odette a little. "Well," said the Pawn, "I had a meeting too." She did not add that her meeting had not resulted in her getting covered in bodily fluids, but both of them were thinking it. "I got a call to go down to Portsmouth. They want me to take a look at something."

"Oh!" said Odette. "So does that mean that I won't…" have to endure your presence for the rest of the day? she mentally finished.

"No, it means you're coming down to Portsmouth with me," said the Pawn. She sounded as deeply unenthusiastic about the prospect as Odette felt. "They checked with your grandfather, and he thought it was a good idea."

"I see."

"He said to be sure to wear your coat, as it gets cold down by the seaside," said Clements.

"Right," said Odette absently. She's not going to be following me around, she realized with a sinking feeling. I'm going to be following her around. Because she is more important than I am.

"We're taking the train down, so you'll need to get changed. Quickly."

Odette nodded unhappily and hurried into her and Alessio's room, where she put on her fourth-best suit. Clements chivvied her out of the suite and down to the lobby. Apparently, there was a car waiting to whip them to Waterloo Station. They were just heading out the hotel's main door when Felicity's mobile rang.

"Clements," the Pawn answered briskly. "Yes? Yes, sir, we'll wait." She snapped the phone shut. "They're sending someone down with a briefing folder; more material came over the secure line. I'll meet them at the lifts. You sit on that couch, and don't go anywhere. I'll be watching you."

Odette sat, reluctantly obedient, and looked on without much interest as a swarm of businessmen were checked in. She glanced over to the bank of lifts and saw that Clements was indeed watching her. She looked down hastily. There was a bowl of apples on the coffee table in front of her, and she took one while she waited.

"Delicious, aren't they?" said a voice beside her, and she turned, startled. A blond woman was sitting on the arm of the couch, also eating an apple. She was stunningly beautiful and had the best-looking skin Odette had ever seen on a non-Grafter. She smiled at Odette and rolled her eyes at the harried-looking hotel receptionists. "I expect they put the fruit out just to cover up for the long waiting times, but what can you do?" Her accent was British and, from what Odette could tell, very upper-class.

"Just have an apple and bide your time, I suppose," said Odette.

"Not a bad motto for life in general," remarked the woman with a smile, and Odette smiled back. "Have you got a busy day coming up?"

"I'm heading down to Portsmouth."

"Well, word around the halls of the Apex is that the negotiations are going along quite well."

Oh, she's Checquy, realized Odette. And she doesn't recoil from me. Finally, someone pleasant. And some pleasant news.

"That's encouraging," said Odette. "I thought I hadn't made the best impression." The woman shook her head, smiling as if she couldn't imagine what had given Odette that idea. "Well, shall I see you at Apex House?" Odette asked.

"Nope, I'll be stationed here for a few days," said the woman. "Security detail. I'm mainly stuck hanging around in the lobby, reading complimentary magazines, watching the door, and being mistaken for a call girl by drunken businessmen."

"We'll try and be as unexciting as possible," said Odette. "I promise."

"I'd appreciate it," said the woman.

"I'm Odette," said Odette. "You probably already know that, though, from the files."

"I do," said the woman. "I'm Pawn Jelfs. Sophie. Good to meet you."

"You too," Odette said, feeling slightly better about the day. On the spur of the moment, she picked up an apple to take to Clements.

Clements guided Odette firmly through Waterloo Station. They'd missed the rush hour, but the crowds were still busy enough that the Checquy agent's threat-detection instincts were on overdrive. She moved like an eel through the throng, avoiding even casual physical contact with people, and every time they were jostled, Odette could see the bodyguard actively restrain herself from taking down some hapless commuter with a chop to the throat. It was apparent that Pawn Felicity Clements was not at ease among civilians.

Odette did her best to remain focused, but she couldn't help getting distracted by the station. The architecture, the people, and the energy were captivating. She kept stopping to take it all in. Judging from Clements's sighs and other irritated mouth-noises, the Pawn wanted nothing more than to take Odette firmly by the hair and drag her to the train, but that would presumably have violated the Checquy policy of remaining unnoticed.

Eventually, after much pained sighing and pointed nudging on the part of Pawn Clements, they were seated in the first-class carriage of the train going from Waterloo to Portsmouth Harbour railway station. Clements disappeared into her folder of official documents, and Odette amused herself by looking out the window at the people walking down the platform.

As the train pulled out of the station, all Odette's concerns were swept away, and she stared out the window, enthralled by the new perspective of the city. Then they were sweeping through the countryside and she didn't care about the awkward silence at all. God, this is a beautiful country. It was so green it almost hurt her eyes.

When they arrived at Portsmouth, she could smell the ocean in the wind. She would have liked a chance to look around the city, but Clements led her briskly to a dark car that was waiting near the entrance of the station. Before the door was even shut, the driver was pulling away, sending the both of them bouncing around in the backseat.

"Where are we going?" ventured Odette once she'd unwedged herself from the corner. The car was moving so fast and taking turns so sharply that all she could tell about the city of Portsmouth was that it appeared to be made up mainly of buildings of some sort.

"The naval base," said Clements. Odette nodded. She was dimly aware that Portsmouth had been a navy port for centuries, but she only remembered it because she'd read Mansfield Park. "The item they want me to look at is under armed guard there." Odette felt a trifle surprised that the item, whatever it was, was being kept at a regular navy base and not some secret Checquy facility. But it's all government, she told herself. You're going to be a government employee yourself.

If they don't kill you.

At the entrance to the base, the Pawn rolled down the window so that the guard could identify the two of them. Salt air rushed in, and it carried with it an odor that prompted both Clements and Odette to wrinkle their noses. Rotting meat, thought Odette absently. Must be a dead fish somewhere nearby. Their names were on the guard's list, and they were driven to an office where they signed in and were given passes. From there, the driver took them to a large warehouse right by the water. He led them through a series of corridors.

"So, is it okay if I observe you while you do this?" asked Odette. "Or is there a room I should go sit in? I would understand if you needed privacy."

"No, I don't think that's a good idea," said Clements. "You don't have the best safety record when it comes to sitting alone in rooms."

"You make it sound like I managed to injure myself while sitting quietly in a corner," objected Odette. "I was fine sitting alone in that room. Up until some guy who decided he hated me came in and attacked me."

"Yes, but I think it's entirely possible that people here will hate you too."

"Oh."

"Plus," said Clements, "I think you might actually be able to provide a useful perspective on the item."

"Really?" said Odette, feeling rather chuffed despite herself. "Why? What is this item?"

At that point, the doors in front of them opened to reveal a preparation room. The far wall was made entirely of glass, and beyond it was the cavernous space of a hangar. The odor, which before had been merely unpleasant, burst out and punched them both square in the face. In the center of the hangar, suspended from gantries, was a dead thing the size of a passenger jet.

"There it is," said Clements.

22

The creature was mottled gray and brown. Its shape put Odette in mind of a lumpy butternut squash, if a butternut squash were several stories high and smelled like the gym socks of a lesser god. It did not appear to have any limbs but was circled by voluminous fronds and frills that draped around it and trailed onto the ground. A web of massive steel cables looped under its body, suspending it, and rolls of fat drooped and bulged through the lattice. A huge scaffolding encircled the middle of it like a belt of iron girders.

The reek was astounding, even through the glass. Odette smelled salt and rot and a dull chemical odor. Water dripped off the beast and puddled on the tarpaulins that had been laid out underneath. A glazed black eye the size of a horse stared blankly at them from the side of the head.

Incredible, thought Odette. I've never seen anything like it.

Workers in blue coveralls clambered about on it. Some of them, suspended by climbing ropes, clung to the sides, and Odette could see that they were spraying something from backpack tanks onto the creature's hide.

"What are they doing?" she asked.

"They're covering it with polyurethane," said Clements. "In case of spores or toxins. It's the same stuff they use at some aircraft accidents to seal in the carbon fibers."

"Where did that thing come from?" asked Odette weakly.

"The ocean," said Clements. "The Checquy believe it was responsible for the sinking of a cargo ship a couple of weeks ago. Two days ago, the coast guard found it, dead, in the shallows of a remote bay, a gigantic column of seagulls circling above it, picking off the flesh. It was moved to the control of the Checquy. They used a few tugboats to tow it here under cover of darkness and then moved it to this hangar for examination."

"But what is it?"

"We don't know," Clements said with a shrug. "A monster? The Checquy science division has gone mad for it. I gather it's like nothing they've ever seen. Samples have been sent to our labs for analysis. Techs all over the country are clamoring to get assigned here. But they want me to take a look at it first, and I thought you might get something out of it."

"This is so cool," said Odette. For the first time, the work of the Checquy didn't seem so frightening. This creature, for all its bizarreness, had been a living animal, and she knew living animals. Now it was a puzzle. And she liked puzzles.

They were given suits of dense rubber, like old-fashioned diving suits, and bulky filter masks. The two women entered the hangar and collared a passing tech, who guided them to one side, where two dozen tables had been set up end to end against the wall, all of them covered with papers, files, photographs, and computers. A swarm of blue-suited Checquy people bustled around, shuffling papers and typing madly. The tech introduced them to Dr. Jennifer Fielding, the head of the operation. It was hard to tell anything about her through her protective gear, but she had a businesslike manner and a rather loud voice that reverberated in her mask.

"Ah, Pawn Clements. You're the psychometrist."

"Yes, ma'am."

"They've prepared a platform for you over by the front of the subject," said the doctor. "Pawn Roff here will take you to it. There's a chair set up for you. Now, I gather that you don't need to be touching the actual subject with your naked skin?"

"No, ma'am. My Sight can pass through most materials. It takes a little longer, but it means I don't need direct contact."

"Excellent; we're still checking the creature for toxins and so on, and this means we won't have to wait. Now, the first thing I want you to obtain is a good overview of what the creature is like inside. We've begun to investigate its interior and have commenced actual excavations into it, but a road map would be extremely useful. Depending on how long it takes you, I'd then be interested in the creature's past. Where it came from and so on."

"I understand, Dr. Fielding," said Clements. "I'll map out the interior, and then emerge. I can sketch out what I find, and then I'll start looking into the past."

"Good," said the doctor. "Now, Miss Leliefeld, when I learned you were coming, I did a quick read-up on your studies, and I'd be very interested in your thoughts on this specimen. If you'd like to come with me, I can show you around." Odette felt rather flattered by this.

Someone in the Checquy actually finds my abilities interesting instead of repulsive.

"Dr. Fielding," said Clements awkwardly. "Are you certain that's a good idea? I was assigned to Miss Leliefeld because—"

"I'm aware of why you were assigned," interrupted Dr. Fielding. "But I can assure you, I do not harbor any ill feeling toward Miss Leliefeld because of her background. I am not a Pawn; I came to the Checquy based on my work, and I was not subjected to any ridiculous indoctrination of hatred for the Broederschap."

To Odette's shameful delight, Clements flushed crimson. "Miss Leliefeld will be completely safe with me," continued the doctor, "and my team is professional enough that anyone with any problems will not act upon them. Now, time is passing, and you have a job to do." The Pawn nodded reluctantly and walked away toward the creature.

"I am sorry about that," said Dr. Fielding to Odette. "Working with the Checquy presents its own unique challenges. The Pawns are brought up in a very regimented environment, and they can have a peculiar perspective on the world. Fortunately, they tend to respond very well to direct commands given with authority."

Odette reflected that she herself would probably respond well to any direct commands given by Dr. Fielding.

"Anyway, let us proceed. What do you think of our find?"

"It's amazing," said Odette fervently.

"I know," said Dr. Fielding, her eyes crinkling in a smile behind her goggles. "That's the thing about working for the Checquy—you get to see the most astounding stuff. That's how they lured me away from a very promising career in academia."

"How did they approach you?" asked Odette curiously. The role of the nonsupernatural Checquy employees was not something she had ever given much thought to.

"Actually, I approached them," said Dr. Fielding. "Albeit unwittingly. I'm a marine biologist, and I thought I was applying for a research grant from some old foundation that dated back to Darwin's time. I submitted all the paperwork, my CV, and a selection of my articles. I had to post them; they wouldn't accept e-mail. I didn't hear back for months, and then they called me down to Walmington-on-Sea for an interview in this dire-looking old building on a backstreet. I sat down, and they wheeled out a glass carboy of sea-water. A massive thing, the size of my torso, with a light shining down on it. And they asked me what I thought." She paused, her eyes distant, locked into that memory.

"And what was it?" Odette prompted gently.

"I saw fronds at first, moving about in the water. Red and gold and mahogany and ebony. Little bunches. And then I peered more closely, and I saw that it was hair. The trailing hair of tiny, naked children flying in the water." Odette felt a shiver go down the back of her neck.

"It never crossed my mind that they were fake," said Dr. Fielding. "They were too perfect. Undeniably real. Tiny, perfect babies that looked at me and smiled and swirled through their own hair. They were boys and girls, and then they were gone, out of the jar, swum away to somewhere else. Inexplicable." She shook her head.

"They asked me again what I thought, and I replied that I didn't know anything at all. From that moment, the Checquy had me, and I never looked back."

"So it's worth it?" asked Odette.

"Oh, absolutely. Of course, there are downsides as well. It can be so dangerous, you know. Horrendously dangerous. You get promoted in this job as much because someone has been killed as because of your talent. But the real downside, at least for an academic like me, is that you can't publish. And you lie to those around you. My family doesn't know what I do; they think I work for a corporation. Of course, I've done more, seen more than they could dream of, but they don't know that." She shrugged. "Anyway, let's get a wriggle on here." She led Odette to the base of the scaffolding, and they started climbing the steep switchbacking stairs.

Close up, the beast seemed somehow less authentic. Odette's mind kept telling her that something that large could not possibly be real. Behind the sheen of polyurethane, its hide looked rubbery. Then, as they neared the top, Odette realized there was a massive gouge in the body. It carved open the back, and she could see the meat, honeycombed with bubbles like a fleshy sponge. There did not appear to be much blood. Perhaps it all drained out, she thought.

"Do we know what happened to it?"

"As best we can tell, it got in the way of a cargo ship, which, as you can see, tore the hell out of it," said Dr. Fielding. "And I suppose it wasn't happy about it, because it attacked and sank the ship before bleeding to death. Later I'll show you its mouth. The teeth are huge, serrated, and made out of some calcium compound that doesn't even chip when it's cutting through iron."

"What have you established so far about the creature?" asked Odette.

"Well, we've found that it's made of flesh and bone." She paused and looked at Odette. "I know that sounds sarcastic, but it's actually a hugely important insight. Another interesting feature is multiple eyes all over the front of its head and several more scattered along the length of its body. Very peculiar, but the preliminary tests have revealed no unusual properties."

"No unusual properties?" repeated Odette incredulously as she looked up at the wall of skin.

"Well, no radiation or internal toxicity," amended the doctor. "Temperature, gravity, light levels, and the rate of time passing all remain normal in its vicinity. None of the attending personnel have reported any medical problems or abrupt shifts in their height, weight, or sexual orientation."

"I see. Can you identify genus? Or even family?"

"We've found that it's tricky trying to taxonomize these sorts of things," said Dr. Fielding. "In the course of my years with the Checquy, we've added two biological kingdoms and identified several thousand new phyla."

"I see," said Odette, somewhat taken aback. "May I ask, Dr. Fielding, why does this fall within the jurisdiction of the Checquy?" She paused, trying to find the right words. "I mean, for all you know, this is a perfectly natural creature that has simply never been seen before."

"It's possible," conceded the doctor. "Although the fact that it's unlike anything ever seen, or even reported, makes us a little suspicious. The fact that it attacked a ship gives us grounds for labeling it malign, which is one of the things that brings it under the Checquy's authority. But if suddenly a whole bunch of them turn up around the world, we'll reclassify it." They reached the top of the scaffolding and walked across the broad platform. In the middle, just above the curve of the creature's back, several people were putting on oxygen tanks.

"What are they doing?" asked Odette.

"Ah," said Dr. Fielding. "This is rather exciting. One of the interesting features of the subject is a line of blowholes along its back. They're very big."

"Oh?"

"Big enough for a person to climb into," said the doctor.

Odette looked at her in awe and delight. "No!" she exclaimed.

"Yes."

"Oh, you have to let me go in!"

I really hope that Leliefeld manages not to get herself into any messy situations while I'm doing this, thought Felicity. If something happens to her while I've got my brain stuck in a dead animal, I am going to get in so much trouble with Rook Thomas.

Pawn Roff, Dr. Fielding's aide, was leading Felicity across the vast hangar to the front of the beast. She could just make out a low platform with a plastic pavilion on top.

"Pawn Clements, we've reviewed your file," said Pawn Roff. "And I applied the risk-analysis template for your powers." Felicity nodded. The Checquy had suffered a few disastrous incidents in which the vulnerable or vacant bodies of Pawns whose minds had temporarily left their bodies were taken over by supernatural squatters. As a precaution, an office in the Checquy had worked up a schema for the employment of abilities like hers. It described what precautions ought to be taken before someone turned his or her Sight on anything.

The risk assessment wasn't always carried out—it depended on how pressing the issue was—but Pawn Roff seemed to be one of those people who liked to have every box ticked.

"What's the evaluation?" she asked.

"I'm afraid the fact that you'll be examining a dead supernatural creature of demonstrated malignancy makes it an automatic category C," said Roff apologetically. Felicity shrugged. Category C meant that she would be supervised by a doctor, a lawyer, and a guard, each of them armed with a handgun and a machete. Once the observation was over, she'd have to submit to weekly medical, toxicological, psychological, and religious examinations for a month. It was inconvenient, but she'd been through worse.

Category E would have meant she'd need to receive a series of nuclear-style decontamination scrubbings after the operation, while category F added mandatory exorcism rituals for all known religions and two weeks of an all-liquid diet. Category G required that all the aforementioned precautions take place on an isolated oil-rig facility in the North Sea with twelve marksmen pointing guns at her from a hundred meters away.

At the level of category S, she would be automatically executed, her remains incinerated, and arrangements made for them to be removed from the planet. And there were nine higher levels of precautions beyond that, moving into the Greek alphabet.

They came to the platform with its little tent. It looked very small and vulnerable with the great corpse of the creature rearing up behind it like an Eiger made of old fish. In a tiny antechamber, they were provided fresh coveralls that were not made of thick rubber but rather a cotton so sheer and breathable that Felicity's scarlet knickers and bra could be seen through it.

This is what comes of thinking you won't be deployed in combat today, she thought dismally. Normally she wore quite plain underwear, since there was always the possibility of being sent into a combat scenario. However, waking up in the glamorous surroundings of the hotel, and somewhat intimidated by Leliefeld's luggage and wardrobe, she'd elected to wear her very best clothing, including her undergarments. Of course, Leliefeld was wearing a suit that looked like it cost three times as much, which had somewhat spoiled Felicity's mood.

Felicity and her guide proceeded into the main area of the tent, where several people, also dressed in cotton coveralls, were waiting. She noted that none of them were wearing exuberantly colored underwear.

"These are your witnesses for today, Pawn Clements. Allow me to introduce Dr. Quis, Ms. Brünnhilde Trant-Erskine-Brown, QC, and Sergeant Patrick Liar."

"Sergeant Liar?" repeated Felicity faintly. Sergeant Liar was a gigantic man and, unnervingly, was already holding both his service pistol and his service machete in his hands, as if ready to execute her at any moment.

"Lyrer, with a Y-R-E-R," he said. He spoke with a gorgeous Irish accent. "Like someone who plays the lyre."

"Well, that's a lyrist, but it's still nice to meet you," said Felicity. "All of you." She shook hands with the other two but not the sergeant, who was unwilling to relinquish his grip on his weapons and who didn't seem delighted to have been corrected about his own name.

There was a groaning sound underneath them, and they all swayed a little as the hydraulics of the platform began lifting them. The plastic roof of the pavilion squashed down a little as it came in contact with the corpse.

Set up in the center of the platform was Felicity's equipment, arranged in her preferred layout: a table with some paper, pens, pencils, crayons, charcoal, and a voice recorder so that she could record her impressions as soon as she emerged from her trance. A thermos of chilled cranberry juice stood by, moisture beading on its sides.

The most important item was a piece of intricate and expensive furniture that looked like a dentist's chair, or would have if Ferrari had been in the habit of making dentist's chairs. It had been specially commissioned by the Checquy for those Pawns whose abilities required them to lie still for a long time.

There were IV drips hanging on a rack and discreet little tanks underneath should a catheter (or worse) prove necessary. Heart, brain, lung, and gallbladder monitors were attached at the back, with the leads all coiled up.

Felicity eased herself into the chair, and Pawn Roff set about fastening restraints around her ankles, knees, waist, and neck. They were uncomfortable, but even more disconcerting was the knowledge that the chair could be electrified if two of the three witnesses judged it necessary. It also contained a series of small explosive charges that would, if detonated, do an astounding amount of harm to the chair's occupant while leaving any bystanders with no greater problem than sourcing an effective dry cleaner.

Dr. Quis, a white man of indeterminate age, facial features, and hair color, applied monitoring leads to her stomach, chest, neck, forehead, and the balls of her feet and then connected them to the machines. The sound of regular beeping filled the little pavilion.

"Is there anything else you need, Pawn Clements?" asked Pawn Roff.

"No, thank you," said Felicity. She set the chair's massaging rollers to "light pummel" and activated the machinery that reclined the seat and brought it up to the depression in the pavilion's ceiling. The armrests lifted up until her bare hands came into contact with the plastic roof.

And here we go.

Felicity closed her eyes and opened her mind. Smell and sound were sucked away, and touch shouldered into the forefront. Her powers were all about physical connections, texture, substance. The light scratchiness of her suit, the liquid crawl of the perspiration on her back. She gathered herself together and pushed forward, out of her body, passing like light through the ceiling. There was a frisson as she moved through the shellac on the creature's hide, and then she was inside.

Odette Leliefeld may think she knows anatomy, thought Felicity, *but she's never had this perspective.*

Much to her regret, this wasn't the first corpse she'd surveyed. When she had begun doing it, at the Estate, it hadn't been easy. She'd felt as if she were drowning in dead flesh. The weight of a body and the flashes of its history that leaked into her psyche had actually prompted her to become a vegetarian. The Checquy, upon learning her reasons for becoming a vegetarian, had firmly told her that she couldn't allow her work to affect her that way; it suggested an appalling lack of self-discipline. They had insisted she keep eating meat.

It still wasn't particularly easy, but she'd reached the point where she could delve around in a murdered corpse for an hour and then go have a hamburger without feeling any guilt or nausea. The key, as when one interacted with kindergartners, was not to acknowledge the immeasurable horror of what you were dealing with.

Now, as she hovered inside the meat of the creature's chin, Felicity took a moment to orient herself. First step, locate the main organs. You're in the head, so check the brain. Navigating one's way through a corpse was, usually, just a matter of following some universal signposts. I just hope this thing has a spine. She sent her mind coursing up a jawbone as thick as a pine tree and then traced her way along the outside skin to the nearest eye.

Okay, and now I just follow the optic nerve to the brain. Mentally humming the theme from Mission: Impossible, she spiraled along the fleshy cable. It's really not a good sign that I'm enjoying this more than the prospect of going back to a five-star hotel at the end of the day, she mused. Rook Thomas never actually said how long I would have to hang out with that Eurotrash Grafter and her creepy little brother. I wonder if—this doesn't feel right, she realized. Where's the fucking brain?

Felicity estimated that she'd traveled about a third of the length of the creature, and not only had she not found a brain, but none of the other optic nerves had converged with hers. I know I'm in a possibly unique, probably supernatural creature, but this really doesn't make much sense. Why would the brain be so far away from the eyes? What kind of creature keeps its brain in its arse? Apart from Pawn Bannister, she amended. If she'd had access to her arms, she'd have folded them in vexation. She settled for thinking vexed thoughts and pressed on farther into the corpse.

Standing carefully on the creature's back, Odette watched as the heels of a Checquy scientist vanished into a blowhole. As it turned out, when Dr. Fielding described the hole as "big enough for a person to climb into," what she'd meant was that it was big enough for a person to wriggle into slowly and laboriously if that person pushed his or her oxygen tank ahead first. This person also needed to be relatively slim, comfortable in enclosed spaces, and willing to be sprayed down with the world's biggest can of lubricant. Fortunately, Odette was such a person.

"You seriously want to go in there?" asked the support Pawn who was strapping an intricate spring-loaded knife to Odette's greasy wrist. Several pieces of equipment had been added to her ensemble, including a slightly larger mask with headlights and a built-in communications system. "Really?" Odette couldn't tell if his tone was genuine incredulity or the sort of snotty goading that suggested she couldn't do this, couldn't live up to the standards of the Checquy.

"Absolutely. It's an incredible opportunity to examine a completely unknown creature." She wasn't certain if she was trying to persuade him or herself.

When Fielding had mentioned the possibility, it had sounded fascinating—a new perspective on anatomy and the mechanics of life that was too good to miss. If this was the kind of work she might get to do with the Checquy, it might all be worth it.

But she also felt she needed to prove something to the Checquy. The knowledge that they disliked her—her especially! And for no reason at all!—had ignited in Odette the desire to show them that she was worthwhile, that she wouldn't hesitate to walk where they walked. For most of the people present, she would be the first Grafter they ever encountered. She was anxious to leave an excellent impression (if only to make up for her disastrous first few).

Finally, there was the knowledge that doing it would really piss off Pawn Clements.

So she'd jumped at the chance. In fact, she'd almost demanded it. Now, as she eyed the dark hole in the creature's hide, it was beginning to seem slightly...unwise.

"Going up a monster's nose? You're 'aving a laugh!" said the man. "'S bloody ridiculous." Which Odette thought was pretty rich coming from a guy who, judging by what she could see through his mask, appeared to be made out of pebbles. "Now, because we're not at all certain how well radio will go through several meters of dead animal, you're going to be spooling this communications cable behind you." A couple of silvery lines were already coming out of the blowhole where the two Checquy monster-spelunkers had gone in.

"We'll be monitoring the feed constantly, and if you ask for help or start screaming, or if we can't hear you breathing into the microphone, then we'll get you out."

"How?" asked Odette warily.

"Oh, we've got people with jackhammers and whatnot standing by. Of course, we'd prefer not to use them. I mean, it wouldn't be a very professional dissection, would it?" Odette smiled weakly. It hardly sounded like a professional rescue either. In fact, the idea of having the Checquy drag her out was far more worrying than the prospect of going in. "You'll be fine," said the guy. He patted her reassuringly on her greasy shoulder and then wiped his gloved hand absently on his coveralls.

Odette gave him the thumbs-up, then awkwardly got down on her knees, holding her oxygen tank. Until she could start pushing herself forward with her feet, she would have to claw her way into the blowhole, pulling herself in by the skin of the tunnel.

The interior of the animal was much as one would expect: close and dark and damp, with an odd smell. It was rather, Odette thought, like trying to enter a really popular nightclub on New Year's Eve. Even with the lubricant all over her and the slicks of thick liquid that dripped out of the walls and roof, it was a damn tight squeeze.

She took a deep breath. You wanted this, she told herself. You asked for it. And it's a good thing that you very definitely do not get claustrophobic.

The irregular tube was not perfectly circular—it was more of a squashed oval wider than it was tall. It was really only just about as wide as Odette herself, so she had to wriggle ahead with her hips and shoulders instead of using her arms and legs. The light from her headlamp did not seem to travel very far. Peering over the squat cylinder of her oxygen tank, she could just make out the white soles of the man several meters in front of her. She carefully scraped some of the viscous material from the tunnel wall into a little sample tube and secured it in its pouch on her sleeve. Then she rolled over (this took some very careful shifting) and examined the ceiling.

The surface had a rubbery texture, and the mucus (at least, she presumed it was mucus) dripping down meant that soon her helmet's mask had multiple disgusting streaks obscuring her view. Odette turned back onto her stomach and then used her well-lubricated hand to try and wipe off the mask. She managed to scrape most of the crud away, but the lubricant coating her glove smeared the faceplate and made everything look hazy.

"The tunnel continues to slope down at approximately forty-five degrees," came a sudden voice in her ear, and, unable to jump in the close confines, Odette settled for a sort of startled spasm.

"Copy that," said another voice, and she realized that the team on the surface had turned on the intercom system. She could now hear the scientists' breathing as it echoed in her helmet.

"Un-understood," she added, and then wondered if she ought to have said, "Copy that," and if all of them were rolling their eyes at her unprofessional, nonmilitary attitude.

As she inched her way along, however, Odette began to brood less about the effort of moving and became focused on examining her surroundings. After a while, the three people inside the monster began to discuss what they were noticing.

The other two were Pawn Wharton, a marine biologist, and Dr. Codman, a zoologist, but Odette's knowledge of general anatomy proved to be far superior to theirs, and so they were all able to bring something to the conversation. Wharton was shooting video, while Codman and Odette collected samples of every solid and liquid they encountered, no matter how gross. The zoologist even bored a few little core samples.

After about ten minutes of exhausting wriggling, they paused to take a rest. Odette put her face on her folded forearms, and tried to ignore how bad her breath was beginning to smell in the confines of her mask. Then she felt a little tremble go through the tube.

"Did you feel that?" she asked. "Are you guys okay?" She could easily imagine one of the scientists deciding that he really didn't like crawling and having a panic attack. It would probably be the worst place in the world to lose control.

"I felt it, but it wasn't me," said Codman.

"Nor me," said Wharton. Both of them sounded wary but calm.

"Feel what?" asked one of the techs on the surface.

"It was like a little shudder," said Codman. "Through the tube."

"Oh. Well, there's no sign of anything up here," said the tech.

"Any thoughts? Odette?" asked Codman.

"Um, maybe a little death spasm," said Odette. "It could be some muscle dying or breaking down." She peered as closely as she could at the surface of the tube and probed with her gloved hands. It felt dense and muscular. I wonder if it could clench together and seal the blowhole shut? The implications for the current occupants of the blowhole were not pleasant.

"Do you want to come back?" asked the tech. Everyone paused. The plan had been to continue going until either their oxygen was one-third expended or they came to a place where they could turn around—a junction or chamber. Having to back out of the tube, while doable, was not an agreeable prospect. If push came to shove, they could try cutting through to another area of the monster. Pawn Wharton had a little chain saw that was apparently designed specifically for cutting through large swaths of flesh.

"That twitch might have just been a one-off thing," said Odette. "If it happens again, we should consider leaving." They cautiously started moving forward once more.

What in the hell was that? thought Felicity.

She had been gliding through the meat and been heartened to find that her optic nerve had merged with four others, which meant that she was getting closer to something, when suddenly she'd been jerked to a stop. For a few bewildering moments, her Sight would not carry her. Not forward, not backward, not in any direction.

It was as if she'd been swimming and the water had suddenly frozen solid around her, holding her fast. Then, just as quickly, it was over. And now that she'd had time to think about it, it made her very worried.

Was it me? She'd never had a moment like that before. Maybe I'm not ready to be doing this. A few days ago, I lost my closest friends. Maybe I should be on leave, or in therapy. Maybe I'm losing it. It was a frightening thought, but not as frightening as the other possibilities. If it wasn't her psyche, then her powers might be going wrong. And if it wasn't her powers, then it might be the monster she was in.

Calm down, she told herself. It might have been a one-off thing. If it happens again, you pull back. She cautiously started moving forward once more.

It was not a one-off thing.

Said the tech over the intercom, "I just felt a little tremor up here on the surface."

* * *

Skimming through the creature's flesh, Felicity had felt it too. She'd been brought to another sudden halt, held by a force that vanished as quickly as it had appeared.

Oh, I don't like this at all, she thought. I'm getting out. She focused her will and sent her mind winging back in the direction it had come from.

There's another!" said Codman.

"They're not death spasms," said Odette doubtfully. "They wouldn't be coming more frequently." The ripples were also increasing in intensity.

They're coming faster, thought Felicity. You have to get out. She gave a moment's thought to cutting away from the nerve and heading directly through the creature's flesh to her body. She wavered—it would get her out more quickly, but the prospect of getting lost was too frightening. Grimly, she pushed on, only to get caught by another freeze. This one lasted longer than any of the others, and she found herself counting desperately. One hippopotamus, two hippopotamus, three—free! She tore herself forward. Get out! Get out!

You know," said the voice of the tech, "we're seeing a dram—"

The intercom suddenly went silent. Even the background noise was cut off. Oh no, thought Odette.

"Hello?" she said. There was no answer. "Hey!" she shouted, and it must have carried through to the man ahead, because he looked back. He held up his gloved hand with his fingers spread.

Stop. Okay. But now what? thought Odette.

Then she felt movement against her feet. With difficulty, she looked back over her shoulder and saw the communication cables slithering down the tunnel toward them. They had been severed or torn free.

Oh no.

Almost there! Felicity thought. She coursed past the eyeball. Almost there!

But the walls slammed down again, and this time they didn't lift. Felicity's soul was caught in the corpse, trapped like a fly in amber.

23

Odette and the two Checquy scientists lay still, tense. More ripples had come, a continuous stream of them that set their air tanks bucking about in front of them. The tunnel walls were now shuddering violently, not keeping their shape but warping and flexing so that it was impossible to move along. Odette could practically feel her teeth rattling in her head.

Someone, she thought, please get me out of here! For a few heart-stopping moments, the roof of the tunnel pushed down on her head, and she cringed, fully expecting to be crushed. Then, mercifully, it lifted a few inches, but she still kept her head as low as she could.

All the team could do was lie flat and wait for things to get better or worse. To try and shout to one another would have put them at risk of biting through their own tongues as they were shaken about. Plus, we must conserve oxygen, Odette thought. Of course, she could shut down most of her breathing and go to sleep, but this was a situation where one needed to remain alert.

It was clear, however, that the movement was not limited to the tunnel. Something was sending quakes through the corpse.

Trapped.

Be calm, Felicity told herself. It went away before; it'll go away again. And this time, you bloody well get out of this cadaver and get yourself back in your own brain.

But it didn't go away. She could still remember the texture of the muscle and the flesh around her and the optic nerve beneath her. If she let herself think about it, she thought she could feel the tons and tons of corpse pressing down and through her.

And it didn't go away.

What if I'm stuck in here forever? she thought. What's happening on the surface? What if there's no one left to help get me out? I'm—I don't know what I am. Electromagnetism? Thoughts? A soul? What if my body dies? Will I die? Or will I be a ghost, locked in a monster? And at that point she lost it.

I want out! I want out! I want OUT!

If she'd been in her body, Felicity would have screamed or cried or torn at her hair and covered her face, but all she could do was think deafeningly loud, incoherent thoughts until she wore herself out and floated, numb, in the darkness.

The creature is alive! thought Odette. That must be it! The idea simultaneously thrilled and horrified her. Somehow, the creature had revived, and, presumably, it was not at all happy to find itself out of the water, strung up in a warehouse, and covered in a chemical skin with people crawling all over the inside and outside of it. It was an astounding development and would have been fascinating to observe from a suitable distance. At the moment, however, her first priority was trying to recall anything she had ever learned about blowholes.

Blowholes close, don't they? They must, to prevent water getting in. She'd already felt the flexing, but she wasn't certain if it would close on them completely. The Checquy will come, she told herself. We just need to wait. They'll kill it, and they'll come get us.

As long as they do it before our oxygen runs out.

And as long as it doesn't break out of its chains and somehow get to the ocean.

And as long as they don't try to kill it in some way that will also inconveniently kill us, like pumping electricity into it or blowing it up.

She thought for a moment of trying to use her spurs to see if her venom would slow the monster down. Not likely, though, she thought. It's much too big for my reservoirs to have any effect. In addition, in the back of her mind was the unappealing idea that she might need to use her octopus venom on herself if things got too horrible.

She felt a rush of air buffet her feet and pass over her. Is that them? she thought. She looked back hopefully, but there was neither a flicker of light nor a burly, cheerful Checquy Pawn with the Jaws of Life and a sippy cup of gin and tonic. Then she squinted. It was difficult to tell with all the shaking, but it seemed like there was less darkness behind her than there had been before. She caught a glimpse of movement and for a moment thought that something was heading down the tunnel toward them. Then she realized that there was no more tunnel. The walls were pinching themselves together, closing up behind them.

Get away! her brain ordered her. GO! She began writhing forward frantically, shoving her oxygen tank ahead of her until it bumped against Codman's feet.

"Move!" Odette screamed. "Move!" He looked back at her, and then beyond her. His eyes widened, and he began moving forward as fast as he could. It wasn't fast enough; there was no way it could be fast enough. Odette kept darting glances behind her, seeing that inexorable closing of the tube coming after them, gaining on them.

She scrabbled forward like a mad rat, shoving against the man in front of her; she watched the end of the tunnel come closer until it was an inch behind her and there was nowhere for her to go and so she flopped onto her back and heaved with all her strength against the cramped space, pulling her knees up to her chest to buy herself a little more room, an extra moment of not being crushed. Codman the zoologist was still crawling away.

And then the roof came down. It pressed on her knees, heavy but not unbearable, not yet. It was enveloping her, and then it was pushing down on her mask, pushing it against her head, pushing on the plastic, and the light on her helmet was smothered, and she heard the first, unmistakable crack of her mask, and she screamed.

Light!

It blossomed into Odette's eyes, which she hadn't even realized were still open. Through the spiderwebbed cracks of her mask, everything around her seemed to be glowing with a soft white light that lifted itself up and away, the pressure coming off her legs and body and face.

For one terrifying, beautiful moment, Odette thought she had died and left behind all the problems she had in the world. But she wasn't dead.

Instead, she found herself in a brand-new, totally incomprehensible situation with some brand-new, totally incomprehensible problems.

The plastic of her mask was riddled with cracks, and there was a little hole. The air that came in was all right, although it did smell like the inside of a fish shop. It's probably an extremely bad idea to take off the mask, she mused. But I can't see anything, and if I'm not poisoned by now, I'm not going to be. So she peeled off the mask to see what was what. She took in her surroundings, sniffed cautiously, and then shrugged. Well, okay.

The blowhole—that claustrophobic slimy tube in a dead animal—had changed. She got to her knees and looked around incredulously. The walls of skin and muscle had stretched around them so that the whole space was now twice as big.

Not big enough to stand up or even crouch in, but it was far less cramped, and patches of soft white light were coming out of the walls. The tunnel was still sealed just behind her, and it appeared to have sealed up ahead of them, beyond Wharton, but a hole had opened up in the floor between her and Codman. It angled down and curved away to who knew where. The slime that had been oozing out of the walls was getting sucked back in, so Odette and the two Checquy operatives lying on the floor were now the dirtiest things in a leathery beige pod.

The two Checquy operatives in question were sitting up, looking as bewildered as she felt. Hesitantly, they pulled off their masks, the light from their helmets no longer necessary in the glowing space. She scooched over to them, carefully avoiding the hole. The three of them established that all of them were all right, if somewhat puzzled to still be alive, and then, to the surprise of everyone, they had a brief, rather trembly group hug.

"Thoughts?" asked Codman once they'd broken the hug and the men were pretending it had never happened.

"I certainly didn't see this coming," said the marine biologist. "What's with the lights?"

"Some creatures do exhibit bioluminescent qualities," said Codman. He poked at an illuminated patch with interest, but the light seemed to be shining through the flesh from a distance.

"And why has it suddenly gotten so comfortable in here?" asked the marine biologist. No one had an answer. Of course, comfortable was a relative term. "Well, we can either stay here, or go down the hole." The pod rocked violently, and they all put their hands against the walls to steady themselves. It was clear that, even if the situation in their particular corner of the monster had undergone a sudden radical change for the better, the overall situation had not.

"I vote for going down the hole," said Odette.

"Any particular reason?" asked Codman.

"Can we assume the Checquy is going to kill this creature?" she asked.

"Yes," said the two men simultaneously.

"Messily?"

"Yes," said the two men simultaneously.

"Then I think it would be better to be closer to the middle," said Odette. "Put as much buffer as possible between us and the conflict." The Checquy operatives exchanged glances and then, as another shudder shuddered through, came to a decision.

"Let's go," said the two men simultaneously. They looked at each other warily. Odette could see the agreement pass between them to stop saying things simultaneously if they could at all help it. She led the way this time, slithering with relative ease down the hole. As they all wriggled along, they felt vibrations through the floor.

"I rather wish I knew what was happening outside," said Wharton as they descended. "If the creature makes a successful break for it and gets to the ocean..." They all paused—it was not a welcome thought.

"Our people will bend heaven and earth to keep it inside the hangar," said Codman decisively. "And there's certainly no way it could escape to the open sea. If worse came to worst, there's an entire military base that could be mobilized to prevent its escape."

"So, theoretically, if it got into the water, they would blast holes in it, and the ocean would come flooding in here?" asked Odette.

"Theoretically," said Codman. The three of them checked their oxygen tanks against the possibility that things might take a sudden turn for the wetter.

The tunnel wound down, coiling tightly. The patches of light were fairly regularly spaced, and, much to Odette's relief, the air remained relatively fresh, though still smelling exactly as if they were inside a giant sea monster. There was also another scent, much weaker, that she couldn't quite identify but that left her feeling uneasy.

As the three moved along, the movement of the creature periodically flung them against the walls or sent them skidding down the tunnel. It did not appear that things were calming down.

"I have good news and bad news," said Odette suddenly. "And I'm not letting you choose which you hear first." The two Checquy agents said nothing. "The good news is that we've come to the end of the tunnel."

"And?" said the zoologist. "Is the bad news that it's sealed?"

"Not...exactly," said Odette. She lay down on her stomach so that they could see past her. The hole had terminated in a large puckered ring of muscle that was clenched closed. There was a horrified silence. "It's an anus," said Odette flatly.

"Well, it's certainly a sphincter," said Codman after a moment.

"Do we try and force our way through?" asked the marine biologist, and the other two winced. "Don't look at me like that. You don't need to read anything into my saying that."

There is no way this conversation is not going to get horrible, thought Odette. *No situation is improved by the presence of a gigantic anus.*

At that moment, the gigantic anus in question trembled and, before anyone could react, unclenched. Everyone was braced for unspeakable developments, but the only thing that poured through was a roar of sound and light. They shrank back. It was horribly disorienting after the close dimness of the tunnel, as if someone had opened a portal to a football game or a rock concert. Odette squinted. There appeared to be a much larger space beyond—one that you could stand up in. On instinct, without opening the subject for debate, she scuttled through and into the larger space.

It wasn't nearly as bad as she'd thought it would be. Her eyes adjusted to the light. The noise was actually music, orchestral music that seemed to be coming out of the walls themselves. It was the sudden strong scent, however, that cut Odette's legs out from under her.

Oranges.

Oh God, how could this be?

She was on her knees, trembling, even as the other two came into the room and stood up. They looked at her oddly and then took in where they were. It was, very definitely, a room. This was not a space in a monster that just happened to be large enough to stand up in. The music and the warm glow put paid to that idea. The walls curved round, but the floor was flat. There were broad ledges and pedestals wide enough to sit or lie upon. One feature in particular drew their eyes.

On the other side of the room, facing the curving wall, was a chair. It appeared to have grown out of the floor and was the most unsettling piece of furniture ever seen. It was wide and high and made up of struts and ridges that were unmistakably bones, covered with padding that looked like muscle and skin. From the roof dangled a mass of tendrils, some fleshy and others glistening like plastic tubes. Their ends vanished behind the chair back.

On one side of the chair, a pale white hand hung down as if it had slipped from an armrest.

As they all took in the presence of that hand, Odette heard two sharp intakes of breath, one on either side of her, and the two Checquy men moved into fighting stances. She heard the snaps of their wrist knives springing out, and Codman held up his coring tool, its little blades spinning. The air around Pawn Wharton suddenly grew hot and dry.

"You needn't bother," Odette said dully. " 'S already dead." Underlying the smell of oranges and salt water was the unmistakable smell of rot. She got to her feet and led them around the chair. She knew what she would see. She'd seen it before.

It was a naked body, slumped and white. White nodules covered its bald head, and the tendrils from the ceiling seemed to have grown into the nodules as well as into points along its arms and spine. It didn't appear to have a gender. Odette peeled off a glove and reached out to the body's neck.

"Don't!" gasped Codman.

"It's fine," she said. The skin was cold, icy cold. She felt for a pulse, found none, and then lifted up the head. Memories flooded back, punching her in the heart: the last time she'd been with her friends, when they were torn out of her life. She snatched her hand away.

Felicity was not happy.

After a while, she'd calmed down. At first, she held out some hope that she would be freed, but after reaching four hundred thirty hippopotamuses, she'd given up counting. Then she'd thought things through and concluded that the creature had come back to life, and that was why she could no longer move. She hung there and brooded.

She had no doubt that the Checquy would kill it eventually, but the potential for disaster was still huge. There was no telling the kind of damage a creature that size could do. Scores of Checquy personnel were in the hangar—the casualties could be horrendous. Leliefeld, with her amazing ability to get into trouble, might get injured or killed.

And there was the stomach-turning knowledge that Felicity had left her own body right next to the creature. Of all the locations that lent themselves to getting one's catatonic body smeared into paste, right below a gigantic monster's chin seemed the riskiest.

I was so close! Felicity fretted. *I bet I'm not ten meters from my body, if it's still there and hasn't been crushed.* All she could do was resolve that once the opportunity arose, she would be ready to escape.

And then the sound came. Though she normally could not register sound with her powers, the vibrations hummed right through her, and she felt a sudden horror. She had heard that tune before.

Bruckner's Symphony no. 8.

So, this is a pilot?" asked Wharton warily. "This person was controlling the monster?"

"I think so," said Odette. "See these cords and tendrils? They

280

are like the material you find in spinal columns, but with a sort of transparent cuticle grown over them to protect them. I think they're plumbed into the monster's sensory organs and muscles. If there's a brain in this monster, then it would probably be completely subjugated."

"And without the pilot, the monster might have gone into some sort of coma or fugue," suggested Wharton.

"Just turned off," said Odette.

"But what is the pilot?" asked Codman. "Do you think it's a merperson?"

"Are there such things as merpeople?" asked Odette in fascination.

"We don't know," said Wharton. "No one in the Checquy has ever found one, but we know that the oceans are far less safe than people think." He was peering closely at the body. "I don't see any gills," he said. "Nothing on the neck, behind the ears, or on the abdomen."

"Would merpeople be listening to classical music?" asked Odette doubtfully.

"I expect they could listen to whatever they wanted," said the marine biologist. "But plumbing a stereo system into an animal seems a little odd."

Codman shrugged. "Just because something's supernatural or ab-human doesn't mean it doesn't have contact with our society. I know there was a flesh-eating ghoul in South Kensington that had an account at Fortnum's."

"Fortnum's was delivering human flesh?" asked Odette in fascinated horror.

"No, I think the ghoul got spices from them," said the zoologist. "And some conserves."

"This is a riveting aside," said Wharton, "but let's focus on where we are."

"You know," said Odette, "I don't think the monster is actually doing anything now."

"What?" asked the marine biologist.

"It's too stable in here," she said thoughtfully. "I mean, we can stand up without any difficulty. I don't care what kind of suspension system this thing has, if the monster were moving around, if it had broken free, we would be flat on our backs." She walked over to one of the ledges and pressed against it. "See how this gives? It's cushioning, for when it's moving."

"But all those tremors, and the opening of the tunnel? If it's not doing something, why did those happen?"

"Maybe it reacted to us coming in," said Odette. "Like automatic doors, or an automatic security system. I doubt that we came in the front door. Maybe the monster was reactivating, waking up, and now it's just idling."

"Waiting for instructions," said Wharton.

"Then maybe you should stop messing around with the dead pilot," suggested Codman. "In case he gives a death spasm and accidentally orders the monster to make a break for it."

"Do we know for sure he's dead?" asked the marine biologist. They both looked at Odette.

"I'm fairly certain," she said. "He's cold, has no discernible pulse, and smells of rotting meat."

"I dated someone like that once," remarked Codman. "A graduate student, a medieval historian."

"Do you think we should make sure he's dead?" asked the marine biologist. "Like slit his throat? Or cut off his head?" He held up his little government-issue chain saw.

"No!" exclaimed Odette. "Cutting off his head might send all sorts of insane signals to the beast."

"I suppose we couldn't just cut through those linkage cords, then?" asked Wharton regretfully. Odette was beginning to suspect that he really wanted to use his chain saw.

"Probably best not. But I have an idea. We don't know how long the Checquy will take to get us out. Presumably there's a way out of here that isn't the way we came in. So let's see if we can't find it." The men agreed, although Wharton looked a little disappointed. "We may have to cut the entrance open," she added, and he brightened visibly.

The search was not as easy as she'd hoped. The walls were

not smooth but rather ridged and corrugated, like the folds of a brain. They were crisscrossed with seams and lines, any of which might indicate an exit or might simply be a quirk of some extremely quirky architecture. The anus through which they had entered had sealed into a tight little knot, and she noted there were several identical little knots around the room.

The problem is that they might lead anywhere, she thought grimly. I don't want to go into the tunnel that leads to the large intestine. Although it would lead out eventually, I suppose, but it wouldn't be pleasant for anyone. There was, of course, always the possibility of Wharton just cutting their way out, but she wasn't at all certain how the creature might react to having various large holes cut through it. And who knows where else the tunnels might lead us? A creature like this, we could end up opening a sac of biological acid or venom or something. Plus, this thing is so big that the chain saw would probably run out of juice long before we got all the way out. Still, she continued to search.

She sat down gingerly on one of the ledges and felt it settle obligingly under her, as if it were the offspring of a water bed and a beanbag. She patted it absently. Think about this logically. Where would you put the entrance to a cockpit? At the far end from the pilot, she decided. That was how it was on airplanes. And since they were situated, as far as she could tell, in the lower back half of the creature, then the far side would be closest to the creature's hindquarters. She swiveled to look at the rear.

And then the world went insane.

Or at least tipped forty-five degrees to the left.

Odette felt somewhat vindicated, since the shelf-thing held on to her, building up a little ledge and tilting itself so that she wasn't flung against the wall. The two Checquy men, however, let out startled squawks as they were sent flying across the chamber.

"What did you do?" Odette yelled at the marine biologist. She guessed that he had prodded at the white body and prompted some sort of response.

"Nothing! What did you do?"

"I didn't do anything!" As one, they looked at Codman, who had gotten wedged upside down in a corner.

"I don't like this sort of thing!" shouted the zoologist. "This is why I studied evolution, so I could do all my work in the lab!" Odette had a tart response ready, but she didn't get to use it because the creature suddenly shifted in the other direction and began a series of undulations that prevented any of them from standing up.

"Should I try and kill the pilot?" shouted the marine biologist. He held up his chain saw.

"No!" shouted Odette and Codman simultaneously. Having someone prancing around with an active chain saw while the ground shifted seemed spectacularly unwise.

"Just hang on to something and try to lie still," said Codman. "They'll kill it soon—listen!"

Even through many meters of living animal, they could hear sounds—extremely peculiar sounds that Odette assumed were the Checquy soldiers limbering up their powers and engaging in battle. There was a muffled explosion somewhere, and a moment later a wave of blinding yellow light swept through the place. It set the walls and floors sizzling and smoking. Odette's own skin flared with a sudden flash of pain, and she realized that she was screaming along with the scientists. No! Stop it! The light died away. The three of them looked at one another in horror. Their skins glistened with burns.

That must have been the Checquy, thought Odette weakly. I've no doubt they can kill this thing. At least, not much doubt. But can they kill it without killing us?

Something was happening. Felicity had been mentally squatting in the darkness, composing her report to Rook Thomas and trying to ignore the little voice in her mind pointing out that she might never get to make it. Then she felt the shifting of the muscles that she was currently occupying. A great deal of movement was occurring.

Be ready, she thought. Not only were the muscles shifting back and forth, but they periodically gave violent shudders. That's got to be the Checquy. They're attacking it. There was a tremendous jolt, and then the walls around her were gone.

Now! Felicity burst away, down, out of the monster onto the concrete floor of the hangar. Free! She coursed to the spot where the observation platform had been set up.

Get in my body.

Get in my body.

Get in my body.

Where in the hell is my body? She didn't find it. All she found was the shattered remnants of the pavilion. Cringing mentally, she gingerly scanned the area for any traces of her corpse.

Nothing.

What's happened? she thought madly. For a ridiculous moment, she wondered if she'd been mistaken about the location. I've gotten lost. But, no, the torn plastic of the pavilion covered the crushed wreckage of the platform and that damn chair. It's gone! They've gone! I've gone! she thought in horrified disbelief.

They took my body. She set out to search the gigantic hangar.

This really is a shitty day.

Oh God, I can't take any more.

Again and again, that searing yellow light swept through the chamber. Again and again, the three of them shrieked and burned. Even the white corpse in the chair was charring, filling the room with a smell that was even worse than the reek of the blackening walls. The miasma of burning rotten meat had prompted the marine biologist and the zoologist both to throw up everything they'd ever eaten in their lives, and it was only because Odette had sealed off her stomach that she didn't join in the festivities.

When smoke filled the chamber, they all yanked their masks on, only for Odette to find that her faceplate had completely shattered. Now the smoke was burning her lungs and eyes. If she tried to suspend her breathing, she would go into a deep sleep, but she knew that the continued tumbling of the chamber and the next burning wave of light would rouse her and her breathing would kick in again.

I think I'm going to die, she thought faintly. Another wave of the light burned across them. But apparently not soon enough. She thought of the venom in her spurs and wondered if it would be wrong to kill herself now.

The yellow light came again, and she could feel her skin scorching. Is this enough pain? And then it passed. No one could blame me, surely. A little scratch or jab with the octopus venom and I could slip away. No more hurt, no more sorrow, no more fear. But then she looked at the two men across the room. She realized, to her dull surprise, that she couldn't desert them by dying and taking the easy way out. And she couldn't kill them. Even if I did it with their permission, if the Checquy found my venom had killed them, it would destroy the negotiations.

There's nothing I can do.

The light flared through again, and she closed her eyes and burned.

24

All Odette knew was the hurt. She was burning inside and out, and she could only lie there, absorb the pain, and wait to die. She didn't think except to wearily acknowledge when something new burned her. She didn't know if the two men were still alive. The room had stopped moving, but still the occasional wave of yellow light washed through or a concussion throbbed in the floor.

A tremendous report shuddered through the chamber inside

the monster, and with an effort, Odette opened her eyes. She saw the walls flex down and down and down. They crumpled and then they tore with a sound that turned her stomach. Fluids leaked in, but then so did a distant flash of daylight. There was the wet, crackling sound of burned meat tearing apart, and then loops of rope poured into the chamber through a tear from above. A man abseiled down and wrinkled his nose.

"Hullo, the three of you! Sorry about the delay, took us quite a bit of work to kill the beastie. We had to call in some naval backup. This whole thing has been rather tedious, really." He looked at the three of them. They stared up at him, dazed. Their suits were smoking, and their exposed faces were burned and crimson. "Been through the wars a bit, eh? I expect you could all do with a draft of something alcoholic." He spoke into his headset. "I have our people, all looking very bad indeed."

I'm sorry, but you can't co—ow! Ow!" Odette opened her eyes just in time to see Pawn Clements grab the doctor by his tie and his belt and swing him smoothly out the door and into the hallway while at the same time relieving him of his clipboard. She kicked the door shut behind her and advanced on the bed. At no time had the Pawn taken her horrified eyes off Odette.

"Sweet bloody hell!" Clements breathed. She sounded utterly distraught. "Oh Christ, look at your face!" Since this maneuver was not possible, Odette settled for staring wide-eyed at the deeply upset Pawn. The other woman was distinctly disheveled and for some reason was dressed in a peculiarly sheer set of coveralls through which her underwear could be seen. Her hair had come partially out of its braid, her face was red, and she was breathing heavily. It was clear that she had just sprinted to the medical facility from somewhere.

"Look at your poor hands!" moaned the Pawn. Odette brought them up with difficulty. She had to concede that they did not look good. They were red, raw, and weeping and had been slathered in antiseptic cream. "Are you in a lot of pain?"

Odette opened her mouth to say something, but the Pawn was flipping through her chart.

" 'Burns, smoke inhalation, possible toxic exposure'!" Clements read aloud. "Jesus, they unleashed Pawn Mnookin on that thing. With that radiation of hers, this could actually be classified as a war crime." The Pawn looked up, aghast. "Are you all right? How do you feel?" Odette felt the rush of happiness that comes when someone is concerned for you.

"I don't know what the hell you could possibly have been thinking," Clements continued without waiting for an answer. "Do you have any idea how much trouble I'm going to get into for this?" Odette's rush of happiness departed abruptly, replaced by the rush of distress that comes when someone is about to tear into you. "I can't believe your selfishness! I'm responsible for your safety, my career is on the line, and the first time I turn my back, you go crawling into a fucking monster? Are you mad? Or is this just a case of suicidal stupidity?"

"I thought that since the other scientists were going in—" Odette started.

"The other scientists were doing it, so you thought you would? What are you, thirteen?" shouted Clements. "The other scientists are expendable. The other scientists aren't diplomatic envoys. The other scientists aren't supposed to go to the country with their senior delegates as guests of the Lord and Lady this weekend. Now look at you! You're going to be in hospital for days—maybe weeks!"

"Well, actually—" began Odette.

"And this could do unbelievable harm to the negotiations," continued Clements. "Do you think something like this sends a good message? 'Yes, we have a member of your family under government protection and she has just been burned, crushed, and poisoned inside a gigantic porpoise.' " She paused, apparently overcome by Odette's idiocy. "Well, I can tell you that that Fielding woman is going to regret ever meeting you."

"You can't punish her! It was my idea to go in there!" protested Odette.

"Yes, and now we've established that you can't be trusted to keep yourself safe. Your decision-making privileges have been revoked. You will be transferred to the Apex hospital, and I will sit in a corner of your room, reading fashion magazines and making sure you don't accidentally stab yourself in the eye with your plastic hospital spork."

Right, that does it!

"You know what?" said Odette, incensed. "You can just shut the fuck up."

"I beg your pardon?" said Clements in a dangerous voice.

"Shut. Up. You are not my boss, and you are not my mother. Yes, if I ever get into the Checquy, it is possible that you will outrank me in some bullshit chess-related pecking order. Although I doubt it, because I can sew a man's head back on and he will live if I get to him in time, while your main qualification is apparently that you can be a real bitch!"

"Do you think I won't beat the shit out of someone just because I'm responsible for her safety and she is suffering from serious burns and"—Clements looked down at the clipboard—"possible internal cookage?"

"I think you won't. Because at the moment, I am the VIP, and you are...my entourage."

"Your entourage?" repeated Clements. Odette could practically feel the heat of her outrage. "Your entourage?"

I may have made a tremendous error here, Odette thought, but I'll get my hits in before she destroys me. She pushed on recklessly.

"Yes," said Odette. "My entourage. And you don't have to worry about the burns. All I need is a night or two in a bath full of some chemicals I have back at the hotel, and I'll come out looking like I've just had some sunburn. So you'll have to give up on your hospital scenario. Sorry about the fashion mags," she added tartly.

"I am not your servant," said Clements through gritted teeth. "I'm here to protect you. And apparently I need to be protecting you from your own moronitude. Let me explain something to you:

You don't need to seek out danger. Thanks to your inspired activities at the Apex, people — people with supernatural abilities — already hate you. Before, they hated the idea of you, and now you go and—" She took a deep breath. "If you do anything like this ever again and I manage to keep you alive, I will proceed to break your ankles." She paused for a moment. "And if you have some sort of weird ankle-based abilities that preclude that, I will simply put a collar and a leash on you."

Ah, Odette, come in," said Grootvader Ernst without looking up. He was seated at the conference table in his suite, a mass of papers laid out before him. A new executive assistant — a replacement for the unfortunate Anabella — was seated a little farther down, looking distinctly nervous at her new responsibilities. *I wonder if she heard what happened to her predecessor,* thought Odette. "You're back earlier than I anticipated."

"They helicoptered us in from Portsmouth," said Odette sourly.

"That's nice. Ria, once you've purchased the train tickets, you can e-mail them to the Chimerae's phones." From memory, he wrote out a list of numbers with a fountain pen. "And they will need accommodations in London."

"Separate rooms?" asked the EA. "Separate locations?"

"No, get them a single hotel room, as central as possible," said Ernst. "One bed. They each only need two or three hours of sleep in a twenty-four-hour period, so they can sleep in shifts. The rest of the time, I want them out in the city, tracking down the targets." He slid a piece of paper covered in his distinctive copperplate handwriting across to Ria. "Here are the details of the accounts to use and the identity for which the booking should be made."

"Yes, sir," said the woman, who appeared to be about the age of Odette's mother. She opened her laptop and began typing away.

"Grootvader, I need to talk to you."

"Of course, sit down," said Ernst. "Give me a moment, we're just about to activate the Chimerae."

"That's one of the things I need to talk to you about, you see—" She was cut off by Marie, who entered the room with a large bottle of water tucked under each arm and one in each hand.

"Hello, Odette," she said. "You're back early. Why are you wearing that insane hat?" Ernst looked up briefly from his papers and raised an eyebrow.

"That hat is insane," he agreed. The chapeau in question was made of an iridescent turquoise straw and had a dense black veil and a brim wide enough to shelter Odette and three other people from the burning rays of the sun (which was not shining that day).

"The Checquy gave it to me," said Odette. "They felt I needed a way to conceal my face from guests in the hotel."

"Well, that was very thoughtful of them," said Ernst absently.

"I get the sense that you're not listening to me," said Odette.

"I'm listening to you, 'Dette," said Marie. She awkwardly deposited her bottles on the table, sat down, lifted one to her lips, and began taking measured gulps, but some still spilled down her mouth onto her designer suit. After a few moments, she asked, "Why do they want you to conceal your face?"

"Because I look like I got microwaved!" exclaimed Odette, pulling off the hat. She was well aware that her face would not have launched a thousand ships—unless they were trying to get away from the sight of her. The cream the Checquy had given her did a good deal to deaden the pain and keep things sterile, but it glistened on her burns and made them look even worse. The EA gave a little gasp, but Ernst and Marie seemed curiously unmoved. He continued his writing, and Marie continued to chug down water like a large man back from a run on a summer's day. "I hope I don't have to explain to you that this is not what I looked like when I left this morning."

"We were notified of what happened," said Marie. "We were going to talk about it afterward. Has Marcel looked at you yet?"

"No, he's still at Apex House," said Odette.

"Well, you're a doctor. Tell us, are you going to die?"

"No," said Odette sullenly. She could see where this was going.

"Will you be crippled in some way?"

"No."

"Are you going to be permanently disfigured?"

"No."

"Then stop complaining," said Marie. "Yes, you look like something out of Italian cuisine, but you'll get over it."

"I had a terrible experience!" said Odette petulantly. "I might have mental trauma."

"No such thing," said Ernst dismissively without even looking up from his papers. "It's just people being soft."

"Soft? Did you hear what happened to me?"

"Yes," said Marie. "You went prospecting in a whale or something, and it turned out not to be dead."

"It wasn't a whale," said Odette. "It was a creature unlike anything I've seen before. Huge."

"That sounds fascinating," said Marie, taking a break from her swilling.

"What was particularly interesting was the fact that in the middle of it was a space with a chair containing a dead naked person with protruding head nodules and pallid white skin."

At this revelation, Marie choked and spat a torrent of water across the table and onto Ernst.

"I'm not going to lie to you," said Odette, "that reaction was incredibly satisfying."

"An...Antagonist?" Marie coughed.

"Yes."

"Do the members of the Checquy understand the nature of their discovery?" asked Ernst intently.

"No, they have no idea," said Odette. "They were talking about mermen."

"Mermen?" repeated Ernst blankly. "Are there such things?"

"No one knows," said Odette. "But the possibility means they'll be looking at this very closely. Grootvader, you have to tell them about the attacks."

"Out of the question," said Ernst. He looked down at his papers and made an irritated sound. The deluge of water from Marie had smeared his notes. He began writing them out again.

"The Antagonists are more powerful and have more resources than we realized," said Odette. "That creature must be how they entered the country, and I've never seen anything like it."

"We have," said Ernst grimly.

"You knew the Antagonists had something like this? Of course you did! You have to tell the Checquy!"

"This problem will be solved shortly," said Marie.

"Are you sure?" asked Odette. "Because at the moment, things are set to become very bad very soon. And why are you drinking like you're a fat person at a rave?"

"I have to make a secure connection to the Chimerae in Wales," said Marie before swigging down the last of the third bottle and reaching for the final one. "It's massively dehydrating."

"I didn't know you had communication implants," said Odette, surprised. The Grafters could install devices that allowed the user to connect to the World Wide Web with his or her mind. Such devices tended to be limited to executive assistants, aides, and bodyguards because they took up so much space in people's bodies. Older, more senior Grafters—those who were important enough to have executive assistants, aides, and bodyguards—were accustomed to conducting their long-distance conversations through the mouths of their entourages. The support staff channeled communications, acting as untraceable speakerphones. "With your combat abilities, how do you have room?"

"Marcel installed them," said Marie. "They're not standard, and they're not complete. This is why I have to drink my own body weight before I do this."

"What's the phone number?" asked Odette curiously.

"I'm not telling you that," said Marie. "I don't want you drunk-dialing my brain at four in the morning because you've lost your purse and need a ride home."

"I only did that once," said Odette.

"You were in Germany, I was in Belgium," said Marie.

"And I was very grateful. We all were." She shut up then. It just happens, she thought. I forget for a moment about everything I've lost, everyone I've lost, and then a simple comment brings it all back.

"I expect seeing that body in the whale was hard," said Marie quietly. She put her hand on Odette's shoulder. "It must have brought back some very painful memories."

"Just of the worst day of my life." Odette shrugged. She sighed. "Anyway, I thought you should know about the creature and the...the Antagonist."

"Thank you," said Marie. "We'll talk about it later." She chuckled. "Your bodyguard must have had a fit."

"She was not best pleased. And that reminds me," said Odette. "I want a different bodyguard."

"Why?" asked Marie.

"Because Felicity Clements is a bitch. She's rude, she's domineering, and I think she's a psychopath. I don't want to have to deal with her, and I don't want her in my suite. If I must have a bodyguard, can you please ask the Checquy for a new one?"

"I don't think that's a good idea," said Ernst. "The Checquy could take it as an insult."

"Good!" shouted Odette. "She threatened to break my ankles!"

"Oh, we've all wanted to break your ankles at some point or another," said Marie dismissively. "Or at least your jaw." Odette found herself making a peculiar gobbling sound of outrage.

"If she actually does break your ankles, come back here and talk to me," said Ernst, returning to his papers. He paused and thought for a moment. "Well, give me a call, anyway."

So your brain was inside a monster," said Alessio in fascination.

"My mind, not my brain," said Felicity. "They didn't saw open my skull or anything."

"And then the monster came alive."

"Yes. They moved my body while I was out," said the Pawn. "Apparently, they were worried that the beast might crush the observation pavilion."

"And did it?" asked Alessio.

"Oh, sure," said Felicity. She sat back in her chair and closed her eyes. "Twenty seconds after they got my body out of there, the whole structure was crushed like an egg. The attending doctor's leg was broken. Then the troops sliced off the creature's lower jaw with my mind in it. After the flesh died and I could get out, I tried to get back to my body, but all I could find were the shattered remnants of the pavilion." Without opening her eyes, she took a sip of Talisker 12. "If I'd had access to my heart, I would have had a heart attack."

The memory of that frantic mental scrabbling through the hangar hung in her head: The fear that she would find her body crushed and ruined. The knowledge that if she had found her corpse, she would have slid back into it, willingly snuffing out her spirit rather than existing as a ghost. Is that something to be ashamed of?

"Eventually I found myself, obviously, but it took a while. I opened my eyes to find my face completely shellacked with my own drool, and a huge hulking Irishman standing over me with a machete at my throat."

"What did you do?"

"I broke his nose," said Felicity tiredly.

"Wow."

"Hmm. It's not as great as it sounds. For one thing, he was the one who'd carried my body to safety, which makes me look pretty ungrateful. And for another, it made everyone think that I'd come back possessed by the vengeful spirit of a whale-monster. I had to talk very fast to persuade them otherwise."

"And now you have to write up a report for your superiors," said Alessio.

"Yup."

"So don't you think you should stop drinking?"

At this, Felicity opened her eyes. She had a wry, withering

remark to make, but then the door slammed open. Leliefeld stalked in, clutching her huge hat. She didn't look at Alessio or Felicity, just stomped across the suite to the bedroom. They heard two more doors slam, and then the distant sound of the bath running.

"I think now is the perfect time to be drinking," said Felicity.

Odette put the toilet seat down and made a mental note to slap Alessio on the back of the head when next she got the chance. Then she put the lid down, sat, and listened to the roar of water pouring into the tub. The room filled with steam and the smell of jasmine. On the vanity was a photo of her and her friends, all dressed up to attend a wedding. She thought of that white corpse she'd seen in the belly of the beast. All of the memories that she spent every day deliberately not recalling came back to her. The horror, the loss. And then, very carefully, so as not to worsen her wounded skin, she put her face in her hands and began to weep.

25

When she awoke in the morning, Odette felt plain awful. She levered herself out of the tub, listlessly washed the slime off in the shower, and wandered out into the living room of the suite, only to find Clements engaged in some weaponized version of yoga on the carpet in front of the television. The Pawn looked up from under her own left armpit.

"Oh, you're up," said Clements. Odette shrugged. With a grunt, the Pawn unbraided her left arm and right leg from each other and rolled up onto her feet. She peered at Odette.

"You weren't kidding about that stuff in your tub," she said appreciatively. "You look like you fell asleep on the beach in Tahiti, but that's it. I don't suppose the two men who were in the beast with you can use it?"

"You have to have had inoculations for two years and take supplements every day," said Odette dully. "Otherwise, your skin comes off in big flakes."

"Figures," said Clements.

"Where's Alessio?" The Pawn looked at her oddly. "What?"

"He's off with the school group," said Clements. "It's three in the afternoon."

"Oh," said Odette. "What am I supposed to do today?"

"Nothing." Clements shrugged. "It's Saturday, so there're no meetings scheduled. You can just stay in."

"You don't have anything to do?"

"I've been having fun with room service," said Clements. "I had a lunch composed entirely of parfaits."

"Well, I don't want to stay in today," said Odette.

"All right," said Clements, raising an eyebrow. "What do you want to do?"

"I want to do something touristy. From the moment I got off the plane, they've been warning us that we couldn't go out. Well, I have a bodyguard, I should be safe, so I'm going out."

"You don't have the best track record when it comes to 'should be safe,'" pointed out Clements. "You managed to bring down spectral wrath upon yourself whilst sitting in a conference room. But fine, where do you want to go?"

"What's your favorite thing to do in London?" asked Odette.

"It turns out that I really like watching repeats of forensic crime dramas and eating parfaits in a five-star hotel."

"Let's go to St. Paul's Cathedral," said Odette. "Alessio's school group got to go there, and I really want to see it."

"Sure," said Clements. "I haven't been there since primary school. It's very cool. Any particular reason you want to go there?"

"No," lied Odette.

St. Paul's Cathedral stood before them, looking as if it did not quite belong in the world. It was as if it had been cut-and-pasted into the city just to make the surrounding buildings look tacky. Odette gazed up the steps, ignoring the lounging students, tracing the columns up to more columns, a gorgeously carved pediment, and then, soaring up into an unexpectedly blue sky, the dome.

You were so right, Pim, thought Odette. It is glorious. She relaxed a little. All the things in my life are just temporary, she thought. This building will be standing long after me and all my ridiculous problems are gone. It was both a comforting thought and a sort of depressing one.

Inside the cathedral, instead of the hushed sound of reverent visitors, the women heard an orchestra that was either tuning up or playing an extremely modern piece of music. A small notice board advised everyone that the Orchestra and Choir of Greater Juster Norton would be performing that evening and apologized for any disruption caused by the rehearsal. The two women walked down to the nave, beneath the gargantuan arches and the soaring ceilings.

In the center, under the dome, the orchestra sat on a broad platform. The musicians were tootling their horns or frowning as they drew their bows across their strings, making all those little sounds that constitute foreplay in the orchestral world. Singers—Odette and Felicity presumed they were singers—were sitting about reading books or peering at their phones. None of them were staring open-mouthed at the magnificent spectacle above them, which struck Odette as astounding, since that was all she could do.

The dome of the cathedral hung in the air, crowning at a height of sixty-five meters. A ring of windows beneath the dome filled the space with light, and its inner surface had been cunningly painted so that it seemed to be lined with gigantic sculptures.

"Ooh," she said, despite herself. She nudged Clements and pointed up to the balcony that ringed the base of the dome. "That's the Whispering Gallery."

"What?" asked Clements over the sound of the orchestra.

Oh, for God's sake.

"That's the Whispering Gallery," Odette said, slightly more loudly. "If you go up there and whisper to the wall, the curve carries your voice around so that someone on the other side can hear you."

"I vaguely recall that."

"You see the top of the dome?"

"Uh, yes," said Clements. "It's right above us."

"There's a tiny little window cut there, and if you climb up, you can look down through it to the floor."

"Is it vomit-proof?" asked Clements. "Because I can imagine nothing that would be more likely to cause vertigo than doing what you just described, and if you throw up on someone from that height, your vomit would literally cut him in half."

"I—I don't think that's the case," said Odette.

"You want to climb it, don't you?" asked Clements. Odette nodded. "Why?"

"Because it's there. And it's cool."

"Well, you can't." Odette looked at her. "Not unless you tell me the truth about why you wanted to come here." The Pawn did not give the impression of budging on this point.

"Fine," said Odette finally. "I like cathedrals. I used to go visit them with someone."

"Your boyfriend Pim," said Clements. Odette stared at her in shock. "I read your file."

"Oh. It's in my file?"

"And Alessio talked."

"That little shit!" exclaimed Odette, then looked around guiltily. Even with the orchestra doing their thing, several cathedral-goers had heard her. She made an apologetic face.

"Marcel too," said Clements. "I'm sorry for your loss." It sounded like an extremely rehearsed phrase, straight out of The Pawn's Handbook for Normal Social Interactions.

Odette resisted the obnoxious urge to say that it wasn't Clements's fault. "Thank you," she said reluctantly. "Anyway, we did all the major cathedrals in Europe and always wanted to go to St. Paul's together." And instead I'm here with you. "Happy?"

"Fine, we can go up," said Clements. "But I'm not whispering any sweet nothings to you."

It was not as if they could have done any whispering to each other anyway. Once they had climbed the spiraling, far-too-broad-and-shallow stairs, they came to the balcony of the Whispering Gallery, where there were a number of visitors. Some were seated on the bench that circled the gallery, staring up at the dome. Some were standing at the iron balustrade (which seemed far too flimsy to Odette), looking down at the orchestra below. Others were walking around gingerly to the exit on the other side of the gallery. One or two could be seen whispering fruitlessly to the wall, their voices drowned out by the sound of the orchestra.

There were also several children trotting fearlessly around, apparently unconcerned that the balustrade could snap away at any moment, allowing gravity to drag them over the edge and send them plummeting, screaming, into the orchestra far below.

Remember, Odette told herself, you may be able to imagine the falls with exquisite, painful detail, but you can cope with heights. You climbed the outside of the Cologne Cathedral. Still, she took a seat on the bench, very close to the entrance. Clements walked along a little ways and then sat herself down. Odette leaned back against the wall and closed her eyes.

Then, delightfully, the noise of the orchestra below faded away. Presumably, they were all tuned up. The natural sounds of a cathedral appeared—the footsteps of visitors, the hushed voices, the breath of the building. After a few moments, the tourists realized their opportunity, and a susurrus of whispers curved around the gallery. Odette could half catch words from the other side of the balcony.

"—ello?"

"Can you hear—"

"—ispering to the—"

"Shall we go up—"

"Odette."

She opened her eyes and looked to the left. Clements was still sitting there, but she was leaning forward, looking at her phone, and very definitely not whispering to the wall. Did I imagine it? she wondered. She looked about the gallery. There were many people of all ages with their faces by the wall, but from the little she could see, none were familiar. Certainly, they all looked perfectly normal, not a white, rubbery-skinned bald person among them. She leaned back carefully.

"Odette, you can hear me." The voice sighed in her ear. It wasn't a question, but despite herself, she nodded slightly. "We've been watching you. We saw you through that secretary's eyes." She felt her mouth twist at the memory of Anabella, possessed at that meeting. "We are coming for you. Not today, but soon."

Odette felt a tremor in her heart, and even she didn't know what emotion she felt. Fear? Rage? Sorrow? She looked down to see that her spurs had slid out of her wrists without her realizing it. Thankfully, no one had noticed, and with an effort, she retracted them. Then, slowly, she turned her head and put her cheek against the wall. She had no idea if her words would get lost in all the murmurs of the visitors or if the owner of that voice could pluck her utterances out as easily as he had cast his message into her ear.

"I warn you," she whispered to the wall, sending her words out to mingle in the dome, "that is a very bad idea. We don't want war. You should leave this place, leave this country. Run away."

If the voice came back with an answer, she didn't hear it, because below them, the orchestra and choir chose that moment to burst into "O Fortuna" from Carmina Burana, and all the whispers were obliterated.

What do I do now? she thought. Should I call Marie? She shied away from the idea. Should I try and identify them, maybe get a picture?

"Miss Leliefeld?" a voice next to her asked, and Odette jumped. It was, of course, Clements. The Pawn jerked her thumb in the direction of the exit and raised her eyebrows questioningly. Odette nodded, and they headed over. Odette, taking care to keep a hand on the balustrade, examined every person they passed. It was useless. Not only were there no people with paper-white skin or nodule-concealing hats that she could see, but there was still half of the gallery that she didn't get a look at. I can't very well insist we make a full circuit, thought Odette. Plus, the whisperer may have left already.

"Miss Leliefeld, did you want to climb to the top of the dome?" Clements asked just outside the gallery exit. Odette didn't answer for several moments. She stood with her eyes closed, ignoring the put-upon sigh and the presumably rolled eyes of the Pawn. She had caught the telltale smell of oranges. It was faint—so faint that no one without exquisitely hand-tuned olfactory senses could have caught it—but unmistakable, and it went down the stairs.

"Let's go," said Odette firmly, opening her eyes. "I'm a bit hungry." The Pawn looked surprised but agreed. Odette led the way, scurrying down the stairs far more quickly than was safe. The startled Clements hurried behind her, obviously too proud to tell her to slow down. They dodged past cautiously slow groups of descending tourists, and Odette mentally cursed her heeled shoes, which were exactly the wrong shape for running down spiraling staircases.

They burst onto the main floor of the cathedral, where crowds of people were meandering about, listening to the music and peering at the curiosities of the cathedral. Odette looked around wildly and saw nothing that stood out. No man in all-enshrouding clothes hurrying away. No civilians staring bewildered in the direction of someone who'd just shoved through them. The scent of oranges was still there in the air, but fainter, rapidly getting washed out by the maelstrom of odors that seeped out of a couple hundred tourists at the end of the day.

"So, was there a specific restaurant you wa—hey!" exclaimed Clements as Odette took off again. She pushed through the crowds, determined to follow the trail as long as she could.

The scent wove back and forth across the nave, detoured down into the crypt, then came up again.

"What are you doing?" asked Clements behind her, but Odette ignored her. She had her phone ready in her hands, the camera function all cued up so she could get, if nothing else, a shot of the Antagonist. But the scent grew fainter, and the renewed blare of the orchestra and the motion of the crowds made it all worse, and soon Odette could not be sure if she was following something real or just her imagination.

Finally, though, she came to a small side door, tucked away behind a column. It was obviously not for use by the public, but when she bent close to the handle, there was the unmistakable tang of oranges on it.

"Are you trying to lose me?" asked Clements as she caught up. "Even after our little talk yesterday?"

"No," said Odette distractedly. She started to open the door, and Clements made a noise of objection. Odette was half ready for an alarm to go off, but the door opened silently, and no outraged priests appeared to ask what on earth she thought she was doing.

The door led outside to a square that scores of people were crisscrossing on their way to a thousand different destinations, all of them leaving clouds of scent in their wake. The wind was blowing, completely and indisputably dissipating any chance of tracking the owner of the voice from the Whispering Gallery. Odette stared at the vista in shock. She'd been so intent on the hunt that it seemed impossible it was suddenly over, suddenly unsuccessful.

"See someone you knew?" said Clements behind her.

"What?"

"Someone you wanted to say hello to?" The Pawn's voice was cold, dangerous.

"No!"

"Indeed," said the Pawn. The disbelief in her voice was palpable. "Lucky for you, you were never out of my sight." Odette could almost feel the leash tightening around her neck.

"So...lunch?" said Clements acidly.

26

Bart Vanderhaegen of the Chimerae stood across from the building that had, before the agonizing deaths of sixteen people, been a charming little Italian restaurant. Now, it was a charming little crime scene that people walked by quickly and talked about in hushed voices. A confusing jumble of warning signs were plastered over the padlocked door. Some were from the police, some from Public Health England, some from the Food Standards Agency. There were skulls and crossbones, and that pointy biological-hazard symbol, and the blue-and-white checkerboard of the Metropolitan Police. All of them combined suggested, very forcefully, that this was not a place you wanted to enter.

Bart turned to his comrade Sander. Where Bart was tall and dark, Sander was slim and pale, with a head that seemed slightly too big for his body. They had both been awoken the evening before when their sleeping sacs split open and poured them onto the floor of a Cardiff flat. It hadn't been pleasant, especially since it had happened to sixteen other soldiers who had also been sleeping, curled up and peacefully adhered to the same ceiling.

There was the usual confusion that ensues when people are woken up abruptly, exacerbated by the fact that these particular people were all trained fighters with the combat instincts of pumas and they had just been dropped, naked and covered in a milky syrup, onto the ground from a height of several meters. If someone had been standing by with a camera, it would have made for an Internet video that was simultaneously the best choreographed, the most confusing, and the least erotic naked group fight scene in the history of the world. The fight had lasted for about thirty seconds before a voice testily cleared its throat in all their minds.

"Ahem." They froze, although they did not necessarily let go of any heads that were locked in their armpits or throats that were clenched in their hands. "You are all Chimerae." Sheepishly, they all released their grips and stood to attention, some of them slipping slightly in the slime on the floor. Now that it had been pointed out and everyone had calmed down, they did all recognize one another.

The voice gave the passwords that identified it as belonging to Marie Lemaier, a representative of Graaf Ernst van Suchtlen. She informed them that they had all been asleep for two years and four months. The good news was that they were not being called forth to wage a guerrilla war against the Checquy. (When they were put under, that had been a distinct possibility.) Rather, negotiations for peace with the Checquy were under way.

"There is a problem, however," said Marie's voice. She went on to explain the situation and ordered the gathered Chimerae to come to London (once they'd cleaned themselves off and put on some clothes) and bend all their efforts to tracking down and obliterating these Antagonists. She made it especially clear that, above all, the Chimerae must avoid the notice of the Checquy. Other instructions were given, and the soldiers snapped into action.

A rota was worked out so that the flat's single shower could be used as efficiently as possible. The first Chimera to emerge from the shower, an enormous man named Jan Kamphuis, was assigned the task of preparing breakfast for the others. He broke open trunks filled with a shiny agar and peeled away the gelatin to reveal perfectly preserved ingredients. Shortly, he was serving up bacon, eggs, waffles, and (him being Dutch) toast with chocolate sprinkles.

Over the course of the night, all eighteen men and women were showered, clothed, fed, and watered. They decrypted and reviewed the files that were e-mailed to their brains and stretched out the kinks that came from being in the fetal position for months. They were issued travel and identification documents, corporate credit cards, and, thanks to a little neurolinguistic alteration, new English accents from all around the country. Four of them were provided with firearms, and everyone had two mobile telephones.

At six in the morning, having established that there was no one watching, the Chimerae filed out of the flat in one continuous stream. They split up into smaller groups, made their way to either Cardiff Central Station or one of various car-rental offices, and then proceeded to London. From there, they spread out into the city seeking traces of their quarry. At St. Pancras Station, Bart, Sander, and Laurita, who had been tasked with a specific mission, waited in a café and were joined by a Grafter who had come over on the Eurostar. She was extremely nervous and kept looking over her shoulder, but she handed them a case and a piece of paper with the address of the Italian restaurant before scuttling off to catch the train home.

Throughout the day, four different cabs drove the three of them by the ill-fated restaurant and they examined it cautiously. Each of them had eyes for a different element, but they all agreed that it looked completely deserted. They adjourned to another café and spent several hours poring over street maps, working out their plans, their fallback plans, and the fallbacks to their fallbacks. A late dinner at a pub in Soho, a leisurely stroll down Oxford Street, and now, at two in the morning, Bart and Sander were loitering on the opposite corner while Laurita, who was by far the stealthiest of them, scaled the back wall and investigated the roof.

"Do you think there's a Checquy in there?" asked Sander under his breath. The Chimerae's hearing was amplified so they could hear each other's barest whispers. Bart shrugged slightly. "Would they have left a guard in there after—how many days was it?" Bart shrugged again. "But they say that sometimes murderers and arsonists return to the scene of the crime. Maybe the Checquy would think it was worth a try."

They had already discussed at length the possibility that Laurita would meet a threat in there, but Sander always felt the need to say something. It was just his way. Bart's way was to say nothing, shrug, and manfully resist the urge to strangle him.

A long pause ensued.

"I like these new phones," remarked Sander finally. "They've gotten very thin in the past three years, haven't they?"

"Gentlemen," said Laurita at a deafeningly normal volume from right behind them. Neither of them jumped, because they were professionals. "Well, it's clear of people," she said. "But they've left behind a couple of cameras."

"Can we disconnect them?" asked Bart.

She shook her head. "Live feed to somewhere," she said. "If we stopped them, the Checquy would know something had happened."

"So we'll have to go in clean," said Bart. The three of them had fibers woven throughout their skin that would render them invisible to cameras. The only flaw was that their clothing and hair enjoyed no such features. "Laurita, you'll stand watch outside."

They made their way around to the back of the restaurant and scaled the walls to the sloping roof. Laurita remained impassive as the two men removed their clothing and retracted every hair on their bodies back into their skin. She had already opened a skylight, and they dropped soundlessly into the room where sixteen people had died. It was dark except for the dim glow that oozed in from the skylight.

"Begin when you're ready," whispered Bart, too quietly for a camera's microphone to catch. Sander nodded. He took up a crouching stance and Bart watched as a ripple went through his comrade's muscles, locking his legs and back into place. The fair man's jaw opened, wider and wider, finally unhinging itself like a snake's. His nostrils flared, and his nose swung up and back into his face. He began to take deep breaths, so long and deep that his rib cage expanded much more than was a normal rib cage's wont. His tongue grew longer and broader and wagged about in the air. It was hardly dignified, but Sander had the smelling ability of a bloodhound and the tasting ability of a Manhattan food critic.

For long minutes, he stood there, drawing in those deep breaths. When he breathed out, however, the air was not released through his mouth. Instead, rows of bladders inflated along his back like balloons. Bart knew that this was so that the particles and traces that Sander had just sampled would not be redistributed to complicate his ongoing search.

The Checquy had scoured the restaurant for any clue of what might have caused the deaths of those people, but they had faced an almost impossible task. Hundreds upon hundreds of people had passed through those rooms, all leaving microscopic vestiges of themselves. With so much to sift through, the Checquy could not find the trail—especially since they had no idea what they were looking for. But the Chimerae knew exactly what they were looking for. The case that the Grafter woman had given them contained ampules of samples that the Broederschap had gathered from the Antagonists. Winnowing out the minute traces of their quarry was still a Herculean task, but then—

"I have it!" exclaimed Sander. He stood up, eyes blazing with triumph. "I've got their trail!"

27

"How do I look?" asked Odette.

"Don't talk to me," said Alessio.

Odette turned to where he sat on the couch. His arms were folded, and he glared at her from under his miniature top hat. He was wearing black morning dress, and with his tails and waistcoat, he looked like he'd stepped out of a period drama and was about to be sent off to Harrow with a young Winston Churchill to learn his Latin verbs, get up to some merry japes, and maybe get flogged before graduating and going off to supervise the empire. Odette thought he looked adorable but resisted the urge to say so. He appeared to be suffering enough.

"I don't have to be dressed like this, you know," said Alessio sullenly. "I looked it up on the web, and it said that since I'm under seventeen, I'm allowed to wear a lounge suit. Then I looked up lounge suit, and it turns out it's just a suit, which I already have. But instead, I'm dressed like...like..." Words failed him.

"You're lucky," said Odette. "You have a uniform; you know exactly what you're supposed to wear. I'm supposed to wear a 'formal day dress of modest length.'"

"What's 'modest length'?"

"Just above the knee or longer."

"Well, that's what you're wearing," said Alessio.

"Yes, but is it right?" She sighed and looked at herself in the mirror. "Is it appropriate?" Her dress, a princess cut in cream and the palest of greens, had cost an astounding amount of money, but she was still agonizing over it. She'd bought it in Brussels and was now worrying that it was not British enough.

It came to just below the knee and had long sleeves and a round collar. It was elegant—at least she was pretty sure it was elegant—and cut in such a way that it bullied her into having excellent posture. She felt like the kind of woman who could reject James Bond at a garden party, a woman who would raise a single wry eyebrow at everything anyone said. But was that the appropriate feeling for Royal Ascot? The problem of what to wear to this occasion had worried her slightly less than the prospect of meeting with the inhuman monsters who had tried to destroy her people, but only slightly.

"The dress covers you," Alessio said with a shrug, "and you don't look like Mr. Bumble sold you to an undertaker, so I don't know what you have to worry about."

"Royal Ascot is a major event in the British social calendar," said Odette.

"Horse races." Alessio snorted dismissively.

"Thousands of people attend every year," said Odette tightly. She anxiously did that thing where you adjust your garments and then panic that you have ruined them. "There is vast press coverage, as much for the fashion as for the races. The Royal Family attends. And we're going to be in the Royal Enclosure as personal guests of the Court of the Checquy."

"What's the Royal Enclosure? A paddock where they keep the King and Queen?"

"It's an exclusive area open only to members," Odette informed him.

"Oh." He paused. "It sounds pretty special."

"It is."

"And that's what you're wearing?"

She looked at him with genuine hatred for a moment.

"Why am I even asking you?" she wondered. "How did my life reach the point where I ask a thirteen-year-old boy for his opinion on fashion?"

He smiled. "That's what you get for not being sympathetic about my school uniform. Anyway, if you're genuinely worried, why don't you ask Pawn Clements if you look all right?"

The Pawn was in her room, getting changed into her Ascot clothes. Odette was secretly curious to see what she would be wearing. The dress code for the Royal Enclosure was strict, but for her entire tenure as Odette's bodyguard, Clements had never worn anything that didn't allow her to free-run through an obstacle course and engage in some kickboxing at a moment's notice.

"Things have been a little cool between us since St. Paul's," said Odette.

"Things have always been cool between the two of you," said Alessio.

"Yes, well, now they're extremely cool." In point of fact, things were glacial. The morning after their excursion to the cathedral, Clements had been called in to attend two meetings even though it was a Sunday. She hadn't said what they were about or who they were with, but she'd returned pale and silent. Odette, in a moment of sneakitude, had looked at Clements's organizer and seen that she'd been meeting with Rook Thomas and Bishop Attariwala. Presumably, Clements had recounted Odette's suspicious dash through St. Paul's because some very firm instructions had been handed down: there would be no more outings. In addition, Odette had been briskly informed that she would not be attending any more meetings at Apex House for a while.

"There's the feeling that you're something of a trouble magnet," Marie had said to her later. "Whatever possessed you to go running around St. Paul's like a mad thing? Were you honestly trying to ditch your minder?"

For a moment, Odette had toyed with telling her about the whispered words of the Antagonist and the trail of orange scent that wound through the cathedral, but she drew back from the idea. If it was known that the Antagonists had tracked her and spoken to her, Odette would likely be put in a stasis coma, shipped back to the Continent, and placed in a Swiss vault until the problem was resolved, no matter how long it took.

"She's exaggerating," Odette had lied awkwardly. "There were crowds, and I wanted to see everything." Marie nodded, rolling her eyes.

"Typical. Well, we'll humor them," the security chief had said. "Once the negotiations are done, I'm sure they'll relax."

And so Odette and Clements had spent the next four days in the hotel, watching television, studying, and glowering at each other. According to the morning meetings in Ernst's suite, the negotiations were moving right along, despite, or perhaps because of, her absence. The Broederschap had provided a full accounting of their assets and holdings to the Checquy, and the legal protections for the Grafters' intellectual property were being laid out.

There was still, however, distinct friction between the two organizations. Rooms went silent when Grafters entered. Flat stares were exchanged in hallways. And there were other, more troubling incidents that might have just been happenstance or might have been superpowered harassment. One of the Grafter accountants reported that during meetings with her Checquy counterparts, she kept hearing the distant voice of her long-dead mother reciting items from a grocery list. Jeroen from the lawyers found that all his credit cards and his hotel key card had been twice magnetically wiped. Alessio had come out in a rash along his shoulders, but Odette couldn't tell if it was natural or the result of supernatural bullying.

Truth be told, she was a little worried about how her brother was getting along with the students from the Estate. He mentioned no names of any friends he'd made, and his descriptions of the field trips were focused solely on where they'd gone.

"Today, we went to the Tate Modern."

Or: "Today, we went to the Rookery."

Or: "Today, we went to an abattoir."

Or: "Today, we went to the National Portrait Gallery."

"And how was that?" Odette had asked, desperate to get some details.

"We were given special versions of those headsets so that we could learn which prominent people had connections to the Checquy."

"Yeah? Was Isaac Newton a Pawn?"

"No, but Christopher Marlowe was killed on the orders of the Checquy, Jane Austen's sister-in-law was a Chevalier, and Francis Walsingham and Dr. John Dee tried to establish a rival organization to the Checquy. We got tested on it," he'd told her.

"I'll worry about Alessio later," Odette murmured to herself now. At the moment, she was more worried about her hat. She was not generally a hat person, and so she did not know the name for the kind of hat it was. It looked, to her ignorant eyes, like someone had taken an extremely broad and shallow fruit bowl, wrapped it in cream cloth, flipped it over, and then added some abstract flower and snowflake shapes to it. When she put it on, though, Odette decided she liked it. For one thing, it was recognizably a hat, and for another, she could use it to hide her eyes if she felt uncomfortable.

"Nice hat," said Alessio.

"Shut up."

"Why are you so tense about this? You've been to big events before."

"I always went shopping with Saskia for these sorts of things!" snapped Odette. She took a breath. Alessio was staring at her with wide eyes.

"Sorry, 'Dette," he said softly.

"It's fine," she said. "I just miss her." She would have loved this.

At that melancholy point, Pawn Clements emerged from her room, looking distinctly ill at ease. She was wearing a fitted black dress that went down to midshin and that seemed specifically designed to prevent the wearer from taking any long strides. She was also wearing a smoldering-red blazer and carrying a hat in the same color.

"You look very nice, Pawn Clements," said Alessio, earning himself a discreet single-fingered gesture from his sister.

"Thank you," said the Pawn distractedly. "I borrowed it from one of my roommates." She teetered a little bit on her heels but recovered and put on her hat, which had an upturned brim and various fluted attachments and so would be useless for hiding her eyes if she felt uncomfortable, although it could probably be jury-rigged into some sort of weapon if necessary. She regarded herself uncertainly in the mirror. She and Odette looked at each other for a moment but said nothing.

"Have you ever been to this thing before?" asked Alessio finally.

"To Ascot, yes, but not the Royal Enclosure," said the Pawn in the doomed tones of one who will be spending time in the company of one's supreme commanders whilst wearing an intricate hat about which one is not entirely confident. "Some friends and I went a couple of years ago. It's cool, very busy." She went to the bar fridge to get a bottle of massively overpriced orange juice and then paused, peering at Alessio's mouse cage. "I think one of your mice is gone," she said uncertainly.

Alessio hurried over and looked in the cage. He opened the lid and took out the only visible mouse. Then he lifted up the little plastic igloo and made an annoyed click with his tongue. Clements was looking about on the floor—not frightened, but certainly not delighted by this development.

"Don't bother looking," said Alessio. "It hasn't escaped. I think it's denatured." He deposited the remaining mouse back in the cage and took up a clipboard to note down the date and time. "Odette, can you confirm for me, please?" She came over and carefully examined the shavings.

"Denatured?" asked Clements.

"It happens to clones," said Alessio. "They unravel."

"And that's what happened to this one," said Odette. She pointed to a corner of the mouse cage. "See the discoloration there? There would have been a puddle of proteins and starches and other stuff where Mouse A(i) dissolved."

"They dissolve?"

"Yeah," said Odette, who realized that she'd been cunningly lured out of her uncomfortable silence. "With clones, it depends on the craftsmanship of the cloner."

"Hey!" said Alessio indignantly.

"It's okay. You're just learning," said Odette, rolling her eyes. "And I'm not that great at it myself. I always got Simon to do mine.

"If you get it right, they don't dissolve, but it's very difficult to get them exactly correct," she continued. "And anything with accelerated aging is inevitably going to break down. When it happens depends on how much you accelerate. You can't hurry Mother Nature. It's one of the reasons we don't clone people. It's bad enough when it's just a mouse that suddenly starts melting. Can you imagine how awkward it would be if the butler suddenly went sploosh?"

"So where's the puddle of proteins and starches?" asked Clements, frowning.

"Ask Mouse A," said Odette drily.

At this, Clements did look upset, and she glanced at her watch. "You're all packed?" she asked.

Odette gestured toward her suitcases by the door. After the races, some of the party would be going to Hill Hall in Suffolk, the country-house retreat of the Court of the Checquy. It was to be a long weekend of Grafters and Checquy making a great effort to enjoy each other's company in a social setting.

Alessio would not be going, since there were various activities he would be attending with the school group from the Estate. They'd arranged for him to join the Ascot trip as a special treat, the irony of which was almost painful. He'd be returning to London in the company of Chevalier Whibley, and then Marie would watch over him for the weekend. While they were away at the races, Odette's and Clements's luggage would be driven up to Hill Hall by some hapless Checquy flunky. Clements had been instructed to pack outfits for dinner, walking, and shooting things (not pheasant, because it wasn't the season, and hopefully not the Grafters). She wasn't nearly as worried about the weekend as she was about the races because there had been no mention of any specific dress code for the weekend, and the press wasn't going to be there.

"If you're ready, then we should go," said Clements. "We have to catch the train."

"We're not being driven?" asked Odette, startled.

"Traffic there is always a nightmare."

"But Marcel and Grootvader Ernst were talking about driving up," objected Odette.

"They went with Sir Henry and Lady Farrier early this morning," said Clements. "They'll be lunching there, but there was no room in the car for us."

"We couldn't take a different car?" Then she rolled her eyes at herself. *If I'm getting used to having a driver, it is time to get out of this hotel.*

"Parking is also terrible," explained Clements. "Lady Farrier has a reserved spot in the closest parking lot, but for everyone else, it's a disaster. To become a member of the Royal Enclosure, you just have to be nominated, but to get one of the good parking places, you have to wait for someone to die." Odette gave a little laugh, but the Pawn wasn't smiling. "So we'll catch the Tube to Waterloo Station, and then there's a race train."

"We're going out on public transport dressed like this?" asked Alessio in horror.

They were, and they did, and while most of the people on the Tube didn't give them a second glance, there was a group of tourists who seemed fascinated by them and who snapped several photos with their mobile phones. Odette took advantage of the shielding characteristics of her hat, but Alessio's mortification and Clements's Checquy-instilled need for anonymity left both of them red-faced and sullen.

The day was hot, and as they climbed the stairs from the Waterloo Tube station to the Waterloo railway station, Odette noticed a few other people dressed for the races. There seemed to be no consistent rules about what shape a hat ought to take, so she relaxed a little. Hundreds of race-goers were milling about: men in suits (morning and otherwise), looking very English and dashing, and women wearing outfits that ranged from the elegant and refined to the surprisingly tarty. Everyone was dressed in his or her best, but some people's best was better than others'.

"Right, that's our train," said Clements, shooing them forward. "We have first-class tickets, but it will still fill up quickly, so let's get seats while we can." The woman seemed to have a thing about getting on trains early, Odette thought. Electronic glass doors slid open, and the blessed touch of air-conditioning lay upon them. The three of them moved to the first-class compartment at the end of the carriage and gratefully sank into seats.

Through the glass doors, they watched more and more race-goers climb into the train. They filled up the seats, and then the aisles, and soon it looked like the train was transporting refugees from a selection of abruptly interrupted weddings. More people entered their compartment too, and all three of them felt compelled to give up their seats to older people.

When they pulled into Ascot Station, the feeling of being festive upper-class asylum seekers was even greater. A crush of people poured out of the train and down the stairs. Odette felt Clements's hand on her wrist, but she could only hope that Alessio was near them. The press of the people and the inexorable movement of the crowd prevented her from looking around without breaking her neck or, worse, her hat. They were buffeted through the station and past some intent-looking uniformed soldiers with submachine guns. She looked a question at Clements, who shook her head. They weren't Checquy guards, just routine security at a major public event.

They followed the throng to a lane that climbed a long, gentle slope. Trees crowded along the sides, and bunting composed of little Union Jacks zigzagged up the path. The crowd spread out, and Odette looked around to find Alessio right behind them. They grinned at each other. Despite herself, she was getting caught up in the festive air.

Television cameras filmed them as they walked up the path, and Odette instinctively ducked her head and then decided to throw caution to the wind. I'm wearing the second-most-expensive outfit I've ever owned, she thought. And this one didn't even require any stem cells. She straightened her shoulders and lifted the brim of her hat a little to smile at the cameras. A weathered-looking woman in blue jeans stepped forward from the side holding some bright flowers, each one's stem wrapped in foil.

"A flower for the young gentleman?" she asked in a lilting accent. "You'll be blessed by God."

"Oh, how nice," said Alessio.

"Touch him, and I'll break your fucking wrist," said Clements. The woman fell back, aghast. They walked on, the Leliefeld siblings exchanging wide-eyed glances.

"I don't think she was a supernatural threat," ventured Odette. "I think she was just trying to sell him that flower for his buttonhole."

"Yes, I know," said Clements absently. "I'd say that to anyone who tried to sell us something."

"Oh."

They came to the end of the lane and there on the brow of the hill, beyond a broad street crawling with people and vehicles, was the huge structure of the grandstand at Ascot racecourse.

For some reason, Odette had thought it would be an old, majestic stone structure. There's something about the adjective royal—you expect everything to look like a castle, she thought. This building looked like the castle of the king of the Internet. It was modern, metal and glass, and stood proudly against the sky. Steel columns climbed up and branched out to support a curving roof of diamond-shaped panels like leaves through which the light shone. Gigantic Union Jacks stretched the height of the building, and golden flags emblazoned with Royal Ascot fluttered gaily in the wind.

Odette was so taken with it that she didn't even notice Clements prodding her along a bridge, across the road, and down some stairs. She had to concede that Clements had been right about the traffic. If they'd driven, their emaciated corpses might eventually have found a parking space. A stretch limousine inched along at the speed of a tectonic plate, followed by three stretch Humvees in pink, gray, and silver.

She drank in the crowds, the clothes, and, above all, the hats. A tiny woman teetered by on high heels wearing a hat as big as her torso and made of rigid corrugated glitter. Odette could practically hear the woman's neck bones crumpling under the weight. At the gate, Clements opened her handbag and handed them pink badges with their names on them. "Don't lose them, or you won't be allowed back in," she cautioned. She looked at her watch and sighed. "I'm afraid we've missed the royal procession. I expect the Court is scattered around the enclosure, along with Graaf van Suchtlen and Dr. Leliefeld."

"Any tips?" asked Alessio keenly.

"Lentus Ultimusque in the fifth is what I heard," said the Pawn, and she ushered them through the gates.

The Royal Enclosure was definitely more than a paddock. They found themselves in a long sweeping garden that curved down toward the grandstand. There were trees and benches dotted about, and white marquees along the sides. They were quite the nicest tents Odette could ever recall seeing, with glass walls and elegant dining rooms inside. Some of them seemed to have their own little outside enclosures of tables and chairs under white canvas umbrellas, barricaded by tasteful little bulwarks of rope and flowerpots.

"What are the tents?" she asked.

"They belong to various clubs—White's, the Garrick Club, the Cavalry and Guards Club. They're by invitation only. That one over there is for guests of the monarch."

"Is there a tent for the Checquy?" asked Odette.

"We're a covert government agency that no one has ever heard of," said Clements acidly. "Having a marquee with our name on it would probably draw questions."

"There's Rook Thomas," said Odette, hurriedly changing the subject.

"Where?"

"Over there, under that orange hat." It was an apt description. The Rook was wearing a teardrop-shaped hat that added a significant amount of height to her silhouette. It swooped up and was adorned with a green rosette and some startling red and green tendrils. It looked like an enormous tropical flower had sprouted from her head.

"Rook Thomas, I love your hat," said Odette when the three of them reached her. It was true that she looked magnificent, although the hat really appeared to be the dominant partner in the relationship.

"Thank you, Odette," said the Rook. "And you all look very nice. Alessio, my condolences on the suit, but at least you blend in. Think of it as camouflage."

"Where is everyone else?" asked Odette.

"I have no idea," said Thomas. "I only just got here twenty minutes ago, after spending several years in my car and then a couple more walking from the car park. I was just going to find a drink and place a bet. You can come with me, or you can have a stroll." Odette shot a look at Pawn Clements, who was standing as close to attention as one could in heels on grass.

"We'd love to come," Clements said. Ten minutes later, Odette and the Rook were sipping from glasses of Pimm's Cup while Alessio and Clements (who was technically on duty and also appalled at the idea of drinking alcohol in the presence of her superior) had lemonades.

Inside, the grandstand was hollow—a tall, long atrium with walkways hugging the walls and escalators leading up. More Union Jacks were scattered around, but the architecture was all so futuristic that the race-goers looked as if they had been Photoshopped in. The Royal Enclosure appeared to take up about half of the building. As the four of them moved through a crowd at the base of an escalator, the Rook paused and looked back, slightly bewildered.

"Are you all right?" asked Odette.

"Yeah, I just..." She trailed off. Her eyes narrowed. "No, I'm fine." She led them through the grandstand and out onto the grass by the racetrack. They placed their bets with the bookmakers according to their own personal systems. Rook Thomas and Clements studied their form books avidly and picked the odds-on favorite while Alessio picked his horse because of its name (Watson's Crick), and Odette was lured by the colors one jockey was wearing (a scarlet Y on white, which reminded her of an autopsy).

"That's the royal box up there," said the Rook, pointing to the middle of the grandstand where a curved structure was bulging out of the wall. "At this very moment, the monarch, the royal spouse, and various royal hangers-on are in there, looking out at us and eating crisps." Odette squinted up. There was a small, tasteful royal crest under the window. The glass was lightly tinted, but she could dimly make out people inside. Well, it's cool to have probably seen the ruler of Great Britain, she thought.

Off to the side, beyond the bookmakers, she could see the other sections of the grandstand. They were far, far more crowded and extended much farther along the track. The people inside looked like battery race-goers. Then the race began, and she was buffeted slightly by the roar of the crowds. The rumbling of the horses drew nearer and Odette found herself shouting wildly with the rest of the people. Alessio jumped up and down and yelled like a mad thing. Even Clements was cheering.

To Odette's delight, her horse came in an unlikely second. She and Clements left Alessio with Rook Thomas while they went to the bookie to pick up Odette's thirty pounds. They returned to find the Rook talking on her mobile phone and appearing extremely perturbed. Alessio was looking on in fascination.

"No, tell them to keep it quiet," she said into the phone. "Threaten them with the Official Secrets Act. Thank God the security guard had the sense not to announce it to the world." She listened for a moment. "No, they'll want this to get out even less than we do."

"What's happening?" Odette asked her brother.

"I don't know, but the Rook is not happy. Really not happy. I learned several new words."

"Well, in that case," said Rook Thomas, "conference the racecourse chief of security in on this conversation." She paused and addressed her companions. "Something has happened here. It looks as if it falls within our purview."

"Here at the racecourse?" asked Clements.

"Here in the enclosure," said Thomas flatly. "A man is dead."

"What are we—" began Clements, but the Rook held up a hand and listened intently to her phone.

"Major Llewelyn, this is Dr. Nicola Boyd. Do you acknowledge my authority?" She nodded in satisfaction and then caught the startled gazes of Odette, Clements, and Alessio. She made a face that meant It's a secret government thing; I'll explain in a moment and turned her attention back to the phone. "Excellent. All right, I think we can agree that we want this to stay as quiet as possible, so no police, no ambulance. Your security guards can keep everyone out of the bathroom for the moment." She paused. "Give them my name and tell them to admit me and anyone accompanying me. I'll be there in five minutes, and I'll be able to tell you if it belongs to me, or if we turn it over to the police. Fine. I'll call you back shortly." She hung up and turned to them.

"Nicola Boyd is one of my working aliases," she explained. "She's something high up in the Home Office. Now, I have to go look at this and decide whether or not it's within our bailiwick." She chewed her lip thoughtfully and glanced around. "I want Pawn Clements for this, and I don't think it would be wise for us to leave you two alone. So you should come with me."

"Is it safe?" asked Odette.

"Yeeeah...probably," said the Rook unconvincingly. "But you've got me and Pawn Clements, so it will be less unsafe than it might otherwise be." She paused briefly and mentally parsed what she'd just said. "Yes, that's right."

"Rook Thomas," said Pawn Clements. "You might want to take off your badge that says Myfanwy Thomas on it."

"Ah, good catch." She led them up the steps and into the grandstand, up a couple of escalators, and down a corridor. They stopped in a comparatively quiet corner in front of a handicapped restroom. Two uncomfortable-looking men in dark suits flanked the door.

"I'm sorry, miss," said one of the guards. "This lavatory is out of order."

And so it needs two security guards? thought Odette. Great cover story.

"Gentlemen, I'm Nicola Boyd. You're expecting me." They nodded in relief, although they looked a little startled at the company she was keeping. Apparently, people didn't usually bring thirteen-year-old boys to crime scenes. "Have you looked inside yet?"

"I found the body, ma'am," said the guard on the left. "It's—it's pretty horrible." He took a deep breath. "I've never seen anything like it, he's all—" Rook Thomas held up a hand.

"Have you told him"—she nodded at the other guard—"what you saw?"

"No, he hasn't, ma'am," said the guard on the right. "Just that there's a dead body. Major Llewelyn ordered him to say nothing else."

"Good," said the Rook. "Now, what's your name?" she asked the guard who'd found the body.

"Ralph," said Ralph. "Ralph Witt."

"All right, Ralph, did you touch anything while you were in there?"

"Just the door handle. And I was sick in the corner," he added apologetically.

"We've all been sick in a corner at some point. But are you sure you didn't try to check the person's vitals or anything?" asked the Rook. "Take a pulse?"

"No, ma'am," he said with certainty. "You'll, um, see why when you go in there." The Rook nodded unenthusiastically.

"Are you prepped?" she asked Clements.

"Yes, ma'am." The Rook and the Pawn opened their purses and took out sealed plastic packages containing surgical masks and latex gloves. The two women donned them after removing their hats and putting them on a nearby chair.

"You two," said the Rook to Odette and Alessio, "will stay out here. Mind the hats." They nodded obediently. "If someone starts approaching you in an odd way, just, um, bang on the door and scream, and we'll come out." She didn't stop to see the Grafters nod.

Just bang on the door and scream? thought Odette incredulously. She looked around and saw no one moving in a manner that suggested supernatural hostility.

"I'll go first," said the Rook. She opened the door a little and stepped through. They heard her gasp and then exclaim, enraged, "Oh, fucking hell!" Everyone froze. "It's fine, Clements, you can come in," she said finally. Clements went and the door shut behind her. There was a silence that some might have described as "ominous."

Then the door opened, making Alessio and Odette jump. Clements emerged, looking a trifle dazed. She pulled off her gloves and mask and walked over to her handbag to pull out another plastic package.

"Here," she said, offering it to Odette.

"Here what?" said Odette.

"Rook Thomas wants you to go in," said the Pawn. "She wants your opinion."

"My opinion? On what?"

"Oh, I wouldn't want to taint your first impression," said Clements. "Here, give me your hat." Odette reluctantly yielded her chapeau and snapped on the gloves and mask. She opened the door hesitantly and moved in through the narrow gap.

Oh. Well, that's a first, she thought. The sight before her left her feeling a little light-headed.

The lavatory was spacious, and very clean. A wheelchair stood next to the toilet, and it was evident that the dead man had moved himself over from one to the other. He was dressed in a morning suit, hat still on his head, and his trousers were down (as was usual, given the locale). He was dead, and Odette could see why Ralph the guard hadn't felt the need to check his vital signs.

Huge glittering crystals sprouted from the walls, ceiling, and floor of the room. They thrust out at the man on the toilet, piercing him all over. One that came from the wall behind the man had gone directly through his right eye. It held his head up, so he appeared to be looking at them with a one-eyed, somewhat reproachful gaze.

Rook Thomas was standing in a crystal-free space near a corner. Her arms were crossed, and she had an expression on her face that suggested she was taking this whole situation extremely personally. "Fucking hell," she said to herself, sighing.

28

All right, Major Llewelyn," said the Rook to the security chief of Ascot Racecourse. "It's definitely ours, and we definitely don't want word getting out about this."

"Is it murder?" asked the major. The Rook looked a little hunted. The gray-haired, dignified man was at least fifteen years older than her, a foot taller, and had a tendency to bark out questions. Odette could see her trying to come up with an answer that wouldn't make things worse.

"Yes," she said finally. "But it's political. National security is at stake."

"Good God. What do you want us to do?"

"Nothing, for the moment," said Thomas. "You know the press, especially here. If word gets out about a death, let alone a murder, let alone a political murder at Royal Ascot, then we'll have no chance of tracking this down discreetly."

"Quite," said the major.

"Keep your men on the door, and don't let anyone in unless I authorize it. I have to go consult with my superiors. Call me if there are any further developments." He nodded, and she led her little entourage away to the escalators before pulling out her mobile and dialing her office. "Ingrid, it's me. The incident at the races is one of ours. Can you please call Chev Whibley, Lady Farrier, and Sir Henry and ask them to meet me at the pink bench on the Royal Enclosure lawn as soon as possible." She was silent as they made their way through the crowd and out onto the lawn by the racetrack. Many benches were dotted about, but only one of them was pink.

"Why's it pink?" asked Alessio.

"Hmm? Oh, some boy once proposed to some girl on one of the benches," said the Rook. "Now they always have a pink bench to commemorate it. They move it around the lawn." At the moment, the pink bench was occupied by a plump older couple, the man looking like John Bull and the woman looking like Mrs. Sprat. There was no room for anyone else to sit there, and they did not seem to be in any hurry to move, so the Rook's party hung around, awkwardly making nonsupernatural-murder-related small talk, until the others appeared.

Sir Henry arrived first with Ernst and Marcel in tow. They had been chatting in the marquee belonging to White's, of which Sir Henry was a member. Lady Farrier materialized shortly after, and then Chevalier Whibley, a gentleman in his fifties with a florid face and a hearty voice. Odette did not know much about him beyond the fact that he spent a great deal of time overseas and had the ability to make wood as hard as titanium. Myfanwy led them away from the plump couple on the bench to a patch of the lawn where no one was standing too close. She hurriedly explained the situation.

"Incredible," marveled Marcel once she was done. "What are the odds of something like this happening here?"

"Around three hundred thousand people come to Royal Ascot over the five days," said Lady Farrier. "That's a lot of people."

"And the Checquy are just keeping these situations quiet all the time?"

"Frankly, unless this had been done on live television, I can't imagine a more difficult situation to keep quiet," said the Rook. "There are hundreds of people wandering around, all of them with phones, all of them keen to share any unusual developments with the world."

"Thank you very much, social media," Chevalier Whibley remarked bitterly.

"And regular media," added the Rook. "If anything odd shows up, like a helicopter with troops, or even a police car with flashing lights, there will be a lot of questions."

"This is another one of those damn murders you're supposed to be stopping, then?" asked Sir Henry.

"Well, given the circumstances, Sir Henry, the odds of it being a copycat crime are extremely small."

"So, what's the situation?" asked Whibley. "Do we evacuate the racecourse?"

"Evacuate seventy thousand-odd people? It would be the biggest story in the world," said Lady Farrier, shuddering. "And what excuse could we possibly give, beyond terr—"

"Don't say it!" exclaimed Rook Thomas and Chevalier Whibley in unison. The Lady shut her mouth and rolled her eyes.

"I'd prefer not to call off Ladies' Day at Royal Ascot unless absolutely necessary," Farrier said finally. "The repercussions would be horrendous."

"If it's necessary to evacuate, we can come up with some excuse," said Rook Thomas. "But I don't know that it is necessary. In all the previous occurrences, there has been one eruption of crystals, and then nothing else."

"You think our murderer just killed this man and then went

back to drinking G and Ts and betting on the horses?" asked Sir Henry.

"Either that or he's left."

"So what shall we do?" asked Chev Whibley. "Just wait until the end of the day and then bring in the investigation team to examine the corpse?"

"That's certainly an option," said Thomas. "But it occurs to me that if the murderer is still here, then this is our best opportunity to catch him." Odette could see that the idea took them aback. These were the mandarins of the Checquy—they were not accustomed to getting their hands dirty. Ernst, by contrast, was nodding approvingly.

"Very wise. One must pursue the quarry while the spoor is fresh," said the graaf.

"Well...quite," said Whibley. "But if we do track down the murderer, isn't there a danger that he might lash out, either at us or the public?"

"That's what we're here to prevent," said Thomas flatly. "But even if we just identify him, we can follow him and snatch him up later."

"And what about the Royal Family?" asked Sir Henry. As one, they all looked up to the royal box.

"We can't evacuate them," said Lady Farrier firmly. "It would raise all sorts of questions and eyebrows. And besides, one of the princes has a horse running today for the Gold Cup."

"Don't they have military protection and bodyguards?" asked Odette timidly. As if on cue, all the Checquy Court members pursed their lips.

"Standard troops don't have any training in fighting the supernatural," said Lady Farrier dismissively. It was clear that she thought non-Checquy security forces would be instantly shredded by any five-year-old with a heightened sense of hearing or a set of prehensile eyelashes.

"One of us will have to secure the royal box, then," said Whibley. "I suppose it should be either Rook Thomas or Sir Henry. They have the most combat-ready abilities."

"I have some daggers sheathed in my torso if you need weapons," offered Ernst.

"Actually, Pawn Mondegreen is there," said Rook Thomas. "She's a lady-in-waiting."

"Lady Pawn Mondegreen," corrected Lady Farrier. "I'll go up and alert her immediately." She walked away briskly with the confidence of a woman who knew she would automatically be admitted to the presence of the Royal Family.

"I'm not familiar with Pawn Mondegreen," said Whibley. "Will she be able to offer adequate protection?"

"With a wave of her hand, she can cause people's bones to dissolve instantly," said Rook Thomas.

"Well, that would probably do it," said Whibley.

"What other presence does the Checquy have here?" asked Sir Henry.

"Aside from us and Pawn Mondegreen?" asked Rook Thomas. "None that I know of. Unless some Pawns happen to have taken the day off to go to the races. I'll have the Rookery text every member of the Checquy to see who's here, but I wouldn't hold out much hope."

"If it's unsafe, perhaps it would be best if we got the members of the Broederschap delegation out of here," said Chevalier Whibley.

"Not at all!" exclaimed Ernst. "We stand beside you as comrades. Your mission is our mission."

"What about the young man?" asked the Chev, nodding at Alessio.

"All the Broederschap stands ready to do service," said Ernst, and he laid his hand on Alessio's shoulder. Alessio looked a trifle startled at this volunteering of his help, but he nodded weakly. "We will bend all our strength to help you track down and kill this person," Ernst declared. Everyone cringed at this heartfelt but unpalatable sentiment and looked around to make sure no race-goer had heard.

"That's very kind of you, Ernst," said Rook Thomas finally, "but we generally try not to kill people unless we absolutely have to. At which point, we kill them absolutely. Our first priority right now is identifying this murderer."

"What are our leads?" asked Sir Henry.

"Damn few," said the Rook. "There doesn't appear to be much of a pattern, except that all the previous murders took place in London or Northamptonshire."

"Security should have lists of everyone who has entered the enclosure," said Chev Whibley. "I'll see about obtaining them and transmitting them to the Rookery. Perhaps they can do an analysis and identify any correlations, such as a home or business address in Northamptonshire."

The Rook explained to him how to reach Major Llewelyn, and Chevalier Whibley hurried off toward the grandstand. Ernst looked over at Odette thoughtfully. "I have an idea that may be of help. Odette, was there any trackable scent in the toilet?"

"Not really," said Odette. "The crystals didn't smell of anything in particular, so there was just feces and the faintest smell of blood."

"You can smell blood?" asked Thomas. "Interesting. Do all of you have super-smell?"

"It's not super-smell," said Marcel. "It's a heightened olfactory capacity keyed to specific biological compounds."

"Right," said the Rook. "Super-smell."

"It's not super," insisted Marcel. "It's equivalent to the best sense of smell possessed by a normal human being, but only for certain substances that we encounter in our work. It helps to diagnose some conditions."

"But there was no trail?" said the Rook. Odette shook her head.

"Perhaps one could pick up the smell of blood if the person walked by," mused Ernst.

"It depends," said Marcel dubiously. "But I suppose it is possible."

"My thought is this," said Ernst. "Marcel, Odette, and I stand at three of the Royal Enclosure exits, and we keep a nose out for anyone smelling of blood."

We're going to be sniffing every race-goer? thought Odette.

"It's ridiculous, but we're in a ridiculous situation," said the Rook. "And it might at least give us a chance. Also, I'd like Pawn Clements to go back to the murder scene and read its history. If she can get a look at the murderer, it could be our biggest break."

"And how long will that take?" asked Sir Henry. Clements straightened slightly under his gaze.

"It depends, sir," said the Pawn cautiously. "We don't know how much time elapsed before the body was found. But not too long, I should think."

"I'll go with her," said Rook Thomas. "Sir Henry, I think you ought to accompany Miss Leliefeld. She has only minimal weaponry, and if the murderer detects any of you at the exits, he might decide to attack." Clements opened her mouth and then shut it again. Apparently, if she couldn't act as bodyguard, then a man who had once sunk a Russian submarine to the depths of the abyssal plain whilst sitting inside it drinking schnapps was an acceptable substitute.

"From what I know of you gentlemen," said the Rook drily to Marcel and Ernst, "I expect you can handle yourselves."

"That sounds like a decent plan, Myfanwy," said Sir Henry. He put out his hand, and, looking startled, the Rook shook it. "You and Pawn Clements go on. We shall work out which exits we will cover."

Myfanwy watched Clements go into the handicapped bathroom and shut the door behind her. The guards outside were under the impression that the Pawn would be engaged in some sort of forensic work, which, technically, she was. Myfanwy sat herself down in a nearby chair, and her phone rang.

"Hello?"

"Rook Thomas, this is Pawn Ball at the Rookery watch office."

"What's the status?" asked Myfanwy.

"We sent out the text messages to all members of the Checquy. The nearest office is in Reading, and, given the traffic, that's over an hour away, if we use cars without lights and sirens."

Myfanwy sighed. "Now, there is a party of three Checquy employees at Ascot today. They are attending in the public areas of the racecourse, but..." He trailed off uncomfortably.

"What?"

"Well, it's their day off, and they're at the races," said Pawn Ball. "They're somewhat intoxicated."

"Oh, for God's sake," said Myfanwy. "How intoxicated are we talking about?"

"Intoxicated enough that they wouldn't legally be able to drive. And one of them was giggling when I spoke to him over the phone."

"Great."

"Plus they e-mailed me photos of what they're wearing, and none of them would pass the dress code for the Royal Enclosure. They couldn't even pass as security guards or waitstaff, especially the ladies."

"All right, well, I suppose we'll hold them in reserve. None of them have any abilities that might help us identify a murderer, do they?"

"I'm afraid not. Two of them are Pawns. One has fireproof skin and the other has the ability to disrupt the part of the human brain that deals with language comprehension."

"No, I suppose that wouldn't be of much use. Look, dispatch the team from Reading. We'll need forensic investigators and a combat team, just in case."

"Understood." And he rang off. Myfanwy sat back in her chair and brooded. She had an idea but was not certain how practicable it was. Earlier, while moving through the crowds, she'd brushed against a person who'd grated on her supernatural ability. Normally, she kept her additional senses firmly closed down to avoid getting distracted by the minutiae of other people's nervous systems. But this person's presence had flickered in the corner of her mind's eye like a cigarette lighter.

At the time, she'd dismissed it. Because of her amnesia, she didn't have nearly the level of understanding of her abilities that the old Myfanwy had possessed. Her previous self had

331

undergone years of training and experimentation with her powers and could do things that were completely beyond the new Myfanwy. For all she knew, that brief flash might have meant that someone was having a stroke, or a seizure, or just an involuntary shudder. She'd dismissed it. But now she wondered if she'd come in contact with the murderer. It was an unpleasant thought, but it opened up a very interesting possibility.

Myfanwy had several secrets in addition to that of working for a covert supernatural government organization. The main secret, of course, was the amnesia. Only a few people were aware that her memories had been stolen from her and that she was masquerading as herself. With the loss of her memories, however, had come a startling development. For all the expertise her old self had possessed, she had always needed to establish physical contact to use her powers. The current Myfanwy could use them at a distance, extending them from her mind out to anyone within a radius of about twenty meters. She looked across at the security guards and knew that, with a thought, she could bring them both to their knees. By shifting the focus of her perceptions, she could view the electricity in their brains, the signals in their spines and muscles, the chemistry in their guts.

So could I track down the murderer with my powers? she wondered. It was a tenuous possibility, very tenuous, but no less likely than the Grafters sniffing out the murderer at the exits. Privately, she doubted that they'd manage it. Expecting the Grafters to pick out the smell of a few drops of blood from hundreds of food- and alcohol-filled passers-by on a windy day was not realistic.

She stood up, having made the decision. "When my colleague emerges from her examination, could you please tell her I've just stepped away?" she asked the security guards. "She can ring me on my mobile." They nodded obediently, and she moved toward the escalators, resolute despite the flaws in her plan, of which there were several. For one thing, there were plenty of areas she wouldn't be able to access: the private boxes, the service areas.

I'll have to go wandering through the crowds, she thought. And hope I'm lucky enough to bump into a serial killer. A methodical approach was clearly needed, so she began at the top. Using her powers to examine people required a good deal of concentration, and so she was obliged to walk very slowly while she did it. She ambled along each of the seating levels, scanning the crowds, trying to pick out that strange flash she recalled.

Nothing. Damn it.

The most crowded areas were around the bars and restaurants, so she headed there next. There were hordes of people waiting patiently (if a little raucously) for drinks. She stood off to the side of the first bar, her eyes narrowed. Her intense focus was disrupted, however, when half a bourbon and Coke was spilled onto her feet by a red-faced young Hooray Henry who was busy drinking his winnings.

"Sorry, miss," he said, but the sincerity of his apology was somewhat marred by his sniggering and that of his equally intoxicated friends. His laughter cut off into a startled howl as, unaccountably, his wrist jerked and he dashed the rest of his beverage onto his own crotch. Myfanwy rolled her eyes and walked away. It was probably a gross violation of some Checquy code of conduct to use her abilities this way, but since she had no memory of ever reading such a code, she felt no guilt.

Myfanwy made her way down through the grandstand, passing by the various bars and food venders, zigzagging along the concourses, and going back down the escalators. She paused to get a glass of orange juice and then walked over to the lawn by the racecourse. Could a person really just saunter around casually right after he killed someone? she wondered.

"Myfanwy!" She jerked around at her name and did a double take that set her hat wobbling. In front of her was one of the few people she knew who had nothing to do with either the Checquy or the Grafters.

"Jonathan!" she exclaimed. "Hi!" Jonathan was her brother—well, the brother of the body she'd inherited. Two years older, some inches taller, but with the same unremarkable brown hair and facial features. Technically, she was not supposed to know him. The Checquy had taken Myfanwy Thomas away from her family at the age of nine, when her powers first manifested. Jonathan had grown up thinking his sister was dead, and it was only when their parents were killed in a car accident and he gained access to their papers that he learned she was still alive. Even then, he had known only the cover story, that she had been struck down by a rare, incurable malady and taken to a secretive research facility where she could at least be made comfortable.

Jonathan and Bronwyn (the youngest Thomas sibling) had spent several months tracking down their long-lost sister. Bronwyn had finally introduced herself to a startled Myfanwy— an amnesiac Myfanwy who had no fond, wistful memories of her siblings but was prepared to fake them, just as she was faking being a Rook of the Checquy. Both Bronwyn and Jonathan remained unaware of Myfanwy's real job and her supernatural abilities. They were under the impression that she was a highly paid administrative consultant who had spent many years in a coma and who now suffered from agoraphobia. It was not the best cover story, but it was the only scenario Myfanwy had been able to come up with that fit all the facts.

"I didn't know you were going to be here," said Jonathan. "That's a great hat." They cheek-kissed awkwardly, partly because theirs was an odd, still-gestating relationship and partly because their respective hats projected in unfamiliar ways and required some careful maneuvering.

"Thank you. You look very handsome. I'm here with people from work."

"Oh, me too," said Jonathan. "The bank has a box, and they asked me along. Apparently, they liked what I did in Hong Kong." He looked around. "Where are your colleagues? I'd love to meet them."

"I appear to have lost them," said Myfanwy. Which is the only break I've managed to catch today. If she and Jonathan had run into each other when she wasn't alone, the situation would have gotten very awkward very quickly. Operatives of the Checquy who had been taken from their families were not supposed to reconnect with them. She looked up at the royal box, worried Lady Farrier might be gazing down at her with a pair of opera glasses, then glanced around anxiously, checking to make sure that none of the others were trying to find her. Then she stiffened.

Fifteen meters away, a middle-aged man in a black morning coat was chuckling at a joke his female companion had made and flaring in Thomas's supernatural senses like a blowtorch.

What is wrong with the universe that it would screw me around like this?

She realized that Jonathan was still talking to her.

"What?"

"Would you like to come up to the box? I'd love to introduce you to some of my colleagues and my boss."

"Oh, that's so kind," said Myfanwy distractedly. She squinted beyond her brother at the man with the flickering aura. He was irritatingly average. A forty-something white male with brown hair and no convenient facial hair or eye patch to help her describe him to the others. She tried desperately to read his name tag but couldn't make it out. "Could we do it in a little bit? I really need to find my work people. There are some foreign visitors—clients—and I'm slightly worried about them."

"Of course, I understand. Can't you call them?"

"I could, yes..." said Myfanwy. "That's a very good and sane point." *Damn it.* "But they don't speak English. And I don't speak Dutch!" she said in a moment of inspiration. "Wait, you don't speak Dutch, do you?" she asked fearfully.

"No, just Mandarin."

Thank God.

"Well, yeah, there you are. I'll go find them and make sure they're taken care of. And then I'll give you a call, and we'll meet your people." She bit her lip anxiously. *The man who might be the murderer was shaking hands with his companion. Is he leaving?*

"Myfanwy?"

"Hmm?"

"Myfanwy." The tone in Jonathan's voice caught her by surprise, and she tore her gaze away from the suspect. Her brother was looking at her with a very serious expression. "Are you all right?"

"I'm fine."

"Are you? You're distracted, you're fidgeting, and you won't look me in the eye. Do I need to be worried about you?" Myfanwy's eyebrows knit in confusion. Then she realized what he was talking about.

Part of the cover story she had concocted for her family was that she had spent many years in a drugged state as part of the treatment for her unspecified condition. At the time, she'd thought it was a good lie. It had gone some way toward explaining why, once she'd been "cured," she'd never tried to contact her brother and sister. But then, in a regrettable fit of creativity, she'd embroidered on the lie and implied to Bronwyn that she still had some residual addiction issues. Bronwyn had dutifully passed this on to their brother, and now he was apparently afraid she was relapsing.

"Oh, no, Jonathan. I'm fine, I swear to you." Despite the ridiculousness of the situation, despite the danger, she couldn't help but be a little pleased. It was a nice feeling, having a protective older brother. He still seemed dubious. "It's the, um, crowds and the noise." You know, my fictional agoraphobia? "I thought I'd be all right, but it's all a little overwhelming."

"Of course!" he said anxiously. "Would you like to sit down? We could go inside, see if there's somewhere quiet." He started to lead her into the stadium, taking her right by the glowing man, and she caught Jonathan's hand.

"Yes, I'll go to the ladies' in a second." She drew him closer to speak quietly. "There's a man behind you—he is the husband of a client of mine. And the woman he is with is not my client."

"Ah. Awkward."

"Yes, that's why I was a bit distracted."

"Are you going to say anything?" he asked.

"Probably not. I'd prefer just to feel really uncomfortable

every time I see her," said Myfanwy. He smiled. Behind him, the suspect was turning to go. "Anyway, I might just head to the bathroom and splash some water on my face. I shall call you once I've found my people."

"Jolly good," said Jonathan. "You don't have any tips for the horses, do you?"

"Totes Pferd in the fifth, I heard."

"Interesting. Maybe I'll go place a bet."

"Go! Bet! And I shall talk to you soon." She patted him on the arm and then took off after the suspect, who was marching up the steps into the grandstand.

It turned out to be quite the worst place in the world to try and tail a man. The dress code meant that they all looked roughly the same. There was some variation, of course, with black morning suits and gray morning suits and gray top hats and black top hats (although colored ribbons on the hats were strictly forbidden). But for a shortish woman trotting along in high heels and a dress whose designer had prioritized looking great over swift movement, maintaining a bead on one specific male was not easy.

To make matters more difficult, the suspect was not sauntering along easily but appeared to be in something of a hurry himself. He had passed through the stadium and was now briskly trotting down the stairs toward the gardens, where even more men in morning suits were clotting together. Myfanwy pulled out her phone and dialed.

"Myfanwy, what is it?"

"Ernst, I have him. I'm on his tail," she said.

"Where are you?"

"I'm passing the big statue of the horse head, and he's moving toward the marquees." She gave the best description she could, even though her quarry was as nondescript as it seemed possible for a person to be.

"Right, I'm coming to you," said Ernst. "Be careful, Myfanwy. Keep your distance from him until I get there."

"I just want one photo of him, and I—bugger. Where is he?" Myfanwy stopped, bewildered. She could have sworn she had not taken her eyes off him, but now he was nowhere to be seen. "Ernst, I need to concentrate. Come find me." She hung up and looked around intently. Where did he go? She shifted her perception, suddenly becoming aware of the crowd's physiologies, but there was no sign of that peculiar flickering from before. She turned around to find that her quarry was right behind her, looking at her intently. It was like realizing you were standing next to a person made of neon tubes.

"Oh! Goodness, hello!" she exclaimed in surprise. "I didn't realize someone was there."

"You are following me," he said.

"I beg your pardon?" she said, and she gave the sort of incredulous laugh that someone who hadn't been doing just that would give.

"If you want to tail someone, I recommend that you don't wear a hat that looks like it belongs to the pope of the jungle. Now, why are you following me?"

"This is dreadfully embarrassing," said Myfanwy, doing her best to look dreadfully embarrassed. "I...the truth is, I thought you were attractive and I wanted to introduce myself." There is no way he is going to buy this. But play it cool. You don't even know that this man is the murderer. "My name is Nicola." She smiled, but he did not smile back. "Perhaps we could exchange telephone numbers?" She held up her phone, ostensibly to get his number but really to get a picture of him, and a sharp pain cut through her hand. "Ow!" she exclaimed, and dropped her phone. She looked down to see that a crystal had erupted out of the casing of the phone and sliced into the palm of her hand. Blood was quite enthusiastically coming out of a cut there.

She glanced up and saw that the man was breathing heavily. His pupils were dilated, and his teeth were bared. It was not a very wholesome look.

"Well, that settles that question," Myfanwy said flatly. He seemed startled, and at that moment she clenched her powers around his nervous system so that the expression froze on his face. "You've probably figured out that I was lying. I actually

338

don't find you attractive at all. Especially because of what you do. You see, it's déclassé to murder people, but it's a particular faux pas to do it at Royal Ascot." He couldn't answer, of course, but the reaction in his eyes was as horrified as she could have asked for. "Let's have a little sit-down on this convenient bench."

Her hand was throbbing, but she ignored it while she twisted his muscles with her mind. He jerkily stepped over and sat down. She bent down to retrieve her phone and then sat next to him, looking through her purse for a handkerchief or something to stanch the bleeding. No one around them appeared to have noticed anything amiss.

"Well, you've successfully murdered my phone," she said sourly. "Congratulations. What did you think would happen when you did that?" Of course, he still didn't say anything, because she had a firm grasp on his vocal cords. She unearthed a half-empty packet of tissues from her purse and clutched it in her hand. "Now we'll just have to wait here for a while. I don't want to try to marionette you through this crowd." His fixed look was peculiar enough to garner some glances from passersby, but she didn't have any experience with manipulating facial expressions. *If I try to give him a smile, I might accidentally break his face. Which I suppose would be a bad thing.* Then she frowned. He might be sitting rigidly, but his brain was a hive of activity. Myfanwy hesitated; she'd never tried turning off someone's thoughts before. *I'm not even certain whether it's pos—*

She felt a hard blow to her lower back, as if someone had punched her.

Her breath rushed out of her. She swayed forward, but something held her against the bench. Something that hurt her deep inside. *I believe I've been stabbed,* she thought in amazement. *One of those damn crystal things. He grew it out of the bench and into me.* This revelation did not upset her nearly as much as she would have expected. She looked down hesitantly and saw, to her distant relief, that there wasn't anything coming out of her stomach. But pain was spreading in her guts. Her head swam and she realized, with a feeling of dread, that she'd released her mental grasp on the man sitting next to her. Falteringly, she turned her head to look at him. Once again, he was breathing heavily; a veneer of sweat shone on his face, but he was able to turn and look back at her.

"Who are you?" he asked in an intense low tone. "What are you? How do you know about me?"

Keep him here, Myfanwy told herself. She couldn't muster up the focus to use her powers on him, but if she could delay him, then maybe Ernst or one of the others would come. So she mumbled something incomprehensible.

"What?" he said, and he leaned closer to her. It was odd that no one in the crowd had noticed anything. Probably because there was no obvious blood, and since she didn't have the breath to scream, people continued to walk by. It was like getting killed in the middle of My Fair Lady.

I'm supposed to say something to him, thought Myfanwy, but she couldn't make her mouth do what she wanted. The man was speaking, but she couldn't hear him.

Her last thought was that she was supposed to call Jonathan.

29

Myfanwy, as long as we're talking, can I get your thoughts on a bit of administrivia?"

"Certainly, Lady Farrier," said Myfanwy. She carefully spooned a dollop of Devonshire clotted cream onto her scone and then placed a teaspoon of strawberry jam into the center.

"Some would call that heresy, you know," remarked the Lady of the Checquy. She herself appeared to be of the "jam, then cream" school.

"I'm not bound by the petty strictures of society," said Myfanwy, and she took a delicious bite. "Anyway, what can I do for you?"

"Do you have any thoughts on possible Rooks?"

"You don't like the job that Andrew Kelleher is doing?" asked Myfanwy, lifting her teacup. "I thought we had agreed to make him permanent."

"No, he's fine," said the Lady. "Apart from the smoking."

"Joshua Eckhart smokes," remarked Myfanwy.

"Not from his eyes," said Farrier.

"Well, you know I've been pushing for Colonel Hall. He's extremely experienced and extremely capable."

"Not a Pawn, though," said Lady Farrier.

"I don't think that should matter," said Myfanwy. "Although, if we're keeping Whibley as a Chevalier—and we should, because he's very good—then we should try and get another woman onto the Court."

"I'll keep that in mind," said Lady Farrier.

"Wait," said Myfanwy, suddenly suspicious. "Why are you asking me this?" She glanced around. They were sitting on a balcony in the Ascot grandstand, looking down on the brilliant colors of the crowds and horses. It all seemed a good deal quieter than it had before. "How did I even get here?"

"Well, you're not here," said Lady Farrier. "I thought you knew that." Myfanwy looked at her in horror. "Think a moment. I'm sure you'll recall getting impaled in the back. I presume it was by the serial killer you were trying to track down."

"Oh God," said Myfanwy, dropping her cup of tea, which unraveled into vapor. It was all coming back to her, like a dream you suddenly remember in the morning. "I'm not awake at all."

This was not the first time Farrier had interviewed Myfanwy in her mind. The Lady of the Checquy possessed the ability to enter (and interfere with) other people's dreams. As a result, she was one of the few people who knew about Myfanwy's amnesia. She had never revealed the amnesia to the Checquy, since she owed the old Myfanwy a debt of honor, but she'd always been cautiously reserved, even after the new Myfanwy had proven herself.

"So where am I really?" asked Myfanwy.

"Currently, you're lying facedown on the conference table in the boardroom at Ascot Racecourse, bleeding all over the place," said Farrier. "Dr. Leliefeld is doing his best to keep you alive. I thought we'd take this opportunity to have a chat in your unconscious mind and make some preparations, just in case." She took a bite of scone.

"You're canvassing me on my possible replacement while I'm dying?" asked Myfanwy.

"There's no better time," said the Lady reasonably. "And we're not absolutely certain that you're going to die. They're working very hard. Did you know that the Leliefeld girl has surgical tools inside her? She just hiked up her dress and two scalpels slid out of a slit in her thigh."

"Yes, it's in her file," said Myfanwy testily. "How bad do I look?"

Lady Farrier shrugged. "I am sorry, truly, but I'm afraid that I have no idea. I didn't see much except the end of a crystal spike coming out of your back."

"Oh God!"

"Don't worry, we covered it up marvelously. Apparently, there wasn't much blood because the crystal thing had absorbed a great deal of it. Graaf van Suchtlen had to carry you through the enclosure, wrapped in his coat, but he told everyone you'd fainted from dehydration."

"Well, that is a relief," said Myfanwy. "Was there a lot of attention?"

"No. Everyone seemed to think it would be in bad taste to take photos of a sick woman, and I arranged for us to use the boardroom. It's private and doesn't look out onto the racecourse, so no one will see us."

"Thank you," said Myfanwy gloomily. "Did they catch the killer at least?"

"No, I'm afraid not. He was gone by the time the graaf found you."

"And none of the people at the exits saw him?" she asked. "No smell of blood?"

"No, but there wouldn't be. Pawn Clements spent thirty minutes reading the history of that bathroom. She watched the crystals erupt out of the wall and impale that man half a dozen times, but there was no sign of the murderer. Then she thought to look at the history outside the room. The man had walked up to the door and put his hand flat against it, and then the crystals appeared."

"That explains why our people never found any evidence at any of the crime scenes," mused Myfanwy.

"I'll pass that on to the investigators if you don't pull through," promised Lady Farrier.

"Oh, good," said Myfanwy. She looked at the scones and shrugged. They might only be figments of the imagination of a dying mind, but that seemed like all the more reason to eat them.

"Hmm," said Lady Farrier. She looked up at the sky and frowned.

"What?"

"I—"

She's waking up!" shouted Odette.

"Well, she shouldn't be," said Marcel tightly. "That chemical could knock out a hippopotamus."

Myfanwy's eyes opened a little. She was facedown, and while her head was cushioned by a bunched-up, formerly white tablecloth, she could feel that the rest of her was lying on polished wood. Her hands twitched, and she felt a warm liquid pooling around them. Her back was wet and hot. As she woke up a little more, her brain pointed out that there was a horrendous pain lancing through her lower back. Instinctively, she thrashed and screamed and felt her powers flash. There were shouts of pain and confusion.

"Jesus!" said somebody.

"It's her!" said somebody else.

"Knock her out again!" exclaimed Odette. Myfanwy felt two firm fingers pressing against her throat, and then she was gone.

Well, that was unexpected," said Lady Farrier. "More tea?"

"Please," said Myfanwy breathlessly. The other woman poured the tea into the cup that was suddenly back in front of her. "It—it didn't seem to be going very well."

"No, I'm afraid not," said Farrier. "When they removed the spike from your back, you started bleeding rather badly."

"How boring," said Myfanwy tightly.

"Well, they seem to be doing a lot of surgery," said Lady Farrier. "And I must say, if you have to get operated on in these sorts of circumstances, I expect that the Grafters would give you the best chance on earth." Myfanwy took a deep breath. Of course, it was only an imaginary breath, but it helped her to calm down. It was difficult to reconcile the serene sunshine of this moment with the bloody, panicked reality she'd just experienced. Be calm. Be cool. Be collected. She was secretly rather grateful to Farrier for bringing her here. It was such a lovely scenario that the possibility of dying abruptly seemed quite absurd.

"Speaking of the Grafters," said Myfanwy, "I suppose I'd better tell you a few things, just in case I don't pull through."

"Oh?"

"Well, it's best to be prepared for the worst." She smiled a little smile. She'd been able to assume her predecessor's life only because the old Myfanwy had been extremely well prepared. "I have some grave concerns about the merger."

For the first time, Farrier's reserve cracked. "What on earth are you talking about? You've been the main force behind this!"

"I know, and on the face of it, everything is going well. Yesterday they provided the list of all the Checquy operatives they'd suborned. There's only a few left, by the way. Most of them were killed at that drinks reception, and then a guard at

Gallows Keep was killed in a car accident a couple of months back. Oh, and a morgue attendant at the Rookery committed suicide a few weeks ago. So the Grafters are showing good faith there. They've turned over huge swaths of information about themselves, and I've had it all checked. It's legitimate. The real estate holdings, the personnel details, the bank accounts and investments—everything is as they said. Of course, inevitably there are some peculiarities. Their finances, for instance."

The personal wealth of the Grafters was substantial, but most of it was in assets that were decidedly nonliquid. Rather, they were gelatinous, viscous, bony, oleaginous, gastric, and cartilaginoid. Broederschap funds tended to be sunk into unique biological items or substances that were rare but that appeared to be of no material use to anyone except the Broederschap. They did not hold stocks or shares, instead investing their money back into their own research and themselves. An astounding amount of money, for instance, had been poured into Ernst's body, but he was not living the lifestyle of the rich and famous. They were discreet, circumspect. "Their cash reserves are less than you would expect, but I'm not surprised that they've lied about the money."

"Well, I am!"

"I anticipated Ernst would have some assets tucked away just in case negotiations were to break down," said Myfanwy dismissively. "I would estimate he's kept fifteen to twenty percent of their wealth off the books, but if anything along those lines ever comes to light, I would urge you to overlook it."

"Overlook it?"

"Once they're part of the Checquy, their finances will be under the same scrutiny that ours are."

All operatives of the Checquy had their finances gone over with a fine-tooth comb by the fiercest and most merciless auditors in HM Revenue and Customs. The unique position of the Checquy and the dangerous repercussions of any corruption meant that every penny every employee earned and spent was accounted for. Random audits of private accounts were an irritating but not unexpected occurrence. As a result, every employee was fanatical about getting a receipt for every transaction, including charitable donations to street beggars.

"If it's not the money, then what are your concerns?" asked Lady Farrier.

"It's what I'm not seeing. There are gaps." Warming to her topic, Myfanwy put down her teacup. "Look, I've plotted all the data they've given us, and some things just don't make sense. For instance, they maintain a research residence in the capital of every Western European country except France? Their facilities in Seraing and Vienna happen to catch fire and be destroyed now? And there are other things. I've identified a lacuna in their population demographics."

"What on earth are you talking about?"

"Odette Leliefeld appears to be the only Grafter between the age of nineteen and twenty-six."

"That's not why you gave her a bodyguard, is it?"

"No, but there are a number of things about that girl that worry me. She has far fewer implants than anyone else in the delegation except the kid."

"She's young," said Farrier. "Perhaps they don't give them too many to begin with."

"Perhaps." Myfanwy shrugged. "But the disparity is notable. Someone should go through the profiles of all the Grafters and compare." The Lady nodded. "Especially given the fact that she was added to the delegation at the last minute, both she and her brother."

"These could all be coincidences," objected Farrier.

"Yes, which brings me to the final point." Myfanwy described the mission in which Clements had lost her entire team, and the possible implications. "Talk to Clements about it. And don't punish her for withholding information—I ordered her to be silent."

"I can't believe you've kept this to yourself."

"I don't know for sure that it means anything," said Myfanwy. "And you know the tensions that exist at the moment."

"So what do you think is going on?"

"I don't know," said Myfanwy. "Not for certain. As far as I can tell, either the Grafters are not committed to the merger, or there's some other party that has followed them. Miss Leliefeld was shocked at the Italian restaurant, but I'm certain it was the shock of recognition. In any case, I don't want you to be caught off guard." She winced and put her hand to her back. In the dream, her skin was smooth and unbroken, but she'd felt a jag of pain. That can't be good. "Lady Farrier?" she asked hesitantly.

"Yes?"

"Could I ask a favor? If the Grafters aren't able to save me, would you mind staying with me here until I...until I go?"

"Of course," said the Lady.

"And just one more thing?"

"Yes?"

"I'm a little tired of tea. I don't suppose we could have some champagne?"

And the Antagonist stood here for half an hour?" asked Bart.

"About that, yes," said Sander. The Chimera tracker rubbed his nose, which was bigger than it had been at the start of the mission but was still within the bounds of plausibility. Bart and Laurita looked around. Over the past three days, Sander had led them through the streets of London, tracking their quarry from the Italian restaurant to a spot on a busy street by Hyde Park. There were tall, impressive buildings in front of them, and the park behind them, but nothing of any particular interest. "He's been back here several times since."

"How can you tell?"

"There's layering and variations in the scent," said Sander confidently. "He came here directly from the Italian restaurant, but he's definitely returned since then. Sometimes it's right after he's bathed, sometimes it's right after he's eaten."

"And it's a male?"

"Oh yes."

"Well, I suppose that's a good thing," said Bart thoughtfully.

"That will mean there are fresher trails, correct?" It had taken the tracker days to lead them to this spot. Trailing an old scent through a city of millions of people had proven to be incredibly difficult, not least because Sander was unable to deploy his full complement of sensory organs in public. They'd had to keep stopping and standing about awkwardly while he froze in the middle of the footpath and dredged up a hint of a scent from the city. On several occasions, they'd had to retrace their steps to intersections and try different routes. Twice, he actually had to lie down on the footpath and sniff, which had gotten them some very suspicious looks. Fortunately, the pedestrians of London were far too polite and jaded to interfere or comment.

"Much fresher trails," said Sander. "It'll be a snap."

"Why would he come and stand here, though?" wondered Bart. Sander shrugged the shrug of a man who was there to sniff the pavement and then kill things, not to reason why.

"I know," said Laurita. She nodded across the street. "That hotel is where the Broederschap delegation is staying." The other two Chimerae digested this thoughtfully.

"How many times has the Antagonist come here?" Bart asked finally.

"At least four."

"Let's get a coffee," said Bart. "I'll contact Marie and let her know. And then we'll resume tracking."

That's it," said Marcel. He stepped away from the table and sat down on one of the chairs that had been pushed back against the wall. Odette moved off and let her shoulders slump, exhausted. Alessio, who had been kneeling on the other side of the table and observing their work, shuffled backward, unmindful of the blood that stained the knees of his suit.

"That's it?" said Sir Henry, standing up and moving forward. "What do you mean, 'That's it'?" He looked incredulously at the boardroom table where the body of Rook Thomas lay, looking very small and vulnerable. She was horribly still. Her dress had been sliced open down the back and blood had ebbed from the wound and onto the table. They had hastily put down cloths and coats to keep it from spreading, and now the place looked like a Crimean War hospital. One tea towel from the adjoining kitchenette was draped over the stab wound, and another lay over the elastic of her knickers, a token effort at dignity. "Is she dead?"

" 'That's it' as in I am finished and she is going to stay alive, at least until she manages to get herself stabbed again when I am not around to accomplish a miracle," said Marcel.

"She'll be all right?" asked Sir Henry. "She's not breathing!"

"Give it a moment," said Marcel. A moment was duly given. The Rook's body twitched, and she drew a raspy breath. And then another, much less raspy one. "I must say, we're very good," said Marcel.

"He means that he's very good," said Odette. She'd assisted Marcel throughout the procedure, but it had been his skills that kept the Rook alive and repaired the worst damage. She stretched her arms up painfully and looked down, crestfallen, at her racing dress, which was liberally splashed with fluids that had once circulated inside Rook Thomas. Another outfit ruined, she thought. Surely this can't happen every time I go out in England.

"Nicely done," said Ernst.

"It's damn outstanding, is what it is!" declared Sir Henry. "Let's have a drink!" he started looking through the cupboards. "It's a boardroom, they must have someth—ah! Here we are." He took out a bottle and brandished it triumphantly. "Old Pulteney, just the thing to celebrate an unsuccessful stabbing." He distributed glasses and poured everyone, even Alessio, a dram. "Cheers!" Everyone drank, and then Alessio started coughing. Sir Henry looked over at the Rook cautiously. "I say, you didn't put anything in her, did you? No new organs?"

"No, nothing like that," Marcel assured him. "Though I had to secrete a great many more enzymes than I normally would. It seems that her powers automatically attack any unfamiliar organism, even if it's benevolent."

"You secreted things into her?" said Clements, looking a little queasy. The Pawn had spent the entire operation standing by the door, her gaze firmly averted from the surgery, ready to prevent any intruders from entering.

"Various anesthetics, sedatives, and cleansing and repair agents," said Marcel. "It helps to have one's tools always to hand."

"And I noticed you breathing on the table and tools?" said Chevalier Whibley uncertainly.

"Marcel can expel an antiseptic mist," said Odette. "In an emergency, it serves to sterilize equipment."

"Also keeps my breath fresh," said Marcel cheerfully. He sipped the whisky. Lady Farrier swept in from an adjoining room and took in the situation. It might have been Odette's imagination, but it seemed as if the Lady's eyes lingered on her thoughtfully for a moment or two. Then she looked at the Rook on the table.

"She's still alive," said the Lady, and it wasn't a question.

"Yes," said Sir Henry. "And likely to stay that way, thanks to Dr. Leliefeld here. And Miss Leliefeld."

"Thank you both," said Farrier. She stepped forward to shake their hands and then noticed the blood. "Well, we'll shake hands later, but rest assured, you have the gratitude of the entire Checquy."

That's nice, thought Odette wearily. Maybe this will help to make up for the disastrous incident with that soldier boy and his leg.

"How long until she recovers?" the Lady asked.

"A few days and she'll be as good as new," said Marcel. "She's lost a great deal of blood, so we'll need to arrange a transfusion. And I'll want to add some agents to the blood to accelerate recovery, but with that and some rest, she'll be fine."

"Marvelous. Well, we can have the blood flown to Hill Hall along with someone to look after her," said Lady Farrier. "It would be a shame to cancel the weekend just because of this." She looked over at Marcel. "It's all right to take her in a helicopter, isn't it?" He nodded. "Good. Oh, where's her handbag?

She mentioned that her car was on the north side of car park seven and that if she didn't make it, we should arrange for someone to come pick it up. I expect one of the Reading team can drive it back to London. Anyway, we'll want the keys."

"I didn't notice a handbag when I got her," said Ernst shamefacedly. "But I wasn't looking."

Lady Farrier sighed. "It's always something, isn't it?"

30

And there's Hill Hall," said Lady Farrier. Odette nodded, entranced. She had been glued to the window of the helicopter for the entire flight from Ascot. The landscape was gorgeous, and she had been mesmerized by the patchwork fields, the slashes of forest, and the towns and villages. Now, as the first helicopter drew down over the estate, she sighed. Ahead of them, the manor house was nestled in a park, around which ran a long, high wall. It really was like entering an elegant past.

Except you're in a helicopter, she reminded herself. And a hideous neon jogging outfit. Before they could leave the boardroom, they'd had to wait for the Checquy team from Reading to arrive, and they'd dispatched a hapless flunky to the local shops to buy some replacement clothes for those whose race-going outfits were stained with blood.

Then they'd discreetly transported the still-unconscious Rook through the service corridors of the grandstand to an exit and suffered in the glacial-pace traffic before finally arriving at the nearest helipad, where there were two helicopters waiting for them. In one of them, Rook Thomas was arranged across three seats and attended to by Marcel, under the watchful eye of Pawn

Clements. Odette, Ernst, and the Lord and Lady had piled into the other one.

The helicopter swept over the estate, and Odette noticed a battered-looking tower of rough gray stone jutting up from one wall.

"Is that part of the fortifications?" she asked curiously.

"No, it's a folly," said Farrier. "The man who had the wall built added it for a bit of decoration."

"Ah. And Hill Hall belongs to the Checquy?"

"It's the country-house retreat of the Court," said Farrier. The helicopter was landing now, on a broad flat lawn at the side of the house. They climbed out and were greeted by a handsome Pawn accompanied by a handsome Dalmatian.

"Thank you, Pawn Dunkeld," said Lady Farrier. "It's lovely to be here." Odette had to agree. It was dusk, and the fading light left the grounds all dark greens and purples. Hill Hall itself was white, and the windows were glowing.

As Pawn Dunkeld ushered them inside, Odette could see three strapping men and an equally strapping woman lifting the unconscious Rook out of the other helicopter and onto a waiting stretcher as Marcel supervised.

The party followed Pawn Dunkeld, who appeared to be something like the majordomo of the place, into a large, high-ceilinged foyer. "Your bags have all arrived and been brought to your rooms and unpacked," he said. "I expect you'll want a bath and a rest. There will be a light, informal dinner in about an hour, but if any of you are feeling too tired after today's events, just ring down and the staff can bring up a tray for you." Odette took this in with delighted incredulity. Judging from Clements's expression, she too felt like she'd stepped into a period drama. One of the staff, a young blond woman in a maid's uniform, guided them up the stairs to their room.

"Does the Checquy seriously have parlor maids and footmen?" Odette asked out of the side of her mouth.

"It's actually a popular posting," said Clements out of the side of her mouth. "People apply for yearlong secondments to Hill Hall.

Everyone here except the head cook and the head groundskeeper has a different, regular job in the Checquy. I gather there's a long waiting list."

"Really? People want to be servants?"

"It's one of those management-training things." Clements shrugged. "You know, learning humility and working as a team. Gleaning important lessons about leadership by being a scullery maid or footman. Plus, there are a lot of intensive advanced courses you can take here that look good on the résumé. Languages, wilderness survival, strategy and game theory, negotiating, pastry-making." Odette mulled it over and resolved to let Ernst know about the true nature of the staff. Not that she really thought he'd bother the housemaids, but he had lived in a time when servants weren't just doing their jobs for the entertainment value.

"But do you actually need a country-house retreat?"

"Probably not anymore," said the Pawn. "It's like Chequers— the official country house of the Prime Minister. I'm sure Hill Hall seemed vital at one point, but now it's handy for entertaining foreign dignitaries and the like. And a nice place to relax. The Court get first pick of the days, of course, but anyone can sign up to use it. I've attended a couple of weddings here."

"Here are your rooms," said the maid with a decidedly amused smile. It was apparent that she'd heard everything. "You share a sitting room, but you each have your own bathroom." She opened the door to Odette's room. "Miss Leliefeld, we've unpacked and prepared all your clothes. You didn't want us to open the two hard leather cases, correct?"

"Yes, thank you, um..." Odette faltered.

"Sarah," said the girl.

She showed Odette around the large room, which was decorated in warm tones that made it feel like the perfect place to fall asleep. Landscapes were hung on the walls, comfortable furniture was set around the room, and a fire flickered in the fireplace. Odette wandered through it, feeling distinctly déclassé in her tracksuit. Her cream heels (the Checquy shopper at Ascot had not gotten anyone shoes) still had some drops of Rook-blood on them and looked demented on the thick red carpet. I've spent my whole life not wearing a tracksuit and ruined heels, and then I come to England, and it's my default uniform, she mused sourly. A set of squashy brown leather chairs and a sofa seemed to draw back from her in horror. It was not pleasant to be the tackiest thing in the room.

Sarah caught her expression and winked, an action that seemed quite un-housemaidly. "If you need anything, Miss Leliefeld, just dial one on your room's phone." She departed, closing the door behind her.

I wonder what she does when she's not being a housemaid, thought Odette idly. She'll probably end up being my boss or something. Then she checked on her luggage. Two cases had indeed been left unopened. One contained the numerous medications she took to ensure that her body didn't realize what had been done to it and go on strike, along with the various chemicals she had to sleep in. The other case contained the set of surgical tools she'd been given for her eighteenth birthday. She didn't anticipate performing any surgeries that weekend, but then she hadn't anticipated performing one at the races either.

All right, first thing I'm going to do is shower and get into some better clothes, she resolved, if only so she could meet her own eyes in the mirror.

He sat on a bench by the river Thames and pondered. Lionel John Dover, formerly of Northampton, now abruptly of no fixed abode and completely unconcerned by that fact.

Nine hours ago, he had been a family man with a well-paying job as a senior manager at a successful company. True, for the past two years, he had been completely insane, but that had not bothered him as much as he would have expected, nor had it interfered with his life.

And then he met that woman.

She knew, he thought. She knew everything. She knew about

the things he'd done, and she'd done something to him, held him pinioned against his will.

So of course he'd had to act, even though it was broad daylight and they were in a crowd.

What was she? Who was she? How could she know about it? About me?

Panicked, he'd hurried away from the racecourse and gone straight to a cash machine. He had taken out as much money as he could, three hundred pounds. That, along with the money in his wallet, gave him four hundred and thirty-seven pounds. Normally he would not have been carrying more than a hundred pounds on him, but he'd been betting and socializing.

He hadn't dared to go to his car. Instead, his mind whirling, he had gone to the train station and bought a ticket to London. Once he got to the city, he visited the nearest Marks and Spencer and bought a complete change of clothes, paying with cash. Nondescript. Designed to blend in. He stuffed the morning suit into the first rubbish bin he could find and walked away.

He'd also walked away from his life, his family. His wife, Catherine. His children, Harry, Jenny, May, and Rupert. His dogs. His job. Everything. And yet, he found that he didn't care. They were the trappings of another man's life, a man who was not impossible and not insane.

Before it all started, he hadn't been a bad man. A stupendously boring one, perhaps, but not bad. He was not given to flights of fancy or possessed of much imagination. He humdrummed his way through life being respectable and upright. Certainly not the kind of man who would kill people.

The first time it happened, he'd been collecting for the Red Cross, of all things. Community service. Knocking on the door of a house on a quiet street in Daventry, he'd felt a burning in his spine, a heat that built unbearably and set him gasping for breath until a pulse surged out of him. It sent him to his knees, and he'd been instantly drenched with sweat. Then he had a sudden awareness of the inside of the house as crystals erupted from every surface and impaled the two people within. He'd seen the house through a thousand facets. He'd felt the man's and the boy's skin, their blood, their muscles and organs, as the blades cut through them.

His mind had fractured then, unable to reconcile the horrific unbelievability of what was happening with the sheer undeniability of its truth.

In a daze, he'd staggered away, gotten into his car, and driven back to his house. No one was home, and he'd stripped down and showered. He'd thrown his clothes in the washing machine and then passed out for hours. When he woke up, the memory of what had happened sent him shuddering. It was undeniably real. His rancid clothes were still in the machine and there were half-moon cuts in his palms from when his fingers had clenched unbearably, but beyond that, the memory of those moments was burned into his brain. He had to dash to the toilet, where he was violently ill. Then, trembling, he turned on the television.

Braced for coverage of the nightmare, he found absolutely nothing. The big story was that some Shetland pony carrying a fat child had bolted from a local riding school, run into town, and come to a halt in the market square. No mention of any murders. No mention of crystals.

Over the next few days, he'd watched the news, read the papers, and scoured the Internet, but there was never any reference to a horrific double murder, let alone a horrific double murder with unexplainable crystals. His psyche, already splintered by the impossibility of what he'd experienced, was shattered completely by the fact that no one else seemed to have noticed.

Lionel Dover had become a different person. The way in which he understood the world had changed. On the outside, he continued to go to work, to spend time with his friends and family, but inside, his thought processes could no longer be considered human.

Eventually, he'd driven by the house and seen no police tape, no bereaved family members wandering around looking shell-shocked. Several weeks later, a For Sale sign went up, and a few weeks after that, people moved in. They did not appear to be aware that their new home had been formerly occupied by a man and a boy who had been killed inexplicably.

Then it happened again. And again. Each time, the sensations were the same. Each time, he braced himself for the world to explode, for word to get out, for the media to go mad, and each time, it was as if it had never happened. No mention anywhere. He was still going home at the end of the day to his wife and children with no consequences whatsoever. He'd stopped caring about what it meant. He was a man who had a home, a job, and a family and who periodically killed people with crystals and felt no concern about any of it. He was madness in the convincing costume of a regular person.

He experimented, cautiously. He went up to London and found that the ability came when he called it—he could direct it to emerge as he wished. But there were times when it came without being summoned, and then there was no way to stop it. He'd feel the burn in his spine, a sure sign that in a few minutes the crystals would erupt, and so he would have to find a person on whom he could unleash them without anyone seeing.

And then that woman had appeared. That impossible woman. Now he sat on the bench by the river and came up with a thousand explanations for her, each one more ridiculous than the last. She was a witch. She was an angel sent to punish him. She was a government operative. She was a figment of his imagination. She was an alien. She was his conscience.

It was all so absurd, he would have thought it was a hallucination.

Except for one thing. His hands closed around his proof.

Much to her surprise, Myfanwy opened her eyes.

Not dead. That's good.

She was in a four-poster bed with a bag of blood hung up next to her, trickling down into a tube in her arm. The blood looked a little more purple than it should have, but she accepted it. On the far side of the room there was a nurse doing some paperwork at an antique desk. A clock on the wall noted that it was ten o'clock; the light coming through the window indicated that it was morning.

Myfanwy quickly took stock of how she felt and was cautiously pleased. No pain. She could wiggle her toes and fingers and — she reached out with her powers and made the nurse drop her pencil — her mind as well. As an added bonus, she knew exactly who she was.

On the downside, she was not entirely certain where she was. The large window showed a little walled garden that could have been anywhere. *Am I in the world's most baroque sanatorium? How long have I been out?* Before she could muster her thoughts to call out to the nurse, the woman walked out of the room. *Marvelous. Well, I suppose I can wait,* she thought. She shifted and felt a twist of pain in her back. *Yes,* she decided hastily, *I think I'll just lie still here for a while.* Then the door opened and her executive assistant entered briskly, holding a stack of files. She was such a familiar sight in such unfamiliar surroundings that Myfanwy felt a little trembly in the lower lip for a moment.

"Good morning, Rook Thomas," said Ingrid in a tone that acknowledged no difference from any other morning.

"Good — good morning, Ingrid. Where am I?"

"One of the rooms at Hill Hall. You were at Ascot yesterday."

"Oh, okay." She felt a rush of relief. "You didn't have to come up here. The traffic this morning must have been a bother."

"I came last night, Rook Thomas. Now, the Rookery has couriered over these reports for you to review and some papers for you to sign."

"All right," said Myfanwy, blinking her eyes rapidly. "Oh, what about my car?"

"It's been delivered back to the Rookery, but I'm afraid that a member of the Reading team had to break in and hot-wire it. They didn't have your handbag, and no one turned it in at the racecourse. New keys are being cut."

"Well, that's irritating."

"The phones and credit cards have been canceled, of course, and your various ID cards are being reissued."

"Thank you." She reached out cautiously, braced for the pain that sparked pointedly in her back and insides, and took the first document. It turned out to be all about her.

The report advised that Rook Myfanwy Thomas had been impaled by a spike of crystal of unknown type that possessed characteristics of quartz and alabandite. The weapon had damaged a couple of major organs, which sent her into shock.

Dr. Marcel Leliefeld and Miss Odette Leliefeld had performed impromptu surgery and repaired the injuries, preempting the death that would normally have occurred from that sort of damage. Examination of the spike did not show any fracturing or chipping.

A photocopy of Dr. Marcel Leliefeld's notes written in glorious copperplate listed the various compounds that had been applied to her during the surgery. The names meant nothing to Myfanwy, but she assumed the Checquy surgeons had reviewed it and would have declared war if something ghastly had been done. More compounds had been added to the blood that was percolating into her. Dr. Leliefeld noted that, provided she remained in bed for the rest of the day and drank plenty of fluids, she would be able to get up to attend that evening's dinner, though she would be restricted to one glass of wine during the meal and one cognac afterward. She should be fully recovered by the next day, and there would be no scarring.

Well, I was bloody lucky there, she thought weakly. She knew that she should probably be outraged at the thought of Grafter materials floating about inside her, but she simply couldn't manage it. For one thing, it would be churlishly ungrateful, and for another, the fact that she was alive and would be able to get up for dinner made it impossible to mind.

There were some distant bangs, and the two women looked sharply at the window.

"Are we under attack?" asked Myfanwy calmly.

"Sir Henry has taken the guests to shoot skeet," said Ingrid.

"Oh, well, as long as none of the guests get shot," said Myfanwy. She turned her attention back to the paperwork.

The next report made her gasp. The first page was a photograph of the murderer.

"What? Do we have him?" she asked Ingrid.

"No," said the EA. "But we know who he is." Myfanwy nodded disappointedly and turned her attention to the dossier. Lionel John Dover of Northampton. I fucking hate you. Most of the file consisted of standard government information—records from the National Health Service, a précis of his finances, details about his family—but there were also two sketches that Pawn Clements had done of him. The first was his face at rest. It was unmistakably him.

She's very good, thought Myfanwy. Of course, she would have to be. If she's summoning up these images, the Estate would have made sure she could draw well so that she could show them to other people.

The second picture, however, was the one that made her hands sweat. According to the caption, Clements had recorded his expression at the moment that he'd unleashed the crystals in the bathroom. It was the same look that Myfanwy had seen when he'd stabbed her through the hand and in the back. The gritted teeth, the staring eyes, the expression of exertion. But in this picture, there was a look of satisfaction on his face that made her want to vomit.

"The pursuit is under way?" asked Myfanwy tightly.

"Yes, Rook Thomas," said Ingrid, "but you know we have to be discreet. There's the fear that if we just started slapping this picture up on television screens and in post offices, we might push him to lash out with his powers in public."

"If we go public, so might he," mused Myfanwy. "God, this job is ridiculous. The monsters and the monster-hunters both have to be circumspect. So, what are we doing?"

"We've spoken with his family—they'd actually gone to the police and filed a missing-persons report when he didn't return home after the races. We've got Checquy people posted in Northampton and searching the area around Ascot. But honestly, he could have gone anywhere. His car was still in the parking lot, but so many attendees traveled by train, he could be anywhere by now."

"Hmm. My concern is that, since he knows someone is onto him, he'll do a Lord Lucan and vanish. Either he'll go on the run in England or he'll bolt out of the country. I don't want this man getting away from us, Ingrid."

"They're doing their best, Rook Thomas."

"I know," said Myfanwy tiredly.

"Do you want some good news?"

"Desperately."

"The BBC's fashion team liked your hat."

Myfanwy looked up at her in confusion. "I beg your pardon?"

Ingrid produced a printout and handed it to her. There, in glorious color, was Myfanwy in her hat. The caption gave no name but described the hat in loving detail. "Oh. Gosh. Does this constitute a security problem?"

"I shouldn't think so. To be honest, Rook Thomas, no one would recognize you without the hat."

"Thanks," said Myfanwy sourly. "Well, that is nice. Remind me to write a thank-you note to that Greek woman who bought it for me."

"Lisa Constanopoulos."

"Right. Oh, and she was one of the people who prophesied the amnesia, so it'll have to be a letter of introduction as well." The intricacies of etiquette in the supernatural world would make Emily Post stab herself in the heart with a fork, she mused. Admittedly, it would be whichever fork was completely appropriate for the occasion.

I'm afraid that the shooting season won't start for several months yet," said Sir Henry. "Pity, too, because we get some excellent pheasant and partridge here at the hall. Still, I thought some sporting clays might be a nice way to spend the morning. Give you a chance to try out the guns."

Odette held her gun carefully. After breakfast, in the library, Sir Henry had presented her, Marcel, and Ernst each with a long, hard leather case with brass corners. Inside, nestled in red felt, were two shotguns. Made of rich, warm wood and gleaming steel, they were works of art. Intricately scrolled initials had been engraved onto the back metal bit, the name for which Odette didn't know. It looked like a weapon for royalty.

"Anderson Wheeler," Sir Henry had said. "Shop in Mayfair. I had them made for you as a welcoming gift. The stock and forend are Turkish walnut, and your initials have been incorporated into the engraving. Lovely things, aren't they?" Odette touched one of the guns hesitantly. The polished wood was flawlessly smooth under her fingertips. She'd never had anything to do with guns, but these were, quite possibly, the most beautiful gift she'd ever received. They were even nicer than the eyes she'd gotten for her twenty-first birthday or the spleen that Pim had made for her for Valentine's Day.

"A custom pair of side-by-side twelve-bores for the gents," Sir Henry had said. "And then I thought a pair of twenty-bores for the lady." He'd gone on, talking about the guns and pointing out the accessories in the case: cleaning rods, snap caps, an oil bottle, and turnscrews.

Now she was standing on the grass with one of her twenty-bore guns in her hands. She was wearing safety glasses and earmuffs, trying to remember everything the gamekeeper, Pawn Farley, had told her.

"Ready?" asked Farley. She nodded tightly. "Pull!" And the target went flying.

Odette tensed and went into the same sort of trance that she entered while doing microsurgery. Her eyes sharpened and the world jumped into razor clarity. She tracked the disc easily, and the muscles in her arms and shoulders activated. Her gun snapped up, almost automatically, and she squeezed the trigger, felt the gun punch back. The clay pigeon shattered, and everyone applauded.

"Well done!" said Sir Henry. "Very good for a first-timer."

"I may have cheated a bit, Sir Henry," she confessed, and she pointed to her eyes. "These are augmented." He laughed.

"Not to worry," he said. "We've been known to deviate a bit from the standard ourselves. Farley, would you show her?" The gamekeeper nodded.

"Pull!"

The clay disc cut through the air, and the gamekeeper stepped forward. Odette saw him tense his shoulders, and then there was a crackling sound in the air. As they watched, a gray cloud coalesced swiftly around the pigeon. The target grew denser and darker until there was a rough brick of dull iron tumbling through the air. It landed with a muffled thunk, lodging itself in the turf.

"My God," said Marcel.

"Of course, we don't do that sort of thing during the pheasant season," said Sir Henry.

"It upsets the gundogs," muttered Farley.

"Very impressive," said Ernst. "May I try? Without the gun?" He handed his shotgun to the startled waiting loader. "As high and as far as you can, please." The man at the thrower nodded and made some adjustments. "Pull."

The disc took off, and so did Ernst. His feet tore up the grass as he blurred across the field. The thud of his shoes against the ground was like a drumbeat. He launched himself meters high into the air, pivoted, and kicked the disc into fragments. As they watched, he twisted on the descent and landed, crouching, in the grass, not even puffing.

There was silence, and a hum of tension hung about the party for a moment. It wasn't clear if a challenge had been made or answered. Then everyone who wasn't Odette started laughing. She rolled her eyes and carefully took her finger off the second trigger of the gun.

This is it," said Sander in a tone of deepest satisfaction. Bart looked around suspiciously. They had stopped at a T-junction.

In front of them, across the road, was Hyde Park, again. Behind them was the maze of streets and houses that Sander had led them through for hours.

"This is what?"

"The house they're in; it's three back on the left. I didn't want to stop in front of it in case they were watching."

"You're certain?" said Laurita.

"Do you want to go sniff the doorstep?" Sander asked tartly. "Yes, I'm certain. Our boy went in there about an hour ago and hasn't come out. Or at least, he hasn't come out the front door. There are four others inside, matching the samples we were given."

Bart nodded. He leaned against a tree and surveyed the road they had just come down. It was lined with tall white houses merging into one another. Behind railings, steps led down to basement entrances. In such houses, neighbors were separated by the thinness of a wall. Sounds might carry through. It was not the ideal place to stage an assault.

"We'll wait until dark," he decided. "I'll alert Marie. We will need the others."

More helicopters flew to Hill Hall throughout the day, carrying other members of the Court of the Checquy. Bishop Attariwala. Chevaliers Whibley and Eckhart. Rook Kelleher. Finally, an hour after sunset, a helicopter roared overhead without landing. A few minutes later, out of the darkness, Bishop Alrich came walking up the drive dressed in a dark suit. Odette watched him through the window of the sitting room. His hair burned in the lights from the house, and she shivered.

"I suppose we should go down," she remarked to Clements, who was sitting on the couch and looking petrified. The Pawn was actually sweating at the thought of a formal sit-down dinner with the Court. This from the woman whose file says she once went bare-knuckle against a neo-druid who was twice her size and armed with titanium sickles, thought Odette incredulously.

"Don't worry, I won't leave you," some unexpected sympathy prompted her to say. Clements shot her a grateful look and then appeared surprised. "Your dress looks great," Odette added. In fact, the dress looked only all right, but the Pawn needed all the encouragement she could get.

The call had gone out.

The Chimerae scattered around London had heard Marie's voice reverberating gently in the bones of their ears. Some had been staking out the various Checquy facilities. Some had positioned themselves as guards at locations that the Broederschap had judged to be high-profile targets. It was a sign of their desperation that three trackers were riding the Tube randomly in the hope that they might stumble upon a trace of their quarry's scent. Upon hearing Marie's message, they had all left their posts and headed quickly to their hotel, where a large (but not really large enough) room was serving as their base of operations.

Laurita and Sander had remained behind to stake out the front and rear of the house in case the Antagonists decided to go for a wander. Bart had explained the situation to the gathered troops. Sentries were deployed to relieve Laurita and Sander, and replacements would arrive every forty-five minutes. By great good fortune, there was a B and B just down the road from the Antagonists' house, and a Chimera named Fawn had taken a room there that had a view of the street. She was now curled up on the windowsill pretending to read magazines and scanning the Antagonists' front door. The Chimera soldier with the most charm and some specialized musk glands had gone around to the local council office and emerged with both the floor plans of the house and a date with the somewhat startled but delighted head planning officer.

With Marie looking through his eyes and making the occasional suggestion through his mouth, Bart, along with two other Chimerae, had composed a plan of attack.

"Well, this will not be quiet or clean," said Amanda, one of the three strategists. She leaned over the building schematics, committing them to memory. "So we must ensure that it's fast. If we're quick enough, we'll be out of there before the neighbors can even call the police."

Bart eyed the blueprints thoughtfully. It was an old building, very narrow, with five stories. He marked the exits. Front door, back door, basement door, he thought. Of course, we do not know their capabilities. For all we know, they could simply vault out of a top-story window and go trotting away down the street.

"Two of our people are equipped with thermal vision," said Franz, the other strategist. "We will identify where in the building they are sleeping, if they do sleep. If they hear us coming, they will try to either fight or flee, which might slow us down a bit. We must give them as little warning as possible."

"The advantage," said Amanda, "is that this house shares walls on either side of it. We need to cover only the front and the back."

"Marie, do you want them captured or killed?" Bart asked the air. He heard a heavy sigh come back through his own mouth. It was a little disconcerting, acting as a speakerphone.

"I'll need to consult with the graaf," she said, and a perfect re-creation of her voice came from Bart's lips. "I'll be recommending execution. I don't think we can take any chances." Was it his imagination, or did he hear a trace of regret in her voice? He shrugged. "But it will be up to him. If the order is to kill them, be sure to bring back their bodies. If you have time, I'd like all their possessions, but the priority is their corpses."

The plan that they formulated called for exquisite coordination. Two snipers would cover the front of the building and two would cover the rear, in case any of the Antagonists elected to try to escape through a window. With eyes that contained both raptor and feline genes, the Chimerae would be able to pick out any movement, even in the dark.

A team of four would scale the building and station themselves on the roof. Two teams of four would position themselves at the front and back doors, and a team of two would enter via the basement. At a signal given by Bart, they would all tear through the place. With the speed the Chimerae could muster up, Bart knew it would sound like a barrage of thunderbolts blasting through the house. To say nothing of the gunfire. He almost pitied the neighbors who were going to be jolted out of their sleep. Every room would be checked. Any Antagonist was to be killed on sight.

It had been a very good plan, and Bart had been quite looking forward to seeing it play out, except that at 4:30 p.m., four Antagonists, two males and two females, had walked out of their front door, nearly giving the posted sentries heart attacks. There was no sign of the unnatural white skin the Chimerae had been warned about. They looked like normal people; they were dressed in normal clothes and had normal faces. They appeared to be in their early twenties, and while the four of them, two black boys, an Asian girl, and a white girl, did garner second glances from a few passersby, it was only because they were all beautiful.

They carried no weapons, but they did have a picnic basket with them, which was the subject of much frenzied debate and speculation among the Chimerae. The consensus was that it contained some sort of weapon of mass distraction, but then the Antagonists spread a blanket on the grass in Hyde Park, opened said basket (prompting some flinching on the part of the Chimera observers), and proceeded to extract an early dinner of cold chicken and various kinds of salad.

"Well, that's fine," said Amanda. "They'll have their little picnic in the park, and then they'll go back to their house, and the plan can still go ahead." Bart said nothing.

Two Chimerae remained stationed by the house, and fresh soldiers were dispatched to the park to maintain a watch on the party of Antagonists, who seemed to be in no hurry to move on, even after they had finished their food and packed the plates back in the basket. Grafter soldiers jogged by the party in running suits and strolled by in business clothes. A pram was hastily procured and a shawl draped over it so that two Chimerae could sit on a nearby bench, absently rocking a pillow masquerading as a baby. Serious thought was given to acquiring a dog to blend in with the many dog walkers, but no one could agree on what would be done with it afterward. The two youngest Chimerae, who happened to absolutely loathe each other, consented, under duress, to lie down in the grass near the Antagonists and make out for a while. With the heavy foot traffic in the park, there was simply nothing to do but wait. The Chimerae could not so much as shout at one of the Antagonists without drawing the attention of witnesses.

"Patience," said Franz after hours had passed and they received a report that the Antagonists had not only failed to move from their spot but had opened a bottle of champagne. They remained lounging on their blanket, chatting easily. There was much laughter. From what the Chimera observers could pick up and relay back to the hotel room, they did not appear to be talking about anything of relevance. No mention of the Broederschap, the Checquy, or any planned attacks. A good deal of the conversation appeared to revolve around a British reality-television show and who was the biggest bitch on it.

"You're sure these are the Antagonists?" Amanda asked doubtfully.

"Sander and two other trackers confirmed it," said Bart.

"Do we want to try entering the house in their absence?" asked Franz. Bart hesitated. It was tempting, but the possibility of raising an alarm was too great. If the Chimerae followed the plan, it wouldn't matter if an alarm was raised. They would still be able to surround the Antagonists and kill them.

Night fell. The other visitors to the park started to depart but the Antagonists made no move to leave; they continued to lounge on the blanket. A park official bustled up to them and pointed out that the park was now closing. One of the females stood up to talk to him, putting her hand on his shoulder and leaning close. He nodded several times and wandered away. The Antagonists toasted one another and settled back down.

To the outrage of the observing Chimerae, the park official then bustled up to them and advised them that the park was now closing. Rather than raise a fuss and thus possibly draw attention, the soldiers meekly withdrew.

Of course, they didn't entirely withdraw, because they were elite warriors on a mission of vital importance who would not be thwarted by a minor functionary, and so the two of them with the best eyesight hid in some nearby shrubbery.

For several hours.

"They have opened another bottle of champagne," said one of the observers over the network in their heads. Back in the room, Bart swore loudly in Dutch.

"It is now two in the morning," said Franz. "Surely they cannot stay in the park forever."

"Screw the plan! Even if they were not the Antagonists, these creatures need to die," said Bart. "Staying in the park after closing time—it is disgusting behavior. The park is closed for a reason. Everyone, we are moving out. We'll kill them in the park, collect the bodies, take the house to check if there are any others or any clues, and then come back here and get room service."

The gathered Chimerae who had been standing around the room, many of them asleep, all snapped to attention. The night concierge of the hotel was a trifle startled to receive a request for four taxicabs, but he arranged it with all the aplomb one would expect from an employee of that establishment. He said nothing as twelve people filed by silently, all wearing long coats, and got into the waiting cabs. The last person in a long coat, a sober-looking man with a Dutch accent, slipped him an envelope that contained an insanely large tip.

The cabs deposited the long-coated people at various points around the boundary of Hyde Park. The Chimerae removed their coats to reveal tight black clothing and submachine guns. Four of them had sniper rifles, which they briskly assembled in the shadows.

Upon a whispered instruction over the network from Bart, they all vaulted over the walls of the park and silently converged near the area the Antagonists were occupying. They took up positions a judicious distance from the party, close enough to shoot them but far enough away that their whispered communications could not be heard by even the keenest of ears. Concealed by trees, bushes, and the darkness, they formed a ring around the picnickers, waiting for an order to be given. Everyone had been fully briefed; muscles were limbered up, talons unsheathed, hair retracted, glands primed, tongues armed, and safeties released.

Only Bart remained outside the park while his soldiers surrounded their quarry.

"Marie, it's almost time," he said quietly to the air. "I need confirmation of the kill order."

"I've conferred with the graaf, and we've agreed," she said, her voice vibrating in his ear bones. "Execute them. Be sure to bring back their bodies."

"Understood," he said. "Chimerae," he said into the darkness, "this will be a terminal interaction. I repeat, they will be luggage, not guests." He leapt liquidly over the wall, moved through the trees and the bushes, and wriggled through the grass until he reached his designated position with his team.

It was a job that would call for versatility and improvisation. No one knew what powers the Antagonists could bring to bear. The Chimerae would begin by shooting their prey from a distance, but there was no certainty that these four could be killed by bullets—even the specialized ammunition the Chimerae carried.

No, I expect this will be mainly knife work in the end, thought Bart grimly. And fist, fang, talon, and venom work. He gazed at them for a moment, the lenses of his eyes obediently zooming in, the hand-tooled rods in his retinas cutting through the darkness. He could see their faces as they laughed and drank. They were lovely. They looked like beautiful young people. That's not what they really look like, he told himself. Those aren't their real faces. As he watched, they seemed to glow faintly in the night.

"Chimerae, every second soldier, identify your proposed target," he whispered. In the event that the Antagonists were not brought down by gunfire, eight soldiers would go in all at once, two to a target. The others would remain as a fallback perimeter, ready to move in as support or pursue any Antagonists who made a break for it. The troops reported which Antagonists they would target.

"On my mark, open fire."

"Three."

"Two."

"O—"

"All right," one of the picnickers called. "We surrender!"

Bart froze.

"Wait," said Marie's voice in the head of every Chimera, warning them to keep weapons trained on the targets.

"We know you're out there," said one of the male Antagonists. They were all standing except for the white female, who was still lounging on the blanket. "You've got us surrounded. It's over. We give up."

"Thoughts?" asked Marie, this time only in Bart's ear.

"I don't like it," said Bart. "I'll go forward, but at the first sign of anything, I'm opening fire."

"Understood," said Marie.

"If anything happens to me, command shifts to Amanda."

"Understood," said Amanda. "And my first order will be to kill them."

Bart stood up and walked forward out of the gloom, his gun at the ready. The Antagonists turned to watch him.

"Congratulations, you tracked us down," the taller man said. Bart wondered if he was the one who had killed the people in the restaurant and then spent all that time standing outside the delegation's hotel. Sander could probably have told him, but the tracker was out there in the darkness, watching, waiting for the signal.

"Obey every order," said Bart. "You will receive no second chances. Now lie down on the ground and put your hands on your heads."

"Yes, well, we've changed our minds," said the Asian woman.

She was dressed in boots and a red velvet minidress that looked as if it had come from the 1960s. "We're not surrendering at all."

"Kill them now!" shouted Bart. But none of the Chimerae, not even him, could move a muscle. It was as if their bodies had been encased in steel. Bart could not even blink. They were like statues.

"Predictable," sniffed the girl in the minidress. "Predictable and pathetic." She looked at him out of a movie-star face and wrinkled her nose. "Why on earth would we surrender to you? You disgust us."

"And I have a special message for that bitch who's peering out through your eyes," said the male who had spoken before. All the Chimerae heard Marie's sharp breath. "What is coming will smash any possibility of an alliance between you and the Checquy. You have brought this upon yourselves." He held up his hand tauntingly, and all the Chimerae tensed, but his hand was empty. "You can do nothing against us." His black skin rippled and became shiny porcelain white.

He snapped his fingers, and all the Chimerae died.

31

Thank you so much for inviting us," said Odette. "I've had a wonderful time here." It was almost the truth. The long weekend at Hill Hall really would have been terrifically relaxing had it not been for two things.

The first was the formal dinners they'd all been obliged to attend each night. These had taken place in a beautiful room with soft light and lovely paintings. The food had been delicious, the conversation had been polite and uncontroversial, everyone had been extremely pleasant, and the horror of it all had nearly driven Clements to self-harm. Making polite chitchat amongst the elite was such obvious agony for the Pawn that Odette had actually felt sorry for her.

The second thing that unrelaxed the weekend was the phone call Ernst had received from Marie sometime in the wee hours of Saturday morning. Odette hadn't dared ask what he'd been told, but it sent him into a cold rage that lasted the rest of the weekend. He'd been withdrawn, sitting silently at meals and spending the rest of the time in his room or the library talking on his mobile phone. Odette and Marcel had apologized discreetly, and Marcel had explained to their hosts that they'd received bad news from home.

"Have we received bad news from home?" Odette had asked when they were alone in the gardens. Marcel explained what had happened to the Chimerae.

"And so Marie had to activate their discretion functions," said Marcel. "Otherwise, the Checquy would have found sixteen armed corpses in Hyde Park and two outside a nearby house, all unmistakably of Broederschap origin. With the discretion protocols, all their DNA unzipped itself, and they liquefied."

"So instead of eighteen corpses in a public park and on the footpath, there will be eighteen sets of uniforms and weaponry, all heavily stained with miscellaneous organic fluids," said Odette. "How do we explain that?"

"We don't have to." Marcel shrugged. "I expect the Checquy will hear about it, but they've no reason to link it to us."

"So what happens now?"

"We don't know," said Marcel. "We aren't sure how they were able to deal with the Chimerae so easily. This is one of the reasons that Ernst is so perturbed. We appear to have run out of options, and the Antagonists seemed to be very confident that their next move would turn the Checquy against us. We cannot flee, we cannot fight, and telling the truth has become increasingly dangerous, since we have been actively lying about a serious threat that has already killed several British civilians. If you think of anything, do let us know."

"You seem very calm," said Odette accusingly.

"I'm very good at not panicking," Marcel said. "But if it makes you feel any better, I am extremely worried about this."

For the rest of the weekend, Odette had fretted and brooded and come up with exactly nothing. Neither, apparently, had any of the other Grafters. And now, after an early supper on Sunday evening, the guests were getting ready to be driven back to London.

"We look forward to seeing you here again soon, Miss Leliefeld," said Pawn Dunkeld. "It's been a pleasure having you all visit." He shook her hand, and she climbed into the back of the car. She sighed. The limo contained her, Clements, Rook Thomas, and Mrs. Woodhouse. Theirs was the last car to depart, and they'd been held up by the Rook's having some final words with Pawn Dunkeld and then making everyone wait while she took a long confidential call from London.

As they moved out of the gates of Hill Hall, Odette looked at her traveling companions. Rook Thomas had her eyes closed, Mrs. Woodhouse was doing something with a tablet computer, and Clements was messing about with her phone. Apparently, there would be no conversation for a while. Shrugging, Odette turned to the window. It was dark outside the car, far darker than she would have expected. The road to Hill Hall was old—someone had told her it dated back to Roman times—and it seemed to have sunk over the centuries. High banks of earth rose on either side, with trees joining above them. It was like driving through a tunnel.

"Rook Thomas, according to Dr. Leliefeld's schedule, it's time for you to have some cranberry juice," said Mrs. Woodhouse. She held out a bottle, and the Rook accepted it.

"Thank you, Ingrid," said the Rook. "There's nothing like having one's every beverage sched—what the hell?" The car had veered violently for a moment, almost swerving into one of the banks flanking the road. The modesty panel slid down.

"Sorry, Rook Thomas," said the driver. "I think something flew into my eye."

"It's fine," said Thomas sourly. She'd spilled the juice down the front of her suit. She took off her seat belt and was in the process of taking off her jacket when the car swerved again. "All right, look, just stop the car," she said in irritation. "If there's an insect, we'll let it out."

The driver didn't reply. Instead, an agonized scream filled the car. Everyone's gaze flew to the front, where, to universal horror, they saw that the driver was clawing frantically at his own face.

Which meant that he had taken both hands off the steering wheel.

"Rook Thomas, seat belt," said Mrs. Woodhouse flatly. The Rook struggled to get her arms out of her jacket as the car began to career back and forth, slamming against the banks. "Quickly."

"What is wrong with him?" asked Odette.

"No idea," said Rook Thomas tightly.

"He's got blood on his hands," exclaimed Clements, craning her neck to peer into the front seat. "I think he's tearing out his own eyes!"

"Rook Thomas, can't you take control of him or something?" asked Odette, clutching at her seat belt. Before the Rook could answer, the car bounced off a bank, and Rook Thomas banged her head against the door of the car. She clutched at her head, her eyes squeezed shut. The car veered off across the road and scraped against the embankment on the other side.

There was a long, bubbling howl from the driver and then two wet bursting sounds, like someone dropping two waxed-paper bags full of water onto the floor. He slumped against the window, and Odette saw, to her astonishment, that a torrent of acrid yellow smoke was flowing out of his face. Unthinking, she gasped, and the cloud seemed to reach out and crawl down her throat.

It was as if molasses had been poured into her brain. Her thoughts grew thick and heavy, and it felt like weights had been attached to her eyelids and wrists. She could feel the car bucking beneath her, but it all seemed very distant and unimportant.

The other women were coughing and gasping, but they were somehow still concerned with who was driving the car. Odette managed to muster up enough focus to admire their determination.

"Take his foot off the damn accelerator!" Clements choked out just as the car jerked, swerved, and ran straight into a bank.

Odette was the first to open her eyes. She could practically feel her system burning away that yellow smoke inside her. Her metabolism was in overdrive, her amplified liver cells enthusiastically scouring the compounds from her blood. *What on earth was that stuff?* she wondered. *I suppose the driver's Checquy powers must have gone bad or something.*

She looked around and saw that everyone else in the car was unmoving, slumped in their seat belts. Everyone except Rook Thomas, who was sprawled halfway down to the floor. She had one arm looped through the seat belt, and there was a good deal of blood in her hair—either from hitting her head or from smacking into something when the car crashed into the embankment. Odette herself seemed to be unhurt beyond a few aches. She undid her seat belt, crawled across the limo to the Rook, and checked the smaller woman's pulse. Thomas was alive, but she wouldn't be happy when she woke up. Odette smoothed her hair aside and checked the cut on her scalp. It was not actually very deep, and the bleeding was minimal. A quick examination revealed no sign of any other injuries.

Well, she won't die from a scalp wound, Odette decided, but she retrieved a clean handkerchief from her purse and applied a judicious amount of pressure nonetheless. *We should get her back to Hill Hall quickly. I don't think Marcel's repair work would have been damaged, but we need to make certain.* With one hand, she dug her mobile phone out of her purse and rang the emergency Checquy number.

"Office of Qualifications and Examinations Regulation, notifications line," said a cheerful voice. "This is Nigel Bonnington."

"This is Odette Leliefeld. There's been a car accident," said

Odette. She heard a pained sigh come over the phone. Sorry to inconvenience you, she thought.

"Are you okay? You sound all right."

"I'm fine. However, Rook Thomas, Pawn Clements, and Rook Thomas's executive assistant are all unconscious, and Rook Thomas is bleeding from the scalp. I'm not certain what other injuries she's sustained, but I'm giving her first aid." She couldn't help smiling a little as she heard the sound of someone having an extremely quick nervous breakdown come down the line. Yeah, suck on that, mate. After a few seconds of compacted panic, Pawn Bonnington spoke. This time, his voice was a little higher in pitch.

"And you're trained to give first aid?"

"I took out my own appendix when I was sixteen," she said. "And I put two new ones in when I was nineteen. I think I can apply pressure to a laceration."

"What's your location?"

"No idea," said Odette. "Fifteen minutes from Hill Hall."

"I'll alert the staff there. Help should arrive soon."

"Great," said Odette. "I'll stay on the line, if you don't mind."

"And the driver?" Bonnington asked.

"Oh, crap," Odette said guiltily, suddenly remembering that there was another person in the car. She carefully lifted the hankie off the Rook's head and saw that the bleeding had stopped. Then she scooched forward. When she peered into the front of the limo, she flinched. The driver was draped over the steering wheel and twitching violently. The airbag had apparently gone off when the car hit the bank. However, while an airbag was generally a good thing for a person in an accident, it had not been good for a man who was in the process of inflicting terrible wounds on his own face. Odette was no stranger to blood, but the mess in the driver's seat was stomach-turning. The yellow smoke seemed to have dissipated—she couldn't even taste it in the air.

"He's in very bad shape," she reported over the phone. "Significant self-inflicted wounds to the face."

"What?"

"I think he had a seizure of some sort," said Odette.

"A seizure?"

"Yes, and then his powers went nuts—smoke everywhere. I think that's what knocked everybody out."

"My God. And you're sure you're all right?"

"Yes, I'm fine," said Odette, "but everyone else is still unconscious." *I hope they haven't been poisoned.* She awkwardly put her hand through the hatch and fumbled at the driver's neck. His pulse was erratic, and his skin was burning hot. *Christ, this is not good.* "I'm going to try to help him."

Getting to him to render said help, however, would be difficult. The car's impacts and scrapings with the embankments had left the sides dented and the doors jammed shut. *I'll have to try to wriggle into the front seat of the car. It wouldn't be easy—the hatch was intended only for the transmission of imperious orders and, possibly, drive-through fast food.* Matters were made even worse by the fact that the front of the car had crumpled in on itself. *Still, I think I can do it.* She put the phone on speaker, laid it on the seat, and was about to start when she heard distant voices outside the car.

Well, that was fast, she thought. *I have to give the staff at Hill Hall credit.*

"Miss Leliefeld?" said the voice over the phone hesitantly.

"Hmm?"

"The driver..."

"Yes?" she asked.

"He's not a Pawn. He's a Retainer."

"What? So?" *The Checquy seemed obsessed with ranks and titles.*

"So he doesn't have any powers."

She froze. *What the hell does that mean?* Then she frowned. *Is that laughter outside?* She heard the voices of young men. They sounded elated.

What the hell does that mean?

Unless it's... oh God.

Antagonists.

She fumbled to take her mobile phone off speaker mode, then froze as she heard footsteps coming toward the car. She knelt on the seats and peered cautiously through the window. It was tinted, so she was certain no one would see her, but it also meant that, on the sunken road in the twilight of the countryside, she couldn't see much. Just silhouettes getting closer.

"Miss Lelie—"

"No time," she interrupted in a fierce whisper. "Let Hill Hall know, men have come. They must have attacked the car, and now they're coming toward us."

"How many men?"

Odette risked another look. "Five, I think."

"Weapons?"

"I can't tell."

"Please hold." Tinkling electronic music ensued.

You've got to be kidding me. She looked up at the sound of someone trying the door handle.

"Bloody door's not opening," said a voice. Odette frowned in confusion—it was not at all the accent she'd been expecting. This was a young man with a very specific London accent. Cockney, it's called, she remembered. So what's the significance of that? Maybe I was completely wrong about who they are.

That would be nice.

"Well, what a fucking surprise," said someone else. "Smash a window, then."

"Nah, wait," said another voice. "Let's have a little play." There was a grunt, and then Odette looked up at the sound of boots landing lightly on the roof of the car. Another pair landed, more heavily, and the roof dimpled a bit. Crap. She hunkered down on the floor and looked around anxiously. The back of the car seemed almost irresponsibly empty of weapons. Her new shotguns were in the boot. There was a little minibar, but all the bottles seemed to be made of plastic.

"Hello, Miss Leliefeld?" came a tiny voice. It was her phone. "Miss Leliefeld?"

"Do you hear that?" one of the voices on the roof said.

"No," said the other one.

"Just move," said one of the figures still on the ground. "Now. Help will be coming."

"Right."

A broad metal blade punched through the ceiling. Odette ducked her head and pressed the back of her hand against her mouth so as not to scream. She looked up and saw the blade directly above her. About ten centimeters of it jutted through the roof. It was as wide as her forearm and made of a dull black metal. As she watched, it began to rip along the roof, leaving a jagged tear behind it.

"Yeah, baby!" came the exultant shout from outside. "Fuck that shit up!"

We're being attacked by hooligans, thought Odette. And apparently they're fucking our shit up. She could feel her muscles tensing into tight springs, and her spurs slid out.

The sword blade was removed, and then two sets of hands forced themselves through the rip. She gave a moment's thought to slashing at them with her spurs, but before she could put thought into action, they had begun to haul back on the roof. A corner of it peeled away with a horrendous metal shrieking, and five male faces peered in. Two of them were black youths, and the other three were white. However, it was not their race that caught her attention.

They had all been mutilated, twisted. There were lines running all over their faces, cicatrices that were swollen and red. One of them had square scars around his eyes. Another had a line running down the center of his face. A third had two lines that began at a point under his chin, angled away from each other, and went up over his shaved head.

All five of them had elected to wear sleeveless T-shirts for the evening's festivities, and she could see similar marks on their arms. One man had continuous spirals curling up the length of his arms, slicing through some tattoos of dubious artistic merit. One of the black men had oblongs of pallid Caucasian skin implanted into his forearms. Another man had lines circling his oversize biceps, outlining the bulging muscles. The sword blade that had cut through the ceiling was projecting out of a slit in his arm.

Odette judged that they would not have looked reputable even before their modifications. Now, they gave the impression of being patchwork thugs. One of the white guys, the one with the sword, squinted at her.

" 'Ere, we've got one that's awake!" he announced, and then he smiled at her broadly. With a shock, she saw that his mouth was full of chromed serrations. "So, darling," he said to Odette, "are you my fanny?"

"I beg your pardon?" she said, completely at a loss.

"Not 'my fanny,' you tosser," said one of the black guys. "Myfanwy."

"Oh, whatever," said the first guy. "Like that's even a name."

"That's not Myfanwy Thomas," said a voice from the shadows by the side of the road. In contrast to the hooligans, this voice spoke with a polished upper-class English accent. "It's Odette Leliefeld. Hello, Odette, good to see you again." Odette frowned. He stepped forward, tall, blond, and handsome. She was fairly certain she had never seen him before in her life, and yet he somehow seemed familiar.

"Who are you?" she asked.

"Plenty of time for explanations later," said the man, smiling. "You'll be coming with us. For now, though, we have some errands to take care of. Lads, that's Myfanwy Thomas." He pointed at the slumped Rook. "Kill the fucking bitch right now."

The youth with the sword blade coming out of his arm drew back, preparing to strike. Odette lunged forward and slashed out with her left spur, slicing across his already scarred cheek.

The men all flinched back at her movement, and then they flinched back even farther when Sword Arm clutched at his face and began a hideous screaming. She'd given him a dose of the platypus venom, and it appeared to be having the effect for which the platypus had evolved it. The other young men around the car seemed suddenly unsure of themselves, but not the tall blond one.

"Anybody else want some?" asked Odette coldly. Sword Arm was now rolling in the dirt, squealing in pain. "You realize he got off lightly, right?"

"Bitch, you are gonna regret fucking up my mate," said one of the other men, the one with the scars twisting up his arms, whom Odette had mentally christened Spiral Guy. "And since you're not that Miff chick, well, you're not even gonna believe what we'll do to you." He bent his hand back slightly, and a blade made of bone slid out of his palm. It was a good twenty centimeters long, and glittered wetly.

"She lives, that's part of the deal," said the blond man sharply. The deal?

"Step back, lads, I got this," said another one of the men. His mouth had scars radiating out from it, and as he opened his mouth, his lips split along the lines, peeling open like the petals of the most disturbing flower in history. A fine crimson mist spewed out of his throat, enveloping Odette.

"You've got nothing," she said coldly. This time she was prepared. Her skin itched, but lenses slid down over her eyes and protected them. She pressed her lips tightly together, and muscles within her sinuses clamped shut. Then, while Mist-Breathing Guy (she was too focused on the task at hand to come up with a better moniker) stood back smugly and his face knit itself back together, she swiped forward with her spur and scored him across the neck.

He stared at her in bewilderment and then crumpled, whimpering. Apparently, he had a different reaction to platypus venom than his mate, although it was still an acceptable result. Odette breathed out. She had never actually used her spurs on a person before. She would have expected to feel something about injecting a man with an excruciatingly painful toxin. She didn't. Perhaps because she didn't have any room to question her actions here. It was simply something that had to be done.

The remaining three thugs didn't feel the need to question her actions either. Instead, they moved forward. Spiral Guy swiped out at her with the blade jutting out of his palm, and she flinched back hastily. Another man held up his hands, and she saw that he'd had extra thumbs added. With a wet crack, his arms split in two at the elbows. He reached behind his back and drew four knives. The black man with the white skin on his arms simply stalked toward her, his oversize muscles twitching slightly. The backs of his fingers were covered in shining, spiky carapaces, like knuckle-dusters made of insect shells.

I don't think I'm going to be able to buy us many more minutes, she thought. Those first two were complete strokes of luck.

Time to bluff.

"Do you think you can just take me down? You want to ask your two friends in the dirt there how easy it is?" she said. "And I'm out of the gentle venom. At least one of you is going to die."

"There's three of us left," said the muscled man, sounding not at all concerned, "plus our friend here." He nodded at the well-spoken blond man. "And you're stuck in the car. And we're gonna watch for your little bitch stingers."

"That's a fair point," conceded Odette. "But you've got to come in the car if you want us, and my little bitch stingers can kill you."

"I'm just going to cut them off," said Spiral Guy brightly. "Or rip them off."

I could probably scramble out of the car and run, Odette thought. Maybe I could lead them away? Except I'm sure at least one of them would stay and kill Rook Thomas. She looked down at the unconscious Checquy people. They weren't her people, but she couldn't leave them.

"This is what I get for working with amateurs," said the blond man. "You three, stop your bloody posturing and immobilize her. I'll take care of Myfanwy Thomas." He stepped forward when a new voice rang out from the trees at the top of the bank.

"Don't move," it said. Odette frowned—she knew it from somewhere. Everyone else froze, and a look of absolute horror erupted on the blond man's face.

"No!" the blond man shouted, absolutely aghast. "Not you! What are you doing here?"

"You, my friend, smell familiar," said the voice. "Where do I know you from?" The owner of the voice stepped forward. It was Bishop Alrich, dressed in a gray suit. He wore no tie, and his free-flowing hair was now a light auburn, almost blond.

"It's just some faggot in a suit," snarled the thug with the knuckle-dusters.

"Yes, quite right," said the blond man, rallying somewhat. "You take him, I'll kill the Rook." He drew a wicked-looking combat knife from inside his coat and moved toward the car. The thugs spread out before the Bishop, who stepped off the bank and dropped several meters to land smooth and unruffled.

"I won't let you kill her," said Odette to the blond man as he approached. Both spurs were unsheathed, and her knees were bent slightly, ready to move. To get at Rook Thomas, he'd have to climb in through the torn roof of the car. She set her mind. If he comes in here, he's getting the octopus venom.

"You couldn't possibly stop me, Odette."

"How do you know me?" she asked. He's not an Antagonist; they wouldn't talk to me like this.

"I'm wounded that you don't recognize me," said the man. "But we'll chat about that later. I really, really want to kill this woman right now." His fist blurred out and cracked Odette on the side of her face before she could react. She staggered, and her back hit the jagged metal where the roof had been torn. Her knees buckled and she went down on the floor of the car. The blond man vaulted in through the hole in the roof easily, swinging his legs in like a farmer going over a fence.

"You won't," she said, and lunged at him, her spurs out. He dropped the knife and caught her wrists easily.

"You're out of your league, Odette. But it sounds like I really need to hurry this up." Outside the car, there were ominous sounds of thuds and tearing. A high, howling scream cut off into a wet gasp. He forced her wrists to the side and slammed his head into hers. The world flashed, and her legs went buttery.

I think I'm going to throw up, she thought fuzzily. Now the

man's grip was the only thing holding her up, and he let her go. She felt herself slither into a puddle. I can't let him...She reached out weakly with her arm, and he planted a foot pointedly on her wrist and forced it onto the floor. He bent over and picked up his knife.

"Finally," he said, and there was a terrible eagerness as he looked down on the Rook. And then the expression on his face changed. Odette made an effort and focused beyond him. Bishop Alrich was perched on the peeled-back portion of the roof. His hair, face, and clothes were bloody, and his hand was closed around the blond man's throat.

"We should have a conversation," said the Bishop. The blond man's face twisted in frustration.

"Damn it! So close. Well, there's always next time." He shrugged, and Odette saw his eyes unfocus as he went limp in the Bishop's hand. The knife dropped to the floor.

"Well, that's disappointing," remarked the Bishop.

32

Before we begin, should Pawn Clements really be present?" asked Sir Henry. Felicity flushed and looked down at her feet. In the wood-paneled conference room, she was the only one standing. At one end of the table was the entire Court of the Checquy. She had been a trifle amused to note that they'd arrayed themselves in the positions of pieces on the chessboard, with the Lord and Lady flanked by the Bishops, who were flanked by the Chevs, who were flanked by the Rooks. Apparently, Rook Thomas was the Lady's Rook. Felicity herself was standing against the wall behind Rook Thomas.

At the other end of the table were four representatives of the Broederschap. Odette looked very small between Marcel and Ernst. Marie, her hair a rich mahogany, was sitting on the other side of Ernst. The distance between the two parties was not great, but it seemed very significant at that moment.

"I requested that Pawn Clements join us," said Rook Thomas. "I have absolute confidence in her discretion, and I believe that she can provide some important information."

"Very well, then," said Sir Henry. "Let us proceed." As one, the Court looked across to the members of the Broederschap. "Graaf van Suchtlen, earlier this evening, an attack occurred. Bishop Alrich observed that it was very specifically targeted at a member of this Court. The leader of the attackers, who has apparently lapsed into a state of catatonia, seemed to know Miss Leliefeld. A Checquy driver with no history of any unnatural abilities suffers a convulsion and vents a chemical weapon out of his skin—a weapon that appears to affect everyone except Miss Leliefeld. And the body parts of the attackers that our people managed to gather up, well, they show evidence of... alterations." His face, which had been serious before, now looked distinctly stern—almost merciless. "This all combines to form a very troubling scenario. We require an explanation. A true and complete explanation. Otherwise, this is going to go to a very, very ugly place."

The graaf's face was expressionless, but he made a movement with his shoulder, like someone shifting to stretch a sore muscle. Everyone tensed, except for Lady Farrier, who rolled her eyes. The atmosphere in the room was icy, and all the occupants of the room, as if by agreement, had their hands flat on the table in front of them. All of them, that is, except Felicity, who had her hands clenched at her sides, and Marcel, who was making notes on some writing paper and seemed quite unaware of any tension.

Felicity wondered anxiously if she was going to be witness to the first executive-level battle since the last time the Americans came for dinner.

"Very well," said the graaf finally. Just saying that seemed to have robbed him of his strength, because there was a pause sufficiently long that Marcel even looked up from his notes.

"Ernst," said Rook Thomas reprovingly.

"I apologize. This is difficult. I am ashamed." Odette looked up at him, startled. "I had hoped that we could resolve this trouble without ever revealing it to the Checquy, but we have failed." He sighed. "For the past several months, we have been the subject of attacks, horrible attacks upon our facilities and our people. There have been deaths, mutilations, and sabotage."

"Why on earth didn't you tell us about this?" asked Chevalier Eckhart. "We could have come to your assistance, even in Europe. Who are these attackers? Do you know?"

"Oh yes," said Ernst, and his voice shook with rage. "We know who they are. Among ourselves, we refer to them as the Antagonists, but in truth they are us. They are a splinter faction of the Broederschap."

"Oh, bloody hell!" exclaimed Rook Thomas in disgust. Everyone stared at her in surprise. The Rook seemed enraged, and she looked up at the ceiling with her mouth twisted. "What is wrong with you people?" It was not immediately apparent to whom she was speaking. She shook her head and, with a visible effort, calmed herself down. "Go on," she said coldly.

"It is the most shameful part, knowing that it is our own family members and colleagues who are responsible for this," said Ernst hesitantly.

"And dare we ask why they are doing this?" asked Lady Farrier. "What is the cause of this schism?"

"You, of course," said Ernst.

"Of course," said Farrier flatly.

"When I announced that the Broederschap would be joining forces with the Checquy, there were some protestations."

"Did you tell them about the pension plan?" asked Chevalier Whibley. "It's index-linked." He realized everyone was looking at him. "My apologies."

"He didn't tell them anything," said Odette darkly. "Just that it would be happening." Grootvader Ernst shot her a look, but she was staring down at her hands and didn't notice.

"And it will be happening," said Grootvader Ernst.

"Grootvader Ernst is accustomed to people doing what he tells them to," said Odette.

"Yes." He nodded. There was a long pause, but no more information was forthcoming. Apparently, he felt that everything had been said that needed to be said. People did what he told them to. He had told them to join the Checquy, and so they would. Odette diplomatically closed her eyes before she rolled them. Then she opened them again.

"There was quite a bit of shock when the announcement was made," she said. "We were informed that one of the heads of the Broederschap had been killed." She didn't add that he had been killed by the Checquy, but everyone was thinking it. "Then we were told that Grootvader Ernst had made peace with the Gruwels—I'm sorry, with your organization. Then we were told that we would be merging with this organization. All of this information was communicated over the course of five minutes."

"Oh, I said it nicer than that!" snapped Ernst.

"Not much nicer!" snapped back Odette. "We've lived in secret for centuries, Grootvader, petrified that the Checquy would track us down and finish the job they'd started in 1677. And then suddenly you expect us to move in with them! Of course people were going to react."

"I expected a reaction, but not this madness." The two of them stared at each other, and Felicity was caught by their resemblance. They might be separated by multiple generations, but there was no doubt that they were related.

"And who are these rebels, these Antagonists?" asked Chevalier Eckhart. "What resources do they have to command?"

"There are five of them," said Marcel, who'd returned to his notes. "Only five now. But they are dangerous."

"It was surprising, at least to me," said Ernst. "I had anticipated trouble from the older members of the Broederschap, those most set in their ways. There are still a few who have been with us since the very beginning, who remember the Isle of Wight and the Checquy. If anyone could be expected to hold on to their hatred, I thought it would be them. But it was not that way at all. Rather, it was the younger people, the apprentices, who would not countenance peace."

"I knew there were people missing from the files you gave us!" exclaimed Rook Thomas triumphantly. "There was a gap in the demographics, from age nineteen to twenty-six."

"Wait, so the five are your friends?" Felicity burst out incredulously. "The ones from the photos? Your boyfriend?" Everyone stared at Felicity, but her eyes were on Odette, who looked back for a moment and then nodded slightly. "You told me they died!" Felicity said accusingly to Marcel. He glanced up from his notes and gave a little shrug.

"They were angry," said Odette brokenly. "So angry."

Paranoia formed a crucial component of every Grafter's makeup. Like twenty-twenty vision or a tolerance for gluten, if you weren't born with it, it was implanted in you at an early age. And the cause of this paranoia was the Checquy.

When the Broederschap troops marched onto the Isle of Wight in 1677, they had anticipated that there would be no real challenges. The closest they had ever come to an inexplicable phenomenon was a regenerative pig they'd stumbled across, and even that was dead after they had tried to see just how regenerative it was.

As a result, when the operatives of His Majesty's Supernatural Secret Service exhibited abilities on the battlefield that made absolutely no sense at all, the Broederschap was shaken to its core. During the campaign, the Grafters captured prisoners and snatched corpses. They frantically dissected them, and what they found (or failed to find) defied even the Broederschap's understanding of science and, indeed, of logic.

The small portion of the Grafters who escaped the purge never felt truly safe. Always in the backs of their minds (and at the beginning of the agenda for every meeting they ever held) was the knowledge that the Checquy was out there, lurking, on their strange gray island.

And so the Grafters kept very much to themselves. If they amassed too much power or wealth or gained any prominence at all, they might catch the eye of the Checquy or some equivalent body. Rather than placing all their eggs in one basket, the Broederschap established chapter houses throughout Europe: in Paris, Madrid, Berlin, Marseille, Hamburg—large cities where they would be lost amidst the population. After a century or two, they also built chapter houses in Belgium and returned circumspectly to their homeland.

Security was always paramount. But despite their scattered distribution across Europe, the Grafters were not isolated from one another. Like many scientists and academics, they thrived on constant collaboration, and information and research results were shared as a matter of course. Younger members acted as couriers, traveling to visit relations and colleagues and carrying materials and heavily encrypted documents within their bodies.

With the advent of telephony and then, much later, the Internet, the Grafters developed ways to take advantage of these new technologies without putting themselves at risk. Certain trusted flunkies were packed full of complex communications equipment and acted as the ultimate secretaries. However, lacking flunkies, the younger members of the brotherhood were obliged to improvise, and one of Odette's friends had come up with designs that allowed animals to fill the flunky roles.

And so Odette had been sitting in her studio in Roeselare, Belgium, listening to the voices of her closest friends come out of the mouths of five members of the lizard family and a tortoise.

"This is insane," said Saskia's voice. "Graaf Ernst has lost his mind if he is honestly thinking there could be peace between us and the Gruwels! He is betraying us, betraying the generations that have worked and died to give us what we have today!"

It was startling to hear such rage in Saskia's normally gentle voice, and it didn't help that it was coming from the passionless face of a tortoise. Saskia, who lived by the seaside in Marseille and could breathe underwater and created beautiful perfumed butterflies with wings like flowers. Saskia, who had taken Odette shopping in Paris for her first gown and taught her to dance.

"What he is proposing—" began an iguana with the voice of her uncle Dieter, but it was cut off by a bright green chameleon.

"He is not proposing anything," declared Pim. Odette could picture him striding around in his studio down the street from hers, as he always did when he was caught up in something. Pim was passionate, innovative, a genius among the Grafters, and Odette loved him with all her heart and all her heat. He had sculpted her spurs for her, and he would kiss her closed eyes and tell her how much he adored her. "He simply told us: 'We will be joining ourselves to the Checquy. Peacefully.' Just like that!"

"As if there could ever be peace with those abominations!" spat Mariette from her home in Brussels. At twenty-one, the only member of the group younger than Odette, Mariette spent as much time studying history as she did the craft of the Broederschap. She had interviewed Graaf Ernst and Graaf Gerd on many occasions and had talked for long hours with the few Grafters who had been alive since the very beginning of the Broederschap. Odette had had a hand in crafting her eyes. "They tried to rob us of our future! The Checquy would have obliterated our people, our families, everything we were if they'd had their way!"

"Well, after our armies tried to invade their country," pointed out Simon languidly. His lizard, a frill-necked variety, had something of Simon's look about it. It might have been the amused expression or the fact that it kept flaring its ruff to get attention. Simon was Odette's cousin, and he never hesitated to push the bounds of either biological science or other people's sensibilities. He had been known to turn up at Broederschap events looking completely inhuman.

"That is not the point!" said Mariette. "After you have won a war, you do not kill every person on the other side! You do not order them to destroy their culture and slaughter their own people."

"Even if they hadn't forced us into hiding," said Claudia's chameleon, "their very nature makes them dangerous." Living in Brussels, Claudia was the one who had designed their reptilian communications network, and she'd secretly gained access to some of the secure records the brotherhood had on its enemies. "I've scrutinized the notes of our handwerksmannen, and there is simply no explanation for what the Checquy are. Their DNA is perfectly normal."

"How can they be so certain?" asked Odette curiously. Even for the Grafters, genetics could be tricky, with unexpected surprises lurking in the coils of code.

"They have twice grown clones of three Checquy operatives," said Claudia, and the reptiles all fell silent. Given a few cells from a living thing, the Grafters could produce an exact genetic duplicate of the original. The prospect of their creating a Checquy-thing in the lab was a disquieting thought.

"Was it done under speed-growth conditions?" asked Pim thoughtfully. The Grafters had the means to rapidly accelerate the aging process, bringing a subject to a particular point in its life span and then allowing it to resume normal metabolism. It was useful because one could see the results of a new process without having to wait years for it to come to fruition. Plus, it saved on lab time and maintenance costs.

"The first batch were speed-grown, yes," said Claudia. "And none of them displayed any sign of the originals' powers. One was a copy of a Checquy man who had patagia and was covered in yellow fur. The clone was a perfectly normal man with brown hair."

"But speed-growth isn't perfect," observed Mariette. She was right. Speed-grown organisms, whether or not they were clones, had various built-in problems. The growing process cut their life spans to a fraction of what they would normally be. At a random point, they would suddenly suffer rapid cellular breakdown, aging in moments, their flesh rotting on the bone.

"Yeah, you know that, and I know that, and, oh, wait, everyone in the Broederschap knows that as well," said Claudia tartly. Even her lizard was rolling its eyes, as only a chameleon could do. Mariette's lizard kept its mouth firmly closed.

"Don't be a snot, Claudia," said the tortoise with Saskia's voice. Odette rested her cup of tea on the tortoise's shell and closed her eyes. It sounded as if Claudia and Mariette were ready to break out into one of their trademark arguments.

"Fine," said the chameleon sniffily. "Anyway, yes, they then did a normal-growth cloning. They spent twenty years raising the clones to adulthood. Same results. No powers, no duplication of unnatural appearances."

"What does that mean?" asked Mariette hesitantly.

"That they're abominations," said Claudia flatly. "Whatever they are, they don't belong in nature. They're not bound by the rules of science."

"Demons," said Simon, and there was no trace of his usual amused tone.

"I had thought the Broederschap was working against them," said the Saskia-tortoise, sounding lost. Odette reached out and, ridiculously, patted the tortoise to comfort it.

"We were," said Dieter. Although he was her uncle, he was only two years older than Odette, and more like a big brother. His laboratory was five minutes' walk away from hers and Pim's, and they had collaborated on several projects together. Also, his father, Marcel, was highly ranked in the Broederschap and a close confidant of Graaf Ernst's. "Papa said that everything was proceeding well."

"And now this!" exclaimed Saskia. "They want us to ally with them, to join ourselves with these atrocities who drove us underground. I simply cannot believe it."

"Believe it," said Claudia grimly. "Because it's happening."

" 'Dette, you've been pretty quiet this whole time," said Pim. "What do you think?" Odette opened her eyes. All the lizards and the tortoise were looking at her expectantly. It was almost worse than having her friends staring at her in person. At least, she would never have used the actual Saskia to hold her teacup. She hastily plucked it up.

"I don't know what to think," she confessed. "I mean, the Checquy is..." She trailed off helplessly.

The idea of the Checquy gave me nightmares all through my childhood, she thought. But that was when they were the monsters under the bed and in the closet. Now I know that they're monsters in suits, in offices. If they're a part of a government, if they take orders from a government, then perhaps they can be reasoned with. But she didn't say that. She didn't dare.

"There are some things one cannot do," said Pim. "Things the graaf cannot ask us to do. And I cannot ally myself with these monsters, who have done so much harm to my people." There was a murmur of agreement among the reptiles. Miserable, Odette kept silent.

"We need to meet," said Dieter. "To discuss this further, face-to-face." Odette looked up hopefully. If there was to be more discussion, then there was the possibility of coming to a sensible conclusion. Dieter will convince them to be reasonable, she thought.

"Let's all meet in Paris," said Pim. "A week from today. And we'll decide what we're going to do."

And?" asked Rook Thomas. "What happened?"

"We went to Paris," said Odette sadly.

Sitting in the lobby café of the Rataxes, Paris's most beautiful hotel, the seven of them had drawn appreciative looks. They may not have been famous, but when you're young, able to control your appearance, and dressed in expensive clothing in an expensive place, you get looked at. Plus, their grave expressions made them stand out even more. Beverages and food were brought to them, and they began an extremely quiet conversation.

"This is where you thought we should have this discussion?" asked Claudia, looking around at the civilians passing through the lobby.

"I thought it would be best if we all remained calm," said Pim. "We can't be productive if we start screaming about the injustice of it all."

"And I like to think that none of us are gauche enough to start screaming here," said Simon. Although it was only midmorning, he was sipping brandy and cream out of a long, thin glass. He was wearing a new suit and a new face that Odette suspected had been specially picked out to go with the suit.

"Fine," said Claudia, folding her arms.

"I'd like to begin, if I may," said Odette hesitantly. Saskia and Pim, who were the unofficial leaders of the group, nodded and smiled for her to go ahead. She'd finally found her courage. "We've all had time to think this over, to move beyond our instinctual reactions. We're educated people, and I think we're all clever enough to, well, to see where we need to go.

"Like you all, the idea of the Checquy makes me deeply uncomfortable. But I'm afraid that we've already come to a place where there's no going back. They know about us, and the rest of the Broederschap is going to join with them. Our teachers, our superiors, our families are going to join with them. Can we really stand against that? Is that what you really want?"

I tried to talk to them," Odette told the silent executives in the conference room, "to make them see that there could be a good ending to all this." She looked down at her hands. "But they wouldn't budge. They felt they had to fight."

Please," pleaded Odette, "I love you all, I can't bear this. I can't bear to watch you ruin everything we have—everything we could have."

"A future like that isn't worth having," said Pim sadly. "They can't order us to join ourselves to this profanity, to give up what makes us who we are."

"We have to act, Odette," said Saskia, taking her hand gently. She was exquisite, in a delicate white dress that bespoke elegance and civilization and calm afternoons. "We have to make the changes, the better changes. Please, please, come with us, darling."

"I can't!" sobbed Odette. "I can't turn on my family! And what about Alessio? You want to bring your fight to him? Why do you have to try and make this worse? Isn't peace better than war? You don't know that a future with the Checquy will be a bad thing."

"We know," said Saskia sadly, and there was a momentary stinging sensation in Odette's hand. Odette looked down and saw a spur stretching out from Saskia's wrist to touch her hand. A single droplet of blood welled on her skin. She looked up at Saskia in horror. "I'm so sorry, 'Dette."

"We all are," said Mariette, and her words seemed to echo in Odette's ears. The lobby and the faces of her friends wavered, twisting and blurring. Pim was gazing at her and his eyes were full of tears.

I love you, he mouthed.

"We love you," she heard Simon say distantly. She felt a kiss on her cheek and Saskia's hand holding hers tightly as she sank into sleep.

I woke up in the lobby of the hotel three hours later," said Odette. "They bribed the manager and told him to keep an eye on me while I slept, that I'd just had bad news. A death in the family. They'd even arranged for a waiter to bring me a coffee and some aspirin when I woke up.

"By the time I was awake enough to think straight, I realized that my friends had been very busy," she continued. "They'd returned to the big Paris chapter house and lifted a lot of things—materials and tools. Then they killed the house and fled."

"They killed the people in the house?" asked Rook Thomas intently.

"No, they killed the living components of the house," said Ernst, real sadness in his eyes. "Two centuries' worth of thoughts, memory, and service, wiped out." He sighed. "That house was a good friend, a member of the family."

"Since then," said Marie, "they've been waging war on the Broederschap in Europe. Infiltrating installations and damaging projects. Some were major endeavors—years of work ruined in a matter of moments. People have been hurt, people have died, and property has been destroyed."

"And now they are here," said Bishop Attariwala.

"They have been for a while," said Ernst. "They have already made some attacks. For instance, those people killed in the Italian restaurant the night of our cocktail party. That was the Antagonists' work."

"Oh God," said Rook Thomas. "Why? Why would they do that?"

"We do not know their purpose in that instance," said Marie. "But it is not the only time you have encountered them."

"What else?" asked the Rook.

"The creature in Portsmouth," said Odette.

"That gigantic sea monster they dredged out of the Channel?" asked Rook Kelleher, an extremely fat white man who was attended by a dozen iridescent butterflies fluttering in the air above him.

"We think it is how they entered the United Kingdom," said Marie.

"Too good for the Eurostar, are they?" asked Chevalier Whibley.

"You know what kind of compounds and equipment our work requires," said Marcel. "They could never have risked shipping it in through conventional means. Using one of our major constructs, they could transport a substantial amount of matériel across the Channel." He snorted. "If they had managed to do it without running it into a cargo ship, they would have had a very useful engine of war as well. Still, I wasn't surprised. That

397

creature was experimental, unique, and apparently a complete bitch to pilot."

"So who was the dead person inside the creature?" asked Bishop Attariwala. "Which of the Antagonists?"

"I think it was Dieter," said Odette weakly.

"My son," said Marcel quietly. There was an appalled silence.

"It had his eyes," said Odette, "but it wasn't his skin, it wasn't his face. He was wearing some sort of white utility epidermis. We have something similar for conducting major surgeries or operating in harsh conditions."

"In order to pilot the vessel, he would have had to link his neurons to the creature's," said Marcel. "When he crashed into the ship, the feedback would have killed him outright."

"That would count as a design flaw in my book," remarked Rook Thomas.

"We probably would have worked out that detail," said Marcel.

"Why did it come alive again in the hangar?" asked Felicity. She was thinking of those horrible moments when she was trapped in the creature's living flesh. "Was that part of their plan?"

"No, we believe it reactivated in response to Odette's presence," said Marcel. "With a living Grafter inside it, it turned back on, although the damage it had taken in the collision with the ship meant it would not have survived for very long."

"And the people who attacked the car this evening?" asked Chevalier Whibley. "Any ideas?"

"I didn't recognize them," said Odette. "None of them."

"They sounded English," remarked Bishop Alrich. "Tasted English too."

"We're having their fingerprints analyzed," said Rook Kelleher. "Two of them were in the system—minor criminals out of London."

"So the Antagonists are recruiting," said Rook Thomas sourly.

"They wouldn't," said Odette. "They might give those men weapon implants, use them as muscle, but there's no way they'd accept them as equals."

"Elitists," said Lady Farrier. It wasn't clear if she disapproved or not.

"Justifiably," said Marcel. "That group of students was our most promising in decades. They're unorthodox, but they're brilliant. All of them." He put a hand on Odette's shoulder.

"And the blond man, the leader?" asked Bishop Alrich. "He was particularly eager to kill Rook Thomas. It seemed almost personal."

"I have no idea who he is," said Rook Thomas. "He was unconscious by the time I woke up in the car, even before the staff from Hill Hall arrived. The holding facility sent me some photos of him, but they rang no bells for me." She flushed a little. "I have a bad memory for faces, though." Lady Farrier snorted at this.

"Currently, he's comatose," said Rook Kelleher. "The doctors at the Rookery have examined him. No Grafter implants, so far as we can tell. No explanation for why he went unconscious. We have him in a secure medical facility in the building."

"He seemed to be calling the shots," said Alrich.

"And he seemed to know who you were," said Odette to the vampire. "He was horrified to see you."

"I can have that effect on people," said Alrich modestly. Odette blushed.

"Well, this is all very well," said Lady Farrier, "but let's move beyond the minutiae of the situation and focus on the big picture. I'm sure you can understand, Graaf van Suchtlen, that these revelations have cast our negotiations in an entirely different light."

"Yes, Lady Farrier," said Ernst soberly.

"We, the Court, will need to discuss the implications of this. If you would excuse us?" The Grafters looked at one another and then began to rise. Marcel gathered up his papers. "Dr. Leliefeld, I wouldn't bother taking those notes with you," the Lady said.

"Oh? Why not?"

"Because this is a dream."

* * *

Odette woke up. She was in the bathtub of her hotel suite, warm in her gel. Unbelievable, she thought. There was absolutely no doubt in her mind that it had been a real meeting, even if it had taken place while she was asleep. She was aware that Lady Farrier could manipulate the dreams of others—she must have reached out to all the attendees' sleeping minds and gathered them together.

Amazing, thought Odette. The advantages were obvious. The meeting could be held in secret, without any chance of surveillance, and if it had gone badly and battle had actually broken out, no one would have suffered any harm. It was a disconcerting thought, however, to imagine that the Lady of the Checquy could simply dip into a person's mind and manipulate it as she saw fit. And I never questioned it, she mused. Just like in a normal dream, I didn't ask how I came to be there.

I wonder what time it is. She opened her eyes and frowned. The lights were on in the bathroom, and she was certain she'd turned them off. Was it her imagination or were there wavery figures standing by the tub? She snapped upright, the slime dripping down her face, and looked around to find three soldiers in camouflage, their large automatic weapons pointed directly at her.

"Evening, miss," said one of them. "Don't be alarmed."

"Don't be alarmed?" she repeated. "What in the hell is going on?"

He held up a finger and then pressed it against his ear. He cocked his head, and nodded a few times. "Copy that," he said into a microphone. "Stand down," he said to his men, and they all dropped their guns. "Well, that's a bit of good news, miss. It seems the members of the Court decided they believed your story, so we don't have to execute you or the young lad in the other room. Sorry to have disturbed you. Have a good night."

33

Felicity woke up to the sound of the phone ringing by her bed. She had been banished from the dream-meeting of the Court almost immediately after the Grafters departed, but rather than waking up, she had slid into a peaceful, natural sleep. Until the phone rang. She fumbled in the darkness, managed to knock over a lamp, and finally put her hand on the phone.

"Yeah?"

"It's Rook Thomas. Can you please come down to room 909?"

"I—of course, ma'am." With an effort, she levered herself out of bed and poured herself into the clothes that she'd left scattered on the floor. She rode down in the lift, yawning hugely and trying not to look at herself in the mirrored walls. To her chagrin, she looked exactly like someone who'd inhaled a biological gaseous anesthetic, been in a car accident, and then gotten woken up at four in the morning.

Mrs. Woodhouse, who let her into room 909, also bore the unmistakable hallmarks of someone who'd had a long, bad night, but she still managed to look several thousand times more together than Felicity did. The executive assistant gestured for Felicity to sit down at a little dining table. Farther in the room, Rook Thomas and Graaf van Suchtlen were seated on opposite couches. There was an odd dynamic to their conversation that Felicity, in her exhausted state, could not quite decode.

"When were you going to tell us about this, Ernst?" the Rook was saying. "When were you going to tell me about the cabal of Grafters working to destroy our peace negotiations?"

"Never," said the graaf without a hint of embarrassment. "Or when they were all dead. Whichever came second." Odette winced. "It was our problem, and we were handling it."

"Well, now they're our problem," said Rook Thomas. "You see, you may not have realized this, but the British government is working toward a peaceful accommodation with the Broederschap wherein you will become a part of this organization and of the British government. Did you think that you would just get a Eurostar ticket, a security pass, a desk in the Hammerstrom Building, and it's all taken care of?

"This is a horrendously complicated undertaking costing huge sums of money and involving hundreds of people throughout the government who are trying to do it all in secret. There are layers upon layers of lies, illusion, and concealment, all woven into this entire nightmarish, convoluted, bureaucratic tapestry.

"And I started that process," said Thomas, "after a conversation with you, Ernst. A conversation in my office during which we agreed that peace between us would be better than the alternative.

"Because, make no mistake," she said flatly, "the alternative is still a very real possibility. The Court has decided that they believe you. Mostly. But if knowledge of your Antagonists were to get out to the greater Checquy, I don't know what would happen."

"They are your troops," said the graaf, "they will obey."

"I really don't know that you're in a position to deliver pompous observations about commanding people's loyalty, Ernst," said the Rook with narrowed eyes. "And while we will try to help you, I can't bring the full force of the Checquy to bear on this issue. They already hate you, and now it turns out that your kids have been running around committing atrocities on British citizens. Yes, the Checquy are loyal. Yes, they are professional. But that doesn't mean that I can order them to do whatever I like. I do not want to be yet another Rook who pushed the Checquy into rebellion against itself."

"I understand," said the graaf. "Of course, we will do everything we can to work with you to eliminate this problem quietly."

"Good," said the Rook. "Tell me, please God, that you have some leads."

"We had warriors here in London tracking them down," said Ernst, provoking a choking gasp from the Rook, "but it proved fruitless. On Friday night, they killed all our agents."

"Those clothes and guns in Hyde Park—those were your people?" spluttered Thomas.

"Oh, you know about those? I suppose that was inevitable."

"Of course it was fucking inevitable," said the Rook. "I just can't believe you had armed soldiers running around London. No other leads?" The graaf shook his head. "Terrific. Well, that brings us to you, Pawn Clements," she said, turning to the dining area. "And your protectee." She gestured for Felicity to join them.

"What about my protectee?" said Felicity as she sat down gingerly on the same couch as the Rook.

"Before the Antagonists make their next attack, before they push us completely over the edge and into war, we think that one of two things could happen: Odette might go to the Antagonists, or they might come for her," said van Suchtlen.

"What?" asked Felicity, startled. "What do you mean?"

"She is one of them," said Ernst simply.

"You think that Leliefeld is a mole?" asked Felicity. "That she's really working for the Antagonists?" The graaf shrugged. "I thought that you had decided she could be trusted."

"We cannot know," he said. "Not definitively. When she came to us the first day, after her friends fled, there was a great deal of doubt. Even Marcel, her mentor, was cautious."

"What about her parents?" said Felicity dazedly. "What do they say?"

"Her parents are not members of the Broederschap," said the graaf. "Her father is the son of Marcel's brother, Siegbert, who died in the war. He was raised as Marcel's oldest son, and he knows some things, but he is not one of us."

"Okay," said Felicity. "But you don't know for certain that she's a traitor."

"No," admitted van Suchtlen. "Not for certain. We have watched her closely and seen no sign of it, but in the end, it doesn't matter. In her heart she loves them, and they love her."

There was no emotion in the graaf's voice. He stared into Felicity's eyes, and she saw nothing but cold calculation. "That is why she was brought here as part of the delegation. We can watch her for any sign of treachery and ensure that she makes no attacks on our places in Europe. Also, they will not strike hard when she is in our custody."

"Not strike hard?" repeated Felicity incredulously. "What about today? What about those deaths in the restaurant? And the sleep-walkers?"

"The sleepwalkers?" repeated Ernst. Rook Thomas hurriedly explained about the civilians getting up in the middle of the night and disappearing, the skin room that had gone up in flames, the loss of Felicity's teammates, and the white-skinned man who had killed them. I wonder if that was Pim, thought Felicity.

"So they have already killed Checquy people," said Ernst. "Myfanwy, I cannot apologize enough. They are unstable, they must be, but I am certain of their love for Odette. That is what the attack on the car was about. They were coming for her. For all their hatred and resentment, they will do their utter best not to hurt her. Having her at the hotel and in Checquy facilities makes it less likely they will strike at those places."

"So you're using her as a human shield."

"We must use every tool at our disposal," said the Grafter. "That is also why we brought Alessio here. His presence is not a sign of good faith for the Checquy, or, should I say, not only a sign of good faith for the Checquy. He is here for us to hold as hostage against Odette's loyalty. There is no one she loves as much as her baby brother. Not even Pim and the others."

"But this is your family," said Felicity, aghast at the extent of the manipulation that had just been revealed. The Checquy used its people, of that there was no doubt. That's why they call us Pawns, after all. But this level of control and deception was something else entirely. "You are using their affection—their love!—as a weapon."

"As insurance," said the graaf. "As a shield, like you said. But if it comes to it, if the only way to win is to sacrifice Odette and Alessio, even if both of them are innocent, I will do it."

"This is the way it has to be, Clements," said the Rook sadly. "We have to use every tool we have, even if we hate doing it. That's the responsibility of our positions. And now it's yours too."

Felicity's mind was reeling. It was loathsome. She wanted to say that she couldn't do it, that she wouldn't do it. But she just nodded.

"What are my orders?"

"You're not going to like them," said the Rook.

The needle itself was no longer than any normal hypodermic, but it seemed as if it ought to be huge, because the syringe attached to it was so very large. In it, a milky blue liquid sat expectantly.

"Now, once I have injected this into you, you absolutely must not get pregnant," said the graaf seriously. "Not for at least seven months. This is not a suggestion."

"Well, I hadn't planned on it," said Felicity wryly. Her tone was an attempt to cover up her increasing unease.

"Planned, unplanned, it must not happen."

"I'm on the pill."

"That is not a hundred percent," he said. "You must be one hundred percent certain."

"And what is this stuff again?" Felicity asked nervously.

"The Antagonists have proven their willingness to use viral and bacterial weapons," said the graaf. "If they come for Odette, or if she makes a break for it, you must be able to resist such weapons."

"But what is it?"

"You wouldn't understand the answer if I gave it."

"But it's Grafter-tech, right? Some bacteria you've cobbled together or a hormone you've twisted about?" She looked at the Rook pleadingly. "Rook Thomas, please, you know what this means. It's everything we've been brought up to despise. Please, please don't ask me to do this." The Rook chewed her lip thoughtfully, and her brow furrowed.

"Pawn Clements?" she said finally.

"Yes?"

"Do it."

"... Yes, ma'am."

So why aren't you just inoculating everyone?" asked Felicity as she squeezed the rubber ball the graaf had given her. The veins in her arm were coming to the surface.

"Because the contents of this little syringe cost about half a million pounds to manufacture," he said carelessly. "And even if we had enough for everyone, I think the members of the Checquy would be uncomfortable having Grafter materials injected into them."

Felicity watched as the needle slid into her vein. A dull ache spread into her muscles. Am I becoming a Grafter by letting him do this? she thought, and felt sick to her stomach. Despite herself, she tried to read the liquid with her powers as it flowed into her, but she found that she wasn't able to. It's alive, she thought. Alive, and inside me.

"It's creepy, I know," said Rook Thomas. "They shot it into me as well."

"You?" said Felicity. The Rook grimaced, and Felicity remembered that the Grafters had performed an entire surgery on her. An injection's not very pleasant, but at least they're not elbow-deep in my abdominal cavity.

"The Antagonists seem to be pretty irritated with me for some reason," said the Rook lightly. "Whoever that blond guy was, he was apparently very focused on killing me, so we thought it best not to take any chances."

"Now you'll have a fighting chance," said the Grafter.

"So what exactly is it that you want me to do?" asked Felicity.

"That's the problem, Clements," said Rook Thomas. "We can't

plan for every eventuality, so we must rely on your personal judgment. Watch her. If you believe Odette is going to do anything on behalf of the Antagonists, if you witness her trying to escape your guard, or if she harms a civilian, an operative of the Checquy, or a member the delegation, then you will do whatever proves necessary to resolve the situation." The Rook's voice was mild. "Personally, I don't believe that will happen. I trust her. She's saved my life twice. But Ernst here thinks it's still a possibility, so keep it in mind."

"Right," said Felicity.

"If the Antagonists come for her," said Ernst, "then you must do everything in your power to stop them. Once they have her, there will be nothing left to prevent them from striking at the Checquy without restraint. And then negotiations will fail. They must not get her."

"And if the opportunity arises," said the Rook, "it would be great if you could acquire one of the Antagonists for us."

Oh, absolutely, thought Felicity. If I see one, I won't hesitate to snatch him up and put him in my handbag.

"If we have even one of them," the Rook was saying, "we can extract the information we need from him or her."

"But if you think Odette might be a traitor, why don't you just interrogate her?" asked Felicity, frowning.

"I am gambling on that point," confessed the Grafter. "I truly hope Odette is not a traitor. Not only is she a valuable and brilliant Grafter, but I love her. She is family. The interrogation that the Checquy has in mind would not be gentle. And the fact that we interrogated her at all would be enough to destroy her loyalty to us."

"If she actually does have any loyalty to you," the Rook remarked to Ernst helpfully. "We're not certain that she does."

"Exactly."

My God, this is getting confusing, thought Felicity. "May I just review this, please?" she asked. "We don't know whether Odette is a traitor."

"Correct," said Ernst.

"If she is a traitor and tries to do something evil, I should stop her."

"Correct," said Thomas.

"But regardless of whether or not she is a traitor, I should stop any attempt by anyone to get her out of Checquy custody."

"Correct," said the Rook and the graaf together. They exchanged glances.

"One final thing," added Rook Thomas. "Please don't kill her if you can possibly help it. Wherever her allegiance lies, her death will leave the Antagonists open to strike at us. And it might actually spur them on."

"Well, it helps that I don't actually want to kill her," said Felicity.

"I appreciate that," said Ernst.

"And I also have a present for you," said the Rook. "Since it seems to be the evening for that sort of thing. Mine is less creepy than an injection of alchemy into your veins, although still wildly inappropriate." Mrs. Woodhouse brought in a small case, and the Rook removed an item covered in bubble wrap from it. She handed it to Felicity, who set about unwrapping it, peeling off the tape and unwinding the plastic until it sat in her hand, small and hard and clever.

"It's a gun," Felicity said stupidly. Despite their abilities, the operatives of the Checquy were not permitted to carry firearms on British soil. Not unless they had actually been placed in a combat setting or were on a security detail. *I suppose I'm both of those*, Felicity thought. Of course, she had received rigorous training in shooting at the Estate, but it was startling to have a gun in her hand. A pistol, small enough to put in a handbag, large enough to put holes in someone.

"I inherited it from a friend," said the Rook carelessly. "If I arranged for you to be officially issued one, I'd have to answer all sorts of questions. And I don't want people looking too closely at you, or at Odette. We still don't know what kind of resources the Antagonists have within the Checquy." She glanced sourly at Ernst and then looked back at Felicity. "I can't very well announce that you are being given a gun to kill treacherous Grafters if necessary, as that would send the wrong message."

But an accurate one, thought Felicity. The world, which had seemed so complex and difficult a few hours ago, seemed infinitely worse now.

They gave you guns?" Felicity heard Alessio's incredulous voice from the living room. She squeezed her eyes shut and snuggled down under her blankets. It was far too early for her to be awake after being awake far too late.

"Shotguns, for hunting," said Odette. "It's not like I got a pair of Glocks." At this, Felicity tensed and put out a hand to the bedside table, where the Glock that Rook Thomas had given her was resting in a drawer. It's there, it's safe, you can go back to sleep.

"Can I see them?" asked Alessio.

Can you shut up? For some reason, this morning the kid's voice was cutting through her brain like a pubescent chain saw.

"The Checquy took them overnight," said Odette. "And then today they're going to a gun-storage place. I guess the shop stores them until you need them. Or until you get a place with a gun safe."

"Were they cool?"

"Extremely," said Odette. "Here, I took a picture on my phone."

"Those are awesome!" squeaked Alessio in a register that put paid to Felicity going back to sleep that morning. Her entire nervous system seemed convinced that his warbling tones presaged some sort of attack. She put on a dressing gown and staggered out into the living room.

"Morning!" chirped Alessio.

"Yeahshutup," mumbled Felicity. She picked up a cup of coffee from the table.

"That's mine," said Odette.

"Yeahshutup," said Felicity, taking a long swig. She focused on Alessio. "It's Monday, don't you have an excursion to run out to?" He opened his mouth. "Don't talk. Just nod or shake your head." He nodded. "All right, good. I'm going to take a shower." She took the coffee with her.

When she emerged from it, Alessio had gone and Odette was sitting at the table, her head bent over something. Felicity looked at her curiously. There was a stillness to the Grafter girl, except for her fingers, which were making tiny, barely visible movements.

She's doing needlepoint, decided Felicity, but then she realized that the other woman was sewing up a raw steak that had been gashed open. The Pawn sat down across from her. As she watched, invisible thread bound the meat together so meticulously that only the thinnest of lines marked where it had been cut open. The focus, the control, the perfection were as magical as anything Felicity had ever seen.

After long minutes, Odette finished and tied an intricate knot that looped and whirled around her fingers like a cat's cradle of silver. When she drew her fingers out, the knot shrank down on itself. She laid her hands down and sighed. Then she looked up, and Felicity saw that her pupils were massively dilated, so much that her eyes seemed black. She blinked several times, and once again, her eyes were blue.

"Impressive," said Felicity.

"Thanks."

"So, we should have a little talk."

"I suppose so," said Odette, looking at her postoperative steak. Felicity felt a little twinge of pity for her. She didn't blame the Grafter girl for not telling her about the Antagonists—she'd clearly been under orders to keep it secret. The fact that her boyfriend and best friends had become international terrorists couldn't have been easy on her either.

"I need a better understanding of the situation with your friends. What happened after you woke up in the hotel lobby?" asked Felicity.

And Odette began to tell the story. By the time she had woken up in the hotel lobby, realized where she was and what had happened, and been able to stop sobbing, her friends had already made their move.

"Pim must have had it all planned out beforehand," she said. "Of course, the Broederschap knew immediately who had done it. Their fingerprints were all over the chapter house. Pim had even used his security pass to open the front door." She shook her head. "They weren't trying to hide what they were doing— they wanted everyone to know. I think that's why they killed the house, as a statement."

"I'm sorry," said Felicity awkwardly. "Did you, um, know the house well?"

"Yes," said Leliefeld. "But I didn't find out about that until weeks later. When I woke up, I knew they'd left me, that they'd left the Broederschap, but that was all. I called Marie in Brussels and she immediately sent a car and some soldiers for me. They put me in the back and drove me to Belgium."

The Broederschap had apparently been very suspicious of her and immediately placed her into a sort of quarantine. She had been screened very carefully, undergone multiple scans and exploratory surgery to check if she had had any new weapons implanted. They injected her with antibodies, "in case of any war bacteria that might be floating around in my system." A number of existing implants had been removed—apparently, despite her surgical and scholarly role, she and the other Antagonists had given each other a variety of unorthodox enhancements. Felicity recalled the photos that she had seen in Odette's bedroom and realized that her dossier had listed nothing that would permit her to breathe underwater or scale a cathedral. So much for keeping my eyes and my brain open, she thought.

Odette had been permitted to keep her spurs, but the venom reservoirs had been drained and the muscles that activated them had been carefully paralyzed. Hours and hours of questioning had ensued.

"It wasn't violent interrogation," Leliefeld assured her. "It was just Marie, Marcel, and I sitting on the veranda with endless cups of tea as they took me through everything I knew and everything

411

I thought I knew and everything I didn't know and everything I didn't realize I'd known. God, it was tedious.

"Of course, there were serious doubts about whether I should be allowed any freedom at all. There was talk of putting me in a penal coma. I really can't blame them. Everyone was already in shock over the announcement about the Checquy, and then this betrayal by their own children. And we were so close, my friends and I, the Broederschap leadership thought I had to be involved, that it was part of some plan.

"I was under supervision for weeks. I wasn't allowed to do any work or research; I just sat around reading novels and watching movies. Then the attacks started, and it was even worse." She took a long breath. "My friends were doing these — these awful things. I was so ashamed of them. And everyone was eyeing me like they expected me to blow myself up or something.

"But then they suddenly decided that they would trust me and let me be part of the delegation. So I received the next set of upgrades right before we left. Great-Uncle Marcel actually did the surgeries himself."

"What were the upgrades?" asked Felicity, half fascinated, half nauseated. "Or is that a rude question to ask?"

"You don't really get to be offended in the Broederschap," said Leliefeld. "Everyone knows about everyone else's anatomy."

"It's like that in the Checquy too," said Felicity. "It's very hard to keep a secret." Not impossible, though, she thought. "And everyone knows what your powers are."

"Sounds familiar. Well, my bones got strengthened, and my second cousin gave me some really nice new kidneys. My spinal cord and nervous system have been augmented and improved, and they put in some fixtures in my throat that allow me greater control over Broederschap constructs and creatures — oral commands and whatnot. They're all still healing and kind of sore. I haven't had time to learn how to use them yet, so they're pretty much off-line."

"So why did they bother to put them in before you came here?" asked Felicity.

"As a sign that they trusted me," said Leliefeld. "It's like your parents giving you back the keys to the car. Only we get new organs. It really meant a lot to me."

"I'm sure," said Felicity. There was a silence.

"What are our plans for today, then?" asked Odette. "Am I back in quarantine? Do we just stay here and watch movies?"

"Far from it," said Felicity. "Once you're ready, we're going to the Rookery to help them track down the Antagonists." She very carefully did not say "your friends."

Last night's attack left us with a few leads," said Clovis, the Checquy security chief, as he led Odette and Felicity through a series of subterranean corridors. Apparently, tucked away in the bowels of the Rookery was a whole series of tiled rooms used when Checquy people needed to be sewn up or when non-Checquy people needed to be cut open. "The first is the catatonic blond man, and the others are the various augmented corpses. Bishop Alrich did manage to leave two of them alive but I'm afraid all of them went into simultaneous seizures at about four a.m. — even the dead ones," he added grimly. "And let me assure you, that gave the morgue attendant a nasty turn. She emptied an entire clip into them."

"She had a gun?" asked Odette, startled. "I thought people in this country didn't carry firearms."

"Oh, everyone who works in the morgue is required to carry a pistol at work," said Clovis. "And we keep a shotgun and a flamethrower on hand, just in case."

"I see."

"Yes, terribly tiresome. Still, as you are no doubt aware, all sorts of information can be divined from a dead body. Your great-uncle is already working on one of them, and he suggested that you, Miss Leliefeld, might be willing to assist with another one."

Please don't ask this of me, Odette thought. It's hard enough that I chose this route, but now you're making me work against my friends directly. It was a ridiculous plea, she knew. She'd set herself against her friends months ago, in that hotel in Paris.

"Absolutely," she said sadly. They arrived at the door of what looked like another medical suite. A tall Retainer in a white coat introduced himself as Dr. Robert Bastion and told them he'd been assigned to assist Odette in her examination. His hair was the same pasty color as his skin.

"It's a genuine pleasure to meet you, Miss Leliefeld," he said. "I'm eager to watch a member of the Broederschap in action."

"Thank you," said Odette. "Now, before we plunge in with scalpels and crowbars, my first concern is booby traps. We'll need to be very careful about activating anything."

"Yes, Dr. Leliefeld warned us not to put them into any scanners, so we brought in one of our people to check them out," said Dr. Bastion. "Pawn Motha can see through flesh. And pretty much everything else. He sketched out the details." He handed Odette a thick sheaf of papers. They were covered in beautifully done pencil sketches of absolutely hideous things.

"Good," said Pawn Clements. "So I don't have anything to do with this task, right?"

"Not right now," said Odette absently. "Ugh, this is a mess." She sighed as she looked through the pictures. Organs, implants, and weapons had been crammed into the man's body, but without the meticulous placement that the Grafters were drilled in. "Clearly, whoever did it was in a huge hurry." Still, they should be ashamed, leaving a subject like this. "What kind of metal or ceramic components did your guy pick up?"

"Not as much as we expected," said Bastion. "Some solid objects in his forearms—no moving parts." He tapped one of the pictures, where three pointed rods were clustered together.

"Okay, looks like weapons," said Odette. "A couple of them had blades implanted in their arms. Have you drawn any blood or fluids?"

"After your great-uncle warned us about the booby traps, we haven't done anything. Fortunately, there was an astounding amount of blood on Bishop Alrich's suit, which we managed to intercept before it was incinerated. The lab results all came back fine, nothing unusual except for some generic antirejection drugs."

"Do we know the identities of the attackers?" asked Odette. "A medical history from before they were modified might be useful."

"We've ID'd four of them," Dr. Bastion told her. "They had no driver's licenses or phones, but their fingerprints were in the criminal database. Assault. Possession of narcotics. One of them robbed an off-license with a knife. They're thugs, essentially. We haven't got a name for the man you'll be examining, though. Not yet."

"Oh, well," said Odette, "that's fine." She peered at one of the sketches and thoughtfully traced a finger around the supernumerary lungs that had been installed. "Fascinating." She looked over to Pawn Clements. "Are you coming in for the autopsy?"

"If you don't need me, I'll pass," said Clements. "I can keep an eye on you from the viewing gallery."

Because they hadn't told her what she would be doing, Odette had not brought her own surgical clothes or tools from the hotel. Asking for them to be fetched seemed unreasonably diva-ish. Instead, she stepped into a changing room and pulled on Checquy-supplied scrubs.

"I'm going to need the most heavy-duty protective garb you can muster up for this," said Odette as she scrubbed her hands and arms vigorously at the OR sink. "I've no idea what I'm going to find in this man."

"Not a problem," Dr. Bastion assured her. "We're used to venturing into unfriendly territory."

Apparently he wasn't exaggerating, because once they'd both scrubbed in, a couple of medical squires proceeded to garb them in a startling combination of heavy plastic and light metal. Stainless-steel plates were strapped to their chests and arms.

"What are these?" asked Odette, plucking at the hoses that trailed out from under the armor.

"They wind back and forth under the armor. You plug them

into the sockets in the examination lab and we pump cold water through them," said one of the assistants. "It gets very warm inside all the layering."

After the armor, they were draped in a series of surgical chemises and petticoats, each one apparently providing resistance to a different possible threat. They were all very thin, but Odette was already feeling the heat. Latex gloves were snapped on, and Kevlar gauntlets slid over them and closed at the wrists with duct tape. Finally, they were robed in surgical gowns with the density of tarpaulins. She found herself crumpling slightly under the weight of it all.

Well, it's not what I expected, she thought, but it shows they're taking it seriously. One of the squires held up an enclosed helmet and waited for Odette to bow her head.

The helmet shut around her head, and Odette heard the faint hiss of oxygen, ensuring she didn't suffocate. The heat inside the getup was vile. She shuffled awkwardly after Dr. Bastion into a little air lock outside the operating room, one of the squires holding the train of her surgical gown like a bridesmaid.

Once she was through, the door hissed shut and then produced various heavy clonkings that indicated it would not be opening again until it was damn good and ready. Then the inner door opened, and they dragged themselves in.

The two-story-high room was brightly lit and lined with tiles that Odette guessed were fireproof, shatterproof, acid-proof, and easy to clean. In the center was the operating table, and on it lay a figure under a discreet plastic sheet. Above the corpse was a lighting array with a camera pointing down. Using sterile gauze, they hurriedly plugged the trailing hoses into the outlets, and a blessed coolness came pumping around them. They slipped antistatic bands around their nondominant hands and connected the trailing cords to the corners of the table the body lay upon.

"It's a fairly standard setup," Dr. Bastion assured her. "Here are the three panic buttons," he said, pointing out a panel near the operating table. "Blue fills the room with a fire-retardant gas."

"Okay," said Odette.

"White fills the room with a paralytic chemical. It took down a weremoose last month, so it should be able to sedate anything person-size or smaller."

A weremoose? thought Odette, nodding automatically.

"And the red button fills the room with fire. Don't worry, though. The really heavy fire will be centered on the table, so if you have to hit the button, be sure to step back as far as possible."

"But the whole room is filled with fire?" asked Odette.

"Only a light fire," he assured her. "And some of the lower layers of the gowns you're wearing are fire-resistant."

"There's no button to summon armed guards?" joked Odette.

"Oh, all three of them summon armed guards," said the doctor. "Plus, we already have a couple up in the gallery." Thanks to the armor, Odette couldn't actually raise her head, but she tilted back at the waist and saw a window beyond which two men with machine guns were standing. She waved awkwardly, and one of them waved back. Behind them were Graaf Ernst, Rook Thomas, Security Chief Clovis, and Pawn Clements.

"We have pistols here as well," said the doctor. "Just reach under the operating table, and you'll find them." Incredulously, Odette felt around and found herself unholstering an alarmingly chunky handgun. "Armor-piercing ammunition," he informed her.

"Okay, well, let's see what we find," she said, picking up the scalpel from the instrument tray. She wasn't sure what to say, but focusing on science and medicine gave her something to hold on to. She paused when she realized that Dr. Bastion's eyes were wide open. "Is everything all right?"

"I'm just rather eager to see a doctor of the Broederschap at work," he confessed. "Do you use a Y-incision or a T-incision? Or just a single vertical cut?"

"Usually I do an asterisk or an outward-spiraling incision," said Odette.

"Oh…By all means, proceed."

34

W hat's that?" asked Dr. Bastion in fascination. It had been twenty minutes, and it was, according to Odette's rough mental tally, the thirty-third time the doctor had asked exactly that question in exactly that tone. She couldn't really blame him—the interior of the body looked like somebody had taken a copy of Gray's Anatomy and engaged in some vigorous cutting-and-pasting.

"I think it's a junction box," said Odette. Crammed deep into the man's torso was a hard, ridged object that looked like the child of an oyster and a chestnut. Clear plastic pipes led out of it, and strands of tissue ran through them to other parts of the body. "See how it's been plumbed into the spinal cord here?"

"Fascinating," murmured Dr. Bastion.

"Hand me those forceps, please," ordered Odette. "We should be able to open it up; these are generally accessible to allow for later modifications and—ah!" The casing opened smoothly and revealed a fist-size mass of tissue, its surface covered with familiar-looking ridges and folds.

"It looks like a brain," observed the doctor.

"It is a brain," said Odette. "A supplementary brain." She peered closely at it, looking for anything unusual. "When they modified this guy, they had to add in a whole bunch of new ligaments, nerves, and muscles to control his implants. See this?" She reached out with a probe and manipulated a nodule of gray matter. The man's left arm convulsed, and with a wet cracking sound, a steel bolt launched itself explosively from his wrist. It shot across the room and lodged itself in the shatterproof tiles. They looked at the bolt cautiously. "Okay, well, I probably shouldn't do that anymore."

"Perhaps not," agreed Dr. Bastion.

"Anyway, when you receive implants, you don't just get

automatic control of them. Some of them, like respiratory or digestive changes, can be wired into your autonomic nervous system. But for weapons or extra limbs, you've got to learn how to use them. It can take months. This type of extra brain is a quick fix to that problem. It's got instructions and commands preloaded."

"Do you have an extra brain?" asked Dr. Bastion.

"No," said Odette. "The control they give is very crude. And it's considered bad form, like cheating. If you want the implants, you must have the self-discipline to train to use them." She thought of her own implants. She'd mastered sheathing and unsheathing her spurs in a couple of days, but it had taken months before she could use her revamped musculature to perform microsurgery. "These sorts of things are generally implanted if we're in a hurry. This gets them active, and then we usually remove them later."

"You remove them?"

"Oh yes. Once the subject can take the time to learn things properly. They're like training wheels. Only, you know, they're brains." She didn't say that the first supplementary brains had been developed for shock troops for the invasion of the Isle of Wight.

Obviously, whoever put the junction box into this guy didn't care about him at all, she thought. Quite aside from the seizure fail-safe. The simultaneous deaths of the men proved that it was no accident or coincidence.

"Dr. Bastion, you said the prisoners were in special cells?"

"Yes," he said. "They were underground and shielded from all means of electronic communication."

"Why?"

"Um, we've had some problems with previous...Grafter... prisoners," the doctor said uncomfortably. "A man in our custody once turned out to be sending information back to his superiors through some sort of antenna on his spine, and then his body was ordered to destroy itself. Of course, this was before we started moving toward peace and amalgamation," he added hurriedly.

Odette raised her eyebrows. The implants he was describing weren't like anything she was familiar with, but she had no difficulty believing they existed. *I suppose they're used for espionage,* she thought, *which is why I've never heard of them.*

"These men were never intended to survive," said Odette grimly. "They had a mission to accomplish and a set amount of time to get it done. Whoever performed the operations on them knew they would have either succeeded or failed by four a.m. and didn't want them to be alive either way." *Probably so they couldn't answer any inconvenient questions.* "Disposable troops."

"Clever," remarked Dr. Bastion.

"Let's keep going," said Odette. "Here, can you help me remove the liver and all these lungs?" The two of them worked briskly for a few minutes, and Odette found herself relaxing a little as she slid into the familiar routine and focus that exploring a body required. She scrutinized every organ closely, paying special attention to the points where they had been joined to the man's nervous system. The placement of the organs might have been sloppy, but the connections were of the highest quality, and there were features she recognized, ones she carried within her own frame. *Pim,* she thought sadly. Then she noticed something in the cavity, a flicker of independent movement that made her freeze. Not wanting to put her face too close to it, Odette opened her eyes wide, sharpened her gaze, and zoomed in.

"Oh, shit," she whispered. *Be calm,* she told herself. *You must be calm.*

How in God's name could they have managed this?

"Something wrong?" asked Dr. Bastion.

"Don't. Move." The Checquy doctor looked at her curiously. "We may be in serious trouble." He started to take his hands out of the torso. "No, don't do that! Just stay still."

"What's the problem?" came Rook Thomas's voice from a speaker. Odette looked up to the gallery and saw the Checquy executive pressed up against the glass, an intercom phone in her hand.

The problem was a small sac tucked away in the folds of a

larger-than-usual large intestine. There weren't any tubes or nerves linking it to other organs; it was just stitched in there, sewn with a cloth ribbon that, before it had spent some time inside an abdominal cavity, had been white. There was even a bow on top. Several ridges of muscle encircled the sac like the rings of Saturn. Occasionally, it gave a little tremble, the muscles flexing softly. Then she noticed something else.

Drawn on the sac with some sort of indelible marker was a smiley face.

"They have left what appears to be a Tartarus gourd inside this man," said Odette tightly.

"What?" exclaimed Ernst.

"What's a Tartarus gourd?" asked the Rook, looking nervous.

"It is impossible!" said Ernst. "They could never have made one—those take years to ripen."

"What are we talking about?" said the Rook.

"And how could they even source a hippopotamus in which to ferment the base stock?"

"Ernst!" shouted Thomas. She took a breath and went on at a calmer volume. "What. Exactly. Are we talking about?"

"It's a biological weapon," said Odette. "Can you see the sac thing there?" She pointed at it, and the camera hummed as it zoomed in. "Those muscles ringing it are designed to tear the sac open and then squeeze to release its contents."

"Okay, well, not to panic. You're wearing armor," pointed out Rook Thomas. "And environmental suits." Behind her, Graaf Ernst was saying something, and she clicked off the intercom to turn and listen. Odette knew exactly what he was telling the Rook. Thomas looked rather startled when she turned back. "So, apparently the Grafters have developed accelerated bacteria that can eat through metal, plastic, and...living tissue. All in a matter of moments. Great." She turned to Ernst. "Why on earth would you people develop those sorts of things?"

"Because of you people," said Graaf Ernst easily, his voice just caught by the intercom. "Don't worry, though, they're very short-lived."

Yeah, just long enough to eat through our armor and then through us, thought Odette.

"Well, any suggestions?" asked Dr. Bastion tightly. Odette had to give him credit, he was handling the situation fairly well, although she could see a sheen of perspiration through his helmet's face screen. His hands, however, were dead still amidst the entrails of the corpse.

"We're thinking," said Ernst. His voice boomed over the intercom—apparently they had switched it over to speaker mode. "And Marie is on her way. But we don't expect that she'll get here in time."

Okay, thought Odette. Maybe we should use the fire button? I'm fairly certain that would kill whatever stuff is in there. She eyed the sac carefully. It's got muscles, so I could try using my octopus venom to paralyze the fibers. Except that would mean taking off my gloves, and I'm not all that keen on that. Plus, there's no guarantee that it would work.

"Maybe we should fill the room?" Security Chief Clovis asked Rook Thomas, who bit her lip. "At the very least, I think we should evacuate all the executives from this observation area." Odette caught a glimpse of Pawn Clements at the window, looking surprisingly concerned.

"This is glass, yes?" said Ernst, tapping at the window.

"Yes."

"It's fine, then," said the graaf dismissively. "We have never cracked a glass-eating bacterium. Nor a stone-eating one. There are a few natural ones out there, but we could never modify them effectively. They always burned themselves out in seconds. It was extremely irritating," he mused. "We really should revisit those projects."

"Anyway," said Rook Thomas, "other ideas?"

"Rook Thomas, this thing is organic," said Odette. "Can you do anything with your powers?"

"There is absolutely no way that Rook Thomas is going in there," said Security Chief Clovis firmly.

"Actually, my powers can reach through glass," the Rook said.

422

She squinted down into the room. "That said, the...what do you call it? Gourd? It's like a little grenade?"

"I suppose," said Odette.

"It's bloody small," said the Rook. She leaned against the glass and closed her eyes. "And complex. Very fiddly." She frowned. "I've got it. No, wait, no I don't." She winced as she said this last part, and Dr. Bastion and Odette exchanged alarmed looks. "I've got it. Oh, bugger!" The two autopsists couldn't help but flinch. "Nope, I've got it!" Everyone heaved a sigh of relief. "Well, don't just stand there—run!"

"Oh!" gasped Odette and Bastion. They jerked their hands out of the corpse's torso and lifted the skirts of their medical gowns. It was impossible to really dash in all the protection garb, so they had to affect a ridiculous sort of high-stepping prancing motion, like dressage horses, while dragging the trains of voluminous material behind them. The hoses of their cooling systems popped out of the sockets, and water jetted into the air.

"Get that door open!" Odette heard Security Chief Clovis shouting. Ahead of them, the air lock shuddered and ground open.

"You need to...hurry...the hell...up," said Rook Thomas through gritted teeth. "I can't...hold it much longer!" On the last word, Odette and Bastion launched themselves clumsily through the door and landed in a tangled mass of nonwoven material, Kevlar, and surgical-grade chain mail. Odette's helmet cracked against the floor. Behind them, the door slid closed.

Odette struggled to look back, clawing her gown material out of the way. Through the window in the door, she saw roaring red flames cascade down from the ceiling. The body on the table was completely engulfed.

That's light fire? she thought.

Meanwhile, showerheads in the ceiling of the air lock had begun drenching her and Dr. Bastion with liquid that smelled strongly of chemicals. By the time the outer door swung open and the little surgical squires peered in, Odette and Dr. Bastion were completely soaked. It took several minutes of laborious unpeeling before the two autopsists could leave and change back into their normal clothes.

By the time they presented themselves to the executives, Marie had arrived at the Rookery and was talking quietly with Clovis. Apparently, the day's meetings had commenced and security had tightened further in light of the previous night's attack. Rook Thomas was not scheduled to attend any meetings that day, but Graaf Ernst's absence had been noted.

"Negotiations would be probably even more awkward if they knew about the rogue Grafters who tried to kill Rook Thomas," remarked Clovis.

"So, not everyone knows about last night? But I called the emergency help line!" asked Odette.

"We gave them a cover story about a training exercise," said Rook Thomas. "Only a handful of people are aware of the truth."

"So what do we do now?" asked Marie.

"To begin with," said Rook Thomas, "let's establish what the situation actually is. Miss Leliefeld, what can you tell us about the charred semi-consumed corpse downstairs?"

"He's a kit thug," said Odette. "They took this guy and weaponized him quickly. Scars unhealed, weapons shoved in. There were painkiller sacs throughout his body preventing him from feeling any of the aches." Although there weren't nearly enough to cancel out my venom, she thought in satisfaction. "I would say he'd been in possession of his implants no more than a week. Still deadly, though. He could have punched through a wall, they'd layered so much cow muscle all through him."

"Cow muscle?" asked Pawn Clements.

"Cows are strong," said Odette. "And convenient. I've got a few pockets of cow muscle in me. Growing human muscle takes too long. Anyway, he'd had bladed teeth installed and some sort of projectile launcher. Multiple lungs, I'm not sure why, maybe they got a job lot or something, and his ribs had been heavily reinforced. Also, his genitals had been, um, enlarged." She flushed a little. "And, of course, there was that Tartarus gourd they left as a booby trap."

"Squirmy little bastard that was," said Rook Thomas. "I was holding on to it right up until the fire was activated."

"That gourd is very concerning," said Marie. "They should not have been able to get hold of one. Those items are incredibly rare and dangerous to make—we haven't grown any new ones since 1976—and there is a strictly limited number in the vaults." She sighed. "I'll have to order an inventory. God knows what else they've managed to snatch."

"Could its contents have survived the fire?" asked Chief Clovis. "Do I need to fill the room?"

"You said that before," remembered Odette. "What do you fill the room with?"

"Concrete," said Clovis. "We've a mass of wet concrete churning above the examination room—if something goes really wrong, we can just pour it in."

"You were talking about filling the room with us in it!" shouted Odette. She looked to Dr. Bastion for support in her outrage, but he just shrugged.

"We can't be too careful," said Dr. Bastion. "We work with dangerous things. Dangerous people. Room two got filled in three years ago when one of the Pawns had a very bad reaction to some routine inoculations. The Pawn and his doctor and a nurse were all entombed in there. It won't be unsealed for another two years."

"Oh," said Odette. Then something occurred to her. "Did someone let Marcel know? Isn't he working on one of the other corpses?"

"Yes, we've pulled him out," said Clovis.

"Anyway," said Marie, who seemed to approve of the Checquy's security measures, "the fact that they all suffered simultaneous seizures is not good news. Odette, did you see anything that might give us a lead?"

"No, I'm sorry."

"You'll need to provide us with files," said Security Chief Clovis. "All the information you have on the Antagonists. We'll want photos—"

"Photos won't do you any good," interrupted Odette. "They'll be wearing new faces. It would have been the first thing they did."

"Sure, right after they murdered the house," said Rook Thomas. "They couldn't just abscond to St. Barts to tan with all the other rebellious rich kids."

"This isn't a tantrum!" said Odette sharply. "They believe this is the right thing to do. To them, the changes you're making—all of you," she said, including Grootvader Ernst, "are unforgivable. They'll die for this if they have to."

"Passionate little clique, aren't they?" mused Clovis.

"They're young." Marie shrugged.

"Be that as it may," said Rook Thomas, "they constitute a significant threat. Which leads me to a point. We can't be pulling any punches. If it comes down to it, we'll kill them rather than risk their escaping. But if we do capture them? Frankly, I don't like the idea of trying to imprison them. Gallows Keep is the most secure facility on these islands, but word would leak out to the Checquy troops eventually."

"We can execute them," said Ernst coldly. Odette felt like she'd been punched in the stomach, and she made an involuntary sound of distress. "But there is another possibility. The Broederschap possesses the means to strip them of their memories and their knowledge." Odette looked away. She could almost feel scaly lips on her own and a writhing mass of slender tentacles pressing at her mouth. She shuddered and noticed that, oddly, Rook Thomas looked a little nauseated as well.

"Well, we'll discuss it if the situation arises," said Rook Thomas finally. "But where is this going? What's their endgame?"

"I don't know," confessed Odette.

"Do they even know?" Clovis snorted.

"I think they want everything to go back to the way it was," said Odette helplessly. She winced under Rook Thomas's scornful look.

"The way it was," said the Rook. "Where they enjoyed immeasurable privileges and no responsibilities."

"They don't know if they're conservatives or radicals," said Ernst. "You almost have to pity them."

"Sure," said Rook Thomas in a tone that suggested no such pity would be forthcoming. "Now, we've got only one lead left, so let's see whether he's of any use at all."

35

Rook Thomas swept through the hallways of the Hammerstrom Building, Odette and Pawn Clements hurrying behind her. Various Checquy personnel stood back against the walls to make a path for the Rook and her entourage. Each person made a hurried obeisance to the Rook, a nod or a slight bow. Then they saw Odette and did a double take (or, in the case of the Pawn with three heads, a sextuple take), followed by a narrowing of the eyes (or, in the case of the Pawn with no eyes, a pursing of the lips). Many of them tried to back even farther against the wall, as if they were in danger of being infected by her.

By the time a pair of massive iron doors leading to the detention area of the Rookery split open in front of them, Odette was completely lost. They had passed through so many security checkpoints and signed so many release forms that she half expected to go through a door and see the crown jewels on display, possibly while still on the monarch.

The part of the Rookery in which prisoners were kept, although it was several stories underground, was quite bright and airy. Or at least the administration area was. A warm light filled the room, and several large displays of flowers were scattered about.

"Hello, Rook Thomas. We weren't expecting you until later today," said the head of the section, a burly woman the sight of whom made Odette's head ache. It looked like someone had taken a blade of unutterable sharpness and sliced her down the middle, from the crown of her head to, presumably, the base of her torso. However, instead of settling for being two parts of a dead body, the woman, whose name was Pawn Camden, had elected to continue going about her business in a position of some responsibility in the Rookery's detention facility.

At least, that was how it appeared. Although Odette doubted that the woman had come to this situation late in life. For one thing, the two halves of her were separated by about four centimeters of empty space and were contained in a business suit. For another, she seemed entirely unconcerned by her situation.

Be cool, Odette thought. Don't stare at her. She could see the gap only down to where it vanished into the woman's collar. She took a cautious step sideways so that she could see into the gap. Huh, fascinating. The inside surfaces of each half of her head, where Odette might have expected to see a cross section of brain and other head matter, was covered in tight, smooth skin. Does that gap go all the way down? How does she hold together? How does she walk? And what about the connection between the two hemispheres of her brain? And her spine? And her bowels? Pawn Camden's eyes blinked in unison, she smiled like one person, and when she spoke, both half-mouths moved simultaneously, producing a strangely choral effect.

"How's the prisoner?" asked Rook Thomas, looking over the file Pawn Camden had handed her.

"Sleeping like a comatose baby," said both halves of Pawn Camden. "Pawn Motha said he was clear of any booby traps—"

"Oh, good, I feel so much safer," muttered Clements.

"—and we've scanned him, done MRIs and x-rays, taken photos and samples. He was deadly still for all of them."

"So...vegetative state?" asked the Rook.

"There have been a few little blips, actually," said Pawn Camden. "Three times, his brain has fired up again, and he's opened his eyes and looked around. The third time, he just rolled over in bed and went back under."

"That's weird," said Odette thoughtfully.

"This is Odette Leliefeld," said the Rook absently.

"Oh," said Pawn Camden, "with the Graf—" She broke off, having turned her head toward Odette and then flinched, which Odette thought was pretty rich. "The, uh, Brotherhood of Scientific Scientists." Odette looked down at her feet, but then guilty fascination dragged her eyes up to the divided woman once again. "It's delightful to meet you," said the Pawn unconvincingly.

"You too," said Odette, equally unconvincingly.

"And this is Pawn Clements," said Thomas. The two women nodded to each other. "So anything else I need to know about this guy?" asked the Rook.

"We're not having any luck mapping his DNA."

"So he's not in any of the databases?" said Thomas.

"It's not that," said Pawn Camden. "The results are odd. Apparently there are gaps in the code, and the films seem almost, I don't know, smeared."

"Huh," said the Rook. She passed the file over to Odette. "Thoughts?"

"I've never seen anything like it," said Odette as she scanned the material. "Very odd."

"I gather from our scientists that we've never seen it either," said Pawn Camden. "Not in any Checquy personnel, not in any manifestations."

"And the other attackers didn't have this issue?" asked the Rook.

"No. Standard DNA."

"But this guy was the normal one among them. No implants, no modifications. What does that mean?" mused the Rook.

"Do we need to worry about his unleashing any powers or anything?" asked Clements.

"The cell is very secure, with all the standard immobilization measures, and we're not getting any odd readings" the bisected Pawn said with a shrug. "He hasn't disconnected any of the monitor sensors. Right now, he's comatose. Dr. Crisp is scheduled to see what he can do this afternoon, but I'm afraid we're not at all prepared for you. The prisoner is still in his cell, Dr. Crisp is out to lunch, and we haven't hosed down the interrogation room yet or gotten the buffet ready for the observation roo—"

"Don't worry, Pawn Camden," Rook Thomas reassured her. "This isn't some snap inspection. I just want to have a quick look at the prisoner. Is he restrained?"

"No. We thought about it, but he's evinced no sign of any special abilities, and they didn't find any trace of Grafter implants in him. He's behind unbreakable glass, but he's just in a bed hooked up to monitors," said Pawn Camden. "If you want to give us a few minutes, we could put him into stocks, or maybe decant him into an oubliette."

"No, I think that'll be fine," said the Rook. "Is he gagged?"

"No, but the cell is soundproof except through the intercom. We're keeping an eye on him and recording everything with cameras and microphones. But orders from Clovis were to keep him isolated."

Of course, thought Odette. Can't have word getting out that one of the Grafters tried to kill the Rook.

"Excellent, Juniper," said Rook Thomas. "Please take us to the observation room." The woman nodded and guided the three of them to a small wood-paneled room with a red chaise longue in the center. One of the walls was glass, and on the other side of it was the cell with the blond man lying in a hospital bed.

"Rook Thomas, here is the control board for the cell," said Pawn Camden, handing her a tablet computer. "It's all very simple. If you wish to activate the intercom or make the glass transparent so that the subject can see you, just use this. And of course, if there are any problems, you can call one of us with the button by the door."

"Thanks, Pawn Camden," said Rook Thomas. The Pawn nodded her half-heads and left the room.

"That was the most insane thing I've ever seen!" Odette burst out, still reeling from the scientific impossibility. Pawn Clements made a little sniffing sound, which Odette decided to ignore. "What on earth happened to that woman?"

"She was born like that," said Rook Thomas, taking the file back from Odette. "She's very nice. Paints gorgeous landscapes; I went to the opening of one of her shows a couple weeks ago."

"Is—is she actually in two pieces?"

"Yes," said the Rook distractedly as she flipped through the file.

"But how does she not fall apart? Or die?"

"I believe it's something to do with magnets," said the Rook with an obvious and, to Odette, astounding lack of concern.

"Magnets?" repeated Odette. "I don't think that can be right." The Rook shrugged. "So how does she go out in the world?"

"A burka," said Rook Thomas. "They're tremendously handy. Lots of our more unorthodox-looking staff wear them." Odette stared at her. "Okay, now, you and Pawn Clements sit there," said the Rook, pointing toward the chaise. "And shut up for a little bit." The two women looked at each other but sat down. Odette's gaze wandered to the adjoining cell.

In contrast to the dark paneling of the observation room, the prison cell was a bright white, not unlike the surgical rooms that she had visited earlier. The only furniture was a hospital bed containing the prisoner. He was curled up, his face buried in the crook of an arm. Various cords had been affixed to his body at strategic points on his head and chest, and they ran to locked cabinets against the back wall. The only movement seemed to come from his breathing, and Odette had to peer pretty carefully to catch even that.

The Rook, meanwhile, was eyeing the tablet computer. Finally, she pressed something on it. There was an audible click and they could hear the sound of breathing coming through the speakers. It was the prisoner.

"Can he hear us?" asked Pawn Clements uncertainly. The Rook shook her head.

"Can't see us, can't hear us," she assured them. "Especially since he's currently in a vegetative state, if I'm interpreting these readouts correctly." She held out the tablet to Odette, who took it and glanced over them.

"Comatose," she agreed.

"Well, that's disappointing," said Thomas, taking the tablet back from Odette and giving her the file again. "I'm going to have a little sift through his physiology and maybe give him a jolt or two to see if that wakes him up. He seemed not to be a fan of mine, so I think a conversation between us might yield some details."

Odette and Felicity sat quietly on the chaise, and Odette flipped through the file. The Checquy had done the usual battery of tests trying to come up with clues to his past, and they'd found nothing very interesting. His fingerprints hadn't tripped any alarms in any databases. No sign of any inoculations, no old fractures. Uncircumcised. His wisdom teeth were intact, as were his tonsils. His appendix was burbling away comfortably. They hadn't even found any incriminating calluses on his hands or feet.

"Interesting..." she muttered.

"What?" asked Clements.

"He's had a vasectomy," said Odette. "A recent one."

"Yes, fascinating," said Clements, edging away slightly.

"Could the two of you shut up, please?" said the Rook. She was leaning against the frame of the glass, her forehead resting on her arm. Presumably, she was reaching out with her powers, examining the prisoner's internal structure, but it looked for all the world as if she were taking a little standing nap.

"Little Myfanwy," said the prisoner suddenly, and Rook Thomas's head jerked up in surprise. "I could feel your familiar touch, your little fingers sliding around inside my face." He hadn't looked up, but Odette could hear the smile in his voice. "And now you're going down, probing in my chest and gut. I wonder, Rook Thomas, will you go even farther down? Find something interesting to play with and explore?" The Rook stepped back, her cheeks flaming.

"And now you've let go," said the prisoner. "Too bad." His voice was a little slurred, as if he'd been drinking.

Could he be one of the Antagonists? wondered Odette. His

English accent is perfect, but all they'd need is a neurolinguistic patch, and there'd be no trace of a European accent.

The Rook looked down at the tablet in her hand. Her finger hovered, and then she pressed at something.

"You sound very calm about all this," said Thomas, and the prisoner cocked his head a little. Obviously, she had switched on the intercom.

"Well, you know how it is," he said. "You take your best shot, and if it doesn't work out, weellll…there's always another time, isn't there?"

"Oh, I don't know about that," said Thomas. "I have to tell you, you're not in good shape at all. I'm not sensing any Grafter additions inside your body, but there's something very wrong with you. I can feel it in your flesh. I don't think you're going to have enough time to come after me and fuck me up. Plus, of course, you're, well, in prison."

"You never know, Myfanwy," said the prisoner. "Things can change, just like that," and he sat up and looked directly at the glass.

"Oh my God!" exclaimed Odette, almost falling off the chaise. Pawn Clements hissed in horror, and Rook Thomas took another couple of steps backward.

The hours since Odette had last seen him had not been at all kind to the prisoner. His face looked pretty much the same, but it was drooping, almost hanging off his skull. The skin of his scalp and neck was sagging too. The color seemed to be leaching out of his hair, clumps of which had fallen out. He was shirtless, and the skin of his chest was gray and mottled. Perspiration was pouring from him.

"Who's that?" said the prisoner.

"That's Odette," said the Rook, and Odette looked at her incredulously. The Rook shrugged.

"Odette," said the prisoner softly. "Right. You made the wrong choice, back in that hotel lobby in Paris."

He is one of them! Odette thought. "Wie bent u?" she asked intently. Who are you? Which of her friends was looking out from behind that mask of skin? Could it be Pim? What had he done to himself? He cocked his head and smirked when she spoke but didn't say anything. He simply stared at the glass.

This doesn't feel right, she thought, staring at the man. Too many things that don't make sense. The accent I can explain, but they would never talk to me like that. I can't see any of them putting on a different face and leading a team of thugs to assault a Checquy Rook. They don't do hand-to-hand combat. And what is wrong with his skin?

"Well, apparently you don't feel like saying anything useful," said the Rook, "so we'll chat a bit later. I can guarantee you'll want to tell us everything." She stared through the glass, waiting for a reaction, but nothing came. Then, suddenly, the man lurched out of bed and flung himself at the glass. The barrier didn't shake, but the bang of his head against it echoed through the observation room. Rook Thomas flinched back in shock, bumping into Odette and Pawn Clements, on the chaise, who had, without thinking, clutched at each other.

"You want answers?" screamed the man, his spit flying. His face was contorted, and he pressed himself against the glass so that his skin squashed and twisted alarmingly. "The answer is, you're going to die!" He drew his head back and smashed it against the glass. The sound was terrible, stomach-turning.

Jesus, thought Odette. All three of them were transfixed by the sight.

"Die!" he screamed, smashing his head forward again. This time, the sagging skin of his forehead split, and blood stained the glass.

"DIE!

"DIE!"

And then he fell back, twitching, to the ground. The Rook warily put her hand against the glass and frowned. Suddenly, she exclaimed, "Hit the panic button! He's damaged himself severely. I think he's fractured his skull."

"Not just that," said Odette shakily. "Look at him. Look!" The man's skin was fizzing and peeling away from his bones.

As they watched, his pectoral muscles tore in several places and they saw his ribs melting like ice cream. His hair was a slick of slime, and his eyes were pouring out onto his face, which lay unchanged over his collapsing skull. She looked at Pawn Clements and Rook Thomas. Both of them were staring incredulously at the rotting mass on the floor. Then the Rook turned to Odette and Clements.

"I totally didn't do that," she said firmly.

36

And here we are again," said Ernst. "Are we actually awake this time?"

"Yes," said the Rook testily. Odette pinched herself surreptitiously, just to make certain. "Although it would certainly save on our entertaining budget if everyone were simply unconscious."

They were seated in the private upstairs dining room of a restaurant in Wapping. The room looked out onto the Thames, and the building appeared to date back several centuries. The floor was made up of gigantic beams of warped wood, and the table could have been older than Graaf Ernst. The Checquy contingent of the party consisted of Rook Thomas, Security Chief Clovis, and Chevalier Joshua Eckhart, with Pawn Clements sitting warily at the end of the table next to Rook Thomas. The Grafters consisted of Ernst, Marie, Odette, and Marcel.

For all the restaurant's battered age, its menu was surprisingly modern and decadent. Rook Thomas drummed her fingers as the maître d' who came with the room recited the specials and they all took their time perusing the offerings before making their selections. She endured Ernst's close questioning of the maître d' as to how wild the wild boar had been before being made into sausage; Marcel's asking to check the sage, dill, and basil before they were washed and used in the meal; and Security Chief Clovis's request to substitute a garlic-and-potato smash for hand-cut vegetable chips, carrots for squash, and lemon juice for béarnaise sauce. Finally the woman left the room, and Myfanwy was opening her mouth but Marcel spoke first.

"Why were we called to this restaurant?" he asked. "Not that I'm complaining, but it was a little abrupt. I was in the middle of examining the only one of those hooligans that didn't have a Tartarus gourd tucked away in him. I'd just started unpacking his cranial cavity and had to leave brains and wires spread out on the table with some plastic wrap from the kitchen draped over them."

"It was a preexisting meeting that we could co-opt," said the Rook. "I wanted Chevalier Eckhart present for this discussion, and this was the only thing in our schedule that I could shoehorn everyone into without raising suspicion." On the official Checquy books, the gathering was still described as a working lunch to brainstorm the integration of incoming Grafter troops into existing Checquy forces, since "a meeting to discuss the actions of supernatural terrorists being kept secret from not only the British government but our own people" did not fit into any billing code.

"So," said Thomas, "there has been a development."

"Oh?" said Ernst.

"Yes. Much to the consternation of the medical staff, the detention staff, and the janitorial staff, the blond man melted," said the Rook. "What does that mean to you?"

"Clone," said Marie promptly. "A botched clone."

"Except that it couldn't be a clone," responded Marcel, equally promptly.

"What about accelerated aging?" suggested Ernst.

"That wouldn't make any sense either," said Odette.

"Hold on," said Rook Thomas. "What's this talk about clones?"

"A clone is a genetically identical copy of a living thing that's produced asexually," said Marcel.

"I know what a clone is," said Rook Thomas. "They made a sheep. So, you clone things?"

"We can," said Marcel. "We don't, though, not usually. Of course, we grow bits of people, but we don't make whole people."

"Why not?" asked Eckhart.

"We prefer to have sex," said Ernst, causing Pawn Clements to choke on her orange juice. "Plus, anyone who wants to clone himself is usually an asshole. You don't want any more of those running around than absolutely necessary."

"So the blond man could have been a clone of one of the Antagonists?" said Rook Thomas.

"No," said Marcel.

"Why not?"

"Because when you clone something, you end up with an embryo that is an exact physical copy." Marcel looked at Marie sourly. "Provided you haven't made any unprofessional errors."

"I made one error!" exclaimed Marie. "When I was nineteen! God! And may I say, that cat lived a long and happy life!"

"It certainly lived a quiet life," remarked Marcel.

"You know, there are cats born naturally that don't have ears!" said Marie. At that point, there was a knock on the door, and their appetizers were delivered while everyone sat in awkward silence.

"Anyway," said Odette after the waitstaff had departed, "cloning is difficult, and even when you do it right, you end up with an embryo that grows into a baby that grows into a child that grows into a person who is a physical copy of the original. Not a mental copy. And the clone ages at a normal rate."

"You can see why we prefer the sex," said Ernst. "Same result, more fun, much less math."

"The blond man was a grown-up," said Odette helpfully. "Older than all of my friends. They didn't have time to grow him, and they certainly wouldn't have the patience to raise him."

"You mentioned accelerated growth, though," said Eckhart. "Could that have been used here?"

"No," said Marcel.

"Possibly," said Odette. "Accelerated growth results in accelerated breakdown, which is certainly what we saw."

"It's very simple," said Marcel. "Much easier than cloning. But if you accelerate the growth of an embryo, regardless of whether it's a cloned embryo or a regular one, you end up with an adult with the mind of an embryo. There's no way to speed-educate it.

"If we are to assume the blond man was a clone, or even a normal zygote that was subjected to accelerated growth," continued Marcel, "then, judging by the rate of deterioration you've described, that man was a couple of weeks old, maximum." He took a sip of wine. "All he should have been able to do was blink a few times and fall over. Possibly he could have soiled himself. But he certainly shouldn't have been capable of masquerading as another person. You can't clone minds or thoughts."

"You did with him," said Rook Thomas, nodding over at Ernst.

"What?" said Odette sharply.

"Oh yes," said the Rook. "I got sent a human heart in a box that grew into a naked man who came into my office, brokered a peace deal, and ate all my frozen pizza." Security Chief Clovis and Felicity listened to this chronicle of supernatural diplomacy with forks paused halfway to their open mouths. "And he didn't dissolve into slime."

"Actually, I did," said Ernst. "Why did you think I left so abruptly that evening?"

"I thought that you had to notify the Broederschap to stand down hostilities. And that you were uncomfortable with the fact that you were wearing my bathrobe. Which I never got back, by the way."

"Both those reasons were true," conceded Ernst, ignoring the point about the bathrobe. "But I also needed to have various nonperishable components of my brain removed and slotted into this pre-prepared cloned body that I had waiting in a house in Mayfair. By the time you were having breakfast, the body you

438

spoke with was a drumful of rotting tissue and liquefying hair and bones that was subsequently poured down the drain into the sewers."

Felicity carefully put her fork down and pushed her plate away.

"So this is a different body?" said Rook Thomas. "It looks exactly the same."

"That's why they call it cloning," said Marcel drily. "And we had to start growing the current body twenty-odd years ago."

"You really plan ahead," said Rook Thomas, sounding impressed. "So could the Antagonists have done that thing you did? Where you get a clone that has your thoughts?"

"That wasn't a clone," said Ernst. "A clone is a copy. That was me. The only me. The procedure with the heart means that you strip core elements from yourself. Your old body breaks down. You see—"

"We get the picture," said Chevalier Eckhart. "So, could they have done it?"

"No. It's classified material," said Marie. "Still extremely experimental."

"The Antagonists have already shown they can get at classified material," said Odette meekly. "Remember the booby trap in that corpse?"

"Also, it's an extremely complex and time-consuming process that you need a special lab for," said Marcel. "And it's horrendously expensive. That heart we sent you cost almost one hundred seventeen million euros."

"And you just mailed it to us?" asked Rook Thomas, aghast. "What if we'd thrown it away? Or incinerated it?"

"It wouldn't have happened," said Ernst comfortably. "We have two men working in the Checquy morgue."

"Had," said Security Chief Clovis pointedly.

"Anyway," said Marie, "the Antagonists have money, but not like that."

"And what would be the point?" asked Odette. "So they maybe have a shot at killing you before they rot away and die? Not their style. They're not suicide people."

At this point, the maître d' knocked on the door, and everyone stopped talking as she led in two servers to collect the plates.

"Your mains should be here shortly," said the maître d' into the silence.

"Thank you," said everyone simultaneously, and then they all were quiet until the door had shut.

"Look," said the Rook, "we simply cannot stop talking every time the servers come in. They're going to think we're here plotting something illegal. So, for God's sake, try to make conversation when they bring the main course."

"About what?" asked Marie.

"What's our cover story?" said Clovis. "We need a context for conversation."

"We're a family out to lunch," suggested Ernst. Felicity looked around the room. Apart from Ernst, Odette, and Marcel, no one looked likely to be related to anyone else. "Here to meet Odette's new boyfriend, Clovis, of whom I do not approve." Odette winced. "It's not a race thing," he said defensively. "It's because he's so much older than her. And he's a drummer."

"How about we're a firm of graphic designers," suggested Odette. "Here to talk about a major project."

"Yes!" said Marie. "Good! We can be artsy and interesting, so no one will expect us to be particularly coherent." Her blond haircut grew abruptly jagged, and streaks of blue poured through it.

"They'll expect our hair not to have changed between courses," said the Rook.

"Of course," said Marie. "Sorry, I got a little overexcited." Her hair snapped back into shape and became a uniform blond again.

"All right, so we're graphic designers," said Chevalier Eckhart. "Fine. Now, back to the actual reason we're here, the mystery of the melting blond man. I've had a thought. What about the self-destruct thing you did with your soldiers in Hyde Park? Could it have been something like that?"

"The Chimerae," said Marie. "They had a discretion function that reduced them to paste."

"I don't think it can be the same thing," said Odette. "The Checquy examined the subject and found no sign of Broederschap implants. That function requires them to have sacs full of chemicals all through them. There's no way those implants could have been missed. I saw the scans."

"Marvelous, another possibility down the drain," said the Rook. "Okay, so, not a clone?"

"No," said Marcel firmly. "Not enough time."

"Not a member of the Antagonists with a self-destructing bowel?"

"No," said Odette uncertainly.

"Could he just have been some man off the street they paid to get a vasectomy, wear someone else's face, and try to kill Myfanwy before bashing himself to death against a window?" asked Eckhart. The lunch party contemplated this possibility.

"It does not seem likely," said Marie finally.

"Where would you even find someone willing to do that?" asked Odette.

"And even if you did find someone like that, how did he dissolve?" mused Rook Thomas. "Plus, he seemed to know me. He was certainly taking the whole thing very personally."

A knock at the door heralded the arrival of the mains. They all composed themselves in a manner that they imagined befitted graphic designers. The food was brought in, smelling delicious. They were all still silent, though, apparently lacking any clue as to what graphic designers might talk about.

"I don't care what you people say!" Felicity burst out suddenly, and everyone in the room jumped. "We are not using a font that does not have fucking serifs!" Odette buried her face in her hands. The servers exchanged horrified looks and left hurriedly.

"Yes...very good, Pawn Clements," said Eckhart. "Good improvisation. Now, shall we eat?" All four Grafters produced large pill organizers and began opening sections. The Checquy people affected not to notice.

"You mentioned something about the melted man's face?" said Marcel as he began his meal.

"Yes," said Security Chief Clovis, "and that is one of the things that is most troubling. It turns out that he was in possession of one Broederschap implant. Everything rotted except his face, which remained relatively pristine." He looked at Odette. "You had mentioned that the Antagonists would be wearing different faces."

"Yes." She shrugged. "It's not a terribly difficult matter to arrange." The Broederschap had 3-D printers that worked in collagen and skin.

"So they can look like anyone?" asked Chevalier Eckhart.

"Well, their faces can," said Odette. "The size of one's skull affects things, obviously, and if I showed up wearing Security Chief Clovis's face, you'd twig pretty early on that something was amiss."

"Of course," said the Chevalier. "But it sounds like it could be a very effective disguise."

"It can be," said Marie proudly.

"Marvelous. My concern is that we can no longer be certain that anyone in your delegation is who they say they are. Is that correct?" This was met with an awkward silence. "I see that it is. The situation is getting increasingly complicated."

"And you have called us here to help uncomplicate it," said Marcel.

"Well, that, and, of course, it gave me a chance to confirm that everyone here is wearing his or her own face," said Rook Thomas. The Grafters looked around uneasily, realizing that the Rook had been using her powers on them. Marie put a hesitant hand up to her cheek as if she could feel Thomas's mind sorting through her skin. "Don't worry. All of you are who you say you are. If you weren't, you'd be lying on the floor awkwardly handcuffing yourself." She took a thoughtful sip of wine.

"Anyway," continued the Rook, ignoring the Grafters' stricken looks, "this does not solve all our problems. It solves barely any of them." She closed her eyes for a moment and seemed to be gathering her strength. When she opened them, she said, "To begin with, we'll need to ensure that there are no moles in your delegation wearing someone else's face."

"We'll set about testing everyone's DNA," said Marie. "Immediately."

"That's not enough," said Chevalier Eckhart. "I want Rook Thomas to read their faces. Is your entire entourage coming to the event tonight?"

"Not everyone was supposed to come," said Marie uncertainly.

"They are now," said Eckhart flatly. Rook Thomas winced.

"And thus the chefs of Apex House will be goaded into a collective nervous breakdown," she said.

"There will be armed guards at the reception," said Clovis. "If Myfanwy identifies someone wearing the wrong face, I will have no compunction about blowing that person's brains into his or her salad."

"If she identifies someone wearing the wrong face, I'll have that person vomiting up his or her lungs," said Marie darkly.

"Until we confirm the identities of all the Grafter delegates, I will have armed guards in every negotiation room," said Clovis. "Don't worry, though, they're extremely discreet. In fact, one of them is actually coating the table in conference room B." At that, Odette took her hands off the surface of the dining table and wiped them on her skirt.

"Now, let's go back to the puddle that used to be the blond man," said Eckhart, blithely putting a spoonful of soup to his lips.

"He was already dying when we came in," said the Rook. "I could read it in his flesh. His organs were falling apart under my mind's touch. I expect that bashing his own head in was simply some sort of gesture. The med staff are about to start testing the remains. Tell me, are they going to find anything?"

"Doubtful," said Marcel. "The effect you've described doesn't leave any identifiable information."

"What about her?" said the graaf, pointing toward Felicity. She flushed as everyone turned to look at her. "Your Pawn who can talk to dead bodies."

"Well, first, that's not what she does," said Rook Thomas tartly.

"Liquids are tricky," said Felicity. "I can try, but the further back in time I look, the longer it will take. The sooner I start, the better."

"How long to look back forty-eight hours?" asked Eckhart.

"With liquid? About twenty-four hours, sir," said Felicity.

"I don't think we have that much time," said Myfanwy. "They said they were building toward something big. We'll have to follow all the other leads first. For instance, why would they perform a vasectomy on the blond guy?" she asked. Felicity looked around with interest. The Grafters seemed particularly bewildered by this revelation. "That was the only modification our doctors found."

"They missed the face?" asked Marcel.

"They noticed he had one. I think they stopped looking after that."

"I can think of only one reason for a vasectomy," mused Eckhart. "Well, two, if you take into account that time we were trying to see how many things Pawn Wampler could grow back. And that was a dare at a stag do anyway." Deathly silence greeted this tangential recollection.

"It doesn't sound right," said Odette finally. "Birth control is one of the very first things we address when we start getting modifications."

"Well, that strongly suggests that he wasn't one of the Antagonists," said Ernst. "I can't think of anything else."

"Well, I suppose that's one more mystery to write down on my list of Stuff That Makes No Sense," said Rook Thomas. She scribbled on a notepad at the side of her plate. Felicity, who was sitting next to her, noticed that the heading actually was "Stuff That Makes No Sense."

"And he had no weapons, not even any spur mechanisms," Odette said.

"I don't know why you children even use those things," sniffed Ernst. "If you're going to poison someone, why not just spit at them? Or give them some doctored schnapps?"

"We're veering off topic here," pointed out Rook Thomas.

"They're discreet, Grootvader," said Odette. "And I managed to take out a couple of attackers with them, so that should make you happy." Ernst didn't say anything, but he didn't look unhappy.

"So, we don't really have any further leads on the Antagonists," said Eckhart sourly. "Unless we get lucky and there's another attack on Myfanwy."

"It's difficult," said Marie, "since they took so much when they absconded. And, of course, they have a great deal of money. That sort of independence always makes it harder." Odette's great-uncle cleared his throat.

"Yes, Marcel?" said van Suchtlen.

"I have been reviewing the portfolios of our runaways. Simon de Wilde's is especially relevant. Owing to his experiments with his own modifications, he requires certain exotic compounds to be applied to his body on a regular basis. These compounds are not common, and they are not cheap, so perhaps this will help us find him. I will pass on the details to Marie and Mr. Clovis."

"Well, that's something," said Chevalier Eckhart.

"Not much," said Rook Thomas. She looked at her watch. "All right, if you'd like dessert, feel free. Clovis, you can put all this on your corporate card and I'll sign off on it. I have some things to get done."

"Yes, you and I have to go talk to the Court," said Chevalier Eckhart grimly.

"Yeah, but first we have to inform the head chef at Apex House that a lot more people are coming to the reception tonight."

"Oh, well, that you can do by yourself," said the Chevalier.

"Are you serious?" asked the Rook. "It was your idea. You have to come tell him."

"Absolutely not. That man terrifies me."

"What's his power?" asked Ernst curiously.

"He doesn't have any power," said Rook Thomas. "He just shouts a lot."

37

Do you have a dress for the reception?" Odette asked Felicity in the car after lunch. "Or do you have to wear a uniform of some sort?"

"I think if a woman showed up to a Checquy reception in a uniform, Lady Farrier would have her assassinated," said Felicity. "The quartermaster has my measurements; they sent over a gown while we were out."

"You haven't even seen it?"

"I'll see it in ten minutes," said the Pawn, "when we get to the hotel."

"I'd put it closer to twenty," said Odette. "The traffic is terrible." Their car was progressing in fits and starts, like an opera singer who had been hit with a hockey stick right in the middle of an aria but who was determined that the show would go on.

"Rush hour." Clements shrugged. "Just be glad you're not out in it." Hordes of pedestrians washed by the car, and the Pawn averted her gaze as if they were all naked.

"You're not a fan of crowds, are you?" asked Odette. The Pawn looked at her and seemed to be weighing something.

"I'm not a fan of the public, really," she said finally. "You know, normal people. They make me nervous. They always have, ever since I moved here from the Estate."

"Why?"

"Oh, I don't know. There's so many of them. And they just wander through life, completely unaware of everything that's going on around them. It's like they're cattle. And we're watching over them."

"Cattle," repeated Odette.

"Or sheep. Sheep that could rise up and burn us all at the stake if they found out about us. We're always told at school how important it is to keep ourselves secret. And mostly it's because of what the knowledge would do to the British people if they found out. But we all know it's also because of what they would do to us." She looked out the window. "So many of them," she mused. "So few of us." Then she frowned. "Huh."

"What is it?" asked Odette.

"I think I know that guy," Clements said, squinting through the glass.

"Yeah? Which one?"

"The homeless gay guy."

"What?" said Odette. "How can you even tell he's gay? Or homeless, for that matter?" she added self-righteously.

"Don't give me that look. He's holding hands with another man," said the Pawn. "And he's dressed like he has no home. Or at least no wardrobe." Odette peered out at the crowd and identified the man in question. She had to admit, Felicity had a point. The man was middle-aged and dressed in sweatpants and a rumpled and heavily stained T-shirt. He had the sort of hesitant, patchy beard that looks decidedly unplanned and the blank stare of one who has been partaking of substances of dubious legality. In contrast, the dark-haired man whose hand he held appeared to be in his midtwenties and was dressed in a beautifully cut blue suit and designer sunglasses.

What an odd couple, Odette thought. "And how do you know him?" she asked as the two men walked away down the street. It was a sign of the slowness of the traffic that the peculiar pair were proceeding far more swiftly than the cars.

"I'm not sure," said Felicity. "I realize this sounds dreadful, but he doesn't look like anyone I would know." She shrugged. "Maybe I don't know him after all."

They settled back as the car made absolutely no progress whatsoever.

"Oh, for God's sake," said Odette after several long minutes.

"Sorry, Miss Leliefeld," said the driver. "It's the worst time of day, and there was an accident on the A4, so traffic's a nightmare everywhere. I thought this route would be quicker."

"It's not your fault, Tom," said Odette. "It's just, I rather

447

need to go to the bathroom." The traffic ahead showed no sign of dissipating and, indeed, appeared to be hunkering down for a long hibernation.

"Tom, I think we'll walk the rest of the way," said the Pawn.

"Are you sure?" asked the driver.

"Yes, it's fine. It's just a few blocks to Park Lane."

The world outside the car was much brighter, warmer, and noisier. Shoppers, tourists, and commuters were all bustling up and down Oxford Street. Felicity seemed to sway against the roar of the city, but then she braced herself and gestured for Odette to follow. They weaved their way through the populace, all of whom seemed to be going in the opposite direction purely out of spite.

"Wait a minute," said Clements. She grabbed Odette's sleeve. "Wait a minute." Her eyes were narrowed in frantic calculation.

"What?"

"I think I know how I recognize that man."

"The homeless guy who might be gay or might just be unbound by the traditional strictures of heterosexual male friendship?"

"I—what?" asked the Pawn, coming out of her thoughts for a moment to cope with this new observation.

"I'm just saying."

"Shut up. I know who that guy was." Her free hand slid inside her coat.

"Who was it?" asked Odette, bewildered by the Pawn's intensity.

"Where are they? Did we pass them?" Clements was scanning the pavement, but the crowd prevented her from seeing very far. "Shit. What should we do?" she wondered, almost to herself. She hadn't let go of Odette's sleeve. "I need a discreet place to call the Rook. Damn it, where's the car?"

"Felicity, who was that man?" Finally, the Pawn looked at her.

"One of the sleepwalkers," she said. "One of the people abducted by your friends."

And then the screams began.

Blocks ahead of them, there was a huge, impossible plume

of...smoke? Mist? Odette couldn't tell. It was boiling up into the sky, already as tall as the buildings around them. Is it a volcano? she thought ridiculously. The column was thick, yellow-green, and impenetrable, and it roiled gently, its whorls and tendrils reaching out.

As she gazed at it, Odette realized that the cloud was expanding, filling the street and washing down toward them. Its size in the sky had made it seem slow, but it was cascading between buildings, surging forward. There were gasps and cries of panic from the crowd, but very distantly, from inside the cloud, came screams of a different kind. It wasn't the sound of people panicking; it was the sound of people in agony.

What did you do? thought Odette, frozen in horror. Oh, Pim, what did you do?

Beside her, Clements was not frozen in horror. She pulled Odette back and pushed her against the wall of a shop. The crowds were rapidly coming to the realization that they should flee. People turned and pressed and shoved against the two women, scrabbling to get away. They spilled off the walk and out of the buildings into the streets. Motorists abandoned their cars and joined in the exodus.

"Clements, we have to go!"

"Wait," said the Pawn, taking out her phone. She looked at Odette calculatingly, and her hand closed more firmly on Odette's wrist. "What is that? What have they done?"

"I don't know, I swear," said Odette. "But it doesn't sound good. We have to try to get away!"

"That's not our first priority." She hit an icon on her phone screen. "This is Pawn Clements. There is an explicit manifestation in the city of Westminster." She paused. "Good. Advise them that there are screams coming from within the cloud." Another pause. "Well, then, please advise Rook Thomas—and only Rook Thomas—that it is confirmed to be the work of the Antagonists. I witnessed a sleepwalker accompanied by a young male in sunglasses wearing a blue Mus and Gloucester suit proceeding along Oxford Street toward Park Lane a few minutes ago...no, you don't need to know what that means. They'll be able to find them on the recordings." She hung up.

"Okay, great, you've done your duty. Now can we run away?" demanded Odette. The cloud was bearing down on them.

"Absolutely," said Clements. She didn't say what they both knew—that they couldn't outrun it and that they would never have been able to even if they'd started running as soon as they saw it. At least it will give us something to do, Felicity thought. The two women turned and joined the stampede fleeing down Oxford Street.

Felicity and Odette were immediately buffeted on all sides. The legendary willingness of the British people to form an orderly queue had, quite understandably, been shattered by the appearance of this nightmare. Images of the Blitz, memories of various terrorist attacks, and the instinctive fear of the inexplicable had all combined to drive the crowd forward like panicked bison. Except they weren't animals. There were no children or elderly people lying abandoned in ditches. As the mob ran, a man off to the side stumbled and fell, and Odette saw two people pull up and stop to help him, dragging him to his feet. The crowd pushed on, but no one was crushed or trampled.

Possessions had been ditched, shopping bags and satchels dropped. A bicycle lay on the ground, its owner presumably having realized that he could make no headway with it. Felicity leapt over it, and her iron grip on Odette's wrist meant that she had to leap over it as well.

"Come on! Come on!" Clements said, panting, which Odette thought was rich, after the Pawn had made them wait. "Come on!"

The wall of fog was casting a shadow over them. Odette risked a glance over her shoulder and saw that it was barely meters away. It was dense, like a yellow-green ocean wave, and there were vague silhouettes of people falling as it overtook them. The screaming was closer too, hundreds of voices strong, so it seemed like the cloud itself was shrieking.

"Come on!"

Then the fog washed over them, and the sun was cut away.

Well, this isn't so bad, thought Felicity, blinking in surprise. It smells of food. I don't see what—IT HURTS! IT HURTS!

Every student at the Estate was, in year seven, year nine, and the final year, teargassed. It was part of their standard training, preparation for their roles as bureaucrats and defenders of the supernatural peace. During the course of her training to be in an assault team, Felicity had been sprayed with CS gas, chemical mace, capsicum, and PAVA, as well as with extracts of poison oak, poison ivy, poison sumac, and poisson meunière. She'd been doused with the odorous secretions of the skunk, the sachet kitty, and Pawn Hurlstone from tech support. She'd also, incidentally, been Tasered, lasered, phasered, grenazered, and set on fire (whilst in her armor).

So she was no stranger to pain.

This, however, felt different. This was pain of a different texture, a different flavor. It felt as if the fog were seeping into her skin and burning as it went. Her eyes were spikes of fire in her head. Felicity curled into a ball on the street, and the world went away, leaving only the hurt.

"I'm sure it does," said Odette's voice from a great distance away. Felicity managed to uncurl herself a little. She squinted up at the Grafter who was bent over her. She hadn't even realized that she was screaming the words out loud. Then a new surge of pain cut through her, and the world went away again. She was lost, deep in an ocean. All of her barriers were breaking down. Her powers swept out frantically, and she was slapped with the histories of the world around her. Images from the past strobed into her mind.

She saw herself and Odette running, and the fog washing over them.

She saw her legs buckle, sending her flying to the ground, and Odette staggering a few steps after her.

She saw other people collapsing, writhing, their mouths gaping open. She could hear their screams now, distantly.

She saw Odette draw herself up and close her eyes, and when she opened them, they had turned completely black—the irises, the whites, everything replaced with flat black orbs. She seemed to be completely unaffected by the fog. The Grafter stood, surrounded by people curled up on the ground. The expression on her face was unreadable.

Felicity saw a man a few meters away lying flat on his back. As she watched, blood and clear liquid began to leak out of his clenched-shut eyes.

She saw herself, curled up on the ground, pressing her cheek against the concrete, her face covered in a smear of tears and snot. Her lips were pulled back from her teeth, and her jaws were open in a scream.

And then, miraculously, the pain began to ebb away. Not all of it—it was still agony—but she could feel a cool sensation sweeping across her skin, under her skin. It let her focus a little, and the years of discipline and practice kicked in. Felicity reeled her senses back into her body. She closed herself off from the people around her, then the pavement, then her clothes.

And now it's just the worst pain you've ever experienced, she thought. There was no way to stop it, but the Checquy had taught her methods to cope with it, just as they'd taught her how to resist torture. Acknowledge it. Breathe through it. Compartmentalize it. Ignore it. The pain is there, it is happening, but you can put it in the background. Focus on the task at hand.

With an effort, Felicity stopped screaming. Her body was tensed against the burning, but she could think. This must be because of that stuff the graaf injected into me. It's counteracting the fog a bit. She could not open her eyes—the pain and the swelling wouldn't let her do that—but there were things she could do.

She sat up, banging her forehead against Odette Leliefeld's jaw. The Grafter had been kneeling over her, although, judging from the surprised grunt, Felicity's head had knocked her off her heels and onto her bottom.

"Leliefeld?" she said tightly, putting out her hand in the direction of the surprised grunt.

"Clements—what's happened? Are you better?" said Odette's astounded voice.

"I am a little better, although it still hurts like billy-oh. You?"

"I'm fine. It doesn't appear to be affecting me."

I noticed, Felicity thought. "What is—your eyes?" she managed to say.

"They're protective lenses," explained Odette. "They're normally slotted away in my skull."

"For this?"

"No, they're actually for swimming, but I seem to be using them for poisonous fog more and more lately."

"Oh...good."

I wonder...Felicity thought. Did she know this was coming? Is she with the Antagonists?

"What should we do?" asked Odette.

But then why would she still be here?

"Do you have anything that can help me?" asked Felicity hopefully.

"No, I'm sorry. Marcel is the one with all the chemical glands. I could only kill you. Or make you feel worse."

"I don't think that's possible. Can you give me my phone?" said Felicity. She felt Odette scrabbling in her pocket and then it was pressed awkwardly into her hand. She pressed the button and ordered it to call Rook Thomas.

"Pawn Clements? I got your message. Where are you?"

"Oxford Street."

"What? In that cloud? We've got people going in there now. There are reports of screams coming from there."

"Those are definitely accurate reports," said Felicity. She briefly held the phone up in the air so the cries of the surrounding injured could be heard. There were distant screams as the fog washed over more people, but around them, there were mainly weak moans and sobbing as the victims lost strength and could only lie curled on the ground.

"Are you all right?" asked the Rook after a moment.

"I'm blind and in some pain," said Felicity, "but the gift our friend gave me seems to be helping."

"Where's Leliefeld?"

"She's right here with me."

"Is she all right?"

"She's a lot better than I am," said Felicity, unable to keep the bitterness out of her voice. "The fog isn't affecting her at all."

"Let me speak to her." Felicity held the phone out and felt it plucked from her hand.

"Rook Thomas, I have no idea what this product is," said Odette. "It seems to have lachrymatory and vesicant properties."

"And it smells of food," put in Felicity.

"Yeah, like erwt—um, I don't know the word in English. Like legumes," said Odette. "I don't know why it isn't affecting me, although I suppose we can guess. Should we try to administer first aid to the victims?" She paused. "Yes, yes, all right." She put the phone into Felicity's hand. "She wants to talk to you."

"Clements, I'm sending in a helicopter team for you and Odette. Keep your phone on."

"Uh, Pawn Clements?" said Odette.

"What?"

"Someone is coming," Odette whispered.

"Did you hear that?" Felicity asked into the phone.

"Yes. Our team isn't there yet." Felicity heard an intake of breath come over the line. "Clements, do you have the gun?" She put her hand to her side. The pistol was still there, snug in its shoulder holster.

"Yes."

There was a pause. Felicity felt Odette's hand on her shoulder. *Is she reassuring me? Or is she going to stab me?* She slid her hand into her coat and closed it around the gun. Very slowly, so as not to make a noise, she thumbed off the snap that kept it in place.

"Oh," breathed Odette softly. "It's Simon."

"Who?" demanded Felicity, scrubbing at her eyes in an effort to rub away the burning. She cracked them open, and through her tears and the fog, she could just make out a silhouette walking toward them nonchalantly. It stepped easily over a woman lying in the gutter.

"Simon, my cousin," said Odette. "He was the one with the sunglasses, the one holding that sleepwalker's hand."

"You recognized him?" asked Felicity. She tensed.

"Not till now. He's wearing a different face, but I just caught his scent." The Grafter sounded as if she was going to burst into tears. "I can't believe it. It's him, it's really him."

"And he just happens to be coming directly toward you?" exclaimed the Rook. It was apparent she could hear everything over the phone.

"And he just happens to be coming directly toward us?" exclaimed Felicity with equal incredulity.

"It's not a coincidence," said Odette brokenly. "That's why the cloud started by our hotel. He's come for me. To take me." There was a terrible yearning in her voice.

"Pawn Clements," said Rook Thomas's voice in Felicity's ear.

"Yes, ma'am?"

"You have the order. Kill Odette Leliefeld. Now."

38

The gun was out. Felicity had dropped the phone and closed her hand over Odette's. In her mind's eye, she could see the movement she would make, sweeping the gun up, pulling the Grafter close, and firing three rounds into her skull. Felicity was braced for the reports—she knew they would be deafening. Then, if she had time and could open her eyes to aim, she would empty the clip at the man, Simon. She could see it all as it would unfold.

But she hesitated.

And the chance was lost. There was the sound of swift steps, and the gun was twisted out of her hand. Despite herself, she yelped.

"A gun?" tsked a man's voice. He had a distinct Dutch accent. "I thought you creatures weren't allowed firearms." There was a distant clatter, and Felicity knew he had thrown her pistol away. Rook Thomas is going to kill me if I lose that gun, she thought dully, with no expectation of being alive long enough for the Rook to kill her.

"Simon," said Odette weakly.

"Odette," said the man, and Felicity could hear the delight in his voice. She struck out blindly in the direction of that delighted voice but hit only empty air. She felt Odette's hand pulled out of hers and then felt the toe of an expensive Italian shoe hit her cheekbone. Combined with the burning of her eyes and skin, it was too much, and it sent her slumping, dazed, to the ground.

"Simon! No! Don't kill her!"

"They have you attended by a Gruwel, one with a gun. That gun is not for me."

"Please."

"Oh, fine," said Simon. "Although it offends me on many levels. Not least because you know how I hate leaving behind loose ends." Felicity heard someone spitting contemptuously but didn't feel anything hit her. "In fact—my God!"

"What?" asked Odette.

"I've seen this Gruwel before. She was one of a team that came and attacked a workshop we'd set up. Set the damn place on fire, and then she and another one vanished into thin air. It was like the universe just sort of folded around them. Horrible." Then he went on in French, a language that Felicity happened to understand. "But enough about the Gruwel. It is so, so good to see you! We have all missed you terribly. You look nice. I like this suit on you very much."

"What is that face you're wearing?"

"It's a simple dermal veneer," he said airily. "You just slap it on. I'm currently wearing a utility skin, but I thought since I'm out in public, I should try to blend in a little."

"Simon, what on earth have you done?"

"Impressive, isn't it? We have created a real pea-souper." He said the last word in English, in a deeply satisfied tone.

"A pea-souper?" repeated Odette. "Oh, for God's sake! You made the fog smell like soup?"

"I know, it is a silly pun, but Pim wanted to make it smell like oranges—you remember his ridiculous trademark. We outvoted him, thank God."

"This isn't a joke, Simon!" shouted Odette. "Look at all these people! Look what you've done!"

"It's war, Odette," said Simon. "You know this. And we needed chaos. It is ideal for you to disappear in."

"You did all this to get me," said Odette dully.

"Well, we would have done it anyway, but it comes in handy for retrieving you."

"You are being ridiculous, Simon," said Odette. "You have to stop this. This is not a war, and..."—she gulped a little—"and I am not coming with you."

"It is a war, Odette. A little war. A guerrilla war. You know how well those work out for everyone. But all it will take to turn it into a big war is the right cut. Like this one."

"I still cannot believe that you want war between the Broeder-schap and the Checquy. You are betraying your own family."

"It is far better than their betrayal of our history—" began Simon hotly, but then he checked himself. "I don't want to have this argument again, and certainly not here. But that war will happen. It is too late to stop it now, and we cannot leave you to be consumed by it. We made a terrible mistake, Odette, leaving you in that hotel. We should have taken you with us. But now, after this, the Checquy will not let you live. You are coming with me."

"I will not!"

"My darling cousin, you really will."

Felicity managed to open her eyes a crack and saw the man, Simon, and Odette facing each other. Simon towered over his cousin, and both had those shining all-black eyes. Suddenly, a long serrated spur slid out of Simon's wrist, and with dizzying speed, he lashed out and sliced at Odette's hand. She looked down at it in stupefaction and then back up at him.

"Again?" she said.

"Don't worry, 'Dette, it's not poison."

"You—you are going…" And she collapsed into his arms. He hoisted her over his shoulder easily and set off down the street.

"No," said Felicity weakly. No. Even through all the pain, a simple fact presented itself: There was no way she could let that man take her charge. Not unless Felicity herself was dead. She dragged herself to her feet. The gun, where's the gun? She scraped away at her eyes, but they kept weeping. Everything was a blur.

"Help me, help meee," moaned one of the people near her, and that spurred others, those who were still conscious and capable, to call out for help also.

"Help!"

"My eyes!"

"Please, oh God, pleeease."

It turned her stomach, but Felicity forced herself to ignore them and take a step forward. And another. The figure of Simon was a distant blurry shadow in the mist, and it was fading. Follow. Half blind, she shambled after them and stumbled into the road. Her feet were heavy and awkward, and she leaned on the cars that squatted along the street. Something shifted limply under her shoe, and she realized that she had trodden on a person. Hurry!

She could barely see the shape of the Antagonist as the fog closed around him and the body slung over his shoulder. They were gone, and she could no more track them down than she could find a missing set of keys in the Indian Ocean.

"No!" She groaned. "Bloody fuck shit bastard!"

She'd had doubts about Leliefeld. Hell, she'd had doubts about all the Grafters. To her, the excuse of the Antagonists had seemed too convenient. It allowed for strikes to be made even as the Grafters insinuated themselves in the heart of the Checquy. She'd been prepared to believe that Odette was secretly an agent of the Antagonists and that the Antagonists were secretly agents of the Grafters. The strategist in her had mapped out all the possibilities.

All those options should have been dismissed when she was given the order to kill Leliefeld. She was a soldier and she followed orders. And yet, they had remained in her mind, including the possibility that Odette—the girl with whom she'd spent the past week, the girl she'd seen at her best and her worst, the girl who'd bickered with her brother and worried about her hat and had brought her an apple—was innocent. And so she'd hesitated.

But the conversation she'd heard between Leliefeld and Simon had wiped out all her doubts. The Antagonists had no reason to leave Felicity alive and lots of reasons to kill her. No one could have known that she would be conscious during Odette and Simon's argument or that she would be able to understand them. That conversation had not been staged for her benefit.

Felicity now believed, now knew, that Odette was innocent and that the Antagonists were working against the Grafters. The problem was that no one else would believe it. The attack was bad enough. But if Odette Leliefeld, the most loathed member of the delegation, vanished without a trace into the fog that had harmed hundreds of British civilians in the center of London, then all of Rook Thomas's efforts at reconciliation would be swept away. The hate was there. War would ensue. The Antagonists would win.

"Damn it!" She fell to her knees, scraping her hands on the asphalt. Her Sight expanded out of her skin like ripples in water. All around her was the wreckage of a terrorist attack. Abandoned cars. Spilled purses and shopping bags. And people, lying helpless. She shuddered away from them and pulled her Sight back in.

Then she took off her shoes and socks.

Felicity ran through the streets.

She couldn't see with her eyes anymore, they had swollen

completely shut, but with every step, she drank in a fleeting impression of the area around her. She read the road beneath her, letting the images well up through the soles of her feet and into her mind.

The world was strobing. For a brief moment, she had an image of the space around her as her Sight spread out to read the present and the past, and then she had to snap back into her mind so as to keep herself running. The pain of her skin and eyes flickered in and out of her senses as she flickered in and out of her body. She was conscious that as she ran, she was gasping in big lungfuls of the fog, and it grated in her chest.

It was not a situation that lent itself to analysis. If Felicity had stopped to think about how she was doing it, she wouldn't have been able to do it. The conscious, meticulous part of her mind had stepped back, and instinct and sensation were controlling her.

She was tracking. Images from a few seconds ago of Simon the Antagonist guttered in front of her. He walked tall, with Odette over his shoulder, her hair hanging down his back. Felicity saw him pick his way down the road, fastidiously stepping over bodies and litter, talking on a mobile phone. She followed in his footsteps.

Other ghosts bled in and out around her as she took in the very recent past. She saw men and women looking up at the cloud as it erupted and then falling down, clutching their eyes. She saw a car crash into another car ten minutes ago, and then she vaulted over the wreckage in the present. She flinched as a man with blood dripping from his eyes staggered in front of her, only for him to vanish when she plunged back, blind, into her own skin.

Then, in the here and now, Felicity heard the Antagonist ahead of her say good-bye and put his phone away. She held her breath so that he would not hear her gasping approach and slowed so that her foot remained on the ground a second longer. She drank in the picture and knew exactly where he was, just a few feet in front of her. Then she screamed out and threw herself at him, driving her shoulder into the small of his back and sending him flying.

Felicity rolled and came to rest down on one knee. For two heartbeats, her hand was flat to the ground as she mapped the scene — Odette lying there and walls there and the Antagonist sprawled there — and then she pushed up like a sprinter in the starting block and moved toward him.

The Antagonist had barely opened his eyes and turned over when he saw the heel of Felicity's bare foot hammering down toward his windpipe. His instincts flared, and he flailed his hand in front of him and swept her leg away. She was thrown off balance and fell on him but managed to drive her knee into his rib cage. He howled and shoved her off. She rolled and came up into a crouch.

"Gruwel!" he snarled.

Felicity didn't answer, but she paused, flexing her toes on the ground. Then she darted forward and struck out with her fists. He stepped back hurriedly, out of reach, and she jabbed at empty air.

She dipped into the past again and saw him in the moments that had just occurred. Her powers could not see him in the present, but a second ago he was standing in front of her, two steps back. He was wheezing, but he smirked at her blind flailing. She saw those long spurs slide out of his wrists and he was stepping forward to attack her now! She jerked her body back and heard the movement of his attack missing her. Felicity reached forward and caught at where his arm should be. She felt his forearm and braced herself automatically, then gripped and twisted and pushed. She sent him staggering.

You can see him only in the past, the analytical part of her mind observed from the backseat. You're operating with a delay, so you'll need to act faster than he does. A second, half a second, can make all the difference in this game.

"So, you've got a few little tricks up your sleeve," she said. She flinched at the feeling of droplets spattering across her face.

"I've got a few up my throat too," said the Antagonist.

What the fuck is this stuff? she thought, and she scruffed at her face with her sleeve. She looked into the past and saw him breathing out a spray into her face. He spit on me? That can't be good. She wrenched herself back into the present. The Antagonist was still speaking.

"...problem is that with your eyes already swollen, I don't expect much got in. But it should be enough, eventually."

What was he talking about?

"I've read your file, Gruwel," said the Antagonist. His voice was moving, and she turned her head to try to follow him, to pinpoint where he was. "When we learned that they'd assigned a guard to Odette, we checked up on you. I know what you are—a soldier, a killer. My cousin is a scholar and an artist, and they put a beast like you behind her so that you could knife her in the back. But now you can barely see," he gloated. "I'm actually mildly impressed that you caught up with us. According to your file, you don't have any abnormalities that make you impervious to the fog, so you must be in a lot of pain. I certainly hope so."

Don't listen to him! Where is he? What is he doing?

A few seconds ago, she saw, he had been crouched, and then extending to leap for—he hit her, but she'd thrown up her arm so that his spur caught in the bunched cloth of her coat rather than slicing through her cheek. His weight made her left leg buckle, and she grabbed his shirt so that they fell together.

Good. If we're grappling, then I know exactly where he is. She clutched at his wrists and tried to deliver a knee to his crotch. She connected, but there was none of the squishing she'd anticipated, nor did Simon's strength waver for even a moment. Did I miss? Then she remembered the white-skinned man from the row house and his novel approach to genital configuration. So, he may have his willy tucked away in his abdomen, she thought. Fine. I doubt he's retracted his skull, and she slammed her head forward in the hope that it would make contact with his nose or forehead.

Instead, her forehead glanced off his chin, which seemed to startle him, because he flinched and she shoved forward against his wrists. He fell back, and she scrambled up. A pause to read the situation as it was a moment ago, and she saw that he was also standing. Her back was against the wall and he was lunging forward, raising his left leg to kick at her.

Dodge! She twisted wildly to the left and heard a crack like a detonation. A hand against the wall and a moment's incredulous peek into the past gave her an image of the Antagonist kicking a hole through the bricks. Cut his legs out from under him! She swung around, crouched down, swept out in a kick that caught his ankle, and (his other foot still being lodged in the wall) brought him flat down on his back.

He's got the weapons, but no training. Take him down quickly, because he just needs to get one lick in with those spurs and you're dead. She heard the breaking of bricks as he wrenched his foot out of the wall, and her Sight strobed flashes of him pushing himself up and turning to face her.

It was ugly, awkward fighting. He had the strength and the spurs, but she had the skills and the Sight. They both had the kind of hate that meant they didn't hesitate and they didn't fight clean. They spat, swore, and slung litter. Again and again they came together and fell back. Felicity's attacks and dodges became more and more rigid as the fog took its toll. It became harder to look into the past, but each time, she managed to get in a blow or twist out of his way. Finally, goaded and frustrated, the Antagonist rushed in toward her. His spurs were low and ichor dripped from them.

She twisted down onto the ground under the spurs and kicked up hard into his stomach. He fell, winded, and she rolled onto him. The Antagonist feebly tried to bring his arms up, but she was quicker. End it! She struck down at his face, her hand a dagger. End it!

It would have killed a normal person, she was sure of that, but it didn't kill him. He shrieked, and she pressed down, scrabbling and clawing until he flung her off. The bubbling, blubbering sounds that came out of his mouth were nothing human, and she braced herself for more, but instead he turned, clutching at his face, and fled away into the city.

I'm not following him, she thought wearily. No one could expect me to. She shuffled over to where Odette lay and knelt down. She'd better be okay, Felicity thought. She was fairly certain that she had trodden on the girl at some point during the fighting, but there was no blood that she could detect.

What do I do now? she thought. Try to pick her up and shamble out of here? It simply wasn't going to happen. The adrenaline and rage that had helped her ignore the pain she was in were fading, and all she really wanted to do was lie down and pass out. Even dying didn't seem like that bad an option. Then she remembered that Leliefeld also had a phone. Was it still on her? She was listlessly pawing through the girl's clothes when she heard a distant sound.

"Felicity Clements!" came a faraway shout. It was curiously muffled, but it had a distinctly English accent.

"Here," she croaked. "Here! Here!" She heard boots on asphalt and felt a hand on her shoulder.

"Pawn Clements, we're here," said a voice. It was muffled by a gas mask.

"It would have killed you to get here five minutes earlier?" She wheezed. A mask was pressed against her mouth, and she breathed cool, clean air.

"Well, you know how it is," said the Checquy man. "Been a bit busy."

"The terrorist who caused this," said Felicity weakly. "He was just here, no more than a minute or two ago."

"We can still catch him?" said the trooper.

"God, I hope so," said Felicity. She put her hand down on the ground for a moment. "He went that way. Fuck him up if you can."

"Can you describe him?" asked the trooper. "What does he look like?"

"Well, he's not lying blinded on the ground," she said testily. "That should make him stick out. He's blond, has a pointy nose, and is wearing a blue designer suit." She took in another deep breath of that glorious air. "Oh, and he's missing an eye."

"Right," said the trooper. He sounded a little taken aback. "Brilliant, we're on it." He spoke into his radio, issued instructions. "So, which eye is he missing?"

"This one," she said, holding up her hand.

39

Alessio looked up as Odette came into the room, and immediately jumped to his feet.

"You're here! It's been crazy, 'Dette! They'd taken us up the Shard to see the city, and there was this green cloud growing across the river, and I realized that it was right where our hotel is. And then the teacher got a call, and we all went down, and there were two men in the lobby who said I had to come with them and they drove me here and put me in this room and told me to stay here and no one's told me anything and it's been hours!"

Odette blinked. Her normally calm brother was evidently completely freaked-out. She hugged him tight and looked around the room critically. They'd been delivered to the Annexe, the Checquy's headquarters for international operations. It was a somewhat squat, unassuming building in the southernmost part of London. It stood only a few meters from a decidedly unsquat, extremely assuming office building that contained some impressive and flashy businesses, including a television production company, a modeling agency, and the editorial offices of a notorious magazine that featured lithe young women wearing mainly hats and gloves, so the Annexe was often overlooked entirely by passersby—which was, of course, the point.

Alessio had been deposited in a sort of break room where Checquy office workers could hold little meetings or presentations.

He'd been supplied with a microwaved pizza, a few bottles of water, a battered edition of Tom Brown's Schooldays, and some old copies of the Beano Annual. An armed guard outside the door had escorted him to the lavatory twice.

"So what's going on?" he demanded.

"I can't tell you right now," she said and looked up at the ceiling meaningfully. His eyes grew wide.

"Are they—are they going to kill us?" he asked weakly.

"I don't know," said Odette. She took his hand in hers and reflected on the past hour.

She'd woken up in the back of a wide ambulance strapped to a stretcher. On the other side was Pawn Clements, looking absolutely dreadful. Her face was swollen from the fog, and there were bruises on her cheeks. A mask covered her nose and mouth, and her skin was mottled red. Two medical personnel, a man and a woman, were leaning over her doing medical things.

"Oh no," said Odette, and they looked at her with distaste burning through their gas masks.

"It's all right for some," said the woman. The fact that Odette had emerged from the fog with absolutely no marks on her—even the cut from Simon's spur had closed up tracelessly—apparently did not sit well with the woman.

"How is she?" asked Odette.

"Not well," said the man. "She's been knocked about, her skin looks like it's been chemically burned, but it's her eyes that are—"

"Don't talk to her," interrupted the woman. "Do your job. And you," she said, turning to Odette, "how do you feel?"

"All right, I think," said Odette.

"Then keep quiet."

What do they know? she thought. What happened? Where did Simon go? Do they have him? What is going on? But they weren't questions she could ask. All she could do was watch as they worked on Clements.

They'd driven to the Annexe, which was apparently the only Checquy office in London that the fog hadn't reached. Both the Rookery and the Apex had been sealed off to prevent fog from getting in, but there was no way that the ambulance could have made it there through the crowds and the carnage.

So instead, they'd maneuvered through the panicked traffic, mounting the curb at several points, and eventually got to the Annexe garage. From there, a team of concerned-looking nurses had whisked Clements away in one direction and three extremely large women had whisked Odette away in another. They'd ordered her to strip for decontamination, and she'd experienced the most intense shower of her life, with seven nozzles jetting carbonated water at her from multiple angles. Afterward, she felt as if she'd gone down two dress sizes. They'd provided her with virulent-yellow scrubs and bed socks in place of shoes and then led her through dingy, linoleum-floored corridors and put her in with Alessio.

The two of them sat silently and held hands.

If they come in and try to hurt my brother or take him away, I will kill them, decided Odette. It was not immediately clear what would happen after she did that—she really couldn't picture any further into the future—but it was a decision that she felt she could stand by.

The door opened, and an Indian man in a suit entered and closed the door behind him. He wore no expression and Odette tensed. Alessio looked at her in alarm as her hand tightened around his. Under the table, a spur slid out of her other wrist.

"I'm Pawn Malhotra. Miss Leliefeld, I'll need you to come with me. Mr. Leliefeld will remain here."

"No," said Odette.

"I beg your pardon?"

"I'm not leaving my brother. Not without some sort of explanation." He opened his mouth. "One that I can trust." He closed his mouth, pursed his lips, and reached into his coat. Odette braced herself, but he produced a mobile phone. He turned away and spoke into it before holding it out to her. She wavered for a moment but then retracted her spur and held out her hand.

"Hello?"

"Odette, this is Myfanwy Thomas."

"What is going on?"

"What's going on? The worst attack on the United Kingdom since the Blitz is what's going on," said the Rook. "Clouds of that stuff erupted in London, Edinburgh, Cardiff, Belfast, Manchester." Odette closed her eyes.

"Jesus."

"Quite. The press are calling it the Blinding. The good news is that it's dissipating. And, for the most part, it's been nonfatal. We've had astoundingly few reports of deaths, and those have been due to car accidents and some heart attacks and falls. It was your friends, though, wasn't it?"

"Yes," whispered Odette.

"They're spiteful little shits, you know. Thousands of innocent people have been affected, and a few appear to have had an especially bad reaction to the stuff. There's panic—the stock market had an epileptic fit before trading was suspended, the roads are jammed, and we're only just getting major rescue teams in. The whole world is looking at us on their television screens and demanding an explanation. Every army on earth is braced to defend against a similar attack. If we get through the next twenty-four hours without war breaking out, I will be astounded."

"I—I don't know what to say."

"I don't need you to say anything, Odette," said the Rook. "I don't know if I can trust you. Last I heard, your cousin was coming to take you away with him."

"He was forcing me!"

"You say. I have no proof of that," said Thomas. "The only witness is currently unconscious in the medical facility of the Annexe. But here's the thing. They tell me that Pawn Clements's eyes have been damaged, very badly. And I understand that you're quite good with eyes."

"I—yes, they're my focus," said Odette, and winced. "They're my specialty, I mean. But Marcel is far more experienced."

"Marcel is here at the Apex," said Thomas. "We can't leave right now, not easily. And he's actually working on someone else, some civilian child. So I want you to fix her eyes."

"What if I can't?" said Odette.

"Try. Try as hard as you possibly can." And the call ended. Odette looked up at Pawn Malhotra.

"All right," she said finally. "Let's hurry."

The Annexe had a little medical clinic, an emergency facility, Malhotra told her as they walked, nowhere near as well equipped as the rooms she'd visited in the Rookery and Apex House. It now formed the core of a hastily established field hospital. Benches lined the corridors leading to the clinic, and members of the Checquy who had been caught in the fog lay on them, unconscious. It was crowded and crude, but it was apparently all that was available. All the public hospitals, it seemed, were crammed full with members of the public. Odette felt a shameful wash of relief that the people she passed were all unconscious. She could imagine the hateful looks she would have gotten. *Has word gotten out that the fog didn't affect me?* she wondered. *Do they know it was unleashed by Grafters?*

Finally, they arrived at the actual clinic. She hurriedly scrubbed her hands and arms and was ritually swathed in a surgical gown by nervous swathers. Her hair was rolled up on her head, and the cap and gloves were put on her.

Clements had been laid out on an operating table with sterile sheets draped over her in strategic locations. She was unconscious and, for the first time that Odette could ever recall, looked vulnerable. In some places, the sheets had been folded back, and Checquy people were applying products to her red skin. The workers were all gowned and scrubbed and looked like fairly standard-issue medical staff. There were three figures, however, who did not look at all standard-issue. Clad in surgical gowns, masks, and caps, they stood against the wall, each of them holding a large gun wrapped in a sterile plastic bag. They all evoked the adjective hulking, and it was clear that they had not taken any oaths to do no harm. Odette glanced at them, swallowed, and took refuge in the familiar problem of surgery.

"How does the damage to her epidermis look?" she asked.

"Well, at first glance, it looks dreadful," said one of the doctors. "But we're not seeing much actual damage. We have reports, though, stating that it was excruciatingly painful."

"For humans, anyway," muttered one of the doctors under his breath. Odette was not supposed to have heard him, but she did, and she shot him a look. He flushed and turned his attention back to Clements's feet.

"Move," said Odette to the nearest doctor, and he shuffled aside. She knelt down close to the Pawn's exposed thigh and took a deep breath. Her eyes refocused, zooming in, so she felt as though she were shrinking and falling into Clements's skin. The mottled red surface filled her vision.

"It's red, but I don't see any blistering or actual burns," she said. "The pores are undamaged, and there's no sign of cellular breakdown."

"Thoughts?" said a doctor meekly.

"It may have seeped through the skin to affect the tissue beneath. Do you have a scalpel?" The doctors and the people with guns exchanged glances and then shrugs. "I'm going to be operating on her eyes in a second; do you expect me to do it with evocative descriptions or with actual tools?" A scalpel was produced, and she ignored the fact that the three soldiers all tightened their grips on their weapons. "I'm just going to make a small incision to check for subcutaneous damage. I'll sew it up later. You won't even know it was there."

Odette made a tiny curving cut and lifted up the flap of skin. She adjusted her gaze and examined the epidermis and the dermis. To the aghast disapproval of the assorted medical practitioners, who were all watching her as surreptitiously as they could, she pulled down her mask and sniffed the wound. Then, before anyone could stop her, she touched the cut with her glove and then licked her finger.

"What the bloody hell is wrong with you?" bellowed the attending physician, grabbing her shoulder and pulling her back violently. The three soldiers all brought their guns up to point at her. The other doctors stampeded to the far end of the room and huddled there together like frightened caribou in surgical gowns.

"Relax," said Odette witheringly. "I'm not your creepy but hot Bishop."

"Are you insane?"

"I'm checking her blood for any poisons or compounds," said Odette coolly.

"Oh. And?"

"And I think she'll be fine—at least, her skin will. It's already improving. As far as I can tell, it's a customized enzyme that acts as a nontoxic, noncaustic trigger of nociception. I can't identify all the elements, but there are chords of sulfur and Murdock's extract over-lying a base note of liquefied kanten along with a distillation from the glands of the Nycticebus coucang."

"I beg your pardon?"

"The slow loris."

"What does all that mean?" asked the doctor.

"That stuff hurts like a bitch, especially your eyes, and it looks like it's causing damage, but it doesn't actually do anything in the long run. Temporary, if extremely painful, blindness."

"You got all that from tasting her blood?" said the doctor skeptically.

"Absolutely," said Odette. "Here, do you want to see if you can taste something different?" She proffered her finger, and the doctor recoiled.

"I'll, um, I'll take your word for it."

One of the advantages of working with the Checquy is that they're quite willing to believe the impossible, mused Odette. Of course it was impossible. She'd tasted something in Clements's blood, but she wouldn't have been able to break it down like that. The truth was, she knew the material because she'd had a hand in concocting it. It was a Grafter weapon that she and Pim had worked on as junior assistants, and she recognized it instantly. Although it's interesting that it didn't have an effect on me, she thought. They must have tailored it that way.

"We'll need a more detailed analysis, of course, but I think the effects will fade away within a week without any residual harm," she said.

"Oh, that is good news," said the doctor in a peculiar tone.

"You don't sound like you think it's good news," remarked Odette as she quickly stitched up the wound.

"No, we do. But will the eyes recover as well?" asked another doctor.

"That I don't know," said Odette dubiously. Exposure to the original formula had been like getting hit in the face with a Siamese cat covered in vinegar—painful, disorienting, and bewildering, but not permanently damaging. However, she recalled some of the people she'd seen in the street. There had been at least one man who had tears of blood pouring out of his eyes. That might have been an allergic reaction. Or the Antagonists might really have tampered with that stuff. "What's the situation with Pawn Clements's eyes?"

"I think you'd better take a look," said the doctor near the Pawn's head. Judging from his voice, he was at least forty years older than her, but he spoke in a tone of respect and awe. "I don't know about the skin, but this doesn't look to me like it's improving at all."

Odette made her way to Clements's head. It did not escape her notice that one of the gun-toting guards had followed her around the room and taken up a position behind her. *Just concentrate on the task at hand, not on the fact that they will likely shoot you if you fuck up.* She gazed down at the aforementioned task at hand, who was still anesthetized but whose eyelids were held wide open with retractors. This gave Felicity a staring, incredulous look, the same staring, incredulous look, Odette suspected, that she would have worn if she were awake and knew that Odette was going to operate on her. With the swelling around her eyes held back by tape, the Pawn had the air of a startled shar-pei.

The Pawn's eyes were red and weeping, but, even more alarming, they were streaked with tiny threads of a dark purple, almost black material. It was not like anything Odette had ever seen before. *What the hell have they done with the formula?*

she thought. I didn't detect any radical changes in it, apart from the fact that they made it smell like soup. Then she noticed a fine dappling of the same color across the Pawn's brow. She leaned forward and smelled the skin around Clements's face.

"It's a different product," she said. "She's had something else sprayed in her eyes."

"Are you going to lick her again?" asked a doctor hesitantly.

"I think best not," said Odette as she zoomed back in on the eyes.

"Should we take a swab to see what it is?"

"How long would it take to analyze it?" she asked.

"The problem is that we don't really have labs here," said the doctor. "The Annexe is pretty much just offices and an armory. We'd have to get the sample somewhere else and then back again."

"We don't have time for that," said Odette. "I don't know if you noticed, but those stains are spreading."

"What?"

"They're growing. Just as I've watched, they've expanded by a couple of microns. We need to go in, now."

There was something almost holy about cutting open an eye. The elegance of the form, the sheer impossibility of its structure. You couldn't help but feel reverence for the liquid beauty of an eye. It was one of the reasons Odette had chosen to specialize in ocular architecture.

She'd rejected the tools they'd offered her. They'd been very good-quality implements, but none had possessed the qualities she required. Instead, to the continued horror of the doctors, she'd hiked up her surgical gown and slid her hand down inside the waistband of her scrubs, to her right leg. A seam opened in her skin, internal muscles rippled, and two scalpels were eased out into her hand. Grown from her own bone, with unorthodox lines to their blades, they were practically unbreakable and beautifully, organically sharp.

"Are those sterile?" asked someone.

"Yes," said Odette. "There are glands that secrete cleansing agents into the pouch." She put the blades down on a sterile field near the instrument tray and held up her hands so an OR tech could remove her no-longer-sterile gloves and put new ones on her. "Now, I know you're all judging me and, um, possibly getting ready to shoot me in the head, but I need you to be quiet while I do this." And she sliced into Felicity's right eye. The scalpel cut easily through the tough coating of the sclera. Long moments passed as she gently twisted the cut open and used the nonbladed end of one of her scalpels to probe inside with minuscule, delicate movements. She paused and drew her gaze in tighter and tighter until the nerves in her head began to burn. The doctors and the guards maintained a petrified silence, barely breathing. Then:

"Oh, Jezus mina!" At her shocked exclamation, the doctors all jumped, and she heard the guard behind her shift into a shooting position, but she reserved all her horror for what she saw inside Clements's eye. It was bad. Very bad.

"It's some sort of organic agent," said Odette. "An edited cancer or maybe a coral. It's bled through the sclera and is growing in the vitreous humor. It's adhered itself to the inner surface of the eye and the hyaloid canal and is increasing exponentially. It's eating her eyes."

Judging by its current size and rate of spread, only a minuscule amount of that stuff had made its way to Felicity's eyes, but it was expanding swiftly. The growths were comparatively small now, but to Odette's heightened vision, they looked vast and frightening—great jagged tendrils that branched out and grew thicker. If it continued unchecked, not only would Clements be rendered permanently blind within the hour, but it was possible that it would continue into her brain and kill her.

"Can you excise it?"

Odette paused. Maybe it was the presence of the armed guards or the unspoken threat Rook Thomas had made, but she sensed that telling the truth would not be good for her.

"What are the odds of you retrieving my tools from my hotel within twenty minutes?" she asked finally.

"That's impossible, I'm afraid."

"I suspected as much," she said. "Okay, what pharmaceuticals do you have available here?" A flunky was dispatched and returned with a tablet computer featuring the Annexe's catalog. Odette scanned it grimly. It was respectable enough for a little clinic, but for her purposes, it would be like working with leeches and a sharp rock.

Okay, think. Are there any compounds here that might buy you some time? Nothing. I have nothing. I can't analyze it, I don't have the tools to cut it out without mutilating her eyes. I have all this knowledge locked up inside me, and I can't do anything with it. They're going to kill me and they might kill Alessio and there's going to be a war and I can't do anything to stop it. I'm useless!

I'm…

I'm…

"I have an idea," she said. "We're going to need all the antirejection drugs you can get. And I'm going to need a hypodermic needle and…" She trailed off, aghast at her own plans. This could either fix everything or make everything much worse.

"Miss Leliefeld?"

She sighed.

"I need you to bring me a mirror."

Are you sure you don't want me to do this?" asked the doctor in the tone of a man who fervently hoped she didn't want him to do this.

"No, it's fine," said Odette. "I can do it." And I wouldn't trust you anyway.

"Would you like one of us to hold the mirror, at least?"

"No, I can lock the muscles in that arm so it'll be steady." She held the mirror up in front of her face and looked herself in the eye. Are you ready? It would have been nice if she'd felt a core certainty, a glow of faith in herself, but there was nothing except the churning doubt and fear. *I'm never going to be ready, so I might as well start now.*

She brought the hypodermic up and pressed the needle into her own left eye.

She'd dulled the sensation in that portion of her face and shut down the eye so there was no pain, but the pressure was nauseating. She watched as the needle slid into the white of her eye while around her the assembled doctors gave a little sigh. The guards even seemed to have forgotten about their guns. Then she slid her thumb into the ring on the end of the plunger and began to draw it out, slowly sucking up a portion of her vitreous humor.

Not too much, not too little, she thought as, bit by bit, she drew out the clear gel that filled her eyeball. She was almost hypnotized by her own movement. Despite her best efforts, a dull ache started to thrum inside her skull.

A little more, she told herself. *As much as you can stand. A bit of pain now might make all the difference later.*

Finally, Odette eased the needle out of her eye. She looked at the hypodermic critically. It seemed such a tiny amount. *But it will have to do.* It was seething, she knew, with Broederschap materials. High-tech bacteria. Specially designed cells. Her own exquisitely edited DNA. For its weight, and the knowledge it represented, that gel was worth billions of dollars. She held out the mirror, and a doctor took it reverently. Then she turned to Clements. She inserted the needle into one of the openings she'd made in the Pawn's right eye and injected a little of the liquid. She'd drawn from only one of her eyes because she needed the other one to finish the procedure. With the amount of vitreous humor she'd taken from her left eye, its vision would be warped and flawed until she could replace it. *If I get the chance.*

The material washed into Felicity's eye and merged immediately. For all its value, Odette's vitreous humor looked exactly like anyone else's. She'd tried to inject it near a smear of the growth, and now she waited anxiously. *Please, please, let it do something.* She knew the potency of her own body.

Her eyes could eliminate cataracts and glaucoma in seconds and scour away parasites in minutes. But this stuff coating the inside of Pawn Clements's eye was a weapon, created to destroy. All Odette could do was hope.

Long minutes dragged by and there was no sign of change. She'd put exactly half of the extracted material into the right eye. Should I put the rest in? If the full amount in one eye has an effect, then one of the doctors can remove more from my other eye, she thought. Hell, they can put me under and drain it all. Depending on how it all turns out, someone can always build me new eyes.

And then she noticed that the spread of the growth had slowed. She counted fifteen of her heartbeats and confirmed that it had stopped completely. Then the tips of the tendrils began to turn white and dissolve. It worked!

"It worked!" she shrieked, and the entire room burst into applause. She quickly injected the rest of the material into the left eye.

It wasn't over. Repair work would need to be done, and Clements would have to be put on a rigorous regimen of antirejection drugs until the Broederschap materials had broken down within her body. But Odette had arrested and possibly reversed the weapon's progress. Thank God, she thought as she accepted tentative handshakes.

I wonder how Clements is going to take this.

40

Felicity awoke, but she could not open her eyes. There was a soft pressure on them that held them closed. She lifted her hands carefully and felt pads covering her eyelids, held down with tape. Okay, be calm. She was afraid to send her Sight down through the bandages, terrified of what she might find.

There was a noise off to the side, and Felicity tensed and her Sight pulsed out. She was lying on a couch, in an office. A desk squatted off to her left, bookcases against two of the walls. There was a chair near the door, and seated in the chair was—she switched her focus to the immediate past—Odette Leliefeld. The Grafter girl was curled up, hugging her knees. A pad and bandage covered her right eye, but apart from that, she appeared to be fine.

"Where are we?" asked Felicity.

"The Annexe. The office of the head of the Southeast Asia section. It appears this was the closest place with an unoccupied couch."

"What about my—" Felicity broke off, frightened to ask in case she got an answer.

"Your eyes are going to be fine," said Leliefeld's voice carefully. "The swelling is already going down."

Felicity frowned, or she would have if the swelling of her face hadn't prevented it. In the course of her career, she'd suffered the occasional injury and seen teammates get hurt. As a result, she'd spent a fair amount of time around doctors, and she knew that they never, ever cut to the chase.

"What aren't you telling me?"

"In addition to the fog, you were exposed to another weapon," began Leliefeld.

"Yeah, he spat on me." There was a startled silence. "And?"

"They asked me to operate," said the voice. Slowly, reluctantly, Leliefeld described what she had found and then, even more slowly and reluctantly, described what she had done to fix the problem.

"You put your Grafter slime inside me!" Felicity felt outrage and nausea. The injection she'd received from the graaf had been bad enough, but it had been sufficiently clinical that she could convince herself it was medicine or an inoculation. But Leliefeld had taken a part of her own body and transplanted—no, grafted!—it into Felicity's eyes. It was disgusting. It was monstrous. Vague memories about the eyes being the windows to the soul floated in her mind. *What does this mean? Will I see things the same way? Can she see through my eyes now? Will it affect my powers?*

"It's technology," said Leliefeld in an unreasonably reasonable tone. "It's natural."

"Natural!"

"If you gave me thirteen months and a lot of slides, I could explain it to you," said Leliefeld. "There is a scientific basis for it. Can you say as much for your powers?"

"I was born with this power!"

"Without Broederschap technology, you would be blind. Blind and maybe even dead."

"I would have been blind because of Broederschap technology!" Clements barked back. "Your cousin spat that shit in my eyes. It's all the same."

"You don't believe that, Felicity. Not anymore. And I don't think you ever really did. After all, you're a Pawn of the Checquy. A tool. You know as well as I do that the line between you and the monsters you fight is very thin. It's the same for me." Her words hung in the air between them. "Anyway, the swelling is going down, and the redness of your skin is fading."

"But what's going to happen?" asked Felicity. "How will this affect me?" Leliefeld explained the nature of the weapon that had attacked her eyes and what the transplanted vitreous humor was doing to it. Apart from its defensive capabilities, it didn't appear to be doing much else.

"You'll be able to take the bandages off your eyes in three days," said Leliefeld, "and you'll be able to see just fine, but you'll have to keep taking the antirejection drugs for a year until the material is absorbed fully and becomes part of you."

"Or what happens?"

"Rejection. Then death. Messy death. The one will follow the other inevitably."

"So I'm going to be blind for three days?" asked Felicity weakly.

"About three days, yeah. They're sending you to some Checquy hospital to recuperate until the bandages come off," said Leliefeld. "I spoke with Rook Thomas to let her know that the surgery was successful. And so that she wouldn't give the order for me to be killed."

Again, thought Felicity guiltily.

"Rook Thomas made it very clear that she wanted you back on duty as soon as possible."

"Seriously?"

"I'll make sure there are some parfaits waiting at the hotel."

Despite herself, Felicity smiled.

"Okay, well, three days with no sight, I can cope," said Felicity. "Plus, I assume the reception was canceled, so I dodged that bullet."

"Oh, no, the Rook also said she wants you to attend the reception. Apparently it was just postponed."

"Of course it was." Felicity sighed. "If the Checquy went around canceling events because of disasters, we'd never have any parties."

"All right, now, don't flinch or anything, I just want to check your vital signs." Felicity heard movement and then felt a cool hand on her brow, by her eyes, at her neck. There was a sound of satisfaction from the Grafter girl, and then the hand was gone. "You're looking good. Are you thirsty?"

"Yes." She felt a cup put into her hands and sat up a little to sip at the cool water.

"They'll run scans and follow-up tests later," said Leliefeld. "But there are a lot of people to look after first. In fact, I have to go help them. Someone will come along in a bit to check on you. You should rest." Felicity heard the other woman moving away, and the door of the office open.

"Leliefeld?"

"Yes?"

"Thank you for saving me," said Felicity.

"Yeah, you too," said Odette.

★ ★ ★

The door opened again and Felicity cocked her head.

"We really should stop meeting when one of us is lying injured," said a man's voice, deep and familiar. She didn't even have to use her Sight to see who it was.

"Chopra," said Felicity, smiling. "You look good."

"Yes, you too."

Felicity hoped that her skin was still raw enough to conceal the blush she felt rising up.

"So, you just happened to be passing by?" she asked.

"Actually, I was called in. I had been on recovery leave until the Rookery could assign me to a new team. Lots of talk therapy, and physical therapy, and combat therapy. But luckily I was at home when the attack hit."

"The fog didn't reach your place?"

"No, I live in Clapham," said Chopra. "The latest reports are suggesting that each manifestation covered an area of only about two square miles, though that's quite enough. It's been bloody bedlam out there."

"Each manifestation?" repeated Felicity. "There's been more than one?" She listened in horror as Chopra explained about the attacks around the country.

"It's the biggest story in the world right now," he finished.

"Any—any idea what it is?" she asked hesitantly. That he had used the word manifestation was telling. It was the term the Checquy used to refer to supernatural events. No suggestion that this was seen as a Grafter action.

"No, but the fact that it happened only in major cities is pretty upsetting," said Chopra. "It's difficult to see it as anything but deliberate. The Liars are probably going out of their minds trying to come up with an explanation, and the press is already throwing the T-word around. God knows what the actual terrorists in the world are thinking. They're probably asking each other what the hell happened and who was responsible."

"Hmm," said Felicity.

"Anyway, how are you feeling?" asked Chopra. "I heard that you got caught up in the manifestation and had to receive some rather, ahem, unorthodox surgery."

"Oh God, so everyone knows?" she asked dismally.

"Word gets around," he said, "even in secret organizations. So now you're a Grafter?" he asked cheerfully.

"Don't even joke," said Felicity. "I asked her if I got any new abilities, and she asked if not getting my eyes eaten away in my skull wasn't enough."

"That's not a bad ability," said Chopra.

"The Grafter materials will break down eventually, but it's still creepy to think they're in me." She jumped a little when his hand slid into hers.

"No one will think any less of you, Felicity," he said, and his grip tightened slightly. It really was a very nice hand.

The next three days passed agonizingly slowly.

Felicity was moved from the couch of the head of the Southeast Asia section, who very definitely needed his office back. A minibus transported her and several other Checquy patients through the subdued streets of London and then up the road to a large house in Oxfordshire.

The house, Bufo Hall, had been in the Checquy for several centuries and had previously been used as the official residence of one of the Chevaliers. During World War II, it had been a convalescent home for wounded soldiers, and it had served so well in that regard that it had simply been kept that way. Now, of course, all the occupants were members of the Checquy. Most of the patients were either soldiers who had been injured in the line of duty or operatives whose unique physiologies and abilities meant that they needed highly specialized care. There were three women and one man who were recuperating after giving birth (the Checquy had an excellent parental-leave policy), and a lad from the Estate whose tonsils had needed to come out and that now spent their time fluttering in the air around him and chirping cheerfully. A few retired operatives were pottering about the grounds, including one elderly lady who kept asking Felicity about the effects of the Blinding on the security of the Raj.

Felicity spent most of her time on the back lawn of the house, which swept down to the Thames. Sitting in a chair with a radio beside her, she listened to the news, most of which concerned the mysterious fog. All British armed forces and police had gone on emergency standby. The nation's airports had shut down for a few hours, which had wreaked havoc on the rest of the globe. The stock market had reeled briefly. The normal world was reacting to the supernatural, even if it did not know it.

Late on the first day came the announcement that the fog did not appear to have any permanent effects, except in some very rare cases. The surgeon general, the four chief medical officers, and the Prime Minister (who seemed desperate to have some good news to deliver) sat together to address the nation. They assured people that the blindness and the rash were only temporary and that every hospital and medical practitioner had received instructions on how to alleviate the discomfort until the symptoms faded. Notably, there was no mention of the source of the phenomenon.

Reactions varied. The vast majority of the world had not experienced the Blinding, and the thrill of a pain they had not felt was fascinating, something they could tut over in the office kitchenette. It was comfortably distant. And yet the footage of the clouds washing over the cities was chilling. London, the capital of the world, where the rich could come to enjoy their money in a civilized and secure condition, had been wounded yet again, but this time there was no explanation. It was a mystery—something that people no longer seemed able to cope with.

Accustomed to having the Internet provide them with an answer to any question at the stroke of a key, many people simply could not come to terms with the fact that this time there was no answer for them. How could such a thing happen?

It nagged at them. It struck at their assumptions about the world.

Theories ran rife. Pundits and experts speculated. People with opinions, both informed and decidedly not, published them online. Each new idea was pounced upon by the press, who were fueled by both the desire to have the answer and the fear of missing out on the latest trend and losing their audience. Everyone was willing to believe the least likely of possibilities.

Inevitably, the crazies came out. Felicity knew that some were actually Checquy-employed crazies, shouting loudly about corporate conspiracies, ley lines, and Mayan calendars so as to muddy the waters, but a depressingly overwhelming majority were genuine.

Then there was the man from Edinburgh who called in to a radio show to describe what he had seen. Felicity listened grimly as he told the obviously disbelieving radio hosts that he had seen a young homeless woman shambling about in the street with her head lifted as if sniffing the air. He claimed that she then began shuddering violently, threw her head back, and a torrent of fog poured from her mouth and eyes. Felicity scowled, certain that the homeless girl was another one of the sleepwalkers.

I suppose that she, along with that man Simon was holding hands with, were just a delivery system for the weapon. She asked to make a call to the office of Rook Thomas and was eventually connected with a harried-sounding Mrs. Woodhouse, who promised to pass on the insight and then promptly hung up. From the hubbub in the background, it was apparent that the Rookery was an absolute madhouse.

It was also apparent that the Liars of the Checquy still had not come up with an explanation that everyone could agree on. The government had yet to make a formal announcement. At first glance, it seemed as if the Antagonists' latest attack had done little to further their cause, but there was a tension in the air that seeped through to even the calm riverside gardens of Bufo Hall. Felicity caught snatches of the staff's conversations as they discussed the fog eruptions. No answers or explanations had come down from the Court. The members of the Checquy were even less accustomed to having no answers than the general populace, and the entire organization was on edge.

Leliefeld did not come to visit her, but she did send a bouquet of sweet-smelling flowers along with a bouquet of prescriptions. The suggested ointments and unguents were diligently applied by the nurses, and Felicity spent two hours in an enormous Victorian bathtub stewing in a mixture of chemicals and herbs. She emerged feeling like she'd been made into a ragout but was advised that her skin looked a thousand times better and that the cuts on her feet were vastly improved.

All the time, she thought she could feel Leliefeld's vitreous humor floating inside her eyes.

Home again, home again, jiggity-jig," said Marie as the elevator doors opened on their floor.

"You know, coming back to this hotel after two days away actually does feel like coming home," said Odette. She paused. "God, that's depressing."

"I'm just looking forward to not sleeping on a cot in a warehouse," said Alessio, yawning. "I am so tired." It was ten at night, and they'd just been about to bed down in the Checquy's contingency facility when word came down that the hotel had reopened and that the Grafter delegation would be transported back to their accommodations immediately.

Odette followed Alessio down the hall to their suite and did her best to ignore the clomping of the two hulking guards behind her. For the past two days, everywhere she went, she'd been shadowed by a selection of Checquy guards. There had been men guards and women guards, guards of every race known to man, but all of them had, without exception, been hulking. It was like having hippopotamuses provide one's personal security.

"Are you coming into the suite?" she asked the current hulking guards, and they shook their heads. "Good night, then," she said and shut the door in their faces. She watched tiredly as Alessio kicked off his shoes, went into his room, and launched himself onto his bed. She couldn't be certain, but she was fairly sure he'd fallen asleep in midair.

"I need a drink," said Odette to herself. She wandered over to the suite's minibar and found that it had been completely emptied of alcohol. Well, thank you, Marcel. At least he hadn't left a pointed note reminding her that she wasn't supposed to be drinking. "I don't care, I am having a drink."

She opened the hotel-room door and found that the two hulking guards were stationed just outside it.

"Hi," she said.

"Miss Leliefeld," said the one on the right. "Is everything okay?"

"I want a drink. An alcoholic one."

"You're not supposed to drink alcohol," objected the one on the left.

"Yes, I know," said Odette.

"It was in our briefing notes," said the one on the right. "Because of your throat surgery."

"I don't care. You are here to...I'm not actually sure what your real purpose is, and I don't really want to know, but I'm one hundred percent certain that it is not to protect me from the dangerous effects of alcohol. I am going down to the bar on the ground floor, and I am going to order one single drink, and you can come and watch me drink it. And then I will return to this room. I promise." The two guards exchanged glances, and she could almost hear the grinding of their mental cogs.

"Yeah, okay," said the one on the right finally.

The Checquy guard posted in the lift looked surprised when they got in but said nothing. They alighted in the lobby and proceeded to the hotel's ground-floor bar, where a few patrons were sitting about. Most were members of the public, but Odette recognized a few Checquy operatives, who were obviously praying that she would not come over and sit with them. Instead, she sat at the bar, the guards hovering obtrusively nearby. She ordered a stinger and took a substantial swallow when it arrived. The alcohol did burn uncomfortably in her throat, but it was completely worth it.

"Pawn Fletcher, Pawn Macdonald, you can go sit over there," said a voice behind her. "You look like you're here to abduct the poor girl." Odette looked around and saw Pawn Sophie Jelfs. The Pawns looked uncertain, but Jelfs spoke with the kind of authority that brooked no resistance. "Odette, you look completely knackered."

"I don't know what that means," said Odette, "but I am willing to bet it is accurate."

"Mind if I sit here?"

"Please." The Pawn sat down next to her and ordered a gin martini. "I see you made it through the Blinding unscathed," said Odette. "I'm glad."

"As luck would have it, it happened on my day off," said Sophie. "I was at home, doing some gardening. So what have you been doing these past few days to exhaust you so?"

"Performing various surgeries at gunpoint and sleeping in a warehouse in an inflatable kiddie pool of slime."

"That would...probably do it," said Jelfs. Odette smiled wryly. "You were in the middle of the fog, right? That's what I heard. It must have been terrifying."

"It was scary," said Odette, "although I got knocked out for most of it. You know what the worst part was, though? The part I'm having nightmares about? It's something that didn't even happen."

"What?" asked Sophie, looking confused. "What do you mean?"

"When it was happening, all I could think of was my little brother. I kept worrying whether the fog had hit him. He doesn't have any implants, you know. No protections. He's just a kid. I looked around and saw all those people lying in the streets in agony, and the thought of it happening to him just, it just—" She broke off and wiped her eyes with a napkin, then took a drink. "He's innocent in all this. When I woke up, it was the first thing I thought of. And I keep playing it over in my mind. It's the worst thing that could happen."

"It didn't happen, though."

"I know," said Odette. "I tell myself that. He was fine. But it's still the thing that makes me sick to my stomach."

In a darkened room, a doctor removed the coverings from Felicity's closed eyes and gently washed her eyelids clean before letting her open them. A faint light glimmered in her gaze, and she could make out the doctor in front of her, so she knew she could see, but still her fingers were tight on the arms of her chair. As he peered into her pupils and photographed her retinas, she was secretly braced for the doctor's scream of horror that it had all gone wrong, that she would go blind, that she must be put down. But instead he sighed with pleasure.

"Everything looks fine."

"Really?"

"Perfect," he said reassuringly. "No sign of any injuries or abnormalities at all." He showed her the pictures, which were of no help except to establish that the inside of her eye looked like a huge orange globe, and then gave her a mirror. As far as she could tell, her eyes looked as they always had—no shift in color, no odd pulsating vessels, no impression of bulging or being about to burst.

Then she peered closely at the rest of herself and admitted that she'd come through it fairly well. The redness of her skin had faded completely, and far more quickly than the radio address had promised. Of course, not everyone has access to a Grafter-sent gift basket of bath salts.

The next morning, a car came and drove her back to the hotel. As it took her through the city, Felicity looked out with wary interest. The last time she had seen these streets, they'd been ghostly and silent, with people moaning or lying still on the ground and the fog swirling about. Now, London had returned to normal. The crowds were bustling, and if there was wariness in the air, at least people weren't hiding in their homes.

The hotel had recovered its haughtiness and was open for business despite being practically ground zero for the outbreak of the fog. The doormen even stood a little more stiffly at attention, as if to say that an inexplicable, possibly terrorism-based disaster was absolutely no reason to let standards slip. One of the lifts had apparently been commandeered for the exclusive use of the Checquy, because as soon she entered the lobby, she saw the guard standing by the doors politely but firmly direct an elderly couple to a different lift. He might be dressed in knickerbockers and a witty allusion to a newsboy's cap, but he'd been in her class at the Estate and could grow razor-sharp tusks from the sides of his jaw and unbreakable horns from his forehead in moments. She'd once caught him cheating off her math test.

"Kevin!" she exclaimed.

"Fliss!" he exclaimed back, then he put on a sober, serious face and spoke in the respectful tones suited to a man disguised in the distinguished but ridiculous uniform of a hotel employee. "How you doing? I heard you got caught in the manifestation."

"Right. Is that all you heard, Kev?" she asked as the lift rose.

"I heard you kicked the shit out of some muppet who managed to get away."

"Anything else?"

"I heard you got the very best treatment in the whole wide world," he said meaningfully. His eyes flicked upward for a moment.

"And is that a problem?" she asked levelly.

"Not for me," he said.

"For anyone else?" she asked. He shrugged. "Yeah, I know how it is."

"They'll get over it. Just don't get involved with anything weird," he advised.

"Course, 'cause nothing weird is likely to happen. My life's just full of unweirdness at the moment. In fact, it's full of unweirdness generally." The lift doors slid open.

"Hey, at least you'll have fun at the party tonight," he said encouragingly.

Oh, right, thought Felicity. The reception. Shit.

41

A note on the table led Felicity to the fridge, where there actually was a little parfait waiting for her.

Well, that's cute, she thought. Admittedly, it contained kiwifruit, which she loathed, but she appreciated the sentiment enough to choke it down. She settled herself on the couch with the parfait and brooded about the prospect of the reception. In the whirl of everything, she had clean forgotten about it.

It's probably ridiculous that I would prefer to fight that bastard in the fog again than go to this bloody function. But it was the truth. Felicity did not enjoy fancy dos. The evening with the Court at Hill Hall had been the second-worst event of her life, surpassed only by the death of her teammates, but still worse than the time she'd had two teeth backhanded out of her head by an elderly woman in a poke bonnet, or the time she was stung into unconsciousness by an ambulatory fern, or even the time she almost had her head pulled off by an insane straw golem that had been wandering around Hampshire pulling people's heads off.

Couldn't Leliefeld have ordered me to have an extra day of bed rest? she thought wistfully. As she sulked and ate her stupid kiwifruit parfait, the door opened and Leliefeld walked in.

"Hello," said the Grafter cautiously.

"Hi," said Felicity. "It would have killed you to botch the surgery just a little?"

"What?"

"Never mind," she said grimly. "Thanks for the parfait. And, you know, the gift of sight."

"My pleasure," said Leliefeld. "In truth, keeping Alessio off the parfait was the harder task. So, you're settled back in?"

"I am on the couch with the shattered remnants of a dessert," said Felicity. "What more could I ask for? I haven't even looked in my room." She narrowed her eyes. "No one went in my room, right?"

"No. We were allowed back in the hotel only after two nights of sleeping on cots in a warehouse."

"I expect it's one of our backup business-continuity facilities," said Felicity. "There are a few dotted around the country. In case of disaster, they can transfer us there to keep doing our work. At least they didn't put you in the abandoned mine in Cornwall."

"Yes, I count myself very lucky, but the place we stayed was also a warehouse for tractor parts. The first morning, I almost got run over by a forklift while standing in the queue for the breakfast buffet."

"Our accountants would never let a warehouse lie fallow," said Felicity sagely. "Budgets are tight, and they can't really offer voluntary redundancies to Checquy operatives. You can't just tell someone whose shadow is a portal to Spain that there's no room in the budget for him and he'll need to move into the private sector."

"It's nice to know I won't have to worry about job security, then," said Leliefeld.

"So, you've spent the past couple of days hanging out in a warehouse?"

"No, we've just been sleeping in the warehouse. Grootvader Ernst volunteered Marcel's and my services to assist with the fog fallout. After I operated on your eyes, I was asked to help analyze the traces of chemicals they've recovered from other victims."

"And?"

"And I have earned an undeserved reputation for genius. Well, slightly undeserved."

"What are you talking about?" asked Felicity.

"I was able to give a lot of useful insights," said Leliefeld. "The Checquy scientists thought it was because I have astounding expertise. Which I do. But it was because I've seen this stuff before."

"Well, it's Grafter-made," Felicity said, shrugging.

"Yeah, but I couldn't let anyone know that. Anyway, the

toxin's not pleasant. It normally has to be processed inside a living creature before it's released."

"That's... disgusting."

"It's science," said Leliefeld. "Everything's disgusting. But I'll admit, this is kind of especially disgusting. The host has to be substantially adapted and needs to be swimming with antirejection products and antibodies. We've always used swine or sheep, but I think that homeless-looking guy Simon was with must have been the delivery system. I have no idea how they managed to get him ready in such a short time, though. It takes months to reach the appropriate levels of chemicals and hormones, and as far as I know, you can't just pump them into the host."

"He was the recipient of an organ transplant," said Felicity. "All the abductees were."

The Grafter's jaw dropped. "That's brilliant," she said. "You find very few animals who are given new organs, but people? That's very clever."

"Yes, very smart," said Felicity.

"So, after that, Marcel and I were in surgery working on people's eyes. Apparently, a small percentage of the populace suffered a horrendous allergic reaction to the fog. We got flown to a few different cities with various large guards escorting us."

"They assigned you new bodyguards?" said Felicity, feeling an unexpected jolt of jealousy. Leliefeld was her charge.

"I don't know that bodyguards is the right word," said Leliefeld. "We were performing the operations with guns pointed at us."

"Oh. Well, did they go all right?"

"I think so," said Leliefeld. "We had to fly in several punnets of eyes from Bruges and Seville."

"I don't know why I ask you questions when I know the answers will inevitably make me feel nauseous," remarked Felicity.

"It wasn't that bad," said Leliefeld. "I mean, installing the new eyes was long and tedious, but it took almost as much time to make sure that the colors matched their previous eyes."

"Is it such a big deal if there's a little discrepancy?" asked Felicity. "People aren't as observant as you think. I know of at least one situation where the Checquy successfully replaced someone's station wagon without his noticing after the original was turned into a column of chutney during a manifestation."

"Well, cars are one thing," said Leliefeld, "but people tend to pay a lot more attention to themselves. It's going to be awkward enough that they'll no longer need glasses without their eyes suddenly going from blue to brown."

"How many people were you able to help?"

"Quite a few," said Leliefeld. "There are going to be a lot of feel-good miracle stories in the press. Anyway, rest assured, no one went in your room, although seriously, I was very tempted."

"Why?" asked Felicity warily. All the classified documents and files she'd been given were locked in the room safe, but she still didn't like the idea of anyone sifting through her stuff.

"Because I wanted to see the dress they got you for the reception tonight!" Felicity stared at her blankly. This sentiment was even more alien than the idea of carrying scalpels around in one's thigh. "Aren't you even mildly curious about it?"

Be diplomatic, thought Felicity, and she managed to pull her upper lip back from her teeth in a sort of approximation of enthusiasm. "Do you want to go take a look?" she said finally.

They regarded the dress in respectful silence. It was the kind of respectful silence heard at ceremonies held to commemorate disasters.

"I'm no expert in dresses," said Felicity finally, "but that... that's not a good dress, is it?"

"I know what I want to say," said Leliefeld, "but I am mindful of my role as a diplomatic envoy here to make peace between our peoples."

"Just say it."

"Look, I'm a trained surgeon."

"Yeah?" said Felicity.

"And as someone who has seen living forms changed and twisted beyond recognition..." She trailed off awkwardly.

"Yeah?"

"I hate to say it, but this dress is the worst crime against nature I have ever seen in my life."

Felicity cringed a little. The dress lay on the bed, malignant and resentful, like an angry jellyfish. It was technically an evening gown, in the same way that dirt is technically edible. The benighted designer was apparently committed to the principle of "accentuate the negative" and had made the assumption that whoever wore it would have cubical breasts. There were folds and pleats where God had decreed that no folds or pleats ought ever to be, and some sort of structure had been built into the back, giving the impression of a prolapsed bustle. The color could perhaps have been described as sky blue, but it was the blue of a sky that would drive even the cheeriest and most tuneful of novice nuns to slash her wrists. It was a blue that had given up.

"Did you offend someone in the quartermaster's office?" asked Leliefeld carefully.

"I don't know," said Felicity. "I think maybe it's intended to establish that I'm there in a functionary capacity."

"It certainly does that," said Leliefeld. "It practically screams 'duenna-slash-janitor.'"

"Perhaps they were worried I would overshadow the higher-ranking guests," suggested Felicity.

"Well, no fear of that," said Leliefeld. "Although they may try to deposit their rubbish in your cleavage."

"The quartermaster's office is more used to sourcing armor and weaponry," said Felicity, spurred by a feeling of defensive loyalty. "I don't think they've had to do much with evening wear."

"I'm sure their intentions were honorable, but there's no way you can wear that," said Leliefeld firmly.

"I don't have anything else even vaguely appropriate at home except a bridesmaid's dress," said Felicity, "and that is fuchsia and has puffed sleeves."

"What about the dress you wore to Ascot?"

"At the dry cleaners," said Felicity grimly.

"If Judas Iscariot were alive, and a woman, and attending formal functions, wearing this dress would still represent a disproportionate punishment for his sins."

"Her sins."

"Right," said Leliefeld uncertainly. "Anyway, I have a spare dress you can wear." Felicity looked at her and tried to think of a diplomatic way to express her thoughts.

"That's very kind of you, but you're too short and your breasts are too small. Any dress that fits you would make me look like a whore or a sausage." Maybe I should look at going into diplomacy, Felicity thought, quite pleased with herself.

"It'll fit you," Leliefeld assured her. "It's very adaptable."

The news channels had not calmed down about the Blinding at all, not even after the unrelated revelation that a married member of the House of Lords had been having a homosexual affair with a married foreign spy. Felicity, Leliefeld, and Alessio all sat on the couch and watched the constantly shown footage of the Blinding. Felicity had listened to the radio broadcasts, but it was different seeing it on television. The image of that yellow-green cloud spreading through the cities was somehow just as terrifying as actually being there. To make matters worse, they were also showing pictures of the victims, focusing on those few who had suffered the very worst reactions.

"Were you able to help that boy?" asked Alessio. They were all looking at one of the most famous photos from the attacks, a small dark-haired child who had been blinded by the fog.

"We probably could have done something," said Leliefeld sadly, "but I'm afraid word came down that too many people had seen the picture, and his getting new eyes would strain the boundaries of a believable medical miracle. There's no mainstream cure for losing your eyes after a biological attack."

"And why not?" asked Felicity.

"I'm sorry?"

"Well, you have a cure, and as you never tire of telling me, your work is based on science," said Felicity. "Why don't you people just go public and make billions?" The two Grafters exchanged glances. "What?"

"You've just described our worst nightmare," said Leliefeld.

"Apart from attending a party with the Checquy," put in Alessio. The two women shot him a look, and he subsided back into the couch cushions.

"There's a lot of dangerous implications in what we do," said Leliefeld. "For the world, and for us."

"Why? After all, it's science, our best friend in the whole wide world."

"You know I don't see it like that," said Leliefeld. "And it's complicated. To begin with, much of our work is still illegal in most countries. We're talking genetic engineering, harvesting organs, cloning, weaponizing human biology. Alessio keeps human stem cells in his thermos."

"For experiments, not for drinking," Alessio assured her.

"Plus, people think that sort of thing is creepy," said Leliefeld.

"It is creepy," said Felicity. "It's incredibly creepy. But you know they would throw those laws out the window if there was the possibility of curing cancer or doubling life spans."

"It's too big," said Leliefeld, shaking her head. "If just one country gained unfettered access to our capabilities, it would become the world's unquestioned superpower. It's the equivalent of the Roman Empire suddenly being gifted with nuclear weapons. You of all people should understand that."

"Yes, but it's different," said Felicity. "I was born with this ability, but anyone could learn how to do what you do." Odette and Alessio both opened their mouths, and she hastily cut them off. "Anyone who's extremely brilliant." The Grafters looked somewhat mollified.

"You have to understand, we are literally centuries ahead of mainstream science," said Leliefeld. "Even if we released the knowledge to everyone, it wouldn't make things better. It would make them worse. Mainstream culture is not ready for what we can do. That's why the negotiations are not just about how much money we can keep and whether we can be called in to help put down a giant malevolent porcupine. Protections are being put in place about the knowledge we possess and what can be done with it. We are not going to be making house calls so that the moneyed classes of Great Britain get a few extra centuries."

"So, no new eyes for the little boy," said Felicity.

"No new eyes for the little boy," agreed Leliefeld sadly. "But Marcel is looking at amping up his other senses, maybe throwing in a little rudimentary radar. People seem quite willing to believe in that sort of thing."

"What about that guy?" asked Alessio as a new picture was flashed up. This one featured a man clawing at his own face. "Did you help him?"

"All right, I think it's time we start getting ready," said Leliefeld.

"But we're not leaving for ages yet," Alessio objected. "And I only take a few minutes to get dressed and ready."

"Well, take them now," said Leliefeld as she turned off the television. "We're going to need the larger room, so you can get changed in Pawn Clements's room."

"But don't touch anything," said Felicity.

The boy grumped, but he hauled himself off the couch and into the bedroom. "I'd like it if he took a bit of time away from the news," Leliefeld said to Felicity. "Plus, the hotel will be sending someone up to do our hair in a bit, and we want to be dressed by then."

"They taught us at the Estate that you do makeup first, then hair, then gown, then shoes," said Felicity cautiously. The Socializing with Civilians class at the Estate had always been her least favorite, but she'd managed to remember the order of preparations through the handy mnemonic Monsters Hate Getting Shot. She and her friends had actually made up an obscene variation, Monsters Hate Getting Shot In The Face, but she could remember only what the Face part stood for, and she didn't anticipate any of that going on that evening.

"Yes, that's how I normally do it," said Leliefeld. "But these dresses are a bit complicated and I want them all settled before any civilians wander in." She sat down in front of the mirror and began dotting foundation onto her face. Felicity expected her to start blending it together, but instead, the Grafter unbuttoned her top and took it off. Despite herself, Felicity ran her eyes over the other woman's body, evaluating and comparing. The Grafter looked as if she went to the gym only when she remembered to, but she had a lack of self-consciousness that Felicity couldn't help but envy. It was all very well having no shirt on when the entire team was getting changed in the back of a truck, but that was part of the job. Felicity had never been the type of girl to strip off casually in the changing rooms.

Then she noticed the scars.

Faint white lines ran down the length of the other woman's arms, and a pink Y-shaped incision ran down from her shoulders and met between her breasts. A single line emerged from the bottom of her bra and continued to below her belt, a few lines stretching across her stomach. Felicity's eyes widened, and then she noticed Leliefeld looking at her in the mirror. Blushing furiously, Felicity glanced away.

"Sorry," she said.

"It's fine, they are noticeable," said Leliefeld. She began dotting foundation down the lines and across her chest. "I'm not embarrassed by them," she said. Thoughtfully, she traced the line running down her chest. "Actually, I'm lucky to have them."

"Sorry?" said Felicity.

"These are pretty recent," said Leliefeld. "Marcel put the improvements in right before we came to London. It was a sign that they trusted me."

"That's great," said Felicity in as convincing a manner as she could manage.

"Twenty-three hours under the knife," mused the Grafter.

"That's a lot of surgery."

"You get used to it. I had my first major surgeries when I was eighteen." She pointed at her face. "The new lenses put into my eyes and modifications to my facial muscles and my skin."

"So that's not your face?" blurted Felicity.

"No, it is my face," said the Grafter firmly. "Just with some alterations behind the scenes." She set about blending the foundation across her cheeks and down onto her chest and shoulders. "My friends and I used to work out modifications for each other, do each other's surgeries, but they were almost always minor cosmetic things, one-offs for an evening." She sounded amused by the memories, but Felicity's flesh crawled at the thought.

"Oh, and Pim gave me these," Leliefeld said, holding up her hands. Two sharp bone barbs slid out of her wrists. Christ! thought Felicity. "Birthday present. Although we all got them." She regarded them for a moment, and then they withdrew back into her skin. Felicity couldn't even see a mark where they had been.

"Anyway, I was scheduled for the next round of major modifications, but then my—then the Antagonists broke away." Leliefeld kept up the blending, but now her voice had gone flat, unemotional. She finished the foundation and opened up a pot of powder that caught Felicity's eye.

"That's an unusual color for face powder, isn't it?" asked Felicity uncertainly.

"It's lavender," said Leliefeld. "My friend Saskia picked it out for me months ago for the Carnevale di Viareggio." She closed her eyes for a moment and put her hands flat on the dressing table. Then she opened her eyes and resumed laying out the cosmetics. "Like the woman in Sargent's painting Portrait of Madame X. The only thing is, it needs to go over the right color of skin." She stared into the mirror and frowned. Her skin grew a fraction paler through the foundation, and she began dusting the powder over herself.

"If you can change your skin, then why are you using makeup?" asked Felicity, curious despite herself. It must be very convenient to have an Etch A Sketch for a face, she thought.

"It's a formal occasion." Leliefeld shrugged. "My mother always says if you're going to a fancy event, you go fancy. It's good to be seen as making an effort." She nodded at the makeup case.

"You're welcome to use anything you like in there, by the way." Felicity felt her face freeze. "Don't worry," the Grafter assured her. "They're all normal commercial cosmetics. Nothing biological. Not even any Botox."

"I suppose I'd better," said Felicity unwillingly. "I just don't normally wear makeup."

"Well, you don't need it," said the Grafter. "You have that great English skin. If you need any help..."

"They taught us how to do it," said Felicity firmly. It was right after jujitsu class and right before algebra. Not wanting to appear too done up—she was only a Pawn, after all, and it wouldn't be appropriate for her to try to look on the same level as her protectee—Felicity quickly brushed on some blush and lip gloss.

Once Leliefeld had applied her more elaborate makeup, she went to the closet and produced two long dress bags. She unzipped the coverings and seemed a little shy as she held up the gowns for inspection. Felicity peered at them and wondered if there was a way she could justify going back to the Blue Dress of Despair.

It was not immediately apparent what the dresses were supposed to look like, but a first glance revealed various problems. To begin with, they were identical, which sent a somewhat disquieting message. Deep purple, the garments had no specific shape and seemed to slump morosely from the hangers with far too much material. Admittedly, the cloth was beautiful, with a texture that cried out to be touched, but...

When she said complicated, I thought they would look nice, thought Felicity. Or at least that they would look like dresses. These look like the winding sheets of morbidly obese fashion editors.

"You want to wear purple?" asked Felicity in surprise, interrupting her own train of thought.

"No, but—you don't like purple?" asked Leliefeld.

"Well," said Felicity. "Um." She pursed her lips and tried to think of a tactful explanation. "The thing is, we don't normally wear purple in the Checquy. It's reserved for the livery of the personal staff of the Court members."

"I see," said the Grafter. "I think I remember something about that."

"But I'm sure it'll be fine," said Felicity hurriedly. Crap, I've just rubbished her party dress, she thought. An hour before we're supposed to leave.

"It definitely won't do," said Leliefeld decidedly. From the little fridge, she took out a polished wooden case that looked as if it contained the world's nicest electric toothbrush or possibly the world's nicest vibrator. Instead, it contained two rows of tiny glass vials nestled in velvet and a slim hypodermic needle made of brass and glass.

What the hell? thought Felicity, taking a step back. Odette drew a few drops of the liquid into the needle and then injected it into a fold of one dress. Dark veins of color spread out from the injection, bleeding throughout the material until the entire garment was a deep, dark, glorious green.

"Better?" Leliefeld asked, and Felicity nodded weakly.

"How did you do that?"

"You mean the colors? Yeah, it's cool, isn't it? What color would you like? I can make it whatever you want."

"But how?"

"The material has chromatophores woven through it," said Leliefeld. "They're color-changing cells. We lifted them from a selection of octopuses and cuttlefish."

"Oh, clever," said Felicity. I'll be wearing a cuttlefish? "Um, well, maybe something light, then?" If they had to be wearing the same shapeless dress, at the very least they could be in different colors, and the instructors in Attire at the Estate had always said pastels suited her.

"I have an idea," said Leliefeld. She spent a few moments filling the hypodermic. Unlike the color for her dress, this one seemed to require extracts from a number of vials. She then shook the syringe hard before injecting it into Felicity's gown. The reaction this time was different, with ripples of pale green expanding through the fabric. Leliefeld regarded the process, frowning, and in a few places injected more of the solution.

Finally, she was satisfied, and the dress was now a soft, delicate sea-foam green. It was nothing Felicity would ever have picked out for herself, but it was lovely. As she watched, the other girl took up a cotton bud, dipped it into one of the vials, and began tracing it over the bodice of the dress. Glittering silver lines appeared in its wake.

"You can do metals."

"They're iridophores," said Leliefeld. "Do you like it? I can do something different if you'd prefer."

"No, it's beautiful," said Felicity, and it was.

"Great. I'll put mine on first, and then we'll do yours." Leliefeld took the dark green dress off the hanger and stepped into it awkwardly. The acreage of material was not easy to navigate through, and she seemed to be having trouble finding the floor. Felicity stepped forward and held some of the cloth out of the way.

Eventually, the Grafter had the dress on, but she was not a prepossessing sight. The garment hung off her in baggy folds and spread out on the floor in drifts of surplus material. It looked like a parachute or a cover for a king-size bed.

"It's ... very flattering," said Felicity finally. *Maybe this is the new look in Belgium.*

"That's tactful of you, but I'm not finished," said the Grafter, sounding amused as she sprayed the dress lightly with perfume. She turned to regard herself in the mirror and ran a gentle finger down her side, stroking the fabric. It drew itself up against her, tightening and holding its shape. Felicity gasped in surprise.

For the next few minutes, Leliefeld sculpted the gown around herself. She drew it in at her bust and waist, tightened the folds around her middle, and corrected the fall of the cloth to the floor. The cloth contracted with a faint whispering sound. When she was finished, the dress looked as if it had been designed specifically for her. The material pooled slightly around her feet, curving a little behind her like liquid. Combined with the faint lavender powder she had dusted on her skin earlier, it was beautifully exotic.

"That's amazing," said Felicity weakly. "So ... it's alive?"

"Yes," said Leliefeld cheerfully. Felicity's stomach turned over at the idea. Suddenly, she had an overpowering urge to wash her hands.

"And it just responds to your touch?" she asked. The Grafter nodded proudly. "But how does it know when to stop? What if someone brushes against you at the party?" Would it fall off if someone hugged you? Would it crush you if you stepped on the hem?

"I just put it to sleep," said Leliefeld. She picked up a different perfume bottle and sprayed a tiny amount onto the base of her gown. "The dress will hold its shape, but it won't react to any more input until I wake it up. Oh, except it automatically absorbs wine stains, which is very handy." She turned around slowly. "Are there any loose folds? It's always hard to tell right at the back."

"No, it looks beautiful," said Felicity truthfully.

"Thank you," said Leliefeld. "Now, let's get you into yours." Felicity froze for a moment, absolutely appalled at the idea but trapped by the unbreakable manacles of Good Manners.

The gown felt like cool silk and closed snugly around Felicity's chest, and she was reminded of an ill-advised hens' night when they'd all worn corsets. Not uncomfortable, exactly, but certainly not something you could relax in. Leliefeld regarded her thoughtfully for a moment and then stepped forward and sprayed the dress with the first perfume.

"Read nothing into this," said the Grafter, and she drew a finger briskly across Felicity's bust and then back under. At her touch, the material gathered itself up, supporting and restraining. It occurred to a shamefully ungrateful part of Felicity's mind that, if Leliefeld wanted to, she need merely flick her wrist, and the gown would clench about the Pawn and crush her to death. For all Felicity knew, it might then soak up all the blood and hoover up the bones.

Of course, nothing of the sort happened, and Leliefeld fussed around Felicity for a few more minutes. She drew out billows and cinched in folds. "You'd better put on your shoes," the Grafter said, "so I can fix the hem." A pair of high heels had been sent along with the Blue Dress of Despair, but Felicity did not bother opening the box, opting for a pair of well-broken-in Kevlar-toed work boots.

"Seriously?" asked Leliefeld.

"Absolutely," said Felicity. "I haven't worn heels in a year except at Ascot, and it was agony." Besides, I want to be able to kick hard if anything happens. "Can you make this work?"

"Sure," said Leliefeld and drew the hem of the gown a little lower to conceal the boots. She then sprayed the garment with the sleep-inducing scent. At last the two of them looked in the mirror. It was remarkable. Although their dresses had begun identical, they were now completely different in color and form.

"Not bad," said Leliefeld, pleased.

"Not bad at all," agreed Felicity. "Thanks." She realized that she felt at ease—more so than she could recently remember being. Unconsciously, she'd been unclenching her powers, letting down the barriers she usually kept up. Because the dress was alive, she didn't need to worry about getting caught up in its history. What an amazing thing. She absently stroked the skirt and was startled when the faintest of vibrations trembled through the material. It was so gentle that the cloth didn't move, but she felt it on her skin.

"Is it purring?" she asked Leliefeld.

"It likes you."

A knock at the door proved to be Alessio announcing that the hairdresser had arrived. A woman in her thirties, she went into raptures over both of them. She worked quickly and did a nice job of arranging their hair into flattering styles. Leliefeld tipped the woman a generous amount, and Felicity tipped her absolutely nothing except an embarrassed smile because she did not have any money, only a corporate credit card.

Alessio was wearing a normal, nonliving tuxedo of which he was extremely proud. Leliefeld and Felicity duly complimented him on it. Just then a Checquy guard knocked and advised them that their car was waiting in the basement parking lot. Feeling very smart indeed, the three of them set off.

42

When the car arrived at Apex House, the two Grafters and the Pawn looked up in fascination. Multicolored lights illuminated the building, with patterns projected onto the surfaces so that one moment it looked as if it were covered in glowing Byzantine mosaics and the next as if it were blanketed with snow.

"Lovely, but it's not very discreet," remarked Leliefeld.

"I expect the public think it's art," said Felicity. "There will probably be a cranky letter or two in the Times about a frivolous waste of taxpayer money." They disembarked and walked through the front doors. The lobby was quiet; there were guards at the desks, but they waved the three of them through.

Felicity knew that the limousines carrying the Grafter delegation had been carefully staggered so that the guests would enter only in small groups. Rook Thomas would scan each individual, checking to see if anyone was wearing someone else's face. Felicity looked around curiously for the Rook but saw no trace of her.

She must be tucked away somewhere by the entrance, Felicity mused. Perhaps in some hidey-hole. It was common knowledge in the Checquy that Apex House had been designed to be a fortress as much as an office, and the building was presumed to possess a multitude of hidden features. The murder-holes in the ceiling, cunningly concealed, were always pointed out to visiting students from the Estate.

In the atrium, the massive central doors stood open, welcoming them into the heart of the building. They proceeded through them and walked along a grand corridor until they came to a shallow flight of broad steps leading down to the assembly hall. Music and chatter floated up to them.

On either side of the doors were four soldiers of the Barghests standing at attention in their dress uniform of crimson and white plate armor. They bore no arms, and as was the custom, their hands were ungloved.

"Do we need to stop?" asked Leliefeld uncertainly. Alessio's eyes were wide as he regarded the forbidding warriors.

"Nah," said one of them, his Cockney accent echoing out from behind his visor. "It's just tradition to have us here. Go on in, have a nice time at the party."

"You might sneak us out some hors d'oeuvres, though, if you get the chance," said another one in a thick Scottish accent.

A nice time? thought Felicity grimly. Please. She looked out on the huge hall with its ceiling of curved golden wood. The far wall was a massive curtain of glass that revealed the carefully cultivated gardens beyond. The room was filled with beautifully dressed people. At one side, an orchestra played by a dance floor on which couples had already gathered. The rest of the room was filled with guests moving about and conversing. It's like walking down the steps into hell.

As they descended the stairs, a rustle went through the crowd, and dozens of faces turned to stare at them.

"Why are they looking at us like that?" said Felicity out of the corner of her mouth.

"Well, I'm hoping they're staring at you because you're gorgeous," said Leliefeld in low tones. "I have a bad feeling, though, that they're staring at me with the expectation that I'll fall flat on my face again."

"You're both idiots," said Alessio serenely. "They're all look-ing at me in my James Bond tux."

"How well does this gown deal with sweat?" asked Felicity, who was feeling very damp in the pits and lower back.

"It absorbs it and uses the salts and nutrients to launder itself," said Leliefeld.

"It will be very clean by the end of this evening, then."

They were not the first Grafters to arrive, and Felicity noted with interest that the normal orders of precedence had been dropped. She saw Sir Henry talking to a tall man with excellent hair. Lady Farrier was actually out on the dance floor, moving in a slow but stately waltz with a nervous-looking young Pawn whom Felicity recognized as having been in the year behind her at the Estate. She also recognized several of the Grafters who had arrived before them.

"Okay, well, now I suppose we mingle," said Leliefeld. "Do you see anyone you know?" she asked Felicity hopefully.

"Not really," said Felicity. "That's the headmistress of the Estate over there, but she seems quite engaged in conversation with your head of security."

"Who are all these people?" asked Alessio nervously.

"Mostly high-ranking Checquy," said Felicity, scanning the crowd. "Heads of departments, some division heads, and chiefs from different regional offices. Quite a few people from the Diplomatic section — your friend Pawn Bannister is right over there." The Grafter siblings automatically turned to look and received a flat stare from the Pawn.

"Well, that wasn't very diplomatic," said Leliefeld.

"He's probably annoyed about losing his minder gig," said Felicity. "Oh, there are also some very important civilians here tonight. That's the chief of the defence staff over there at the bar, and there's the archbishop of Canterbury talking with Bishop Alrich." At the mention of the vampire Bishop, she heard Alessio give the tiniest moan.

"Who's the blind man who's just coming in?" asked Leliefeld.

"I don't know," said Felicity, "but the dog he's escorting is the ruler of one of the Channel Islands. Let's see, who else is here? There's the chancellor of Oxford, the chief constable of Police Scotland, the first minister of Wales, and the mayor of Stowmarket. Oh, and Lady Farrier is now dancing with the chief rabbi." A waiter bearing a tray of drinks materialized by them.

"Thank God," said Leliefeld.

"Miss Leliefeld, I brought you a grapefruit juice specially," said the waiter.

"Huh?"

"Rook Thomas informed us of your throat problems," said

the waiter. His expression did not change as the Grafter woman unwillingly accepted the proffered drink. Felicity, in a move of solidarity that even she didn't expect, took a glass of orange juice. Alessio made a move toward a glass of wine, but a hissed remark from his sister redirected him toward a soft drink.

"Evening," said Security Chief Clovis as he came up to them. "Ladies, your gowns are beautiful."

"Thank you," said Leliefeld. Felicity smiled weakly.

"Are you enjoying the party?" asked the security chief.

"It's much bigger than I expected," said Leliefeld. Then her eyes widened. "Is Sir Henry talking to who I think he's talking to?"

"Who? Wait, that's the Prime Minister!" exclaimed Felicity.

"He looks pissed off," said Leliefeld.

"Yes, well, a terrorist attack on one's soil will do that," said Felicity.

"But why is he here?" asked Alessio. "Shouldn't he be doing prime-ministerial things about the Blinding? Like figuring out what the source was?"

"We already know what the source of the fogs was," said Clovis.

"You do?" asked Alessio in surprise. "What was it?"

Felicity caught a glimpse of Odette's horrified face. The Grafter girl's eyes were wide as she looked at Clovis pleadingly. *So, Alessio doesn't know about the Antagonists.*

"Oh, I'm afraid it's classified," said Clovis awkwardly. "But we do know it falls within our area of responsibility, and we are obliged to inform the Prime Minister of the truth. As far as the public are concerned, the Prime Minister is currently in camera at Number Ten consulting with the heads of the various intelligence agencies, most of whom are also here, eating little pastries filled with salmon."

"So the world thinks the leaders of the United Kingdom are addressing matters of dire national security, and instead they're attending a ball," marveled Leliefeld.

"They're doing both," said a voice behind them, and they turned to see Rook Thomas. She was wearing a magnificent glistening black dress that fell from her shoulders like a waterfall of crude oil and trailed behind her for several feet. It was obvious, even to Felicity, that this was genuine couture. Two large bodyguards, a man and a woman, stood behind her, dressed in purple so dark it was almost black. Felicity suspected that they were there partly to underline the status of the Rook (who was perfectly capable of defending herself against pretty much everyone in the room) and partly to prevent people from stepping on her dress.

"Good evening, Rook Thomas," they all said in unison. Felicity automatically bobbed a little curtsy.

"Good evening," said the Rook. "You all look very nice. Good tux," she said to Alessio, who stood a little taller. "Odette, you are surprised that the great and the good have gathered here for drinks and dancing when disaster has just struck?" Leliefeld flushed a little. "All sorts of important things can happen at a social event." For a moment, the Rook's eyes went distant and her face went serious. Then the look was gone, and she smiled again. "Plus, I find that people tend to be a little more open at these kinds of things. A little more courteous. It's as if they want to live up to their clothes." She looked at her own gown. "Or possibly down to them. I was rather hoping that tonight's event might help the Checquy and the Broederschap relax around each other. If nothing else, there's an open bar."

Felicity looked around. There was definite tension in the room, and not a great deal of mingling between Checquy and Grafters. People were staying with their own little groups. Conversations were hushed, and what laughter there was was brittle. Eyes were constantly moving about, evaluating.

"So who else knows about the source of the fog?" Leliefeld asked, still staring at the Prime Minister. "Does it get shared throughout the government?"

"This sort of information is closely held," said Rook Thomas. "But with something this big, it's very important to inform the highest authorities and not allow them to blame it on an existing threat, like terrorists. We don't want bombing strikes ordered in the Middle East because some kid in Doncaster can't stop bursting into fire. So as soon as we knew who was responsible, we advised the Croatoan, our American equivalent, and they advised the president."

"So, I expect the Prime Minister is not happy with us?" asked Leliefeld. It was not clear if by us she meant the Grafters or the Checquy.

"It probably doesn't help that what happened is all over the Internet," said Alessio sagely.

"That's true," said Clovis. "We're just fortunate that the attack wasn't unequivocally supernatural. The fog clouds were horrible, but not inexplicable. Even the conspiracy nuts haven't quite dared to claim it's something spooky. They're all busy criticizing the Prime Minister and accusing him of being either incompetent or a terrorist himself."

Felicity looked over to the aforementioned Prime Minister, who was talking with Sir Henry and Lady Farrier. She automatically started to read his lips but caught only the words *fucking disaster* before she realized what she was doing and looked away hurriedly.

"What would the Checquy have done if it had been explicitly unnatural?" asked Leliefeld curiously.

Chief Clovis took on a lecturing tone. "The Internet has proven to be both tremendously inconvenient and tremendously useful for us. It's much more difficult to keep a secret contained. However, the public's skepticism has also increased." The security chief smiled. "I know of at least two instances where footage of real harpies fighting in the Shetlands was criticized online for being poorly executed. People didn't even call it a hoax—to them, it was simply low-quality CGI."

"The Rookery also has Liars who deal with public perception," put in Rook Thomas.

"Liars?" said Alessio in puzzlement.

"The Tactical Deception Communications Section," corrected Chief Clovis patiently. "They send out disinformation after any manifestation that has gotten significant public notice."

"Fascinating," remarked Leliefeld.

"Has the Broederschap encountered many other supernatural elements?" asked the Rook. "You must have, surely."

"Very few," said Leliefeld. "And it's never been pretty." Felicity thought of Marcel's story about the woman in Paris who killed all those Grafters. And Marcel had hinted at other, even worse incidents.

"I was hoping that you would be able to tell us more about what the supernatural scene is like on the Continent," said Rook Thomas. "We know so little."

"We probably know even less," said the Grafter girl ruefully. "We have always been extremely cautious about anything to do with the supernatural. Almost reclusive."

Rook Thomas nodded thoughtfully and then looked over as her executive assistant came to them through the crowd. "Hello, Ingrid, you look stressed. I take it something is going to ruin what's left of my evening?"

"Rook Thomas," said Mrs. Woodhouse urgently, "the Prime Minister has decided he is going to make a speech. Now."

"Oh, hell," said the Rook, looking pained. She held out her hand and took a glass of champagne from the tray of a waiter who had just appeared at her shoulder and who looked rather surprised about it. The Prime Minister, flanked by the Lord and Lady of the Checquy, waited by the orchestra. As the song came to an end, Sir Henry stepped forward to a microphone.

"Good evening," said the Lord, and the conversation in the room died away. "And the warmest of welcomes to you all. The Checquy Group is delighted to host tonight's festivities at Apex House, an evening in which old friends and colleagues join together to welcome new allies. Now, I give you the Prime Minister of the United Kingdom of Great Britain and Northern Ireland." Applause swept through the room as the head of the government stepped forward.

"Distinguished guests," began the Prime Minister. "It is, as always, a privilege to spend time at a gathering such as this." Felicity's mind wandered a bit as he went on to praise the

Checquy for its centuries of steadfastly defending the kingdom. There was applause, but Felicity saw that the Rook remained tense.

"The reception tonight was meant to be a celebration," he went on, "marking the first steps toward reconciliation and union between old adversaries. This merger is an exciting idea, an inspiring idea, and I am confident that it will result in something greater than the sum of its parts. It is a tremendous pity that tonight's pleasure should be marred by tragedy.

"The heinous attacks on innocent civilians have, once again, brought the world's eyes to our country for the worst of reasons. I have received messages of sympathy and support from nations around the world. In times of misfortune, the importance of friends and allies cannot be overestimated. That is why the work toward the joining of the United Kingdom and the Broederschap is, in these dark days, a thing of hope."

"This isn't too bad," said the Rook in a low, cautiously optimistic tone.

"It is provident to have you all here tonight," said the Prime Minister. "In the days ahead, all of you will be called upon to lend your strength and courage as we work to track down the enemy that has struck at our people with such cowardice and spite. I say all of you because these attacks have come from the world that the Checquy polices. Indeed, we are already aware of the identity of those responsible."

"Oh, shit," said Thomas.

"The attacks were the work of rogue elements from within the Wetenschappelijk Broederschap van Natuurkundigen. They are a small group of extremists, zealots who have torn themselves away from their families and their oaths and who are determined to use terror and cruelty to prevent peace."

"Well, that was a nice secret while it lasted." The Rook sighed. She threw the rest of the champagne down her throat and looked about for another waiter.

Around the room, reactions were mixed. The civilian guests were, for the most part, confused and antsy as they absorbed this information. The Grafters were looking about warily and seemed to be drawing together into tighter clumps. Among the Checquy, however, there was the sound of angry muttering.

Felicity became aware of pointed and none-too-friendly stares directed at Leliefeld and Alessio. As she watched, the Grafter girl put out her hand and drew her little brother in closer.

Scents suddenly hovered in the air, musk and compost and electricity. Felicity felt a strange sensation run through her stomach, as if, for a moment, the liquids there had sloshed a little to the left. The glass in her hand hummed a little, vibrating in harmony with a sound she could not hear. A wave of humid air washed over her, followed by a cooler one from a different direction.

Whether or not they realized it, the Pawns of the Checquy were letting their feelings get the better of them.

Automatically, Felicity moved closer to the two Grafters, and she found herself casually standing with her legs shoulder-width apart and her knees and elbows slightly bent. She was ready to defend them.

And then the tension in the room was gone, dissipated. The resentment and the outrage remained, of that she had little doubt, but the moment was over. A decision had been made. The Pawns of the Checquy were too disciplined, too civilized, to turn on their guests. The civilians did not appear to have noticed anything, and the Prime Minister had continued to speak without a break.

Felicity looked at Rook Thomas and saw that the woman's face was absolutely blank. She must have been ready to do something pretty damn dire if it came down to it. Clements didn't care to imagine what that could be—everyone in the Checquy thought they knew what Thomas's powers were capable of, but some startling rumors had been going around. For a few moments, the Checquy had teetered on the brink of disaster.

And what would I do, she thought, if some Checquy Pawn did make a move against that girl and her brother? Would I stand between my people and their worst enemy?

And at that moment, she knew she would. She absolutely would. She had been given a task: she was responsible for Odette Leliefeld. If anyone lays a finger on her, they'll lose it.

"All of us will work together," the Prime Minister was saying solemnly. "I expect full cooperation between security personnel, the military, elected officials—indeed, every organization represented in this room. Most encouragingly, our new friends in the Broederschap have already pledged their services and their expertise to both track down their treacherous former comrades and assist the victims." This announcement was met with cautious, measured applause.

"This will take a tremendous amount of organization," the Prime Minister went on. "Everything will be coordinated through a central authority. It has been decided that my longtime friend Bishop Raushan Attariwala will oversee our efforts, and he, along with the Lady and Lord of the Checquy Group, will be reporting to my office."

"And there's the icing on my fucking cake," said the Rook.

"This rare opportunity to share the truth is a gift that I am grateful for," said the Prime Minister. "All of us will have to turn to each other in future days for support, both emotional and professional. But I am confident that, with God's grace, we will emerge from this challenge, as we always have, stronger and wiser."

The applause that greeted this sentiment was heartfelt but hardly thunderous. The audience appeared to be contemplating the immediate future and not finding it especially palatable.

But at that point, the orchestra struck up a lively tune, waiters once again started circulating with drinks (which were noticeably more intricate, and presumably more alcoholic, than the previous wines, champagnes, and fruit juices), and a few people began to dance, although they did not seem particularly enthusiastic about it. The chatter that resumed in the hall was of a different tone than before.

Felicity was not at all certain what she should do. The Rook was talking to her EA in low tones, and Mrs. Woodhouse was taking notes very swiftly on a small tablet. Leliefeld was still tense and was answering Alessio's questions with an abstracted air. The boy looked utterly shocked by the Prime Minister's revelations, and as Leliefeld told him more, he seemed about to burst into tears.

Oh, crap, comforting distraught kids is so not in my job description, Felicity thought awkwardly.

Rook Thomas, Sir Henry has invited you for drinks in the Reading Room in fifteen minutes."

And here it comes, thought Myfanwy grimly.

"Thank you, Marilyn," she said. "Please let him know that I'll head there immediately—this dress hampers my progress a little." The Lord's EA smiled and nodded. It would not do for various key figures to leave the party all at once; it would draw notice. "Ingrid, it will be closed-door; could you please stay here and keep an eye on the situation?" Her assistant nodded. "Menaz, Sewell," she said to her bodyguards, "let's go."

As she moved through the room, she caught snatches of conversation. Light touches of her power on the bodies of the guests revealed tensed muscles, churning stomachs—even some trembling hands.

The Prime Minister's revelation about the Antagonists has hit them hard, she thought. And it will spread. The news has already escaped this room. The waiters are telling the kitchen staff and they're telling the security guards. It will be all through the Checquy by this time tomorrow. This could throw everything into the toilet.

As she left the room, Myfanwy looked back, and her eye was caught by the figure of Alessio standing small in the crowd. For a moment, he wasn't a boy in a suit at a party he was too young to be at. Suddenly, Myfanwy pictured him as one of those children who were dressed in suits before being put into coffins. Guilt flushed her face. So much relies on the choices we make, she thought. That boy there, and all the boys and girls at the

Estate, and all the people in the Checquy, and all the Grafters, and everyone else. So many lives relying on me.

When they arrived at the Reading Room, one of the guards checked and confirmed it was empty before Myfanwy went in alone and closed the door behind her. The room was dim, and most of the light came from a fire crackling in a large fireplace, with a few lamps contributing a negligible glow. Dark oak bookshelves lined the walls, and the gilt lettering on the books' spines caught the flickering light.

She settled herself in a leather-covered armchair, taking a moment to arrange her dress's train about her feet. *Honestly, I can't wear a nice dress without some ridiculous bullshit ruining the evening.* She closed her eyes and thought.

Earlier that evening, she had sat in a concealed chamber that opened off the corridor to the assembly room. The room was small, designed to hold one or two soldiers. It, and others like it, had been built against the possibility that the Apex might someday be besieged and breached by an enemy. Checquy warriors could be salted throughout the building to burst out to attack intruders. The Rook had sat gazing through a cunningly hidden spy hole as, in dribs and drabs, the Grafters walked by on their way to the party. She had gently run her powers over them with the softest touch she could muster. There had been some extraordinary features and designs in the bodies of the guests but none was wearing any face but his or her own.

Immeasurably relieved, she had immediately reported her findings to the Lord and Lady. *Did they tell the Prime Minister? Is that why he made his announcement?* she wondered. *Or did he simply think revealing privileged information would make him look powerful?*

The door opened, and the Prime Minister entered, accompanied by the forbidding figure of Bishop Raushan Attariwala. The Bishop's eyes tracked Myfanwy as she stood and walked up to greet the head of His Majesty's Government.

"Excellent speech, Prime Minister," said the Rook.

"Thank you. It's going to mean a hell of a lot of work for a lot of people, I know," he said. "But this situation must be addressed immediately."

"I quite agree, sir," said Myfanwy. At that point the door opened again and Sir Henry entered.

"Sorry about the delay, Prime Minister," said Henry. "Had to wait a bit after you'd departed. Didn't want tongues wagging, not that they'll lack for things to talk about."

"Will the rest of the executives be coming?" asked the Prime Minister as he settled himself into one of the seats.

"We thought it best not," said Sir Henry. "The absence of the entire Court from the reception would draw questions. We'll brief them later. Now, drinks. Port, Myfanwy?"

"Yes, thank you, my Lord," said the Rook.

"Prime Minister?"

"Please."

"Raushan?"

"I'll take it," said the Bishop, "but you know I'll just be holding it in my hand for the look of the thing."

"Of course," said the Lord of the Checquy. "And a tonic water in case you actually get thirsty?"

"Much obliged."

"Surely the Belgians must have pictures of these extremists," said the Prime Minister. "Since they're former operatives of the brotherhood."

"Yes, indeed," said Myfanwy. "They have already provided us with detailed files."

"When do you propose to make the photographs public?" asked the Prime Minister.

"We have been advised," said Bishop Attariwala heavily, "that there would be little point."

"Little point?" repeated the Prime Minister incredulously. "Raushan, if we can show the public that we have already identified the culprits, it will do a great deal to reassure people."

"We quite understand, Prime Minister," said Bishop Attariwala. He looked over to Rook Thomas. "It seems, however, that these targets are quite capable of changing their appearance."

The PM's face twisted in distaste. "I really loathe this sort of shit," he said. "It's difficult enough running a normal country without all these abnormal issues cropping up."

"That's why you have us, sir," said Myfanwy.

"Yes, it appears to be doing me a mountain of good," he replied sharply. "Your function is to keep this kind of thing from affecting the citizens of this country. I would not say that you are succeeding at the moment." The Rook flushed. "These attacks have come as a result of this...amalgamation that you have brought to us?"

"Yes, sir."

"And you think it possible that these radicals might still have contacts among their old allies? Even within the Checquy itself?"

"Yes, sir," she said quietly.

"I cannot take this risk. The Checquy must not be divided against itself, Rook Thomas. The nation cannot afford that. And it cannot afford to have an enemy that is willing to use unnatural weaponry against the public. The clouds of gas were plausible—just. But Sir Henry advises me that the extremists are escalating. They are angry and they are reckless. The next attack might be impossible to explain away. It would change the world forever."

"I don't believe they would do that, sir," said Rook Thomas.

"Oh?" said Bishop Attariwala. "Why not?" His eyes narrowed. "After all, from what we've heard of these 'Antagonists,' they could have unleashed monsters like at the Isle of Wight, or worse. Why are they being so discreet?" He pursed his mouth sourly when he realized that he had described the suffering and mutilation of hundreds of innocents as discreet.

"The same thing that keeps the Checquy discreet," said Myfanwy simply. "Upbringing."

"What?" asked the Prime Minister, bewildered.

"It's the Estella principle," she said. "If you take a child and teach it to hate and fear something from before it can understand language, it will be supremely difficult for the child to overcome that. Like graduates of the Estate, these Antagonists have been brought up to keep themselves secret at all costs.

"The Broederschap taught them to be afraid of more than just the Checquy," continued the Rook. "The Antagonists will be frightened of revealing too much in public, in case they draw the attention of other predators."

"Marvelous, so they just reserve the patchwork thugs for attacks on Court members," said Sir Henry.

"They don't hate the public," said Myfanwy. "They just hate us."

"This all sounds very speculative, Thomas," said the Prime Minister dubiously. "I was not elected to take chances with the well-being of this nation. And you were not appointed to your position to do so either."

"No, sir."

"Any more attacks of this sort, and drastic steps will have to be taken. It is not essential that the Checquy merge with this brotherhood, but it is essential that this problem be solved."

"I understand, Prime Minister."

"Two days, Miss Thomas. That is all I can give you."

"Sir."

"Sir Henry, Raushan, is this acceptable to you two?"

"Very reasonable, Prime Minister," said Bishop Attariwala. The Lord of the Checquy nodded.

"Forty-eight hours from now, then," said the Prime Minister. "If the problem isn't solved one way, you solve it the other. Quickly and quietly. It is now"—he looked at his watch—"ten past nine. At eleven past nine on Sunday, the Grafters will no longer be a problem."

"I'll begin making the arrangements," said Rook Thomas quietly.

"I expect we'd better get back to the party, then," said Bishop Attariwala finally. "Myfanwy, you and I will have a little chat later."

"Yes," said Thomas. She rose as the men left and then placed a telephone call. "Ingrid, can you please come to the Reading

Room, and bring Security Chief Clovis." She sat down again, brooding in the shadows.

Two days. The Prime Minister has given me two days. But that presupposes that the Antagonists won't do anything in the meantime. If there is another attack, then all bets are off.

Why are they delaying? Is it to build up tensions in the Checquy? If that was their goal, then it was certainly succeeding. When the Prime Minister had revealed the true nature of the Antagonists to the guests at the reception, there had been a moment when she had genuinely feared the Checquy would turn on the Grafters present.

What would I have done then? she wondered. Would I have used my powers against my own people? To protect a peace they don't want? Or would I have stood aside and let them kill our guests in front of civilians? And what was she to do now? The tension would only heighten as word of the Antagonists coursed through the ranks.

It would take so little, even now, Myfanwy thought. A simple strike, a simple wound, placed precisely, and this peace will be smashed forever.

She wondered if the Antagonists had agents within the Checquy who were feeding them information. The Grafters had possessed such spies, after all, although Ernst had finally turned over the names. They knew when we'd be leaving Hill Hall, she mused. They had attackers waiting for me on the road.

Suddenly, ridiculously, she wished she could speak with Thomas—the first Myfanwy Thomas, the woman who'd worn this body before she herself came into existence. Thomas had been shy and meek, but she'd possessed years of experience and training. She would have given good advice, or at least been someone Myfanwy could confess her fears to, could show weakness to.

I have to ensure that nothing happens in the next two days. How can I make the Antagonists wait? And then the revelation came to her.

Odette! They won't strike without retrieving her. Christ, look at the effort they went to before. Thank God Clements was prevented from killing her when I gave the order or we'd have no leverage at all!

I need to place her somewhere beyond their control, somewhere they cannot access but that raises no questions. I can't simply put a hundred bodyguards around her — Ernst and the Broederschap would know there was a problem, that the Checquy does not trust them. And I can't send her overseas, or the Antagonists will feel free to strike on British soil. Myfanwy turned the problem over and over in her mind, certain there was a solution.

There was a knock on the door, and her EA entered, followed by Security Chief Clovis. Myfanwy explained the situation quickly, and they both looked horrified.

"So, Rook Thomas," said Ingrid. "The Prime Minister..."

"Yes?"

"He's given you two days to eliminate the Antagonists."

"Yes," said the Rook.

"And if you don't, he means to shut down the negotiations?"

"In a manner of speaking."

"Which would mean war," said Clovis grimly.

"Maybe," said the Rook. "Although if I manage to make all the arrangements I need to, it might simply mean a quick, discreet one-sided slaughter."

As they emerged from the Reading Room and made their way back to the reception hall, Myfanwy kept turning the problem of Odette over in her head. There must be a way, she thought. But if there isn't, I need to prepare for every other eventuality.

"Ingrid, I'll need to talk to the team leaders of the Barghests immediately," she said. "All of the domestic ones." I'll need them ready if Sunday comes and we have to eliminate Ernst and the Broederschap.

When they came to the assembly room, she looked about automatically for Odette. I'm going to feel really bad if she's still standing alone with no one to talk to except her kid brother and Clements.

The room still seemed to be somewhat subdued and there wasn't much cross-pollination between groups. Finally, she saw the Grafter girl talking to a tall man in his late twenties. Judging by their postures and hands, it seemed to be quite a civil conversation. At least, no one was getting slapped or stabbed.

"Who is that?" she wondered aloud.

"He's a Pawn," said Ingrid. "Louis Something. He works in Analysis and Assessment." As they watched, the Pawn stepped out on the dance floor and extended a hand to Odette. She took it, and even from a distance they could see that she was both nervous and delighted. The two began to waltz, easily and beautifully.

"Did you tell him to do that?" asked Myfanwy.

"No, I didn't," said Ingrid. "I don't think anybody ordered him to do that." She was smiling as she watched the two dancers. "So maybe there's hope for us all yet."

Yes, maybe, thought Myfanwy grimly, the ultimatum she'd just received replaying in her head. But not much.

43

It had been a pretty good evening all in all, thought Odette in satisfaction. Some low points, certainly, but the high points had outnumbered them.

And the Prime Minister's speech was very encouraging, she thought. He really put his support behind the negotiations. After that, she and Alessio had milled around a bit, and Alessio had continued to interrogate her frantically about the Antagonists. Of course her brother had known them all, but he'd been ignorant about their turning against the Broederschap. He'd been told a milder version of the story that had been given to Clements—that they had been killed by a supernatural enemy. He was particularly distraught to hear about Dieter, whom he'd known well. Odette had tried to keep her answers reassuring, but it was hard to sugarcoat the fact that his family was responsible for the atrocities they'd been watching on television all evening.

People had begun looking at the two of them with increasing distaste, and Alessio was almost in tears when, with impeccable timing, the headmistress of the Estate, a well-rounded woman with a German accent, swooped down and engaged him in conversation about his studies and the field trips. Odette, grateful for the break, had looked around for Clements and seen her a few feet away, talking to an acquaintance. Felicity had nodded permission for her to mingle, so Odette drifted through the crowd, listening to snatches of conversations.

"...either have to apply for emergency funding or dig into some of the bequests. I simply have no idea to what extent the government will pay for all this..."

"...I think there were traces of nut in that little pastry thing, does anyone have an epi-pen..."

"Hush, there's a Grafter walking by."

"I love her dress."

"Yeah, but God knows what's squirming underneath."

At that last remark, Odette had moved away, focusing on keeping her countenance calm, her complexion unflushed, and her spine straight. You never thought it was going to be easy, she told herself. And one speech from the Prime Minister isn't going to change minds instantly. For a moment, she considered taking refuge in one of the little clots of Grafters, but then decided against it.

I've sculpted bones, delivered babies, and held off a gang of thugs, she told herself. I'm not going to be intimidated by some snobs at a cocktail party. Taking even herself by surprise, she abruptly turned a sharp ninety degrees to the left and stood expectantly by a little clump of Checquy operatives. Their conversation died away awkwardly.

"Good evening," she said brightly. "I'm Odette Leliefeld. It's a lovely party tonight."

Now make pleasant conversation, you fucks.

And make pleasant conversation they did. It was clumsy and stilted at first—none of them had actually met or chatted with a Grafter before—but she had to give them credit, they rallied magnificently. As it turned out, they all worked in Analysis and Assessment: three Pawns (two men and a woman), and three Retainers (two women and a man). They'd discussed trivial things to begin with: the orchestra, the food, the men's suits. Then they'd moved on to other, more important topics: the attacks on various British cities, the merger, the ladies' dresses. Everyone had taken care not to say anything that could be considered offensive, but Odette had taken extra care to condemn the attacks and mention that she'd been caught up in one.

"So, what are your preternatural abilities?" she asked during a lull in the conversation, and there was a pause. "Oh God, have I committed some supernatural faux pas?"

"No," said Pawn Grasby, whose first name she had forgotten. "Not at all. It's just that we're used to everyone knowing what we can do."

"I can summon and command wasps," said Pawn Harriet Collinge, whom Odette suspected of being a little bit tipsy. "Roger disrupts mathematics, and Louis can draw wasps to him."

"Very cool," said Odette. "Wait, so you can both do things with wasps? Are you two related?"

"Oh, no," said Louis. "Sorry, she does the thing with insects. I can attract white Anglo-Saxon Protestants."

"That must come in handy," said Odette.

"What about you?" asked Pawn Grasby curiously.

"Oh, I'm a regular little Swiss army knife," said Odette. "But nothing as impressive as maths, or, um, white people."

"Oh, come on," said Harriet.

I should give them something, thought Odette. Something they can understand.

"Okay, well, I can rearrange my muscles," she said. She held up her arm and concentrated, and they watched as ripples moved underneath her skin. There were some polite comments, although she suspected that they were used to much more impressive effects among their own. "It lets me perform incredibly tiny microsurgery better than any robot, but it takes a bit of time to arrange the muscles properly. Though I don't think of that as the coolest thing I can do..."

"All right, then, what's the coolest thing you can do?" asked Monique, one of the Retainers.

"It's going to sound terrifically nerdy," Odette cautioned them.

"We're analysts," said Roger, "we like nerdy things."

"We prefer them," said Harriet.

"I performed a heart transplant on an unborn baby."

There was a startled silence.

"That's actually way more cool than controlling insects," said Monique.

Then the extremely nice Pawn Louis Marshall had invited her to dance. She'd been conscious of everyone's eyes on her and him and was thankful that her dress had obligingly absorbed her perspiration, which had been copious. Then more couples had joined them on the dance floor, and suddenly it felt as if a dam had broken. The music swelled, and the party began.

At one point, Great-Uncle Marcel had tangoed by with the headmistress of the Estate. Odette saw Marie whirling with a man whose suit had steam pouring out the collar and sleeves. Odette herself moved from partner to partner, being as charming as she knew how to be.

The tempos changed, and she blessed her mother for insisting that she take dance lessons. She essayed a pavane with a man whose skin chimed whenever she brushed against it; she cha-cha'd with a man who was attended by a troop of hummingbirds that fluttered above him; and she did the twist with Harriet. There were even some slow dances. And always, she took the opportunity to say some pleasant words and leave a better impression than she formerly had.

Finally, a Pawn of the Checquy, with much urging from her comrades, had stepped up to the microphone and begun to sing. As far as Odette could tell, her voice was not supernaturally gifted—no strange emotions or sensations touched her from the sound—it was simply a lovely voice singing "At Last," written by Mack Gordon and Harry Warren. The lights dimmed overhead, and the room was full of dancers. A hand touched her arm, and she saw that it was Grootvader Ernst, dapper in his tuxedo.

"Kun je je voorvader deze dans?" he asked. Would you grant this dance to your ancestor?

"Met alle plezier," she replied with a smile. With all pleasure.

He was, of course, a good dancer. Centuries of practice ensured that. And there was a courtly dignity to the slow but stately steps he led her through.

"A big evening," he said. "Are you having a good time?"

"I am," said Odette. "They're just people, once you get to talking to them."

"Most people are," he said. "I am very proud of you, Odette. You have been a credit to us this evening."

"I think it will all work out, Grootvader." He didn't say anything but nodded, his face solemn. As the song drew to a finish, she stepped back and gave him a little curtsy. Then they joined in the applause for the singer.

"And that is the end of the evening, I believe," said Grootvader Ernst. "We shall make our thanks, and then it will be time to go back to the hotel." Making the thanks actually took another half hour; Odette circumnavigated the room, speaking with everyone she had danced with and then thanking the Court members. Alessio was nodding off on a chair against the wall and submitted to being guided up the stairs. Eventually she found Clements waiting by the door. The Pawn was quiet in the car but acknowledged that she'd had a good time.

The delegation was decanted at the front of the hotel. Yawning receptionists at the desk stood up straight when the elegant party glided by. As they walked through the lobby, Odette saw Pawn Sophie Jelfs sitting in the bar. I'm so glad she wasn't killed in the attack, she thought, and she smiled, putting on an expression of exaggerated relief. The Pawn looked exhausted and her hair was messy, but she held up a drink in toast and smiled back. She raised her eyebrows at Odette's dress and made an impressed face.

In Pawn Clements's room, Odette helped Felicity take off her dress. As the gown shivered and unclenched, the Pawn slumped a little and took a deep breath. "Thank you for lending me the dress," said Clements. "And putting all that work into tailoring it for me."

"It really was my pleasure," said Odette.

The Pawn gave the garment a wistful little stroke and then handed it back to Odette, wished her a good night, and closed her bedroom door. Odette wandered back into the room she shared with Alessio and carefully hung up the dress. She looked over at the bed, where her little brother was already asleep. Worn out by the revelations of the evening, he'd drifted off almost as soon as his head hit the pillow. Odette gave a moment's thought to picking up the tuxedo components that he had scattered across the room but then snorted and walked away. I'm not his mother, and if he shows up looking crumpled at some other event, that's his problem. It's how he'll learn.

In a fit of hypocrisy, she stepped out of her dress and just let it lie on the bathroom floor. But at least my dress will straighten itself out, she thought defensively. Once it's had a good meal of applesauce and been dusted with some paprika and cuprous sulfate.

As she ran her bath and added the various chemicals and powders, she thought wistfully of sleeping in an actual bed. There really is something extremely comforting about a pillow and a blanket, she mused. And you hardly ever wake up to find that your sheets have congealed into a solid around you. One of her fellow students had once mixed the chemicals wrong, and the staff had had to chisel him out. She contemplated just falling into the tub but remembered that she still had her makeup on. And the strategic underwear that she'd worn to suit the dress.

If Alessio came in to wake her up and found her in that, they'd both be scarred for life.

"Oh, fine. I'll be responsible, then," she said to no one in particular. She even remembered to put her headphones on before sinking blissfully into the steaming slime. I am going to sleep forever. And tomorrow is Saturday, she thought blissfully as her heartbeat slowed. I don't have to do anything.

Wake up!" the voice thundered in her ears. She thrashed in the slime, her brain jolting into action. As she opened her eyes, something floated down through the murk and clonked her on her forehead. She clutched at her forehead and instinctively opened her mouth to make a noise, and the slime rushed into her mouth. Oh, gross! Fuming, she clamped her mouth shut and scrabbled around for whatever had hit her. It was her phone. Apparently, her jerkings had yanked the cord of the headphones and pulled the phone into the tub. I may have to murder someone, she thought. When she surfaced, she saw that the murderee would be her brother. She spat out the mouthful of slime, which, though it smelled delightful, tasted like a combination of shampoo, antifreeze, and Bloody Mary mix.

"It's Saturday morning," she said acidly.

"Grootvader Ernst has called a meeting," said Alessio.

"It's Saturday morning."

"Everyone except me has to be there," he said.

"It's Saturday morning."

"It's in fifteen minutes, so you'll be eating breakfast there," he said, leaving the bathroom.

"But . . . it's Saturday morning," she said to the cruel, uncaring empty room.

Odette was well aware that she was not looking her most impressive as she entered the royal suite. A frantic shower had gotten most of the slime out of her hair, but it was still damp, and, in a moment of resentful rebellion, she had pulled on jeans and a T-shirt. It's Saturday morning, after all, she thought sulkily. They can't expect me to be wearing a business skirt the morning after a party.

As it turned out, everyone was dressed casually, which rather took away from her rebellious gesture. Even Grootvader Ernst, behind his newspaper, was wearing a button-down shirt without a tie or cravat. There was a contemplative silence in the room that suggested that nobody was particularly thrilled to be awake. Much yawning took place behind hands. Odette helped herself to the buffet that had been laid out and then slumped into her chair at the conference table. She realized that, in the present company, she would not be able to have her illicit coffee without receiving pointed remarks about her throat.

Resting her chin on her hand, she took a mouthful of scrambled eggs and looked resentfully up the table to where Grootvader Ernst sat. He was reading the Times, the front page of which was completely devoted to the attacks. Too tired even to turn her head, Odette moved her eyes in their sockets and saw that almost everyone was staring at their leader. He turned a page.

Thank God we were summoned early to watch you read the paper, she thought. Then everyone jumped as he scrunched the paper down and regarded them all.

"It is early," he said, "but there are things I want us to deal with immediately."

And that is as close as we are going to get to an apology.

"Last night went very well. I am proud of you all. You conducted yourselves admirably, and I am confident that the Checquy has come to terms with the problem of the Antagonists. It seems that we drastically overestimated what their reaction would be to our, ahem, insurrection. Last night I spoke with the Prime Minister, and he assures me that they completely understand the situation. He was especially grateful for our work in the aftermath of the attacks. Marcel's and Odette's efforts with the casualties have not gone unnoticed, and they have put us in a very strong position in the negotiations."

Well, if you want to take a selfless act and make it selfish, I suppose that's your privilege, thought Odette.

"Now, it is important that we continue to build upon this excellent foundation. I am aware that this is the Saturday morning after a long and exhausting week, but we must strike while the iron is hot and before the tumor spreads." The meeting attendees were quickly given assignments. To Odette's bewilderment, she received no task. Even Alessio has something to do this weekend, she thought. Her brother was going off with the school group for a day of various activities that would culminate in a night at the theater to see a production of A Midsummer Night's Dream. The next day, he'd go to the Victoria and Albert Museum, Sir John Soane's Museum, and then some famous restaurant.

No explanation was given for Odette's lack of orders, and when she offered to assist people, she was politely but firmly rebuffed.

"The Checquy provided the placements for the day," said Marie as she bustled off to address a million pressing tasks. "And you're supposed to stay in the hotel. Maybe they want you to keep an eye on your damaged bodyguard. Anyway, it's a day off. Enjoy it!" Odette nodded glumly. It was too late to go back to sleep, and even if she'd wanted to, the bathtub of gel would be cold. She returned to the suite, where Alessio was just heading out the door.

"Clements went down to the Checquy security floor," he said hurriedly. "She said she'd be back in a bit."

"Okay, you have a good time," said Odette. "I'll see you tonight." She turned on the TV and saw nothing but footage about the attacks. I don't need to see any of that. She sat on the couch and thought crabby thoughts about the world in general.

For God's sake, you're in a five-star hotel. There's a million things to do. Full of resolve, she stood up. World-class gym, a pool, excellent room service, a spa. And Clements to drag along to them all. To her mild surprise, that final prospect didn't depress her spirits at all. She picked up the phone and dialed Clements's number.

"Hello?"

"Hi, it's Odette. Are you busy?"

"No, we were getting a briefing, but it's over," said the Pawn. "Are you all right?"

"Yeah, I'm fine. What are you doing now?"

"I was going to—nothing," said Clements. "I don't have any plans."

"Well, I was kind of at a loose end," said Odette. "You want to go to the gym?"

"Oh," said Clements. "Okay, sure. Come meet me here and we'll go together."

Odette changed into exercise clothes and made her way to the elevator, stopping by Marie's suite to let her know that she was going off the floor, that she was taking her minder, and that she wouldn't leave the hotel or talk to strangers.

"That's good," said Marie absently. She was staring intently at her computer screen and typing feverishly. "You could do with some more time at the gym."

44

The two guards at the elevator nodded to her when she approached and waved off her explanation. "Clements alerted us to your intended movements," said one of them, pointing at his earpiece. As he spoke, the elevator slid open. Inside was a man wearing civilian clothes and a bored expression. Odette recognized him as one of the Checquy guards. He didn't have any weapons, but presumably he didn't need them.

"Going down," he said.

"So you're guarding the elevator all day?" she asked.

"This hotel has six elevators," he said grimly. "And as of last night, each one has a Checquy guard in it. Plus two in the service elevator."

"It looks like a plum posting," she said.

"This is what happens when you lose the poker game."

She made a sympathetic face and disembarked on the Checquy floor. It was very different from the Grafter floor. Still nice (although not quite as nice), but it had a different air about it. Probably because there aren't armed guards at every junction, she thought. Also, many of the doors were open. As she passed by, Odette couldn't help sneaking a peek in. They were in an almost military state of tidiness. Many rooms contained people doing things on computers, and all of the people looked startled when they saw her walk by.

Clements was standing in a room with another Pawn, a woman in shorts and a tank top who appeared to be covered in thorns. Despite herself, Odette looked at the twin beds, checking for signs of shredded sheets, but they were both immaculate. Maybe she can retract them, she thought. The thorny woman gave her a level look and nodded silently before Clements hurriedly ushered Odette out of the room.

"She's just coming off the night shift," the Pawn explained. "Best to leave her to sleep."

"Ah," said Odette.

"The Rookery upped security overnight, so they're hot-bunking it." She caught Odette's look of complete incomprehension. "That's where we schedule the shifts so that beds are always occupied."

"Well, if they're short of beds, it's fine if they want to share the ones in our suite," said Odette in the generous tones of a person who knew no one would be sleeping in her bathtub. "We're not using them during the day, after all."

"I'll let them know," said Clements. "So, you want to go to the gym? You don't want to go out?"

"I'm having a day at home, apparently," said Odette. "Everyone else got assignments. I was assigned to stay in the hotel."

"Which means I'm having a day at home as well," remarked Clements. "Well, then, the gym it is, I'll just—" She paused as her mobile rang and she saw that the call was from a private number. "One second, I'll just see who this is."

"Hello?"

"Pawn Clements, this is Rook Thomas. Don't say anything."

"..."

"Good. Shortly you're going to be assigned to a mission. Request permission to take Odette with you. Present it as your idea. Now hang up."

Clements terminated the call, and stared at her phone.

"Wrong number?" asked Odette.

"Survey," said Clements.

"Pawn Clements!" came a call down the corridor, and they looked over to see a Pawn leaning out of a doorway. "They want you in the ops room." Clements turned her gaze back to Odette.

"Why don't you come with me?" she said.

The operations room was actually a suite with an armed guard posted outside. She regarded Odette warily and had to mutter something into a throat microphone and, presumably, receive an answer in her earphone before they were let in. Inside, a number of people sat at desks that obviously did not belong to the hotel. They were all talking on headset telephones in low tones and typing madly. Whiteboards with grids marked on them lined the walls. Odette caught a glimpse of her own name paired with Clements's. One of the bedroom doors opened, and a man in tactical armor came out. She caught a glimpse of gun racks and other weaponry before the door closed. Were those halberds? she thought incredulously.

Clements led her over to one of the other bedroom doors and knocked. A call of "Come!" came, and they came. It was quieter in there; only two people sat at desks typing. The bed was covered in stacks of files. Near a low desk stood an extremely short person. As in, coming up to just above Odette's waist.

Alessio could have rested a drink on his head, although, judging by the man's manner, his muscles, and the two pistols in his shoulder holsters, that would have been the second-to-last thing Alessio ever did (the last one being dying messily while apologizing profusely). The short man was talking on one phone and scrolling madly on another. He glanced at them and held up an imperious hand for them to wait. Clements nodded, and they both stepped back and waited. And waited. Finally, Odette turned to Clements.

"He's not, like, a dwarf, is he?" she whispered. Clements looked at her and raised an eyebrow. "I mean, he's not a mythological dwarf? Like in Tolkien?"

"There's no such thing as mythological dwarfs," said Clements. "Commander Derrick isn't even a Pawn. The Checquy recruited him because he's brilliant at what he does. He arranged the security for that pop star who got drunk and made all those comments that managed to offend every major religion."

"Right!" said Commander Derrick, finishing his call. "Both of you sit down." They sat. He spoke with an Irish accent and had a deep, growling voice. "So, Pawn Clements, you're wanted at a site in the Scottish Lowlands. Some sort of manifestation in a church in a little piece-of-shit village up north. A few civvy deaths. They've got it contained to the building, but the Rookery wants you to scope the place out before they send in the team." The Pawn's brow wrinkled as she took in the order.

"A car will be along in a few minutes to take you to the nearest helipad," he continued. "They'll fly you to London City Airport, and from there a private jet will take you to Dundee. Briefing file will be in the car."

"Yes, sir," said Clement. She seemed a little uncertain and looked over at Odette. "Um..."

"It's all right, Pawn Clements," said Odette. "I know that you need to go. You have responsibilities."

"We'll assign another minder for her," said Derrick. "No problem."

"Yeah," said Clements. "Unless...you'd like to come along?"

"Oh!" said Odette, startled. When she thought about it, the idea was tremendously exciting. Certainly it would be far more interesting than staying in the hotel, and she was rather touched that Clements would invite her. She didn't have to ask me along. "Would that be allowed?"

"Buggered if I know," said Commander Derrick sourly. "I'll have to check with the Rookery, and that'll probably take longer than we can afford. Clements is supposed to be departing shortly. Maybe if we get permission, we can send you up after her."

He put a headset on and muttered some words into the microphone. As he waited for an answer, he stared at them. Odette heard a tinny little response come through the headset, and Derrick looked surprised.

"They say it's fine with them if it's all right with the Broeder-schap."

"I'd need to get permission from Grootvader Ernst," said Odette. "Although I really don't think he'd have any objection. He's always saying we should get out more. Do you know if he's in a meeting at the moment?" she asked Commander Derrick. He muttered into his headset and then shook his head at her.

"He's receiving a haircut from the hotel hairdresser."

"Thank you."

Odette was put through to Grootvader Ernst by his assistant and he approved the idea immediately. "It sounds like an excellent plan," he said. "It will do you good to get out of the city and away from the paperwork and tension here. Combat can be very invigorating."

"I'm just going as an observer. I don't think I'll be engaging in actual combat," said Odette doubtfully.

Although once this is done, I really should learn how to fight, she mused. I expect the Checquy will insist on it, regardless of whatever role I move into. Apparently even the librarians are death machines.

"Good to see combat done, anyway," said Grootvader Ernst. "Do me proud. Endeavor not to get killed or eaten. Oh, and don't forget to wear your coat."

535

"Yes, Grootvader." She sighed. "But be sure to let the Checquy know that you've given your approval. And you should probably make it clear to them that if I get hurt at all, you won't hold the Checquy responsible," she said and hung up.

"Is it likely to be dangerous?" Clements asked.

"You're a Pawn of the Checquy," said Derrick. "What kind of fuckin' question is that?"

"Not for me, sir," said Clements. "For her."

"Oh, well, I don't expect so," said Derrick. "You won't be going into the actual church, and she'll be staying in the command center. Plus she'll be surrounded by armed troops — the Rookery just sent up an additional lot of soldiers. Hard-pressed to find a safer place for her."

Clements looked a little relieved at this news. Then, with remarkable alacrity, the Pawn hustled Odette out of the operations suite, down to the front entrance of the hotel, and into a waiting car. As the car swiftly took off, Clements began reading through a file that had been waiting for them in the backseat.

"Can I take a look?"

"It's classified," said the Pawn, and she paused. "But then, so are you, and you're going to the site." She handed over the folder.

As she read it, Odette began to feel less and less certain about everything.

In Muirie, a village tucked away in the Central Lowlands of Scotland, no fewer than fifteen people were believed to have been killed by forces unknown over the course of the previous night. Believed was the operative word, since no bodies had been recovered, but the moans had endured for several hours before stopping abruptly shortly before dawn.

What in God's name happened? thought Odette. She skimmed over the history of the village itself.

Muirie was a small community of about two hundred houses clustered around a dour-looking church. Historically, its primary industries had been agriculture and a sort of willful illiteracy. The earliest mention of the place dated from a history of Macbeth, the king of Scotland, who had been struck down with food poisoning whilst passing through (an anecdote that was somehow left out of the play). Apparently, between bouts of vomiting, the monarch had expressed his mild incredulity that the town continued to exist, and that had been in 1050.

Since then, the village had grown somewhat in size, and the demographic had shifted from subsistence-level barley and cabbage farmers to information technology and legal professionals, who were drawn by Muirie's quaint alleyways, authentic gray stone houses, and the willingness of the local council to let newcomers tear the guts out of the homes' interiors and renovate (for a suitable fee).

The place had one village store (now stocked with a selection of gourmet ingredients) and no fewer than five exquisite little restaurants serving food of extremely specific ethnic origins. The village's children were bused to a nearby town for school, and most of the residents spent at least two hours a day commuting between their homes and their jobs in Perth (which boasted reliable Internet connections and legal problems that didn't exclusively involve sheep). Some residents predated the arrival of the young, wealthy professionals. These proto-Muirites tended to be older, somewhat weathered-looking, and prone to making pointed remarks about the kind of limp fancies who felt the village shop needed to stock six kinds of salt.

The church, as far as the Checquy could tell, was the origin of the problem. It was a squat structure that (judging from the photos) had not been so much built as laboriously chiseled out of a single sullen boulder of granite. As a result of its rugged construction, the building had withstood the centuries easily, and the village's new denizens had resisted their natural urge to renovate the interior, feeling that it was their duty to preserve it for future generations whilst simultaneously not attending services. It had caught the eye of a visiting academic, who exclaimed over its untouched qualities and returned a few months later with a team of archaeology graduate students and permission to use them.

The archaeologists had been laboring away inside the church with their little brushes and their distilled water and their digital cameras, and though they hadn't discovered anything astonishing, they were getting some insights into the history of the place and had found some nice examples of local craftsmanship. Then, on Friday afternoon, around the time that Clements had been grimly surveying her assigned dress, something had happened. It was not immediately clear what, but the caretaker's wife, who had been gardening out front, had heard a brief flurry of shouts coming from within, followed by faint moans and a sound like that of "a large dog when it laps at a bowl of water on a hot day."

Thoroughly unnerved, she had gone home and told her husband. The caretaker had rolled his eyes upon learning that his wife hadn't even dared to enter the church. He declared that he would stroll along over there, poke his head in, and make sure that everything was all right.

He did not return.

His wife waited for the rest of the afternoon. She calmly tried his mobile phone and got no response. She calmly called the pub, which had seen no sign of him. She then calmly decided to lock all the doors and draw the curtains and call the village constable.

The village constable, who was just sitting down to his tea, listened patiently to her story while his wife brought him a nice piece of fish. Fortunately, he had recently attended a course in Aberdeen for small-town police at which a woman (actually Pawn Lillian Wyldeck of the Rookery) had briefed them on what they should do if something a bit...unusual should pop up. He dug out the card with Miss Wyldeck's number and was assured by the calm voice on the other end that he'd done the right thing to call. He should go down to the church and keep an eye on it, she said, but he should by no means enter it nor let anyone else do so. Assistance was on its way.

The nearest Checquy contingent was two hours from Muirie, in Dundee, and they were all taken up in the nationwide alert about people's eyes melting in public places. Two junior operatives (a Pawn and a Retainer who were in need of some experience) were sent in a fast car to take stock of the situation. In the meantime, a police team was dispatched from the much closer city of Perth with very specific orders not to enter the building. They had quietly established a perimeter around the church and waited for the big boys to arrive from Dundee. Then one bright young spark on the team, eager to make a name for himself, had pointed out that this was daft, that they didn't know for certain what was wrong, and that people might be hurt in there. There was no strange sound that he could hear, and he was going in!

The bright spark led three of his team into the church. They opened the doors, and blinding light flooded out into the darkness. The four officers rushed in and the doors shut behind them. This time, there weren't even any screams. The rest of the police decided to wait quietly for the arrival of someone who was being paid enough to deal with this shite.

The two Checquy operatives who eventually arrived might have argued that they weren't being paid enough to deal with this shite either, but they did anyway. It turned out that the big boys from Dundee were actually young ladies, but the police still jumped to obey their orders. Their obedience mainly stemmed from the young ladies' assurance and authority, although it probably helped that the Pawn could influence the minds of men as a result of her astounding ability to emit pheromones, while the Retainer could influence the minds of men as a result of her having big knockers.

The Retainer approached the church cautiously, heard the aforementioned lapping sound, and backed away. Then she and her colleague made some phone calls.

Various things happened in quick succession:

1. The Checquy duty officer in Dundee reassured the Pawn and the Retainer that they had done the right thing.
2. Then that officer called and woke up her boss.
3. The boss, Pawn Mungo Kirkcaldie, called the Rookery.
4. The villagers were roused, herded onto the village cricket pitch, and given a garbled but alarming story about spores, toxins, and bacteria that might have been unearthed in the church. The villagers, who could imagine the value of

their homes dropping with every detail, conferred amongst themselves and decided to keep their mouths shut and not argue until they knew the extent of the problem. They were then evacuated to a lonely point in the countryside where hastily mobilized army troops were setting up a temporary quarantine and testing facility (one that featured no mobile phone reception so as to ensure the rest of the world did not take an interest).

5. A Checquy team, led by a yawning Pawn Kirkcaldie, left Dundee for Muirie.

6. Rook Myfanwy Thomas, who had gone to sleep only fifteen minutes earlier after finally getting home from the reception for the Grafters, got woken up.

This has been going on for many hours," said Odette, looking up from the file.

"Yeah," said Clements. There wasn't much more to tell; that was the point when Pawn Felicity Clements had been ordered to the site to assist in reconnaissance.

"Shouldn't the Checquy have moved in by now, rescued the people?"

"We have to be strategic about these things," said Clements, looking out the car window. "If Checquy operatives just charge in without planning, you end up with large swaths of the countryside that don't support life. There can be fallout."

"Like, nuclear fallout?"

"If only," said Clements. "There are fields in Cumbria where, for every hour you stand on them, you lose a year off your life span. In Bridewell, there's a house whose second story, if you ascend to it, will destroy your credit rating. And a pond on the Lizard Peninsula whose water melts your teeth together." Odette could feel her brow knitting in bewilderment, but she kept her mouth shut.

"Those people in the church, maybe they're alive, and maybe they aren't," said Clements, turning to her. "But the people outside, including the Checquy people, are definitely alive, so they get first priority. Checquy operatives are rare enough that it's irresponsible and unpatriotic to just throw our lives away." She looked out the window. "We're here."

They hurried through a hospital and up to the roof, where the helicopter was waiting for them. They lifted off and away, Odette looking down in delight at the city beneath them. Within minutes, they landed. They were met by a man in uniform coveralls who led them to a jet waiting on the runway. The craft was small, pointy, and exquisite inside, and it did not have to wait in line to take off. Instead, it weaved its way between the larger, bewildered-looking planes on the tarmac and zipped off into the sky without apology.

The flight up to Dundee went by swiftly, or at least it seemed that way to Odette, who was drunk on the landscape beneath her. Clements spent most of the time rereading the briefing files. At one point, the Pawn called the Rookery and asked for more information on the church, which was obligingly faxed through to the jet since no one's phone could display the floor plan on a useful scale.

From Dundee, another helicopter took them to Muirie. Odette looked curiously down at the town as they flew over it. "It doesn't seem particularly malevolent," she remarked. "Dour, but not malevolent." They were dropped off at one end of a shinty field, where a Retainer in body armor met them, ducking slightly as he ran up to help them out of the helicopter. As soon as they had disembarked and moved away, the aircraft took off.

"Welcome to Muirie," said the man. "I'm Peter Burrows, site manager."

"Pawn Felicity Clements and Miss Odette Leliefeld," said Clements, and they all shook hands. He didn't give Odette any wary looks, which she thought was nice.

"I'll take you to Pawn Kirkcaldie," said Burrows. "We're all ready for you." He led them off the pitch and through the village. There were only a few actual streets in the town but an abundance of little alleyways weaving between the houses.

"Quaint," remarked Clements as he led them through.

"I believe it's one of the reasons people like to live here," said Burrows. "Everyone loves a snickelway." Odette shot Clements a bewildered look.

"It's a word from the city of York. It means little streets and alleyways," the Pawn explained.

Some of them were very narrow, and several times the three of them had to go single file. Doorways opened off the alleys, presumably into the two- and three-story houses, all adjoining, that rose above them. Gray stone walls merged into gray stone walls and led up to steep slate roofs. Eventually, Burrows brought them to a courtyard with a few tables scattered under a large oak tree. "We've commandeered the pub as a base of operations—it's the only place big enough," he explained. "Except for the church, which is, of course, not available."

The main room of the pub was aggressively old-timey, with heavy beams across the low ceiling and creaky floorboards. Several tables had been pushed together to form a big one, and a group of armor-clad soldiers were eating at one end. On the other side of the room was an administrative area where people looked at computers, talked on radiotelephones, and perused large pieces of paper. Burrows introduced them to Pawn Mungo Kirkcaldie, a big military-looking man in his forties.

"Pawn Kirkcaldie, this is Pawn Felicity Clements and Miss Odette Lilyfield," said Burrows. Odette bit her tongue at his mispronunciation of her name.

"Ah, Clements, excellent," said Kirkcaldie. "Good to have you here, we've been waiting on you. And Miss Lilyfield, welcome. We'd better get on with it." He walked them over to a map pinned to the wall. "We've got troops ringing the church; they're on the roofs of the surrounding buildings and in the street," he explained, pointing out the positions. "They're mostly concentrated at the front, where the doors are, and the rear, where they've got that one biggish window. We're lucky there's not a lot of stained-glass windows in this building—the original builders of the church seemed to think windows were a wicked popish extravagance—so there's really only two points of access and escape.

"So, Pawn Clements, we want you to sashay over and take a peek in the church. Give us an idea of what's where before we go inside. I understand you need to be touching the building?"

"It'll make it easier and faster," said Clements. Several Pawns came over to strap some armor onto her and give her a headset. A Retainer handed her a nasty-looking submachine gun.

"Easy and fast is what we want," said Kirkcaldie, and he led them over to the front windows of the pub. "Now, that's the church over there," he said, pointing through the glass. "We'll send you across the street so you can lay hands on the back wall. There'll be sharpshooters covering you, but I'm also sending Pawn Pickhaver here." Pawn Pickhaver was a large man with a large chin and a large gun. "He has a trick where he can solidify light, so he can raise some walls around you if necessary, give you a bit of extra protection. Not that we expect any trouble."

"Fine," said Clements.

"Miss Lilyfield, you'll be staying in here with me," said Kirkcaldie firmly.

"I understand, sir," said Odette.

"We've heard from the historians at the Rookery and Apex House," said Burrows. "So far, their searches have revealed nothing ever happening at Muirie."

"No history of supernatural activity at all," mused Kirkcaldie. "Well, this town's had a pretty good run up until now."

"Not just no supernatural activity," said the aide-de-camp. "I don't think anything has ever happened here."

"Well, spontaneous shit happens," said Kirkcaldie. "That's what keeps us in work, eh? Let's get a move on, then. Clements, can you give us a running commentary?"

"I'm afraid not, sir," said Clements. "I've got to leave my body entirely to scan something outside it."

"Right. Then to begin with, just make quick forays and then zap back into your body to give us sketches of the situation. Once we've got an overview, we'll work out what we want in detail."

"Understood, sir. You don't need to know what's happened in there, do you? No past events?"

"Nah, just give us the present situation," said Kirkcaldie. It was clear he'd been briefed on Clements's abilities. "We'll figure out the past later. You take a look, tell us what you see, then we'll work out a strategy and go in."

Clements agreed, nodded to Odette, and then proceeded outside with Pawn Pickhaver. Burrows handed Odette a headset so she could hear Clements's commentary. She watched through the window as the two Pawns ran across the street, keeping low. When they reached the church, they crouched down against the wall. Clements knelt and placed her hand against the stone while Pickhaver stood ready with his gun.

"We're established. Going through the wall now," Clements said.

"Sentries, stand ready," ordered Kirkcaldie. There were several minutes of tense silence, followed by a couple of minutes of bored silence, followed by a minute or two of increasingly worried silence.

"I'm back," said Clements suddenly.

"What did you see, Clements?" Kirkcaldie asked.

"The place is empty, sir. The people have vanished."

"No bodies?"

"Negative."

"No bones, even?" said Kirkcaldie hopefully.

"Nothing, sir."

"Well, that's creepy as anything," said Burrows in a vexed tone.

"The place seems undisturbed," said Clements. "The aisles are mostly clear. There are some backpacks and cases between the altar and the pews. I'm guessing they belong to the archaeologists." She described tools lying about as if dropped, but "I'm not seeing anything," said Clements finally. "No life at all. Some small puddles of something."

"Blood?" asked Kirkcaldie intently.

"I couldn't tell. There's some spotlights on stands pointed out toward the door," Clements reported. "It looks as if that's the light the cops saw last night."

"When you go back in, try the ceiling," advised Kirkcaldie. "Bad shit always tends to drop down on you from the ceiling. It's like getting attacked by clichés."

"Copy that. I'll do one more sweep, then?" asked Clements.

"Please. And then we'll send in the troops."

"Yes, sir." Odette watched in fascination as Clements's body slumped a little against the church wall. After a few moments, however, the Pawn stood bolt upright.

"Sir, a big flagstone in the floor had moved while I was gone!" she reported frantically.

"Oh, the crypt!" exclaimed Kirkcaldie. "Of course!"

"Sir, something came out!" said Clements.

"What? What is it?" demanded Kirkcaldie.

"I'd have to look into the past to see it," said Clements tightly. "Which means I'll—" She broke off as something slammed against the rear wall of the church, punching a hole through the stone right by the two Pawns. Then something reached through the hole, grasped the stunned Pickhaver, and pulled him, shouting, into the church.

45

Felicity reeled. The horrendous noise and the impact of the hole being punched in the wall of the church had hit her like a thunderclap, and chips of stone had smacked her in the face. Dust was in her mouth, her ears were ringing, and her senses were smeared between her body and an area inside the church just in front of the altar. The horrible quickness with which Pickhaver had been snatched away had stunned her. Automatically, she peered after him and caught a glimpse of him being dragged so quickly by that thing that his body whipped back and forth against the pews. Then down he went into the crypt.

I should look in the crypt, she thought foggily. Get a better view of the thing. It had been man-size and skittered along on all fours. Then she heard a voice cutting through the ringing in her ears.

"Clements!" Kirkcaldie's voice was blasting. "Fall back to the pub immediately!"

Right, thought Felicity dazedly. The pub, right. Just let me get my bearings. She felt her muscles twitch as her entire consciousness settled itself into her brain, and then she was up and running toward the pub. She was distantly aware of Kirkcaldie giving other orders over the headset, but all she could concentrate on was getting across the grass to the street, and then across the street to the pub, And then I'll be safe, and Leliefeld will be safe, and—

The grass in front of her burst open, and a shape erupted out of the hole and landed in front of her. Felicity skidded to a stop, stumbling over her feet. It stalked toward her and she saw that it was human-shaped and green and yellow and black, like a poisonous frog. Its skin was wrinkled and caught the light as though it had been shellacked with slime. The seemingly feature-less face was covered with a membrane that glistened and moved.

Then flashes lit up at its sides and shoulders, and it twitched as if stung. She saw Checquy troops advancing with guns. Unfortunately, their bullets did not appear to be doing much harm. The creature was, most thoughtlessly, failing to crumple or even get punctured. It was, however, getting irritated, and it gave a wet, bubbling snarl through the membrane on its face. So it has a mouth somewhere behind that stuff.

She realized with a start that she was still clutching her gun. Maybe at closer range it will do some damage, she thought. Or at least buy me a couple of minutes. But by the time she brought it up, one of the Pawns must have managed to unlimber his powers, because a bolt of orange lightning lanced across from the pub and buried itself in the creature's body, which shuddered as it smoked. For a few moments, crackles of electricity danced across its skin, but then it resumed moving toward Felicity. She scrabbled backward and brought up her gun.

"You think that's all we've got, beastie?" she heard Pawn Kirkcaldie say over her headset. "Checquy, bring that thing down." And the Pawns let loose.

It was madness. Trails of green smoke wound over its body, raising blisters and bubbling skin. Frost spread in fern patterns on the monster's chest. The grass underfoot grew longer and twisted around the creature's feet, then a squealing scraped through the air as veins of copper spread through the vegetation and turned to rigid metal cuffs shackling its ankles. Patches of color were leeched from its skin.

A pair of razor-sharp hatchets whirled down from a nearby rooftop, buried themselves in its shoulder blades, then whipped through the air back to the hands of their owner, who threw them again and again. And not all of the Pawns' powers could be seen. For a few moments, for no apparent reason, the creature frantically clawed at its own face. Then it was slapping at the air at things no one else could see. Meanwhile, bullets continued to spray it, and Felicity fired her own weapon into its chest. Another bolt of reddish-yellow lightning erupted and the creature went to its knees. Finally, it fell backward, its feet still locked in those metal shackles.

Then, almost like an afterthought, a nearby Volvo was jerked away from its parking place and came cartwheeling thunderously across the road to land, nose-down, directly on top of the monster.

The echoes from the attack died away. *I will never use the word overkill again,* thought Felicity weakly.

"Nice job, people," said Kirkcaldie in her ear. "Very nice. Now let's take a breath, then we'll enter the church and see if that thing has left any victims alive." The troops on the ground began walking toward the wreckage, and several others descended from the rooftops, one of them backflipping easily down three stories and landing like a cat.

I'm going to have to scout out that crypt, thought Felicity. But first I could do with half a pint of something. She was rather pleased with herself. She hadn't been killed, she'd managed to get some shooting in, and she hadn't been ill. Maybe I'll make it a full pint.

Suddenly there were bursts of dirt and grass and tarmac all around as one, then four, then a dozen of the creatures came out of the ground.

Bloody hell!

The street went apocalyptic as each Pawn acted instinctively to attack the creature nearest to him or her. Light and sound exploded. A wave of cold swept over Felicity and, for a few hideous moments, everything looked upside down.

Then everything righted itself, and the world made sense again. Except for all the supernatural shit going down. Kirkcaldie was screaming something over the airwaves, so loud that Felicity had to tear her headset off, but now one of the creatures was looming right in front of her, its back to her as it held up a squirming Pawn with both hands and crushed the man's neck. Damn you! thought Felicity, and she suddenly had the barrel of her gun against the nape of the creature's neck and was pulling the trigger and emptying the clip. To her astonishment, the creature fell to the ground. Automatically, she slapped a fresh clip into her weapon. One clip left after this, the professional part of her mind reminded her.

Okay, what next? she thought, looking around.

Apparently, disaster was what was next, because other Pawns did not appear to be faring at all well against the creatures, who were now vaulting up onto roofs and going after the snipers. Pawns and Retainers were scattering, shouting to one another to fall back.

So extremely bad, thought Felicity. Leliefeld! I've got to get her out of here! Between Felicity and the pub, however, was a supernatural free-for-all, and the Checquy was not winning.

She would have to find a way around. Then she realized that the pub's windows were shattered and a cloud of black smoke was belching out.

Oh, I'm in so much trouble, she thought. The creatures, fortunately, were focusing on the Checquy troops who were attacking them and ignoring the one who was standing there, aghast. She saw one soldier, the man who had been shooting lightning, get pulled, yelling, into one of the holes in the ground.

All right, you can't help them armed only with moral outrage, she told herself. You need to fall back, find Odette, and keep her safe. Holding her gun low, she scuttled to her left, her eyes fixed on the gap between two houses. She ducked as a high-pitched whine filled the air behind her, and a human voice rose up in agony. As she hurried into the passage, she heard the unmistakable sound of a car exploding behind her.

Felicity ran down the curving alleyway, and the noise of the battle grew quieter. She paused, gasping for breath, and leaned back against the wall.

I will be calm.

Now prioritize.

First, check communications. She put the headset back on. There was only static. "Hello?" she said quietly into the microphone. "Pawn Kirkcaldie? Leliefeld?" No answer. Oh God, please don't let her be dead. Quite aside from the political ramifications of Leliefeld's death and the fact that it was Felicity's job to keep her alive, she actually liked the Grafter. It was impossible not to like someone when she saved your sight and sculpted you a dress and you saw her worried out of her mind about her little brother.

And what did I do for her? thought Felicity. I brought her here. It had been on orders, but still.

Second, take stock of equipment. She had two clips left, one in the gun, one on her belt, but since bullets seemed to have no effect unless you put the gun right against the napes of the creatures' necks, Felicity was not encouraged. One combat knife strapped to her thigh. You need to find yourself more weapons, locate that girl, and get her out of here. Do it now!

She looked up, startled, as something vaulted over the alley above her head. It was followed by two other somethings. She caught a flash of yellow, green, and black. The sound of gunfire echoed down to her.

I need to put some distance between me and the chaos and then circle around back to the pub. If Leliefeld isn't there, then at least my phone will be. She hurried down the alleyway, ignoring the passages that sprouted off it. Finally she came to a doorway set into one of the walls. It was locked, but she smashed the lock open, horribly aware of the noise, and slid into the house.

It was nice. Jarringly so, after the insanity outside. The owners had obviously spent a good deal of time doing the place up and selecting that couch to go with that rug to go with that chaise. She picked up the phone hopefully and was disappointed but not surprised to find it dead. Next step, look for weapons. There was a study upstairs with wooden bookshelves and a computer, but the desk was lamentably empty of handguns. Nor was there anything hidden in the bedside table, or even under the mattress of the master bed. It was a long shot, I suppose. The inhabitants of this house and, she feared, most of Muirie's denizens were too liberal to have shotguns. Okay, so improvise.

The kitchen provided two very nice large cooking knives, which she taped to her forearms. The leg from an exquisite antique table became a very passable (if somewhat curvy) club. She couldn't, however, find a map of the village, which would have been useful. From there, she hesitated. Streets or snickelways? If she used the streets, she'd probably find the pub much more quickly, but she'd also probably get killed much more quickly. Snickelways it is, she decided, and she let herself out the way she'd come in.

The alley was quiet except for the occasional distant screams, blasts of automatic gunfire, and, once, a sound like harps that shimmered through the passageways. Still only static over the radio. She took a moment to orient herself, using the plume of smoke rising into the air in the distance as a handy reference for the location of the pub. Then she set off at a trot, combat knife and club at the ready.

Felicity turned a corner and came to a T-junction, only to find herself in the middle of a standoff. On one side, a few feet from her, was a creature, poised to lunge. Facing it from several yards away was a woman in tactical armor. Behind her, filling the alleyway, was a roiling mass of water that stood like a wall.

"Oh, I beg your pardon," said Felicity.

"Pawn, fall back!" the woman barked. The water behind her grew still for a moment, and then a torrent poured forth, a deluge that, Felicity saw in astonishment, split around the woman before coming together and hammering its way down the passage. Felicity stepped back hurriedly and watched the wave sweep toward the creature. Then she realized that the cascading water was also pouring toward her. She turned to run but the flow swept her feet out from under her and sent her skidding and bouncing against the walls on either side.

By the time she was able to get to her feet, the torrent had died away, but she felt strangely disinclined to go back and see how it had all worked out. Instead, she took a different route and found herself facing an actual thoroughfare. She peered cautiously around the corner and couldn't see anything either threatening or promising.

This looks like it might go to the pub. Or at least in the general direction of the pub.

She proceeded cautiously, taking care to glance behind her every few seconds. Then a sound caught her ear.

There was a wet coughing off to her left, and she saw one of the creatures emerge from a snickelway opposite. She looked about and saw no escape routes on her side. The creature caught sight of her and stiffened. Think quickly. She ducked her head and, much to her own surprise, hurled herself through the window of the nearest house. She rolled to her feet, a little unsteadily, and then couldn't help but scream as the creature burst through the wall and skidded past her into the kitchen. Why didn't it just come in through the broken window? she wondered blearily. It was probably asking itself the same question as it pried its way out of the wreckage of the cupboards. The monster shook its head, almost human in its attempt to clear its thoughts.

They're resilient, she thought. I'll give them that. But not too bright. Then the thing focused on her, and she scrambled away up the stairs. She rounded the landing, bounded up the next flight, and then turned, club at the ready. She'd lost her combat knife in the trip through the window but tore the kitchen knife off her left arm.

Come on!

"Well, fucking come on!" she shouted. There was nothing there, no monster coming up the stairs. No sound of any movement in the house. Well, what does that mean?

And then it burst up through the floor directly behind her. Its hands closed around her head—No!—and in her horror, her mental defenses slipped and her powers flared. She had a fleeting impression of liquid pouring onto her face, and then she was back in her head, back in the present, and she stabbed behind her with the horrendously expensive Japanese cooking knife in her hand. To the surprise of everyone concerned, the knife actually went into the creature a little bit. Not a great deal, but enough that the beast let go of Felicity's head.

Felicity dropped to one knee, retrieved her club from the floor, and whipped it up as she stood, bashing the creature in the chin. Not that she believed for a minute that would kill it. Without stopping, she changed her grip on the club, took a step to the side, and twisted to hit the monster in its knee. It buckled, and she spun around, using her momentum to whack the creature square in its lack of a face. The monster toppled backward into the hole it had emerged from, its yellow fingers scrabbling at the rim. Again. She brought the club down on one of the hands, and this time it fell.

Keep going! She turned and ran up the next flight of stairs, heading for the roof. There might be creatures on the rooftops, but there's definitely one behind me and it's in a shit mood. She scrambled through a tiny bedroom with slanting ceilings and out through a dormer window. She dropped lightly onto the roof of the house next door and clung to the tiles as she made her way across the rooftops. Finally she let herself down in another alleyway. She wasn't sure if her recent movements had set her back or forward on her route, so she jogged until she found herself, purely by luck, on the pitch where the helicopter had dropped them off. Okay, now I just go to the pub the same way as before.

And then?

There was the temptation to turn her back on the village and run off into the countryside. The smoke hung thick in the air. Gunfire echoed, and she felt the occasional gut-churning sensation of a Pawn lashing out with his or her powers. Felicity didn't know what pushed her to walk back into it. Maybe it was the thought of abandoning her fellow Checquy operatives. Maybe it was years of lessons about duty and responsibility. Maybe it was because her charge Odette was in there. Maybe it was because her friend Odette was in there.

Maybe it was all those things.

So she went back in.

Now that she was oriented, she made her way to the pub with relative ease. She was just approaching the last corner before the courtyard when something rushed out of a side passage. Felicity dropped to her knee and held her last knife low, ready to stab up, but it held out a hand.

"Stop! Checquy!" It was a man, in armor. A tall black man with a shaved head, he had a distinctly military air about him. A long gun was slung across his back, and he was holding a submachine gun identical to Felicity's. "Trevor Cawthorne." A Retainer, she thought. Must have been recruited from the army. He held out a hand.

"Pawn Clements," she said, taking his hand and pulling herself up. "Felicity."

"Yeah, you scouted the church," he said. "I thought you would have got killed in the first confusion." Felicity shrugged. "Nice club, by the way."

"Thank you."

"Is that—that's not from a Clavell desk, is it?"

"Well, it was," she said.

"Shame," he tutted. "Wouldn't care for some ammunition, would you?" He drew a couple of clips out of his vest and handed them over. "You have to be right up to the creatures to have any effect, right in their faces, but not as close as you need to be with a club." Felicity gratefully accepted the clips and retaped her kitchen knife to her forearm. With a reloaded gun in one hand and her club in the other, she felt a little better. "You're keeping the club?" he asked.

"Sentimental value," said Felicity.

"Fair enough. So, why are you soaking wet?"

"Fortunes of war," she said. They quickly exchanged stories. Cawthorne was a sniper and had been on one of the roofs on the far side of the church. After those creatures had burst out of the ground all around the church, one had sprung up onto his roof and dragged his spotter down and toward a hole in the earth. He had hesitated only briefly before shooting the woman dead.

"A mercy, I think," he said. He pressed his lips together and closed his eyes for a moment. "I hope." He had seen a Pawn on the next roof grow several extra arms and grapple with another monster for a few minutes. He had shot at it, but his bullets had no visible effect, and then the creature tore the Pawn apart.

"Have you heard anything over the radios?" she asked.

"There was a few seconds' worth of shouting over the air from the chief, then static." After that, Trevor had beat a hasty retreat and was making his way through the alleyways back to the pub when he ran into Felicity.

"You didn't meet up with any other Checquy?" she asked.

"I saw two," he said, "both of them involved in fights. I went to help one, Sally, but the creature walked through her gunfire, snatched her up, and bounded up onto the roofs before I got within twenty meters. The other one was Jimmy Hourani; he was spraying that acid mist of his at three of the monsters. I fired a few bullets at them, but it's best not to get too close when the conflict gets, uh, eccentric. Some of my Pawn mates can get a bit carried away. Jimmy started flooding the alleyway with that stuff, and I got out of there. I take it you're heading to the pub too? For the backup radio and satellite phones?"

"Oh, yeah," said Felicity. "Those would come in handy. But I'm also looking for a girl from our side. She was in the pub with Pawn Kirkcaldie when things got edgy."

"Right, the guest you brought." Cawthorne nodded. "I heard about it over the radio when you arrived. She was some kind of VIP?"

"Well, she's an I, anyway," said Felicity. The Retainer's eyebrows went up. "And a P as well," she conceded.

"Let's see if she's around, then," said Cawthorne. "Shall I lead the way?" They proceeded around the corner and into the courtyard. The back door of the pub hung on its hinges, and they waited for a moment, listening for any sounds, before they ventured in, guns at the ready. Felicity found herself praying as she went in. Please. She didn't even know what she was praying for.

But this certainly wasn't it, she thought. The front room of the pub was empty except for the corpse of a soldier sprawled awkwardly on top of the beer taps. There was, however, a gaping hole in the middle of the floor. Damn it, they came up in here as well. The windows had been blown out, but there was no sign of the thick black smoke she had seen pouring out of the building, nor of any fire. The place was riddled with bullet holes, however. Through the windows, they could see that the area around the church was now deserted, no sign of either the monsters or any Checquy people. Acrid smoke from burning cars wafted over the street.

"It's not looking good for the chief," said Cawthorne. "Or any of the lads and lassies who were in here." He shook his head over the dead man. "Pawn Lenton. At least he went down fighting." Felicity looked at the corpse—instead of hands, long stone blades projected from his wrists, scraps of that yellow and green skin fluttering on the ends.

"The others?" asked Felicity. "Any sign?"

"Either scattered or down the rabbit hole," said the Retainer grimly.

Did they take Odette? she thought.

"Can you stand guard for a sec?" she said.

"Why, do you need to go to the lav?" he asked. "Because I think we can find a slightly more secure place than a building with a gaping hellhole in the floor."

"No, I'm going to take a peek into the past."

"Fine," he said. "But make it fast, and move back from the hole a bit. If something comes out, I want to shoot it before it snatches you." She nodded and sat where Odette had been sitting. Cawthorne watched as her body stiffened and her eyes went distant, and then he turned his attention back to the rest of the world.

Felicity returned to her body a few minutes later to find that Cawthorne was kneeling down by the windows, his long rifle out at an angle. He held his finger to his lips and gestured for her to get low. She joined him, and he pointed down the street to where one of the monsters was prowling. She lifted her weapon.

"Any problems while I was gone?" she whispered.

"Just our friend down the lane there," he replied in low tones. They watched tensely as the creature moved along the street. Finally, it entered one of the snickelways and vanished from sight. They relaxed slightly.

"So, what're the results of your trip into the past?"

"As soon as the creatures emerged outside, Pawn Kirkcaldie ordered his aide to take Odette out the back. A few moments later, that hole opened up in the floor and three of the things came out." She didn't mention how relieved she had been that Odette had escaped. "Four of our people were pulled down into the burrow, including Kirkcaldie, I'm afraid." His face was grim. "The smoke I saw came from a Pawn. A creature pulled his arm off, and it poured out of him. Then his body evaporated."

"Cutler," he said. "A good man. Good friend. But your girl got away?"

"Yes, or at least away from here. But I don't know where she went," said Felicity.

"Can you track her with your powers?"

"I could, but it would take a while. However, I have another way." She backed away from the window, retrieved her handbag from where it lay in a corner, and produced her mobile phone. "I'll give her a call."

"That reminds me," said Cawthorne. There were several large plastic cases in the kitchen of the pub, and he cracked one open. "Satellite phone. And more ammunition. But I think we should find somewhere a little more secure before we start making calls."

"I don't think there's anywhere particularly secure in this place," she said with feeling, but they made their way back through the snickelways to a nearby house and briskly broke in. From a bedroom on the second floor, Felicity began to dial.

"Wait. Text her," suggested Cawthorne. "If she's hiding, the ring might give her away." Felicity nodded and thumbed in a message.

RU OK? Is it safe to ring you?

The answer came back straightaway.

Yes.

Felicity called her immediately.

"Clements?"

"Odette!" exclaimed Felicity. Thank God.

"You're alive! Are you all right?"

"Yes. Where are you?" asked Felicity. Odette explained that she and Burrows were in the attic of a house on the outskirts of the village. "Do you have an address?" For all the good it will do. As it turned out, she did have an address, the apparently resourceful Burrows having snatched some mail from the letterbox before they'd hidden. "Okay, hold on a sec." She turned to Cawthorne, who had been talking intently on the satellite phone.

"The Checquy is aware of the situation. They're sending backup troops," he said. "They should be here within the hour, and then they'll march through and kill everything that's not us."

"Okay, so, we'll just hole up here and wait?" she said.

"Probably easiest," he agreed. Felicity put the phone back to her ear.

"Odette, reinforcements are on the way. We're going to wait until they arrive. Okay? Odette?"

"Felicity, there's something moving about downstairs," came the whispered reply. "I think there's more than one." She sounded terrified.

"Keep quiet," said Felicity. "We're on our way."

"We are?" said Cawthorne in surprise.

"We are," said Felicity firmly. She slung the gun back on her shoulder and took up her club. "Let's go."

How are we going to find them?" asked Cawthorne, following her down the stairs. "This place is a maze."

"Internet directions," said Felicity, holding up her phone.

"It won't have the alleys on it," he warned. "We'll be using the streets."

"Then you'll want to have your big gun ready," she said, and she opened the front door. According to her app, Odette's temporary address was two minutes' drive away. "Let's run."

They ran, taking care to keep to one side of the street. Out of the corner of her eye, Felicity saw a flicker of green and yellow as a creature let itself down from a roof.

"Keep going!" Cawthorne said to her as he stopped and turned to face it. "I'll take care of it!"

"Thanks," gasped Felicity as she ran on, but she didn't think he heard her. Behind her, there were rifle reports, then silence. She couldn't even look back to see what had happened; she had to keep on running. Then she heard footsteps and tried to speed up. She fumbled for her gun, ready to swing around and fire.

"It's me!" shouted Cawthorne from behind her. "Keep running! They don't respond well to getting shot in the middle of the face!" He drew level to her. A bit fitter than me, she acknowledged. Rounding the corner onto Odette's street, they saw two creatures prowling about outside one of the houses. "Machine guns!" barked Cawthorne. "Faces!" The creatures whirled toward them, and the two Checquy operatives slowed as they brought up their guns and fired.

Cawthorne was correct—the middle of the creatures' faces, like the napes of their necks, seemed vulnerable to bullets. The two they shot fell to the ground almost instantly.

"That's Odette's house!" Felicity wheezed. There were creature-size holes in the wall—Why make more than one hole? she thought—and the two operatives eased their way through them. Maybe those we killed made the holes, she thought hopefully. Cawthorne silently touched her hand and pointed upward. There were more holes punched in the ceiling. They're really not very clever monsters. She heard movement above but couldn't tell if it was human or otherwise. Guns at the ready, they went up the stairs.

The landing was empty, but there were no holes in the ceiling. So they might not have gotten into the attic yet, she thought. She was about to call out quietly for Odette when two of the creatures stalked out of a bedroom into the hallway. Ohhhh, shit. The two pairs looked at each other, and then Cawthorne said from behind her, "Shoot 'em."

Felicity immediately pulled the trigger, but, with that horrible quickness, the creatures had ducked back into the bedroom.

Advance or wait? she wondered. There was a crash behind her. She whirled to see that one of the creatures had punched through the wall of the corridor, emerged between the two operatives, and smacked Cawthorne's gun out of his hand. Now the Retainer was backing away, holding his hand against his chest in a manner that suggested all was not well inside. The creature stalked toward Cawthorne, ignoring Felicity. The sniper looked at her and mouthed, Run! Then the monster slapped out, slamming him against the wall.

Run, she thought. What a good idea. Instead, she stepped forward, aimed the gun at the nape of the creature's neck—I've been here before—and fired. The creature jerked, went to its knees, then fell facedown on the floor. Cawthorne slid down the wall next to it and looked up at Felicity.

"Where's the other one?" he said weakly. Felicity whirled around and saw the second monster coming into the hallway. She fired—or she would have if she'd had any bullets left. Just as she dropped the gun and clasped both hands around her club, a noise came from the ceiling above them.

Everyone, including the monster, looked up.

Then they looked back at each other.

The creature cocked its head, gathered itself, and leapt up, punching through the plaster. Felicity heard Odette screaming. "No!"

Where's the ladder? Where's the hatch? She saw it set into the ceiling down the hall and ran to it. Behind her, Cawthorne was calling something, but she was too focused on pulling the steps down and scrambling into the dim attic.

Burrows was dead, she saw that immediately. His body lay broken by the hole in the floor. Odette was farther back, where the roof angled down. The creature prowled toward her. The Grafter girl was brandishing a scalpel in one hand, and a spur projected from her other wrist. She looked terrified.

The creature turned to Felicity, and Odette made a break for it. As she darted forward, the beast spun and raked her back with its fingers. It had no claws that Felicity could see, but under its touch, the material of Odette's coat parted, and then there was a horrendous fanning spray of bright red blood. Odette collapsed facedown onto the floor.

"No! Motherfucker!" Felicity screamed and lunged forward. There wasn't room to swing her club, but she jabbed it at the creature's knee. The club glanced off and she lost her grip on it, but it made the creature pause, and she wrapped her arms around its wet neck and hauled it backward, tangling her legs around it so that it came down onto her. Her breath was knocked out of her. The monster scrambled to get up, but Felicity twisted and kicked out wildly, not letting it find purchase. "I will kill you," she said through gritted teeth. She scrabbled with one hand for the knife taped to her other arm. Then out of the corner of her eye, she saw Odette moving a little.

Still alive, she thought.

"Get away!" Felicity said, wheezing. Odette didn't get away. Instead, the Grafter got to her knees and crawled over. She put her hand to the struggling creature's chest and felt about. Then she put the point of her scalpel to the middle of its torso and shoved up. The blade merely scratched across its slimy hide. "It's useless — go!" Odette set her face and pushed her sleeves back, and Felicity saw the muscles in her arm jerk and shift unnaturally under the skin. The Grafter winced in pain, and then she bore down on the blade once more. The instrument slid into the monster.

The creature stopped its struggles for a moment, as if surprised, but then resumed them. It flung its head back and missed giving Felicity's skull a hammer blow by centimeters.

"A lovely effort," said Felicity through clenched teeth, "but please go!" Odette pulled the scalpel out and held up her other hand, and her spur slid out. She plunged it into the cut, and her brow furrowed. Poison, thought Felicity. Maybe... The creature tensed, and then kept fighting. Felicity's muscles were tiring, and the monster's strength was getting the better of her. "More!" gasped Felicity. "Use everything!" Odette pushed the other spur in. The creature was pushing up off the floor. Odette's face twitched, and the monster faltered. "Again!"

And it all stopped.

Oh, thank Christ, thought Felicity. The monster lay limp, not even twitching. With an effort, she rolled it off her. Odette was on her knees, breathing heavily, her head bowed. She helped Felicity sit up, and then the two women held each other tightly.

It was unclear who was more shocked by the hug, but neither let go immediately.

When they drew back, Felicity saw blood all over her hands.

"Your wound!" she exclaimed in horror, running her hands over Odette's back. "Lie down on your stomach, we need to get pressure on it!"

"It's fine, it's not me," said Odette. "It's just my jacket."

"Your jacket?"

The Grafter girl held up a fold of her coat. "It's woven crab cells," she said. "It can solidify into armor, although apparently it's not quite strong enough to resist these things."

"You nearly gave me a heart attack," said Felicity. "Are you okay?" She noticed that the Grafter's right arm was hanging weakly.

"I think I tore some muscles in my arm," said Odette. "I had to rearrange them to get the scalpel in, and I couldn't do it properly. They're not designed to give extra strength but I wrenched them into a position that let me do it." Felicity winced.

"Are you right-handed?"

"Usually," said Odette. She wrinkled her nose. "But not at the moment."

"Okay," said Felicity. "Let's go downstairs." With an effort, she got to her feet and scooped up her club. "Come on." Cawthorne was still sitting where she'd left him, his eyes closed, but he opened them as the women came down the stairs.

"Oh, you got her," he said. "Good." Felicity made the introductions, and Odette one-handedly examined his injuries. The diagnosis was not good, but it was not as bad as it might have been. Broken forearm from where the monster had slapped his gun away. Broken ribs and possible concussion from getting thrown into the wall.

"You'll live," she said.

"Lucky old me."

Odette bent down and examined the corpse of the monster on the floor, prodding carefully with a combat knife she borrowed from Cawthorne.

"What are you doing?" whispered Felicity fiercely. "These are inhuman creatures that may have been locked away for centuries; we have no idea what kind of toxic crap is inside them."

"This one is wearing a wristwatch," Leliefeld pointed out.

"I beg your pardon?" As Felicity looked on, the Grafter poked at the thing's hide with her knife and, after a bit of effort, managed to saw through it. "Odette, this is not the time or the place to conduct an autopsy." Leliefeld ignored her, making two cuts and peeling a corner back with the point of the knife.

"I think this hide is actually clothing," she said. "It looks like it's been welded to the skin and strengthened with a sort of resin."

"Oh, crikey, you're right," said Felicity. "Look, there's that tacky trademark thing on the chest." Odette carefully made an incision at the creature's hairline and peeled back the membrane. A thick clear syrup drained out, and a man's face was revealed, his features twisted in pain.

"That's one of the missing graduate students," Felicity said.

"Are you sure?" asked Odette.

Felicity nodded. "I remember his picture from the file."

"So they're civilians," Odette said. "And maybe the Pawns that got snatched away. Locked into these suits."

"Tragic," said Felicity.

"Since they're normal people, that might explain why they're so vulnerable in the middle of the face," mused Odette. "Whatever's capturing them, it can't layer that stuff over their eyes, or they wouldn't be able to see. Apparently they can see through the liquid and the membrane, but the hide is too tough." She poked gingerly at the membrane. "It's much stronger over the mouth and nose. I suppose the eyes are the only weak spot."

"Good to know. But we should get out of here," said Cawthorne, and he struggled to his feet. "The gaping holes in the walls and the floors are probably a good signpost to other creatures that we're here. And the gunshots probably gave the game away as well."

"Agreed," said Felicity. "But we need to let the Checquy know about this. Killing them may not be necessary if there's a possibility these people can be saved."

"Let's make the call from somewhere else," said Cawthorne. "And I can tell you now that if we see any of them before backup gets here, I'm shooting them."

"Agreed," said Felicity.

"Agreed," said Odette.

They let themselves out the back door and decided to find a place that was easily defensible and then wait for rescue to arrive. After shuffling along painfully for a while, they came to a passage where two houses leaned so close together that the sky above was just a narrow strip of smoky blue.

Cawthorne sat with his gun pointing in one direction, the women sat with Felicity's gun facing the other way. Felicity was about to call the Checquy when faint voices came through over Felicity's headset and Cawthorne's earpiece. A voice identified as Pawn Bourchier was advising all Checquy operatives in Muirie that backup troops had arrived and were moving in. Anyone needing medical attention should advise. Various Checquy people chirped in from around the village, but there were very few injured. It sounded like most of the combat teams were dead.

"This is Pawn Clements," said Felicity. "Party of three, serious injuries on...one?" She looked to Odette, who shrugged and nodded. "Also, we have important information about the threat." She explained its true nature. Bourchier did not sound best pleased with this revelation but thanked her for the information. He advised that he would send medics to treat Cawthorne.

"Do you know where you are?"

"We're in the snackwallets," said Odette.

"The what?" said Bourchier.

"Or whatever the hell you call them," said Odette sourly.

"The snickelways," said Felicity.

"The what?"

"The fucking alleyways," said Felicity.

"You would be astounded at how little that narrows it down," he said.

"No, we wouldn't," said Felicity. "We're off Broy Lane, just next to number ten."

"Roger that, we're on our way. Sit tight."

They sat.

46

Early the next morning, before the sun had even begun to rise, the plane lifted off from Dundee bearing two extremely tired women.

"You know, the doctors could have taken a look at your arm," said Felicity.

"The painkillers were enough," said Odette, but she shifted uncomfortably in her seat. "Besides, I'll need to get Marcel to reweave the musculature. A regular doctor would probably..." She trailed off.

"Fuck it up?" suggested Felicity.

"It's best to get a certified repair agent to work on these things," said Odette.

"Otherwise it might void the warranty?" asked Felicity.

Once the troops had rescued them from the snickelway and brought them to the encampment a mile outside Muirie, doctors had swarmed over them. Cawthorne was spirited away, and the doctors had been aghast when they finally took Odette's coat off and saw the gnarled muscles that wound up her arm and across her shoulder. She had waved them off (left-handedly) and ordered a special cocktail of painkillers that had them blinking in bewilderment. By the time she and Clements had been checked over and debriefed, it was too late to go back to London. They'd slept uneasily on camp beds and were woken at four in the morning and transported back to Dundee.

They were dozing in their plush seats when word came through from the cockpit that the troops had finally infiltrated the church crypt and found the source of the problem. The pilot didn't have many details: "A humanoid, very quick, and coated in layers of secretions." The Checquy had "subdued it," which could have meant any number of things but definitely meant that the problem was over.

This briefing complete, Felicity was just drifting off again when her phone rang.

"Hello?" she said, without opening her eyes.

"Pawn Clements, this is Trevor Cawthorne."

"Hi," she said in surprise. "How's your arm?"

"In a cast," said the Retainer. "But still attached."

"And your brain?"

"Light concussion."

"Glad to hear it," said Felicity.

"Thanks. I have some news for you and Miss Leliefeld," he said.

"I'll put you on speaker," said Felicity, plugging her phone into the console. "It's Cawthorne," she explained to Odette.

"The historians finally found something in the records about Muirie," said Cawthorne.

"We already know the monster's been taken care of," said Felicity sleepily. "I don't really care about its provenance."

"I think you might," said the Retainer. "The mention of Muirie was in the Checquy burial records."

"What?"

"A Pawn Hamish Reid was buried in the crypt of the Muirie church in 1502."

"No," breathed Felicity, coming completely awake.

"Served in the Order of the Checquy from 1460 until his death. Regular hero—helped put down some big monsters in his time. The records say he could sweat a sort of paste, 'livid in hue, that bent men's minds to his will and gave them vigor.' It sounds like a junior version of the crap that was coated all over the people we fought. The Pawn was laid to rest in his home village."

"So you think that a dead Pawn of the Checquy, decorated for service to his country and buried with full honors several hundred years ago, suddenly started snatching innocent people and turning them into his drones?"

"I think people can change," said Cawthorne. "Especially if they've been buried alive for a few centuries."

"If Pawn Reid wasn't dead, not the way they thought, then who knows how his powers—and his mind—might have warped?" put in Odette.

"This is one of the reasons the Checquy has developed such intricate burial procedures," reflected Felicity.

"Oh?" asked Odette.

"Yeah, Rook Thomas instituted them a couple of years back. It was one of the things that got her into the Court. Before her, people were just buried any old how. Now their bodies get shot in the head and incinerated, and the ashes are spread from four different mountains around the country," said Felicity. "It's a very beautiful ceremony."

"She got a program under way to retrieve all the Checquy bodies that have ever been buried," said Cawthorne. "But apparently, they haven't disinterred everyone yet. Anyway, I thought you might like to know."

"Thanks for that, Mr. Cawthorne," said Felicity. "And thanks for everything else." Odette chimed in with her thanks, and the Retainer said all the appropriate things before disconnecting. The two women drifted into sleep.

I still can't believe how well that worked out!" exclaimed Odette as the car drew up in front of the hotel.

"I still can't believe we survived," said Felicity.

"That's what I mean," said Odette.

"I am completely exhausted. When I get back to my room, it's a hot shower for me, followed by a hot bath, followed by a hot meal, followed by bed."

"Throw in a massage from a hot masseur, and I'll follow your lead," said Odette. "Even once they're repaired, my muscles are going to be aching for days." Leaning on each other, they limped through the lobby. Dressed in their Checquy-issued plain tracksuits, they caught some disapproving glances from the staff and other guests. God knows what they think of us, thought Felicity. Before, we were in evening gowns. Today we look like we've been in a bareknuckle boxing match. It took all her strength to push the elevator call button, and the wait seemed interminable.

Finally, the doors slid open, and the inevitable Checquy security guard eyed them flintily for a moment before recognizing them and stepping forward to help them in. They slumped on his shoulders, and he awkwardly leaned them against the wall and pushed the buttons for the Checquy and Grafter floors.

"Hold the lift!" came a voice, and a blond woman slid in. The Checquy security guard stiffened a little. "My shift is over, I might as well go up instead of sitting in the bar all day," the woman said. "Odette, you look exhausted. I heard you were going out to a site. Looks like it was a rough one."

"Sophie, it was amazing," said Odette, smiling. "Insane and terrifying, but amazing. I don't know how you people can do this every day."

"Well, we don't do it every day," said Sophie wryly. "Some of us just pull guard duty in the lobby of a five-star hotel."

"Do you two know each other?" Odette asked Felicity.

"I don't think so," said Felicity.

"Ah, Pawn Felicity Clements, this is Pawn Sophie Jelfs," said Odette. "She's one of the security guards for the delegation."

"Good to meet you, finally," said Pawn Jelfs.

"Thanks," said Felicity. "You too." She leaned back against the wall of the lift and then noticed the elevator security guard was frowning. "Are you all right?"

"I don't recall a Pawn Je—" he started, but Pawn Jelfs snapped up her arm and chopped the side of her hand into his throat. Then, with the same dizzying speed, she held up two tiny aerosol cans and sprayed them into the faces of Felicity and Odette. They crumpled to the floor.

47

Odette opened her eyes and felt incredibly happy.

Saskia!

Her delight was instinctive, rooted in her heart. Her friend's arms were around her, holding her close, and she could smell Saskia's familiar perfume. Then she remembered everything and felt her face crumple into tears. No! No, no, no.

"Je suis là, 'Dette," she crooned. I'm right here. "Nous sommes tous là." We are all here. Despite herself, Odette held her friend tight in a one-armed hug and pressed her face into Saskia's shoulder. She felt a kiss on her hair. "It's all right, Odette. You're home." Odette allowed herself one more moment of that comforting embrace, one more moment not to have to worry about anything at all, and then she drew back.

"It's really you," Odette said in French.

"It really is."

And it was. Sitting on the end of the bed, barefoot, Saskia looked completely unchanged from when Odette last saw her that horrible day in the hotel. Her friend's hair was pulled back loosely from her face, and she was wearing a short skirt and a T-shirt with a cardigan over it. So completely inappropriate for a terrorist, Odette thought fondly.

"You're wearing your own face," said Odette. "I'm glad."

"Yes, we have different ones for when we go out—they're very simple, clumsy things," said Saskia. "Not a real face, but an overlay. Very clever; we even have ones for different races. Gloves too. Pim came up with them." Odette nodded and looked around to take stock of the situation. She was sitting up in a queen-size bed made up with soft cotton sheets. The room was hardly bigger than the bed and had no windows, but a gentle light glowed from overhead.

Am I in a cell? she thought. I don't think so. The walls

were the sort that were put up in offices when the renter had a large space to fill and wanted to create rooms. A metal frame covered with plasterboard. Unless there's some sort of material reinforcing it, I could kick through it, she decided. There was a print on the wall, an ink engraving of buildings she recognized from Prague. Nice picture.

"It's not a cell," Saskia said, and Odette started. She was no longer used to someone who knew her so well. "It's just a room we had available. We have to make do with what we've got, I'm afraid."

Odette looked down at herself. She was wearing a fresh T-shirt, plain orange. A peek under the blankets revealed that she was wearing her original underwear. On her left thigh there was a fresh bandage. Her right arm was in a sling, one of those rigid polyester ones that held the injured limb against her. When she tried to wiggle her fingers, however, she couldn't.

"Simon took a look at your poor arm," said Saskia. "He said you must have done something to your muscles without any prep at all?"

"Yeah," said Odette. Saskia raised her eyes to heaven and shook her head.

"I expect you had your reasons, but it will take a good bit of work to rearrange and repair them," she said. "One of us will get to it once we have a free moment. In the meantime, it will need to remain immobilized. Believe it or not, a sling is actually the best thing for it. That, and a little judicious paralysis to make sure the muscles move as little as possible."

Odette nodded but carefully flexed some other muscles. Her spurs remained firmly, and pointedly, sheathed. Saskia was looking at her with calm eyes.

"We've taken a few precautions, Odette," she said. "Don't be hurt, please. We love you, but you're still torn, and we can't take any chances. Not that it would make a huge amount of difference. The reservoirs for your spurs were completely drained," she sniffed. "Do I want to know what you were doing?"

"I was fighting something," said Odette. I was saving

the life of someone who saved my life, she didn't say. Saskia nodded.

It was odd, almost like a dream. Saskia was so calm and so obviously delighted to see her. Odette simply had no idea what was going to happen. *What do I say? Are we going to talk about what they've done?* Then she caught sight of the shoes that were standing by the door. Black heels with a cream canvas sheath coming up from the leather and metal buckles.

"Nice shoes."

"Vivienne Westwood," said Saskia, pleased. "I've gone very London since we arrived. It really is amazing to be here, despite everything. Have you been able to see much during your stay?"

"A bit," said Odette. "Mainly I've been working."

"Oh, too bad," said Saskia sympathetically. "I really do love this city. So much culture, things I never thought I'd get to see with my own eyes. Of course, I've done a lot of shopping too. All the lovely brands, and I got some marvelous cloth from Joel and Son. But also the museums and the galleries. I got that print on the wall just for you. Pim and I spent two days going through Kew Gardens, and then we went in at night and took samples from at least a hundred plants."

"You've been busy," said Odette. It was jarring. Her thoughts of the Antagonists had been muddled, her memories of who they were overlaid by visions of them plotting in a smoke-filled room or surreptitiously laying explosives. The Checquy should have been staking out the tourist spots and boutiques, she thought. "How long have I been under?"

"Not long," said Saskia. "An hour, maybe?"

"From the hotel?"

"We moved quickly," said Saskia. "We had to, since we have one more thing to do, and we don't want the circumstances to change."

"What are you talking about?" asked Odette, dreading the answer.

"We need to have a talk," said Saskia seriously. "All of us. Can you stand up?" Odette swung her legs over the side of the bed and shakily stood up. Her leg trembled a little under her. "We took your scalpels out," said Saskia delicately. "The muscles are still probably a bit wobbly. Let me help you." Odette braced herself against the wall as Saskia brought her a skirt and put it on her. It was knee-length, black, well cut.

"Thanks," said Odette. "Let's go." The floor was carpeted, and they both remained barefoot as Saskia took her arm and led her out the door into a hallway with more of those dividing walls. The carpet looked as if it had been freshly laid. It was all very sterile.

"So, where are we?"

"In the City," said Saskia carelessly. "We rented a floor in one of those dull office buildings. We were lucky to find it; real estate in this town is insane."

"You're in an office building?" asked Odette incredulously.

"You actually can't do much better," said a voice behind them. Odette shuffled around awkwardly to see him. He wasn't wearing the face he'd sported during the Blinding. Instead, he was just as Felicity had described him: shiny white skin, nodules along his head. At least he's wearing clothes.

"Simon," said Odette. She reached out and took his hand.

"'Dette. We finally got you." He leaned forward and kissed her on both cheeks. His lips felt strange on her skin. But his eyes were the same, with so much merriment and genuine delight that it made her want to cry.

"It's good to see you too, although..." She trailed off awkwardly.

"I know, not ideal circumstances," he said, grinning.

"You replaced your eye."

"Twenty minutes' work." He shrugged. "Anyway, let's keep moving, I expect the others are waiting."

"You were saying this was such a good location," Odette said.

"Right, yes," said Simon. "Very convenient. It's got all the space one could need, air-conditioning, lots of power outlets, easy access to public transport, reserved parking, and Claudia got the owner to set us up with good Internet connections."

"You've gone corporate."

"Actually, we do have a little company," said Simon. "Registered and everything. Of course, it doesn't really do anything, but the corporate credit cards are handy, and I've set up an account with a furniture rental place that has proven very useful."

"And there's a nice Indian restaurant downstairs that delivers," said Saskia.

"I understand you've stayed in some other London places too," said Odette.

"We were in a hotel for the first couple of nights," said Simon, "and then Claudia moved in here and got set up. The rest of us rented a house by Hyde Park that was rather pleasant, although we had to abandon it and come here after the Chimerae tracked us down."

"I was thinking more of the other place, the one that burned down."

"Ah yes, that was insane. I actually took on a team of Checquy! Can you imagine?" Odette didn't point out that it had been half a team. Or that he had apparently been turning civilians into human bombs there.

"You have a surgical suite here?"

"Our last one," said Saskia. "There's another one gestating in a house in Madrid."

"Let's move into the conference room," said Simon, and he opened a door at the end of the hallway. The conference room was large—it appeared to take up half the floor—and mostly dark, with dim pools of light dotted about. A narrow band of windows looked out onto the city, but thick blinds cut out almost all the light, showing just silhouettes of the buildings around them.

A long conference table covered with familiar detritus stood before the windows. Odette recognized the laptops that Simon used and Saskia's sketchpads. Pim's tablet computer sat on a pile of newspapers. A deep plastic tray filled with pink jelly marked the place where Mariette must have been accustomed to sitting—her father had created a biological computer for her. A figure was hunched over at one end of the table. The person

573

was seated in darkness, but cords of light glowed on the head. As they approached, the figure sat up and turned toward them, and Odette recognized the face.

"Mijn God, Claudia!" Her friend's eyes were gone. Instead, many clear plastic tubes poured from her sockets. They spread out and back, draping over her head and hanging down over her shoulders to trail away into the shadows. Odette saw, inside the plastic, the white and black strings that made up synthetic nerves, as well as some copper wires. "What in God's name have you done to yourself?"

"Odette," said Claudia, and her voice chimed oddly. "It's good to see you."

Odette refrained from stating the obvious. It took all her strength, but she managed it.

"No, I actually can see you," said Claudia. "I'm looking through Saskia's and Simon's eyes." Odette turned to look at the other two. They nodded. "I really wish you wouldn't nod," said Claudia peevishly. "It's like watching that damn movie with all the little handheld cameras. If you could all just sit, that would be great. Odette, sit next to me. Saskia, could you please sit across from her?" Odette sat automatically, her back to the window, and Claudia fumbled for her hand, found it, and squeezed it. "I'd hug you, but moving around like this is a pain in the ass. And the eyes."

"What is this?" asked Odette.

"Communications," said Claudia simply. "Surveillance. We had access to a couple of agents within the Checquy, but to stay abreast of all the developments we've had to turn to other, more direct means of observation."

"You hacked into the brotherhood's communication structure," said Odette tiredly. "I saw what you did to Ernst's secretary."

Claudia nodded slightly, and the wires shifted on her shoulders. She put a hand up to her face. "Ow! Damn it, I have got to remember not to move my head," she said. "Honestly, I can't wait until I get all this stuff removed and my eyes are out of the refrigerator and back in my head. Anyway, yes, Odette, I did that."

"All this, just for that one trick?" said Odette. Which was pretty juvenile anyway. "After that, you know the brotherhood stopped using internal telephones."

"They thought they did," said Claudia. "But actually, I've been looking through a lot of people's eyes. It's not easy, but I can activate anyone's communications implants without their knowing. I can see what they see and hear what they hear. Mainly it's been secretaries, but the secretaries learn all the important things anyway." Odette thanked her lucky stars that she'd never had the phone implants put into her. "Plus, I can surf the Net with this, which makes up for the inconvenience a little bit. I've been watching a lot of movies."

"You still had at least one Checquy traitor on your side, though," said Odette. "Didn't you? Sophie Jelfs."

"We had someone keeping an eye on you, certainly," said Claudia. "And I was looking through her eyes too."

"In fact," said Odette, "you've had quite a few new people working for you. You've even been making them, somehow. Like that clone who led the attack on the car at Hill Hall."

"Saskia, could you please nod for me?" asked Claudia. "It's killing me not to be able to bob my damn head. And don't roll your eyes like that because I'm looking out through them."

"Who was that man?" Odette asked. "What was he?"

"So you haven't figured it out?" said Saskia.

"Don't gloat, Sas, it's really annoying."

"I'm sorry, really," said Saskia, "but I was so pleased with the idea, and I finally get to share it with someone."

"The rest of us stopped being impressed a while ago," said Simon drily. "Especially since it meant tying ourselves to a tremendous pain in the ass."

"It was still brilliant," said Saskia defensively. She turned back to Odette. "From the very beginning, we knew we were going to need more information, more help. We were only six people, after all. And then we lost Dieter on the trip over here."

"I saw his body in that whale creature," said Odette.

"It was quick," said Saskia sadly. "But I'm sorry that I can't say it was painless. He collided the vessel with a ship, and the feedback killed him. Losing him meant that, more than ever, we needed an ally. Someone who hated the Checquy as much as we did and who could bring us information about them."

"Oh my God, Saskia, I can't take any more lead-up," said Claudia. "Just bring her in." Saskia shot Claudia a sour look, which was totally wasted since she couldn't possibly have seen it. She sighed, got up, and strode away into the darkness.

"You seem to be giving an awful lot of orders," said Odette suspiciously.

"It's one of the things that comes with not being able to do stuff for yourself," said Claudia. "Plus, she's been so self-congratulatory about it."

"So, where are the others?" asked Odette. "Mariette and Pim?"

"Pim's over in the surgery," said Simon. "He's wrapping up a little project. And Mariette is out—you'll see them later."

"Well, that will be good," said Odette. She was still trying to come to terms with the situation. Every few moments, they would all slide into the easy, casual tone they'd enjoyed before everything happened. They were eager to show off for her, but the conversation seemed very careful, as if they were trying not to shock her. I guess it's strange for everyone. A door opened in one of the temporary walls, and an arm of light cut into the darkness as Saskia returned, accompanied by a familiar figure. As they approached the table, Odette found herself clenching her left hand into a fist. Her right hand trembled a little but remained obstinately unclenched.

"Pawn Sophie Jelfs," said Odette, and her disgust could be heard in her voice. Saskia looked at her with surprise, taken aback by the contempt. Odette realized she was as outraged by Jelfs's treachery to the Checquy as she was by Jelfs's treachery to her.

"Not quite," said Jelfs.

"I beg your pardon?" said Odette coolly.

"You can call me Sophie if you like, I suppose," said the woman. "But I'm not a Pawn, and my last name isn't Jelfs." Odette kept her mouth shut. There's something here I'm not seeing, she thought.

"My real name is Gestalt," said Sophie, a small smile twisting around her lips. "Rook Gestalt, although I've been informed that my rank was stripped from me."

"That can't be," said Odette. "Rook Gestalt's female body was killed. Fell out a window." Sophie's face soured. "There are only three Gestalt bodies left, and they are all imprisoned."

"Well, you're wrong on a few counts," said Sophie. "First, my female body didn't just fall out a window. I was shot by a girl who was acting under the control of Myfanwy Thomas. Then I fell out the window. And there aren't three of my bodies in Checquy prisons, there are four. And now there are a few more bodies running about, thanks to my friends here." She gestured around the table. "They very obligingly grew me some new ones, including this one." She tapped her own chest.

"But you can't clone Checquy powers," objected Odette. "The Broederschap tried for centuries. All it got was regular people. Unless"—she turned to Saskia—"did you manage it somehow?" Saskia shook her head.

"You're quite right," said Simon. "You can't clone powers. If you clone Gestalt, any of Gestalt's bodies, all you get is a new person. One that's completely unconnected to the hive mind."

"Useless." Sophie sighed.

"But there is an exception," said Saskia. "A child whose parents are both part of the Gestalt hive mind will be part of the Gestalt hive mind too."

"That fourth body I mentioned?" said Sophie. "The one in prison? It's a baby I made. My female body and one of my male bodies had sex and conceived it. I suppose really it's a toddler now."

"I understand that," said Odette. "It's disgusting, but I understand how it works. However, the female Gestalt is now dead. So how could any new ones be conceived?"

"You can harvest eggs from a dead body," said Saskia. "Gestalt's female body, Eliza, was retrieved by the Checquy after it fell out the window."

"After it got shot and fell out the window," said Sophie testily. "It's not like I got drunk and just toppled out."

"The body was not in good shape, to say the least," said Saskia delicately. "But the Checquy had put it in the fridge almost immediately, and that bought us some time."

"I thought the Checquy destroyed the bodies of their dead," said Odette. "They're burned, and the ashes are scattered from some mountains."

"Bitch Myfanwy Thomas's little initiative, yes," said Sophie. "But before they do all that, they examine the hell out of the bodies. It's the Checquy's last opportunity to unravel the mysteries of their people."

"One of the Broederschap's moles among the Retainers was in the morgue," said Claudia. "We got in contact with him, and he smuggled Saskia in."

"Walking into that place was absolutely terrifying," confessed Saskia. "But I retrieved as many eggs as I could from the corpse. Most of them had deteriorated and were no longer viable, but there were still quite a few we could use, especially once I applied some rejuvenation techniques."

"And the sperm?" asked Odette. "It takes two parties to make a baby."

"Checquy prisons are still prisons," Sophie said with a shrug. "And no prison is completely cut off from the world. All sorts of things can get smuggled in or out if you have enough money or the creativity to come up with some interesting threats for the guards."

"We had both," Simon put in. "And there was a guard who had already sold his soul to the Broederschap."

"There I was, rotting in four different prisons around the country," said Sophie. "I had no idea that there were some people fiddling around with my female remains. And I was extremely surprised to receive an invitation to meet with some mysterious people. The message said that they might be able to arrange my freedom in exchange for helping them to harm the Checquy. All I had to do was provide a little bit of semen, and they'd arrange a meeting. What did I have to lose? I provided the product and then waited. To be perfectly honest, I thought they were going to break one of my bodies out, or maybe smuggle a representative in."

"So why did you think they wanted the semen?" asked Odette, frowning.

"I thought they were freaks." Gestalt shrugged. "After all, like you and the Checquy, I assumed that the death of Eliza meant the end of any new bodies. But then, a few days later, I was suddenly more." Her eyes glowed. "I was aware of a new body to slide into. I opened my eyes, and I was here, sitting up in a metal box filled with jelly."

"Just a little child," said Saskia. "A lovely little boy with white-blond hair. He opened his eyes and immediately started talking terms."

"The last time I made a deal with the Grafters, I wasn't asking for much," said Sophie. "Power, wealth, the opportunity to kick arse. This time, I was much more strategic."

"The deal was simple," said Simon. "We would provide Gestalt with more bodies. Bodies outside the prison system. Gestalt would use them to act on our behalf as well as sometimes directing our troops, disposable soldiers who would be equipped with Broederschap weapons."

"Gestalt has been far better than the British criminals we started out with," said Saskia. "Much more competent, much more organized, much more disciplined. It was easier to modify the new bodies and put in the enhancements as they grew. Plus, it turns out that common criminals are not the most professional people on earth. You saw them, Gestalt was leading them at the assault near that ostentatious country house."

"The Sophie-body was stationed in the hotel," said Claudia, "to both observe the delegation and keep an eye on you."

"And I provided valuable insights and knowledge about the Checquy," said Gestalt. "Let's not forget that."

"We worked out the details over a few hours," said Claudia, "and then the body broke down."

"Well, we had accelerated the growth drastically," said Saskia.

"This body, the Sophie body, took quite a bit longer to grow," said Gestalt. "But as a result, it's going to last longer."

"Not that much longer," objected Odette. "It's inversely proportional. Do you know what that means? The more you accelerate the growth, the less time the body will last."

"Thank you, yes, I know how math works," said Sophie. "And you may recall I've already been in a couple of bodies that have rotted away abruptly." She shuddered. "But that's where we come to the point of payment for my services."

"We're realistic about Gestalt's commitment to the cause," said Saskia.

"Fucking over the Checquy is a bonus," said Sophie. "And I still want to kill that bitch Thomas. But it's not my end goal."

"So what is your end goal?" asked Odette.

"Being alive," said Sophie. "Being free. With bodies that won't just fall apart after a few days or weeks."

"All of the Gestalt bodies we created were grown at an accelerated rate," said Saskia. "And we took care to ensure that they could not make any more without our help." Odette recalled that the Gestalt body that had rotted away in the Rookery prison cell had been given a vasectomy.

"All the males were neutered, and this Sophie body has no viable eggs," said Gestalt, "thanks to a couple of injections from my friends here." The woman did not look best pleased at this fact. "But there are two new ones out there in the world," she said with a look of utter satisfaction. "Pure and clean, without any modifications or accelerated growth."

"We agreed to create two zygotes that have been implanted in civilian women," said Saskia. "They will grow at the normal rate and develop into a male and a female. After the normal gestation period, they'll be born, with a normal life span ahead of them."

"I can feel them now," said Gestalt, closing her eyes. "Little lights in the darkness."

"It is impressive," said Odette. "Why didn't you use the Gestalt bodies to do the suicide bombings in the cities? Why did you have to use civilians?"

"We obtained Gestalt's services relatively late in the piece," said Simon. "And besides, the systems we implanted required special conditions. They had to be the right blood type and possess specific hormones and antibodies. We could only use people who had successfully undergone organ transplants."

"And even then it was not easy," said Saskia. "These were extremely complex designs that Claudia stole from the Broederschap archives, well beyond even our skill levels. Several of the candidates rejected the implants."

"But how did you find them?" asked Odette, curious despite herself.

"It's not just people I can hack with these things," said Claudia, stroking the cables that poured out of her skull. "Hospital records, government databases, it's all extremely useful. Except for the Checquy, of course, who haven't even plugged their mainframe computers into the web."

"That's really quite sensible of them," said Simon. "I always roll my eyes whenever I read about government computers getting hacked."

"I don't understand how you could do it," said Odette.

"Well, the delivery system was difficult; there were some missteps," said Simon. "But the product itself was a rather clever tweaking of the original toxin. 'Dette, I think you'd really appreciate the changes I made." He sat back and folded his arms, the picture of a white, rubber-skinned person pleased with himself. "And do you know, I believe that rendering it nonfatal actually makes it a more effective weapon. Sometimes we get so caught up in the physical aspects of our technology, in the meat, that we ignore the psychological applications."

"I'm not talking about the technical expertise, Simon!" shouted Odette, and they all jumped. "I'm talking about maiming people!"

"We tried to keep the civilian carnage to a minimum, really," said Claudia.

"Are you serious?"

"It could have been worse," said Simon. "So much worse."

"This comes back to the choice," said Saskia. "The choice

between us and the Broederschap." She was calm, her chin resting on her folded hands. "It's a choice you couldn't make, and we don't blame you for that."

"I made it," said Odette.

"Not really."

"I did!" shouted Odette. "I did! It was the hardest thing I've ever had to do in my life, and it broke my heart, but I made my choice!"

"Odette, can you honestly say that you gave yourself entirely to Ernst's cause?" said Saskia. She sounded so reasonable. "That you committed completely to seeking us out and destroying us? Did you do everything in your power to help them catch us? Did we become your enemies?" Odette hung her head.

"No." It was true. She'd held back. In her heart of hearts, she hadn't made them her enemies, and she'd secretly hoped that they wouldn't get caught. I didn't want the attacks, I didn't want people dying, she thought. I just wanted my friends to retreat, to live their lives away from this.

"You couldn't choose against us," said Saskia. "You couldn't choose against the rest of the brotherhood. So we're removing the choice for you."

"What?"

"You won't have to choose, Odette. That's our gift to you." Odette felt Simon's hand on her shoulder. "Today, the ridiculous peace between the Checquy and Broederschap will die."

"What are you going to do?" asked Odette weakly.

"Don't fool yourself," said Gestalt. "It won't be pretty."

"Actually, it was you who gave us the idea, Odette," said Simon placidly.

"Me?" said Odette, her mind reeling. "No, I never—what are you talking about?"

"We were floundering about before," said Claudia. "All that rage, and we had some good concepts, but we didn't have an end point in mind."

"Striking at the Broederschap was the easiest thing for us to do," said Simon. "We thought that if we demonstrated our feelings, showed how appalling this was, our colleagues and our family would reconsider. But that wasn't realistic. They're too much under the thumb of Ernst."

"You kept it up, though," said Odette softly.

"Every little piece of stress helps to destabilize," said Saskia. "Who knows which straw will break the camel's back?"

"So we moved our focus to the Checquy," said Claudia. "A much larger organization with greater diversity. And when Gestalt joined us, she provided us with better insights into their weak points. Their indoctrinated hatred for the Broederschap. The pressure they face from the British government. We tried to take out Rook Thomas, the one who was really making the merger happen. Gestalt thought that if we removed her from the equation, it would all break up."

"It was a good idea," said Gestalt, inspecting her nails.

"And if you hadn't botched it, it might have worked," said Claudia.

"Botch is a very strong word," said Gestalt, looking over at Odette pointedly. "In any case, I like to think it shook her up a bit." Odette kept silent. She was not about to share any information, especially information that Gestalt might enjoy.

"I was always against it, anyway," said Saskia. "You know if you kill her, you'll just make her a martyr to the cause."

"Which brings us to today's attack," said Claudia. "It's very last-minute, but one of the advantages of our being a small group is that we're very flexible."

"What are you going to do?" whispered Odette. She was still reeling from the suggestion that she was the origin of their plan.

"There's a group of Checquy children in town," said Simon.

"No," breathed Odette.

"They're here for a field trip."

"No."

"We're going to kill them."

"No!" She slammed her hand down on the table.

"That's the reaction we're looking for," said Simon. "Gestalt told us about your terror when you thought Alessio might have been caught up in the fog attacks. She said that you were distraught at the very idea of it." Odette shot Gestalt a poisonous look. The blond woman winked at her.

"Mariette is there now, waiting for the students to arrive," said Saskia. "Then, when she judges it appropriate, she will unleash a poison that will wipe out the group."

"This will hit them hard," said Simon. "According to Gestalt, Grafters killing Checquy children will strike a particular chord in the Checquy mentality. It dates back to the Isle of Wight. They have some oral tradition that they all have to experience."

"Now, I didn't think it would be necessary," said Saskia. "We really, really thought the fog attacks would push them over the edge. That the mutilation and terror would kill the negotiations immediately. Frankly, I thought the Checquy would kill the delegation as well."

"Including me," said Odette.

"We tried to snatch you, 'Dette," said Saskia. "We really did."

"Killing those children will hurt them like nothing else could," said Simon.

"In an ideal world, we'd destroy their training ground," said Claudia. "Kirrin Island would be full of little corpses if we could manage it. But it's impossible." She shrugged awkwardly. "It's too well guarded."

"Our attack today may not even get them all," said Saskia. "I expect there will be some little monster who doesn't need to breathe air or is actually a living song or some such ludicrous atrocity. But that's not a bad thing, really. Traumatized witnesses ensure that the story doesn't die. A kid, scarred for life by what he's seen, that will whip the Checquy into a frenzy like nothing else.

"And it will be public, so the regular people will be outraged too. The Checquy will have to scramble around, produce fake families to mourn the loss. Unless they decide to pretend that they're orphans. Which just adds to the pathos, really."

"And Alessio?" said Odette weakly.

"We will do everything we can to protect him," said Saskia.

"We do understand—he's the real reason you didn't come with us."

"But he's not," said Odette faintly. "He wasn't the only reason."

"We care about him too, 'Dette."

"I can't believe you would kill children," said Odette. *This can't be happening. They can't mean this, not truly.*

"They're not really children," said Claudia. "They're not humans. Humans can't do what they do."

"We are in no position to say what humans can and cannot do, Claudia!" said Odette.

"Don't cheat yourself, 'Dette," said Saskia. "We are human. It's human to make tools. To fix broken bones, and straighten teeth, and remove cataracts. Humans figure out new ways to do things, organ transplants and fighting disease and doing research." She gestured around the room to her comrades, and Odette noticed herself included in the group. "We're just ahead of the rest of them.

"But I'll tell you what humans don't do," she said in a poisonous tone. "They're not born with fangs, or mirrors for skin, or with the air around them turning to bronze. They don't swim through the earth. Those creatures aren't human. They're vermin, they're cockroaches. And the targets? They're baby cockroaches. That's all."

"And you!" Odette exclaimed to Gestalt. "Doesn't this concern you? These people you've allied yourself with—they don't think of you as human."

"I don't think of myself as human either," said Gestalt. "I'm something more. But then, I'm something more than the rest of the Checquy too. I've always known that."

"The Checquy killed us," said Saskia calmly. "They would have wiped us out. They don't get any mercy."

"Everyone in the delegation will be finished," said Odette. "They'll destroy them."

"And that's a loss," said Claudia, "but this is war. And it will put everyone else in the Broederschap—all our people in

Europe—on our side. They'll be able to evade the Checquy. There are fallback plans. I've seen them. I've read the files."

"And then?" asked Odette. "Do you think they will just leave us alone? After what you're going to do? They will never stop coming."

"The Broederschap hid before," said Simon. "For centuries."

"They thought we were dead," said Odette.

"And they were fine with that," said Claudia, and her voice shook with barely controlled rage. "The Checquy felt no guilt, no doubt about what they had done. They nursed their spite and their hatred for generations, even when they thought they had won."

"They didn't find us because they weren't looking for us," said Odette. "Now, they'll know."

"We've learned a lot since then," Simon observed. "Look, they've been trying to track us down this whole time." He gestured around the room. "We've been right in England, in London, and they haven't caught us. They never will."

"You would make us fugitives!" said Odette. "Forever."

"It would be better than joining ourselves with them," said Claudia.

They cannot be convinced, Odette thought in despair. "Where is Pim?" she asked finally.

"Why are you doing this?" asked Saskia.

"What?" asked Odette.

"Why won't you acknowledge the truth? You hate them too, Odette!" said Saskia. "You can't pretend you don't. You can't pretend to me. I know you too well."

"Where is Pim?" said Odette coldly. "I want to talk to him." This time, I can make him see, she thought. I know I can. And if I can convince Pim, then the rest will follow.

"He'll be here in a moment," said Claudia finally. "He's just finishing up with that Checquy-thing that Gestalt brought in with you."

Felicity!

48

Felicity knew immediately what had happened.

I failed.

I failed at every single thing they ordered me to do.

I did not prevent the Antagonists from seizing Odette.

I did not capture a member of the Antagonists.

I did not keep her safe, and alive, and in Checquy custody.

I failed.

Compared to all these failures, the fact that she was lying paralyzed on a surgical table did not seem quite so bad.

Although it was bad enough.

The paralysis was ghastly. She could not move at all, not anything. Her chest rose and sank by itself, so presumably her body was being permitted to keep up basic functions, but she was just an occupant. A passenger. Fortunately, her eyes were open so she could see, but she could not move them, and she could not blink. If they were drying out, if they were burning, she did not feel it.

What she could see was not good. The room was distressingly familiar. The featureless white walls that blended into the ceiling and (she assumed) the floor, the glow that came from everywhere. Back in a skin room, she thought grimly. She heard movement from somewhere in the direction of her feet, a clinking of metal. So, I can hear, she thought. I can hear, and I can see, but I can't feel anything. She couldn't even tell if she had clothing on.

What about my powers? she thought, and she tried to use her Sight to read whatever she was lying on. Nothing. She could not even use her Sight to detect if she was wearing clothing. She remembered Odette saying that some of the surgical suites could grow their own tables and tools. Either they've paralyzed my powers, she thought, or I am naked and lying on something that is alive. She was not certain which she found more distressing.

"I know you're awake," said a voice from beyond her feet.

It was a man's voice with the same accent as Odette's. "I know that you can see and hear but do nothing else. Don't worry, I'm not going to torture you."

Well, it's nice of you to let me know, thought Felicity.

"You won't feel a thing."

Somehow, that does not make me feel any better.

"There's nothing you can tell me that I need to know," said the voice. "Gestalt has only the vaguest of recollections about you. She could us tell practically nothing about your powers besides what we read in your files."

I can't have heard that right, thought Felicity. The male Gestalts are in prison, and the female Gestalt is dead.

"But we do know that when some of the Checquy Pawns are sedated or unconscious, their powers will activate to protect them. So we have to be very careful. I don't know if you're one of those, but just to be certain, I have sedated various parts of your brain so you can't activate your abilities."

Okay, so that explains that. But it still doesn't tell me if I'm naked or not.

"Anyway, you should know," said the man, "if I get the slightest impression that you are pulling some Checquy magic, I will immediately slice open your carotid artery, and you will die right here in this room, on this table."

Understood, she thought.

"Honestly, I don't know what Gestalt was thinking, bringing you here at all," he said.

Gestalt must be that woman Odette knew. Pawn Sophie Jelfs, thought Felicity. How is that possible?

"Still, I thought I'd better take a quick look over and inside you, just for safety's sake. I know you've been attending Odette for a while now." He talked on, more to himself than to Felicity, although he addressed all the remarks to her. "Gestalt thought we might be able to use you somehow to spur on the Checquy after tonight. 'Adding insult to injury,' she said. To be honest, I think she's just excited to be out in the world. She gets a little overwhelmed by the freedom of it all."

She sprayed me in the face, Felicity remembered. And Odette too, I think. So Odette wasn't a mole. She's not a traitor. I'm so glad.

"After all, we can just grab a Checquy person whenever we need one," the man was saying. "For God's sake, they do go home, some of them. Not the Court, apparently, they've all been staying tucked away in their fortresses for the past few weeks, but the rank and file go to their houses and apartments."

Not this little black duck, thought Felicity. I never get to go to my place. Had to put my dog in the boarding kennels.

"Anyway," said the man, "I have to make sure there are no surprises tucked away. And see if I can get a clue about the nature of your powers. I admit the whole idea is fascinating."

Good luck, thought Felicity. The scientists at the Estate spent years trying to figure it out.

"You've got quite a few scars, you know," he remarked.

I do know that; I was present when I got them.

"Good musculature."

Why, thank you.

Then he was moving around, up into her field of vision, peering down into her face but not her eyes.

Oh, I know you! I saw you in the photos. You're Pim, the boy Odette gets all teary-eyed about when she thinks no one sees.

I'll give you credit, you're quite a cutie.

He reached out and touched her face, and she could see the crescents of her cheeks rise up a little at the very bottom of her vision.

He's opened my mouth.

Then he was coming closer, and his face was intent. His eyes were a smoky gray.

You are yummy, thought Felicity. Odette has good taste in terrorists.

"You used to throw up your food," he said finally. "Years ago. They repaired your teeth, and did a pretty good job of it, but I can still see traces." He still hadn't looked her in the eye. "But I don't think that's particularly relevant to our situation here. You don't have hollow teeth filled with cyanide, and no foldaway fangs.

"Now, I just want to take one quick look under your skin," he said. "No big cuts, but if your powers are touch-based, then maybe your epidermis will show something interesting."

Sure, knock yourself out, thought Felicity. I'm just gonna lie here and work on my haikus, since I have nothing better to do. He moved down so that he was just barely in her field of vision.

"Just a small incision on the palm, and I can peel it back and s—merde!" There was a fizzing sound, and an acrid smell wafted through the air.

Oh, good, she thought. I get to smell things too. Then a cloud of bottle-green smoke was billowing up from somewhere and filling the room. It grew denser and denser until she couldn't see anything. Even the radiant light from the walls and ceiling was blotted out. Did that come out of me? she wondered. Good.

In normal circumstances, the prospect of a torrent of apparently poisonous gas emanating from her might have been mildly concerning, but she'd already accepted the entire situation as hopeless. Now, anything that might screw over her captors was good.

"God!" Pim was choking, coughing, wheezing, and, from what she could tell, swearing a lot in a language she didn't know. Guess something went wrong. She felt a little bit of satisfaction at the thought. See? Not in control of everything, are you?

Eventually, however, the smoke grew thinner, and light began to shine through again. She couldn't see Pim, but the weak sound of coughing seemed to be coming from somewhere near the floor. All she could do was stare up at the ceiling, which was not in good shape. There were gray splotches from which no light shone, and sections where the skin was drooping down limply. Pim's retchings went on for a while, and when his face finally appeared in her field of vision, his skin was red, his eyes were weeping, and he did not look happy.

"So, it seems that someone from the Broederschap injected a few things into you," he said tightly.

Oh, yeah, the inoculations, remembered Felicity. They seemed like a long time ago.

"I should have guessed. Stupid of me. Do you know what they did?" he asked. "They put some weapons into your system. Some very, very nasty products. Very clever too; they reacted to the bone scalpel I was using. The Broederschap prefers to use bone blades—they're sharper and better than steel ones. But the shit in your veins could read it. If you got shot with a normal bullet or cut your legs shaving with a metal razor, nothing would happen. But as soon as your blood comes in contact with Grafter-grown bone, fssss!"

No kidding. I wonder if Rook Thomas knew about this?

"It's designer stuff, masterpiece product," he said. "And meant to kill me. Maybe kill the whole group." His face was stern.

Is it going to kill me? she wondered. Is my blood all poisoned and toxic?

"Marcel came up with the original in the seventies, I think," said Pim. "He must have perfected it since. It may even react specifically to the bone of one of us. Very clever old man." He shook his head.

"Unfortunately for him, it was in the files Claudia grabbed. And I made a vaccine for it. It took a while to activate, but it worked. We are prepared for all of their weapons. So fuck Marcel, and fuck them all. Their hidden weapon failed." He was smiling now, and it wasn't a particularly nice smile. Then there was the sound of a phone ringing. He turned away to answer it and spoke some words in Dutch. He hung up and turned back to Felicity.

"Hmm. I will come back to you in a bit," he said.

So I'll be alive then?

"I want a much closer look inside you. But for the moment, my girl is waiting to have a talk."

Oh, Odette'll be thrilled to see you, she thought. I'll just stay here, shall I?

She heard him walk away.

Wanker.

49

"All right," said Claudia. "Pim will be here in a minute." She hadn't had to pick up a phone or anything; she had simply cocked her head and moved her lips a few times. Odette nodded, leaned forward in her chair, rested her elbows on the table, and put her hands over her eyes. The others in the room sat solemnly, except for Sophie Gestalt, who picked up a magazine and flipped through it.

Odette's head was churning. There were so many things she needed to say to Pim, and she needed to get them absolutely perfect.

If I just say it the right way, then I can convince him, she told herself. I can tell him about Felicity and how she's actually a good person despite being Checquy. That most of the Checquy actually seem like good people despite being Checquy. I can tell him about how she and I worked together to fight monsters who hurt people but who were really themselves people who had been hurt. And that it was the most amazing thing I've ever done.

And I'll explain to him that all the things we love in humanity, the big ideas and the little kindnesses, they're so delicate. They're so easily smashed. That what the Antagonists are doing makes the world a worse place. And the Checquy helps to keep the world stable. They keep peace.

I can make him see that it's not too late. I know I can.

She heard the sound of a door opening and closing. I won't look up, she thought. Not yet. She heard his footsteps coming closer and the little sounds of other people turning in their chairs to see him.

"Odette?" Pim said finally.

"Yes?" she said.

"Aren't you going to look at me?"

"Oh, sure," she said, and she looked up.

She was relieved to see that he was still the same, that he hadn't changed his face. The face she loved. Despite herself, despite all her concerns, she was so happy to see him. And then she felt a hand close around her heart.

His mouth was opening to say something, but his expression was confused as, without meaning to, Odette found herself standing up. What am I doing? she thought. Her limbs had moved without her conscious effort. And now her joints were locking. Everyone was looking at her warily, and she wanted to say that it wasn't her, that she didn't understand either, but she couldn't speak. Her body took a long, deep breath—more breath than she thought she'd have room for—and her jaws forced themselves wide open.

She screamed.

It was a sound unlike anything Odette had ever heard before. It had parts of her own voice woven into it, at least at the beginning, but they were overlaid with the voice of someone else—a different woman. The two screams twined around each other, almost like a duet. And then the sound rose up and up, and all traces of Odette were lost, left behind. There was only that strange voice, that woman's voice she did not know, coming out of her. And she couldn't stop.

Pain sparked all through her body. Her wrists stung, and she felt as if she were being stabbed all over her torso, in her eyes, in her muscles. A wave of agony washed through her. Her eyes rolled up, and she saw that she wasn't the only one affected.

Next to her, Claudia was shuddering, and the cords that emerged from her eyes clacked and rustled against each other. Inside the clear plastic, Odette could see, the tiny nerves grew black and broke. Blood flooded through the tubes and then it, too, turned black.

It's destroying our implants! Odette realized dazedly.

Simon had his hand on her wrist, and she felt his rubbery white surgical skin become liquid. No, I don't want to see! Odette thought, and she had enough control left to close her eyes. He was shouting something, but she couldn't understand the words, heard only the sound of his voice falling away into gurglings. His hand slid off her and he crumpled to the floor, tearing down one of the blinds as he fell.

She opened her eyes a crack and saw that Saskia was crawling across the table to her. Her once-beautiful eyes were now bloody red. Black lines around her neck showed where gills had been hidden, ready to open and let her breathe in the ocean. Now they were rotting inside her. Her elbows buckled, and she fell on the table. Saskia's spurs were unsheathed. They were beautiful little blades, sculpted to be razor sharp, and they were dripping with venom. With all her strength, she pulled herself closer and closer to Odette. Her eyes had lost their focus, but they were still fixed on Odette.

Yes! thought Odette. Please! Do it! Kill me! Anything to stop this!

But instead, the elegant little weapons fell away from Saskia's wrists, trailing strings of muscle and ligament. She stared at her forearms and then looked up at Odette. They were both thinking of the same thing, Odette knew: The little sacs tucked away in Saskia's forearms. Carefully cocooned in layers of bone and Kevlar, and full of poison. Odette felt her own sacs shred and disintegrate inside her arms, but they were empty, drained in that attic in Muirie.

She saw the moment when Saskia was killed by her own body. Her friend's torso stiffened and then thrashed as the venom rushed through her. Then she was still. Odette had no idea what toxins Saskia had carried in her—she'd kept changing them, going for the more and more exotic.

But still Odette kept screaming.

And Pim was turning, stumbling, trying to get away from her. Run! she thought desperately. I love you! Get out! He shambled into the shadows, where she saw him totter and fall. A dark shape that lay still.

They're all dead, she thought dully. Am I going to be allowed to die too? She could feel her implants being destroyed, but the pain no longer registered. It was just a sensation. Her muscles were breaking down, and her eyes were losing focus. Her skin burned.

Finally, the screaming stopped. There were no echoes—there hadn't been any sound for a long time. Odette staggered on her feet, then fell backward, sprawling on the floor. She felt wetness under her hand and didn't want to know what it was from. All she could do was suck air in through her burning throat.

She discovered that she could cry. So she cried until her tear ducts stopped working. And then she lay there, breathing.

"Well, they didn't see that coming," croaked a voice. It took all her strength, but Odette managed to flop herself over. Her limbs were rubbery and smacked on the floor. Beyond the mess that was Simon's body, she saw the source of the voice. It was Gestalt. The blond woman lay on her back, but she turned her head to stare at Odette. "Judging from your reaction," she said, "I don't think you saw it coming either."

Odette couldn't even shake her head, but she found that she could speak, sort of. Her voice was raspy.

"I don't even know what it was," she said. "I—I think my great-uncle put something into me. A weapon." She was thinking of the surgery that she had gotten at the last minute before coming to England and that, in her naïveté, she had been so thrilled to receive. They trusted me, she thought. But trusted me to do what?

Gestalt opened her mouth to say something, and clear liquid ran out of her throat and over her lips. She spat. "Please excuse that," she said. "I was going to say, congratulations, you're a soldier. A Pawn. They use you. It's how it works. You wouldn't believe the number of people I sent off to their deaths."

"Did they know you were sending them off to die?" asked Odette bitterly.

"Not always. But whatever your family put in you, it certainly did a number on Grafter organs. My spine is killing me."

"They put implants in you?" asked Odette. "In that body?" Her gaze flickered up and down Sophie.

"Oh, yes," said Gestalt. "Quite a few. Of course, in all the bodies, there was always that phone thing so the one girl could look out through my eyes."

"Claudia," she said weakly. Claudia, who was sitting dead in her chair, still plugged into the wall.

"Whatever," said Gestalt. "They had to put a different face on the other body, the male I used at Hill Hall. It was too recognizably a Gestalt's. And in this one they jacked up my reflexes a bit. So I could take out that Pawn in the lift and spray you two down."

"I suppose those implants don't seem like the best idea now," remarked Odette.

"Oh, it's just a body," said Gestalt.

"And you've got your new ones, your free bodies, don't you?" Gestalt didn't say anything, but she looked pleased. "And you think that you can trust my friends? How can you be sure that those zygotes haven't been tampered with?"

"They're clean." Gestalt coughed. "I've had enough bodies now to know the difference."

"So what, then?" said Odette. "Your bodies will grow up and meet and have more Gestalt babies?"

Gestalt managed a sort of shrug. "Something like that."

"You realize that all your new bodies are the result of incest?" said Odette.

"Of course I do," said Gestalt. "I did have sex with myself." Odette winced. She couldn't help but be disgusted by the idea.

"It's not the religious taboos I'm thinking of," said Odette. "It's a small gene pool you're drawing from, and it will be getting smaller all the time."

"I'll be very organized about it," said Gestalt. "But I'm not relying on immortality. Every new baby is another generation I'll get to live. And who knows what clever science the world will come up with in the next couple of lifetimes?"

Oh yeah, thought Odette weakly. Clever science is terrific. Look where it got me.

"Maybe I'll study it myself," Gestalt mused. "One of my bodies could do a degree. I'll have a lot of time since I'll have no Checquy to worry about. Now, if you'll excuse me," said the rotting woman, "they're serving spaghetti Bolognese at the Gallows Keep prison tonight, and it's my favorite." Her eyes glazed as the mind of Gestalt withdrew from the Sophie-body.

And then Odette was alone. She imagined a blond man with Sophie's eyes coming awake in a small locked room somewhere in Scotland.

I'm going to die here, she thought. I'm dying alone with the corpses of my best friends. She closed her eyes.

And then she remembered Alessio and the attack that was to be made.

There's nothing I can do, she thought weakly. I can't stand up; I don't think I can even scream for help. She wished suddenly that Gestalt hadn't left. I could have tried to persuade her to alert the authorities. Her imprisoned bodies could have told the guards. Word might have gotten through. Gestalt might have bought herself a few privileges in prison—something to make the time pass faster until the new bodies were ready.

But there was no guarantee that Gestalt would have agreed to any such thing. They would probably want as little attention paid to their doings with the Antagonists as possible.

They're going to win, she thought. The Antagonists' attack on those children is going to smash the negotiations. There will be no chance of peace—they were right about that. And Pim and Saskia and Claudia and Simon would have considered dying to be a small price to pay. Look at everything they were willing to do. Claudia, plugged into the wall. Saskia letting her friend use her eyes. Simon working away in those suites, turning innocent people into weapons. Simon walking over the bodies in the fog to retrieve me. Felicity told me how jauntily he'd moved, taking out his mobile phone and calling the others to let them know their beloved friend was being brought back to them.

Calling them on the phone.

Simon has a phone.

In front of her, Simon's body was withered and black. His surgical skin had proven to be especially vulnerable to that horrible scream. Brown liquid had soaked through his suit and spread out in a puddle around him. Odette tried to move her arm, and ribbons of fire shot across her shoulders. This is what rotting muscle feels like, she thought. It feels like shit.

All her Grafter muscles were dead, but she knew that there were still thin cores of her own, natural muscle buried underneath. So, it really will be all me. She strained, and her arm moved a little. Just a little. Progress, she thought. Now, a little more. Every few minutes, she managed to jerk her arm a little closer to the edge of Simon's coat. Sweat soaked her clothes. She was horribly aware that time was passing, that at any moment, Mariette might begin unleashing something horrible on a group of schoolchildren in a museum.

Finally her fingers closed on the cloth and she managed to walk them up his coat, scrabbling against the wet material and then pulling it open. Then, in a moment of divine mercy, his phone slid out of his inside pocket. It took as much concentration as performing micro-surgery on an infant's eye, but Odette found a way to bat the phone toward her until it was lying by her face.

I did it!

Now, what's the damn number? It was growing hard to think, but she managed, with all the strength of her will, to recall her brother's phone number and dial. It rang and rang again. If it just goes to voice mail, thought Odette, then I am going to…to… well, I'll probably just die here in a puddle of slime, knowing that it's all over.

"Hello?"

He's alive! " 'Lethio," she said, her tongue thick in her mouth.

"Odette? You sound terrible," he said cheerfully. "Whose phone are you using?"

"Where are you?" she said, gasping. "Are you okay?"

"What's wrong?" he asked.

"Are you okay?" she said. She would have screamed it if she could.

"I'm fine," he said defensively. "I'm with the school group, we're at the Victoria and Albert Museum."

"Gimme teacher right now. Now." He must have detected her urgency, because after a few scuffling sounds and some distant conversations, the phone was passed over.

"This is Cathy Tipper" came a voice. It was a very gentle voice.

"Pawn Tipper?" Odette asked intently. She wanted to make sure that she was talking to someone who had actual powers to protect her brother.

"Yes," said the teacher.

"Pawn, 'm Odette, 'Lethio's sister. I'm with the delegation." She paused for breath. "There will be an attack on you, in the art museum. Any moment. Unnerstand?"

"Understood," said the teacher.

"P'tect 'em. Get 'em out."

"Yes," said the teacher. She snapped out orders in a drill sergeant's tone, something about formation and securing vulnerables. Odette had the impression that the orders were being given, not to any other teachers or accompanying guards, but to the students. "They'll be safe," the teacher said, coming back on the line. "Now, where are you? Hello?"

Odette could hear the voice faintly, but she couldn't answer. The phone lay by her face, but all she could do was draw long, slow breaths. Eventually, the voice on the phone stopped. Odette missed it a little. It was nice to have some company. She felt the sunshine move onto her face, and she closed her eyes. The warmth poured onto her eyelids and took the chill off the sweat and the slime. She felt as if she were floating in the light.

I wonder why I'm dying so much more slowly than the others did, she thought absently. She had no idea how long she'd been lying there, drifting in and out of consciousness. She remembered a period when her legs had twitched violently and woken her up, but that had stopped after a while. Good-bye, spine. She barely realized it when she wet herself.

Maybe she slept. She had visions. They might have been dreams, or perhaps they were memories fluttering up as her brain began to shut down. But they were all good images, of simple things. A pond, a vase, a dress, a kiss.

She was awake but lost in a reverie, so she didn't hear the door open or the faltering steps that came across the carpet. As if from very, very far away, she heard Felicity's voice saying her name, and, somehow, though she could not move, she smiled.

50

Felicity lay on that table for hours, they later told Odette. She'd lain there long enough for the paralytic chemicals Pim had injected into her to wear off. Long enough for Felicity to roll herself off the table in the suite and put on a shirt.

The skin room she'd been in was not looking healthy. Whatever poisonous smoke had come out of her veins had left the place looking decidedly seedy, but the sphincters that held the door shut remained firmly clenched. Felicity tried cutting her way out with a bone scalpel, and then with a bone knife. Finally she picked up an alarming-looking surgical saw and hacked her way out into a very corporate hallway.

Exhausted, clutching the walls, she sent her Sight gliding through the offices. She saw the corpses lying about and Odette sprawled on the floor, just barely alive. She hobbled through the hallways as quickly as she could and made it to the conference room. The smell was horrific, all the corpses slumped in pools of fluid. And there was her friend, lying very still.

"Odette, are you all right? What happened to you?"

"Flsssss," Odette bubbled.

"Good to see you too, babe," said Felicity, coming closer. "Although you look really bad." She sat down beside the Grafter and gingerly took her friend's sticky hand. Then she picked up the phone that was lying by Odette's face. It was odd-looking—much chunkier than most phones today. Then she saw that there was still a call in progress, and the counter on the bottom of the screen showed it had been going on for a few hours. She tentatively put it up to her face.

"Hello?"

"Hello? Who is this?" said a startled man's voice on the other end.

"Who is this?" she asked.

"I'm Constable Alan Summerhill," said the voice. "I'm with the police. We believe that a crime has taken place, and we are trying to track the location of your phone. May I have your name and location please?"

"I'm Felicity Clements," she said. "I don't know the location; I was abducted." She bit her lip, wondering what to say. If the police came, the carnage around her would inevitably result in the Checquy appearing eventually, but they might not be able to contain this situation. She looked down at what remained of Odette. Fuck it, she needs help now. "I'll look around for something that might show where I am."

"Ah, are you Felicity Jane Clements?" said Constable Summerhill.

"Yes..."

"Pawn Clements, I'm Pawn Summerhill," he said. "Rookery Communications section. Wasn't sure whether you were a civilian."

"I quite understand," said Felicity.

"What's your situation?" asked Summerhill. "Are you in immediate danger?"

"No," said Felicity, looking around the room. Everyone else, including Pawn Jelfs, was most definitely dead. "But I have Odette Leliefeld from the Grafter delegation here, and she's in critical condition." She looked down at Odette. "Extremely critical condition."

"You were taken by the group responsible for the Blinding?"

"Yes," said Felicity, "but they're all dead here. Five of them. Advise Rook Thomas immediately. It looks like—I don't know—

some sort of toxin attacked them? Or maybe it was a suicide-pact thing." Odette, did you agree to kill yourself with these manky terrorists?

"Understood. Now, the phone you're using is preventing us from tracking your location."

"It's big and chunky," she said.

"Probably some paranoid hacker product," he said. "They run the call through all sorts of clever connections on the Internet. I expect that any other phones you might find there would be similarly tedious, so we're going old-school. Are there windows? Can you see anything that will give you a clue about your location?"

"Yes, we're in an office building, a few stories up. I think we're in the City."

"Okay," said Pawn Alan. "Do you see any familiar buildings?"

"No, not really," said Felicity helplessly. "I can see across the street, and it's just some other office building."

"That's okay. Can you get out of the office?"

"I don't know," said Felicity. "And I don't want to leave my friend here. She's in very bad shape."

"Okay," said Alan. "Is there any furniture?" In the background, Felicity could hear people giving orders about prepping medical care.

"Yes, there are some chairs and laptops and things."

"Excellent; we have a procedure that we've found works very well in this situation. It will help us identify your location quickly, but I need you to do exactly as I say."

"Okay," said Felicity seriously.

The pedestrians walking on Barrington Road looked up in surprise as an office chair burst out of a fourth-story window. The chair spiraled down crazily as a woman put her head out through the hole.

"Falling glass! Everyone look out!" she screamed. The people below scattered out of the way as the shards rained down. Then they looked up indignantly. "Please, call the police!" she shouted frantically. "There's a man in here with a gun, and he's insane! Help us!" Then she vanished back into the building.

Approximately twenty-two calls were immediately made to the local police, who had been alerted, through various back channels, that a call of that sort was expected and that some extremely important people wanted the address as soon as possible. The civic-minded members of the public were assured that help was on the way. Most of the civic-minded members of the public hung around warily to see what happened. A few of them shared their story on the Internet.

Interest flared, especially when several police vehicles arrived, lights flashing. Large men with large guns emerged, to the gratification of the waiting citizenry, and rushed inside. By the time the press arrived, three ambulances were in place and some victims had been removed, two of them covered with sheets. The ambulances screamed away, to which hospital, no one seemed to know.

This is hardly subtle," remarked Felicity as the ambulance sped through the streets. The medic who was taking her pulse smiled a little.

"A madman with a gun is a handy story," he said. "It allows for all sorts of things. Armed officers running around. Sites sealed off. Ambulances. Of course, the media will go absolutely insane, and the government will have to answer some awkward questions, but when we're in a hurry, that's a price worth paying."

"Odette—the girl in the other ambulance—do you know how she's doing?"

"She didn't look good, but we have someone very talented with her. Now, lie back and take some deep breaths."

The world swam before Odette's eyes, but she was alive. Alive, and feeling slightly more so than before. Patches of gentle warmth touched her cheeks, her body just below her breasts, her hips. The sensation soaked through her, and she felt stronger, and very safe. Her eyes focused a little, and she was looking up at a plump older man with gray hair.

"You...you have twelve arms," she said blearily. "And two heads."

"No, you're just seeing double," the medic assured her.

"Am I going to die?"

"No," he said cheerfully.

"I know medicine," she said. "I should be dying."

"I cheat a bit," he confessed. "You're not going to die from these injuries. As long as I've got you," he said. "And I'll stay with you until we've got you stabilized. I gather there are quite a few Belgians clamoring for you to be delivered back safely to the Apex so they can take care of you."

"Is it safe for me to sleep?"

"Absolutely."

So she did.

51

Time passed. Odette found herself back in the medical wing of Apex House, only this time she was a patient. The medic from the ambulance, Pawn Eustace Brigalow, stayed with her, keeping her alive. She was placed in a private room that immediately became much less private as surgical-masked Grafters swarmed in, partially to say hello and congratulate her but mainly to examine her body. Scans were taken, samples were drawn, and Pawn Motha was brought in to look at her and report what he saw. Odette found it difficult to care.

One afternoon Marcel came to her and described the repairs that would be undertaken on her body. There seemed to be rather a lot. Many of her organs would need to be replaced, and her skin and bones had suffered significant damage. I wonder if there will be any of the original me left.

"Marcel," she said. "What happened to them—to me? What was that?"

"We'll talk about it later," he assured her. "There will be lots of time to talk."

Alessio was not permitted to visit her. It was judged that since he had been spending so much time amongst the pupils of the Estate, he was likely to bring an infection in with him. Odette and her brother spoke on the telephone but kept the conversations light. He was having a decent time and would be going up to the Estate for a visit. He assured her that he was okay and that all the other students from the field trip were fine, but he would give her no more details. Odette suspected that he had been ordered not to tell her anything too upsetting.

Grootvader Ernst came twice, but the visits were cold and awkward. Odette had no doubt that whatever had been done to her, whatever had been put into her, had been at his command.

One frequent visitor was Felicity. They didn't talk about the abduction or the events in the conference room, only about very frivolous things. Felicity had moved back into her flat with her dog and was coping very badly with the lack of room service. The housemate who had been in hibernation had woken up. The negotiations were going well. On a different note, Felicity had gone out for dinner with a Pawn from her old combat team, but Trevor Cawthorne, the sniper from Scotland, had given her a call to tell her he'd be down in London in a few weeks and asked if perhaps they could get together for a drink. Felicity wasn't entirely certain how she felt about these developments.

The surgeries began. Most of the time, it was Marcel repairing her body. Crates and canisters had been shipped in from the Grafter houses around Europe. Equipment and materials. Every morning, Odette was wheeled to the OR and lifted onto the table. Marcel would open her up and begin the day's work. Occasionally, he would be assisted by a member of the delegation; a few times, a specialist was brought in from Europe to advise on a particular component. The Checquy attendants were aghast at the amount of work that had to be done on her, but to Odette, it seemed almost comforting. For her, a surgical table was a familiar place to be.

Once, she'd woken up to find that a dozen members of the Checquy medical staff were looking on in fascination as Marcel explained what he was doing in her chest cavity. She recognized a couple of them from when she'd tried to assist in that one Pawn's emergency surgery. She looked around, rolled her eyes, and went back to sleep.

Most of the time, though, she was awake while her great-uncle did his work inside her, and it was just the two of them present. A mirror was set up so that she could observe. He would demonstrate techniques on her internal organs and test her on what she'd learned. He also told her about his life and his experiences in World War II. Then, one day, he described the woman in Paris whose screams had killed her grandfather Siegbert.

"It was from her that I took the components that were put into you, Odette." During that long, torturous journey from Paris to Belgium, while his brother and his wife lay in a cart and watched themselves rot, he had kept the woman's head and neck in a sealed jar, preserved in alcohol. "Such a weapon was too valuable not to keep." In the years since, he had tested the components secretly, wondering if the effects could be duplicated. "In the end, those nodes in the woman's throat proved to be unique," he said regretfully. "I do not know why they did what they did. They were a mystery, just like the Checquy. And I put them into you."

"You put Gruwel parts inside me," she said tightly. It was lucky that she was lying on a surgical table with everything below the neck paralyzed or she would have attacked him. "You made me a monster and a murderer. You made me kill them! You made me kill the people I loved best! How could you? How could you?"

"Ernst and I decided that we had to take every possible chance to remove the Antagonists," said Marcel. "We have seen hatred like theirs before, an unwillingness to move on, to forgive. It is poisonous. And so I grafted the nodes from the woman's throat inside you. I installed a supplemental brain and plumbed it into your eyes and gave it override control over your limbs so that when you saw Pim and Saskia in the same place, you would kill them."

"Pim and Saskia?"

"They were the leaders," he said. "I know them, Odette. They were my students, my relations. All of the Antagonists were talented, but Pim and Saskia were the sine qua non of the conspiracy."

"And why didn't I die?" she asked dully. "All my friends died, so why didn't I?"

"They had far more implants than you," said Marcel. "They made themselves into monsters for hatred of the Checquy. Simon and Claudia were the most obvious, but all of them seethed with weapons and tools under their skin. They must have begun as soon as they pillaged the Paris house, operating on each other. They took themselves too far from what they had been. It made them vulnerable. Plus"—and here he paused for a moment— "I made some modifications to your system, as much as I could, to shield you."

"Oh," said Odette in a small voice.

"I could not do much. The weapon affects Broederschap materials, the substances that allow our craft to function. And I am a Grafter, I have to use the tools I know. If I had removed all the Broederschap organs, you would have noticed. But I replaced some of your augmented organs with standard human ones." They were both quiet for a while, and then he set about putting in her new heart.

Finally, her body was repaired. Better than it had ever been. Odette looked at herself in the mirror and saw exactly the same person. On the inside, she knew, she was stronger, faster, with greater control. Her spurs were tucked away inside her arms, but they were new. Her old ones, the ones Pim had sculpted for her, had shattered inside her during the scream. The new ones had been made by a distant relative who lived in Bratislava. Everything about her was bespoke, specially made. Her whole body was couture.

Inside her mind, though, she felt broken. She had enough control of herself to ensure that she didn't dream, but she was still haunted by memories of what had happened.

And then she was summoned to meet with Rook Thomas and Grootvader Ernst to make her report.

Odette went to the Rookery and was led up to Rook Thomas's office. Ernst embraced her, holding her tight, but she was stiff in his arms. She could not forget that it had been he who had given the order to make her into a weapon.

She told them everything. They sat silently, and Rook Thomas took some notes, but they did not ask any questions. Odette suspected that they knew it all anyway. When she was finished, Rook Thomas told her what had happened when Mariette attacked the school group at the V and A Museum.

As a result of Odette's phone call to Alessio, the class had broken down into small groups, with various combat- and defense-powered students assigned to protect those who were more vulnerable. The students had then begun to make their way through the building to a multitude of exits, planning to regroup at a prearranged location. Alessio's group had been accompanied by the teacher, who was especially eager to ensure the safety of her politically significant charge. As they moved through the fashion gallery, Alessio had recognized Mariette. She was wearing a different face, but she had on an armor-coat that was identical to the one Odette had worn. He very quietly pointed her out to his teacher.

So I suppose it was a good thing, in the end, that I explained everything to him, Odette thought.

The students in his group formed a protective ring around Alessio, and Pawn Tipper had engaged her discreet but devastating abilities. The public had been none the wiser, simply seeing the girl in the suit fall victim to a heart attack. None of them imagined that she had been struck down by a silent word from the teacher's lips. Investigation of her corpse had revealed smoke grenades filled with an intricate and deadly toxin.

Odette bowed her head and accepted the fact that it was over. The Antagonists were done. Ernst and Rook Thomas remained respectfully silent while Odette absorbed this idea. Then she looked up.

"Is that all?" Odette asked. "Do you need me for anything else?"

"Not today," said Ernst. "You may go."

How could they do it?" Odette asked suddenly, and Felicity looked up from her unenthusiastic contemplation of her bowl of muesli. They were having breakfast in the hotel restaurant. Felicity was no longer Odette's minder—Odette didn't seem to have a minder anymore. Apparently, if you murder your friends and relations for the sake of national security, the government will finally trust you. But Felicity and she still spent a good deal of time together. The things they'd been through set them both apart from their respective organizations. So they shopped, and walked, and talked. Odette had explained everything to Felicity, how she'd been used. The Pawn hadn't said anything, for which Odette was profoundly grateful. But now, this morning, Odette needed answers. "How could they do that to me?"

"You're a Pawn," said Felicity. "A Pawn of the Checquy. You might not have taken the oath yet, but that's what you are. You're a tool, to be used and directed for the good of the people. Sometimes you'll be a scalpel, cutting out disease. Sometimes you'll be a sword, and you'll take on threats with all the strength you can muster. And sometimes, Odette, you'll be a stiletto, a hidden weapon that slides quietly into the heart."

"I'm honored," said Odette. She stared down at her food. "I just can't stop thinking about it, Felicity. All I can see is them dying. I'll be walking or taking a bath or watching television, and I'll remember Saskia getting poisoned by her own body. Or Claudia's brain shutting down. Or Simon's skin putrefying. It's been weeks now, and it doesn't stop. I want it to go away!"

"It won't ever go away entirely," said Felicity. "I wish it did. But with things like this, with wounds on the inside, sometimes it's just a case of getting through the day. Or the hour. Or the minute. Sometimes the hard times come every other minute, and they'll keep slapping you so that you can't ever relax. And sometimes you'll go for weeks and maybe even months before it gets you, right when you least expect it. But it never goes away entirely." Odette sighed. "Although it does get easier, Odette. And it's easier when you have comrades."

Later that day, Odette went for a walk in Kensington Gardens. The weather was getting colder, and the sky was gray. She looked in the Serpentine Galleries, which Saskia had mentioned visiting, and then stood in the wind and looked at the water. It gets easier, she told herself.

She sat down on a bench. It gets easier. And then she found that, despite herself, she was weeping, and she couldn't stop. She sat, crying, while people hurried by, averting their gaze out of embarrassment, or courtesy, or distaste. She wept because of the sorrow and the guilt of watching her dearest of friends die, watching her beautiful boy die, and knowing that it was because of her, that she was the vessel of their destruction. She wept because of their rage and their fanaticism and because, in her heart of hearts, she knew that their deaths had been for the best.

A little old lady came walking by with two Scottie dogs in little tartan coats. She sat down on the bench by Odette and silently took her hand. Nothing was said between them, but they held hands until Odette ran out of tears. The lady gave her a clean handkerchief, and Odette mumbled something thankful.

Then she went back to the hotel and hugged a startled Grootvader Ernst for real.

* * *

Lionel John Dover stood on the footpath under the dim light of a lamppost and looked up at the house. Maybe this is it, he thought. It was different from the two places he'd visited before. Those had been little town houses, new and sterile. This was an old house in an expensive neighborhood. The trees along both sides of the street were huge, and they reached across to each other to make a tunnel of leaves. Beyond a low stone wall and a garden, the house stood large and beautiful. If he squinted, he could just make out the number 1841 carved in stone above the door. Light glowed behind the curtains on the ground floor.

Please, finally, answers.

At the thought, his hand tightened around his talisman, his proof. It was such a small, ridiculous thing to pin all one's hopes on, but over the past weeks, a woman's designer handbag had given direction to his life. It was the only clue as to what had happened at Ascot. There had been a woman, and she had known about him. She had.

He wasn't certain that she'd died. There hadn't been time to finish it at the racecourse, and then there'd been no outcry, no coverage, even though he'd done it in public, in broad daylight. Of course, there had never been any coverage for any of the other times he'd done it. But she had existed.

He had the photos to prove it.

The woman's wallet made as little sense as she had. For one thing, it was stuffed full of different forms of identification and credit cards with many different names. There were driver's licenses and identity cards for Colonel Amanda Connifer, Dr. Nicola Boyd, Mlle. Jeanne Citeaux, Ms. Myfanwy Thomas, Dr. Iris Hoade, Mrs. Susan Katzenelenboygen. Each of them had a different address, but the same woman was in all of the photos.

For hours, he'd looked at these photos. In most of them, she stared straight ahead with the usual glassy expression one found on government-issued identification. But in one of them, she gazed out at him with the same wry spark he'd seen in her eyes at the racecourse.

She knew, he thought. I have to find out what she knew.

I'll get her to tell me what I am. And then—then I'll be free. He hadn't unleashed the crystals on a living person since Ascot. If she knew, others might know, and they might come for him. It had taken all his self-discipline, but he'd restrained himself. He'd left no clues for them to follow, whoever they were. No bank transactions, no phone calls, no drained corpses impaled on crystals. The weeks of living rough had taken their toll on his appearance, he knew. Surviving on handouts, staying in the shabbiest of hostels and shelters. Always moving. But always, burning in his mind, the knowledge that she was out there. And, after her, freedom.

He moved across the road. Dressed all in black, he merged well with the shadows. The old-fashioned lamps of the neighborhood lent a charm to the area, but they didn't cast much light. He passed between the open gates and stepped off the pebbled drive onto the grass to keep from making noise. Crouching low, he moved between the bushes of the garden and scuttled to the side of the house.

A quick look through a window showed him nothing useful. Light came down the hallway, but that didn't mean anything. At the first two places, there had been lights on timers. One of them had a television that turned on by itself, which had nearly given him a heart attack. When it suddenly began blaring pop music at him, he only just barely stopped himself from exploding it with crystals.

He continued around the side of the house to the back, where a broad deck jutted out into the garden. There was a door that led, as far as he could tell, into the kitchen, and some French doors with curtains drawn, and a laundry-room door that, unbelievably, was unlocked. He eased it open, centimeter by centimeter, wary of squeaks, but it was silent.

The laundry was unremarkable, but there were things about it that gave him hope. A half-empty box of washing powder. A pair of still-damp socks draped over the rim of a basket. Most encouraging, there was a litter tray on the floor in the corner of the room. He went down on one knee and sniffed. The litter had been used, and recently. This is real, he told himself, and he felt a thrill.

The first two places, the addresses belonging to Amanda Connifer and Iris Hoade, had been...disappointing. He'd broken in, kicking the doors open or smashing windows instead of using his crystals to shred the locks out of the doors. There had been an alarm at one, and he'd exploded it with a glance. Each place initially gave the impression that the owner had just stepped out. Art on the walls, books on the shelves, bottles in the fridges. Even a toothbrush in a glass by the sink. It was all very convincing. In one, the toilet paper in the lavatory had actually been ripped unevenly. He'd torn the first place apart, desperate for some clue about the woman. Every drawer had been tipped out, every book flipped through. He'd found nothing at all. No documents, no personal letters, not even any photos. Finally, he'd realized that it was a sham, a false home. Even the clothes in the drawers had never been worn. The second place had been the same. But now, now...He clenched his fists, and little crystals blossomed on the wall without his realizing it. Perhaps the house of Myfanwy Thomas is the real one.

He stepped into the kitchen and froze. Somewhere in the house, nearby, a person was moving. Light seeped out from under a door, and a shadow passed by. He could barely breathe as the footsteps stopped and there was the sound of the person sitting down on a couch. A sigh; the rustle of a book being opened. It's her! he thought. It has to be. It took all his self-control to walk slowly and silently to the door.

His heart was pounding in his chest. It would be so easy to reach out his hand and push out his mind...he could practically see the crystals erupting out of the walls and floor and ceilings. They would stab out unerringly, transfix her, and she would bleed down into the minerals and into him, everything that she was. But he couldn't do it. He hadn't come for her death— at least, not right away.

I know she can stop me moving, he thought. But she can't stop me from doing it. She'll give me the answers. I'll make her.

And then! He put the handbag down on the counter and stepped through the door.

It wasn't her.

He wanted to howl at how much it wasn't her. This woman was tall, and black, and beautiful. She was dressed in jeans and a long-sleeved top, bright silver jewelry at her neck and wrists, and she seemed completely unperturbed by his sudden appearance in her house.

"Oh, hi," she said, putting down her book.

American, he noted dully. The disappointment had left him dazed.

"You're looking for Myfanwy, right?"

"I—yes," he said. He'd been thrown by the way she said it, to rhyme with Tiffany.

"She's actually not here at the moment," said the woman.

"Oh no," he said automatically. "I'm so sorry, please excuse me, I—I should have checked ahead."

She waved a hand dismissively. "Don't worry about it. You know what, have a seat. You want a cup of tea?" Out of habit and sheer befuddlement, he nodded. "Great, I'll get it. How do you like it?"

"Just with a little bit of milk, please," he said. He gingerly sat down on a chair. The room was pleasant, if a little odd. A deep red carpet and dim lighting made it feel cozy, but the shelves were empty of books, and there were hooks on the walls but no artwork.

"You want sugar?" she called from the kitchen.

"Thank you, no." The whole thing had that familiar dream-like feel in which everything was so ridiculous that he began to question what was real. He wished that he hadn't left the handbag on the counter in the kitchen—it would have been reassuring to have it in his hand.

Myfanwy Thomas is real, he told himself. And the woman implied that she is still alive. This must be her housemate. She must think I'm here for a date or a casual hello. It seemed tenuous, especially given his shabby appearance, but it was all he could think of. So what do I do now? He brooded over it while from the kitchen came the sounds of tea being made. All right, so I'll have the tea and make polite conversation, and then I'll torture this woman into telling me everything she knows about Myfanwy Thomas. And then I'll kill her. He leaned back, pleased to have a plan.

"Here's your tea," said the American woman. She sat back down on the couch and looked at him expectantly. He took an experimental sip.

"It's very good," he assured her.

"Thank God," she said. "Nothing scarier than making tea for a Brit." She took a long drink from her own mug and shrugged. "For me, it's like wine. I don't know if it's good, I just know if I like it or not."

"I suppose if you don't like it, it's not good," he said.

"Yeah, you would think, but I've had expensive wine that still tasted like ass to me," she said. She smiled, rolled her eyes, and took another drink. To be polite, he did the same. There was a pause, which was agony to him, but she seemed quite comfortable.

"And you're from America?" he asked finally.

"Yeah. I'm based in Texas but I'm originally from Michigan," she said.

"Marvelous. You know, I'm dreadfully sorry, but I didn't catch your name," he said.

"Oh, jeez," she said. "Of course. I'm Shantay. Shantay Petoskey." She did not ask who he was, which only added to the unreal nature of the whole thing.

"So, Myfanwy isn't here?" he asked casually, taking special care to pronounce it as she had.

"No, she's up in Scotland," said the woman. "I'm heading up there tomorrow. I was going to stay in a hotel, but then she mentioned you might be stopping by the house, and I said I'd mind the place for tonight, just on the off chance."

I might be stopping by? he thought. She knows! She must know!

"Well, that's grand," he said. His eyes narrowed; he took

a long sip of tea and willed stakes of crystal to grow out of the couch cushions and impale her through her thighs. He felt the thrumming in his brain and skin as the energy built, and then he braced himself for the moment of sudden violence.

Which didn't come.

"Yes, it's nice to be able to do a friend a favor," she said cheerfully. He was bewildered. He had felt the crystals erupt, but he hadn't seen any go through her, and she was still drinking her tea. He clenched and tried to call forth another spike, this one through her back. His nerves hummed, and he knew it was happening, that the crystals were stabbing out, but instead of screaming as she was pierced, she was checking her mobile phone with pursed lips. "Anyway," she said, putting down the phone, and he jumped, still bewildered that she was not transfixed, "let's get down to business." She put down her cup and shook her hair about her face, and suddenly, impossibly, she was metal. A statue in silver, sculpted by Praxiteles.

"Don't worry," she said, and her voice had the musical timber of a flute. "This is really happening."

"But, but—" He was hyperventilating. It was impossible. Again.

"They've been waiting for you to show up here," said the silver woman. "Apparently, you broke into a couple of other places, but by the time they got there, you were gone. Myfanwy said you would never stop and that it was inevitable you would come here.

"I was actually metal under my clothes the whole time," she said. "Just in case you tried anything funny. Which you did." She shifted over on the sofa, and he saw broken-off stumps of crystal jutting out of the back and seat cushions and a good deal of little shards and powder. "Your weapons ripped the shit out of my clothes, but they can't go through my skin. We tested ahead of time."

"I—what?"

"Yeah, they had a chunk of your crystal handy—you left it inside my best friend's torso, remember?" She didn't wait for an answer. "When I offered to stay here, they wanted to make sure you wouldn't be able to kill me. So they tried that chunk against my skin. Turns out they couldn't push it through at all. I didn't even feel it. Lucky I was visiting, eh? Otherwise, they'd just have blown this place up when you entered, and Myfanwy's quite fond of it."

"You—you're…"

"You actually do have my sympathies," she said, standing up. "I mean, no offense, but you're my worst nightmare. Not to fight, but to be. I can't imagine suddenly developing these sorts of powers and not having anyone to guide me. No structure, no understanding but what you make for yourself. We would have tried to help you." There was pity in her voice, but then it hardened. "However, you're being dominated by your abilities. You either can't or won't control yourself, and we can't have that. And besides, you tried to kill my friend."

"Who are you?" he finally managed to gasp out.

"We're the government," she said. She turned, gripped the sofa, hauled it up into the air, then spun back and flung it at him. He threw up his hands to shield himself and braced for a horrible, bone-crushing impact that never came. After several heart-shredding moments, he opened his eyes and saw a wall of crystals bisecting the room, the sofa suspended in the middle of them. They must have erupted from the walls, floors, and ceiling and caught the couch in mid-tumble. Through the smoky surface of the mineral, he could see a vague shape moving toward him.

Got to get away! he thought frantically. He turned toward the kitchen and caught a flicker of motion in the corner of his eye. There was a sound like breaking mirrors as several of the crystals shattered and fell. Despite himself, he turned back and saw, through a jagged gap in the wall, the statue-woman drawing herself up after the blow she'd struck against the barrier. In her hands she held an ugly-looking black sledgehammer. She gazed at him through narrowed cabochon eyes, then brought the hammer back over her shoulder and began to swing it again.

He didn't wait to watch her batter more of the wall. Instead, he scrabbled through the door to the kitchen, animal in his terror. Instinctively, he called up the crystals, which surged along the floor in front of him and then punched up and shattered the back door out of its frame. He leapt forward, and the crystals dissipated into powder that burst in a cloud around him. I didn't know I could do that, he thought vaguely, but there was no time to consider the implications. He was out in the back garden with no idea where to go. Behind him, the house had lit up, and the side pathway that he had taken before was filled with light. Before him, the garden stretched into darkness, the trees and shrubs offering a million possibilities to hide and escape.

He scrambled forward off the patio, his feet slipping on the wet grass as he fled. Over the hammering of his heartbeat, he could hear footsteps. The woman called something to him but he ignored it. There was a whirling sound behind him, and something clipped one of his legs. His knee crumpled, and he tumbled sideways, landing in a fishpond.

Blowing and gasping, he sat up and saw the silver figure approaching him. The sledgehammer that she'd thrown at him was lying on the grass to his side.

"God, I love this country," said the woman, and he looked up at her. She was beautiful and horrible and impossible. "Every time I come here, I get to kick some ass. At home, it's all paperwork and meetings."

"I—I..." He couldn't seem to make words.

"You know, Myfanwy actually spoke up for you," she said. "And that was after you stabbed her. She thought you should be imprisoned, maybe rehabilitated, but the Court outvoted her, and I think they're right. So here we are." She lifted her hand and he saw that she was holding some sort of black-and-yellow weapon. A stun gun. "Now, I'm not entirely certain what will happen when I use this on someone sitting in a pond, but we'll play it by ear, shall we?" She pointed it at him and he found himself screaming and slashing up his arm to shield himself. A fan of crystal spun up out of the ground and knocked her arm aside. The Taser flew into the shrubbery.

"Aw, crap!" she exclaimed. "I really should have seen that

coming. It's my own fault for talk—" She was cut off as a crystal column erupted from the grass and sent her flying. There was a distant crash as she landed in the hedge. Groaning, he levered himself out of the water. His knee grated under him and he was shivering, but he was also exhilarated.

I can't kill this woman, he thought. And I can't outrun her either. But maybe, maybe I can stop her.

The silver woman stumbled out of the bushes. She was still perfect, there were no scratches on her metal, but her shirt had a few tears, and her silver hair was tangled. With a scraping sound that set his teeth on edge, she combed her fingers through it and picked out a twig. She did not look best pleased.

"Let's do it the hard way, then," she said. "That's always much more fun anyway."

He didn't answer. Instead, he fanned his fingers out over the ground and concentrated. Go!

From under his palms, four rivers of crystal snaked through the grass toward her and then burst up into glittering eight-sided pillars two feet across. They weren't there to cut but to smash at her, to fling her out, away. She sidestepped two of them, spun around the third, and then continued her spin to slam her forearm into the fourth column and break it. She caught it as it fell and flung it directly at him.

You can do this, he thought. He stepped forward, toward the hurtling shaft, and put out his hands. As the missile touched his fingertips, it exploded silently into a cloud of powder. Yes! Coughing, he stepped back and heard thudding. Through the cloud, he caught a flash as she shot toward him.

Now!

Jagged spikes slid out of the grass in her way. Barely breaking stride, she ducked and dodged around them.

More!

Talons of glass curled out of the ground and down from the tree branches above them. They clutched at her, scraped her skin and caught her shirt, but she tore free.

Stop her!

A faceted wall of mineral rose up before her, and she lowered her shoulder and plowed through it with a hideous cracking sound. Fragments scattered across the lawn.

And now I'll...I'll...he had no more ideas. As she came toward him, violence in quicksilver, he hesitated.

And he was lost.

Hello, Ingrid? It's Shantay Petoskey. Is our girl there?"

"Just a moment, please, Bishop Petoskey." The American woman took up her cup of tea, which was still warm, and drank. She'd given up smoking years ago, and she was in someone else's house, but if there'd been a cigarette handy, she'd have snatched it up without hesitation.

"Shan? What's happened?" The Rook's voice was anxious.

"Hey, I'm fine. He did come to your house, though."

"Oh, Jesus."

"Yeah," said Shantay. "He had your purse from the race-course. Did you cancel all your cards?"

"Is he dead?"

"I'm sorry, Myfanwy. He was rabid; I had to put him down." The Rook sighed. "Yeah, okay. Thanks, Shan."

"Don't thank me too soon," said Shantay. "It's a good thing you got all your stuff out of the house, because your couch is ruined, and you'll need to get your kitchen redone."

"Great, well, the Checquy can pick up the tab for that," said Myfanwy sourly.

"Fortunes of war," said Shantay. "But I actually kind of like what's happened to your backyard. You might want to think about keeping that. Very alternative-ice-sculpture chic."

"I dread to think," said the Rook. "Anyway, I'll send a cleanup team around immediately. Do you want to go to a hotel tonight? I can have a car come and pick you up."

"Nah, I'm fine. The guest room's untouched, and it's a bit late," said the Bishop.

"Then I'll see you at Balmoral tomorrow."

It's a lovely day," said Odette. "I didn't think it would be. The weather reports all agreed that it would storm."

"There was supposed to be a thunderstorm today," said Felicity, "but Celia from the Finance section can control the weather in a mile radius around her. They brought her up from London so we could have a nice day here and take advantage of the Balmoral gardens for your grandfather to kiss hands."

"Kiss hands?" repeated Odette.

"It's what they call it when a government minister formally takes office. Now it's just a term—they don't actually kiss the monarch's hand."

"Someone better tell Grootvader Ernst that," said Odette. "Because they did it in his time and—oh! Too late." They watched as Ernst rose from his knees. Once again, he is a warrior and a general, she thought, happy for her grootvader.

"And now he's kissing the King on both cheeks," said Felicity, sounding very cheerful. "Splendid!" The startled-looking monarch was smiling broadly. "Royalty is always rather fond of tradition."

Tradition was certainly the flavor of the day. The delegation of Grafters had come to Aberdeenshire to officially join themselves to the Checquy, committing themselves and their people back in Europe to the service of the British Isles. Dressed in their best, they had knelt on red carpets laid out on the lawn and taken an oath of citizenship and then an oath of fealty, and, when they had risen, they had been embraced by cheering Pawns and Retainers. Several of the embraces had been stiff and perfunctory, but most had been genuine.

"Your ancestor looks very pleased," said Felicity. "I hope he's not disappointed that he wasn't made a member of the Court."

"No," said Odette. "I think he's quite satisfied with the fact that they're making him a duke."

And once again a nobleman, she remembered. For all her life, and the lives of her family going back generations, Grootvader Ernst had been their leader, respected for his power, his age, and his foresight. But his lost noble status, his fiefdom long since stripped from him in the horrible aftermath of the Isle of Wight, had been abstract knowledge to the Grafters, less real than their fear and hatred for the Checquy.

"Once, we were nobles," a Grafter mother might say, knowing that it was a nice thought but nothing to compare to being a member of the Broederschap.

But that wasn't true for Grootvader Ernst, I'd bet, thought Odette. *It's so easy to know that he's old without realizing, really understanding, that he was alive in those days. That the man who sits at the head of the table with a however-many-greats-grandchild on his knee and a beer in his hand was the man who rode horses to war, sat with his dogs in a great hall, bargained with kings, and invaded a nation.*

And for him, noblesse oblige, the obligations and responsibilities of nobility, would be real, and eternal. Is that why he did what he did? Is that why he joined us to the Checquy? Not so that he could become a duke again, but so that he and his people could be of genuine service? She watched him talking with the King, and her heart was filled with love, not just for her liege lord and leader, but for her great-grandfather, who had taught her so much about honor and duty. Then she frowned.

"Felicity, that guy over there, the one who's right up by the front. He's not in the Checquy, is he? I mean, he's wearing a dress military uniform."

"No," said Felicity, biting her lip slightly to keep back a laugh. "He's not in the Checquy."

"It's just that he was at the reception," said Odette. "He was one of the men I danced with."

"Yeah, he's one of the VIPs."

"Oh? I suppose that would make sense," said Odette thoughtfully. "He's cute, isn't he? We danced quite a few times. Chatted a bit. It was very nice."

"You hit it off?"

"Oh, well, I don't know," said Odette, blushing a little. "He said we should go shooting sometime."

"Really?" said Felicity.

"Yeah. I said I had some really nice shotguns but that I'd only ever shot clay pigeons, and he said he'd be happy to teach me."

"Odette?"

"Hmm?"

"He's third in line to the throne."

"Oh. *Really*."

ACKNOWLEDGMENTS

This book took longer to write than I'd expected, but it would have taken much, much longer if not for the support of a multitude of people. There are too many to thank each one individually, but I am supremely grateful to all of them.

Whenever I require inspiration to write about public servants who do extraordinary things, I need only look at my colleagues at the Australian Transport Safety Bureau. Especial gratitude to Brett Leyshon and Dave Grambauer, who blithely shared harrowing insights from their days in medicine, which I promptly stole. Also, many thanks to my colleagues in the operational search for MH370.

The Internet really is an extremely handy little thing. Periodically I will throw out a question on Facebook or Twitter, and an answer will come winging its way back. My thanks to all the people who gave me advice and encouragement, whether we've met or not.

Liesbeth van Alphen and Frank de Jong had me to stay with them during my time in the Netherlands and ferried me about without a word of complaint. They, along with Eva Lemaier, were also the recipients of frantic messages asking for Dutch vocabulary (obscene and otherwise) and guidance on pronunciation. (I also shamelessly pillaged their lists of Facebook friends for cool names.)

Nikki Keene kindly answered all my questions about Royal Ascot, even the inane ones. (Any differences between my descriptions of the racecourse and reality are entirely the fault of reality.) Her and Boyd Allen's hospitality means all the more since they had never met me before in their lives.

Kimberley Stewart-Mole fed me and watered me and squired me around Cardiff.

Erik and Katy Davis let me stay with them in London, and in return I stole their home and stored three Checquy agents in it. My discussions with Erik about the nature and impact of terrorism greatly informed my thoughts about the Antagonists, and his guidance on how to storm a room with armed troops was invaluable.

Hillary Noyes furnished me with some ghastly symptoms to inflict upon innocents, and her Pomeranian, Wallace, was the inspiration for Grenadier.

Stuart and Fiona Anderson Wheeler also dared to have me in their home. My friend since high school, Stuart advised me on shooting and showed me some stunning examples of shotguns, which I promptly gifted to Odette.

The staff of Foundry Literary + Media, Little, Brown and Company, and HarperCollins Australia continue to be incredibly kind, incredibly patient, and incredibly incredible.

Finally, of course, I must thank my parents, Jeanne and Bill O'Malley, for absolutely everything.